THE
Half-Stitched
Amish
QUILTING CLUB
~TRILOGY~

THE
Half-Stitched
Amish
QUILTING CLUB
~TRILOGY~

WANDA E.
BRUNSTETTER

SHILOH RUN PRESS

An Imprint of Barbour Publishing, Inc.

The Half-Stitched Amish Quilting Club © 2012 by Wanda E. Brunstetter
The Tattered Quilt © 2013 by Wanda E. Brunstetter
The Healing Quilt © 2014 by Wanda E. Brunstetter

Print ISBN 978-1-63058-884-7

eBook Editions:
Adobe Digital Edition (.epub) 978-1-63409-541-9
Kindle and MobiPocket Edition (.prc) 978-1-63409-542-6

Note: The words to the following songs used in this book were written by Wally Nason: "Never," "Falling Star," and "You Saw Me." Used with permission by Nasun Music Group, 2011.

Scripture is taken from the King James Version of the Bible.

Scripture is also taken from the HOLY BIBLE, NEW INTERNATIONAL VERSION®. NIV®. Copyright © 1973, 1978, 1984, 2011 by Biblica, Inc.™ Used by permission. All rights reserved worldwide.

All German-Dutch words are taken from the *Revised Pennsylvania German Dictionary* found in Lancaster County, Pennsylvania.

This book is a work of fiction. Names, characters, places, and incidents are either products of the author's imagination or used fictitiously. Any similarity to actual people, organizations, and/or events is purely coincidental.

Cover photography: Brandon Hill Photos

For more information about Wanda E. Brunstetter, please access the author's website at the following Internet address: www.wandabrunstetter.com

Published by Shiloh Run Press, an imprint of Barbour Publishing, Inc., P.O. Box 719, Uhrichsville, Ohio 44683, www.shilohrunpress.com

Our mission is to publish and distribute inspirational products offering exceptional value and biblical encouragement to the masses.

 Member of the
Evangelical Christian
Publishers Association

Printed in the United States of America.

CONTENTS

The Half-Stitched Amish Quilting Club 7

The Tattered Quilt 323

The Healing Quilt 635

About the Author 949

The
Half-Stitched
Amish
Quilting Club

DEDICATION

To all my dear Amish friends who live in Indiana.
Each one of you is special to me.

A special thanks to Wally Nason, Mel Riegsecker, Dan Posthuma, and
Martha Bolton for your creative suggestions.

The LORD is nigh unto them that are of a broken heart;
and saveth such as be of a contrite spirit.
PSALM 34:18 KJV

PROLOGUE

Shipshewana, Indiana

Emma Yoder's hands shook as a single thought popped into her head. *What if I fail?*

She eased into a chair at the kitchen table and drank from her cup of chamomile tea, hoping it would calm her jangled nerves. When she glanced at the battery-operated clock on the far wall and realized it was 9:45 a.m., her stomach tightened. Half an hour from now she would begin teaching her first quilting class—and to folks she had never met. Some she'd spoken to on the phone, but a few of the reservations had been made by relatives of those who'd be attending.

Emma had made many quilted items to sell on consignment at one of the local quilt shops and had taught several of her family members how to quilt. But teaching strangers would be different. Those who'd signed up for her six-week class could be from all walks of life. Would they understand everything she taught them? Would her instructions be clear enough? When the classes were complete, would she be able to find more students? All these questions swam around in her head, but she refused to let doubt take over.

The back door opened, bringing Emma's thoughts to a halt. Her daughter, Mary, who'd recently turned thirty-two, stepped into the room and sniffed the air. "Umm. . . Do I smell peanut butter cookies?" Mary asked, pulling out the chair beside Emma and taking a seat.

Emma nodded. "I baked a few dozen this morning. I'm just waiting on the last batch." She motioned to the cooling racks, filled with fresh cookies. "I'm planning to serve them to my quilting class, but feel free to have a couple if you like."

"No thanks. I'm still full from breakfast." Mary's brow wrinkled. "Are you sure you really want to do this, Mom?"

In an effort to keep Mary from knowing how apprehensive she felt, Emma smiled and said, "*Jah*, I'm very sure. Learning to quilt will give my students an opportunity to create something beautiful and lasting." She took another sip of tea, letting the smooth taste of chamomile roll around on her tongue and then settle her uneasy stomach. "Perhaps after my students learn the basics of quilting and make a small wall hanging, they might want to try something larger." Emma felt more optimistic as she talked. The thought of sharing her love for quilting gave her a sense of excitement and purpose.

Mary opened her mouth to say something more, but a knock on the front door interrupted them.

Emma jumped, nearly knocking over her cup of tea. "That must be one of my students. Surely none of our friends or relatives would use the front door."

"Would you like me to answer it?" Mary asked.

"*Jah*, please do. Show them into my sewing room, and as soon as I take the cookies from the oven, I'll be right in."

Mary, looking a bit hesitant, pushed her chair away from the table and hurried from the room.

Emma opened the oven door and took a peek. The cookies were a nice golden brown, perfectly shaped, and smelled as good as they looked. She slipped on her oven mitt, lifted the baking sheet from the oven, and quickly transferred the cookies to a cooling rack.

As she stepped out of the kitchen, she nearly collided with Mary. "Are my students here?" Emma asked.

"Jah, but Mom, are you truly certain you want to teach this quilting class?" Mary's face was flushed, and her dark eyes reflected obvious concern. "I mean, you might reconsider when you see how—"

"Of course I want to teach the class." Emma gave Mary's arm a gentle pat. "Now go on home to your family. I'll talk to you later and tell you how it all went."

"But, I—I really think you should know that—"

"Don't worry, Mary. I'll be just fine."

Mary hesitated but gave Emma a hug. "Come and get me if you need any help," she called as she scooted out the back door.

Drawing in a quick breath, Emma entered her sewing room and halted. A man and a woman who appeared to be in their midthirties sat in two of the folding chairs, scowling at each other. To the couple's left sat a middle-aged African-American woman with short, curly hair. On their right, a pleasant-looking Hispanic man held a baby girl on his lap.

Sitting across from this group of people was a young woman wearing a black sweatshirt with the hood pulled over her head. A look of defiance showed clearly in her dark eyes, accentuated by her heavy black makeup. On the young woman's left sat a big burly man with several tattoos and a black biker's bandana on his head.

Feeling a bit overwhelmed, Emma grabbed the edge of her sewing machine to steady herself. *Ach, my! No wonder Mary looked so flustered. Such a variety of unexpected people have come here today! What in the world have I gotten myself into?*

CHAPTER 1

Three weeks earlier

As Emma stepped into the spacious sewing room her late husband had added onto their house, a sense of nostalgia settled over her. Ivan had passed away thirteen months ago after a massive heart attack. Emma still missed his cheerful smile and easygoing ways, but she was getting on with her life—keeping busy in her garden and flower beds, working on various quilting projects, and of course, spending time with her beloved family. One thing that bothered her, though, was feeling forced to rely on her grown children so much. Mary and her family lived on the property next door, and ever since Ivan's death, they'd been helping Emma with numerous chores, not to mention contributing money toward her financial obligations. But Mary and her husband, Brian, had five children to support, and Emma's oldest daughter, Sarah, who lived in LaGrange, Indiana, had eight children. Emma's sons, Richard and Ethan, had moved their families to Oklahoma two years ago, and they each had two boys and four girls. All of Emma's children had been giving her money, even though none of them could really afford it. Emma had sold only a few quilts lately, so with the hope of earning enough money to be self-sufficient, two weeks ago she'd placed an ad in a couple of local newspapers and put some notices on several bulletin boards in the area, offering to give quilting lessons in her home. So far, she'd only had one response, and that was from a woman who wanted to reserve a spot for her granddaughter. But Emma was hopeful that more reservations would come in.

Pulling her thoughts aside, Emma took a seat at her sewing machine to begin piecing a quilted table runner. Sewing gave her a sense of peace and satisfaction, and as her foot pumped the treadle in a rhythmic motion, she began to hum. While many of the Amish women in the area had begun using battery-operated sewing machines, Emma preferred to sew the old-fashioned way, as her mother and grandmother had done. However, she did have a battery-operated machine as well, which she would let her quilting students use when she was teaching them. She also planned to borrow one of Mary's sewing machines.

Emma had only been sewing a short time when she heard the back door open. "I'm in here!" she called, knowing it was probably Mary.

Sure enough, Mary entered the room. "Brian's off to work at the trailer factory, and the *kinner* just left for school, so I'm free to help you pull weeds in your garden or flower beds today."

"I appreciate the offer," Emma said, "but I'd planned to get some sewing done today. I also want to line out everything I'll need when my quilt classes begin."

Tiny wrinkles creased Mary's forehead as she took a seat in one of the folding chairs near the table Emma used to cut out material. "Are you sure you want to do this, Mom? What if no one else responds?"

Emma shrugged. "I'm not worried. If the good Lord wants me

to supplement my income by giving quilting lessons, then He will send students. I'm trusting, waiting, and hoping, which to me are all connected like strands of thread that form strong stitches."

Mary's lips compressed as she twirled around her finger the ribbon strings attached to her stiff white head covering. "I wish I had your unwavering faith, Mom. You're always so sure about things."

"I just try to put my confidence in the Lord. Remember, Hebrews 11:1 says, 'Now faith is the substance of things hoped for, the evidence of things not seen.'" Emma smiled, feeling more confident as she spoke. "I believe God gave me the idea to teach quilting, and if my choices and desires are in His will, then everything will work out as it should. And if for some reason no one else signs up for this class, then I'll put another ad in the paper."

Mary leaned over, and her fingers traced the edge of the beautiful Double Wedding Ring quilt draped over one of Emma's wooden quilting racks. Emma planned to give it to a friend's daughter who'd be getting married this fall, and it was nearly finished. "You do such fine work, Mom. Thanks to your patient teaching, all the women in our family have learned to quilt, and I'm sure the younger girls will learn from you as well."

Emma started the treadle moving again as she pieced another strip of material to the runner that was nicely taking shape. "It gives me pleasure to teach others, and if teaching quilting classes will add to my income so I won't have to rely on my family for everything, then so much the better."

"Families are supposed to help each other," Mary reminded. "And we don't mind at all, because we love you."

"I love you, too, and I appreciate all the help you've given me since your *daed* died, but I feel guilty taking money from all of you when you have growing families to raise. I really want to make it on my own if possible."

"If you're determined not to let us help you financially, then I suppose you could consider getting married again. I think Lamar Miller might be attracted to you, and from what I've seen, I believe he'd make a good—"

Emma held up her hand. "Please, don't even go there. I loved your *daed* very much, and I'm not the least bit interested in getting married again."

"You may feel that way now, but someday you might feel differently. Lamar's a lonely widower, and I don't think he'll wait forever to find another *fraa*."

"I'm not asking him to wait. Maybe he'll take an interest in Clara Bontrager or Amanda Herschberger. I think either of them would make Lamar a good wife."

"Aren't you interested in him at all?"

Emma shook her head.

"Well, I'm sure he's attracted to you. Why, it wasn't more than a few weeks after he moved here from Wisconsin to be close to his daughter that he started coming around to see you."

"I know, and I wish he would quit." Emma peered at Mary over the top of her metal-framed glasses, which she wore for reading and close-up work. "It's time for me to make a new start, and I'm excited about teaching the quilting classes. Fact is I can hardly wait to see who God sends my way."

Chapter 2

Goshen, Indiana

The mournful howl of the neighbor's dog caused Ruby Lee Williams to cringe. The infuriating beagle had been carrying on all morning, and it was grating on her nerves. Of course, everything seemed to irritate her these days: the phone ringing, a knock at the door, long lines at the grocery store, the TV turned up a notch too loud. Even a simple thing like the steady hum of the refrigerator could set her teeth on edge.

Ruby Lee poured herself a cup of coffee, picked up the morning's newspaper, and took a seat at the kitchen table, determined to focus on something other than the dog next door, now alternating its piercing howls with boisterous barks. It was either that or march on over to the neighbors' and demand that they do something with their mutt.

"But that wouldn't be the neighborly thing to do," she murmured. For the past two weeks, the Abbots had attended the church Ruby Lee's husband, Gene, pastored, and she didn't want to say or do anything that might drive them away. It was bad enough that Ruby Lee felt like running away.

Inside their newly purchased home, everything was finally in its place after moving a month ago from the parsonage, which was owned by the church. Both Ruby Lee and Gene were in their late forties, and thinking a new house would be where they would retire, they'd decided that a one-story home would be the most practical. But they'd instantly fallen in love with this older brick house, even though it was a two-story and would mean climbing stairs to their bedroom. Compared to all the homes they'd looked at over the winter months, it was hard to pass up a place that was in such good condition and so reasonably priced. The house was solid, and the freshly painted rooms cheerful— not to mention the hardwood floors that shined like a basketball court. Ruby Lee was thrilled with the large windows throughout the house and the charming window seats that had been built into most of the rooms. With the exception of the kitchen and two bathrooms, she could sit on the seats in any of the rooms and enjoy looking out at different parts of their yard. The front and back yards were neatly manicured, and the lovely flower beds were weed free—at least for the moment. With the exception of the sometimes-noisy neighbors' dog, this house was perfect for her and Gene's needs. Now if everything else in their life would just fall into place as nicely as the moving and unpacking had done, Ruby Lee could finally relax.

This morning Ruby Lee had e-mailed her friend Annette Rogers, who lived in Nashville. She'd intended to unburden her soul but had ended up sending a casual message, asking how Annette and her family were and mentioning the beautiful spring weather they'd been having in northeastern Indiana. Ruby Lee had been there for Annette when she'd gone through breast cancer surgery five years ago, but things were now going well in her friend's life, and Ruby Lee didn't want to burden Annette with her own problems. Besides, she hoped the issues they were facing at church might soon work themselves out.

Maybe I just need a diversion, she thought. *Something other than directing the choir, playing the hymns and choruses every Sunday, and heading up the women's ministries. What I need is something fun to do that's outside of the church.*

Ruby Lee turned to the ad section of the newspaper and scanned a few columns, stopping when she came to a small ad offering quilting lessons. *Hmm. . . I wonder if this might be something I should do. I could make a quilt for one of our elderly shut-ins or maybe a quilted wall hanging for our home. Now that all the boxes are unpacked and I've arranged the rooms, I need something—anything—to take my mind off of the church troubles.*

Elkhart, Indiana

"Hey, sweet girl," Paul Ramirez said to his nine-month-old daughter, Sophia, as he carried her from the Loving Hands Daycare Center out to his van. "Were you a good little girl today?"

Sophia looked up at him with her big brown eyes and grinned. "Pa-pa-pa."

"That's right, I'm your papa, and I love you very much." Paul smiled. He knew Sophia was pretty young to be talking yet and figured she was probably just imitating him because he said *Papa* to her so often. Then, too, from what he'd read in her baby book, some children started saying a few words at an early age.

Paul opened the back door of the van and secured Sophia in her car seat. Then, handing the little girl her favorite stuffed kitten, he went around to the driver's side. With just a few weeks left until school was out for the summer, Paul was looking forward to the time he'd have off from teaching his second-grade class. He could spend more time with Sophia and more time with his cameras, as well. Perhaps he could combine the two. Maybe when he took Sophia to the park or out for a walk in her stroller, he'd see all kinds of photo opportunities. It would be good not to have to worry about who was watching Sophia during the day when he was teaching, too. It'd be just the two of them spending quality time together.

Paul swallowed around the lump in his throat. *If Sophia's mother were still alive, it would be the three of us enjoying the summer together.* Lorinda had been gone six months already. Every day he missed seeing her pretty face and listening to her sweet voice. Yet for Sophia's sake, he'd made up his mind to make the best of the situation. Thanks to his faith in God and the support of his family and friends, he'd managed to cope fairly well so far, despite his grief over losing his precious wife. The hardest part was leaving Sophia at the day care center every day. This morning when he'd dropped her off, the minute he'd started walking across the parking lot, she'd begun to cry. By the time they'd reached the building, Sophia was crying so hard, the front of Paul's shirt was wet with her tears, and it was all Paul could do to keep from shedding a few tears of his own. It nearly broke his heart to leave her like that. He wished he could be with her all the time, but that simply wasn't possible.

Paul looked forward to spending this evening with his sister, Maria, and her family. Maria had invited Paul and Sophia to join them for supper, and he was sure that whatever she fixed would be a lot better than anything he could throw together.

By the time Paul pulled into Maria's driveway, his stomach had begun to growl. He hadn't eaten much for lunch today and was more than ready for a substantial meal. If not for Maria's frequent supper invitations, he would have almost forgotten what a home-cooked meal tasted like.

When he stepped into his sister's cozy home a few minutes later, he was greeted with a tantalizing aroma coming from the kitchen.

"Umm. . . Something smells awfully good in here," he said, placing Sophia in the high chair Maria had bought just for the baby to use whenever they came for a meal.

Maria turned from the stove and smiled, her dark eyes revealing the depth of her love. "We're having enchiladas tonight. I made them just for you."

Paul gave her a hug. "I know I've said this before, but you're sure a good cook, Maria. Your enchiladas are the best. All I can say is *gracias* for inviting Sophia and me here for supper this evening."

"You're more than welcome." Maria patted Sophia's curly, dark head. "It won't be long and she'll be off baby food and enjoying enchiladas, tamales, and some of our other favorite dishes."

Paul gave a nod. "How well I know that. She's growing much too fast."

"That's what kids do," Maria's husband, Hosea, said, as he strode into the kitchen, followed by three young girls. "Just look at our *muchachas*." He motioned to Natalie, Rosa, and Lila, ages four, six, and eight. "Seems like just yesterday and we were changin' their *pañal*."

Lila's face reddened as she dipped her head. "Oh Papa, you shouldn't be talkin' about us wearin' diapers like that, 'cause we don't wear 'em no more."

"That's right," Maria agreed. "And can't you see you're embarrassing our girls?"

"Aw, they shouldn't be embarrassed in front of their uncle Paul," Hosea said with a chuckle.

Maria handed him a platter full of enchiladas, and he placed it on the table.

"You know, Paul, you're absolutely right about Maria bein' a good cook. She's always liked spendin' time in the kitchen, so I knew soon after I met her that she'd make a good wife." Hosea winked at Maria, and she playfully swatted his arm.

"Lorinda enjoyed cooking, too." Paul's throat tightened. Watching Hosea and Maria together and thinking how much he missed his wife made him almost break down in tears. Even during a pleasant evening such as this, it was hard not to think about how Lorinda had died after a truck slammed into their car. Paul had only received minor bumps and bruises as a result of the accident, but the passenger's side of the car had taken the full impact, leaving Lorinda with serious internal injuries. She'd died at the hospital a few hours later, leaving Paul to raise their daughter on his own. Fortunately, the baby hadn't been with them that night. Maria had been caring for Sophia so Paul and Lorinda could have an evening out by themselves. They'd eaten a wonderful meal at Das Dutchman in Middlebury and had been planning to do a little shopping on their way home to Elkhart. That never happened.

"Paul, did you hear what I said?" Maria gave his arm a gentle tap.

"Huh? What was that?"

"I asked if you've talked to any of Lorinda's family lately."

"Her mama called the other day to see how I'm doing, and said she'd be sending a package for Sophia soon," Paul replied. "Ramona sends a toy or some article of clothing to Sophia on a regular basis. I know it's hard for her and Jacob to be living in California, with us so far away, but they're good about keeping in touch, same as our folks do."

"Yes, but Mom and Dad only live in South Bend, so you get to see them more often," Maria said.

"That's true."

"Are Lorinda's folks still planning a trip here sometime this summer?" Maria asked.

Paul nodded. "As far as I know."

"That'll be nice." Maria smiled. "It's good for Sophia to know both sets of her grandparents."

"What about Lorinda's sister? Have you heard anything from her since the funeral?" Hosea asked.

Paul shook his head. He wished Carmen's name hadn't been brought up. "I doubt that I'll ever hear from her again," he murmured.

"Well, that's just ridiculous! That young woman's confused, and she's carryin' a grudge against you for no reason." Hosea shook his head. "Some people don't know up from down."

Paul went to the sink to get a glass of water, hoping to push down the lump that had risen in his throat. "Can we talk about something else—something that won't ruin my appetite?"

Maria's eyes brightened as she leaned against the counter and smiled. "I saw an interesting ad in the newspaper the other day."

"What was it?" Paul asked.

"It was put in by a woman named Emma Yoder. She's offering to give quilting lessons in her home in Shipshewana."

"What got you interested in that?" Hosea asked. "Is my pretty little *esposa* plannin' to learn how to quilt?"

Maria shook her head, causing her short, dark curls to bounce around her face. "You know your wife doesn't have time for that. Not with my part-time job at the bank, plus taking care of our girls." She winked at Paul. "I was thinking you might want to take the class."

Paul's eyebrows shot up. "Why would I want to take a quilting class?"

"Well, Lorinda liked to sew, and since she started that pretty pink quilt for Sophia and never got it finished, I thought maybe—"

Paul held up his hand. "It would be nice to have the quilt done, but I sure can't do it. I can barely sew a button on my shirt, and I'd never be able to make a quilt."

"But you could learn, and it might even be fun," Maria said.

"Huh-uh. I don't think so. Besides, I have enough to do with my teaching job and taking care of Sophia."

"Say, how about this?" Hosea thumped Paul's shoulder. "Why don't you let Maria sign you up for the class? Then when you get there, you can see if the Amish woman, or maybe one of her students, might be willing to finish the quilt Lorinda started."

Paul rubbed his chin as he mulled the suggestion over a bit. With a slow nod, he said, "I'll give it some thought, but right now I'm ready to eat."

———

Goshen

Star Stephens sat at the kitchen table, staring at the words of a song she'd begun working on earlier this week. *Can't seem to look behind the right door; maybe that's 'cause I don't know exactly what I'm looking for. Can't seem to shake the hand that I've been dealt; a road of bitter regret, headed straight to hell. And it doesn't really matter to those who really matter. . . .*

Star tapped her pen as she thought about her life and how she and Mom had left their home in Minneapolis and moved to Goshen, Indiana, six months ago. Mom needed to take care of Grandma, who'd been having health problems because of emphysema. From what Mom had told Star, Grandma had been a heavy smoker for a good many years. As time went on, Grandma got worse, and two weeks ago she'd passed away, leaving her rambling old house and all her worldly possessions to Star's mom, her only child. Star had never met her grandfather, whom she'd been told had drowned in a lake when Mom was three years old. Grandma never remarried. She'd raised her only daughter alone and supported them by working at a convalescent center as a nurse's aide. Star hadn't met her own father either. All she'd ever had was Mom to rely on, and their relationship had never been all that good. They'd moved around a lot during Star's childhood, and Mom had held more jobs than Star could count. She'd done everything from waitressing to hotel housekeeping but never kept one job very long or stayed in one place more than a few years. Mom seemed restless and had drifted from one boyfriend to another. She'd also been self-centered and sometimes had lied to Star about little things. Star had learned to deal with Mom's immaturity, but it irritated her nonetheless.

"What are your plans for today, Beatrice?" Mom asked when she entered the room wearing a faded pink bathrobe and a pair of floppy, lime-green bedroom slippers that were almost threadbare and should have been thrown out months ago.

"My name's Star, remember?"

Mom blinked her pale blue eyes as she pushed a wayward strand of shoulder-length bleached-blond hair away from her face. "I know you've never liked the name Beatrice, but I don't see why you had to change your name to Star. Couldn't you just be content with being called Bea for short?"

Star shook her head determinedly. "For cryin' out loud! I'm twenty years old, and I have the right to do as I want. Besides, I like the name Star, and that's what I want to be called—even by you."

Mom scrutinized Star and then slowly shook her head. "You need to get over the idea that you're going to be a star, because that's probably never gonna happen."

Star's jaw clenched as she ground her teeth together. Mom had never understood her desire to sing or write songs. In fact, she'd actually made fun of some of the lyrics Star had written, saying she should get her head out of the clouds and come down to earth. Well, what did Mom know about all that, anyway? She could barely carry a tune and didn't care for the kind of music Star liked. Other than appreciating the roof over their heads, the two of them really had very little in common.

Mom stared at Star a little longer. "I wish you hadn't gotten that stupid star tattooed on your neck. It looks ridiculous."

"I like it. It's who I am."

"And I suppose you like those ugly purple streaks in your hair?"

"Yep."

"What about that silly nose ring? Doesn't it bother you?"

"Nope."

Star could see that Mom was about to say something more, so she grabbed up the notebook and headed for her room, stomping up the stairs and slamming the door. She tossed the song lyrics on the dresser and flopped back onto the bed with a groan. As she lay there, staring blindly at the cracks in the ceiling, she thought of Grandma and all the times Mom had brought her here to visit. She'd say she was leaving Star at Grandma's for a few weeks because Grandma had asked her to, but Star had a hunch it had been more for Mom's benefit. She figured Mom had just wanted her out of her hair for a while so she could be with whichever boyfriend she had at the time. A woman as pretty as Mom never had any trouble finding a man, and it was no surprise when she'd married Wes Morgan shortly after Star turned eight. Tall, blond-haired, good-looking Wes had turned on the charm and promised everything but the moon.

Star clutched the edge of her bedspread tightly between her fingers. *I hated that man, and I'm glad he's dead!*

Tears stung her eyes as she thought back to the times she'd spent with Grandma, which she now realized had been the happiest days of her life. *Oh Grandma, I miss you so much.*

Grandma had been pretty ill the last two weeks before her death, and it had grieved Star to watch her suffer. But at least they'd been able to share some special moments, talking about the past and the fun times they'd had. Star had even shared with Grandma her dream of getting some of her songs published, and Grandma had never once put her down. She missed the words of encouragement Grandma had offered, even in her weakened condition. She longed to see Grandma's cheerful smile and be held in her loving arms.

Three days ago, Star had been looking through Grandma's room, searching for Grandma's old photo album. She remembered it being filled with pictures of Mom when she was young and a few older photos of Grandma and Grandpa when they were newly married. There'd also been some pictures of Star from when she'd come to visit. Star had finally found the album in Grandma's dresser, and when she'd opened the drawer, an envelope had fallen out. Written on the outside in Grandma's handwriting was Star's name. Grandma had never hesitated to call her only granddaughter *Star*, because she knew how much Star disliked her given name.

Inside the envelope, Star had found a note stating that Grandma had paid for a six-week quilting class in Star's name. It had puzzled Star at first, but then she'd read the rest of Grandma's note and realized that since Grandma had always enjoyed quilting, she wanted Star to learn how to quilt as well. She'd even said she hoped if Star learned to make a quilt that she would think of her and remember all the happy times they'd had together.

At first Star thought learning to quilt was a dumb idea, but after contemplating it for a while, she'd decided to give it a try. Maybe Mom would appreciate her quilting instead of nagging all the time about Star needing to do something sensible with her life. Not that Mom had ever done anything levelheaded with her own life. It seemed as though Mom was always searching for something she couldn't find.

As Star shook her negative thoughts aside, a few more song lyrics popped into her head. She leaped off the bed, grabbed her pen and notebook, and took a seat at the desk. *I'll never give up my desire to become a songwriter,* she thought. *And someday I'll show Mom that I can be a real star.*

CHAPTER 3

Shipshewana

Look over there, Stuart! Do you see that colorful Amish quilt hanging on the line in the yard across the road?" Pam Johnston nudged her husband's arm.

"Don't poke me when I'm driving. You might cause an accident," he grumbled, adjusting his baseball cap.

Pam wished he hadn't worn that ugly red cap today. It looked ridiculous! Of course Stuart didn't think so. He wore the dumb thing a good deal of the time. She was surprised he hadn't tried to wear it to work. Truth was the only time Stuart dressed halfway decent anymore was when he was at work, managing the sporting goods store in Mishawaka.

"I really wanted you to see that quilt," Pam said, rather than bringing up the subject of Stuart's baseball cap.

"Yeah, it was nice."

"How would you know that? You didn't even look when I called your attention to the quilt, and now we've gone past it."

Stuart shook his head. "I can't look at everything and keep my focus on the road ahead. You want us to get in an accident?"

"Of course not, but you could have at least glanced at the quilt. I'll bet you would have looked if it had been something you'd wanted to see."

Stuart mumbled something unintelligible in response.

Pam sighed. "I wish I could make an Amish quilt. It would give me a sense of satisfaction to be so creative."

No comment. Not even a grunt.

She nudged his arm again. "Did you hear what I said, Stuart?"

"I heard, and if you don't stop poking me, I'm going to zip right out of Shipshewana and head back to Mishawaka."

"I'm not ready to go home yet. Besides, you said we could stop by Weaver's furniture store and look for a new coffee table."

"Yeah, okay, but that's the last stop I'm going to make. There are other things I'd rather be doing than shopping for furniture."

"Like what?"

"There's gonna be a baseball game on TV this evening, and I don't want to miss it."

Pam looked at Stuart with disgust. It was always the same old thing with him. "When you're not working, you're either hunting, fishing, watching some sports event on TV, or putting your nose in one of those outdoor sportsman's magazines. You obviously would rather not be with me."

"That's not true. I'm here with you right now, aren't I?"

"Well, yes, but—"

"I've spent all morning and part of the afternoon traipsing in and out of every shop in Shipshewana just to make you happy."

She glared at him. "It's kind of hard for me to be happy when in almost every store you said you were bored and wished we could go home."

Stuart tapped the steering wheel with his knuckles. "Never said I was bored. Just said I could think of other things I'd rather be doing."

"Oh, I'm sure you could."

For the next several minutes, Pam said nothing, but as they turned into the parking lot of Weaver's store, she reached into the plastic sack at her feet and pulled out a newspaper she'd picked up when they'd first arrived in town. "Before we go inside, I want to talk to you about something."

Stuart turned off the engine and looked at her, blinking his hazel-colored eyes. "What's on your mind now?"

"Remember how our marriage counselor suggested we do more things together?"

"Yeah. . .yeah. . . What about it?"

"She said I should do something you like, and then in turn, you should do something I like."

"Uh-huh."

"I went fishing with you two weekends in a row." *Which I absolutely hated*, she mentally added. "So now it's your turn to do something I want to do."

"Just did. Came here so you could do some shopping."

"Shopping doesn't count. All we've bought so far are some bulk foods items at E&S."

"But we went into nearly every other store in town just so you could look around."

Ignoring his sarcastic comment, Pam held the newspaper in front of Stuart's face and pointed to the ad she'd circled. "An Amish woman who lives here in Shipshewana is offering a six-week quilting class."

"So?"

"I've always wanted to make an Amish quilt, and I really would like to take the class."

"Go right ahead; I have no objection to that."

"I thought maybe we could attend the classes together."

He tipped his head and looked at her as though she'd lost her mind. "You want me to go to a quilt class?"

She nodded. "It would be fun."

"Oh, you think? You'd better speak for yourself on that, 'cause I think it would be boring." Stuart shook his head forcefully. "No thanks. I'll pass. It's not the kind of thing a man like me would do."

"Oh, so do you think sewing is just for women?"

"Yeah. That's exactly what I think." Stuart drummed the steering wheel with his fingers, emphasizing his point.

"Well, if sewing's only for women, then fishing's only for men."

He shrugged.

"I hated fishing, Stuart," she said resentfully. "Now it's your turn to do something with me that you think you'll hate."

He gave an undignified snort. "Give me a break, Pam!"

"I went fishing to make you happy. Can't you do the same for me?"

His eyebrows furrowed. "Six weeks? Do you really expect me to sit in some dumb quilting class for six whole weeks with a bunch of women I don't even know?"

"You'll know me, and I don't expect you to just sit there."

"What then?"

"You can learn to quilt, same as me."

His eyes narrowed as he stared at her in disbelief. "I can't believe you'd expect me to learn how to quilt. That's the dumbest thing you've ever asked me to do."

She folded her arms and glared at him. "I can't believe you would expect me to hire a sitter for the kids so I could sit in your boat at the lake and hold a fishing pole all day. But I did it for you, so why can't you do this for me?"

"You only went fishing two Saturdays. If I went to the quilting class for six weeks, it wouldn't be fair."

"What are you saying? Do you expect me to go fishing with you four more times? Is that what you're saying?"

"Yep. That's exactly what I'm saying."

Pam sat mulling things over. "Agreed."

"Huh?"

"I'll do it."

"You'll go fishing with me four more times?"

"Yes, that's what I said.'

"And you won't complain about anything?"

Pam nibbled on her lower lip. No complaining? Now, that would be really difficult; especially since she hated the bug-infested woods.

"Well, what's it gonna be?"

"If you promise to go to the quilt classes every Saturday for six weeks, then for the next four Saturdays after that, I'll go fishing."

"And you won't complain?"

"I'll try not to."

"It's a deal then. Now are we done with this discussion?"

Pam swallowed hard as she gave a slow nod. She couldn't believe what she'd just agreed to do. Maybe after the quilting classes were over, she could think of some excuse not to go fishing with Stuart. Better yet, maybe she could talk him out of going fishing, period. Well, for now, at least, she'd be getting her way. As soon as they got home, she planned to call the number in the ad and reserve two spots for Emma Yoder's quilting classes.

CHAPTER 4

Stuart couldn't believe Pam would even want to make an Amish quilt, much less expect him to make one, too. Some women were hard to figure out, and his wife was certainly one of them. Maybe the idea of quilting was just a passing fancy. Could be that after she'd attended a class or two she'd change her mind and decide that quilting wasn't something she really wanted to do.

Six whole weeks! That's just plain dumb. I catch on to things really fast, though. Bet I'll have the whole process down pat after the first couple of weeks, and then I won't have to go anymore. 'Course, if Pam does decide to stick it out, she'll expect me to go along, even if I am able to quilt something sooner than that.

Stuart gripped the steering wheel a little tighter. This was really a no-win situation—at least for him. On the other hand, if he stuck it out the entire time, then Pam would have to keep her end of the bargain and go fishing with him four more times. It might be worth it just to watch her try to deal with the whole fishing scene again.

Stuart chuckled to himself. The last time they went fishing, it had been comical to watch Pam swatting at bugs, primping with her hair, and struggling with the line on the fishing pole when she'd caught a fish. He could still hear her hollering when she'd tried to reel it in: *"Help! Help me, Stuart! I don't know what to do with this fish!"*

That day could have been kind of fun if Pam hadn't whined and complained about every little thing. Why couldn't she just relax and enjoy the great outdoors the way he did? If he'd known she was too prissy to get dirty and deal with the bugs once in a while, he'd have thought twice about marrying her. Of course, during their dating days he'd been attracted to her beauty and brains and hadn't thought much about whether they had a lot in common. He just felt good being with her back then.

Just look at her now, Stuart told himself. *She's sitting over there in the passenger's seat, looking so prim and perfect. Not a hair out of place on her pretty blond head, and I'll bet there isn't one wrinkle on her slacks or blouse. We're sure opposites in what we like to do, how we dress, and in so many other ways. No wonder our marriage is in trouble. Even with the help of our counselor, I have to wonder if there's really any help for me and Pam.*

Topeka, Indiana

"How'd it go with your probation officer yesterday?" Jan Sweet's employee Terry Cooley asked as Jan climbed into the passenger side of Terry's truck.

Jan shrugged and clipped on his seat belt. "Went okay, I guess. During our sessions, she always asks me a bunch of stupid questions, but I'm just keepin' it real."

"That's probably the best way, all right. So, are you ready to head home now or what?"

"Yeah, sure thing." They'd just completed a roofing job at a home near Tiffany's Restaurant, and Jan knew it was too late in the day to start tearing the roof off the Morgans' house in LaGrange. "Guess we'll get an early start on Monday mornin'," he told Terry.

"Sounds good to me. I'm kinda tired anyways."

"Same here."

They rode in silence for a while, and then Jan brought up the subject that had been on his mind all day. "You know, I really hate relyin' on you for rides all the time. Sure will be glad when I get my license back, 'cause I like drivin' my own truck to work." Jan thumped his knee. "And man, I sure do miss ridin' my Harley. I like the feel of the wind in my face and the freedom I have when I'm sailin' down the road on my motorcycle. Know what I mean?"

Terry nodded. "Just hang in there, buddy. As long as you don't do anything to blow it, you won't have too much longer to go."

"Three more months seems like forever." Jan groaned. "In the meantime, when I don't have far to go, I'll keep ridin' that old bicycle I bought at the secondhand store. And when I need to travel farther, I'm thankful for friends like you who are willin' to give me a lift."

"Hey man, it's no big deal." Terry grinned and pushed his shoulder-length, flaming red hair away from his face. "If the tables were turned, I'm sure you'd do the same for me."

"You got that right." Jan appreciated a friend like Terry, who was not only a hard worker, but liked to ride motorcycles, as well. The two of them, both single, had become good buddies despite their age difference. Although Terry was only twenty-eight and Jan had recently turned forty, they had a lot in common and saw eye to eye on many things. When Jan moved to Shipshewana and started his roofing business three years ago, he'd been glad to find Terry.

"So what'd your probation officer have to say during your session yesterday?" Terry asked.

Jan squinted his eyes almost shut. "Said I should try to find some kinda creative outlet."

"How come?"

"She thinks I'm uptight and need to find somethin' that'll help me relax."

"You mean somethin' other than a few beers?"

Jan grimaced. "It was a few too many beers at the biker bar that caused me to lose my license, remember?"

"Yeah, but if you hadn't gotten picked up for drivin' your motorcycle too fast, you wouldn't have gotten nailed for driving under the influence."

"True, but I've learned my lesson. No more drinkin' and drivin', and no more speedin'." Jan pointed to a grocery store on his left. "Would you pull in over there? I'm thirsty, and I'm all out of bottled water."

"Sure thing." Terry put on his signal and turned into the store's parking lot. "Guess I'll go with you, get some water, and see what I can find to snack on."

"I'll grab us the waters while you look for whatever you wanna munch on."

"Okay. Thanks, bud."

When they entered the store, Jan went to the cooler and grabbed two bottles of water. As he waited for Terry, he studied the bulletin board on the wall near the front entrance.

His gaze came to rest on a handwritten notice offering quilting classes. Learning to quilt would sure be creative, and it might even help him relax. Jan had never admitted it to anyone, but he'd done a bit of sewing in the past and had even embroidered a few pictures he had hanging in his bedroom where no one else could see them.

He pulled off the section of paper with the phone number on it and stuck it in his shirt pocket. He didn't know if he'd take the quilting class or not, but he'd give it some thought.

CHAPTER 5

Shipshewana

I still think this is a really dumb idea, and even though I agreed to come here with you, if this class is boring, don't expect me to do anything but sit and listen," Stuart mumbled as he pulled his black SUV onto the graveled driveway leading to a large white farmhouse on the outskirts of town.

Pam wrinkled her nose. "That's not fair. I shouldn't need to remind you that I went fishing with you not once, but twice."

"That was different." He scowled at her. "It's easy to fish, and it's something both men and women do."

"Some men sew, and some men cook. We've been through all this before, Stuart."

"I cook every time you want something barbecued."

"That's not the same thing, and you know it."

"It is to me."

"By the way, have you looked in the mirror lately?"

"Yeah, this morning when I was brushing my teeth. Why?"

"Well, you didn't look close enough, because you obviously forgot to shave."

Stuart rubbed his stubbly chin. "Guess I did."

"I'm not real pleased with your choice of clothes, either. You could have worn something more appealing than that stupid red baseball cap, faded jeans, and a red-and black-plaid flannel shirt. Oh, and I hope you won't tell any corny jokes today. We're here to learn how to quilt, not put on a show or try to make people laugh."

When Stuart and Pam had begun dating and he'd joked around, she'd thought it was funny, but not anymore. Now it irritated her—not to mention that when he did it in public, she was embarrassed.

"All right, already! Would you stop needling me?" Stuart yelled.

Pam frowned. They sure weren't starting off on the right foot today. She hoped Stuart didn't humiliate her during the quilting class. Since he didn't want to go, no telling what he might say or do.

"It looks like you're not the only man here," she said, motioning to an attractive-looking Hispanic man with a dark-haired, rosy-cheeked baby exiting the silver-colored minivan parked beside Stuart's SUV. Although he was dressed in a casual pair of jeans, his pale blue shirt looked neatly pressed. That was more than she could say for Stuart.

Stuart grunted. "The guy's obviously not with his wife. I wonder what's up with that."

"Maybe she couldn't come today. Maybe he cares about her so much that he's willing to take the class in her place."

"You think so?"

"I guess we'll soon find out." Pam opened the passenger door and stepped down, being careful not to let her beige-colored slacks brush the side of their dusty vehicle. It really needed a good washing.

She'd just closed the door when a blue, midsize car pulled in. A few minutes later, a middle-aged African-American woman stepped out of the vehicle. "Are you here for the quilting class?" she asked, smiling at Pam.

"Yes, I am," Pam replied, admiring the pretty turquoise dress the lady wore. "I'm eager to learn how to quilt, and being taught by an Amish woman is a good guarantee that I'll be taught well. From what I understand, most Amish women are expert quilters."

The woman nodded. "That's what I've heard, too."

Pam glanced over at Stuart, thinking he might be talking to the Hispanic man, but no, he stood in front of their vehicle with his arms crossed, staring at the ground. *Maybe I made a mistake forcing him to come here,* she thought. *I probably should have come up with something else I wanted to do that he would enjoy, too. Well, it's too late for that. We're here now, so we may as well go in.*

Pam went around to the front of the car and took hold of Stuart's arm. "Are you ready to go inside?"

"Ready as I'll ever be," he muttered.

"Well, hold that thought," she whispered, again hoping he wouldn't embarrass her during the class.

They started for the house, and as they stepped onto the porch, a small red car in dire need of a paint job pulled in. When a slender young woman dressed in a pair of black suede boots, black jeans, and a black sweatshirt with the hood pulled over her head climbed out of the car and headed their way, Pam couldn't help but stare. The girl didn't seem like the type who'd want to learn about quilting, but then neither did the Hispanic man. She guessed everyone who'd come must have their own reasons, and she hoped Stuart would now see that quilting wasn't just for women.

Pam was about to knock on the door when Stuart nudged her arm. "Look who's joining us now." He motioned toward a tall, burly-looking man with a short brown beard, riding in on a bicycle, of all things! He wore blue jeans; a tight white T-shirt; and a black leather vest. A black biker's bandana was tied around his head, and his brown ponytail hung out from the back of it. The man had a mean-looking black panther tattooed on his left arm and the name *Bunny* on his right arm. He wore black leather boots—the kind motorcyclists wore—and looked like he belonged on the back of a Harley instead of on a beat-up blue and silver bike.

When I signed us up for this quilting class, Pam thought, *I certainly never expected there would be such an unusual group of people taking the class.*

The young woman wearing the hooded sweatshirt barely looked at Pam as she stepped up to the door and knocked before Pam even had a chance to lift her hand. A few seconds later, a thirty-something Amish woman answered the door. She wore a very plain dark blue dress and a stiff white cap perched on the back of her dark brown hair, which had been parted in the middle and pulled into a bun at the back of her head. The woman stood staring at them with a strange expression. After several awkward moments, she said she was Emma Yoder's daughter, Mary, and then she led the way into an unexpectedly large room, which she told them was where the quilt class would be held.

Pam tried to take it all in with one swooping look. The room held a long table, several folding chairs, some wooden racks with colorful quilts draped over them, and three sewing machines. One of them was a treadle and appeared to be an antique. The four gas lamps flickering overhead completed the picture of plain, simple living.

"If you'll all take a seat, I'll get my mother," Mary said before hurrying from the room. The poor, red-faced woman looked about as uncomfortable as Pam felt right now.

Pam and Stuart quickly found seats, and everyone else did the same. Stuart turned to Pam and glared at her. "Why didn't you tell me it would be like this?"

"I didn't know." She glared right back, grabbing Stuart's ball cap and plunking it in his lap. Didn't he have any manners at all? Between the angry look on Stuart's face and the stony expression from the biker, as well as the young woman dressed in black, the room seemed to be permeated with negative vibes.

Pam glanced over at the dark-skinned woman and was relieved when she smiled. At least someone in the room seemed friendly. She couldn't tell much about the demeanor of the Hispanic man, because he was occupied with his baby.

They all sat quietly for several minutes until a slightly plump, rosy-cheeked Amish woman with gray hair peeking out from under her stiff white cap and wearing a plain rose-colored dress and a pair of metal-framed glasses, entered the room. She looked a bit overwhelmed as she stood beside the antique sewing machine, gripping the edge until her knuckles turned white. Maybe she, too, hadn't expected such an unusual group.

Emma released her grip on the sewing machine and took a deep breath, hoping she could find her voice. When she'd placed the ads and bulletin board notices for the quilting classes, she hadn't expected those who came would be from such varied walks of life. And she certainly hadn't figured any men would attend her classes! No wonder Mary had looked so worried when she'd come to get her.

Thinking back to the phone calls she'd received, there had been one from a man, but he'd said he wanted to make a reservation for Jan. Emma had assumed it was for the man's wife or a friend. And come to think of it, another woman who'd called had said she wanted to reserve a spot for her brother; although at the time Emma had thought maybe she'd misunderstood and that the woman had said, "her mother."

"Hello," she said, smiling despite her swirling doubts and the reeling in her stomach from the nervousness she felt. "I'm Emma Yoder. Now would each of you please introduce yourself, tell us where you're from, and state the reason you signed up for this class?" Maybe the introductions would put them all at ease.

The English woman with golden-blond hair hanging slightly below her shoulders was the first to speak. "My name's Pam Johnston. That's Johnston with a *t*. I enjoy sewing and have always wanted to learn how to quilt." She turned in her chair and motioned to the man with thick brown hair sitting beside her. "This is my husband, Stuart, and we live in Mishawaka. Stuart manages a sporting goods store, and I'm a stay-at-home mom to our children: Devin, who's eight, and Sherry, who is six." Pam wore an air of assurance, but Emma sensed it might be just a cover-up for a lack of self-confidence.

Stuart gave a nod in Emma's direction then glanced at his wife as though seeking her approval. "She's the one who actually wanted to come here. I just came along for the ride."

"That's not true." Pam shook her head. "My husband also wants to learn how to quilt."

"Yeah, right," Stuart mumbled. His tone was clipped, and the look he gave his wife could have stopped any of Emma's clocks from ticking.

Emma quickly turned to the African-American woman wearing a full-length turquoise dress with a loosely knit brown sweater. "What's your name, and what brings you to my class?"

"I'm Ruby Lee Williams, and I live in Goshen, where my husband pastors a church. We have twin sons who are twenty and attending a Bible college in Nampa, Idaho. Of course, they'll be out of school for the summer in a few weeks, but they've both founds jobs there, so they won't be coming home until Christmas." She grinned, looking a bit self-conscious. "I guess that's a lot more than you asked me to share."

"No, that's okay," Emma said. After all, Ruby Lee really hadn't shared any more than Pam. "Would you mind telling us why you're taking this class?"

"I came here to learn how to quilt because I thought maybe—"

"What church does your husband pastor?" Pam interrupted.

"It's a community church," Ruby Lee replied.

Pam gave a brief nod. "Oh, I see."

"So what brought you to my class?" Emma asked Ruby Lee.

"Well, I just thought it would be kind of fun and that maybe I could make something for our new home or perhaps a quilt for someone I know."

Emma smiled and turned her attention to the young woman wearing black jeans and a black hooded sweatshirt, which she kept firmly in place on her head. It was really too warm to be wearing a sweatshirt—especially indoors. "Why don't you go next?"

"I'm Star, and I also live in Goshen. My grandma used to quilt, and before she died, she paid for me to take this class because she wanted me to learn how to quilt, too."

"You have a very pretty name." Ruby Lee smiled at the young woman. "What's your last name, Star?"

Star lifted her gaze, as though studying the cracks in the ceiling. "You can just call me Star."

"Is that your real name?" Pam asked before Emma could voice the question. She'd never met anyone named Star before. Besides the dark clothing she wore, her coffee-colored eyes were accentuated by heavy black eyeliner.

"It's real enough for me." Star lowered her gaze, and when she gave a nod, the shiny gold ring on the side of her nose caught the light coming through the window.

"I thought maybe it was a nickname," Pam said.

Star lifted her chin and stared straight ahead. It didn't take a genius to see that the young woman had some issues she needed to deal with.

Feeling even more uncomfortable, Emma turned to the tall muscular man with the short-cropped beard and tattoos on his arms. "And who are you?"

"Name's Jan Sweet. Now ain't that sweet?" He slapped the side of his leg and chuckled, a rich, warm sound. "I live here in Shipshewana and have my own roofin' business. I got a DUI three months ago when I was ridin' too fast on my Harley; had my driver's license suspended for six months; had to do thirty days jail time; and paid a hefty fine. I'll be on probation for three more months, at which time I'll get my license back." Jan paused to draw in a quick breath. "My probation officer suggested I do somethin' creative, so when I saw your notice on a bulletin board, I signed up for the class."

"Jan Sweet? What kind of a name is that for a man?" Stuart, who had been staring at the tattooed man, snickered. "Sounds more like a girly girl's name to me."

Jan's brown eyes narrowed as he eyeballed Stuart. "Better watch what you're sayin,' buddy, or I might just have to show you how much of a man I can be." His tone had grown cold, and the muscles on his arms rippled slightly.

"Oh, I–I'm sure my husband was only kidding," Pam was quick to say. She bumped Stuart's arm with her elbow. "I think you owe Mr. Sweet an apology, don't you?"

"Sorry," Stuart mumbled without looking at Jan.

"Yeah, well, some people oughta keep their opinions to themselves," Jan growled. "You hear what I'm sayin'?"

Emma could tell by the smirk on Stuart's face that he still thought his comment about Jan's name was funny. And Jan looked downright miffed. How on earth would she handle things if the animosity kept up between these two men? Did she have the nerve to ask one or both of them to leave? Would that even be the right thing to do? Could God have sent this group of unlikely folks to her home for another reason besides learning how to quilt?

Emma turned her attention to the Hispanic man holding the baby. "What's your name, and who's the cute little girl on your lap?"

"I'm Paul Ramirez, from Elkhart. I teach second grade, and this is my daughter, Sophia. She's nine months old." Paul bent his head and kissed the top of the baby's head. "My wife, Lorinda, started a quilt for Sophia, but she was killed in a car accident six months ago, so the quilt was never finished. I came here hoping someone might be able to finish it for me." He removed the small pink quilt from the paper sack he'd brought along.

"Oh, I think you should be the one to finish it," Emma said, understanding the look of pain she saw on the young man's face. Perhaps completing the quilt his wife started would give him some sense of peace.

"I—I don't know a thing about sewing, but I guess with your help I can try." Paul motioned to the baby. "I won't bring Sophia with me when I come next week, but I couldn't find a babysitter today. Since I didn't think I'd be staying for the whole class, I brought her along." One look and Emma could see how much that adorable little girl meant to Paul.

"She's a cute little tyke," Jan spoke up. For such a big, tough-looking man, he sure had a tender expression when he smiled at Paul's baby.

Emma still couldn't believe she'd ended up with such an unusual group of people, but Lord willing, she would teach them all how to quilt, and maybe a bit more besides.

CHAPTER 6

When Emma took a seat in a rocking chair and draped a colorful quilt across her lap, everyone gathered around. Then, as Emma began to explain the history of Amish quilts, Star glanced over at the biker dude. In so doing, the hood of her sweatshirt slipped off, and she quickly put it back in place. She couldn't believe that Jan had blabbed all that information about himself, or for that matter, that he'd been stuck with a girl's name. It didn't fit his rough exterior. But then, the fact that he kept smiling at the baby girl sitting on her daddy's lap didn't fit the way Jan looked either. Maybe he wasn't as tough as he appeared. Maybe he had a soft spot for kids. He sure didn't seem the type who'd want to learn how to quilt, but then neither did the other guy, Stuart.

Guess I don't really fit the mold either. Even though I told them about Grandma signing me up for this class, some still might be wondering what a girl like me is doing here.

Star pulled her gaze away from the biker and focused on the Amish woman holding another colorful quilt she said was the Lone Star pattern. *Now that one fits me,* Star thought. *I'm a lone Star who no one but Grandma has ever really loved.*

To keep from giving in to self-pity, Star studied her surroundings. While she'd seen many Amish people when she'd gone to the Shipshewana Flea Market, this was the first time she'd been in one of their homes. Upon first entering Emma's house, she'd noticed how neat and clean it was. From what she could tell, not one thing was out of place. A wonderful aroma permeated this home, too—like freshly baked cookies—which gave the place a homey feel. In some ways, Emma's house reminded Star of her grandmother's place but with one big distinction—the absence of electricity. The oversized sewing room was dimly lit with only the light coming from the windows and the few gas lamps suspended from the ceiling.

How weird it would be for me to live without electricity, she thought. *No TV, computer, dishwasher, hairdryer, or microwave.* Star was sure she'd be bored if she couldn't go online and post messages on forums to people she didn't really know or download favorite songs to her computer. Yet something about being here in this simple, plain home, gave Star a sense of peace. She was glad she'd followed through with Grandma's wishes and come to the class. If nothing else, it would be a nice diversion.

"And this colorful quilt is called the Double Wedding Ring," Emma said, breaking into Star's musings. "It's a quilt that's often given to young couples when they get married."

"I wish someone would have given me and Stuart a lovely quilt like that when we got married," Pam spoke up. A look of longing showed on her perfectly made-up face.

"Perhaps after you learn how to quilt, you can make one of your own," Emma said, as though to offer encouragement.

"That would be nice." Pam looked over at her husband. "Don't you think so, Stuart?"

"Uh-huh. Whatever," he mumbled, pulling one of the newer type smartphones out of his pocket.

"There seems to be a sense of unity in the balance and blending of the many parts and colors in your quilts," Ruby Lee interjected.

Emma nodded, peering at Ruby Lee over the top of her glasses. "I believe you're right about that. Also, quilting not only holds the layers of fabric together, but it's important for the design and appearance of the quilts."

Emma showed the class a few more quilts, including Weaver Fever, Ocean Waves, and one called Dahlia. "The Dahlia pattern has a three-dimensional effect from the gathered petals surrounding the center of each star-shaped flower," she went on to explain. "Since I have a love for flowers, Dahlia-patterned quilts are one of my favorites."

"That's the one I like," Ruby Lee said cheerfully, "because since we moved into our new home, I'm enjoying all the pretty flowers blooming in my yard this spring."

"I like flowers, too," Pam agreed, "but I still favor the Double Wedding Ring quilt."

"This one might fit you, Jan," Emma said, holding up a quilt made with both light and dark brown material, which she identified as the Log Cabin pattern. "Now this quilt is often made from various scraps. Its narrow, log-shaped pieces often vary in length, and smaller pieces of material can be used that aren't large enough for other patterns."

Jan shrugged his broad shoulders. "Well, I ain't much into campin', but I guess the house I live in could be considered my cabin."

"I like to camp," Stuart interjected. At least he was paying attention again.

Emma reached for another quilt. "This is called Tumbling Blocks, and it's also referred to as Baby Blocks. By using a single diamond shape, with varied placement of colors, the quilt creates an optical illusion of hexagons, cubes, stars, or diamonds." She motioned to the small quilt Paul had brought along. "My Tumbling Block pattern is similar to the quilt Paul's wife started for Sophia."

Paul's forehead wrinkled. "I'm still not sure I'll ever be able to finish that quilt."

"Don't worry about it for now," Emma said patiently. "You may feel differently once you learn how to quilt."

Star glanced at Stuart. He was back to fiddling with his phone. The guy was probably surfing the web or playing some game. She looked away, and her mind began to wander again as she continued to peruse her surroundings. Across the room sat an old treadle sewing machine. Star knew this because she'd seen one in an antique shop when she and Grandma had gone shopping during a visit to her home a few years before she'd become so ill. Grandma had been interested in antiques, and the strange-looking milk bottles on her kitchen counter were some of the old things she'd collected. An antiquated roll-top desk sat in the bedroom where Star slept. In the attic, she'd also seen several old pieces of furniture in dire need of repair, as well as a battered-looking trunk, which she hoped to go through someday.

When Stuart exhaled a noisy, deep breath, Star looked at him in disgust. Slouched in his chair with his eyes half closed, still holding his phone in one hand, he looked about as bored with all of this as she used to feel during high school math. The poor guy obviously did not want to be here. His wife, on the other hand, sitting straight in her chair with an expectant look, was no doubt eager to learn everything there was about quilting. The prissy little blond's makeup was perfectly done, as were her fingernails, painted with a pale lavender polish that matched her gauzy silk blouse.

I wonder if she paints her nails to match everything she wears, Star thought with disdain. *I can't figure out why some people have to look so perfect, while others don't seem to care how they look at all.* She glanced back at Stuart, noting a dark stain—probably from coffee—on his shirt. He and Pam sure didn't fit—at least not in the way they dressed. Emma and the others were okay, she guessed. At least they seemed more down-to-earth than Pam, although Star would have to wait until she'd spent more time with these people before drawing any real conclusions.

"Now that I've explained some of the history of quilts and shown you several of the designs I have here, I'll explain what we're going to do with the quilted wall hangings you'll be learning to make," Emma said. "I have lots of material you can choose from, and I think it would be good for everyone to use the same simple star pattern for your first project. Then hopefully, once you know the basics of quilting, you'll be able to make a larger quilt on your own. Or in Paul's case, he should be able to finish the baby quilt his wife started. Of course you may all use whatever color material you like, which will make each of your wall hangings a bit different and unique."

When Paul's baby started to fuss a bit, Star jerked her attention to him, noticing how attentive he was to the little girl, as he gently patted her back. It couldn't be easy for Paul, losing his wife and having to raise their child alone. Star hoped he would do a better job of it than Mom had done with her. A baby needed to know she was loved and that her needs came first, not the other way around.

During Star's childhood, she'd felt more like Mom was her big sister, rather than her mother. Mom sometimes seemed like a silly schoolgirl— especially when she was around one of her boyfriends. Maybe Mom's immaturity stemmed from the fact that she'd only been eighteen when Star was born, but by now she should have grown up and quit acting so self-centered.

Emma set aside the last quilt she'd shown them and had just risen from the rocking chair when a thumping noise drew everyone's attention to the window behind Emma. A white goat with its nose pressed against the glass stared in at them. *Ba-a-a-a! Ba-a-a-a!*

"Get away, Maggie! Go on now, shoo!" Emma tapped on the window and flapped her hands at the goat. When the critter didn't budge, Emma turned to the class, her cheeks turning red. "I'm sorry for that interruption. Maggie can be a real pest sometimes. She often gets out of her pen and causes all kinds of trouble. Even pulled some clothes off my line the other day, and then I had to rewash them."

"Want me to put her away for you?" Stuart asked, practically leaping out of his seat. "I'm a sportsman, and I know a lot about animals."

Emma looked a bit hesitant but nodded. "You can try if you like. My grandchildren next door helped me plant a small garden two weeks ago, and I would hate to see Maggie running through and ruining it."

"Sure, no problem. I'll put her right back in the pen." Stuart slapped his ball cap on his head and moved quickly across the room.

Pam followed and grabbed hold of his arm. "I don't think that's a good idea, Stuart."

"Why not?"

"Chasing after a goat isn't the same as shooting a deer. The animal might butt you."

Stuart pried Pam's fingers loose from his arm and adjusted his ball cap, which was slightly askew. "Duh! I'll just catch the critter and put her back in the pen."

"Be careful," Pam called as he sauntered out the door.

Star exchanged glances with the biker. Did he know what she was thinking?

Jan grinned tightly and gave her a wink.

Smothering a giggle, Star moved over to the window, eager to see how the know-it-all hunter would go about capturing the goat. Everyone else followed, including Emma, all jockeying for a position at the window.

As soon as Stuart stepped onto the porch, the goat leaped over the railing and darted across the yard. Stuart did the same.

I wonder what that guy's trying to prove, Star thought. *He could have just as easily taken the stairs.*

Star glanced back at Jan, who now stood beside her wearing a big grin. Like Star, he probably thought they were in for a pretty good show. Amused and a bit skeptical, she was eager to see what would happen next, although she kept her thoughts to herself.

As Stuart approached the four-legged creature, Maggie let out a loud *Ba-a-a-a!* and leaped onto the picnic table. Stuart leaned forward with his arms outstretched. He was almost touching the goat's neck when it jumped into the air, nearly hitting Stuart's head with one of its hooves. Fortunately, the ball cap took the brunt of the impact and flew into the air. After Maggie's feet hit the ground, she looked back at Stuart as if to say, "All right now. Catch me if you can!"

Red-faced and shaking his fist, Stuart scooped up his hat and raced across the grass in hot pursuit of the goat. Round and round the yard they went until Stuart made a sudden leap for the critter. It darted between Stuart's legs, and he ended up facedown on the ground, unfortunately in a puddle of water—no doubt from last night's rain.

Everyone but Pam started laughing; it really was a comical sight. Star thought it was worth coming here just to see that.

Pam gasped as the goat turned around and made a quick lunge for Stuart's ball cap. A few seconds later, Maggie was running across the yard with the cap in her mouth.

"I'm real sorry about this," Emma said, turning to Pam with an apologetic expression.

Pam slowly shook her head. "It's not your fault. My husband should never have gone out there thinking he could capture your goat."

"If someone will hold Sophia, I'll go out and see if I can help Stuart round up the goat," Paul said.

"I'll hold the baby." Jan eagerly spoke up before any of the women could respond.

"Why don't you let one of us hold the baby and you can go help the men catch the goat?" Pam suggested.

Jan shook his head. "I ain't in the mood to chase after some stupid goat that obviously don't wanna be caught." He glanced at Paul's little girl and smiled. "Besides, I'd much rather hold the baby."

Paul hesitated but then handed Sophia to Jan. As Paul went out the door, Jan took a seat in the rocker and began rocking the baby while gently patting her back.

Star vacillated between watching the burly biker speak in soft tones to the baby and Paul out in the yard helping Stuart chase after the goat. It seemed odd that Jan would rather be holding a baby than helping the men prove their valor, but something about seeing Jan's tender look as he held little Sophia touched a place in Star's heart. Growing up, no one other than Grandma had looked at her in such a gentle way.

Having never known her real father and being stuck with a jerk for a stepfather, she hadn't experienced what it was like to have loving parents. She supposed in her own way, Mom loved her, but she'd never expressed her love so that Star believed or felt it. Mom had always seemed to care more about meeting her own needs than she did Star's. If it hadn't been for Grandma, Star might never have known what it felt like to be loved at all. Maybe if Mom could have been at home more with Star, things might have been different. Then again, she doubted it.

After Mom married Wes, Star had thought that her mother's days of working as a waitress would be over, but the lazy bum never held a steady job, so Mom had been forced to continue working full-time in order to pay the bills. *I never liked that man,* Star thought bitterly. *He was abusive to Mom and treated me like I wasn't even there. He probably wished I wasn't so he could have Mom all to himself. The two years he lived with us were horrible, and I hope Mom never gets married again!*

"Well, would you look at that!" Ruby Lee shouted. "Paul almost has that ornery goat eating right out of his hand."

Star turned her gaze to the window again. Paul stood near the edge of the yard, holding several pieces of grass, and Maggie the goat was moving slowly toward him. When Maggie drew closer and took the grass in her mouth, Paul put his hands around the goat's neck and led her easily to the pen. Meanwhile, Stuart stood near the porch holding his battered-looking baseball cap and shaking his head. So much for the great white hunter!

When the men returned to the house, Emma, still chuckling a bit, apologized to Stuart for the rumpled cap. "I think maybe we all need a little break," she said. "Let me go to the kitchen and get some refreshments."

"I'll go with you," Ruby Lee said, quickly following Emma out of the room. Star figured their teacher probably needed a break as much as those in her class did right now. Hopefully after some refreshments, everyone would calm down and relax.

Jan seemed reluctant to give the baby back to Paul, but when Paul sniffed the air and said the baby's diapers needed to be changed, Jan scrunched up his nose and quickly handed Sophia to her father.

"Babies will be babies." Pam nudged her husband's arm. "Isn't that right, Stuart?"

"Huh?" He was fooling with his phone again.

"I said, 'Babies will be babies.'" Pam glared at him and pointed to the phone. "Would you please put that thing away? I suppose you're checking the scores on some stupid sporting event."

Stuart shrugged and put his phone back in his pocket. Star hadn't expected him to give in so easily. Was he always so compliant or merely trying to avoid a fight?

"So what do you do for fun?" Star asked, turning to Jan.

"I ride my Harley." He gave her a sheepish grin. "Well, I did before I lost my license."

"I've never ridden a motorcycle," she said.

"You oughta try it sometime. It's really a lot of fun." He frowned as he slowly shook his head. "Sure beats ridin' a beat-up bike that you have to pedal everywhere."

"Well then, maybe you ought to get one that's not so beat-up," Stuart interjected.

Star held her breath, waiting for Jan to make some wisecrack, but he just ignored the man. Didn't even glance his way. It was probably a good thing, because if he'd said something derogatory, the two men might have ended up going toe-to-toe again.

It would serve Stuart right if Jan punched him in the nose, Star thought. *He's got a big mouth and oughta know when to keep quiet. Maybe Mr. High and Mighty needs someone bigger than him to put him in his place.*

Paul returned from the bathroom, where he'd gone to change the baby, just as Emma and Ruby Lee entered the sewing room, bringing with them a plate full of peanut butter cookies, a pot of coffee, and a pitcher of iced tea. They also had cups, glasses, and napkins, which they set on the table. The atmosphere in the room seemed more relaxed after everyone had been given a treat.

Emma smiled at Paul and then Stuart. "I want to thank you both for rounding up my goat, which I'm sure saved my garden."

"No problem," Paul said.

"Yeah, I was happy to do it," Stuart added with a satisfied smile. Had he forgotten so quickly that the goat had gotten the best of him? Didn't he care that they'd all been laughing as they'd watched his antics from the window?

What a jerk, Star thought. *He's right up there with Mom's boyfriend, know-it-all Mike. Only I think Stuart likes to show off so he'll get attention.*

As they ate their refreshments, everyone shared a little more about themselves. Star was surprised to learn that Jan liked the same kind of music as she did, and that he was a self-taught harmonica player. Of course, she didn't think playing the harmonica was all that difficult. One of the geeks at the coffee shop in Goshen had a harmonica, and he'd told her once that it was really nothing more than knowing when to suck in air and when to blow it out.

When everyone had finished their cookies and drinks, Emma showed the class how to use a template and begin marking the design on the fabric, using dressmaker's chalk or a pencil.

"When you're done marking, you'll need to cut out the pattern pieces," Emma said. "In the next step, which is called 'piecing,' the pieces you've cut will be sewn together, and then onto the quilt top, which will also need to be cut," she continued. "Now, the pattern pieces are usually pieced onto the quilt top by machine. Then the backing, the batting, and the quilt top are layered, put into a frame, and quilted. When that is done, the binding will be put on, and the project will be finished."

Stuart, still obviously disinterested in the whole process, leaned back in his chair, which he'd positioned near the wall. With his arms behind his head, he closed his eyes and dozed off. Star was sure he was sleeping, because she heard soft snores coming from his side of the table.

That guy shouldn't even be here, she thought. *He oughta be home taking a nap or doin' whatever he does to occupy his time. He's probably one of those geeks who likes to sit around watching some game on TV and doesn't help his wife at all.*

"Wake up!" Pam bumped Stuart's arm, jolting him awake so he nearly fell out of his chair. "We didn't come here so you could sleep."

"I can't help it. Chasing that stupid goat wore me out." His face still shone with the sweat of his exertion.

Pam wrinkled her nose. "You shouldn't have gone out there then. All you succeeded in doing was getting your ball cap nearly ruined and your jeans wet and dirty. Oh, and by the way, you'd better give me your handkerchief so I can wipe those smudges off your face. I can't believe you didn't wash up before you ate Emma's cookies."

Like an obedient little boy, Stuart reached into his jeans pocket and handed her his hanky, but he didn't look the least bit happy about it. Star almost felt sorry for the poor sap. Of course, if Stuart had stood up to Pam and put her in her place, they'd have probably had a blowup.

Star's forehead wrinkled as she frowned. All married couples seemed to do was fight—just one more reason she was never getting married. It wasn't worth the pain and disappointment.

"Hey, Stuart, I want to thank you for givin' us all such a good laugh," Jan said with a smirk. "You were quite entertaining with that goat out there in the yard. In fact, you looked downright silly."

"Well, no thanks to you! At least Paul was man enough to help out."

Stuart stood and took a step toward Jan. "You chose to sit in here with the women and a baby in your arms. So you shouldn't be laughing at me."

Jan stood, too, and moved toward Stuart until they were almost nose to nose. "So you think me sittin' in the house holdin' Paul's baby is funny, do ya?"

"Well, since you asked. . ."

Jan bristled. "Hey, I'm talkin' here, and I wasn't done, so kindly don't interrupt!"

"You're totally out there, you know that?"

"Oh, you should talk. You know why guys like you have to prove their manhood?" Jan's eyes narrowed as he pointed at Stuart. "Because you're afraid."

"Oh yeah, right," Stuart said gruffly, shifting his stance. Then he drew his shoulders back and stood to his full height, which Star figured probably wasn't more than five feet ten. "For your information, Mr. Tattoo Man, I'm not afraid of anything."

Jan's face reddened, and he took another step toward Stuart. Like the ferocious-looking black panther on his arm, Jan looked ready to attack. "Why, I oughta—"

"What are you gonna do—sit on me?"

"If that's what it takes to shut you up."

Emma's eyes widened; Pam's mouth dropped open, as did Paul's. Ruby Lee folded her hands as though praying, and Star just sat there shaking her head. Men could be so juvenile sometimes—always having to prove how tough they were. Well, if she had to choose sides, she'd go with the biker. The baseball-cap geek acted like a big know-it-all. He probably thought he was smarter and better than Jan. At least Jan seemed real and down-to-earth. He'd proven that when he'd spilled his guts about driving under the influence and doing time in jail. It was doubtful that Stuart ever had so much as a speeding ticket, and even if he had, he'd probably never admit it.

Star leaned forward, waiting to see who would land the first blow, but before either man could raise a hand, Ruby Lee left her seat and stepped between them. "I think you both should calm down. We came here to learn about quilting, not watch the two of you act like a couple of silly schoolboys trying to one-up each other."

The men, both red-faced, stood a few more seconds looking peeved, but finally returned to their seats.

Emma, talking fast and appearing to be quite shaken, began explaining more of the things they'd be learning over the next several weeks. Everyone listened, and thankfully there were no more nasty comments from either Stuart or Jan. Star really felt sorry for poor Emma.

I'll bet she never expected anything like this would happen during her quilt class.

By the time class was over, Emma had given each person some material and a template for their star-shaped pattern, along with instructions on how during the week they should mark, cut, and pin the pieces together.

Everyone told Emma good-bye, and as they headed out the door, Jan looked over at Paul and said, "You're a lucky man to have such a cute baby."

Paul smiled and nodded. "Yes, I feel very blessed."

Star glanced at Stuart and Pam, who were arguing again about the goat escapade as they headed to their car. *I'll bet that man's wishing he didn't have to come back here again. Maybe he's wondering what sort of excuse he can make up to get out of learning how to quilt. It'll be interesting to see whether he shows up for the class next week. Bet he doesn't. Bet prissy Pam comes alone.*

CHAPTER 7

I can't believe you," Pam said through tight lips.

"What's that supposed to mean?" Stuart asked as he directed his SUV onto the highway.

"The way you acted during the quilt class was absolutely inexcusable!" She narrowed her eyes as she stared at him, hoping he'd realize how angry she was. "Emma Yoder seems like a very nice lady, but after today, she's probably wondering why she ever agreed to teach us quilting."

"If you're talking about the goat escapade, I was only trying to help. It wasn't my fault that crazy critter thought my baseball cap would make a great morning snack. Besides, if you'll recall, Emma thanked me for helping out."

"I wasn't just talking about the goat or your stupid cap. I was mostly referring to the fact that throughout the entire class you were either nodding off or saying something rude."

His thick eyebrows furrowed. "What are you talking about, Pam?

I never said anything rude."

"You most certainly did."

"Such as?"

"For one thing, the way you talked to the biker was terrible. When he introduced himself, it wasn't right to make fun of his name. Why did you have to insult him like that?"

Stuart gave a nonchalant shrug. "Well, what can I say? Jan's a dumb name for a guy. Besides, he had it coming, the way he was ribbing me about how I chased after the goat."

"When you made an issue of his name, you had no way of knowing he was going to say anything to you about the goat. And even if you think Jan's name is dumb, you didn't have to make a big deal about it and say it sounded like a girly girl's name." Pam gripped the straps of her purse tightly, trying to keep her emotions under control. "Then getting on his case about staying in the house with the women while you were trying to round up the goat made things even worse. In fact, the way you acted today made you no better than him."

"I was only stating the obvious. Do you have a problem with it?"

"As a matter of fact, I do."

"Yeah, well, I wasn't gonna let some tattooed bully push me around."

"Jan hardly seems like a bully. I think he was just defending his pride."

"Oh, and I wasn't?"

She sighed. "You're impossible, Stuart."

"Give me a break. I'm no more impossible than you." He glanced over at Pam and frowned. "I can't believe you'd expect me to learn how to quilt or sit in that boring class with a bunch of weird people."

"They're not weird; they're just different. And you need to get over your prejudices."

"I'm not prejudiced."

"Whatever you say." Pam knew she should stop right there, but she couldn't. "So, let me ask you something, Stuart. How does it feel to be Mr. Right twenty-four hours a day?"

He stared straight ahead. "I think we should find something else to do together. Something other than quilting."

"Like what?"

"I don't know. Anything that doesn't involve sitting in some dimly lit room, listening to an Amish woman bore us about the history of quilts. I'm surprised everyone wasn't sleeping."

"Emma was only giving us some background on quilting so we'd have a better idea of what makes up the different quilt patterns. We've got homework to do this week, and next Saturday she'll be teaching us the next step involved in making our wall hangings, so I'm sure the class will be more interesting."

"For you, maybe," he mumbled. "Wish now I'd never taken you fishing!"

"You know what?" Pam shot back. "That's one thing I can agree with you about. I wish you'd never taken me fishing either!"

Soon after her quilting students left, Emma went to the kitchen to fix some lunch. The morning hadn't gone at all the way she'd planned, and she couldn't get the thought out of her mind that God had sent her some very unusual people to teach.

Am I really up to the task? Emma asked herself as she removed a loaf of whole-wheat bread from the bread box. *Is there more than quilting I should teach these people?* With the exception of Ruby Lee, who'd appeared to be fairly bright and cheerful, the others in the class seemed to have some serious issues they were dealing with. She was concerned about Star and

Paul because they'd both recently lost a family member, although, from what Emma could tell, Paul seemed to be dealing with his wife's death fairly well. Perhaps he'd found comfort in his baby girl, and maybe he had a strong faith in God. When he'd leaned forward to pick up a toy the baby had dropped, Emma had noticed a silver chain with a cross around his neck. She figured he probably wore it as an indication of his religious beliefs.

Star, on the other hand, had been dressed almost completely in black. Was it because she was mourning her grandmother's death, or did she just prefer to dress that way? With the exception of the goat incident, when nearly everyone had been laughing, Emma hadn't seen Star laugh or smile during the two-hour class.

Emma paused to chuckle, thinking how funny Stuart had looked, running around the yard chasing Maggie after she'd grabbed hold of his hat. For Pam's sake, Emma had tried not to laugh, but with everyone else laughing as they watched out the window, she just couldn't help herself.

"A day without smiling is a wasted day," Emma murmured as she took a can of tuna fish from the pantry. That used to be one of Ivan's favorite sayings, and he'd lived up to it by looking on the brighter side of life and having a cheerful smile and a good sense of humor. Emma tried to be cheerful, too—especially since Ivan died. Laughter was good medicine for the soul, and looking for things to be joyful about had helped Emma through the worst of her grief.

Turning her thoughts to Star again, Emma wondered if the somber young woman might be angry with someone. Or perhaps she was just unsure of herself. Whatever the reason, Emma hated to see Star or anyone else look so sad.

It touched Emma's heart to know that Star had come here because her grandmother had wanted her to learn how to quilt as a remembrance of her.

Emma knew all about things that made a person remember a loved one. She thought about Ivan and how he'd died a few weeks before her sixty-fifth birthday. He'd made something special for Emma—a finely crafted quilt rack, which she'd found three days after her birthday, hidden in the barn behind a stack of hay. Ivan had attached a note to the gift, telling Emma how much he loved her. The love and respect she and Ivan had felt for each other would always be with her, and every time she looked at the quilt rack he'd made, she would think of him fondly.

Knowing she needed to finish making her lunch, Emma removed a jar of mayonnaise from her propane-operated refrigerator, letting her thoughts go to the muscular man with the black leather vest and tattoos who'd come to her class to learn how to quilt. With the exception of his encounters with Stuart, Jan had seemed nice enough. And he'd certainly looked content when he'd held Paul's baby. However, Emma had a feeling the man with the girl's name had a painful and perhaps shameful past.

Then there was the married couple, Stuart and Pam. Not once during the morning had they said a nice word to each other. Stuart seemed to have a need to prove his manhood, and he'd obviously been bored and probably felt forced to come to the class.

I wish Stuart could have met my Ivan and heard how kindly he spoke to me. Emma grimaced. *Of course, Pam wasn't very kind to Stuart either. Those disgusted looks she gave him, not to mention her unkind words, makes me wonder if she loves her husband at all.*

Perhaps after a few weeks of getting to know each of her students, Emma could get them to open up and share what was on their hearts. If she knew more about these people, she would know what things from her own life she could share that might help them, too.

With her sandwich made, Emma took a seat at the table and bowed her head. *Dear Lord,* she silently prayed, *if I'm supposed to do more than just teach this group of people how to quilt, then please give me wisdom, a sensitive heart, and of course, Your direction.*

The back door opened, and Mary stepped into the room just as Emma finished her prayer.

"*Wie geht's?*" Mary asked.

"I'm a little tired but otherwise fine."

"How'd the class go?"

Emma motioned to the chair beside her. "If you'd like to take a seat while I eat my sandwich, I'll tell you about it. And you're welcome to join me. I can make another sandwich for you."

"No, you go ahead. I had a bowl of soup before I came over here." Mary pulled out a chair and sat down. "So how'd it go with the class? Were you able to teach that. . .uh. . .rather unusual group anything today?"

"I'll admit I was taken aback when I saw the people who'd come to my class. From the phone calls I'd received, I'd really thought I would be teaching all women."

"And I bet you didn't expect one of them to be dressed all in black with a ring in her nose."

"No, I sure didn't."

"When I answered the door for you this morning, I was more than a little surprised by the group waiting on your porch."

Emma took a bite of her sandwich and sipped some water. "I was, too. And I certainly never expected someone like Jan Sweet to join the class."

Mary tipped her head. "Jan Sweet?"

"Jah. He was the big, tall, muscular man dressed in biker clothes."

"Oh, so his name is Jan?"

Emma nodded. "One of the other men, Stuart, teased Jan about his name. Said it was a girly girl's name, and Jan didn't take that too well."

Mary's eyes widened. "What happened?"

"Jan pretty much told Stuart to keep his opinions to himself." Emma frowned. "For a minute there, I was afraid Jan might hit Stuart or something."

With a worried frown, Mary placed her hand on Emma's arm. "*Ach*, Mom. Do you really think you ought to be teaching these people? I mean, what if—"

Emma held up her hand. "As you well know, God made everyone, and we're all uniquely different."

"Jah, some more than others." The worry lines in Mary's forehead deepened.

Emma chuckled. "Be that as it may, God cares for them just as much as He does you and me. I'm sure that He looks beyond what people are to who they can become, and I have a feeling way down deep in my heart that God brought the people who came here today for more than just learning to quilt."

"What other reason could there be?"

Emma took another drink of water and blotted her lips with a napkin. "Well, after just one meeting, I could sense that most of them are dealing with some kind of a painful or distressing issue. And with God's help and His words of wisdom, I hope I'll be able to say or do something that might help them all spiritually or emotionally, in addition to teaching them how to quilt."

Mary's face relaxed a bit. "One thing I do know is that you have been blessed with the ability to sense when people are hurting. You proved that many times during my childhood, and especially during my teen years when I had a problem and didn't share it until you wormed it right out of me."

Emma grinned. "Well, I hope I won't have to worm anything out of my students, but I would ask you to pray that the Lord will give me insight and wisdom in knowing what to say and when to say it."

Mary nodded. "I'll be praying for you, as well as your students."

CHAPTER 8

For the last three days, Jan and Terry had been roofing a house in LaGrange, and by the time Jan got home from work each evening, he was too tired to do anything but fix a quick bite of supper, play a few tunes on his harmonica, and fall into bed. The roof on the house in LaGrange had been steep, and he was glad to have it done. Every muscle in his legs seemed to hurt from the energy it took to keep his balance on that high-pitched roof.

But Thursday morning it was raining too hard to begin his next job in Middlebury, so Jan was at home, just him and his dog, Brutus. He'd acquired the black and tan German shepherd two years ago when it was a pup. Brutus had proved to be a good companion, although due to Jan's busy work schedule during the warmer months, he didn't spend much time with the dog.

A roll of thunder sounded in the distance as Jan poured himself a cup of coffee and took a seat at the kitchen table. Brutus, sleeping peacefully under the table, didn't budge; he just began to snore.

Jan decided that today would be a good opportunity for him to begin working on his quilting project. With Saturday only two days away, he wanted to be sure he'd done his homework as Emma had instructed. What she'd asked them to do seemed easy enough, so he was sure he could get it done quickly. He figured once he finished the wall hanging, he might try to make a full-sized quilt. He could donate it to one of the local benefit auctions. There always seemed to be plenty of those going on in the area, since that's how many of the Amish raised money to help with medical expenses. One thing for sure: Jan couldn't wait to tell his probation officer when he saw her next week that he'd found something creative to do.

He thought about Emma and smiled. Through his job and living in Shipshewana, he'd met other Amish people, but he hadn't gotten to know any of them very well. Emma Yoder seemed like the type of person who easily made friends, and her patience with those in the class last Saturday made him think she was easygoing and accepting of others.

Emma kinda reminds me of Mom, God rest her soul, Jan thought as he gulped down his lukewarm coffee and headed to the living room to get the material he needed. *She's even got that same perky smile and soft way of speaking Mom had. Wish I could say the same for my dad.*

Jan's mother had died from a brain tumor when he was seventeen. A year later, his dad split for parts unknown, never to return. Jan was an only child, and since he had no intention of living with his drunken uncle, Al, he lit out on his own, doing whatever odd jobs he could find and living in the back of his beat-up van. Jan ended up in Chicago for a time, where he'd bought a motorcycle, joined a club, and met the girl he thought he would marry. When things went sour, he stuck around for a while but finally moved on, doing everything from slinging hash at a diner in Sturgis, South Dakota, to boring factory work in Springfield, Missouri. Several years later, while living in Grand Rapids, Michigan, Jan learned the roofing trade under the guidance of a motorcycle buddy who had his own business. After a few years, Jan became restless, so he moved on and eventually ended up in Shipshewana, where he'd opened his own business. It was the first time he'd stayed in one place for more than a year, and since he really liked it in this quiet, quaint little town, he felt sure he would stay.

Jerking his thoughts back to the present, Jan was about to grab his sack of material when someone knocked on the front door.

"Now I wonder who that could be," Jan mumbled, ambling across the room. With the rain coming down as hard as it was, he couldn't imagine anyone being out in this weather. He could hear the rain from inside as it pelted his roof.

When Jan opened the door, he was surprised to see Selma Nash, the elderly woman who lived in the house next door, standing on his porch. She held a black umbrella in one hand, but it hadn't done much to protect her clothes, because the skirt of her dress and sleeves on her light-weight jacket were wet.

" 'Mornin', Selma. What brings you to my door on this rainy spring day?" he asked, offering her a smile and hoping it would wipe away the deep frown that graced her wrinkled face. "Is everything okay?"

Selma's frown deepened. "No, young man, everything's not okay."

"No?"

She shook her head.

"What's wrong?"

"I'm getting sick and tired of your dog tearing up my flower beds. If you don't do something about it, I'm going to call animal control and have that mutt hauled off to the pound!"

Jan's eyebrows shot up. "Brutus is here in the house with me. Fact is, he's sleepin' under the kitchen table right now, so I don't see how he can be diggin' in your flower beds."

Selma lowered her umbrella and gave it a little shake. "Now don't you play games with me, Mr. Sweet. I know the mess Brutus made wasn't done just now. He did it yesterday while you were at work."

"How do you know it was my dog and not someone else's?" Jan questioned. "There's several other dogs in this here neighborhood, you know."

"Humph! I know it was Brutus."

"How can you be so sure? Did you actually see him diggin' up the flowers?"

"No, but I saw him wandering around my yard soon after you left for work, and it wasn't long after that when I noticed that my flower beds had been torn up." She shook the umbrella a little harder this time, sending a spray of water in Jan's direction.

He stepped back, but not before getting hit in the face with a few drops of liquid sunshine. "I ain't believin' that my Brutus tore up your flower beds, but I'll do my best to keep my eye on him from here on out."

She pursed her lips and tipped her head back as she stared up at him, her milky blue eyes narrowing into tiny slits. "And just how are you planning to do that? With you working all day, that mangy mutt of yours is free to do whatever he wants. You know, there are laws about controlling your pets."

Jan couldn't argue with any of that. When he put Brutus outside every morning, he had no idea what the dog was up to all day. But he didn't think Brutus wandered very far, because when he arrived home from work, the dog was usually lying on the front porch waiting for him. Since the house he'd bought a few years ago was in the country and on nearly an acre of land, Jan had never felt the need to chain the dog up or build him a pen. Now, with Brutus being under suspicion with the neighbor, Jan figured he'd better do something about the situation. He sure didn't want the old lady calling animal control and having Brutus hauled off to the pound.

"I'll tell you what," he said, smiling at Selma. "I'll build Brutus a dog pen just as soon as I find the time. Until then, I'll keep him in the garage when I'm gone. Is that okay with you?"

"Yes, I suppose that will keep him from digging up my flowers again, but what about the pansies he's already ruined? Are you going to buy me some new ones?"

Jan hated to shell out money for flowers he wasn't sure his dog had wrecked, but he didn't want to rile the old lady anymore than she already was. So rather than argue about it, he reached into his jeans' pocket and pulled out a twenty-dollar bill. "Think this'll cover the cost of some new posies?"

She gave a quick nod. "It was pansies your dog destroyed, Mr. Sweet, and you'd better see that it doesn't happen again."

"No, it sure won't."

Selma lifted the umbrella over her head and hurried away, muttering something under her breath about wishing she had a better neighbor—someone without a dog.

When Jan returned to the living room, now out of the mood to work on the wall hanging, he spotted Brutus lying on the sofa. "Mrs. Nash would probably pitch a fit if she knew I allowed you to be on the furniture." Jan plopped down beside Brutus and reached out to stroke the dog's silky ears. "Lucky for you I didn't invite her in."

Brutus grunted and nuzzled Jan's hand with his wet nose. Jan was glad for the loyalty of the dog, because he knew some people couldn't be trusted. With the exception of his biker buddies, Jan didn't allow himself to get close to many people—especially women. He hadn't lived forty years without learning a few things about the opposite sex. He'd been burned once by a cute little thing who'd promised to love him forever, and he'd vowed sometime ago that he'd never let it happen again.

Deciding to watch TV for a while, he reached for the remote under his sleeping dog's paw. As he did, he looked closer and noticed some dirt caked on the pads of Brutus's front feet.

"Brutus, was that you diggin' up the flower beds next door?"

Oblivious to the words of his master, Brutus started making muffled barking noises as he continued to sleep.

Jan smiled to himself as he watched the dog, still dreaming and now making digging motions with his two front feet. How comical it looked with those paws moving while his muzzle quivered as if he was trying to bark. All Jan could do was chuckle as he thought, *Think I'd better get that dog pen built as soon as I can.*

Goshen

Ruby Lee stepped into the sanctuary to practice the songs she'd picked out for Sunday. A knot formed in her stomach. It was hard to believe she and Gene had been here for ten years already. It was also difficult to believe that the joy they'd felt when Gene had been asked to take this church was now far removed. At least for Ruby Lee. Gene went about his ministerial duties, acting as though nothing was wrong, but she was sure that deep inside he was hurting—probably more than her, truth be told. She'd seen her husband's pained expression when he'd come home from the last few board meetings. She'd heard his concern when he talked about the future of their church. If she only knew of something that might make things better. If she could just take away the pain and frustration tugging at her and Gene's hearts.

Ruby Lee knew she should go to the altar and leave her burdens there, but she didn't feel like praying today. Oh, she'd brought this problem to the Lord many times already. Nothing had changed, and it was beginning to affect her ability to minister to others. She felt as if her faith was being tested and wondered if an end was in sight.

With a sigh of resignation, Ruby Lee took a seat at the piano and opened the hymnbook. Besides the lively choruses they sang every Sunday to open the worship service, they always did a few traditional hymns. Ruby Lee's favorite was "Rock of Ages," one of the songs she'd decided to play this Sunday.

" 'Rock of ages,'" she sang as she played along, " 'cleft for me. Let me hide myself in thee.'"

She certainly felt like hiding these days—hiding from the church people—hiding from her friends—and yes, even hiding from God. With the problems the church had been having, her faith in those who called themselves Christians had begun to dwindle little by little, week by week. But she couldn't let on. She had to keep her chin high and put a smile on her face so no one would know about the deep ache in her heart. After all, she was the pastor's wife, and it was her duty to set a good example to others. It wouldn't be right to let anyone in the congregation know how truly miserable she felt. It might jeopardize Gene's ministry.

As Ruby Lee's fingers glided easily over the piano keys, she continued to play the rest of the song. No longer able to sing, her thoughts went to the quilting class she'd attended last Saturday. Emma Yoder seemed like such a pleasant, patient person. The kind she could easily make her friend.

In two days she would be going to Emma's house for another lesson, and Ruby Lee wondered how things would go. *Too bad I'm not Emma's only student,* she thought wistfully. *It would be easier to learn quilting if the others weren't there, asking so many unnecessary questions and making catty remarks, the way Stuart Johnston did last week.*

It didn't take a genius to see that Pam and Stuart's marriage was strained—maybe even in deep trouble. During Gene's years of preaching, he'd counseled many couples with marriage problems. Some listened to his advice, and others continued down the same old path that had brought them to his office for counseling. A good marriage took commitment and a desire to meet the needs of one's spouse. When selfishness and always wanting to have one's own way took over, it spelled trouble. And from what Ruby Lee had seen during the quilt class, both Pam and Stuart had issues they were dealing with—issues that had affected their marriage.

Then there was the young woman who called herself Star. From the way she talked, and her whole demeanor, it had been obvious to Ruby Lee that Star had a chip on her shoulder and probably needed to let her defenses down. Ruby Lee wondered why Star had worn a black sweatshirt with the hood up on her head the whole time they'd been in class. Was she trying to make some kind of statement, hiding something under that hood? Or could the defiant young woman be one of those "gothic" people Ruby Lee had seen around town? Star was a pretty girl, so why she would hide her natural beauty was a bit baffling to Ruby Lee. Perhaps Star needed some counseling, too.

The biker with the big biceps probably had a few issues as well. But with the exception of his encounter with Stuart, Jan had seemed fairly easygoing. And even though Jan looked like the type who might punch someone in the nose if they looked at him the wrong way, Ruby Lee had a hunch that he was a really just a big ole softy with a heart of gold.

The young Hispanic schoolteacher who'd recently lost his wife seemed fairly stable, yet Ruby Lee figured he must still be hurting pretty bad. Who wouldn't hurt if they'd lost their spouse and been left with a baby to raise? It was a shame that Paul's little girl would grow up never knowing her mother.

I should be very kind to these people, she thought. *I'm a pastor's wife, and it's my duty to set a good example to others. But how can I do that when I feel so angry and depressed myself?*

Ruby Lee leaned forward, resting her forehead on the piano keys. *If You will, God, please give me a sense of peace.*

———

As Star left the Goshen Walmart after working the early-morning shift where she stocked shelves, she frowned. It was raining hard, and by the time she reached her car, she was soaking wet.

Well, let it rain, she thought. *I have no place but home to go today anyway.* Still, she didn't care for this drenching wet weather. It was depressing, and when it rained, she didn't like being cooped up inside.

Star thought she might spend the rest of the day cutting out the pieces for the star pattern that would be in the center of her wall hanging. After that was done, she hoped to get some more lyrics written on the song she'd started a few weeks ago. Maybe someday she would find a way to get some of her music published. Maybe someday her musical abilities would be recognized. But for now, she'd have to be content with playing her guitar and singing her songs at the coffee shop in downtown Goshen on Friday nights. Some of the kids from the local college hung out there, and a few performed on the little stage; although no one but Star sang original songs.

Who knows? Star thought as she started her car's engine and pulled out of the parking lot. *Maybe the right person will be sitting in the coffee shop some night, and I'll get discovered.*

She let go of the steering wheel with one hand and slapped the side of her head. *Dumb. Stupid. Like that's ever gonna happen. I'm just a nobody who no one cares about. It's just like Mom always says: I'm full of big ideas that will never come true. And now that Grandma's gone, I'll probably never find anyone who truly loves me for the person I am. I'll always be lost—like a falling star that nobody ever noticed.*

Some new words to one of the songs she'd been working on popped into Star's head, and she began to sing in a whispered tone: "It's hard to breathe; it's hard to sleep; it's hard to know who you are when you're a lost and falling star."

CHAPTER 9

Mishawaka, Indiana

I'm ready to work on my quilt project now," Pam called to Stuart, who sat on the sofa in the family room watching TV with his feet propped on the coffee table.

No reply.

"Stuart, are you listening to me?"

Still no response.

Pam pushed her son's toy truck out of the way with her foot and stepped in front of the TV.

"Hey! You're blocking my view." Stuart gave Pam a determined, angry look and waved her away.

She stood firm, both hands on her hips. "It's the only way I can get your attention."

"What do you want?" He peered around her to look at the TV.

She moved to the right so his view was still blocked. "I said I'm ready to work on my quilting project now."

"That's nice. Would you please move out of my way?"

Pointing a finger in his direction, Pam felt her face heat. "The next quilt class is only two days away, and you promised we could work on our wall hangings together this evening."

Stuart shook his head. "I never promised anything of the sort. You said you wanted to work on your quilt project, and I said that was fine with me." He pointed to the TV. "I'm watching a baseball game. At least I was until you interrupted me."

Pam's irritation mounted. "If you don't work on your project tonight, you won't have the first phase of your wall hanging done before Saturday."

"I'll work on it tomorrow night."

"Tomorrow's Devin's piano recital, and afterwards, we're taking the kids out for ice cream. Remember?"

"Oh yeah, that's right. Okay then, I'll work on the stupid wall hanging Saturday morning—before we head to Shipshewana." He yawned and stretched his arms over his head. "Or maybe I won't work on it at all. Maybe I won't even go this week. I might sleep in on Saturday."

She narrowed her eyes. "You'd better not go back on your word."

He leaned to the left, craning his neck to see the TV again. "Oh, great! I missed that last play, and now the other team is up to bat."

Pam gritted her teeth. "Why is it that baseball is more important than me?"

"It's not."

"Yes it is. If it wasn't, you'd turn off the TV, come into the dining room, and cut out the material for your star pattern. We can visit while we cut and pin the pieces in place."

Stuart's face tightened and tiny wrinkles formed across his forehead. "Look, Pam, when you went fishing with me, you didn't have to do anything before we went."

"And your point is?"

"I didn't expect you to dig worms for bait or even get the fishing gear out of the closet. I did all those things for you. All you had to do was sit in the boat and fish."

Her irritation increased. "Are you saying you think I should work on my quilt project and yours, too?"

A smile played at the corners of his mouth. "That'd be nice."

"Oh sure! Then you can just show up at Emma's on Saturday with a big smile on your face and let everyone think you'd done what she asked."

He shrugged.

"If you don't want to do your homework, that's up to you, but don't expect me to do it for you!" Pam turned on her heels and stomped out of the room. She didn't think any amount of counseling or doing things together would save their marriage. They were heading down a one-way street, and unless a miracle transpired, she feared their journey might end in divorce.

Elkhart

"Could this week get any worse?" Paul grumbled while his daughter fussed in her playpen. A parent/teacher conference one night and a meeting with the school principal the next evening was just too much for one week. Both times Paul had asked Carla, a teenager from church, to watch Sophia. Carla seemed capable enough, but both evenings when he'd arrived home, Sophia had been sobbing. It was bad enough that he had to drop his little girl off at the day care center every morning before school. He wished he didn't have to leave her with a sitter whenever he had to be away during the evening. He wished, too, that his sister, Maria, could watch Sophia all the time, but with her part-time job at the bank, plus caring for her three active girls, that just wasn't possible. On the days Paul took Sophia to day care, she still cried as soon as he pulled up in front of the building. It nearly broke his heart when she reached her little arms out, as though begging him to stay.

Paul hoped Maria could watch Sophia on the remaining Saturdays he'd be attending the quilt classes so he wouldn't have to take her along, like he'd done last week, or worse yet, leave her with a sitter she didn't know. Even though Sophia had been good during the two hours they were at Emma's, it had been hard for Paul to concentrate on all that Emma had been trying to teach them. It was important for him to learn some quilting techniques, since he'd decided that he would definitely try to finish the quilt for Sophia, and he hoped by doing so it might bring him some closure.

Tonight, Paul was thankful to be home, but he had some papers to grade. Sophia was in the dining room with him, but she wasn't happy being in the playpen rather than on her daddy's lap, like she was accustomed to doing most evenings. Still, it was better than having someone else watch her.

"Oh Lorinda," Paul whispered, rubbing a sore spot on his forehead. "How I wish you were here with me right now, holding our precious baby daughter."

Shipshewana

Emma had just taken a seat in front of her treadle sewing machine when she heard the back door swing open. A few seconds later, her eight-year-old granddaughter, Lisa, skipped into the room.

"*Daadi* built a bonfire out back, and we're gonna roast hot dogs and marshmallows soon," the blond-haired, blue-eyed little girl announced. "Would you like to come over and eat with us, *Grossmammi?*"

Emma smiled and gave Lisa a hug. "I appreciate the offer, but I've already had my supper."

"Then come for some marshmallows." Lisa grinned up at Emma and smacked her lips. "They taste *wunderbaar gut*."

"I think marshmallows are wonderful good, too, but I'm busy sewing right now. Maybe some other time when your daed builds a bonfire I can join you," Emma said.

Lisa's lower lip protruded in a pout. Emma hated to disappoint the child, but if she didn't get the piecing done on this quilt, she'd never have it finished in time for the benefit auction that would be held in a few months. She also hadn't quite completed the quilt for the fall wedding she would attend. Still, she didn't want to pass up an opportunity to be with some of her family.

She patted her granddaughter's arm. "I'll be over later on, after I get some sewing done. How's that sound?"

A wide smile stretched across Lisa's face. "Sew real fast, grossmammi!"

Emma smiled as the rosy-cheeked little girl scampered out of the room. It was nice living so close to Mary and her family. Not only could they be there whenever she had a need, but almost always someone was at home next door for Emma to visit when she felt lonely. Other times, especially during the warmer months when her windows were open, it was nice just hearing her grandchildren on the other side of the fence, laughing and playing in their yard. It made her feel connected to them.

For the next hour, Emma worked on the quilt. As she sewed, she thought about her upcoming quilt class. She hoped it would go better than last week's had, and that everyone would take an active interest in the things she planned to teach. Last Saturday, when Stuart had fallen asleep, she'd been worried that he might be bored or hadn't understood what she'd been trying to explain. Even though Emma knew a lot about quilting, she wasn't sure she'd presented the information clearly or interestingly enough. She would make sure to go a little slower this week and not let her nerves take over. And hopefully there would be no interruptions, like Maggie getting out of her pen, or Stuart and Jan exchanging heated words and nearly getting into a fight. Emma had found that most unsettling.

Emma's thoughts came to a halt when she heard the wail of a siren, which seemed to be drawing closer all the time. When she saw red lights flashing through the window and realized they were coming up the driveway that separated her home from Mary's, she became very concerned.

She sniffed the air. *Is that smoke I smell?*

Hurrying to the window, Emma gasped as two fire trucks pulled in. Moving to the side window, she noticed smoke and flames coming from the shed where her son-in-law kept their wood and gardening tools. The shed wasn't far from the barn, and Emma feared that if they didn't get the fire out soon, the barn might also catch on fire.

With a quick yet fervent prayer for everyone's safety, Emma rushed out the back door as the sound of crackling wood reached her ears.

CHAPTER 10

Goshen

Star had just sat down at the kitchen table to cut out her pattern pieces when Mom entered the room.

"I just looked over the movie schedule," Mom said, holding the newspaper out to Star. "That new romantic comedy we've seen advertised on TV is playing at Linway Cinema 14. Would you like to go?"

Star shook her head. "No, I'm good. I'm just gonna hang out here tonight."

"Doing what?"

"I'll be busy cutting out the pattern pieces that will make up my wall hanging. Gotta have this first part done before Saturday." She pointed to the black-and-gold material she'd chosen.

Mom's eyebrows drew together as she frowned. "I still think it's a dumb idea for you to waste your time on that quilt class."

Star gritted her teeth. *Not this again. So much for trying to impress Mom with something I'm doing.* "Grandma wanted me to go, or she wouldn't have reserved a spot for me."

Mom looked at Star like she still didn't get it.

"I miss Grandma, and taking the class so I can learn how to quilt makes me feel closer to her," Star said.

"You can miss her all you want, but I'm the only parent you have, and you ought to appreciate me and be willing to spend some time together when we have the chance."

"I'd spend more time with you if we liked more of the same things." What Star really wanted to say was, *"Yeah, like all the time you spent with me when I was growing up?"* But she couldn't get the spiteful words out of her mouth.

"What kind of things are you talking about?" Mom asked.

Star placed her scissors on the table and looked up at Mom. "I like to play the guitar, sing, and write songs, and you don't like music at all," she said, trying to sound nonchalant. One thing she didn't need this evening was a blowup with Mom. They had those too often as it was.

"That's not true. I just don't care for the kind of music you sing and play."

Star's defenses began to rise, despite her resolve to keep things calm. "And just what do you think's wrong with my music?"

"It's slow and the lyrics you write are depressing."

"Maybe that's because I feel depressed a lot of the time."

Mom folded her arms and glared at Star. "You have nothing more to be depressed about than I do, but I don't go around singing doom and gloom."

Star clenched her piece of material so tightly that her knuckles turned white. "It's not doom and gloom. I'm just expressing the way I feel."

"And how is that?"

"Alone and unloved."

"You have no call to feel unloved. Ever since you were a baby, I've taken care of you. That's more than I can say for—"

Star lifted her hand. "Let's not even go there, Mom. I've heard the old story so many times I know every word by heart."

"Well, good. Then you ought to appreciate the sacrifices I've made for you and get that chip off your shoulder."

"Yeah, okay, whatever." Star figured there was no point in saying anything more. Mom had raised her single-handedly and thought she deserved the Mother-of-the-Year award. Anything more Star had to say would only fall on deaf ears.

Deciding this might be a good time to change the subject, Star said, "You know, Mom, it wouldn't hurt you to do something creative, something different for a change. I've actually met some rather interesting people at the quilt class. I really think I'm gonna enjoy getting to know them all better, too—especially Emma; she really seems nice."

"You, making friends? You've pushed people away most of your life. What's different now?"

"Well, there must be a reason Grandma wanted me to learn how to quilt. Who knows—maybe it goes beyond quilting; and to tell you the truth, I'm kind of anxious to find out."

"Is that so?" Mom put her hands on her hips. "Well, we'll just see how long that lasts."

"Boy, Mom, you can be so negative." Star flipped the ends of her hair over her shoulder. "I really don't care what you think. I have a feeling that Emma's classes are just what I need right now. Learning to quilt could even be a positive thing for me."

"You've got to be kidding! It sounds to me like you're putting more faith in this Amish woman than you ever have with me."

It's kinda hard to put your faith in someone who thinks more about themselves than she does her daughter, Star thought. With all the little lies Mom had told over the years, Star didn't see how she could be expected to have much faith in her. Of course, in all fairness to Mom, Star had to admit that since they'd moved to Goshen, Mom had seemed a bit more settled and not quite so flighty. Star hadn't caught her telling any white lies either, so at least that much was good.

Mom tapped her foot as she continued. "You really don't know the half of it. I gave up a lot to give you a decent life, and—"

"Before you say anything more and get yourself in an uproar, just listen to what I have to say," Star interrupted.

"Okay, sure; go right ahead."

"As I was going to say about Emma. . .she truly listens when people talk, and she seems genuine, too. She reminds me of Grandma in a lot of ways. She alone would give me a reason to continue going to the classes."

Seeing that she had Mom's attention, Star rushed on. "Then there's this biker dude, who I'm pretty sure is nothing more than a big ole teddy bear. There's also a very pleasant African-American woman who's a preacher's wife, and a Hispanic schoolteacher who has the cutest baby girl. It's a shame the poor guy's wife passed away six months ago. Oh, and there's a married couple attending the class. I can't figure them out yet, but they made the time in class quite interesting. It's almost funny to watch 'em pick on each other."

"Those people sound unique all right, but I still think you're all talk about this and won't follow through." Mom shrugged. "But you go ahead and do what you want; you always have."

Star's defenses rose. "Just forget it, Mom. You can't see past your own issues, but mark my words: I'm gonna prove you wrong about this, because I'll not only finish the class, but I'm gonna learn to make a beautiful quilted wall hanging, 'cause that's what Grandma wanted me to do!" Star picked up her scissors and started cutting another pattern piece.

"So are you going to see the movie with me or not?" Mom asked, waving the newspaper in front of Star's face.

"Didn't you hear me the first time? I said no. I'm going to spend the evening working on my quilt assignment."

Mom stared at Star with a look of disgust. "Fine then; I'll see if Mike wants to see the movie with me!"

"That's a really great idea," Star mumbled as Mom hurried from the room. "He's probably better company than me anyway." Trying not to let the tears clouding her vision spill over, she squared her shoulders. *Boy, just once I'd like to be the one who says, "I told you so."*

Shipshewana

By the time Emma reached Mary's yard, she was out of breath and panting. She gasped when she saw how the fire had gotten out of control. And if the wind started to blow, the house could be in danger. Maybe Emma's own home, as well.

Don't borrow trouble, Emma told herself as she hurried to Mary and her family watching the firemen battle the flames. *We just need to trust God and pray for the best.*

"Is everyone okay?" Emma asked, touching Mary's arm.

"Jah, we're all fine," Brian said before Mary could respond. "I'm afraid I wasn't watching close enough, and some of the sparks from our bonfire caught the shed on fire." He wiped the sweat from his forehead and pushed a lock of sandy brown hair aside. "I tried putting it out with the garden hose, but it didn't take long for me to realize that I needed the fire department, so I sent Stephen to the phone shack to make the call while I kept the water going."

"After the fire trucks got here," Mary continued, "Brian and the boys wanted to help, but they were told to stand aside and let the fireman take care of the situation." Tears gathered in the corners of her dark eyes. She appeared to be terribly shaken.

"While one group of men works at getting the fire out, another group is keeping the house and barn wet so they don't catch fire," Brian added.

Emma was glad the fire department wasn't too far from where they lived. Remembering back to the time in her early marriage when she and Ivan had lost their barn and several of the livestock because they'd lived so far from help made her glad that they'd moved closer to town several years ago, where help during a crisis was readily available.

"Where are the little ones?" Emma asked Mary, noting that the children were nowhere in sight.

"Lisa and Sharon were frightened, so I sent them next door to our neighbors," Mary replied.

"You could have sent them to my house." Emma felt a little hurt that Mary had chosen to send the children to their English neighbor's rather than over to her.

"I knew as soon as you heard the sirens you'd be coming over here," Mary explained.

Emma nodded. Even if the children had been at her house, she probably would have come. But she would have told them to stay put while she went to check on things. She'd never been one to sit around and wait to find out how things were going. She guessed it was just her curious nature, coupled with the need to help out whenever she could.

"Mary, why don't you go with your *mamm* back to her house?" Brian suggested, wiping more sweat from his brow. "There's no point in you both standing out here in the cool evening air."

Mary shook her head determinedly. "I'm not going anywhere until I know that our house and barn are safe from the fire."

CHAPTER 11

When Emma woke up on Saturday morning, she felt so tired she could hardly keep her eyes open. She'd spent most of yesterday helping Mary clean her house and get rid of the lingering smell of smoke. They'd also fed the men who'd come to help Brian clean up the burned wreckage left by the fire. They'd lost the shed, but thankfully, the barn and house hadn't caught fire. Sometime next week a new shed would be built, and Brian planned to move the fire pit farther from their outbuildings.

Emma had been glad to hear that. The thought of losing a house to a fire sent chills up her spine. When she was a girl, one of her friends had died in a house fire, and several others in the family had been seriously burned. Emma had never forgotten that tragedy and hoped no one she knew would ever have to go through anything like that.

A knock sounded on the front door. Emma glanced at the clock on the kitchen wall. It was ten minutes to ten, so she figured one of her quilting students had arrived a little early.

When Emma answered the door, she was surprised to see Lamar Miller on her porch, holding his straw hat in one hand.

"*Guder mariye*, Emma," he said with a friendly grin.

"Good morning," Emma replied without returning his smile. She didn't want to appear rude, but at the same time, she didn't want to encourage Lamar in any way.

"I heard about the fire at Brian and Mary's and wanted to make sure everything was okay," Lamar explained.

"Except for some frazzled nerves, everyone's fine. It could have been so much worse. Brian will have to replace their shed, of course, but other than that, nothing was damaged."

"That's good to hear," Lamar said with a look of relief. He shifted his weight slightly and cleared his throat. "The other reason I came by is I'm heading to the bakery to get some doughnuts and wondered if you'd like to go along."

She shook her head. "My quilt class begins at ten o'clock, and my students should be arriving soon, so I'll be busy all morning. But *danki* for asking," she quickly added.

Lamar placed his straw hat on his head and pushed it down, as though worried it might fall off. "Guess we could wait till this afternoon, but by then there may not be any doughnuts left."

"That's okay; you go ahead. I'll be busy with other things this afternoon, too."

"Oh, I see." Lamar's shoulders drooped.

"Maybe another time," Emma said, although she didn't know why. She really had no intention of going anywhere with this persistent man. "Oh, and danki for your concern about the fire next door."

"I'm glad it was only minor damage." Lamar's face brightened a bit. "Maybe I'll stop by the next time I'm heading to the bakery."

Oh, great, Emma thought as she watched Lamar amble across the yard toward his horse and buggy. *I hope I have a good excuse not to go with him the next time he drops by.*

Lamar had just pulled out of Emma's yard when the Johnstons' SUV pulled in, followed by Ruby Lee's car. A short time later, Star's dilapidated-looking vehicle came up the driveway, and then Jan pedaled in on his bicycle. Everyone was there but Paul.

"Let's all go inside and take a seat," Emma suggested. "As soon as Paul gets here, we'll begin today's lesson."

Everyone agreeably pulled up a chair at the table.

"How long do we have to sit here waiting for the school teacher?" Stuart asked, glancing at his watch with a look of agitation. "I don't have time to twiddle my thumbs all day, and I'm sure not going to stay past noon because we've gotten a late start."

Pam's eyebrows squeezed together as she shot him a disgruntled look. "Oh, stop your complaining. I'm sure Paul will be here soon."

Stuart folded his arms. "Well, he'd better be."

Pam looked at Ruby Lee and scrunched up her nose. "All he ever does is complain."

Ruby Lee quickly changed the topic of conversation to the weather they'd been having this spring. That seemed to help the atmosphere some.

Emma was about to suggest that each person show what they'd done on their quilt project this week when a knock sounded on the door. She was relieved when she opened it and found Paul on the porch.

"Where's your baby girl?" Jan asked when Paul entered the room with Emma and took his seat. "I was kinda hopin' she'd be with you again."

"My sister, Maria, is taking care of Sophia today," Paul replied.

"Maria and her family were out of town last week, so that's why I brought Sophia along."

"Oh, I see."

Emma couldn't help but notice Jan's disappointment. He was obviously hoping Paul would bring the baby with him. Emma would have enjoyed seeing little Sophia again, too, but she knew it would be easier for Paul to concentrate on learning if he didn't have the baby to care for.

"Sorry I'm late," Paul said. "We were almost ready to go out the door when Sophia made a mess in her diaper. Of course, in all fairness to Maria, I had to change the baby before I dropped her off. Never thought there'd be so many messes to clean up with a baby in the house." He shook his head. "And none of those messes are fun."

"I've always figured that God gives us children to make us humble," Emma said with a chuckle. "I can't count all the times one of my children made a mess on either their clothes or mine, and it was usually on a Sunday morning when we were almost ready to leave for church."

"Where's your church located?" Paul asked.

"Oh, we don't worship in a church building the way Englishers do," Emma said. "We hold our services every other week, and the members in our district take turns hosting church in their home, barn, or shop."

"You have church in a barn?" Star asked.

Emma nodded. "Sometimes, if that's the biggest building available and we know a lot of people will be attending."

Stuart snickered and plugged his nose. "I imagine that must smell pretty raunchy with all those dirty animals in there. Do the horses' neighs and the cows' moos accompany your singing?" he asked with a smirk.

Pam's elbow connected with her husband's ribs, causing him to jump. "Stuart, don't be so rude! I'm sure there are no animals in the barn when the Amish hold their worship services."

"That's right," Emma agreed. "If we do choose to hold a service in one of our barns, the animals are taken out and everything is cleaned before the wooden benches are brought in."

Ruby Lee quirked an eyebrow. "You mean you sit on wooden benches, not padded chairs?"

"Yes. We have backless benches that are transported from home to home in one of our bench wagons whenever we have a church service, wedding, or funeral."

Tiny lines formed across Pam's forehead when she frowned. "I can't imagine sitting in church for a whole hour on a backless wooden bench."

"Actually, our services last more than an hour," Emma said. "They usually go for three hours, and sometimes longer if we're having communion or some other special service."

"Three whole hours?" Stuart groaned. "I could never sit that long on a wooden bench with no back."

"You sit that long on the bleachers when you go to some stupid sporting event," Pam said, her elbow connecting with Stuart's ribs once more.

Not only must the poor man's ribs hurt after all that jabbing, Emma thought, *but he's probably embarrassed by his wife's behavior. Should I say something or just ignore it?*

"Sitting on bleachers can't be compared to wooden benches." Stuart stood and moved his chair away from Pam. "When I'm watching a game, I jump up and down a lot. Besides, there's more to see at a baseball or football game than there would be in a barn." He shook his head slowly. "Sure am glad I'm not Amish."

"Stuart!" Pam's cheeks turned bright pink; she looked absolutely mortified.

Emma wanted to say something right then, but for the life of her, she couldn't think what. She noticed how uncomfortable the others looked, too, as they squirmed in their chairs.

"Say, why don't you just keep your opinions to yourself?" Jan spoke up. "The Amish have their way of doin' things, and we Englishers have ours. And who says anyone has to have cushy padded pews in order to worship God?"

"What would you know about it?" Stuart shot back. "When was the last time you stepped foot in a church?"

Jan leaned forward and leveled Stuart with a look that prickled the hair on the back of Emma's neck. "I might ask you the same question, buddy. So you wanna make somethin' of it?"

Oh no, not more trouble between these two men. Emma knew she'd better say or do something before things got out of control.

"Now, now," Ruby Lee said, before Emma could find her voice. "We didn't come here to talk about church. We came to learn more about quilting." She looked at Emma and smiled. "Isn't that right?"

Emma nodded, relieved that after Ruby Lee's comment both men seemed to relax a bit. "Before we begin the next step in making your wall hangings, did you all get your pattern pieces cut out this week?"

Everyone but Stuart nodded. "With all my responsibilities at the sporting goods store, I didn't have time to get anything done on the quilt project this week," he mumbled.

Pam crossed her legs, and her foot bounced up and down as she shot him a look of disdain. "That's not true, and you know it! You would have had plenty of time to get all your pattern pieces cut out if you hadn't watched so much TV. But no, just as soon as you came home every night, on went the stupid sports programs."

"Well, at least I'm not sitting around all day watching a bunch of melodramatic soap operas," he shot back.

"I don't do that!" Pam said with a huff. "When I'm not cleaning, cooking, or doing laundry, I'm in the car running the kids to and from school. Oh, and don't forget, I drive Devin to and from his piano lessons and soccer practice every week."

"I go to all his games."

"Sure you do, but it's not the same as—"

Emma cleared her throat loudly, hoping to put an end to the Johnstons' bickering. "Shall we begin with the next phase of making your wall hangings?"

"How's he gonna begin the next phase when he hasn't done the first phase?" Star asked, pointing at Stuart. It was the first time the young woman had said more than a few words since she'd entered Emma's house this morning. "I hope we don't have to sit here and watch while he does what he should've done during the week."

"That's for sure," Jan spoke up. "We all paid good money to take this class so we could learn how to quilt." He leveled Stuart with a look Emma thought could have stopped a runaway horse in its tracks.

Before Stuart could respond, Emma intervened. "Now if everyone will please lay their pattern pieces on the table, I'll be able to see how things are progressing."

Emma wasn't surprised at how neatly Pam's pink and Ruby Lee's blue pieces had been cut out and pinned, but she never expected Jan's dark green pieces to have been done with such precision. Paul's pieces were yellow, and both his and Star's black and gold pieces were a little off-center, but nothing a little readjusting and pinning wouldn't fix.

Emma smiled. "You've all done quite well."

"All but him." Pam motioned to her husband. "He did nothing at all."

Stuart's eyes squinted as he sneered at her. "That's it. Just keep on reminding me about it!" His face turned red, and his voice rose with each word he said. "Things always go so much better between us when you throw things up in my face. And it's even better when you have an audience, isn't it? I'm sure it makes you feel real good if you can get others to take your side."

"You're impossible," Pam mumbled, turning her head away.

Emma squirmed nervously. A lot of anger and tension seemed to be going on between Pam and Stuart. She knew she had to say something to help ease the tension, and her mind grappled for the right words. Then, remembering something Ivan had told her once, she looked first at Pam and then Stuart. "Tolerance is what we all need for each other. Things go smoother if we're kind to everyone we meet."

Neither of them said a thing in response.

"Love God, yourself, and others. That's what the Bible teaches," Ruby Lee put in.

Paul gave a decisive nod; Star rolled her eyes toward the ceiling; Jan shrugged his broad shoulders; and Stuart and Pam both stared at the table. Emma figured not all her students went to church or had a personal relationship with God. Although most Amish didn't evangelize the way many English believers did, most, like Emma, tried to set a Christian example through their actions and words. Emma determined in her heart that she would try to show her students the love of Jesus and would begin doing that today.

CHAPTER 12

Emma was about to show the class what they needed to do next when she heard a knock on the back door. "Excuse me a minute while I see who that is," she said, hurrying out of the room.

When Emma opened the door, she was surprised to see Lamar holding a rectangular cardboard box. *Oh dear, what does he want now?* She'd told him earlier that she would be teaching her class until noon, so she couldn't imagine what he was doing here again.

Before Emma could voice the question, Lamar smiled and held the box out to her. "I know you still have guests, and I didn't mean to interrupt, but when I got to the bakery and discovered they had chocolate and powdered-sugar doughnuts on sale, I bought a dozen of each. Knowing it was more than I could eat, I decided to bring most of the doughnuts here, thinking you could share them with the people in your quilting class."

Emma, still feeling a bit put out for the interruption, took the box of doughnuts, thanked Lamar, and said she needed to get back to her students.

"Oh, of course. Sorry for the intrusion. I'll be on my way."

Emma nodded and stepped back into the house, almost shutting the door in his face.

"Who was that?" Pam asked when Emma returned to her sewing room.

"Oh, it was just Lamar Miller—a man in my community. He was on his way home from the bakery and stopped by to give me these." She lifted the box of doughnuts. "We can take a break soon, and I'll share them with you."

"Yum. . .doughnuts sure sound good," Stuart said.

"I'd better pass," Paul said. "I had some of my sister's homemade tamales for breakfast this morning, and I'm still feeling kind of full."

Jan's eyebrows shot up. "You had tamales for breakfast?"

Paul nodded. "I could eat them any time of day."

"Did you invite the nice man who brought the doughnuts to join us?" Ruby Lee asked Emma.

Emma's face heated as she shook her head. So much for setting a good example for her quilting students. They probably thought she'd been rude for not asking Lamar if he wanted to come in and share the doughnuts. Well, they didn't understand. If she'd invited him in, he would have seen it as an invitation to come here again—maybe even during one of her classes. It was bad enough that he'd been hanging around so much lately—doing little chores she hadn't asked him to do and trying to have conversations she'd rather not get into. A few weeks ago, Lamar had stopped by when she wasn't at home and mowed her lawn. Emma knew he had done it because he'd left his straw hat on one of the fence posts, and she'd discovered his name on the underside of the brim. Emma figured she'd better do something to discourage him soon or she might be looking at a marriage proposal.

"Are you all right, Emma?" Ruby Lee asked. "You look upset."

"I'm fine," Emma said, not wishing to discuss her thoughts. "I'll take the doughnuts to the kitchen until it's time for our break." She hurried from the room, feeling more flustered than ever.

When Emma returned, fully composed, she overheard Paul talking to Jan about Sophia and how he hoped the quilt he wanted to finish after he learned the basics of quilting would be a keepsake for the baby. He explained that when Sophia was old enough he planned to tell her what a wonderful mother his wife had been.

Paul paused and reached into his pocket for a handkerchief as several tears trickled onto his cheeks.

Everyone in the room got deathly quiet. Obviously no one knew what to say.

"I'm sorry. I know Lorinda's in a better place," Paul said after he'd dried his tears and blown his nose. "But I—I miss her so much, and it pains me to think that Sophia will never know her mother." Pausing to take a deep breath, he continued. "Then this past week was sort of a nightmare, with meetings, grading papers, and Sophia protesting through it all. The weekend just couldn't get here fast enough."

Emma stepped forward and placed her hand on Paul's shoulder. "It's never easy to lose a loved one. My husband's been gone a little over a year, and I still miss him and wish he could come back to me." She swallowed hard, hoping she wouldn't give in to her own threatening tears. "When the death of a loved one occurs, everything changes, and you find yourself doing things you never thought you could do."

"I miss my grandma, too." Star's forehead creased, and she opened her mouth like she might say more, but then she closed it and dropped her gaze to the floor.

Emma's heart ached for the members of her class who were so obviously grieving. Even though she still missed Ivan, she'd found joy in life again. She hoped she could share some of that joy with her class.

As Emma showed the class how to stitch the patterned pieces together, using one of the battery-powered sewing machines, Ruby Lee thought about how flustered Emma had seemed right after the Amish man brought the doughnuts by. At least she assumed he was Amish. While Ruby Lee hadn't actually seen the man, she'd heard the distinctive *clippety-clop* of horse's hooves and the rumble of wheels as the buggy pulled away.

Could there be something going on between Emma and that man? Ruby Lee wondered. *If so, I guess it's really none of my business.*

Ruby Lee's role as a pastor's wife often put her in a position to know other people's business—sometimes more than she wanted to know. She always kept quiet about the things she heard, knowing it wouldn't be good to start any gossip. But there were others in the congregation who didn't seem to care about that. Some, even those with well-meaning intentions, spread gossip like wildfire.

Ruby Lee winced. For the past several months, Gene had been the subject of gossip within their church, yet he wouldn't do anything to stop it. He just continued to turn the other cheek and tried not to let the rumors and grumblings bother him. It was all Ruby Lee could do to keep from stepping into the pulpit some Sunday morning and chastising those who had gossiped and complained. The congregation needed to know that Gene had the church's best interests at heart and that he didn't deserve to be unjustly accused.

"And now I'd like each of you to spend the next half hour working on your quilt project," Emma said.

With a sense of determination not to think about anything church-related, Ruby Lee picked up one of her pattern pieces and pinned it to another, making sure it was positioned correctly. She'd signed up for this class so she could forget about the church and its problems and was determined to do just that.

"Hey, watch out there, junior," Jan said, pointing at Stuart. "You're gonna stick yourself with a pin if you're not careful."

Stuart frowned. "Just worry about yourself; I'm doing fine over here."

Jan shrugged his shoulders. "Whatever. I'm just sayin'—"

"How does this look?" Ruby Lee asked, holding up the two pieces of material she'd sewn together and hoping to diffuse any more arguments between the men.

"That's exactly right." Emma smiled. "You know, I just thought of something."

"What's that?" Pam asked.

"My grandmother used to say that God stitches the fabric of our lives according to His purpose and perfect pattern in order to shape us into what He wants us to be, just as you are all shaping your quilt patterns here."

"That's a little over the top, don't you think?" Star spoke up. "I mean, comparing God—if there really is a God—to us making a quilted wall hanging? That seems pretty far-fetched to me."

"Of course there's a God," Ruby Lee was quick to say. While her faith in other Christians may have dwindled in the last few months, she'd never doubted God's existence.

"I think anyone who doesn't believe in God must have a problem," Paul put in. "Why, I can see the hand of God everywhere."

"That's right," Emma agreed. "God's hand is in the flowers, the trees..."

"A baby's sweet laugh," Paul said, picking a piece of thread off his jeans.

Star shrugged her shoulders. "You can think whatever you like, but I'm not convinced that God exists, and I *don't* have a problem."

"Everyone has some kind of problem or somethin' they're tryin' to hide," Jan said. "Some of us just hide it better than others." He looked right at Star. "What's your problem, anyway?"

"I just told you, I don't have a problem." Star stared back at Jan defiantly. "Even if I did, I wouldn't discuss my personal life with a bunch of strangers."

"We're not really strangers," Pam interjected. "This is our second time together, and—"

"And with the exception of you and me, none of us knows each other at all." Stuart removed the green baseball cap he'd worn today and pulled his fingers through the top of his hair, causing it to stand straight up. "Of course, there are days when I'm not sure I really know you all that well either."

Pam blinked a couple of times. "I hope you're kidding, Stuart. We've been married ten years, and we dated two years before we got married. If you don't know me now, then I guess you never will."

Oh no, here we go again. They're going to start arguing now. These two really do need marriage counseling. Ruby Lee pushed her chair away from the table. "I don't know about anyone else, but I'm hungry. Is it all right if we have those doughnuts now, Emma?"

"Yes, of course. I'll get them right away." Emma scurried out of the room, and Ruby Lee was right behind her.

"What can I do to help?" she asked Emma as they stepped into her cozy kitchen.

"You can get some napkins and the box of doughnuts, and I'll get the coffee and cups." Emma smiled. "Maybe these doughnuts will sweeten everyone up and we'll end our class on a pleasant note today. Oh, and be careful not to get any of that powdered sugar on yourself." Nodding toward the doughnuts, she added, "There must be a hole in the bottom of the box, because I see some powder drifting out from underneath, and I'd hate to see any of it get on that pretty pink blouse you're wearing today."

Ruby Lee nodded, appreciating the warning and, even more, the compliment from Emma.

When they returned to Emma's sewing room, Ruby Lee was glad to see that with the exception of Paul, who was talking on his cell phone, everyone was visiting. It seemed like they all might be warming up to each other a bit. She placed the doughnuts and napkins in the center of the table and took a seat.

"I have coffee to go with the doughnuts," Emma said as she set a tray with the coffeepot and cups beside the doughnuts. "Go ahead and help yourselves."

"I don't really care much for coffee," Pam said. "Do you have something else to drink?"

"There's chocolate milk in the refrigerator, or you can have water," Emma replied.

"Chocolate milk sounds good to me." Pam started to rise from her chair, but Emma shook her head.

"Help yourself to a doughnut while I get the milk."

By the time Emma returned from the kitchen with a glass of chocolate milk, Paul was off the phone and everyone had begun eating their doughnuts. Paul mentioned that he'd called his sister to check on Sophia and was relieved to hear that she was doing just fine. Then the talk around the table turned to the weather.

"Sure has been raining a lot this spring," Ruby Lee commented. "I hope the sunshine we're having today keeps on, because I would hate to have flooding like we did two years ago."

"I remember it was so bad that some of our roads were closed," Emma said. "One of my friends had so much water at her place that she couldn't even get to her phone shack."

"Phone shack?" Pam looked surprised. "Don't you have a phone in the house?"

Emma shook her head. "Most of us share a phone with other family members or two or three close neighbors, and it's in a small wooden building we call our 'phone shack.'"

"Oh, I couldn't handle not having a phone in the house," Pam said, slowly shaking her head.

"And I couldn't do without my cell phone." Stuart reached across Pam to take another doughnut and bumped her arm just as she was about to take a drink.

The glass tipped, and chocolate milk spilled all over the front of Pam's creamy-white blouse. "Oh no!" she gasped. "Just look what you've done now! My new blouse is ruined!"

"I–I'm sorry," Stuart sputtered. "I didn't mean to bump your arm."

Red-faced, Pam jumped up from the table, her eyes flashing angrily. "Get up, Stuart; it's time to go home!" With that, she raced out the front door.

Stuart, looking thoroughly embarrassed, grabbed his and Pam's quilt projects, stuffed them into the canvas tote Pam had brought along, and turned to Emma. "Sorry, but I'd better go." Before Emma had a chance to respond, he hurried out the door.

CHAPTER 13

Tears burned Pam's eyes as she slid into the car feeling humiliated and angry with Stuart. How could he have been so careless and bumped her arm like that? Didn't he ever watch what he was doing?

"Are you okay?" Stuart asked as he took his seat behind the wheel and fastened his seat belt.

"No, I'm not okay!" She sniffed and blotted the tears from her cheeks. "I just bought this beautiful blouse, and now it's ruined."

"I'm sure it'll be fine once we get home and you've washed it."

"I. . .I doubt it. Chocolate's hard to get out, and it'll probably leave a nasty stain."

"If it does, you can buy a new blouse."

"No, I can't. This was the last one they had in my size in this style."

"Then buy one in another style."

She shook her head. "I like this one. Besides, I'm not like you. You'd be happy if the baseball cap, faded jeans, and red-checkered flannel shirt you wear so much of the time were the only pieces of clothing you owned. Don't you ever get tired of wearing those things? Wouldn't it be nice if just once in a while you'd dress in clothes that are a bit more tasteful—especially when we go someplace together?"

"You're exaggerating, Pam. I don't wear a flannel shirt and ball cap all the time. I sure don't wear 'em to work."

"Don't you realize how embarrassing it is for me when you dress like a slob?"

"It's all about you, isn't it?" Stuart slashed back. "Did it ever occur to you that I just might be comfortable in these clothes? Or should I say *rags*, which is probably what you think of them anyway. Now buckle up. We're heading home."

Pam said nothing as he started the engine and pulled out of Emma's yard. What was the point? She was sure her blouse was ruined and equally sure that Stuart didn't really care. He didn't care about his sloppy appearance either.

They rode in silence until they were almost out of Shipshewana; then Stuart looked over at Pam and said, "This isn't working out. I want—"

Pam's heart hammered and her mouth went dry. "A divorce? Is that what you want?" She knew they were just holding on by a thread.

"Whoa! Who said anything about a divorce?"

"You said things aren't working out, so I assumed you meant—"

"I was talking about the stupid quilting class." He gave the steering wheel a whack. "I'm bored with the class, I'll never catch on to sewing, and I'm getting sick and tired of hearing you talk about me to anyone who'll listen. You make it sound like I'm the world's worst husband, and you're saying it to a bunch of people we don't even know." He groaned. "Why do you always have to make me look bad? Is it so you can make yourself look good?"

"Certainly not." She folded her arms and stared straight ahead. "You're just too sensitive, that's all."

For a few seconds, their conversation ebbed as traffic came to a halt in both directions. Pam watched as a mother duck, followed by seven scurrying ducklings, crossed the road in front of them to get to the area where water had formed a small pond after the recent rain. *If only life were as simple as crossing the road to get to the other side, where something good awaited you.*

Picking up their conversation as if they'd never seen the ducks, Stuart continued talking as traffic moved once again. "Humph! You think I'm too sensitive? You're the one who lost it when I bumped your arm and the chocolate milk spilled on your blouse. It's not like I did it on purpose, you know."

"So you said."

"Look, Pam, this whole quilting thing is only adding more stress to our marriage, and it's sure not helping our relationship any. I think you should go without me next week."

She sat quietly for several seconds, letting his words sink in; then with a quick nod she said, "Okay, I'll go by myself, and you can stay home and watch the kids instead of asking our neighbor girl to babysit them."

"Why can't Cindy watch them again? She said she'd be available to sit with the kids for all six weeks."

"It would be a waste of money to pay her when one of us isn't going."

A muscle on Stuart's right cheek quivered, the way it always did whenever he was irritated with her. "Fine then. I'll watch the kids!"

Pam was pretty sure Stuart wanted to do something else next Saturday—probably go fishing with one of his buddies. Well, that was too bad. If he wasn't going to keep his promise and take the quilting class with her, then he could stay home and deal with the kids.

She leaned her head against the seat and closed her eyes, allowing her thoughts to drift back to her childhood. Back then, the only thing she should have been worried about was having fun with her friends—deciding what to do for the day and what games they would play. Those should have been days filled with mindless entertainment, doing things kids enjoyed, like lying in the grass with no cares in the world and watching the clouds overhead form into all sorts of characters and shapes. It was a phase in her life when time schedules shouldn't have been that important yet. Unfortunately, Pam's childhood wasn't that simple. As far back as she could remember, she'd felt like she had the weight of the world on her back. She'd never had those carefree days of youth. Instead, Pam constantly had her nose in a book and strived to be a straight-A student so Mom and Dad would be proud of her and say something that would let her know they approved. The hope of gaining their approval gave Pam the determination and drive to keep striving for perfection.

School books make lousy friends, she thought. Even with all the studying Pam had done, none of it seemed to have really mattered to anyone. The good grades were rewarded, but with money or clothes, not words of affirmation or a loving hug.

During Pam's childhood, she'd never even had a close friend. Heather Barkely, whom she'd met at aerobics class a few years ago, was the first real friend she'd ever had.

What was worse than not having any close friends, and the one thing she'd really despised about school, was going back in the fall after summer vacation. When the teacher would ask if the students wanted to share their summer adventures with the rest of the class, Pam envied hearing about the family outings most of them had. Sure, her parents had given her many things, and she'd learned at a very young age how to put on a good front. Pam had been clever about fooling her parents and others when she'd pretended to be pacified with the so-called treasures they'd bought for her. And she appreciated that she'd been given nice clothes. At least that was something she was complimented for during her teenage years—that, and her good looks—especially from the boys.

Maybe this is why it bugs me so much about the way Stuart dresses, she thought. *I just want him to look as nice as I do so people will be impressed.*

Stuart hadn't been such a slob before he'd married her. What had happened between then and now to make him change in his appearance?

Focusing on the scenery as they continued the drive home, Pam kept all those forgotten feelings from the past to herself. If she told Stuart any of this, he wouldn't understand. He didn't seem to want to communicate with her on any level these days.

———

Star noticed that as soon as Stuart and Pam stormed out of Emma's house, the sewing room had become so quiet she probably could have heard a needle drop on the floor. Even Ruby Lee, who was usually quite talkative, sat drinking her coffee with a strange-looking stare.

Emma, looking more flustered than she had when the man with the doughnuts came by, stood near the window, looking out at her yard.

Star watched outside as a wasp flew around the overhang above the window, no doubt trying to find a place to build its nest.

Several more minutes went by; then Jan leaned close to Star and said, "I can't say as I care much for know-it-all Stuart, but that wife of his is sure one whacked-out chick. You know what I'm sayin'?"

She gave a nod, glad that Jan saw things the way she did—at least where prissy Pam was concerned.

"I guess she had a right to be upset, but I'm sure Stuart didn't bump her arm on purpose," Paul spoke up. "Although I think she could have been a little more understanding when he said he was sorry."

Would you have been understanding if someone had spilled chocolate milk all over your clean shirt? Star thought, although she didn't voice the question. Seeing the way Pam and Stuart argued only confirmed in her mind that she was never getting married. Most of the men she'd known had been jerks, and even though Star didn't care for Pam's uppity ways, she'd actually felt a bit sorry for her when she dashed out of the house in tears.

"Women like Pam Johnston are never understanding; they're just high maintenance," Jan muttered. "Believe me; I know all about whacked-out, high-maintenance chicks."

"Biker babes?" Star asked.

"Some yes, some no." Jan reached for a doughnut and took a bite, followed by a swig of coffee. "The first biker babe I ever met was probably the most whacked-out chick of all."

"In what way?" Star asked, her curiosity piqued.

"She could never make up her mind. One minute she wanted to get married; the next minute she didn't." A pained expression crossed Jan's face as he slowly shook his head. "She took off one day without a trace—just like my old man did after my mom died."

"How old were you when that happened?" Star questioned.

"I was seventeen when Mom died from a brain tumor." Jan went on to tell that his drunkard father had split a year later, and then he'd lit out on his own. "I eventually learned the roofing trade and ended up in Shipshewana, where I started my own business," he said.

"Losing your mother, and then having two people you loved run away must have been very painful." Ruby Lee reached over and touched Jan's arm. Her eyes, the color of charcoal, looked at him with such compassion that it made Star feel like crying.

It wasn't bad enough that the burly biker had lost his mother, but then some fickle woman hurt him so badly that he still carried the scars of her rejection. To top it all off, having his dad take off had probably left Jan feeling a lot of animosity. Star could sure relate to that, since her own dad had done the very same thing. The only difference was Jan had known his dad for seventeen years, whereas Star had never known her dad at all.

"Yeah, it was all very painful, but I learned how to cope." Jan swiped some crumbs from the front of his T-shirt. "You know Bunny was the only girl I ever really loved." He pointed to the tattoo on his right arm. "I even had her name put here. But of course, that was when I thought she was gonna marry me. Now I realize what a jerk I was for believin' her. Shoulda never got involved with her in the first place."

Guess I'm not the only one in this room with hurts from the past, Star thought. *It's too bad people have to disappoint each other. If everyone had a heart of love the way Grandma did, the world would be a better place. I'm thankful I had her, even though we didn't get to spend nearly enough time together.*

Emma turned from the window and joined them at the table again. "No one is perfect. We all make mistakes, but we have to forgive and move forward," she said.

Star grimaced. *That's easy enough for you to say. You've probably never made a mistake in your life. Well, walk in someone else's shoes for a while, and then see what you have to say about forgiveness.*

CHAPTER 14

As Jan pedaled home from the quilting class, he thought about his comments concerning the woman he'd once loved and wondered if he'd said too much. The way everyone had looked at him made him wonder if they thought he was some dumb guy who'd never gotten over his first crush. Or maybe they'd felt sorry for him because he'd been jilted. Either way, he figured it would be best if he didn't say too much more about his personal life during the quilting classes. It was bad enough that during their first class he'd told them about his DUI. He'd signed up to learn how to quilt, not spill his guts about the past and hash things over that couldn't be changed. Looking back on it, he figured he'd blabbed all that because he'd been uncomfortable the first day, unsure of what to expect and a bit embarrassed because he didn't know how people would respond to a guy like him taking a quilting class.

Jan knew that he needed to quit worrying about what others thought. He also needed to forget his former life and look to the future.

He'd been doing a pretty good job of that until he'd started blubbering about Bunny.

"Yikes, I'd better watch what I'm doin'," he muttered, nearly losing his balance as he caught sight of some pretty azaleas blooming in a yard along the way. "Better pay closer attention to handlin' this stupid bike and quit gawkin' around, or I might end up on my backside."

Continuing on, Jan pictured some azalea bushes around his small house. Maybe a few flowers would help it look a little homier and not so plain. He had a lot of yard space he could work with and really needed something to give the place some charm.

Vr. . .oom! Vr. . .oom!

"Now that there's what I really need to be thinkin' about," Jan said as a motorcycle roared past. He could hardly wait to get his driver's license back so he could take his Harley out and start riding again. He missed the exhilaration of zooming down the road with the wind at his back. He missed the power of the motorcycle underneath him.

Hang on, he told himself. *Just a few more months and I'll be home free.*

When Jan pedaled up the driveway to his house, he noticed right away that his garage door hung open. He glanced toward the house and grimaced when he saw Brutus lying on the front porch.

"Oh, great," he muttered as the dog greeted him with a welcoming bark and a wagging tail.

Jan parked his bike, stepped onto the porch, and bent to pet the dog's silky ears. "Hey, boy. How'd you get out of the garage, huh?"

Brutus whimpered and nuzzled Jan's hand with his nose.

Jan took a seat on the top porch step as he contemplated the situation. When he'd put Brutus in the garage this morning before leaving for Emma's, he'd thought he had shut the door.

I either must've forgot or didn't close it tight enough. Should've paid closer attention, I guess.

Brutus ambled across the porch and picked up an old dilapidated slipper in his mouth. Then he plodded back and dropped it at Jan's feet.

"Now where'd that come from?" Jan scratched his head. "Sure isn't mine. Brutus, did you steal this from someone in the neighborhood?"

Brutus gave a deep grunt as he flopped onto the porch and stuck his nose between his paws.

Jan squinted. "Well, if you did steal it, then I guess I'd better get started buildin' that dog pen right away, 'cause I can't have you gettin' me in trouble with more of the neighbors."

———

Goshen

As soon as Ruby Lee stepped into the house, she knew something was wrong. The newspapers that had been scattered on the coffee table when she'd left for the quilting class were still there, as well as Gene's empty coffee cup, which sat in the middle of the strewn-out papers. Gene was a perfectionist and rarely left things lying around. His motto was "When you're done with something, put it away." He'd started a rule in their house back when the boys were small that when a person was finished with their dishes, they were to take them straight to the kitchen sink.

Gene was so meticulous that whenever he finished his coffee, he would rinse the cup out and put it right in the dishwasher. Since he'd obviously not done that this morning, nor had he picked up and folded the newspaper he'd been reading after breakfast, he'd either been called out because of an emergency or was upset about something and forgot.

Ever since they'd been having problems at church, Gene hadn't been acting like his usual self at home. He seemed less talkative, became easily distracted, rarely played his guitar, and had become moody and despondent. At church, though, he went about his business, unwilling to let anyone in the congregation know how he really felt. Ruby Lee had tried talking to him about it but couldn't get him to open up. If something didn't happen to change the church situation soon, she feared he might have a nervous breakdown from holding his emotions inside.

I wish I could get through to him, Ruby Lee told herself as she bent to pick up Gene's cup. *I need to convince him that he should leave the ministry or at least seek a new church.*

Ruby Lee took the cup to the kitchen, and as she was placing it in the sink, she spotted Gene out the window. He was sitting on the grass in the middle of the backyard with his legs crossed, staring up at the sky. It wasn't like him to do that. For that matter, since he usually called on members of their congregation most Saturdays, it seemed strange that he was home at all.

Ruby Lee went out the back door and knelt on the grass beside him. "What are you doing out here?" she asked, touching Gene's arm.

His forehead gleamed like polished ebony as he lowered his head and gave her a blank stare. "What do you mean?"

"Well look at you, hon. How come you're sitting here on the grass staring up at the sky?"

"I was talking to God. Oh, yes, indeed."

Ruby Lee tried not to act surprised by his statement, but she'd never known him to talk to God in this manner. Not that it mattered where, when, or how a person talked to God, but with the exception of the prayer they said at meals, Gene usually went to the church to pray. He'd told her on more than one occasion that he felt closer to God when he was on his knees in front of the altar. Ruby Lee would sometimes join him there, and they'd pray and meditate together, but she hadn't done much of that lately. Maybe, like her, Gene just needed a change of pace. That was why she'd decided to take the quilting class. So far it had been a nice diversion, giving her something other than their church problems to focus on.

"Gene, I've been thinking about something," she said softly.

"What's that?"

"I think we should consider looking for another church. Or better yet, let's get out of the ministry altogether. Now that we've moved from the parsonage and are in our own home, we're not tied to the church. Since we both like to sing and each of us plays an instrument, maybe we could teach music lessons."

Gene shook his head. "I'm not leaving the ministry, Ruby Lee. God called me to it, and I'm not going back on my promise to serve Him."

"I'm not suggesting you stop serving God. I just think there are other ways you can serve besides pastoring a church full of ungrateful people. Even moving from the parsonage to our own place here, we can't seem to escape all the gossip. And if things keep going as they are, you're bound to cave in." *And so will I.*

" 'Though he slay me, yet will I hope in him,' " Gene quoted from Job 13:15.

Ruby Lee swallowed hard. "Yes, that's what I'm afraid of."

He gave her arm a gentle pat and lifted his gaze to the sky again.

Sighing deeply, Ruby Lee rose to her feet and headed back to the house. *Sweet Jesus, we need Your help in this. Please protect my man and make everything all right for us again.*

CHAPTER 15

Shipshewana

Emma had spent a good deal of Wednesday afternoon shopping in Shipshewana, and had also stopped to see her friend Clara Bontrager. During their visit, the subject of Lamar came up, and Emma dropped a few hints about Clara and Lamar maybe getting together. She'd even gone so far as to say she thought they would make a good couple. Clara had completely vetoed that idea, however, saying that she'd been corresponding with Emmanuel Schrock, an Amish man from Millersburg, Ohio, whom she'd met when they'd both visited Sarasota, Florida, the past winter.

"I actually think Lamar is interested in you," Clara had said.

"Jah, I know," Emma mumbled, talking out loud, as she flicked the reins to get her horse moving a bit faster. "I just hope he realizes that I'm not interested in him."

Not quite ready to go home, she decided to stop by a place she and Ivan used to go when they were courting. It was near a pond about four miles from where she lived. If she went there now and didn't stay too long, she should still have plenty of time to get back before supper. Besides, she'd only be cooking for herself this evening, so it really didn't matter what time she ate.

Heading on down the road, Emma slowed her horse to watch an English man on his tractor mowing his acreage. She smiled, noticing the tree swallows as they swooped and dove at the bugs flying out of the grass from the mower. The birds brought up another scene in her mind from long ago. This scene was of Ivan, strong and capable, walking behind their mules as he worked in the fields. She couldn't help smiling back then, either, as the birds followed after her husband, looking for an easy meal.

As Emma guided her horse and buggy off the main highway and onto a narrow, graveled road, more memories flooded her mind. When she and Ivan had come here, either alone or with friends, they'd often shared a picnic supper, fished in the pond, or taken leisurely walks along the wooded paths. Not too much had changed since then, except the trees were much taller now. Back then everything had been more overgrown, of course, and not nearly as many people used the pond as they did now. Even so, coming here gave her a peaceful, nostalgic feeling.

Emma stopped her horse and buggy in a grassy spot, climbed down, and secured the horse to a tree. She was about to take off on foot in search of her and Ivan's special spot when Lamar pulled up in his open rig.

"Wie geht's?" he called.

Oh no. What's he doing here? Emma forced a smile. "I'm doing fine. How about you?" she asked, a little less enthusiastically.

"Real well, thanks." He climbed down from his buggy and lifted a fishing pole out. "Came here to do a little fishing. Would you like to join me, Emma?" he asked with a twinkle in his eyes.

She shook her head. "I'm going for a walk and need to be alone." *There, that ought to discourage him.*

A look of hurt replaced Lamar's twinkle, causing Emma to regret her choice of words. It seemed like she was always saying the wrong thing when she was with Lamar, and even though she wanted to discourage him, she didn't want to hurt his feelings.

"There's a spot up the path that used to be my husband's and my special place," she said, pointing in that direction. "I like to go there sometimes and spend time alone, thinking about the past and thanking God for the wonderful years Ivan and I had together."

Lamar gave a brief nod. "I understand. My wife, Margaret, and I had a good life, too."

From the look of longing Emma saw on Lamar's face, she figured he probably missed his wife as much as she missed Ivan.

"I'll let you get to your walk now. Nice seeing you, Emma." Lamar flashed her a quick smile and headed off toward the pond.

Emma turned and started up the path, seeking her place of pleasant memories and solace. The afternoon breeze carried the scent of wildflowers, and she noticed several bees dancing on the flower blossoms. What a lovely day it was for a walk.

Emma found what she was looking for a short way up the path. The area was overgrown, but she recognized the leafy branches of the huge maple tree, where several clumps of wild irises grew nearby. A large boulder sat beneath the tree—the perfect place for young lovers to sit and make plans for the future. It was here that Ivan had first declared his love and told Emma he wanted to marry her. It was here that Emma had agreed to become his wife. And yes, it was even here in this very spot that the birds still seemed to sing their sweetest, as if to serenade her every time she came to visit this special place.

Emma took a seat on the rock and looked up. Even after all these years, her and Ivan's initials were still there—carved deep in the wood with Ivan's pocketknife.

Tears welled in Emma's eyes. "Dearest Ivan, oh, I still miss you so much."

As a young woman, Emma had been courted by a few other men— one in particular, whom she'd rather forget. But she'd never loved anyone the way she had Ivan, and she thanked God for the precious years they'd had together. She wished all couples could be as happy as she and Ivan had been.

As Emma continued to contemplate things, she thought about Pam and Stuart Johnston and wondered how they'd been getting along this week. Had Pam managed to get the chocolate stain out of her blouse? Had she accepted Stuart's apology and forgiven him for bumping her arm? Emma was sure Stuart hadn't done it on purpose. *I wonder if they ever have any fun together, without all that strife.*

Emma closed her eyes and whispered a prayer. "Dear Lord, please be with that troubled couple and heal their marriage. When they come to my class next week, help me to be an example of Your love—to Stuart and Pam, as well as the others in my quilting class."

When her prayer ended, she opened her eyes just in time to see a butterfly, with its colorful wings of yellow and black, flitting around her head. Emma smiled, feeling peace and never tiring of God's almighty showcase.

Mishawaka

As Pam stood in the laundry room staring at the ugly chocolate stain on her blouse, a sense of bitterness welled in her soul. Not only had Stuart's carelessness ruined her new blouse, but he'd reneged on his promise to attend the quilting classes with her. It wasn't right to make a promise and then break it, but Stuart didn't seem to care. Well, maybe she'd enjoy the class more without him, and maybe after being stuck at home watching the kids this Saturday, he'd change his mind and agree to go with her for the three lessons after that. If he didn't, she wouldn't be going fishing or camping with him ever again. Not that she wanted to go anyway. She disliked sleeping in a tent, and sitting in a boat for hours on end was just as bad. She hated everything about spending time in the dirty, bug-infested woods.

When Pam first married Stuart, he'd mentioned wanting to go camping together, but she'd had no idea he meant in a tent. She'd suggested they get an RV, which had many of the conveniences she was used to at home, but Stuart shot that idea down, saying he preferred to rough it, and that he thought sleeping in a tent was a lot more fun.

Fun for him, maybe, Pam fumed, tossing her blouse into a bag of cleaning rags. That's all it was good for now. She would never wear it again—not even around the house. *I should go find that stupid flannel shirt of his and throw it in this bag, too. It would serve him right for ruining my blouse.*

The sound of children's laughter drifted through the open window of the laundry room, reminding Pam that Devin and Sherry were playing in the backyard. They'd gone outside shortly after they arrived home from school, and Pam figured they'd stay out there until she called them in for supper.

She glanced at the small clock she kept on the shelf above the dryer. It was almost four. Stuart should be getting home from work in the next hour or so. Since it was a warm spring evening, she hoped he'd be willing to cook some hot dogs and burgers on the grill. Those would be good with the potato salad she'd made earlier. If he wasn't willing to barbecue, she'd have to broil the meat in the oven.

"Gimme that! Gimme that right now!" Devin's angry voice pulled Pam's thoughts aside. When she looked out the window, she saw Sherry running across the yard with a basketball. Devin was right on her heels.

Pam waited to see what her son would do, but when he pushed his sister down and the children started shouting and hitting each other, it was time to intervene.

"What's the problem here?" Pam asked after she'd rushed out the door and up to the children.

Devin pointed to the ball.

"Now, just say what you mean, because I don't understand pointing," Pam said, trying to keep her voice calm.

"She took my ball and won't give it back!" Devin's brown eyes flashed angrily as he glared at his little sister and made a face.

Sherry's lower lip protruded, and her blue eyes filled with tears. "He wouldn't let me play with it."

Devin wrinkled his freckled nose. "You can't play basketball 'cause you can't throw the ball high enough to reach the hoop."

"Can so."

"Can not."

"Can so, you stupid head." Sherry raised her hand like she might slap her brother.

"I'm not a stupid head. You're a—"

Pam stepped quickly between them. "That's enough! There will be no more hitting, and it's not nice to holler and call each other names."

Sherry tipped her blond head back and looked up at Pam with a most serious expression. "You and Daddy holler at each other."

A feeling of shame washed over Pam. Her daughter was right; she and Stuart did argue a lot.

Determined not to set a bad example for Devin and Sherry, Pam decided right then that she wouldn't argue with Stuart anymore—at least not in front of the children. Of course, she would need help controlling her tongue, because Stuart seemed to know exactly how to push her buttons.

Pam crossed her fingers and said a quick prayer. Maybe the two gestures didn't mix, since crossing one's fingers was superstitious, but if she was going to keep from arguing with Stuart, then she'd need all the help she could get.

She took the ball from Sherry and handed it to Devin. Then she reached for Sherry's hand and said, "Why don't you come in the house with me? You can help me bake a cake for dessert tonight. How's that sound?"

The child nodded and walked obediently with Pam toward the house. They stopped to look at the tulips blooming around their deck. Pam was happy to see all the other flowers that were sprouting up and starting to bloom in the various nature gardens she'd created. All the pretty flowers and shrubs added just the right touch to their charming Cape Cod home.

When they stopped on the patio to bring in a plant Pam needed to repot, Sherry pivoted toward Devin and stuck out her tongue.

"That's not nice," Pam scolded, turning the girl toward the door. She couldn't imagine where her daughter had picked up such a bad-mannered gesture.

"I saw you stick your tongue out at Daddy once," Sherry said as they stepped into the kitchen.

Setting the plant near the window, Pam flinched. She really did need to set a better example for the children. Opening the curtains so the plant would get more sunlight, Pam sighed deeply and leaned her head against the window. *It's gotten so bad that even the kids are imitating us now.*

Shipshewana

For the last three days, Jan had been working late, and by the time he got home from work, all he wanted to do was sleep. But Brutus had other ideas. Locked safely away in his new dog pen, which Jan had built a few days ago, the poor dog seemed to want Jan's attention as soon as Terry dropped him off at the house.

"Oh. Oh. Looks like Brutus got out," Terry said as he pulled his truck into Jan's yard that afternoon.

Jan rubbed his tired eyes and squinted. Sure enough—there lay Brutus on the front porch. "For cryin' out loud!" Jan opened the door and hopped out of the truck. When he stepped onto the porch, he noticed a blue cotton shirt lying beside Brutus.

"What's up, man? You look upset," Terry said when he joined Jan on the porch.

Jan grunted and pointed to the shirt.

"Where'd that come from? Is it yours?"

"Nope, but I'll bet somebody's missin' it, and only Brutus knows where it belongs."

Terry's brows lifted high, and then he leaned over the porch railing and spat on the ground. "Not only is your mutt an escape artist, but looks to me like he's also a thief."

Jan reached under his biker's cap and scratched the side of his head. "Guess I'd better find out how he got out of his pen and make sure it don't happen again."

CHAPTER 16

Mishawaka

W hew! That was quite a workout we had today, wasn't it?" Pam asked her friend Heather after they'd finished their aerobics class for the day.

Heather nodded and pushed a loose strand of jet-black hair behind her right ear. "It got my heart pumping pretty good. That's for sure."

"Do you have time to sit at the juice bar and visit a few minutes?" Pam asked. "I really need to talk."

"Sure, no problem. Ron's working late at the office like he usually does on Fridays, so I don't have to be home for a couple more hours."

They both found seats at the bar and ordered cranberry juice over ice.

"What's up?" Heather asked. "Even after that workout we just had, you look kind of stressed."

Pam drew in a quick breath and blew it out with a puff of air that lifted a piece of hair that had stuck to her sweaty forehead. "I've been stressed for several weeks, and it's only gotten worse."

"What's wrong? Are the kids getting on your nerves?"

"It's not the kids; it's Stuart. Despite the fact that we've been seeing a counselor for the last month, things aren't any better between us."

"But you're taking that quilting class together, right?"

"Well, we were, but Stuart hated it so much he said he didn't want to go again."

"Then maybe you shouldn't force the issue."

Pam took a drink of juice and frowned. "I'm not trying to force him to take the class, Heather. At first he agreed to go if I promised to go fishing with him four more times."

Heather's eyebrows squeezed together. "I know how much you hate to fish, so why would you even agree to do such a thing?"

"I agreed to it because our counselor said we should do some things together, and also because I wanted Stuart to learn how to quilt with me."

"But why? You had to know he wouldn't like it. I mean, most men I know wouldn't be caught dead with a needle and thread in their hands. And Stuart sure doesn't seem like the type who'd want to learn how to sew."

Pam wrinkled her nose. "You're right about that. All he ever thinks about is hunting, fishing, and sports. And since I don't enjoy any of those things, I decided it was time for him to do something just for me. . . something that would prove how much he loves me. But I'm beginning to think he doesn't love me at all."

"Has he said he doesn't love you?" Heather asked.

"No, but he rarely says so anymore. And when he does, it's usually because he wants me to do something for him. I can tell by the way Stuart acts that whatever love he used to feel for me has dried up and blown away." Tears welled in Pam's eyes and threatened to spill over. "I cook all his favorite foods, dress in stylish clothes, and work out here every week so I can keep my figure, but he barely notices me. When we were dating, he paid me compliments about my looks, and there wasn't anything he wouldn't do for me. But that's over now—just like our marriage."

"You don't think there's another woman, do you?"

Pam shook her head. "I just think he's selfish and so into himself that he doesn't see me or even acknowledge my needs. Besides, with the sloppy way he often dresses, I doubt any other woman would be attracted to him. I know I wouldn't have been if he'd looked like that before we started dating."

"Have you tried talking to him about the way he dresses and how he treats you?"

Pam flipped the ends of her hair over her shoulder. "Oh, dozens of times. He just shrugs it off and says I'm too demanding. The other day he even said I was a high-maintenance woman and that I should quit putting so many expectations on him."

"What'd you say to that?"

"I said he was insensitive and only thinks of himself."

Heather drank the rest of her juice. "Maybe you and Stuart should go away by yourselves for a few days and see if you can talk things through. A little romance wouldn't hurt either," she added with a grin.

Pam rolled her eyes. "If I suggested going away by ourselves, Stuart would probably want to go camping—in a tent, of all things."

"Just put your foot down and tell him you want to stay at a nice hotel or a bed-and-breakfast. I hear there's some lovely B&Bs between Middlebury and Shipshewana."

Pam shook her head. "I doubt he'd go for that."

"Well, you won't know if you don't ask. A little time alone might do wonders for your marriage."

Pam sighed deeply. "That would be nice, but it would have to be on a weekend, and with the quilting class taking up most of my Saturdays, we couldn't even think about going away by ourselves until the last class is over."

Heather gave Pam's arm a gentle pat. "Well, my good thoughts are with you, and remember, I'm here anytime you need to talk."

"Thanks, I appreciate that."

"Is everything okay?" Blaine Vickers, one of Stuart's employees, asked as he joined Stuart in the break room. "You've been looking kind of stressed-out all day."

"I am stressed," Stuart admitted.

"Did something happen here at work?"

Stuart shook his head. "Everything's going along fine here in the store. What has me stressed is what's going on at home."

"A little trouble in paradise?"

"More than a little; and our home is anything but paradise these days."

"I'm a good listener if you want to talk about it," Blaine said.

"Pam and I started seeing a counselor about a month ago, but it's not helping. Things just seem to be getting worse."

Blaine gave Stuart's shoulder a light thump. "Well, give it a bit more time. There's never been a city built in a day, you know."

"I don't think any amount of time will make Pam enjoy the same things I do." Stuart scrubbed his hand down the side of his bristly face. He really should have shaved this morning. It wasn't good for business to have the store manager looking scruffy, but he'd been upset with something Pam said and left the house in a hurry. Pam was always nagging him about the way he looked and dressed, and even though he knew she was probably right, it irritated him to have her telling him what to do all the time. He had to admit at times he deliberately wore clothes she didn't like just to get back at her for harassing him.

"Maybe if you did more things your wife enjoys, she'd be willing to do some things you like to do."

"I doubt that's ever going to happen, but I did try something she wanted me to do."

"What was that?"

"You're probably not gonna believe this, but Pam actually talked me into going to some quilting classes with her."

Blaine's dark eyebrows lifted almost to his hairline. "Are you kidding me?"

Stuart shook his head. "She promised to go fishing with me four more times if I attended the six-week quilting class."

"I can't believe you'd agree to that. You've got more guts than I do."

Stuart thumped the side of his head. "More to the point, I think I was just plain stupid."

"So you're actually going to learn how to make a quilt?"

"Well, I was supposed to be making a quilted wall hanging, but—"

"What will you do with the wall hanging when it's done?" Blaine asked as he poured himself a cup of coffee.

"If I were to finish mine, it would probably look so horrible I'd end up throwing it in the garbage." Stuart grimaced. "Pam's such a perfectionist; hers will probably be good enough for any wall in our house. You know, I thought at first that quilting would be easy, but after the second lesson, I realized there's a lot more to it than I'd expected."

Blaine sat staring at Stuart, slowly shaking his head. "You must love your wife a lot if you'd be willing to sit through six weeks of classes, playing with a needle and thread."

"We made an agreement that I'd take the quilting classes with her, and then she'd have to go fishing with me four more times, but I—"

"That sounds tough. Besides the sewing thing, which I could never do, I'm not sure I could sit with a group of people I don't even know while they carried on about material and quilts all day."

"The class is only two hours every Saturday, and after the way things went last week, I decided I don't want to go back."

"So you're reneging on your promise to Pam?"

Stuart shrugged. "If you want to call it that, then, yeah, guess I am."

Blaine shook his head. "Oh boy, no wonder your marriage is in trouble."

"What do you mean?"

"It means if I'd made a promise to Sue and backed out, she'd never let me hear the end of it." Blaine took another swig of coffee. "Was it really that bad sitting in class with a bunch of women?"

"This may surprise you, but I wasn't the only man in the class."

"Now that is a surprise. How many other men were there besides you?"

"Two. There's this big biker fellow who likes to throw his weight around and a young Hispanic schoolteacher whose wife recently died. There are also three women taking the class: Pam; Ruby Lee, an African-American woman who's a pastor's wife; and Star."

"Star?"

"She's a young woman with a nose ring and an attitude that reeks of defiance."

"Wow! Sounds like you've gotten yourself hooked up with quite an unusual bunch of people."

"Yeah. That little quilting club is pretty unique." Stuart lifted his coffee mug and took a drink. "And from what I could tell, almost everyone there has some sort of problem."

"Problem with quilting you mean?"

"Nope. A problem with some issue in their life."

"Show me someone who doesn't have problems, and I'll show you someone who's no longer livin' on this earth," Blaine said with a snicker.

"Yeah, you're right, but some problems are more serious than others." Stuart groaned. "I'm just afraid if Pam and I don't get our problems solved soon, we might be headed for a separation—or worse yet, a divorce."

Shipshewana

"You can just drop me off here," Jan told Terry as they approached his driveway late Friday afternoon. "Need to check my mail, and since I know you have a heavy date this evening, you can just be on your way."

"It's not a heavy date. Dottie and I are going bowling and out for pizza." Terry thumped Jan's shoulder. "Want us to fix you up with Dottie's friend Gwen? I think you'd really like her."

"Not tonight, man," Jan said. "I've gotta work on my wall hanging."

Terry looked at Jan with disbelief. "I can't believe you'd pass up a night of bowling and pizza with a fine-looking chick to stay home and keep company with a needle and thread."

Jan shrugged his shoulders. "What can I say? Think I've found my creative self, like my probation officer said I should do. And you know what—it's actually kinda relaxin' and fun."

Terry snorted. "I can think of lots of other creative things to do besides prickin' my finger with the sharp end of a needle."

Jan chuckled. He didn't figure Terry would understand. "I'll see you on Monday mornin'. Have a good weekend, bud."

"Yep. You, too."

As Terry's truck pulled away, Jan headed for his mailbox by the side of the road. He'd just taken out a stack of mail when Brutus bounded up, wagging his tail.

Jan frowned. "You're out again? How in the world are you doin' it, Brutus?"

Woof! Woof! Brutus's fast-moving tail brushed Jan's pant leg.

"Well, come on. Let's see where you dug out," Jan said as he tromped up the driveway with the dog at his side, tongue hanging out. He could have sworn Brutus was smiling, but then, somehow the dog always looked like he was grinning about something. He was one of those dogs that panted no matter what the weather was like. Even on the coldest days of winter, his tongue would often be hanging out the side of his mouth.

When Jan reached the dog pen, he discovered a hole where Brutus had obviously dug his way out. He shook his finger at Brutus. "Bad dog!"

Brutus lowered his head and slunk through the grass until he reached the house; then he leaped onto the porch with a grunt and a thump. When Jan caught up to him a few seconds later, he discovered a canvas gardening glove lying on the porch near the door.

"Now where'd this come from?" he muttered. "Brutus, did you steal this glove from one of our neighbors?"

The dog's only reply was another deep grunt as he flopped down and rolled onto his back.

"This has gotta stop," Jan said with a disgruntled groan. "Before I do anything else, I'm gonna dig-proof your dog pen."

Goshen

"Where are you going, Beatrice?" Mom asked when Star entered the kitchen wearing her favorite pair of jeans and black hooded sweatshirt.

"I'm goin' to the music store to get some new strings for my guitar; then I'll grab a bite to eat someplace and head over to the coffee shop." Star frowned. "And would you please stop callin' me Beatrice?"

Mom emitted a disgusted sound as she lifted her gaze to the ceiling. "Can't you find something else to do on a Friday evening besides hang out with a bunch of wannabe musicians?"

"I wish you'd get off my case. It's what I enjoy, it's the way I am, and it's better than hangin' out here all evening watching you act all sappy when Mike shows up." Star paused and cleared her throat. "I sure wish you'd dump that creep."

"Mike is not a creep." Mom's nose crinkled as she scrutinized Star. "Don't you want me to be happy?"

Star groaned. "I don't see how you can be happy with a guy like Mike."

"What's wrong with him?"

"For one thing, whenever he comes over here, he just makes himself right at home. Either heads to the kitchen and helps himself to whatever he wants or expects you to wait on him hand and foot. It irritates me when he starts hollering, 'Hey, Nancy, would you get me a beer?'" Star lowered the pitch of her voice to imitate Mike. " 'Oh, Nancy, my shoulders are all knotted up. Could you rub 'em for me, huh?' "

Mom opened her mouth as if to defend her man, but Star cut her off.

"Oh, and don't forget how Mr. Wonderful flops on the couch to watch TV. The guy acts like he owns the place." Star frowned deeply. "And he's always tellin' me what to do, like I'm a little kid and he's my dad."

Mom shook her head. "Oh, come on, Beatrice; it's not that bad."

"Yeah it is."

"Mike asked me to marry him."

"What?" Star gasped, as her mouth dropped open. "I hope you told him no."

Mom sank into a chair at the table. "I didn't say no, but I didn't say yes either. Just said I'd give it some thought and let him know in a few weeks."

Star took a seat, too, and clutched her mother's arm. "If you marry

Mike, I'll have to move out, because I won't stay in the same house with another crummy stepfather!"

"I'll admit Wes wasn't a good husband or stepfather, but Mike's different. He's kind, easygoing, and the restaurant he manages here in Goshen pays him real well."

"Yeah, I know all that, but I still don't like the guy, and I hope you'll think this through and say no."

"Whether I marry Mike or not is my decision, Beatrice, not yours."

Star clenched her fingers until her nails bit into her skin. "Why do I have to keep reminding you, Mom? I go by Star now, not Beatrice. You know how much I hate that name."

"I realize that, but your father insisted on naming you Beatrice after his mother."

"Well, it's a dumb name, and he was a jerk if he liked it." Star leaned forward with her elbows on the table. "Tell me about my dad."

"A few weeks after you were born, he decided that he didn't want to be a father, so he took off down the road and never came back." Mom blinked her eyes rapidly. "I've told you all this before."

"Yeah, but you've never told me much about him. I want to know everything—what he looked like, what he did for a living, where you two met, that kind of stuff."

Mom pushed her chair away from the table and stood. "That's all in the past, and I'd just as soon forget it. Right now I'm going to my room to change out of my waitress uniform, because Mike will be coming here for supper soon."

"Figured as much, and it's all the more reason for me to be gone." Star leaped out of her chair, picked up her guitar, which she'd set in the corner, and headed out the door. *Mom might think Mike's a great catch, but I'm sure he's just like all the other men in her life—nothing but a loser!*

Mishawaka

"Where are the kids?" Stuart asked when he entered the living room where Pam sat in front of her sewing machine near the window. "On a nice day like this, I figured they'd be outside playing."

"Devin's over at his friend Ricky's, and Sherry's upstairs, sick in bed."

Stuart's eyebrows shot up. "What's wrong with her? She wasn't sick when I left for work this morning."

"I got a call from her school shortly after noon saying she was running a fever and had vomited during recess, so I went right over and picked her up."

"How's she doing now?" he asked.

"About the same. I've been checking her temperature regularly, but it hasn't gone down yet."

"That's not good. How come you didn't call me at work?"

"I didn't want to worry you. Besides, there was nothing you could do."

"Did you at least call our pediatrician?"

Pam could hear the irritation in Stuart's voice. Well, she was irritated, too. Didn't he think she was capable enough to take care of their daughter or smart enough to know when to call the doctor? How was she supposed to have any confidence in herself when all he did was put her down or question her intelligence?

"Of course I called Dr. Norton," she snapped. "I'm not stupid, you know."

"Never said you were. Just wanted to be sure our little girl gets well."

Pam folded her arms stiffly, feeling more defensive. "I want that, too, Stuart. Despite what you may think, I am a good mother."

Stuart's eyes flashed angrily. "Give me a break, Pam. I never said you weren't a good mother. Just like always, you're putting words in my mouth."

She blew out her breath in a lingering sigh. "This conversation is getting us nowhere."

"It would be if you'd tell me what Dr. Norton had to say. Or were you even able to get past the receptionist so you could speak with the doctor directly?"

"I wasn't able to talk to her at first, but she did return my call."

"And?"

"She said Sherry's symptoms sound like the flu that's been going around and asked me to let her know if the fever spikes or if Sherry's stomach doesn't settle down soon. If it's the twenty-four-hour flu bug, then I'm sure she'll feel better by tomorrow."

"I hope so." Stuart shifted his weight from one foot to the other. "Uh, I hope you don't expect me to watch the kids tomorrow if Sherry's still sick."

"Well, you did say you'd stay with them while I go to the quilting class."

"Yeah, I know, but that was before Sherry got sick. You know I don't do well with the kids when they're sick. For that matter, they don't do so good with me, either. It's you they want when they're not feeling well."

"Maybe you could take the quilt class in my place," Pam suggested.

His eyes widened. "Huh?"

"If one of us doesn't go, we won't know the next step in making the wall hanging, and I don't want to get behind."

"Then why don't you just quit the class?" he asked.

She shook her head determinedly. "No way! I paid good money to take that class, and I really do want to learn how to quilt. Please, Stuart, say you'll go in my place."

"Huh-uh. I don't think so."

"It's pretty ridiculous and selfish that you don't want to go there alone, but yet you won't stay with the kids either." Pam's chin trembled. "Don't you care about anyone but yourself?"

" 'Course I do."

"Then prove it."

Stuart sat mulling things over then finally nodded. "I may be crazy, but all right, I'll go. Maybe it won't be so bad this week."

Elkhart

"Sleep well, precious one," Paul whispered as he placed Sophia in her crib and bent to give her forehead a kiss. "Pleasant dreams."

Sophia looked up at him through half-closed eyelids and smiled.

Paul's heart clenched. He had to admit he was a bit overprotective of his daughter, but she was all he had left of Lorinda. His baby girl had her mother's dimpled smile, and oh, so many things about Sophia reminded him of Lorinda.

He tiptoed quietly from the room and made his way down the hall, swallowing past the lump in his throat. Today would have been Lorinda's twenty-fifth birthday. If she were still alive, they'd have celebrated the occasion with some of their family. Paul would've bought a bouquet of yellow roses, Lorinda's favorite flower. And Maria probably would have fixed enchiladas and baked a carrot cake with cream cheese frosting— also Lorinda's favorite. They'd have laughed and played games, and if Lorinda's folks had been able to come, they would have shared humorous stories from Lorinda's childhood. But it wasn't meant to be. Lorinda was spending her birthday in heaven instead of here with her family.

Paul ambled into the living room and sank onto the sofa. So many memories—so many regrets. If he'd just seen that truck coming, maybe he could have avoided the accident. Of course, as Paul's priest had told him on more than one occasion, the trucker, who'd only sustained minor

injuries, had admitted that he'd run the red light, so if anyone was to blame, it was him.

Then why does Carmen blame me? Paul wondered. *Is she angry because I followed my family when they moved to Indiana? Does she think if we hadn't left California, Lorinda would still be alive? Well, accidents happen there, too—probably even more than here because it's so heavily populated.*

Paul had tried talking to Carmen on the day of Lorinda's funeral, but she'd barely said more than a few words in response, and those she had spoken were hurtful: *"Lorinda would still be here now if it weren't for you."*

Paul leaned forward and let his head fall into his open palms. If Carmen hated him, that was one thing, but did she have to take it out on Sophia? By not keeping in contact, she was cutting herself off from her only niece. And that meant, short of a miracle, Sophia would never get to know her mother's sister. Where was the fairness in that?

Of course, many things in life weren't fair. Look at all the problems some of his second-grade students had gone through with their families this past year. Little Ronnie Anderson's folks had ended their ten-year marriage in an ugly divorce; Anna Freeman had lost her grandma to cancer; and Miguel Garcia had been diagnosed with leukemia. Life was hard, and many things weren't fair, but Paul knew he must keep the faith and trust God to help him through each day. Sophia needed him even more than he needed her. Together they would take one day at a time, and Paul would remember to be thankful for all of God's blessings.

CHAPTER 17

Shipshewana

Emma was surprised when her students showed up for class on Saturday morning and Stuart was alone.

"Where's your wife?" Ruby Lee asked as they all took seats around Emma's sewing table.

"Our daughter came down with the flu, so Pam stayed home to take care of her," Stuart said. "I'm here to learn what I can so Pam doesn't fall behind."

Emma wasn't sure if Stuart's distraught look was because he was worried about his daughter or irritated that he had to come to class. During the first two classes, it had been obvious that he'd felt coerced into coming, and he hadn't shown much interest in learning to make a quilted wall hanging at all.

"It's too bad about your daughter and also Pam missing the class," Emma said.

Ruby Lee clucked her tongue noisily. "I missed many events when my boys were young and came down sick, but then that's just a part of being a mother."

"If Sophia got sick, I'd stay home with her," Paul interjected, "even though I'd probably have to rely on my sister for help, because I'm sure I'd be a basket case if my little girl became ill."

Star folded her arms and frowned. "Nobody ever cared when I got sick—except for one time when I was visiting Grandma and came down with a bad cold. She fussed over me like I was someone special. Even served me breakfast in bed. It felt nice to be taken care of that way and to feel like I meant somethin' to somebody."

Emma's heart went out to Star. She'd obviously had a rough childhood, and with the exception of her grandmother, the poor girl probably hadn't felt much love at all.

"Are you sayin' your ma didn't take care of you when you got sick?" Jan questioned.

Star lifted her shoulders in a brief shrug. "Mom took me to the doctor whenever I was really sick, but when she was at work and I had a cold or the flu, I pretty much had to fend for myself."

"You mean she left you at home alone?" Paul asked with a look of disbelief.

"Yep."

His forehead wrinkled deeply. "I would never leave my little girl alone! What was your mother thinking?"

Star tipped her head and looked at Paul as though he were a complete idiot. "She didn't leave me alone when I was a baby. I went to day care back then. She didn't start leaving me alone till I was in school and old enough to manage on my own while she was at work."

How crazy is this? Star thought. *Now I'm defending my mom? Guess there's something to the saying that a person can talk bad about someone in their family, but no one else had better do it.*

Emma came around behind the table and placed her hands on Star's shoulders. "I'm sorry you had to be alone when you were sick. I'm sure you must have been lonely and scared."

"Yeah, well, I appreciate your sympathy and all, but it won't change the past. Now can we forget all this doom and gloom and get on with our lesson?"

Emma, taken aback by the young woman's abruptness, quickly took a seat on the other side of the table. "Before we begin, I'd like to see how each of you did on your quilting projects this week."

The students placed their unfinished wall hangings on the table, and Emma looked them over. She was disappointed to see that very little work had been done to Pam's and nothing at all on Stuart's.

As though sensing her disappointment, Stuart said, "Pam did a little more sewing on her project before Sherry got sick."

"What about you, man?" Jan spoke up. "Doesn't look like you've done a thing since last Saturday."

Emma tensed, thinking Stuart might lash out at Jan, but she was surprised when he lowered his gaze to the table, removed his ball cap, and mumbled, "I didn't do anything to it 'cause I wasn't planning to come back to the class again."

Emma nodded slowly. "I had a feeling that might be the case."

"It's not that I have anything against you people," Stuart was quick to say. "I just don't feel comfortable about using a needle and thread. Besides, with the way Pam's talked about our problems, I figured you all probably think I'm a terrible husband."

No one said anything. Then Emma finally spoke. "Marriage is about loving the other person enough to do some things just for them—even things you don't want to do."

"Guess you're right." Stuart pulled his fingers through the top of his hair, making it stand nearly straight up. "So maybe I'll change my mind and stick it out through the whole six weeks. Then I'll see if Pam keeps her end of the bargain and goes fishing with me."

"I wouldn't count on that," Jan spoke up. "Most of the women I've ever known say they'll do one thing and end up doing just the opposite."

"Men are no better," Star interjected. "All my mom's *wonderful* boyfriends have been losers—promising this, promising that, and never keeping their word on anything."

Emma figured the conversation was becoming too negative and might lead to a disagreement, so she suggested that everyone take turns using the battery-operated sewing machines so they could get more of their pattern pieces sewn together.

While they worked, Emma was surprised to see how much more easygoing and relaxed Stuart seemed to be. He even cracked a few jokes.

"I may not be so good at sewing," he said, "but there's one thing I know I can do better than anyone else."

"What's that?" Ruby Lee questioned.

"I can read my own handwriting."

Ruby Lee chuckled; Paul grinned; Star rolled her eyes; and Jan just shook his head.

Stuart held up the few pieces he'd managed to sew. "Now look at this mess. Good grief, it takes too many pieces of this little material to make up each point of the star, and to make things worse, I can't even sew a straight seam!"

"You'll get a feel for it," Emma said. "It just takes practice."

Stuart placed his material on the table and pointed out the window. "Those cows I see in that pasture across the way remind me of a story someone told me at the sporting goods store the other day."

"What was it?" Paul asked.

"Well, a guy and a gal were walkin' along a country road, and when they came to a bunch of cows, the guy said, 'Would you just look at that cow and the bull rubbing noses?' He glanced over at his girlfriend and smiled. 'That sight makes me want to do the same.' The girlfriend looked that fellow right in the eye and said, 'If you're not afraid of the bull, then go right ahead.'"

Stuart's joke brought a smile to everyone lips, including Jan's.

Emma wondered if perhaps Stuart felt freer to express himself when his wife wasn't with him. If so, it was a shame, because God never intended for married couples to put each other down or argue about petty things.

———

Ruby Lee had a hard time keeping her mind on the straight line she was trying to make while using Emma's battery-operated sewing machine. Gene was having a meeting with the church board this morning, and she couldn't help but worry about how things were going. Would they listen to what he had to say or insist on having their own way? She knew that earlier this week Gene had talked to each of the board members individually and hoped he'd been able to make them see that he wasn't trying to get the church into debt. He just wanted to see the congregation take a step of faith so it could grow and reach out to more people in the area.

Resolving to put her concerns aside, Ruby Lee looked over at Emma and said, "How are things with your goat? Maggie, is it?"

Emma nodded.

"Is she still getting out of her pen?"

"Not since my son-in-law fixed the latch on the gate. But then, knowing that sneaky little goat, she might just find a way to open it."

"Boy, I can sure relate to that," Jan said with a grunt. "My German shepherd, Brutus, has turned into the neighborhood thief, so I had to build him a dog pen. He's managed to dig his way out of it a couple of times, but I fixed that by diggin' a small trench all the way around the pen and then puttin' some wire fencing in the ground."

"That was good thinking," Star said, giving Jan a thumbs-up.

"Yeah, but it didn't solve the problem, 'cause the other day Brutus got out again." Jan's forehead creased, but the stress lines disappeared under his biker's bandanna. "Since I didn't see no sign of a hole anywhere, I'm guessin' he had to have climbed over the top."

"My folks used to have a dog that did that," Stuart spoke up. "Dad put some wire fencing over the top of the dog pen, and that solved the problem."

"Guess I might hafta do that if Brutus keeps gettin' out. Sure can't have him runnin' all over the neighborhood stealin' other people's things. I just don't have the time to be chasin' all over the place, tryin' to find out who the items belong to that Brutus keeps takin'. If he doesn't quit it, I'm either gonna be the laughin'stock of the whole neighborhood, or no one will be speakin' to me." Chuckling, he added, "Guess there's a positive side to all of this though."

"What's that?" Paul asked.

"I'm actually gettin' to meet some of my neighbors when I go around lookin' for the owner of the things Brutus has taken."

That comment got a good laugh from everyone.

"I heard about a cat that was a kleptomaniac," Ruby Lee said. "After talking to an expert on the subject, the people were told that the cat was probably bored and needed more attention. I guess the cat stole more than a hundred items before the owners finally figured out what to do about the problem."

"Lack of attention could be why your dog's getting out of his pen," Star said. "I visited a website once when I was doin' a research paper for twelfth-grade English. The whole thing was about pets that escape from their pen and run off. Some animal psychologist came up with the idea that when a dog does that, it's also in need of more attention."

Jan nodded as he popped a few of his knuckles. "I've been pretty busy with work lately, and so I haven't spent much time with Brutus. Guess I'll need to take more time out for him and see if it makes a difference. Maybe it'd be a good idea if I take him with me when I make my rounds through the neighborhood tryin' to return all of the things he's taken."

"I've always wanted a dog," Star said wistfully. "But Mom and I have moved around so much it just never worked out for me to get one. I may get a dog when I have a place of my own someday though."

"Another reason you don't want your dog running all over the place, Jan, is to keep him from getting out on the road where he might get hit by a car," Emma said. "That's why I asked my son-in-law to fix the gate on the goat pen. Maggie's a bad one, but I would hate to see anything happen to her."

"That's right," Paul interjected. "On my way here this morning, I saw a German shepherd lying dead in the road. Apparently someone hit the poor dog and then fled the scene, because I didn't see anyone standing around or even a car parked near the shoulder of the road."

"What'd the dog look like?" Jan asked, concern showing clearly on his face.

"Traffic was almost at a standstill, and from what I could tell when I passed the animal, it was black and tan."

Jan's eyebrows shot up. "That sounds like my Brutus. Where exactly did you see the dog?"

"He was on the main road coming into Shipshewana, near the 5 and 20 Country Kitchen," Paul replied.

"That's not far from my place!" Jan leaped out of his chair then turned to Emma. "Sorry, but I've gotta go." Leaving his quilt project on the table, he rushed out the door.

"That poor man sure looked upset," Emma said. "I hope his dog is all right."

Ruby Lee nodded. "Some people's pets are very important to them— almost like children. When my boys were six years old and their cat died, they insisted their dad do a little burial service in our backyard."

"Did he do it?" Star asked.

Ruby Lee nodded. "The boys carried on so much that Gene could hardly say no."

"My kids have been after me to get them a dog, but pets are a lot of work, and I'm not sure they're ready for the responsibility." Stuart's stomach growled, and he covered it with his hands, probably hoping to quiet the noise. "Oops. . .sorry about that. Pam was busy caring for Sherry this morning, and she didn't have time to fix me anything for breakfast. So I just grabbed a cup of coffee and headed out the door."

"Why didn't you fix yourself something to eat? You look capable enough to me," Star said, looking thoroughly disgusted with Stuart.

Stuart shrugged. "Never thought about it 'cause Pam has always made my breakfast."

"Well, there's a first time for everything. Maybe you oughta help your wife out once in a while," Star muttered.

"I do plenty of things to help out."

"Uh, let's take a break, and I'll bring out a treat. Then we can continue working on the wall hangings after that," Emma said with a cheerful smile.

Ruby Lee was quite sure that Emma felt the tension between Star and Stuart. If she had to guess, she'd say that Star was probably angry with someone who'd treated her mother poorly.

"A treat sounds good to me," Stuart agreed. "Have you got any more of those tasty doughnuts you served us last week?"

Emma shook her head. "No, but I do have an angel cream pie I baked yesterday, and there's a pot of coffee on the stove. I'll head out to the kitchen to get them right now."

"I'll go with you." Star left her seat and followed Emma out of the room, leaving Ruby Lee alone with the men.

"Sure hope I get the hang of sewing," Stuart said, motioning to the little he'd done on his wall hanging. "I feel like I'm all thumbs." He held up his hands. "Sore thumbs at that, from getting stuck with the pins so many times. No wonder I've seen women use those little thimble contraptions to cover their fingers."

"I've pricked my finger a few times, too," Paul said with a chuckle. "Makes me appreciate all the sewing my wife used to do."

Ruby Lee was about to comment when her cell phone rang. It was a number she didn't recognize, so she was tempted to let the call go into voice mail. But something told her to answer, as it might be important.

"Hello," Ruby Lee said.

"Is this Mrs. Williams?"

"Yes."

"My name is Joan Hastings. I'm a nurse at the hospital in Goshen, and I'm calling to let you know that your husband's here in the emergency room."

"Oh, can I speak to him?" Ruby Lee asked, thinking Gene must be with one of their parishioners who'd been hurt or had become ill.

"He can't talk to you at the moment," the nurse replied. "He's being

examined by one of our doctors."

Ruby Lee's heart started to pound. Gene was in the emergency room being examined by a doctor? Something terrible must have happened. "W–was he in an accident? Is he seriously hurt?"

"He's having trouble breathing and complained of feeling dizzy when he first came in. We've run some tests to see if it's his heart, and—"

"I'll be right there!" Hands shaking, Ruby Lee ended the call and turned to face Paul and Stuart. "W–would you please let Emma know that I had to go? My husband's been taken to the emergency room." Without waiting for either man's reply, she gathered up her sewing and rushed out the door.

CHAPTER 18

Mishawaka

Pam glanced at the clock on the kitchen wall. It was eleven o'clock, which meant the quilting class would be over in an hour.

She opened the refrigerator and poured herself a glass of iced tea, wondering how Stuart was doing. She hated to see him go alone but knew her place was at home, taking care of the kids. Although Sherry was feeling a little better this morning, she wasn't well enough to leave with a sitter. Poor little thing hadn't been able to keep anything down until early this morning when Pam had given her some ginger tea and a small piece of toast.

A niggle of guilt settled over Pam as she remembered that she hadn't fixed Stuart any breakfast—although once in a while, he should be able to manage on his own. After all, he had to have known she was busy taking care of Sherry, and he wasn't completely helpless in the kitchen—just lazy and too dependent on her.

Pam glanced out the window to see what Devin was up to. She

didn't see him jumping on the trampoline, but then she remembered he'd said something about playing in the tree house. Stuart had built it last summer so that he and Devin could climb up there once in a while and have a little father-son time. Trouble was Devin was the only one who used it. Pam had seen Stuart go into the tree house just once, and that was right after he'd built it.

If he didn't spend so much time in front of the TV watching sports, he might take more of an interest in the kids, Pam fumed. *Doesn't he realize how quickly they're growing? Soon they'll be grown and moved out on their own, and then it'll be impossible to get back those wasted years when he should have been doing more things with his family.*

Knowing she needed to focus on something positive, and confident that Sherry was still sleeping, Pam decided to take her iced tea outside on the porch where she could enjoy the breeze that had come up a short time ago.

Stepping outside and taking a seat in one of the wicker chairs, Pam glanced toward the pink and purple petunias she'd planted in her flower garden last week. They were so beautiful and added just the right splash of color to the area where she'd put them.

Pam's thoughts halted when she heard a whimpering noise. Glancing up at the tree house in the maple tree, she realized it must be Devin. She set down her glass and hurried across the yard.

"Devin," she called. "Are you okay?"

More whimpering followed by some sniffles.

Heart pounding, she climbed the ladder to the tree house where she found her son huddled in one corner, tears rolling down his flushed cheeks.

"What's wrong, Devin?" she asked, kneeling on the wooden floor beside him. "Are you hurt?"

He shook his head. "I–I'm scared 'cause Daddy might leave and never come back."

"Now why would you think that?"

"My friend Andy's dad left, and Andy never sees him no more." Devin sniffed and swiped his hand over his damp cheeks. "If Daddy left, I'd really be sad."

Pam slipped her arm around Devin's shoulders and drew him close. "Your daddy's not going to move out of our house."

"Are—are you sure?"

"Yes, I'm very sure," Pam said with a nod, although secretly she'd been worried about that very thing.

Shipshewana

"What did you say this is called?" Star asked when Emma placed the pie on the table and asked her to cut it into even pieces.

"Angel cream pie," Emma replied. "My grandmother used to make it, and she gave me the recipe when I got married."

"Speaking of grandmothers—you sort of remind me of my grandma. Not in the way you look, but the way you treat people. Your kindness and sense of humor make me think of her, too."

Emma smiled. Even though Star was wearing that black sweatshirt again, it was good to see that the hood wasn't on her head today. The young woman had a pretty face, and it was nice to see her tender expression when she spoke of her grandmother—although Emma still didn't understand why Star had purple streaks in her hair, wore a nose ring, and had a tattoo on her neck. But then, there were many things she didn't understand—especially when it came to some Englishers. Even so, Emma knew God had created everyone, and that each person was special to Him.

"I miss my grandma so much." Star's eyes suddenly filled with tears. "She always did nice things for me. Not like my mom, who only thinks of herself."

"What about your father? Where is he?" Emma questioned, wondering how any mother could only think of herself. It wasn't the Amish way to be selfish like that.

"Beats me. I've never met him. He ran out on us when I was a baby, and Mom ended up marrying some loser when I was eight years old." Star's forehead creased as she frowned. "His name was Wes Morgan, and he was really mean to Mom."

"Was he mean to you as well?"

"Not really. He pretty much ignored me. Wes died a few years after they were married, when he stepped out into traffic and got hit by a car. Mom and I have been on our own ever since."

"I'm sorry," Emma said, gently touching Star's arm.

"Yeah, it hasn't been easy, but I'm glad Wes is out of the picture." Star wrinkled her nose. "Now Mom's thinkin' of marrying this guy named Mike."

"I take it you don't care much for Mike?"

"Nope. Don't like him at all. He hangs out at our place all the time, expects Mom to wait on him, and tries to tell me how I should live." Star motioned to the pie. "All the pieces are cut now. Is there anything else you want me to do?" she asked, abruptly changing the subject.

Emma handed Star a serving tray. "You can put the pie on this, along with some plates and forks." She gathered up five plates and forks, which she then handed to Star. "Before you take these out to the others, I want you to know that you're welcome to come by here anytime if you should ever need to talk."

Star blinked a couple of times and stared at Emma with a look of disbelief. "Really? You wouldn't mind?"

"Not at all. I'm a good listener, and perhaps I may be able to offer you some advice."

"Thanks. I might take you up on that offer sometime." Wearing a smile on her face, Star picked up the tray and headed into the next room. Emma followed with another tray that held the coffee and mugs.

When Emma entered her sewing room, she was surprised to see only Paul and Stuart sitting at the table. "Where's Ruby Lee?" she asked.

"She got a phone call saying her husband had been taken to the emergency room, so she had to leave," Paul explained.

"I'm sorry to hear that," Emma said, feeling concern. "I certainly hope Ruby Lee's husband will be okay."

Goshen

When Ruby Lee entered the room where Gene had been examined, she found him sitting on the edge of the table buttoning his shirt.

"What happened?" she asked, rushing to his side, wanting to help with the buttons.

He waved his hand. "Don't look so worried; I'm not going to die. The doctor said I had an anxiety attack, but I'm feeling much better."

"What brought that on?" she asked. "Did something happen during the board meeting to upset you?"

"Yeah. The subject of adding on to the church came up again, and we ended up in an explosive meeting. I think all the bickering got to me, because my chest tightened up and I felt woozy and like I couldn't breathe."

Ruby Lee clutched his arm. "This whole mess with the church isn't good for your health. Surely you can see that. How much longer do you intend to put yourself through this, Gene?"

"I'm fine. There's nothing to worry about."

"You might be fine now, but what about the next time? You could end up really having a heart attack if you keep subjecting yourself to all this conflict with the board members. Won't you reconsider and look for another church? And what about me? I don't know what I would do if I lost you—especially over something like this."

He shook his head. "I've told you before, God called me to shepherd this flock, and until He releases me from that call, I'm staying put."

"What about the plans you have for adding on to the church? Are you going to keep fighting for it or let the idea go by the wayside?"

"I don't know. I'm trusting God to give me further direction, and I feel confident that everything will work out as it should—for our church building, our congregation, and for us, Ruby Lee."

I wish I had your optimism, she thought. *If I believed for one minute that it would do any good, I'd speak to each of the board members right now and give them a piece of my mind!*

Shipshewana

By the time Jan turned onto the road his house was on, he was out of breath from peddling his bike so hard. After he'd left Emma's, he'd gone to the intersection where Paul had seen the dead dog, needing to know if it was Brutus who'd been hit by a car. But the only sign of the accident was a large bloodstain on the pavement. The body of the dog was gone. He could hardly look at the crimson spot without imagining his faithful pet lying there lifeless. It had been all he could do to call the Humane Society and ask if they had his dog. He'd been told that a German shepherd had been killed and brought in earlier today, but since there were no tags or license to identify the dog's owner, they'd already disposed of the body.

It's just as well that I didn't see the dog's remains, Jan thought. *If it was Brutus, I don't think I coulda stood seein' him lyin' there, dead.*

Another thought popped into his head. *Maybe I'll find Brutus at home, safe in his pen, and then all my worries will have been for nothin'.*

Even though Jan hardly ever prayed, he found himself thinking, *Please, Lord, don't let my dog be dead.*

Anxious to see if Brutus was there, Jan didn't bother to stop at the mailbox. Instead, he pedaled quickly up the driveway and halted the bike, letting it fall in front of the dog pen. It was empty. No Brutus in sight.

"Brutus, where are you boy?" Jan called, hoping against hope that the dog might be somewhere on the property or at least close by. This was one time he wished Brutus was roaming the neighborhood, looking for something he could carry off and bring home.

Still no response to Jan's call.

Jan clapped, hollered the dog's name several more times, and gave a shrill whistle. Nothing. Not a whimper or a bark.

"Oh man," he moaned. "Brutus is dead, and it's all my fault. If I'd only done somethin' right away to keep him in his pen, this wouldn't have happened. Now it's too late, and I've lost my best friend."

Jan tried his best not to get choked up, wondering what his friend Terry would think if he stopped by and saw him blubbering like a baby. But Jan couldn't seem to help himself. That four-legged animal had gotten inside his heart, and he was miserable without him.

Jan looked up and noticed his cranky neighbor, Selma, peeking around the curtain in her kitchen window. Did she know Brutus was gone? When she found out he was dead, she'd probably be glad. He wished that he'd had the smarts to get a license and some ID tags for Brutus. At least then the Humane Society could have called and let him know when the dog was brought in.

Jan felt so miserable he was tempted to go in the house and drown his sorrows in a few beers. But what good would that do? It wouldn't bring Brutus back, and it would only dull the pain for a little while. No, he was better off without the beer and may as well face this thing head-on. It wasn't like the dog's death had been the only disappointment he'd ever had to face. Jan had faced a lot of disappointments along the way.

CHAPTER 19

W hen Emma woke up on Sunday morning, it was all she could do to get out of bed. She'd been extremely tired when she went to sleep last night and felt a strange tingling sensation along part of her waist. This morning her symptoms had increased, and her ears were ringing, too. She figured the fatigue could be from working too hard and not getting enough sleep, but she didn't like the constant irritation bothering her stomach. Maybe she hadn't gotten all the soap out when she'd washed clothes the other day. Could she be having an allergic reaction?

Maybe I shouldn't go to church today, Emma told herself as she ambled out to the kitchen. *Might be best if I stay home and rest—just in case I'm coming down with something contagious. But I'll need to let Mary know.*

Emma filled the teakettle with water and set it on stove, and while the water heated, she got dressed. She'd just set her head covering in place when she heard the teakettle whistle.

Returning to the kitchen, she poured the water into a ceramic teapot, dropped a tea bag in, and went out the back door.

When Emma entered Mary's yard, she was greeted by her fourteen-year-old grandson, Stephen, who was leading one of their buggy horses out of the barn.

"Guder mariye, Grossmammi," he said cheerfully. "Are you comin' over to our house for *friehschtick?*"

Emma shook her head. "No breakfast this morning. I just need to speak to your mamm."

Stephen pointed to the house. "She's probably in the kitchen. Would you tell her I'll be in as soon as I get Dan hitched to the buggy?"

"Jah, I sure will." Emma, feeling even wearier than before, stepped onto the back porch. When she entered the kitchen, she found her two young granddaughters, Lisa and Sharon, setting the table, while Mary stood at the counter cracking hard-boiled eggs.

"Guder mariye, Mom," Mary said, turning to smile at Emma. "Will you be joining us for friehschtick?"

Emma shook her head. "I'm not feeling like myself this morning, so I'm just going to have a cup of tea and stretch out on the sofa."

"Are you *grank?*" Mary's dark eyes revealed the depth of her concern.

"I'm not sure if I'm sick or not. Just feel really tired, and my skin feels kind of prickly right here." Emma touched the left side of her stomach.

"Have you checked for any kind of a rash?" Mary questioned.

"Jah, but I didn't see anything. Why do you ask?"

"I'm wondering if you might be coming down with shingles again. It seems to me when you had them before you mentioned your skin felt prickly at first."

Emma frowned. She'd come down with shingles a week after Ivan died and had been absolutely miserable. "I do hope it's not shingles again. I sure don't have time for that right now."

"Nobody has time to be grank, Grossmammi," Lisa spoke up. "But when it happens, there ain't much you can do about it."

"Isn't," Mary corrected. She looked back at Emma. "If you're not feeling well, would you like me to come over to your house and fix you something to eat before we leave for church?"

Emma shook her head. "I'll be fine with the tea, and maybe I'll have a piece of toast."

"All right then, but I'll be over to check on you sometime after we get home," Mary said.

"Stop by if you must, but I'm sure I'll be fine." Emma patted the top of Lisa's head and then turned toward the door.

Lingering on Mary's porch to take in the quiet of the morning, Emma leaned her head on the railing post and breathed in the heavy scent of lilacs that had been blooming along the fence for the last week. Overhead in the trees, the red-winged blackbirds sang, *Jubile-e-e! Jubile-e-e!* Pausing to enjoy peaceful moments like this could make up for any day that had started out wrong.

Emma's weariness increased, so she didn't linger long. Approaching her own back porch, she'd just made it to the first step when a wave of dizziness caught her off-balance. She quickly grabbed for the railing, thankful that she was able to keep from falling over.

Please, just let me get into my house.

The wooden boards creaked beneath her feet as she took each step slowly, inching her way up, still wavering. At the door, she closed her eyes for a minute, steadying herself and breathing deeply. Relieved when the dizziness started to fade, she was able to enter the house.

When Emma stepped into the kitchen, she checked the teapot. The tea was plenty well steeped, so she poured herself a cup, fixed a piece of toast, and took a seat at the table. Then she bowed her head for silent prayer.

When she finished eating, she put the dishes in the sink and took the rest of her tea to the living room.

Emma yawned. Unable to keep her eyes open, she removed her head covering, stretched out on the sofa, and closed her eyes. The gentle breeze blowing softly through her open living room window, the smell of fresh air, and the melody of birds singing outside in the maple tree at the corner of her yard were all she needed to lull her into a deep slumber. The last thing she remembered hearing was the distant sound of her goats in some unknown conversation with each other out in their pen.

Sometime later, Emma was awakened by a knock on the door. Still half-asleep and thinking it was probably Mary or someone from her family, she called, "Come in!"

Emma was surprised when Lamar stepped into the room.

She sat up quickly, smoothing the wrinkles in her dress and setting her head covering in place. "Ach, I didn't expect it was you."

"Sorry if I startled you," he said. "I spoke to Mary after church, and she said you'd stayed home because you weren't feeling well."

"I'm just a little under the weather. I don't think it's anything serious."

"You look *mied*," he said with a look of concern. "Have you been doing too much lately?"

Emma's spine stiffened as her defenses rose. "I have not been doing too much, and I'm feeling less tired after taking a nap."

"I'm worried about you, Emma."

"Well, you needn't be. I'm fine."

Lamar shifted his weight a few times as though uncertain of what to say next. "Well, uh. . .guess I'll be going."

"I appreciate you stopping by," Emma said, knowing she couldn't be rude.

Lamar was almost to the door when he turned back around. "If there's anything I can do for you, please let me know."

She gave a brief nod.

When Lamar went out the door, Emma leaned her head against the back of the sofa and moaned. *Won't that man ever take the hint? I am not interested in a relationship with him, and I don't want him to do anything but leave me alone.*

Goshen

As Ruby Lee stood at the back of the church with Gene, greeting people as they filed out of the sanctuary, a knot formed in the pit of her stomach. Gene had preached a meaningful sermon this morning, and yet not one person had even uttered an *amen*. Normally their church was a lively place where people often shouted *amen* and *hallelujah*. Not today, however. You could have heard a feather fall all the way from heaven the entire time Gene had been preaching. Was it his topic—stepping out in faith—or was it the fact that there had been so much gossip circulating about their pastor wanting to get the church into debt?

Whatever the case, Ruby Lee couldn't help but notice that some of the congregation had slipped out the side door rather than going through the line to greet their pastor and his wife. This only confirmed to Ruby Lee that she and Gene ought to leave this church, because she was quite sure that's what most folks wanted them to do.

Why couldn't Gene see that, too? Did he enjoy going through all this misery with no end in sight? Did he think the Lord would bless him for his diligence and playing the role of martyr? Ruby Lee knew that if Gene was going to stay here, then she had to as well because her place was at her husband's side. She was glad their boys were away at college and couldn't see how their father was being treated. She was sure it would have hurt them as much as it did her, and they probably would have been more vocal about it than she had been. It surprised her even more that only a short time ago these same church people who were now ignoring them and saying hurtful things about them had been their good friends. Or at least she'd thought they had been.

Drawing in a quick breath and plastering a smile on her face, Ruby Lee reached for the next person's hand. "Good morning, Mrs. Dooley. May God bless you, and I hope you have a good week."

Mishawaka

Pam tiptoed down the stairs. She'd just checked on Sherry and found her sleeping peacefully upstairs in her room. After Sherry had finished eating a little oatmeal for breakfast, she'd climbed back into bed with her favorite stuffed animal and fallen asleep. So far no one else in the family had gotten sick, and Pam hoped it stayed that way. Stuart thought maybe they should have moved Sherry to the spare bedroom next to theirs, but Pam had decided to sleep in Devin's room, which was across the hall from Sherry's, while Devin slept in the guest room downstairs.

Feeling the need for a little time to herself, Pam went to the living room, grabbed a book she'd been wanting to read, and curled up on the couch. Stuart and Devin were in the yard playing catch, so the house was peaceful and quiet.

Pam had only been reading a few minutes when Stuart entered the room and bent to nuzzle her cheek.

"Stop it. I'm busy right now," she mumbled.

"Doesn't look like you're busy to me. Looks like you've got your nose in a book."

"That's right, and it's the first minute I've really had to myself since Sherry got sick on Friday, so if you don't mind—"

Stuart flopped onto the other end of the couch. "How's our little gal doing?" he asked, lifting one of Pam's feet and starting to rub it.

"Better. She kept the oatmeal down that I gave her earlier."

"That's good to hear. Unless she has a relapse, you should be able to go to the quilt class this Saturday."

"Yes, but I wish you were going with me."

"I'm considering it."

Her eyebrows lifted. "Really?"

He gave a nod. "I felt more relaxed there yesterday than I did the week before."

"How come?"

He cleared his throat a couple of times. "Well, it was nice to have the chance to just be myself."

"What are you saying—that you couldn't be yourself when I was there?"

"Yep, that's pretty much the way it was."

Pam clenched her fingers tightly around the book, irritated with his answer. "Why can't you be yourself when I'm there?"

"Because I'm not comfortable with you telling everyone our problems and trying to make it look like I'm responsible for everything that's gone wrong in our marriage."

"I don't do that."

"Yes you do, and it makes me feel awkward and stupid."

"Fine then, I won't say a word about anything at the next quilt class. Will that make you happy?"

"Yeah, sure...like that's ever gonna happen." He picked up her other foot and began rubbing it, probably hoping it might soothe her tension, as it had when he'd rubbed her feet many times before.

Pam's irritation mounted, barely appreciating the foot massage, which at any other time would have been so relaxing that she'd have fallen asleep.

"I could keep quiet throughout the whole class if I wanted to."

"Great. I'll go with you next week, and then we'll see."

She set the book aside and gave a nod. "It's a deal!"

Stuart pushed her feet aside and stood. "Now that I'll have to see in order to believe."

Pam wrinkled her nose and caught herself just in time before sticking out her tongue.

After Stuart left the room, she bolted upright. "Oh, great. What did I agree to now? Can I really keep quiet throughout the whole class?"

Chapter 20

Shipshewana

On Monday morning, Emma still wasn't feeling well, but she forced herself to get out of bed, fix breakfast, and do a few chores. She really needed to get some laundry done, but she wasn't sure she had the energy for it.

Emma stepped into her sewing room, took a seat in the rocking chair, and leaned her head back, feeling ever so drowsy. It had been a long time since she'd felt so fatigued. She was almost at the point of dozing off when she heard the back door open. A few seconds later, Mary entered the room. "I came over to see how you're doing," she said.

Emma sighed. "Not as well as I'd like to be. I'm still awfully tired, and I haven't even washed my clothes yet."

"I'll do it, Mom."

Emma shook her head. "You have enough of your own work to do."

"My laundry is already out on the line, and I really don't mind helping you."

"Oh, all right. You can wash the clothes, but I'm going to help you hang them on the line." Emma didn't know why it was so hard for her to accept Mary's help. She never thought twice about helping others, yet when it came to being on the receiving end, she usually wanted to do things on her own. Even so, she appreciated her daughter. In fact, all her children would make any parent feel grateful. No matter how busy they were, they never hesitated to drop what they were doing if help was needed elsewhere. Emma just didn't want to become a burden.

Mary smiled. "If you're feeling up to helping, that's fine with me."

Emma followed Mary to the basement and took a seat on a folding chair while Mary filled the gas-powered wringer-washer with water.

"It was nice of Lamar to stop by and check on you yesterday," Mary said as she put some towels into the washer. "When I spoke to him after church, he seemed concerned about you not being there."

Emma rubbed a spot on the front of her dress where some tea must have dripped.

"Lamar seems to be a very nice man," Mary continued. "I also think he's lonely."

Emma folded her hands and began to twiddle her thumbs. She didn't care for the way this conversation was going. "If he's lonely, then he needs to find something to occupy his time. Keeping busy has helped me not to be so lonely since your daed died."

"From what I can tell, Lamar keeps plenty busy with the hickory rocking chairs he makes. Besides, staying busy is no guarantee that a person won't be lonely."

"I suppose you're right." Despite Emma's activities in her yard and with her quilting projects, she still felt lonely at times—especially in the evenings, which was when she and Ivan used to sit out on the porch or in the living room to relax and visit after a long day. Oh, how she missed those special times.

"I think Lamar would probably like to find another wife," Mary said.

Emma clenched her fingers into a tight ball. "Jah, well, that's fine. It's just not going to be me."

Star had just gotten off work, and instead of going straight home, she decided to drive over to Shipshewana to see Emma. She wanted to talk to her more about Mom's new man friend—tell her what happened yesterday when Mike came over. She was still upset and needed someone to share her feelings with, and it sure couldn't be Mom. Had Mom taken Star's side yesterday when Mike jumped her about wearing dark-colored clothes and too much eye makeup? No! Had Mom told Mike to get his shoes off the couch when he'd sprawled out to watch TV for the day? Of course not! Mom pretty much let Mike do whatever he wanted, even though they weren't married.

"And I hope they never are," Star mumbled as she started her car's engine.

As she pulled out from Walmart, she began to sing the lyrics to one of the songs she'd been working on. "Never gonna be the princess, holding tight to Daddy's neck; never gonna be the apple of his eye. Never gonna walk the aisle hand in hand; a sweet vignette. Never gonna answer all the whys."

Tears pricked the back of Star's eyes, and she blinked to keep them from spilling over. No point giving in to self-pity, because it wouldn't change a thing. If Mom ended up marrying Mike, there wasn't anything Star could do about it. She just needed to take one day at a time and try to focus on other things. Maybe someday one of her songs would be discovered and she'd become a real star; then she wouldn't need anyone—not even Mom.

Star continued to sing as she drove toward Shipshewana. When she pulled into Emma's yard sometime later, she saw Emma and a younger woman hanging clothes on the line.

Seeing that Emma wasn't alone, Star was hesitant about getting out of the car. But when Emma looked her way and waved, she knew she couldn't turn around and leave. That would be rude. So Star turned off her car's engine, stepped out, and headed across the yard.

When she reached the clothesline, Emma smiled and said, "What a nice surprise. What brings you by here this Monday morning?"

Feeling suddenly shy and more than a bit uncomfortable due to the other woman's curious expression, Star dropped her gaze to the ground and mumbled, "Just got off work."

"I didn't realize you worked in Shipshewana," Emma said.

"I don't. I work at the Walmart in Goshen." Star dragged the toe of her sneaker along a clump of grass. "Thought maybe it would be a good time to visit with you awhile, but I can see that you're busy right now."

"I'm not too busy to talk." Emma placed her hand on Star's arm. "Besides, you just drove probably half an hour to get here, and I surely can't send you away."

Emma's gentle touch felt warm and comforting. It made Star think of Grandma again, but she wasn't sure how to respond. She really did need to talk to Emma but didn't want to do it in front of the other woman.

"Oh, silly me," Emma said. "I don't believe you've met my daughter. Star, this is Mary. She lives next door and came over to help me with the laundry."

"We did meet briefly on the first day of your quilting class, but we weren't introduced." Mary held out her hand. "It's nice to meet you, Star."

Star, feeling a little more relaxed, shook Mary's hand. "Yeah, I remember now. Nice to meet you, too."

"What kind of work do you do at Walmart?" Emma asked as she hung one of her plain blue dresses on the line.

"I stock shelves in the wee hours of the morning."

"That must be nice in some ways," Mary said, "because it gives you the rest of the day to do other things."

"Yeah." Star bent down and picked up a wet towel from the wicker basket. "This looks like fun. Think I'll help, if you don't mind."

Emma laughed. "We don't mind at all, but I'm surprised you would think hanging out the laundry is fun."

"Well, fun might not be the best word for it," Star said, "but it's different. With the exception of the time we've spent living in my grandma's house, Mom and I have always washed and dried our clothes at the Laundromat." Star pointed to a sheet flapping in the breeze. "Do you hang things out when the weather is nice and then use the dryer when it's raining or snowing?"

Emma shook her head. "Oh no. We don't have automatic clothes dryers, but if we did, I'd really miss the fresh scent that clings to the sheets. For me, it's almost like sleeping in the outdoors when I cover up at night and smell the earth's sweet fragrance on my bedding."

"Oh that's right. I forgot you don't use electricity in your homes. So what do you do about washing your clothes? Do you have to wash 'em in a big round tub with a washboard?"

"Some of the washing machines we use in this community are run with a generator, but Mom's machine is run by a gas-powered motor that's set up outside, and the drive shaft is run into the washing area," Mary explained.

"Oh, I see." Star couldn't imagine living without the benefit of electricity and doing without all the modern conveniences. She did remember, though, how good the sheets smelled when she'd stayed at Grandma's house a few times before Grandma had become so ill.

That must be what Emma meant about the fresh earthy scent. Grandma probably hung her clothes out to dry sometimes. Funny how I'd forgotten that little memory of Grandma's sheets until Emma spoke of it.

They visited about other things until all the clothes were hung, and then Mary said she needed to do some things at her home, so she bid them good-bye.

"Would you like to take a seat on the porch?" Emma asked. "All that bending and stretching left me feeling rather worn out."

Star nodded. "Then I guess we should both have a seat, because I'm kinda tired, too."

As they walked to the porch, Star couldn't help but notice Emma's slow-moving gait. "Are you feeling all right today?" she asked, reaching out to steady Emma as they took seats on the porch swing.

"I've been feeling rather drained for the last few days. Just don't quite feel like myself." Emma smiled, although the usual sparkle in her blue eyes wasn't there. "I stayed home from church yesterday to rest, but I guess it didn't help because I don't have much energy this morning either."

"Maybe I oughta go so you can take a nap." Star started to rise, but Emma shook her head and motioned for her to sit back down.

"There's no need for you to rush off. I can rest right here while we visit."

"Okay, if you're sure." Star seated herself again and tucked a lock of hair behind her ear as a breeze lifted it from her shoulder. It was warm out today, and she was wearing jeans and a black tank top instead of

WANDA &. BRUNSTETTER

her usual hooded sweatshirt. She was glad the job of stocking shelves at Walmart didn't require that she wear a uniform. She wouldn't feel comfortable dressed in one of those.

"How was your weekend?" Emma asked.

Star shrugged. "Could have been better. At least Sunday sure could have."

"What happened?"

Star began telling Emma how Mike had acted—controlling the TV remote, telling Star how she should dress, and complaining because he thought she wore too much eye makeup and too many rings on her fingers. He'd also griped about the small gold hoop in her nose, saying it looked ridiculous.

"I finally left the house and went for a walk just to get away from him. Don't know what I'm gonna do if Mom marries that guy." Star pursed her lips. "Mom's so gullible when it comes to men, and I'm not sure she's making a right decision where Mike is concerned. Fact is, she's made many poor choices and hasn't always been honest with me about things either. It really makes me mad."

"People are human, Star, and sometimes due to circumstances or just plain immaturity, they make poor choices." Emma sighed. "I made some poor choices myself when I was a young woman during my courting days."

Star tipped her head. "Courting? Is that the same thing as dating?"

"Well, I believe it's a little different," Emma said. "Courting is done with the intention of discovering if you want to be with the person forever. Dating is not as serious. At least that's how I understand it."

"Well, dating or courting, I can't imagine a nice lady like you making poor choices."

"I did though. When I was seventeen, I chose the wrong boyfriend."

Emma stared into the yard as though remembering the past. "His name was Eli Raber, and he had a wild side to him. Eli liked to drink, smoke, and run around. He also had a bright red car he kept hidden behind his daddy's barn."

Star leaned forward, listening intently as Emma went on to tell that Eli had it in his mind to leave the Amish faith and wanted Emma to join him.

"I almost did, too," Emma admitted. "Had it not been for Ivan coming along when he did, I might have run off with Eli and gotten into who knows what kind of trouble." She smiled, and some of that sparkle returned to her eyes. "Ivan was so kind and polite. He had good morals and was a dependable worker—helping his father in his harness shop. It didn't take me long at all to realize I'd found a good man."

"Hmm. . . I see."

"Does your mother love Mike?" Emma asked.

"I guess so. At least she says she does."

"Is he in love with her?"

"Supposedly, but then who knows? He could just be putting on an act to impress her."

"Does he have a steady job?"

"Yeah. He manages a restaurant in Goshen, and from the gifts he brings Mom, I'm guessin' he makes pretty good money."

"And is this man kind to your mother?"

"He seems to be—so far, anyway. According to Mom, Mike doesn't drink, smoke, or do drugs either."

"Then perhaps marrying him is what your mother needs."

"Maybe so, but it's sure not what I need."

"What do you need, Star?"

Star drew in a deep breath, and when she released it, her bangs lifted up from her forehead. "I need someone who won't look down their nose at me and criticize everything I say or do. I need someone who'll be my friend. I need someone who'll care about me the way Grandma did."

Emma placed her hand gently on Star's arm. "I care about you."

"Even though I dress weird and say things in a different way than you do?"

Emma chuckled and motioned to her head covering. "Some people probably think I dress weird, too."

Still not quite comfortable talking about her life, Star pointed to the pretty flower arrangement in the corner of Emma's yard. "That's an unusual flowerpot. Did you get it at the Shipshewana flea market?"

Emma explained that one morning, rather than throwing her husband's old work boots out, she'd planted carnations in them. "It's a beautiful reminder of how hard Ivan worked to provide for me and our family," she said. "I have the other boot in another nature garden out back, where I can see it when I'm looking out the kitchen window. I planted petunias in that one."

Emma went on to tell Star that the rock in the front yard where the boot sat had been found by her husband while they'd been walking through the woods together one afternoon during their courting days.

Emma paused for a minute, and Star looked at her intently, thirsty to hear more.

"After Ivan and I got married, we lived on a farm, where we worked hard and soon became busy raising our children," Emma continued. "No matter how busy things got, one thing we remembered to do was to make time for having fun." She chuckled. "I can still recall a little joke I played on Ivan one time that had us all laughing."

"What was it?"

"On his forty-ninth birthday, instead of throwing the newspaper away after he'd finished reading it, I hid the paper for a whole year. Then the following year on his birthday, I replaced the current newspaper with the one from the year before. It was hard to keep from laughing as I sat across from Ivan at the breakfast table, slyly watching as I finished my cup of coffee and he read the paper."

"Did he catch on?" Star asked.

"He never noticed it was year-old news until he was almost done reading the entire paper." Emma giggled as she touched her cheeks. "You should have seen Ivan's expression when he commented about the articles sounding like news that had happened a year ago. And, oh my... I laughed so hard, I thought I was going to pop the seams in my dress."

"How'd he take it when he realized it was an old newspaper?"

"He actually took it quite well. Even laughed about it and told the rest of our family how I'd fooled him real good on his fiftieth birthday."

Star smiled and leaned back in her chair, noticing the laugh lines that had formed around Emma's eyes. Something about being with Emma made Star feel good. She hadn't felt this relaxed or lighthearted in years.

"You know, Star," Emma said, "those are the kinds of joys, even though they're simple, that help to keep a person grounded."

Star was quiet for a moment, thinking how wonderful it must be to have such happiness being with another person. "I like you, Emma Yoder. Yeah, I like you a lot."

Emma slipped her arm around Star's waist and gave her a hug. "I like you, too."

CHAPTER 21

"Y ou look like you've eaten a bowl of sour pickles for breakfast," Terry said when Jan climbed into his truck that morning. "Are you dreadin' going to work that much?"

"It's not the work I dread; it's the comin' home."

"Since when have you ever dreaded that?"

"Since my dog was killed."

Terry's eyes widened. "Brutus is dead?"

Jan nodded soberly.

"Oh man, how'd that happen?"

"He got out of his pen and was hit by a car."

"But I thought you fixed the pen so he couldn't get out."

"I thought that, too, but I guess he must've climbed the fence and gone out over the top."

"I'm real sorry to hear that. Did you bury him out back?"

Jan shook his head. "It didn't happen here. Paul—one of the guys who attends the quiltin' class on Saturdays—said he saw a dead dog on his way to Emma's that looked just like Brutus. It was over by the 5 and 20 Country Kitchen."

"Did you see the dog?"

"Nope. By the time I got there, the body was gone. Figured someone from Animal Control had probably hauled it off." Jan nearly choked on the words. "And I was right, 'cause when I called the Humane Society, they said a dead German shepherd had been brought in."

"How do you know it was Brutus? Did they identify him by his tags?"

"Didn't have any. I stupidly let the dog run around without a collar and never even bothered to get him a license or an ID tag. The description of the dog was the same, though, and when I came home on Saturday, Brutus wasn't in his pen or anywhere in the yard." Just talking about losing the dog made Jan feel sick. He'd been struggling with his emotions the entire weekend.

"That don't actually prove the dead dog was Brutus."

"Maybe not, but since Brutus didn't come back, it's pretty clear to me that it had to be him."

"Guess you're probably right," Terry said as he pulled out of Jan's driveway.

As they headed down the road, a thought popped into Jan's head. "Say, would you mind makin' a quick stop before we head on over to LaGrange to start our next roofin' job?"

"Sure. Where do you want me to stop?"

"At the Amish woman's home who teaches the quiltin' classes. She lives a short ways from here."

"Why do you wanna go there?" Terry asked.

"When I found out about the dog that had been hit, I left Emma's in such a hurry I forgot and left my quiltin' project on her table. If I don't pick it up, I won't be able to work on it this week."

"I still don't get why you're takin' that class, but to each his own, I guess."

"You got that right." Jan frowned when Terry lit up a cigarette. "Thought you'd given up that nasty habit."

"I've been tryin' to, but when I get stressed-out I need a smoke."

"What's got you feelin' stressed?"

"My folks." Terry groaned. "After being married thirty-five years, they're talkin' about splittin' up."

"That's too bad, man. Now you know why I've never gotten married. Too many complications, and it seems like there ain't much commitment anymore."

"Yeah, but I know some couples who've made it work."

"Guess that's true. Emma Yoder's a widow, and I'll bet you anything she and her husband had a good marriage. Even with him gone, her face lights up like a jar of lightnin' bugs whenever she mentions his name."

"Yeah, well I hope my folks get their act together soon, 'cause I sure don't wanna see 'em go their separate ways. They've been married too many years to throw in the towel."

"Maybe they oughta see a marriage counselor. That's what the couple takin' our class is doin'; although I ain't sure it's done 'em much good." Jan bumped Terry's arm. "Turn right here. That's Emma's house up ahead."

When they pulled into Emma's yard, Jan was surprised to see Star sitting on the front porch by herself. What was even more surprising was that she wasn't wearing her black hooded sweatshirt.

"You wanna come up to the house and meet Emma and Star?" Jan asked, turning to Terry.

"Naw, you go ahead."

"Okay. I'll just be gone long enough to get what I left." Jan hopped out of the truck and hurried across the yard.

"I'm surprised to see you here this mornin'," he said to Star as he stepped onto the porch.

"Came to talk to Emma awhile." She smiled. At least he thought it was a smile. Her lips were curved slightly upwards. "I'm surprised to see you here, too."

"I'm on my way to work, but I wanted to come by and get the quiltin' project I left when I ran outta here on Saturday."

"So what'd you find out? Was it your dog that had been hit?" she asked.

"It must have been, 'cause when I got home Brutus wasn't in his pen, and there ain't been no sign of him since."

"That's too bad." Star's somber-looking face let Jan know that she felt his pain. He figured behind that defiant attitude lay a heart of compassion. Out of all of Emma's other students, Star was the one who seemed the most real. Probably didn't have a phony bone in her body. Jan kind of liked her because she had spunk. Didn't care what anyone thought of her either. Too bad she wasn't a couple of years older, or he might consider asking her out. 'Course, he'd known a few other guys who'd dated younger women, but then he wasn't really looking to get serious about anyone again. Right now with all the roofing jobs he had lined up for the summer, he had enough to occupy his time.

"Did you check at the Humane Society to see if the dog had been taken there?" Star asked.

He nodded, unwilling to admit that he hadn't bothered to get Brutus any form of identification.

"So, where's Emma?" he asked, quickly changing the subject before he ended up blubbering about how much he missed Brutus.

Star motioned to the door. "She went to the kitchen to get us some iced tea."

"Guess I'll go inside and ask about my stuff, and then I need to be on my way."

"Before you go, you might like to know that you weren't the only one who left the class early the other day," Star said.

"Oh?"

"Yeah, Ruby Lee got a call from the hospital, sayin' her husband had been taken there."

"That's too bad. What was wrong with him?"

Star shrugged. "I'm not sure. Ruby Lee took off like a shot after she got the call. Hopefully it wasn't serious and she'll be back for the class this Saturday."

Jan couldn't help but notice the look of concern on Star's face. It was refreshing to meet a young woman who cared about people. He looked forward to getting to know her better in the coming weeks—maybe some of the others in the class as well. It seemed that joining their little quilting club was one of the few things he'd done right lately, rather than adding to the list of bad decisions he'd made.

———

Carrying two glasses of iced tea, Emma left the kitchen. She was just passing through her sewing room when she nearly collided with Jan.

"Oh my! You startled me. I—I didn't realize you were here."

"I'm on my way to work and decided to stop by and get my wall hangin'," he explained, looking a bit embarrassed. "I left here in such a hurry on Saturday I forgot to take it with me."

"Yes, I was sorry about that," Emma said, noticing the look of sadness in Jan's eyes. "Did you find out whether it was your dog that had been hit?"

Jan nodded soberly. "I'm sure it must've been Brutus."

"You must miss him very much."

"Yeah, I sure do, but it's my own stupid fault. Shoulda made sure his pen was secure all the way around and over the top, 'cause I'm convinced that must be how he got out."

"Blaming yourself will not bring the dog back, and it won't help you feel any better about losing him, either," Emma said gently.

"I know that." Jan hung his head. "Guess it's a good thing I'm not tryin' to raise any kids, 'cause I'd probably bumble that, too."

Emma set the glasses of iced tea on the sewing table and impulsively reached out to touch Jan's arm. "I'm really sorry for your loss."

"Thanks. I appreciate that."

"You know, Jan, a lot of accidents have happened within my Amish community, and even within my own family unit." Emma paused a moment to gather her thoughts. "One time when I was a little girl, one of my friends drowned in her uncle's pond."

Jan's eyes widened. "That's a shame."

She gave a nod. "It was a shock to everyone, and at first Elsie's parents blamed themselves for not keeping a close enough watch on her."

"I can understand that."

"They weren't the only ones who blamed themselves. Elsie's uncle Toby blamed himself because he should have put a fence up around the pond."

Jan gave a nod. "Guess they were all to blame then, huh?"

Emma shrugged. "I'm not sure if anyone was really to blame, except for my friend, who knew she couldn't swim and shouldn't have gone anywhere near that pond. The point is, blaming didn't bring Elsie back, and until her folks and her uncle came to accept Elsie's death and moved on, there was no healing for any of them."

"But they did finally accept it. Is that what you're sayin'?"

Emma nodded. "They still grieved and missed Elsie, of course, but when they stopped blaming themselves and accepted her death, knowing she was in a better place with God, then healing began in their hearts."

"But Brutus is a dog. He wouldn't have gone to heaven. Right?"

Emma turned her hands palm up. "Only God and those who are with Him right now know whether there are animals in heaven or not." She smiled up at Jan and gave his arm another gentle pat. "The main thing to remember is that your dog isn't suffering, and if you focus on the good memories you have of him, it'll help to heal the pain you feel so intensely right now."

Jan, his eyes now glassy with tears, smiled and said, "Thank you, Emma. I'm sure glad I stopped by here today, and I look forward to seein' you on Saturday for another quiltin' lesson."

Emma nodded. She hoped, Lord willing, that she'd be up to teaching the class.

CHAPTER 22

Elkhart

F or the last couple of days, Paul had been trying to reach Carmen, but here it was Wednesday, and she hadn't returned any of his calls.

Should I try again before I leave for school? he wondered, glancing at the phone. *Guess there's not much point. Carmen obviously doesn't want to talk to me, or she would have responded to at least one of my calls.*

Paul didn't know why it bothered him so much that Carmen had cut them out of her life. It wasn't as if she was Sophia's only aunt. It just hurt to know that she blamed him for Lorinda's death and didn't care enough about Sophia to come for a visit—or at least keep in contact with them.

He glanced at Sophia sitting in her high chair, patiently waiting to be fed. Not only would his precious little girl never know her mother, but it looked as if she wouldn't know her aunt Carmen either.

Paul had spoken to Lorinda's mother last night, asking about the trip they were planning to make to Indiana sometime this summer. When he'd mentioned that he hoped Carmen might come with them, Ramona had dismissed it lightly, saying Carmen had just started a new job and wouldn't be able to take time off for any trips this year. While that might be true enough, it didn't excuse Carmen for refusing to answer his calls.

Carmen was two years younger than Lorinda and had always been very independent. She'd gone to college right out of high school, and after she'd graduated and landed a job as a reporter for one of the Los Angeles newspapers, she'd rented an apartment several miles from her folks. Ramona had suggested that Carmen live at home for a while so she could save her money for other things, but Carmen wouldn't hear of it. She wanted to be out on her own. Carmen's career seemed to come first, and as far as Paul knew, Carmen didn't have a serious boyfriend.

Oh well. . .it's none of my business what Carmen does. I just wish she'd open the lines of communication with me again, Paul thought as he took a seat beside Sophia to feed her a bowl of cooked cereal.

Sophia looked up at him and grinned. "Pa-pa-pa."

Paul leaned over and kissed her soft cheek. "That's right little one, and you can always count on me."

Goshen

After Gene left to make a hospital call on one of their parishioners, Ruby Lee had felt the need for some fresh air and sunshine, so she'd left the house right after breakfast and headed for the Pumpkinvine Nature Trail.

As she walked briskly along trying to clear her head, she spotted a clump of violets growing along the edge of the path. Seeing the flowers caused Ruby Lee to think about her friend Annette, whose favorite flowers were violets. She'd e-mailed and called Annette several more times, but no response. Was Annette mad at her? Could she have said or done something that may have ruined their friendship? It didn't make any sense. Even though Ruby Lee had originally decided to keep her frustrations to herself, she desperately needed to talk to someone about the church's problems and the way Gene had been responding to them. She'd hoped Annette might offer some sympathy and understanding— maybe even give her a suggestion or two. If Annette lived closer, Ruby Lee would pay her a visit, but a trip to Nashville wasn't possible right now. Ruby Lee had commitments at church, not to mention finishing the quilt class she'd enrolled in.

Refusing to give in to self-pity, which seemed to be right at the surface these days, Ruby Lee picked up the pace and hurried on.

Concentrating on the soothing motion of Rock Run Creek, which ran beside the trail, and the gentle breeze whispering through the canopy of trees overhead, she tried to relax. She had only gone a short ways when she spotted a young, dark-haired woman with a ponytail, who was dressed in a pair of black shorts and a matching tank top, running along the trail in the opposite direction. As the woman approached, Ruby Lee realized it was Star; although she almost didn't recognize her without that usual black sweatshirt.

"Hey, sister! I'm surprised to see you here on the Pumpkinvine Trail," Ruby Lee called. It felt good to see a familiar face—someone who wasn't likely to judge.

"Hi, how's it going? How's your husband doing?" Star asked.

"He's fine. We were worried at first that it might be his heart, but everything checked out okay." Ruby Lee chose not to mention that the doctor had told Gene he'd had an anxiety attack. Star would probably want to know why, and Ruby Lee didn't feel like talking about it—at least not with her.

"Do you come here often?" Ruby Lee asked as Star turned and

started walking in the same direction as her.

"Once or twice a week." Star picked up a stone and threw it in the water. "Or whenever I need to run and take out my frustrations. It's great here, isn't it?"

"Yes, it really is a beautiful place. I come here frequently, and for the same reason as you," Ruby Lee admitted. "Only I don't run."

Star stared at Ruby Lee, as though in disbelief. "I can't imagine you having any frustrations."

Ruby Lee blinked her eyes. "What makes you think that?"

"You're always so happy-go-lucky during our quilting classes—like you don't have a care in the world. Except for last Saturday when you got the call about your husband, that is. I could tell you were pretty upset."

"Well, we all have our share of troubles, so there's bound to be times when we're upset and need to do something to help relieve our stress."

"That's for sure."

"I wonder how Jan is doing," Ruby Lee said, quickly changing the subject. "He seemed really upset on Saturday when Paul told him about seeing that dead dog on his way to Emma's."

"I saw Jan on Monday," Star said. "I dropped by Emma's to talk to her about some things I've been dealing with at home, and while I was there, Jan stopped by to pick up his quilting project."

"Did he say anything about his dog?"

"Yep. Said when he got home Brutus wasn't in his pen, so he's almost sure it was his dog that was hit."

"That's a shame."

"Yeah. Poor guy called the Humane Society, and they said they'd disposed of the dog's body, so Jan couldn't even go there to see whether it was Brutus or not. Jan tried to hide it, but I could tell he was taking it pretty hard." Star's expression was one of compassion, causing Ruby Lee to see a different side of the young woman.

As they continued to walk, they talked about Emma and how sweet and kindhearted she seemed to be.

"Emma's full of good advice, too," Star said. "Even shared with me some things about her past."

"Is that so?"

"Yeah, but I guess it's not my place to be blabbin' any of the things she told me."

"No, you're right. When someone confides in us about something, it's best not to tell anyone else."

"So what do you think of Stuart and Pam?" Star asked, taking their conversation in a little different direction.

"Well, it's really not my place to say, but I believe they're both very unhappy in their marriage," Ruby Lee replied.

"I got that impression right off the bat. Think they'll finish taking Emma's classes?"

"I don't know. I guess we'll have to wait and see how it goes." Ruby Lee motioned to a nearby bench. "Shall we take a seat?"

They sat quietly for a while, watching the squirrels run back and forth across the path. Then Ruby Lee asked Star a few questions about herself and was surprised to learn that the young woman not only sang and played the guitar, but had composed a few songs.

"Why don't you sing something you've written for me?" Ruby Lee asked.

Star's dark eyes widened. "Here? Now?"

"I wish you would."

"But none of my songs are completed yet. I just have a few lines written on each of them," Star said.

"That's all right. I'd like to hear some of the lyrics you've come up with."

"Well, okay." In a hesitant voice, Star began to sing. "Can't seem to look behind the right door; maybe that's 'cause I don't know exactly what I'm looking for. . . ." As she continued into the chorus, her tone grew stronger. "It's hard to breathe. . . . It's hard to sleep. . . . It's hard to know who you are when you're a lost and falling star."

When Star finished the song, she turned to Ruby Lee and said, "It's not much, but at least it's a beginning to something that I hope I'll be able to complete."

"Oh, I'm sure you will, and Star, you certainly have a lovely voice," Ruby Lee said truthfully. "The words to your song were well written, but my only concern is that they evoke a message of sadness and hopelessness. Is that the way you really feel?"

Star nodded solemnly. "Nothin' ever goes right for me, and I—I feel kinda lost, like I don't know what purpose I serve here on earth."

Ruby Lee placed her hand over Star's, unable to speak around the lump in her throat. Here was a young woman without hope, and Ruby Lee, a pastor's wife and professing Christian, couldn't think of a thing to say but, "I'm sorry, Star."

"That's just how it is—life stinks!" Star leaped to her feet. "Guess I'd better finish my run and head for home. Mom's probably havin' a hissy fit wondering why I'm so late gettin' home from work this morning. See you on Saturday, Ruby Lee." She turned and sprinted in the opposite direction, leaving Ruby Lee alone on the bench, feeling even worse than when she'd left home. Oh, how she wished she had shared the love of Jesus with Star right then. She'd seen Star's need and how quickly she covered up her emotions, and yet she'd missed the perfect opportunity to tell the confused young woman about God's love. Was it because she felt so hopeless and sad herself? Truth was, Ruby Lee really needed someone to encourage her today, but Star, not even knowing Ruby Lee's need, hadn't been able to do that. Worse yet, Ruby Lee hadn't met Star's real need either.

Shipshewana

Emma cringed as she directed her horse and buggy toward the health food store. Every move she made and every bump in the road made the lesions on her stomach rub against her clothes and hurt like the dickens. While Emma was getting dressed that morning, she'd discovered several painful blisters and realized she had in fact developed another case of shingles. She'd immediately gone to the phone shack to call her naturopathic doctor but was unable to get an appointment until tomorrow. So she'd decided to head to the health food store near the Shipshewana Flea Market to find a remedy that might help with her painful symptoms. If her blisters continued to hurt like this, she wondered how she could teach the quilting class on Saturday. She would have asked Mary to take over for her, but Mary and her family had left this morning for Sullivan, Illinois, to attend the wedding of Brian's cousin, and they wouldn't be back until Saturday evening.

When Emma arrived at the health food store, she guided her horse up to the hitching rail and gritted her teeth as she climbed down. Just the slightest movement caused pain, making her wish she'd asked someone else to make the trip for her. Emma really wished she could be home in bed.

When she entered the store, she headed for the aisle full of herbal preparations, where she found some pills labeled as help for the pain and itching of shingles. She also discovered a bottle of aromatic oils to dab on the blisters.

"Need some help?"

Emma jumped at the sound of a man's deep voice. Surprised, she turned and saw Lamar beside her. "I...uh...came here to get something that might help with shingles' pain."

Lamar's eyebrows furrowed. "For you, Emma?"

She nodded slowly. "The eruptions came out this morning. Now I know why I haven't felt well the last few days."

"I had a case of shingles a few years ago," Lamar said. "My doctor gave me a B-12 shot."

"Did it help?"

"I believe so. He also gave me a shot to help prevent any nerve pain."

"I couldn't get in to see my doctor today, but I'll go there in the morning." Emma motioned to the bottles on the shelf. "In the meantime, I think I'll use one of these." She sighed deeply. "I hope I'm feeling better by Saturday. I can't imagine trying to teach my quilt class feeling like I do right now."

"I'd be happy to fill in for you," Lamar offered.

Emma tipped her head back and looked up at him in surprise. "Oh, I doubt you'd know what to do."

"You're wrong about that." Lamar smiled. "My wife used to run a quilt shop, and I helped out there. In fact, I even designed some rather unusual quilt patterns for her to make."

Emma's mouth fell open. "Are you serious?"

"Sure am."

"I appreciate the offer, but I think I'll be able to teach the class." At least she hoped she could, because despite what Lamar said about having helped his wife, she couldn't imagine how things would go if he tried to teach the class in her place. But when Saturday came, if she felt like she did now, as much as it would sadden her, she'd have to cancel the class.

CHAPTER 23

Mishawaka

When Stuart entered the kitchen on Friday morning, he found Pam sitting at the table drinking a cup of coffee.

"Where are the kids?" he asked after he'd poured himself some coffee and joined her at the table.

"They're still in bed. I figured I'd let them sleep awhile so I can have some quiet time to myself."

"Guess you won't get much of that once school's out for the summer."

"No, I sure won't."

Stuart blew on his coffee and took a sip. "Since tomorrow's Saturday and I have the day off, why don't you get together with one of your friends? You can go shopping all morning and then out to lunch while I keep an eye on the kids."

Pam shook her head. "Tomorrow's the quilting class, remember?"

He snapped his fingers. "Oh yeah, that's right. I almost forgot."

"It sounds to me like you did forget," she said, scowling at him.

197

He shrugged. "Okay, so maybe I did. There's no big deal in that, is there?"

"Well, that all depends."

"On what?"

"On whether you just conveniently forgot."

"I didn't conveniently forget. Things have been busier than usual at work this week, and my brain's tired; that's all."

"Are you sure you didn't suggest I go shopping with a friend so you wouldn't have to go to the quilting class with me?"

"No, that's not how it was."

"Would you rather go without me again?"

Stuart's irritation mounted. "Are you trying to put words in my mouth?"

"No, I just thought—"

Knowing that if he didn't get out of there immediately he'd start yelling, Stuart pushed away from the table. "I've gotta go or I'll be late for work."

"But you haven't had your breakfast yet."

He gestured to the table. "I don't see anything waiting for me. . . unless it's invisible."

Tears welled in her eyes. "You don't have to be sarcastic. I was waiting to start breakfast until you'd had your coffee."

"Well, I don't want any breakfast!" Stuart hauled his coffee cup to the sink and rushed out the back door, slamming it behind him. It seemed like every time he tried to have a conversation with Pam, they ended up in an argument. He was tired of it, and her turning on the tears didn't help. He was sure she did it just to make him feel like a heel, and it wasn't going to work this time. If things were ever going to be better between them, Pam needed to get off his back and quit antagonizing him all the time.

Shipshewana

After Jan ate a quick breakfast, he went out to the garage to get some tools for the roof he planned to strip today. Terry would be here to pick him up soon, and then they could be on their way.

When Jan entered the garage, his gaze came to rest on his motorcycle, parked beside his truck. Oh how he wished he could ride it right now. Just head on down the road and leave all his troubles behind. But he knew he couldn't do that. He had a responsibility to complete a roofing job, not to mention the quilting classes he'd paid good money for and really did want to finish. Besides, if he rode the Harley and got stopped by the police, he'd probably have his license permanently suspended. No, he could hold out for a couple more months until he got his license back. No sense taking any foolish chances on his bike. He'd done that already, and just look what it had cost him.

Jan ambled across the room and took a seat on the cycle. Gripping the handlebars and closing his eyes, he let his mind wander for a bit, wondering just where his life was going. With the exception of work and riding his motorcycle, he really didn't have much purpose—not like he would if he were a married man raising a family. But he'd given up on that idea several years ago, convincing himself that he was better off alone. Besides, he figured living a quiet, boring life was better than a life full of complications. Had he been wrong about that? Should he have taken a chance on love again? Was it too late for that now?

Brutus sure kept me on my toes, he thought, redirecting his thoughts. *At least the dog gave me a reason to come home every night.*

Jan wondered if he should get another dog to take Brutus's place. Maybe a pup he could train from the get-go would be better than a full-grown dog with bad habits, like stealing and escaping from his pen.

But do I really want to go through that puppy stage? he wondered. *All the chewin' and numerous trips outside till it's housebroken. On the other hand, puppies are cute and have that milky-sweet breath. Guess I'll have to think on it a bit more before I jump into anything I might later regret.*

Woof! Woof!

Jan's eyes snapped open. Had he been so deep in thought that he was hearing things, or was that a dog barking outside the garage?

Woof! Woof! Woof!

Jan leaped off the bike and jerked open the garage door.

Brutus, tail wagging like a windshield wiper at full speed, bounded up to Jan with a toy football in his mouth, which he promptly dropped at Jan's feet. Then he sat down in front of Jan, tail still wagging, as if waiting for some sort of praise at the gift he'd just delivered.

Jan, unable to stop the flow of tears, squatted on the ground and let the dog lick his face. He'd never been one to show much affection, but he couldn't resist giving Brutus a gigantic bear hug.

"Where have you been all this time, boy? I thought you were dead." Relief flooded Jan's soul, and he nearly choked on the words as he tenderly scratched the fur on his dog's neck and then behind his ears. "I don't know whether to scold you or feed you a juicy steak dinner."

The dog whimpered, and then he nuzzled Jan's hand with his nose and leaned in for more attention.

Other than some mud caked on his paws, Brutus looked to be in fairly good condition. Jan figured someone must have taken the dog in—maybe some family with a kid, which would explain the toy football at least.

Jan was really stoked to know that Brutus wasn't dead, but he knew the dog could end up that way if he didn't get him secured in his pen while he was at work during the day. He planned to get him a collar, a license, and an ID tag, too. No way was he going to ruin a happy ending by being so careless again. So after Jan had given Brutus some food and water, he put him in the garage while he went to work covering the top of the dog pen with chicken wire. He'd just finished the last section when Terry's truck pulled in.

"Hey, man, isn't that a little like lockin' the barn door after the horse has escaped?" Terry called after he'd stepped out of the truck and headed toward the dog pen.

"Good news! I was wrong about Brutus. He showed up this mornin', and he's in my garage right now." Jan gave Terry a wide smile. "Now ain't that a kick?"

"Oh man, that's really great. Where was he all this time? Do you know?"

Jan shook his head and stepped out of the pen, appreciative that his good friend was truly happy for him. "I think when he got out he must've been roamin' around lookin' for more things to steal and some family probably took him in. Maybe that's why he couldn't come home all these days."

"What makes you think that?"

Jan explained about the good condition Brutus was in and how he'd come home with a kid's toy in his mouth. "And now that I've made his pen escape-proof, I'm sure it won't happen again. Talk about learnin' a good lesson." Jan pointed to the sky. "I think Someone up there must be lookin' out for me."

Terry thumped Jan's back. "I'm sure glad Brutus is back home again, 'cause you've been pretty hard to work with these last several days."

Jan shrugged his broad shoulders. "What can I say? I missed my dog. Never thought I would, but boy, I sure did!"

Terry gave Jan's back another good thump. "Well, if you'd get yourself a wife, you wouldn't need a dog."

"Like I've told you before, I'll go out on a date now and then, but I ain't gettin' seriously involved with any woman. Havin' a dog is trouble enough."

———◦———

Goshen

Ruby Lee took a seat in front of their computer and logged into her e-mail, hoping she might find something from Annette.

A sense of relief washed over her when she discovered an e-mail with Annette's address in the sender's box. It was titled "Letting You Know."

Ruby Lee brought the message up and soon realized it had been sent from Annette's daughter, Kayla:

Dear Ruby Lee:

It's with regret and great sadness that I'm writing to let you know my mother passed away two weeks ago.

Ruby Lee gasped. "What? Wait a minute! No, this just can't be!" Tears sprang to her eyes as she continued to read Kayla's message:

Mom's cancer came back, but she didn't go to the doctor or tell anyone until it was too late. We've all been in shock—especially Dad. He's so depressed, he can barely cope. Someone in the family should have let you know sooner, but we couldn't find Mom's address book, and I just got into her e-mails today and discovered several you had sent to her. I apologize for letting you know this way.

Sincerely,

Kayla.

P.S. Please pray for our family—especially my dad.

Ruby Lee's head swam with swirling emotions—anger, shock, and grief—because Annette hadn't let her know that the cancer had returned and she was just now learning that her friend was dead.

"This just can't be true! Girlfriend, I would have been there for you if I'd known," she wailed. Hadn't Annette wanted her support? Ruby Lee couldn't imagine going through such a terrible ordeal all alone. And now her friend was gone? It was too much to take in.

Tears streamed down Ruby Lee's face. Trying to get a grip on what she'd just learned, she closed her eyes in continued disbelief. *My problems are nothing compared to what Annette must have gone through. Oh how I wish she'd responded to my phone calls and e-mails. If I'd only known, I would have dropped everything and gone to Nashville to be with her.*

Ruby Lee let her head fall forward into her outstretched palms and sobbed. "Dear Lord, where were You through all of this? Why'd You let my best friend die? If only I could have been there for her."

As quickly as she said the words, Ruby Lee felt remorse. "Guess I should have tried harder to get ahold of you, Annette. Oh, I'm so very sorry." The tears continued to flow as she tried to sort out this unwelcome news.

Shipshewana

For the last few days, Emma had spent much of her time on the sofa with an ice bag pressed against her stomach. Of all the things she'd been doing to help with the pain and itching of the blisters, the cold compress seemed to help the most. She'd seen her naturopathic doctor on Thursday, and he'd given her a B-12 shot and some lysine capsules. Those things had helped some, but she was still quite miserable—although not as bad as she had been the first time she'd come down with shingles.

As much as Emma hated to do it, she knew she had to call her quilting students and cancel tomorrow's class because she was in too much pain to teach them right now.

Gritting her teeth in determination, Emma stepped out the door. She was halfway to the phone shack when a horse and buggy pulled into the yard. A few seconds later, Lamar stepped down.

"Wie geht's?" he asked, walking toward her.

"Not so good," Emma admitted. "I was just heading out to call my quilting students and let them know I won't be able to teach the class tomorrow." She sighed. "Hopefully by next week I'll feel well enough, but I'm in too much pain to do it this week."

Lamar's usual smile turned into a frown. "I told you the other day that I'd teach the class for you. Are you too full of *hochmut* to accept my help?"

She planted both hands against her hips and winced as a jolt of pain shot through her left side. "I am not full of pride! I just wasn't sure you knew enough about quilting to take over my class."

"I know a lot more than you think, and since you're in no shape to teach the class yourself, you ought to at least let me try."

Emma contemplated his offer a few seconds and finally nodded because, really, what other choice did she have? She just hoped it didn't prove to be a mistake.

CHAPTER 24

Star was surprised when she pulled her car into Emma's yard on Saturday morning and saw a horse and buggy parked at the hitching rail. Had Emma invited one of her friends to join them today, or had someone from her Amish community dropped by for a visit? If that was the case, Star was sure whomever was here would leave as soon as Emma started teaching the class.

Just as Star got out of the car, Paul's van pulled in, followed by Ruby Lee in her vehicle. A few minutes later, Stuart's SUV came up the driveway. This time Pam was with him.

They all started walking toward the house, and Jan pedaled up on his bicycle. He must have seen the horse and buggy, too, because he turned his head in that direction.

"Look out!" Paul shouted just before Jan's bike crashed into the fence. Jan, unable to keep the bike upright, landed on the ground with a thud!

"I'm okay. Nothin's broken. I'm just fine," he said, after he'd stood and dusted himself off. Jan's red face let Star know he was a bit embarrassed. She couldn't blame him. She'd be embarrassed, too, if she'd done what he did.

He squinted as he studied his bike and then took a look at the fence. "Seems like they're both okay, too."

Star stepped up to Jan. "How's it going?" She knew that, having just lost his dog, he must still feel depressed.

He grinned. "It's all good! Brutus ain't dead after all! He came home yesterday mornin'."

"That's great news." Star was pleased to see the smile on Jan's face. "I'm sure you were really glad about that."

"You got that right," Jan said with a nod. "And I covered the top of Brutus's pen with heavy chicken wire so he won't get out again when I'm gone. Like I told my friend Terry, I've learned a good lesson from this."

Everyone else said they were happy for Jan, too—everyone but Ruby Lee and Pam. Ruby Lee, though silent, did give Jan's arm a little pat, but Pam said nothing at all. Star wasn't surprised. From the first moment she'd met Pam, she'd thought her to be quite high and mighty and into herself. People like that were hard to take. People like Pam needed to learn a lesson in humility.

Star hadn't cared much for Stuart at first, either, but at least he didn't dress and act like he was better than anyone else, and he'd been a lot easier to talk to last week when Pam wasn't with him. Too bad the snooty woman hadn't stayed home again today.

"Guess we'd better get into the house," Paul said, knocking on the door. "Don't want to keep Emma waiting."

A few seconds later, the door opened, and they were greeted by a pleasant-looking Amish man with gray hair and a long, full beard to match. He introduced himself as Emma's friend, Lamar Miller. Star realized then that he was the man who'd brought the doughnuts by Emma's, because Emma had mentioned his name.

When Star and the others followed Lamar into the sewing room, she glanced around. "Where's Emma?"

"She came down with shingles earlier this week and isn't feeling up to teaching the class today." Lamar's sober expression showed that he was truly sorry about that.

"That's too bad. Emma said she was feeling tired when I visited her the other day, so that must have been the reason for it." Thinking Emma's illness meant the class had been canceled, Star turned toward the door.

"You don't have to leave. I'll be teaching the class today," Lamar announced.

"Oh?" Star whirled around. "What qualifies you to teach the class?"

Lamar's cheeks reddened. "I used to work with my wife in her quilt shop. Believe me, I know what I'm doing."

Star, a little unsure, looked at Jan. When he gave her a smile and a nod, she pulled out a chair at the table and took a seat. Everyone else did the same.

With the dubious expressions she saw from the others, Star was sure she wasn't the only one in the room who thought it was a little strange that this Amish man could be capable of teaching a quilt class. But it was only fair to give him the benefit of the doubt.

She glanced over at Pam, who still hadn't said a word since she and Stuart arrived, which was strange, since all the other times Pam had been here, she'd had plenty to say. Star figured Pam and Stuart may have had a fight on their way here and weren't speaking. Well, that suited Star just fine because the less snooty Pam had to say, the better it would be for everyone. It wouldn't hurt her to sit and listen for once, instead of yammering away at Stuart so she could hear herself talk or make a point.

"From what Emma has told me, I understand that each of you has been working on a wall hanging," Lamar said, redirecting Star's thoughts. "Now, I'm going to start by showing you a couple of patterns I designed myself, and then I'll let you get to work on your projects."

"You've designed some quilts?" Ruby Lee asked, eyebrows lifted.

A wide smile stretched across his face. "I've always been somewhat of an artist, and as I said, when my wife opened a quilt shop, I helped her sometimes. It didn't take long before I was designing some new patterns." Lamar reached into a large cardboard box set on one end of the table and withdrew a quilted wall hanging made from white and three shades of blue material. "I call this one Goose Feathers on the Loose." He grinned. "Makes me think of the time one of our geese was chasing the dog. She flapped her wings so hard that she left a trail of feathers."

Laughter, as well as oohs and aahs came from everyone but Pam and Ruby Lee. They both, however, let their fingers trail over the design of feather-like stitches.

"Here's another one I created," Lamar said, removing from the box a quilted pillow top in various shades of brown, designed to resemble some type of bird tracks. "This one I call Pheasant Trail, because some of the menfolk in my family like to hunt."

"Those are both really great," Stuart said. "You're sure talented, Lamar."

Star nodded in agreement. "I'll say!"

"Thank you," Lamar said, blushing slightly. "It gives me pleasure to make nice things."

"So, is designin' quilts what you do for a living?" Jan asked.

"No, it's just a hobby. My real craft is making hickory rocking chairs, and I'm only doing that part-time these days."

"Well, you certainly could design quilt patterns full-time," Paul said, "because these are really unique."

Lamar gave a slight nod in response, and then he asked everyone to bring their wall hangings out and lay them on the table so he could see what they'd done.

They all did as he asked—everyone but Ruby Lee. She just sat, staring out the window as though occupied with her own thoughts at the moment. She'd been so pleasant and talkative when Star had met her on the Pumpkinvine Trail the other day. Something was definitely wrong with her today.

"Mine doesn't look so good," Stuart mumbled. "Some of my stitches are crooked, and some look like they're only half-stitched 'cause the sewing machine kept skipping or something. My wife said I didn't have the tension set right, but even after she fixed it for me, things weren't much better." He pointed to the few pieces he'd sewn onto his wall hanging. "The thread broke on me a couple of times, too."

"Some people who are first learning to sew end up having to take a lot of their stitches out," Lamar said. "You just have to watch and see that your stitches are straight, and that the tension is set right when you thread your needle and put the bobbin in place. We'll work on the projects for a while, and then I'll serve you some doughnuts that I bought fresh at the bakery this morning."

"That sounds good to me, so I'll keep trying," Stuart said. "But I'm still not sure I can sew a straight stitch." He motioned to Pam's quilted project. "Hers looks pretty good, though, wouldn't you say?"

"Yes, it's coming along real well," Lamar said after he'd inspected the pieces Pam had stitched onto her wall hanging.

Pam smiled but didn't say a word.

"What's up with you today?" Star asked. "Do you have a sore throat or laryngitis?"

Pam reached into her purse, pulled out a notebook and pen, and wrote a short message. *"My throat's fine. I promised Stuart I wouldn't say anything today."*

Star looked over at Stuart and frowned. "You asked your wife not to talk to anyone?"

His face turned red as he shook his head. "I didn't mean she couldn't say anything at all. I just meant I didn't want her talking about our problems or putting me down." He nudged Pam's arm. "Say something so they know you can talk."

Pam glared at him. "You're so stupid."

Star laughed. She just couldn't help herself. She looked over at Jan, and then he started laughing, too. Paul, Lamar, and Ruby Lee weren't laughing, and of course neither was Stuart. He looked downright miffed.

"No, you're stupid, Pam," Stuart mumbled.

"Would you two please stop?" Ruby Lee's hand trembled as she pointed first at Stuart, and then Pam. "You need to appreciate each other and stop quarreling all the time. Have you ever stopped to think about how things would be if something happened to one of you? Worse yet, what if one of you died, leaving the other alone?"

"That's right," Paul chimed in. "Once your mate is gone, it's too late to make amends for anything you may have said or done that was hurtful. I'm so thankful for all the good times my wife and I had together before she died. Lorinda and I didn't have the perfect marriage, but we had a good one, and we loved each other very much. You need to remember that things can change in a blink," he added, looking right at Stuart.

Stuart lowered his gaze and gave a little grunt.

"Do you have any idea how I felt when my wife died?" Paul continued. "It was like a part of me had died, and to make things worse, my wife's sister blamed me for the accident. She's made no contact with me since Lorinda's funeral—not even to see how Sophia, her only niece, is doing."

Paul's pained expression let Star know how much his sister-in-law's accusation and avoidance had hurt him. "What makes her think the accident was your fault?" she questioned.

"She said I should have been paying closer attention, and thinks if I'd seen the truck coming, I could have somehow gotten our car out of his way." A muscle on the side of Paul's cheek quivered. "I've spoken to my priest about this, and he says Carmen needed someone to blame."

"People often like to blame others for the bad things that happen to them," Lamar interjected. "I believe it's our human nature."

Paul nodded. "Sometimes people blame themselves. One thing I've learned through all this, though, is that life's too short to hold grudges or play the blame game. Good communication and a loving relationship with your family—that's what's really important."

"I'm a widower, too," Lamar said, "and my wife, Margaret, and I always tried to keep the lines of communication open. I'm thankful for the happy years we had together, which has left me with lots of good memories. Other than my children reminding me of what our love created, the memories I have of my wife are all I have left to hold on to."

Pam frowned and folded her arms, as though refusing to budge. "Well, if Stuart took more interest in me, it would be easier to make our marriage work."

Ruby Lee sucked in her breath as tears welled in her dark eyes and dribbled onto her flushed cheeks.

"Are you okay?" Star asked, touching Ruby Lee's arm. "Are you upset about something today?"

Ruby Lee gave a slow nod.

"Would you like to talk about it?" Pam asked. "Tell us what you're feeling right now?"

Ruby emitted a soft little sob and covered her mouth. "I—I can't go on like this. My faith is wavering, and I...I'm almost beginning to doubt that God is real." She sniffed deeply. "If. . .if He's truly the heavenly Father, then I don't think He cares about His people."

The room got deathly quiet. Star couldn't believe what Ruby Lee had just said. She'd thought the happy-go-lucky woman was strong in her beliefs. Up until now, she'd never let on that her faith in God had faltered. For Star to think God might not exist was one thing, but Ruby Lee was a pastor's wife. As far as Star was concerned, Ruby Lee had no right to be saying such things.

No one said anything at first; then Paul spoke up. "I suspect you're speaking out of frustration, Ruby Lee. Please tell us what's wrong. Is it your husband? Is he ill?"

"No, he's fine—at least physically." Between sniffles and sobs, Ruby Lee shared with the class about the problems they'd been having at her husband's church because he wanted to add on to the building. Then, after wiping her nose on the tissue Pam had handed her, Ruby Lee told how her friend had passed away two weeks ago, and she'd just found out about it the other day. "So much drama! I...I can't take this anymore," she said tearfully. "I used to be able to pray and feel some peace, but lately there just are no peaceful feelings for me."

I had no idea poor Ruby Lee's been going through so much, Star thought. *Sure wish she woulda said somethin' to me about all this the other day.* She glanced at Pam and noticed that even her eyes were glassy with tears.

Maybe the prissy woman did care about someone other than herself.

Rising to her feet and looking at Lamar, Ruby Lee said in a quivering voice, "I—I'm sorry, but I can't stay. I made a mistake coming here today." She grabbed up her quilting project and rushed out the door.

CHAPTER 25

Emma yawned and stretched her arms over her head. She didn't know how long she'd been asleep, but it seemed like she'd been lying on her bed for a good long while. The ice bag that had been pressed against her stomach when she first lay down was now warm, so she assumed that several hours must have passed.

She reached for her reading glasses lying on the table beside her bed and slipped them on after she sat up. Looking at the alarm clock, she realized it was half past noon.

Emma removed her glasses and ambled over to the window. There were no cars in the driveway, so she figured all her quilting students must have gone home. Lamar probably had too, since she didn't see any sign of his horse and buggy.

Emma redid her hair into a bun at the back of her head and put her head covering in place. Smoothing the wrinkles in her dark green dress, she made her way to the kitchen. When she stepped inside, she opened her mouth in surprise. Lamar stood in front of the stove, stirring something that smelled delicious.

At her sharp intake of air, he turned from the stove. "Oh good, you're up."

Leaning on the counter for support, all Emma could do was squeak, "Y–you're still here?"

He smiled and nodded. "Figured when you woke up you'd be hungry, so when I found some leftover soup in the refrigerator, I decided to heat it up for your lunch. Oh, and I added some canned peas and carrots that I found in your cupboard," he added with a sheepish grin. "Hope that's okay with you."

Emma gave a slow nod. "When I looked out my bedroom window, I didn't see your horse and buggy, so I figured you'd gone home."

"Nope. I put Ebony in the corral and moved my buggy to the back of your shed where it's in the shade." Lamar turned back to the stove and gave the kettle of soup a few more stirs. "I think it's about ready, so if you'll take a seat at the table, I'll dish you up a bowl."

Emma, unsure of what to say, stood staring at the back of Lamar's head. She wasn't used to having someone take over in her kitchen like this, and she sure hadn't expected Lamar to fix her lunch.

As though sensing her discomfort, he looked over his shoulder and said, "As soon as I serve up your soup, I'll be on my way."

Not wishing to be rude, Emma smiled and said, "Why don't you stay and join me? Unless you have other plans, that is."

"Nope. I have no plans at all for lunch." Lamar smacked his lips. "This sure smells good. Can't guarantee what it would taste like if I'd made it from scratch, though." He chuckled and went on to tell Emma about some of the blunders he'd made in the kitchen since his wife died.

"I may know how to craft a sturdy hickory rocking chair and design a quilt pattern, but I still don't know my way around the kitchen that well," he said. "One day I spent almost an hour searching for some salt I'd bought, only to find that I'd put it in the refrigerator by mistake." He shrugged his shoulders. "Finally decided to quit worrying about things so much and just do the best I can, because one thing I've discovered is that a day of worry is more exhausting than a week's worth of work."

Emma nodded. "That's true enough."

Lamar ladled some soup into two bowls, and Emma set out a basket of crackers and a glass of water for each of them.

Once they were seated, they bowed their heads for silent prayer. When they were both finished, Emma picked up her spoon and was about to take a bite of soup when Lamar said, "It's pretty hot. Better give it a few minutes to cool."

Emma set her spoon down and ate a few crackers instead, since she really was quite hungry and didn't want Lamar to hear her stomach growling.

"How are you feeling?"

"How'd it go today?"

They'd both spoken at the same time; so Emma motioned to Lamar and said, "Sorry; you go first."

"How are you feeling?" he asked. "Are your shingles blisters still causing you a lot of pain?"

"Jah, but I'm feeling a bit better than I did yesterday, so that's a good sign." Emma's throat felt dry, so she reached for her glass of water and took a drink. "How'd things go with the quilt class today?"

In response to Emma's question, Lamar's forehead wrinkled. "I think I did okay with the lesson, but that group of people you're teaching are sure a bunch of half-stitched quilters."

"What do you mean?"

"They've all got problems, Emma, and with the exception of Pam, none of 'em can sew all that well."

"I know they have problems, but then who doesn't?"

"True."

Emma went on to explain that some of her students had opened up to her, and she'd been trying not only to teach them to quilt, but to help with their problems at home.

"From what I can tell, they've got plenty of those." Lamar took a bite of his soup. "It's cool enough to eat now," he announced.

Emma began eating, too, and as they ate, they talked more about the people in her class.

"That couple—the Johnstons—seem to be having trouble with their marriage," Lamar said.

Emma nodded. "They're seeing a counselor who suggested they do more things together."

"Is that why they're taking the quilt class?"

"Jah, and hopefully it'll help bring them closer."

"Even Paul, who seems to be fairly stable, opened up to the class and told how painful it is that his sister-in-law blames him for his wife's death."

Emma frowned. "How can that be? From what Paul's said, his wife was killed when a truck slammed into the side of their car."

"That's right, but I guess Paul's sister-in-law thinks he could have done something to prevent the accident."

"That's *lecherich*," Emma said with a shake of her head.

"It may be ridiculous, but as I told Paul today, some people have to find someone to blame when things don't go as they'd like."

"Unfortunately, that's true. Some even blame God for all their troubles."

"What about the big fellow with the girl's name tattooed on his arm? Why's he taking the class?" Lamar asked, moving their conversation in a little different direction.

Emma explained about Jan's probation officer suggesting he find something creative to do, and then she told him the reasons the others had given for taking quilting lessons.

"Ruby Lee had some problems today," Lamar said, frowning.

"With her quilting project?"

He shook his head. "She shared with the class that her best friend had died two weeks ago, and she'd just found out about it."

"Oh, that's a shame."

"Jah, and she also mentioned that they've been having problems in their church, and it's affected her faith in God."

"What kind of problems?"

Emma listened intently as Lamar repeated all that Ruby Lee had shared with the class. "She ended up leaving early, and I felt bad because I wasn't sure what to say in order to help with her distress."

"It's okay, Lamar. You don't know those people very well." Emma pursed her lips. "As soon as I'm done eating, I'm going out to the phone shack and give Ruby Lee a call. I just hope I'm up to teaching the class next week, because if anyone else shares their problems, I really want to be there for them."

"I can understand that."

"Changing the subject," Emma said, "Sometime I'd like to see those quilt designs you've created."

Lamar smiled and pushed back his chair. "No problem there. I brought two of 'em with me today to show to your class."

He left the kitchen and returned a few minutes later with a cardboard box, which he placed on the counter. "This one I call Pheasant Trail," he said, holding up a quilted pillow slip.

"Ach! That's beautiful," Emma said, amazed at not only the design of what looked like a trail made by a bird, but also the pretty shades of brown material that had been used.

"This one I call Goose Feathers on the Loose," Lamar said, reaching into the box again and retrieving a wall hanging done up in white and a few shades of blue. Emma thought it was even prettier than the other.

"That feather design is beautiful. You certainly are creative," she said. "I never imagined you had the ability to do that."

Lamar's thick eyebrows furrowed. "What are you sayin', Emma—that I'm *dumm?*"

"No, no, of course you're not dumb. I just meant. . ." She paused and fanned her face, which suddenly felt very warm. "I'm just surprised, that's all, because I've never known a man who has the kind of talent you have or enjoys working with quilts."

Lamar's frown was replaced with a smile. "I think your students were a bit surprised as well," he said with a twinkle in his eyes.

"I'm sorry that I doubted your ability to teach the class. You obviously know quite a bit about quilts."

"At least from the designing end of things, I do," he said with a nod. "Of course, working with my wife in her quilt shop, I learned a lot about making quilts, too."

Emma leaned closer to the table and started eating her soup. She wondered what other things she didn't know about Lamar.

Goshen

Soon after Star got home from the quilt class, she decided to work in her grandma's flower beds. They were getting overgrown with weeds, and it didn't look like Mom was going to tackle them anytime soon. When

Mom wasn't working, she was busy entertaining know-it-all Mike, with whom she was spending the day. He'd come by for Mom right after breakfast, saying he wanted to take her shopping at the mall in South Bend, and then they would see a show and go out to dinner after that. Why they couldn't have gone to the mall in Goshen, Star couldn't figure out, but at least with Mom and Mike being in South Bend, it was better than him hanging around here all day. Now Star would have the run of the house.

Star had just finished pulling weeds in one flower bed and had moved over to start on another when their nineteen-year-old neighbor boy, Matt Simpson, came out of his house and sauntered into Grandma's yard.

Oh great, Star thought. *Here comes Mr. Pimple Face, who can't even grow a beard.*

"What are you up to?" he asked, kneeling beside Star on the grass.

"I'm weeding the flower beds. What's it look like?"

"Hmm. . ."

"I'd appreciate it if you'd move back, 'cause you're invading my space."

"Hey, don't mind me. I'm just tryin' to be friendly," he said, moving back just a bit.

Star stabbed her shovel into the ground and pulled up a weed. *Maybe if I ignore him, he'll go away.*

"Say, what are you doin' for supper this evening?" Matt asked.

Star kept digging and pulling at more weeds, hoping he'd take the hint and leave.

"Hello. Uh. . .did you hear what I said?"

"I heard you all right, and quit winking at me."

"I wasn't. The sun was in my eyes, and I was squinting, not winking." He leaned closer again. "What are you doin' for supper?"

"I really don't know. I'll probably fix a sandwich or something."

"I thought maybe you'd like to go out for a burger and fries."

"With you?"

"Yeah."

She glared at him. "Get lost, creep. I wouldn't give the time of day to someone like you."

His blue eyes flashed angrily, and he pushed some of his auburn hair out of his eyes. "What's that supposed to mean?"

"It means, no. I'm not interested."

"Why not?"

"Because you're a loser, and losers are nothing but trouble. I ought to know; I had a loser for a dad and another loser for a stepdad." She grimaced. "Losers are losers; that's all they'll ever be."

Matt frowned. "Sorry about your loser dads, but it's no reason for you to compare me with them, 'cause I'm not a loser!"

"Oh, yeah? Then how come you're still living at home, sponging off your folks, and won't look for a job?"

"Who told you that?"

She shrugged. "Let's just say it's common knowledge."

"For your information, I do have a job."

"Oh really? Doin' what?"

"I have a paper route now, and I've got enough money in my wallet to take us both out for a burger and fries. A milkshake, too, if you want it."

She grunted. "Give me a break. I'm not goin' anywhere with you!"

Matt wrinkled his freckled nose. "That suits me just fine, 'cause unless you were willing to wear something sensible on our date, I wasn't plannin' to take you out anyways."

"I wear what I feel good in, and if you don't like it, that's just too bad."

"Why do you have to be so mean? Are you tryin' to hurt me so I'll leave you alone?"

She gave a nod. "That's what I do best. . .I push people away—especially losers like you."

Looking more than a little hurt, Matt stood and shuffled out of the yard. "You know," he yelled over before going into his house, "I knew your grandma, and I can't believe you're even related to her! And you know what else? You're nothin' like her, even if you are pullin' weeds in her garden the way she used to like to do!" With that, he stormed into his house and slammed the door.

Star flinched. She knew she'd been hard on Matt, but if she'd given the poor sap even a hint of niceness, he might have thought he had a chance with her. "Like that'll ever happen. If I was gonna go out with someone, it would be with a guy like Jan, who at least has a decent-paying job and likes some of the same things as me. Not that he'd be interested in someone as young as I am." She stabbed the shovel into the dirt again. "But if he did ask me out, I'd probably say yes."

CHAPTER 26

Shipshewana

Shortly before noon on Wednesday of the following week, Emma stepped outside and headed for the phone shack to check her messages. She hoped she might hear something from Ruby Lee. She'd tried calling her on Saturday and then again on Monday. Both of those times, though, she had to leave a message on Ruby Lee's answering machine. Could Ruby Lee be out of town, or was she avoiding talking to Emma?

I wish I'd been able to teach my class on Saturday, Emma thought as she approached the phone shack. *Maybe I could have said something to help Ruby Lee when she shared her troubles with the others.*

Emma was almost to the shack when the door opened suddenly and Mary stepped out. "Ach, Mom, I didn't know you were out here!" Mary said, jumping back, her eyes going wide.

"I came to make a phone call," Emma replied. "Sorry if I startled you."

"No problem. I'm done with the phone now." Mary moved aside. "How are you feeling, Mom? Are you still in a lot of pain?"

Emma shook her head. "I'm doing better every day. I don't think this bout with shingles is quite as bad as the first time I had them."

"I'm glad to hear that."

"I plan on teaching my quilt class this Saturday," Emma said. "I appreciated Lamar's help last week, but I don't want to impose on him again."

Mary smiled. "I know I've said this before, but I think Lamar is really a very nice man, and I also wanted to tell you that—"

"I'd better get my phone call made," Emma said, quickly changing the subject. She wasn't in the mood to hear more of her daughter's thoughts about Lamar, because she had a hunch that Mary wanted to see her get married again. Why, she couldn't imagine. Didn't Mary realize that no one could ever take Ivan's place in Emma's heart? For that matter, could Mary so easily accept a stepfather? Maybe she thought if Emma married Lamar, then the family wouldn't have to help her so much.

All the more reason for me to show them that I can be independent, Emma thought.

"Would you like to come over to my house for lunch after you're finished with your phone call?" Mary asked.

"I appreciate the offer, but I'd better pass. I have some chicken noodle soup simmering on the stove, and after I eat, I'm going to take a nap. I want to make sure I get plenty of rest between now and Saturday."

"That's probably a good idea."

Mary gave Emma a gentle hug, said good-bye, and headed for home.

Emma stepped into the phone shack and dialed Ruby Lee's number. Again, no one answered, and Emma had to leave another message.

"Hello, Ruby Lee, it's me, Emma Yoder. I've been trying to get in touch with you," she said. "I hope you'll be at the quilting class on Saturday. In the meantime, if you'd like to talk, please give me a call."

When Emma left the phone shack, she stopped at the goat pen and watched Maggie and the other goats frolic awhile. She was glad Maggie couldn't get out and make a pest of herself any longer. It had just made more work for Emma whenever the goat messed things up in her yard.

After Emma arrived back at the house, she discovered that a tear in her front screen door had been fixed. She figured Mary's husband must have done it, maybe while she was taking a nap earlier in the week. Emma had been so out of it lately, she hadn't noticed much of anything.

She paused to run her fingers over the spot where the tear had been and noticed what a fine repair job it was. She'd have to thank Brian for his thoughtful gesture right away.

Emma entered her house and went to the kitchen to check on the soup. Seeing that it was thoroughly heated, she turned off the stove and headed for Mary's house.

"Did you change your mind about joining me for lunch?" Mary asked when Emma entered her kitchen a few minutes later.

"No, I just came over to tell Brian thanks for fixing the tear in my screen door."

Mary shook her head, "Brian's still at work, and no, Mom, it wasn't him. Lamar fixed the tear in your screen."

"How do you know that?" Emma asked, raising her brows.

"Because I saw him do it."

"And you never said anything about it to me?"

"I was going to mention it when I spoke to you a bit ago, but you said you were in a hurry to make a call, so I decided it could wait."

"Oh, I see." Emma was thankful the screen had been fixed, but she wished it had been Brian who'd done it and not Lamar. Now she felt obligated to repay him in some way, because he'd done three nice things for her in one week.

———

Goshen

Since Mom was working at the restaurant and Star had gotten off work earlier this morning, Star had the house to herself again. That was fine with her. She was thankful Grandma had left this old house to Mom, because it was a place she could just relax and be herself. When Star was alone, she could sing and play her guitar without Mom telling her to tone it down. She could work on writing more songs without any negative comments. This morning, however, Star had decided to go through some of Grandma's things that she'd found in the attic.

As she sat on the floor in the dusty, dimly lit room looking through a box of pictures she'd found in an old trunk, tears sprang to her eyes. She'd never seen any of these photos before, and it was hard seeing pictures of herself when she was a girl, sitting on Grandma's lap. Those had been happy days, though, when Star felt loved and secure. But seeing the pictures made her miss Grandma even more.

If only I could feel that kind of love from Mom, she thought. *But then, under the circumstances I guess she did the best by me that she could. It couldn't have been easy raising a child alone. Maybe that's why Mom married Wes. She was hoping to give me a father.*

Anger boiled in Star's chest. *That creep was anything but a father to me, and he sure wasn't the kind of husband Mom or any other woman needed. He should have been put in jail for all the times he hit Mom. But no, Mom had either been too afraid of him to file a report, or maybe she was just plain stupid and liked to be smacked around. Who knows? Maybe Mom thought Wes was the best she could do and didn't realize that she deserved better.*

Star swiped at the tears dripping onto her cheeks. The past was in the past, and it didn't make sense to cry over what couldn't be changed. At least they were rid of Wes now, and even though she didn't care for

Mike, she had to admit, he was a better choice for Mom than the wife abuser. Even so, Star hoped Mom wouldn't marry Mike, because then Star would feel forced to move out of Grandma's house—the only place that had ever truly felt like home.

Bringing her troubling thoughts to a halt, Star reached into the trunk and pulled out a few more photos, stopping when she came to a picture of Mom holding a baby in her arms. Star knew the baby was her, because she'd seen other baby pictures of herself. But part of this picture had been ripped away. Could there have been someone else in the photo? Had Mom, or maybe Grandma, torn the picture like that?

Was my Dad in the other half of this picture? Star wondered. *Should I show this to Mom and ask her about it or keep it to myself?* Knowing Mom and the way she avoided the subject of Star's real dad, Star figured if she showed the picture and started asking a bunch of questions, Mom would get real mad. However, if it was her dad, then Star really wanted to know, because she'd always wondered what he looked like and whether she resembled him or not. Maybe Mom had some other pictures of him hidden away somewhere that Star didn't know about.

Star started to put the picture back in the trunk but changed her mind. She'd keep it in her wallet for now—until she decided whether to mention it to Mom or not.

CHAPTER 27

Mishawaka

While Pam prepared supper on Friday evening, tears welled in her eyes as she reflected on the things Ruby Lee had said during the last quilt class, things about appreciating each other and not quarreling all the time. She could still hear the tone of almost desperation in Ruby Lee's voice when she'd said, *"Have you ever stopped to think about how things would be if something happened to one of you? Worse yet, what if one of you died, leaving the other alone?"*

Maybe I don't appreciate Stuart enough, Pam thought as she reached for some garlic powder to sprinkle on the ground beef patties Stuart would soon be putting on the grill. *Maybe it would help if I try to be a little nicer to him and show more appreciation for the good things he does.* That was one of the things their counselor had suggested, only Pam hadn't put it into practice. But then, neither had Stuart.

"Daddy wants to know if the patties are ready," Devin said, dashing into the kitchen at full speed and nearly running into the table. He was still in high gear, since today had been the last day of school and the kids' summer vacation had officially begun.

Pam dabbed at her eyes so Devin wouldn't see her tears. "Slow down, son. You know you're not supposed to run in the house."

"Sorry," the boy mumbled, "but Daddy said I should hurry 'cause the barbecue's ready and he don't wanna waste the gas."

"Yes, the patties are ready, and I'll take them out to him right now." Pam picked up the platter and headed out the back door, hoping her eyes weren't too red from crying. She found Stuart on the patio, fiddling with the control knob on their gas barbecue.

"Here you go," she said sweetly, handing him the platter.

"Thanks." Stuart put the patties on the grill and then stood off to one side where he could keep a watch on things. "What else did you fix to go with the burgers?" he asked.

"I made macaroni salad, and we'll have chips, dip, pickles, and olives. Oh, and I baked some chocolate cupcakes for dessert."

"Sounds good." He offered her a crooked grin.

Pam's heart skipped a beat. He hadn't looked at her that sweetly in a long time.

Maybe there was some hope for their marriage, after all.

She leaned close to his ear and whispered, "I appreciate your help fixing supper tonight."

"No problem. I'm glad to help out. And you know how much I enjoy barbecuing. Besides, it's a nice way to celebrate the kids' last day of school." Stuart slipped his arm around Pam's waist and pulled her close. It felt nice to have him show her some attention.

They stood like that for several minutes, until Stuart had to flip the burgers. "You know, I've been thinking it might be fun if I took Devin on a camping trip this summer. . .just the two of us. It would give us some father-son time, and I can teach him how to fish."

"Why can't we do something as a family?" she asked. "Something we'd all like to do."

He quirked an eyebrow. "Such as?"

"We could take the kids to the Fun Spot amusement park. Or better yet, why don't we make a trip to Disney World in Florida?"

Stuart shook his head. "A trip like that would take too long. I've only got a few days of vacation time left this year—just long enough for a few camping trips."

Irritation welled in Pam's soul. "Camping! Camping! Camping! Is that all you ever think about? Don't you want to do anything Sherry and I might enjoy?" She clenched her fingers so tightly that her nails dug into her palms. "Don't you love me, Stuart?"

"You oughta know I love you, but I enjoy being in the woods, and since you don't like to camp, I thought I'd take Devin." He paused long enough to flip the burgers again. "Can't you and Sherry do something together? You know—some little mother-daughter thing like shopping or going to a movie?"

She shook her head. "I want us to do something as a family."

"Then go camping with us."

"I don't like camping—especially in a tent. Worse than that, I don't like being at home while you run off and do whatever you like with no consideration for what I might want to do."

He frowned. "I'm taking that stupid quilt class, aren't I? I'm doing it because I love you and want to make you happy."

"The class is not stupid!"

His eyes narrowed. "I just said I love you, and all you heard was my comment about the class being stupid?"

"You didn't think it was stupid when you went two weeks ago

without me. Why was that, Stuart?" Pam's voice rose higher with each word she spoke. "And why did you enjoy the class when you went alone but hate it when I was with you?"

"Lower your voice," he said. "The kids or the neighbors might hear you hollering and think there's a problem over here."

"Were you just showing off for Emma and the others in the class, trying to impress them? Or were you trying to make me look bad—like I have all the problems and you're Mr. Nice Guy?" she hissed, not caring in the least who might be listening or what they thought. "And who cares if the neighbors hear us and think there's a problem? There *is* a problem. Don't you get it?"

"I know there's a problem, and no, I wasn't trying to make you look bad. I told you before how it was. Don't you believe me?"

"No, I don't! What I believe is that you'd rather be alone or with other people than spend time with me." She stamped her foot and scowled at him. So much for trying to make things work with Stuart. He was absolutely impossible! "You're just like my father, you know that? He spent more time away from home than he did with me and Mom, and I hated him for it! They made me work hard in school, forcing me to get straight As. And yet when I did, all I got for my hard work was money and some really nice clothes. What I wanted was their unconditional love and to be with them as a family, but Dad never cared about any of that. All he cared about was himself!"

Stuart looked stunned and seemed unable to speak. "You. . .you've never told me any of that before," he finally said. "I always thought you loved your dad, and that everything was perfect in your home when you were growing up."

Pam gulped on a sob. "I did love him, but things were far from perfect. I've never admitted it to anyone before, but now you know."

Stuart reached his hand out to her, but she quickly pulled away. "I've lost my appetite. The rest of the food's on the kitchen table. You and the kids can eat whenever the burgers are done."

"What about you? Aren't you going to eat with us?"

"I'm not hungry. I've got a headache, and I'm going to bed!" Pam whirled around and dashed into the house. Tired of every conversation turning into an argument, she just wanted to be alone.

Goshen

"It's nice to be home, isn't it?" Gene said as he and Ruby Lee entered their house and headed for the kitchen. "I'm sure our own bed will feel really good tonight."

Ruby Lee nodded. Sunday, after another tension-filled church service, Gene had suggested they take a few days off and go somewhere to be alone so they could think and pray about their situation. They couldn't really do that at home—not with the phone ringing at all hours of the day. Even in their new home, people often dropped by unannounced. So Ruby Lee and Gene had booked a room at a lovely bed-and-breakfast outside Middlebury and spent the last four days in solitude. While nothing had been definitely decided, Ruby Lee thought Gene might actually be considering leaving the ministry. If that's the way he chose to go, she'd be relieved. She was tired of trying to help people with their problems, only to be kicked in the teeth. She, and especially Gene, deserved better than that.

"Guess I should check our messages," Gene said. "Unless you'd rather do that."

She shook her head. "You go ahead. I'm going to see what I can throw together for supper." She opened the refrigerator door. "We have plenty of eggs. Does an omelet appeal to you?"

"Sure, that's fine."

When Gene punched the button to replay the messages, Ruby Lee recognized Emma's voice as the caller of the first message, asking if Ruby Lee was okay and saying if she needed to talk, to please give her a call. Following that were a couple of advertising calls, including one from a man who wanted to tune the piano at the church. Two more calls from Emma said pretty much the same as the first one had, but Emma ended the last message by saying she was feeling better and hoped to see Ruby Lee at the quilt class on Saturday.

"Are you going to call her back?" Gene asked. "She sounded eager to talk to you."

"Tomorrow's Saturday, so I'll see her then." Truth was, Ruby Lee had debated about not going to the class tomorrow morning. It would be hard to face the others after her outburst last week. But she wanted to finish her wall hanging and needed help with the next step, so she would swallow her pride and go. After all, it wasn't like she was the only one who'd ever had a display of emotions during one of their classes. Truth be told, it had felt somewhat healing to share her grief and frustration with her newfound friends. Maybe later she would share even more.

CHAPTER 28

Look what Mike bought for me when we were in South Bend the other day," Mom said, holding her left hand out to Star after she'd taken a seat beside her at the breakfast table. "We had to have it resized, so he wasn't able to give it to me till last night."

Star blinked at the flashy ring on her mother's finger, noting how huge the diamond was. "Is it real?"

"Of course it is, silly. Do you really think Mike would give me a fake?"

"So what'd the guy do, rob a bank?" Star nearly gagged, watching Mom wiggle her finger as she stared at the prisms within the diamond catching the light.

"What? No, of course not." Mom smiled widely. "He's been saving up to buy me a really nice engagement ring."

Star wrinkled her nose. "I suppose that means you've decided to marry the creep."

"Mike is not a creep. He's a steady worker and a good man. A much better man than any other I've ever known, and we're planning to be married in September."

"That's just great. Super awesome, in fact. Yeah, this is the best news I've had all year."

"You don't have to be sarcastic about it. Just what have you got against Mike anyway?"

Star held up one finger. "He's bossy." She held up a second finger. "He's opinionated." A third finger came up. "He's a control freak."

Mom flapped her hand. "Oh, he is not. When have you ever seen Mike try to control me?"

"Not you, Mom; although he does expect you to wait on him a lot. It's the TV he really likes to control." Star frowned. "As soon as he comes in the door, he grabs the remote, and on goes the TV. From then on, he's in charge of whatever we watch. Not only that, but he doesn't like anything about me."

"That's not true, Star."

"Oh, isn't it? The last time he came over, didn't you hear how he was on my case about the clothes I wear and the kind of music I listen to?"

"He has a right to his opinion." Mom stuck the end of her finger in her mouth and bit off a hangnail. "You already know how I feel about the way you dress, so you shouldn't be surprised that Mike doesn't care for it either."

Star slapped her hand on the table, just missing her glass of orange juice. "I don't care what he thinks! I don't want another crummy stepfather!"

"He's not going to be a crummy stepfather or a crummy husband either. Despite what you think, Mike is good to me, and—"

"Well, I hope he does better by you than Wes did. 'Course anyone would be better than that wife abuser." Star picked up her glass of juice and took a drink. "What about my real dad? Did he abuse you, too?"

Mom's forehead wrinkled. "Now what made you ask that question?"

"You've never really given me all that much information about him, so for all I know, he could have treated you even worse than Wes."

"I've told you all you need to know about your dad. He didn't abuse me physically, but he was wild and undependable. And being a new father, he proved that when he ran out on us when you were a baby."

Star reached into her jeans' pocket, pulled out her wallet, and removed the picture she'd found in Grandma's attic the other day. "Was it my dad's picture that was ripped away from this?" she asked, handing the photo to Mom.

Mom stared at the photograph in disbelief. With a slow nod, she said in a whisper, "Yes, it was your dad. I tore him out of the picture."

"Why?"

Mom picked up her coffee cup and took a drink before answering. "I. . .I didn't want any reminders of the guy around. The day I tore that picture, I was very angry with him."

"Was he really that bad?"

Tears gathered in the corners of Mom's eyes. "Can't you let this go? I'd rather not talk about it. I just want to focus on my future with Mike."

It was obvious that the subject of Star's real father was a touchy one. Mom had no doubt loved him at one time, and when he'd pulled up stakes and deserted them, it had probably broken her heart. From what Star had seen all these years, whenever the subject of her dad came up, Mom still held a lot of hurt and anger toward him, so maybe it was best if she just dropped the subject. After all, what was the point? If her dad didn't care enough about her and Mom to stick around and support them, then he really wasn't worth knowing.

"Could I have the picture back?" Star asked. "It's a good one of you and me, don't you think?"

"You're right. It is." Mom handed the picture to Star and smiled. "So what are your plans for the day?"

"I'm goin' to Emma Yoder's quilting class. Today will be our fifth lesson, and I'm hoping Emma's well enough to teach the class again because she explains things better than her Amish friend did. Although he was quite an interesting guy and knows something about designing quilt patterns," Star added.

"Well, before you go, there's something else I wanted to say about Mike. I think you should know that—"

"I've gotta go now, Mom, so hold that thought till I get home from Emma's," Star said, glancing at the clock on the far wall. She gulped down the rest of her juice, grabbed her sack with the quilt project in it, and raced out the door. She would deal with Mom marrying Mike when the time came, but she didn't have to like it.

Middlebury

As Stuart and Pam passed through Middlebury on their way to Shipshewana, Pam kept her head turned to the right. Maybe if she pretended to be looking at the scenery they were passing—scenery she'd seen many times before and knew almost by heart—Stuart would stop trying to make conversation. She was still upset with him for wanting to take Devin camping, while she and Sherry sat at home by themselves. Sure, she could probably think of something the two of them could do together, but Pam wanted to do more things as a family. Maybe if she continued to whine about it, Stuart would change his mind. Or maybe if she gave him the cold shoulder long enough, he'd wake up and realize how insensitive he was about her needs.

"When I checked the weather report on the Internet this morning, it said we might be getting some rain next week," Stuart said.

Pam silently focused on the black, box-shaped buggy up ahead. The little Amish girl who sat in the back looked out at Pam and waved. She was so cute that Pam waved back and smiled, despite her gloomy mood.

"Wish it would have rained today." Stuart grunted. "Then I wouldn't mind being cooped up in Emma's house all morning with a bunch of people I'd rather not know."

"That's not what you said after you attended the class without me," Pam mumbled. "You seemed quite interested in what all had been said and done that day. And to be honest, I really don't want to talk about the weather."

"Why do you have to be so critical of everything I say and do?" he questioned.

She gave no response.

"You know, sometimes I wonder why we ever got married. All we seem to do is fight."

"Then I guess we made the biggest mistake of our lives when we tied the knot, huh?"

"Maybe we did, but we loved each other, and I wish we could start over."

"I'd be happy to start over if you agreed to spend more time with me."

"What do you think I'm doing right now?"

"You're only doing it out of obligation. You take no pleasure in being with me, do you?"

A muscle in Stuart's cheek twitched. "Just stop it, Pam. You're putting words in my mouth again, and I'm gettin' sick of it, because we've been through all this before."

"That's a really dumb answer, Stuart."

"Can you give me an example of what a better answer would be? I mean, what exactly is it you want me to say?"

"How about, 'I love you, Pam,' and—"

"I've told you that many times."

She bumped his arm. "I'd appreciate it if you didn't interrupt when I'm talking."

"Sorry," he mumbled. "Go ahead and say what you were going to say, but let me remind you that you're one of the biggest interrupters I know."

Pam turned her head away. "Never mind, Stuart. Like all the other times, this is getting us nowhere."

"Just say what you were gonna say and be done with it!"

"What's the point? You're not going to change your mind about going camping with Devin."

"I don't know why you should begrudge me a little quality time with my son."

"*Our* son, Stuart." Pam placed her hand on her stomach. "I carried him for nine whole months. I've also nursed him back to health whenever he's been sick."

"I realize that. When I referred to Devin as *my* son, it was just a figure of speech."

"Whatever." She stared out her window until another thought popped into her mind. "You know what, Stuart?"

"What?"

"Maybe Sherry and I will do something together—something she'll think is really fun, like going to a baseball game. She likes sitting with you and watching the games on TV. Maybe then you'll realize what it feels like not to join us." Pam really didn't want to take Sherry to a game, but it was the only thing she could think of at the moment that might make Stuart realize how she felt.

"Sure, go ahead," he muttered. "You and Sherry can do whatever you want while Devin and I are camping."

Pam clenched her teeth. She'd be glad when they got to Emma's so she could make conversation with someone sensible—someone like Emma, who seemed to care about everyone's needs.

Shipshewana

Emma hummed softly as she placed needles, thread, scissors, and six small quilting frames on the table in her sewing room. She was glad she felt well enough to teach the class today and looked forward to showing her students how to quilt the patterned pieces they'd already put together. It gave her a sense of satisfaction to teach others the skills she'd learned at a young age. And being able to listen to and offer helpful suggestions about her students' personal problems made the class even more rewarding.

Glancing at the battery-operated clock on the far wall, Emma saw that she had about ten minutes before class started. That should give her just enough time to walk to the end of the driveway and get the mail.

With that decided, Emma hurried out the door. She was almost to the mailbox when a horse and open buggy pulled onto the shoulder of the road. Lamar was in the driver's seat.

"Guder mariye," he said with a friendly wave. "How are you feeling, Emma?"

"I'm doing better," she replied with a nod. "What brings you by here this morning?"

"Just thought I'd stop and see if you were feeling up to teaching your class today." His eyes twinkled when he smiled at her. "If you're not, then I'm more than willing to take over for you again."

Emma bristled. "I told you when you came by yesterday that I'm feeling better and can manage the class on my own."

"I know, but today's another day, and I thought even though you were doing better yesterday, you might not feel up to teaching the class today."

"I'm fine," Emma said a bit too sharply. She didn't know why this man got under her skin so easily. She knew she should appreciate his concern, but at times like now, Lamar seemed overly concerned and almost intrusive. Emma's irritation made no sense, really, because when Ivan was alive, she'd never minded if he'd shown concern for her well-being.

"I'm glad you're feeling better, but since I have no other plans this morning, I'd be happy to at least give you a hand with your class."

Emma shook her head so vigorously that the ribbon ties on her head covering swished around her face. "I appreciate your offer, but I'm sure I can manage fine on my own," she said, pushing the ribbons back under her chin.

"Oh, I see."

Emma couldn't help but notice the look of defeat on Lamar's face. Was it because he was lonely and needed something to do, or did he enjoy quilting so much that he really wanted to help? Either way, she wasn't going to change her mind about this. She saw too much of Lamar as it was, and if she let him help in the class today, he might end up taking over the lesson. Worse yet, he might think she was interested in having more than a casual friendship with him.

Just then, much to Emma's relief, Stuart and Pam's SUV pulled onto the driveway.

Emma gave them a friendly wave; then she turned to Lamar and said, "Some of my students are here now, so I really must go." Without waiting for Lamar's response, Emma grabbed the mail from the box and hurried toward the house.

CHAPTER 29

After all Emma's students arrived, they followed her into the sewing room and took seats around the table.

"It's good to see that you're back, Emma," Paul said warmly.

Everyone nodded in agreement.

"How are you feeling?" Ruby Lee asked.

"I'm doing much better," Emma replied. "Last week I was in a lot of pain and wouldn't have done well if I'd tried to teach the class. I'm sorry I couldn't be here."

"Ah, that's okay. It was nice of your friend Lamar to take over for you," Jan said. "He seemed like a real nice fellow, but we're all glad you're feelin' better and can teach the class today."

"Yes, I appreciated him filling in for me, but I'm also glad to be back." Emma smiled, looking at each one. "I missed all of you."

"We missed you, too," Star said sincerely. It was nice to see that even though she wore the black sweatshirt again, the hood wasn't on her head. Emma also noticed that Star seemed more relaxed around the others than she had when she'd come to the first quilting class.

"Today I want to teach you how to do the quilting stitches on your wall hangings. So if everyone will lay their work on the table, I'll tell you what we'll be doing next."

Once everyone had done as Emma asked, she explained that the process of stitching three layers of material together was called *quilting*.

"But before we begin the actual process, you'll each need to cut a piece of cotton batting approximately two inches larger than your wall hanging on all sides," she said. "The excess batting and backing will then be trimmed even with the quilt top after all the quilting stitches have been completed."

Emma handed some batting to each of her students. "Now, in order to create a smooth, even quilting surface, all three layers of the quilt need to be put in a frame," she continued. "For a larger quilt, you would need a quilting frame that could stretch and hold the entire quilt at one time. But since your wall hangings are much smaller than a full-sized quilt, you can use a frame that's similar to a large embroidery hoop." She held up one of the frames she'd placed on the table earlier.

"That suits me just fine," Jan spoke up. " 'Cause I've done some embroidery work before and know all about usin' a hoop."

Emma smiled. "It's important when using this type of hoop to baste the entire quilt together through all three layers. This will keep the layers evenly stretched while you're quilting. Just be sure you don't quilt over the basting, or it will be hard to remove those stitches later on."

Emma waited patiently until each person had cut out their batting. Then she said, "The next step is to mark out the design you want on your quilt top. However, if you just want your quilting to outline the patches you've sewn, then no marking is necessary. You'll simply need to quilt close to the seam so the patch will be emphasized."

Emma went on to tell them about needle size, saying that it was best to try several different sizes to see which one would be the most comfortable to handle. She also stated that the use of a snuggly fitting thimble worn on the middle finger of the hand used for pushing the quilting needle was necessary, since the needle would have to be pushed through three layers of fabric repeatedly. She demonstrated on one of her own quilt patches, showing how to pull the needle and thread through the material to create the quilting pattern.

"The stitches should be tiny and even," she said. "Oh, and they need to be snug, but not so tight that they'll create any puckering."

Stuart frowned. "That looks way too hard for me. My hands are big, and I don't think I can make tiny stitches or wear that thimble thing you mentioned. It was hard enough sewing the pattern pieces together on the sewing machine."

"For now, rather than worrying about the size of your stitches, just try to concentrate on making straight, even stitches," Emma instructed. "Don't worry when you're doing your best, and remember, I'm here to help you."

"Okay," Stuart mumbled. It was obvious that he still wasn't comfortable using a needle and thread. But at least he was here and trying his best. Emma had to give him credit for that.

"Yeow!" Jan hollered. "My thimble fell off, and I just pricked my finger with the stupid needle! Think I'd do better without the thimble." He stuck his finger in his mouth and grimaced. "That sure does hurt!"

Stuart snickered.

Jan glared at him. "What are you laughin' at, man?"

"I'm not laughing."

"Yeah, you were."

"I wasn't laughing at you."

"I think you were."

Stuart, red-faced and looking guilty said, "I was just thinking that a big tough guy like you with all those tattoos on your arms shouldn't even flinch if he pricks his finger."

Emma held her breath, wondering how Jan would respond.

"Well, what can I say," Jan said. "I may be a big strong man, but I bleed like anyone else."

Emma breathed a sigh of relief.

"I haven't gotten the hang of using the thimble yet either," Paul interjected, looking over at Stuart. "Even though I know it's supposed to help, to me it just gets in the way and feels kind of awkward. You know what I'm saying?"

Stuart nodded and went back to work on his quilting project.

After the first hour had passed, Emma went to the kitchen to get some refreshments. It always seemed like things went better in the class after she'd given her students a snack.

When she returned to the sewing room, she served them coffee, iced tea, and some rhubarb crunch that she'd baked last night before going to bed. As they ate their refreshments, Emma asked each one how their week had gone.

Pam was the first to respond. "It was okay, I guess. Probably would have been better if Stuart and I hadn't argued so much." She cast a quick glance in his direction, and he glared at her.

"Knock it off, Pam. Nobody wants to hear about the problems we're having."

She dropped her gaze to the table and mumbled, "Well, we wouldn't have those problems if we'd both stayed single."

"You've made a good point," he said with a nod.

Emma, feeling the need to intervene, quickly said, "Did you two ever stop to think how your life would be if you hadn't gotten married?"

Neither Pam nor Stuart said anything.

"Think about it," Emma continued. "If you hadn't married each other, you wouldn't have your two precious children."

"I hadn't really thought about it before, but that's true." Stuart looked over at Pam. "That's somethin' to be grateful for, right?"

She gave a slow nod.

"Just remember," Emma said. "It's important for you to work at your marriage if for no other reason than for the sake of your children."

Pam's chin trembled a bit. "Thanks, Emma. You've given us something to think about."

Emma smiled, pleased that they'd made a little progress. She turned to Paul then and asked about his week.

"It went pretty well," he replied. "It was nothing like the stressful one I had previously. I took Sophia shopping for new shoes yesterday afternoon, and I can't believe how big she's getting. Her shoe size actually went up a notch," he added with a proud-father grin. "Plus, she's growing out of her clothes faster than I can buy new ones."

"That's what kids do," Stuart said with a chuckle. "They grow up way too quick. It seems like just yesterday when our two were babies, and now they're both old enough for school."

Paul smiled. "Sophia's saying a few words now, too. She calls me 'Pa-Pa-Pa,' and has even learned the word *no*. It probably won't be too long before she's trying to walk." Paul's face sobered. "Too bad my wife's sister won't be around to see any of Sophia's childhood."

Emma went over to Paul and placed her hands on his shoulders. "I know it must be hard for you to have your sister-in-law cutting you and Sophia out of her life, but just keep praying for her and trusting that someday her eyes will be open to the truth, and she'll make amends."

"I know I need to keep praying," Paul said. "In 1 Thessalonians 5:17, it says we are to pray continually. It's just that sometimes it's hard—especially when we don't see answers to our prayers."

"Oh, God always answers. Sometimes He says yes. Sometimes, it's no. And sometimes He just wants us to be patient and wait." Emma looked at each one in the room. "Prayer is always a good thing, and for me, when I combine quilting and prayer, I can feel the love of God surrounding me."

"I've never believed much in prayer before," Jan spoke up, "but when I thought Brutus was dead, I prayed to God."

"So your prayer was answered then," said Emma.

Jan gave a nod. "Made me wonder if I oughta start goin' to church." His face reddened a bit. " 'Course, I'm not sure how folks would feel about a tattooed biker like me showin' up at their church." He looked at Ruby Lee. "What do you think? Would a guy who's rough around the edges be welcomed in your church?"

"Why certainly," she replied, "but then I'm not sure how much longer Gene and I will be there, and—"

"What do you mean?" Star interrupted. "I thought your husband was the pastor of your church."

"Well, he is. . .right now, at least." Ruby Lee went on to tell the class that she and her husband had taken a few days off and stayed at a B&B near Middlebury where they'd talked things through and prayed about their situation. "It didn't solve the problems we've been faced with at the church," she said, "but it did give us some time alone to reflect and spend some much-needed time in prayer."

Emma took a seat beside Ruby Lee, grateful for the opportunity to speak to her about this. "I'm glad you were able to do that, Ruby

Lee. After talking with Lamar and hearing how things went last week, I knew you must be hurting, so I tried calling you several times. Now I know why you didn't return my calls."

"That's right, and I didn't call when we got home last night because I knew I'd see you today."

"I just wanted to see if there was anything I could do and let you know that I've been praying for you," Emma said, giving Ruby Lee's arm a gentle squeeze.

Ruby Lee smiled. "Thanks, Emma. I appreciate that."

"And you know," Emma added, "God doesn't want us to lose faith in Him or become full of despair. He wants us to trust Him and keep praying as we wait and hope for the best."

"I know," Ruby Lee said quietly. "I'm working hard at trying to do that."

When everyone had finished their refreshments and begun quilting again, Emma turned to Jan and asked, "How'd your week go?"

His face broke into a wide grin. "Pretty good. I've been spendin' more time with Brutus in the evenings, and he seems to be much calmer now. We try to get in a walk around the neighborhood before it gets dark, and I'm actually gettin' to meet more of my neighbors in a positive way now."

"I'm glad your dog came back," Emma said sincerely.

"Yeah, me, too. While he was gone, I really missed the mutt."

"It made me sick to see that dead dog lying by the side of the road and then wondering who it belonged to and if some child would go to bed that night missing his dog," Paul said.

"Yeah," Stuart interjected. "People ought to keep a closer watch on their pets."

Emma turned to Star to check in on her week.

"It was terrible. . .especially this morning when I found out that my mom's definitely gettin' married again—to that guy I don't even like."

"I know you're not happy about this," Emma said, "but do you think your mother's happy?"

Star shrugged. "She seems to be."

"Then maybe you should be happy for her, too," Pam put in.

"I'd like to be, but I can't imagine Mike livin' in the same house with us, criticizing everything I wear, making fun of my songs, and tellin' me what to do all the time."

Emma gave Star's shoulders a reassuring squeeze. "Maybe it won't be as bad as you think."

"Guess we'll have to wait and see how it goes." Star frowned. "If Mike keeps tellin' me what to do and tries to act like he's my dad, then I'll probably end up movin' out on my own."

"I'll be praying for your situation," Emma said.

"Thanks. Like Jan, I've never held much stock in prayer, but I guess it wouldn't hurt to have a few prayers goin' up just in case there is a God and He might actually be listening."

"Oh, there's a God all right," Paul interjected. "He is the One true God, and without my faith in Him, I'd never have made it this far since Lorinda died."

"Same with me after Ivan passed," Emma added. "Psalm 71, verse 3 tells us that God is our rock and our fortress. I'm real thankful for that."

Ruby Lee nodded, and so did Paul, but everyone else remained quiet as they continued to quilt. Emma hoped they were all taking the words of the psalm to heart and that any of her students who didn't know the Lord in a personal way would someday make that decision.

For the rest of the class, things went along fairly well. Then shortly before it was time to go, Paul said, "Oh, I almost forgot. I brought some pictures I took of Sophia the other day. Would anyone like to see them?"

"Of course we would." Ruby Lee smiled. "Who doesn't like to look at baby pictures?"

Paul reached into the sack he'd brought his quilting project in and pulled out a manila envelope. Then he removed two eight-by-ten photos of Sophia and shared them with the class.

"So, you took these pictures of your daughter?" Stuart asked, passing them on to Pam.

Paul smiled. "I sure did, and I was pretty pleased with the way they turned out."

"Well, let me tell you, Paul," Pam said, "these are just as good as the pictures we had professionally done of our kids last Christmas. I think they're amazing."

"Thanks." Paul fairly beamed. "I've been interested in photography since I was eleven years old when my parents gave me a camera for Christmas. I still have that camera, but these days, I use a digital. You know, these new cameras today can almost do the work for you."

"Say, man, you have a real talent there," Jan said after he'd been shown the photos. "If I had skills like that at takin' pictures, I'd be snappin' photos all the time."

Emma couldn't miss the tender look on Jan's face when he studied Sophia's picture. It was too bad he had no wife or children. Emma figured Jan probably liked it that way, because she knew that some folks, like her, preferred to remain single. It wasn't that she liked not being married, for she'd certainly enjoyed the years she and Ivan had together. She just wasn't open to the idea of getting married again.

"I'm sure my parents had no idea the camera they gave me would introduce me to a hobby I enjoy to this day," Paul went on to say.

"Would you like to see some pictures of my twin boys when they were little?" Ruby Lee asked. Before anyone could respond, she had her wallet open and the pictures passed around.

Next, Pam shared some photos of her and Stuart's children, and then Star pulled a picture from her wallet. "Here's one of me when I was a baby," she said, handing it to Pam.

Pam squinted at the picture. "You were a cute baby, and I assume that's your mother holding you on her lap?"

Star nodded.

"What happened there?" Stuart asked, looking over his wife's shoulder. "It looks like someone's picture's been torn out."

"Yeah. My mom ripped it out 'cause it was my dad, and I guess she was really angry with him." Star frowned. "That creep gave me an ugly name, and then before I was even old enough to remember what he looked like, the bum bailed. I used to wish he'd come back so I could get to know him, but maybe it's best that he didn't, 'cause if he didn't care enough about my mom to want to marry her, then he probably didn't care about me."

Everyone in the room became quiet. Even Emma didn't know what to say. No wonder this poor young woman hid behind her dark clothes and seemed so confused about things. She'd never known her father and was obviously deeply troubled about him running out on them when she was a baby. Who could blame her for that? Oh, how she wished there was something she could do to make things better for Star.

"Can I see the picture?" Ruby Lee asked.

Pam handed it to her.

Ruby Lee studied the photo; then she looked over at Star and smiled. "You were a beautiful baby, and you're a lovely young woman now."

"I agree," Emma said, giving Star a tender hug.

Star blinked a couple of times like she was holding back tears. "Thanks. No one's ever said that about me before."

"I'd like to see the photo, too," Jan spoke up. "Whoever that bum of a father of yours was didn't know what he was doin' when he walked out on you."

Ruby Lee handed Jan the photo. He sat several seconds, staring at it with a peculiar expression while shaking his head as though in disbelief. He glanced away then back again, as if to clear his vision. Then he looked over at Star, and in a voice barely above a whisper, he asked, "Is your real name Beatrice Stevens?"

Star nodded, squinting her eyes. "Yeah. How'd you know that?"

Slowly, Jan reached into his back pocket, removed his wallet, and pulled out a picture. "Take a look at this." His hands shook as he handed it to Star, but he didn't make eye contact with her. "It's the same picture you have, only as you can see, in my picture I'm not ripped out."

Star blinked and stared at him as though he'd taken leave of his senses. Everyone else sat without saying a word.

"Bunny was my girlfriend," Jan said, his eyes turning glassy.

"Bunny?" Star repeated.

"Yeah. Bunny was Nancy's nickname. I started callin' her that when we first started dating 'cause her nose twitched whenever she got upset." Jan paused and swiped his hand across his forehead where sweat had beaded up.

Star sat rigid, refusing to look at him.

"Bunny and I met when we both lived in Chicago. We dated awhile and then moved in together. Several months later, I found out she was gonna have a baby, so I asked her to marry me." Jan stopped talking again, and there was a break in his expression. Emma sensed the strong feelings that had swept over him. Drawing in a couple of deep breaths, he continued. "At first, Bunny said she'd have to think about it. Then, as the time got closer to our baby bein' born, she finally agreed to marry me but said she wanted to wait till after the baby came." Jan's voice quavered a bit; then it steadied. "When our little girl was born, we named her Beatrice after my mom."

Star's hands had started shaking now, too, and her voice squeaked as she stood and pointed at Jan. "You. . .you're my dad?"

"It's really a shocker, but yeah, I think I am," Jan said as though hardly believing it himself.

"So you're the mangy cur who walked out on me and my mom!"

He shook his head vigorously. "No, no! That's not how it was. There's something you need to know. I didn't run out on you and your mom. She must have changed her mind about us gettin' married, 'cause without even tellin' me where she was goin', she just took you and split."

Star's eyes narrowed as she glared at him. "You're a liar! Mom would never do something like that."

"No, please listen; I'm not lyin'. I wanted to marry your mom and wanted more than anything for us to be a family. But Bunny had other ideas, and they obviously didn't include me."

Star and Jan seemed oblivious to everyone else in the room. Emma was so shocked by all of this, she simply couldn't think of a thing to say.

"Now you wait just a minute," Star said, her voice high-pitched and intense. "Mom may not have always had her head on straight when it comes to men, and she has been known to lie about a few things, but when it comes to the story she's always told about my dad runnin' off, that's never changed. So I don't think she was lying."

"But you don't understand. I loved Bunny back then, even though she was always headstrong and kinda hard to figure out." Jan left his seat and took a step toward Star. "I probably wasn't the best catch a girl could want, but I had a good payin' job, and there wasn't much I wouldn't have done for you and Bunny. And I want you to know that I did everything I could to find you both. But your mom—well, she did a good job of hidin' from me.

"When I contacted Bunny's mom, even she didn't know where Bunny had gone." Jan drew in a deep breath and released it with a moan. "I can't believe we've been here at Emma's house all these weeks, and I had no clue a'tall that my own flesh-and-blood daughter was right here in front of me. All these years of wonderin', and now, here you are." He seemed to be taking in every detail about Star as though seeing her for the very first time. "You even have the same color eyes as mine, but I can see now that you've got your mother's nose."

Backing up as though to put some distance between them, Star planted both hands on her hips and glared at him. "Stop looking at me that way! Seriously, it's creepy."

Reaching out to touch her arm, he took a step closer, but she backed up even farther. "Don't touch me! I don't want anything to do with you!"

"It must be fate that brought you two together," Pam spoke up, as though trying to calm Star down. Or perhaps she saw this as some kind of happily-ever-after scene she was witnessing. Well, it wasn't. Emma could certainly see that.

"I think it was divine intervention," Emma said, finally finding her voice and walking over to place her hand gently on Star's arm. "It was the good Lord who brought you and your father together."

"Well, I wish He hadn't!" Star pointed at Jan. "You know what? I'm glad you never showed up in my life before, because if you had, I might have hauled off and punched you. I don't believe for one minute that my mom left you." Star grabbed up her things and raced for the door.

"Please, don't go!" Jan called. "I've waited all these years to meet my daughter, and I sure don't wanna lose her now!"

The door slammed behind Star.

Jan groaned and flopped into a chair, letting his head fall forward into the palms of his hands. He sat like that for several minutes; then he lifted his head and turned toward Emma with a look of bewilderment, as though seeking an answer. . .advice. . .anything. The pain on his face was undeniable.

"What was I thinkin'?" he mumbled, shaking his head. "This sure didn't turn out the way I'd imagined it would if I ever found my daughter. No, this went down bad. Yeah, really bad."

CHAPTER 30

I blew it! I really blew it!" Jan slapped his knee and groaned. "I should never have blurted that out like I did. I probably scared the poor kid half to death. Worse than that, she doesn't believe a word I said. I think she hates me."

"Were you telling the truth about not being the one who ran off?" Stuart questioned.

Jan's jaw clenched. "'Course I was tellin' the truth. I'd have no reason to lie about somethin' as important as that!" He scrubbed his hand down the side of his face, fighting the sudden urge to start howling like a baby. "Trouble is, I have no proof. It's Bunny's word against mine."

"Maybe it would help if you spoke to Star's mother yourself," Paul suggested. "You could remind her of how it all happened."

Jan tapped his fingers along the edge of the table. "If I thought for one minute that Bunny would tell the truth, I'd do it. But I have a gut feeling she'd keep on lyin' about all that happened. Besides, I'm pretty sure that after all these years, Bunny probably don't wanna even see the likes of me." He slowly shook his head, feeling worse by the minute. "I've never understood why she hated me so much that she'd just take off with our baby without even tellin' me she was leavin' or where she was goin'. I thought Bunny loved me and wanted to get married, but somethin' must have happened to change her mind." It was all Jan could do to keep his emotions under control.

"I think the best thing you can do is to wait until next week and see what Star has to say then," Ruby Lee said.

"Don't think I can wait that long. Besides, what if Star don't come back? She may never wanna see me again." Jan looked over at Emma with a pleading expression. "Can you help me out here? If you have Star's address, would you tell me what it is?"

Emma shook her head. "I wouldn't feel right about giving you that information without asking her first. And, Jan, I think you really do need to give Star some time to sort things through. Like Ruby Lee said, you can talk to Star again next week. I feel sure she'll be here."

"Maybe Star will talk to her mother, and she'll find out that you were telling the truth," Paul said in a tone of reassurance.

Jan grunted. "Boy, you don't know how bad I'd like to see it go that way, but unless Bunny's had a change of heart, she ain't likely to admit she was wrong."

Emma gave Jan's arm a reassuring pat. "I'll be praying for you this week, and I hope you'll pray, too. Try to remember that God is with us no matter what situation we may face."

Goshen

Star felt so stressed by the time she got to Goshen that her body trembled and she could hardly breathe. She really shouldn't have driven anywhere feeling this upset, but she just wanted to put some distance between her and Jan. She also needed time to calm down before she talked to Mom, so she decided to stop and jog a ways on the Pumpkinvine Trail.

As Star jogged along, her legs threatened to buckle. She still couldn't believe the burly biker was her dad. And as she thought about everything Jan had told her about Mom taking off, her frustration and confusion increased. She didn't know whether to believe him or not. All these weeks she'd seen Jan as a really nice guy—the kind who loved kids and dogs.

Was it all just for show? she wondered. *Or has Jan changed from how he was when he and Mom were dating?* At the moment, Star was angry with both of her parents: Jan for abandoning them when she was a baby, and Mom for refusing to tell Star much about her dad or letting her see any pictures of him. Of course, even if she had seen a picture of Jan from back then, he'd no doubt changed a lot, and she probably wouldn't have recognized him. But if Star's mom had told her his name, she would have figured things out a lot sooner. After all, how many men had a name like Jan Sweet?

Stopping to catch her breath for a minute, Star kicked at a clump of weeds along the edge of the path with the toe of her sneaker and jumped back as a baby rabbit ran into the higher brush.

"Oops. Sorry little fellow. Didn't mean to scare you like that," she murmured, momentarily enjoying the short interruption.

I still can't believe Jan's really my dad, Star thought, as she started running again. *All the times he's been sitting beside me at Emma's, making small talk and acting so friendly as we worked on our quilting projects, and I never had a clue.*

Deciding to pick up the pace, Star panted as she jogged harder. While a trickle of sweat rolled down her forehead and into her eyes, she knew it didn't matter how fast or how hard she ran. The unexpected, shocking news she'd received today was inescapable. She had half a mind to head back to Emma's and give Jan a well-deserved punch. But what good would that do? It wouldn't change the past, but oh, it sure would make her feel better.

Sides aching and gasping for air, Star knew she couldn't run any farther, so she headed back toward her car. She really needed to go home and talk to Mom.

When Star entered Grandma's house sometime later, the phone was ringing. She raced across the kitchen and grabbed the receiver. "Hello."

"Star is that you?"

"Yeah, who's this?"

"It's Emma Yoder." She paused. "I was worried about you and wanted to see if you're all right."

"Yeah, I'm fine. Never better," Star mumbled.

"You don't sound fine. The tone of your voice says you're still upset."

Emma's soothing tone caused Star to relax a bit. "I. . .I still can't believe what happened today," she said. "I mean, what are the odds that Jan Sweet would turn out to be my long-lost father?"

"Are you still angry with him?" Emma asked.

"Sure. Why wouldn't I be? He ran out on us, Emma. Big, sweet, lovable Jan ran out on his wife and baby. And I'm supposed to be okay with that?" Star's voice had become shrill, but she couldn't seem to help it. She was still so angry she could spit.

"What did your mother say when you told her about Jan?"

"I haven't told her yet. I just got home from the Pumpkinvine Trail, where I went to try and jog off my frustrations."

Another pause. Then Emma said, "Jan wants to talk to you, Star— and to your mother, too. He was really upset after you left and asked if

I'd give him your address or phone number."

Star grabbed the edge of the counter as fear gripped her like a vise. She wasn't ready to talk to Jan yet. Not until she'd spoken to Mom. "You didn't give it to him, I hope."

"No. I told him I couldn't do that without your permission."

Star breathed a sigh of relief. "Oh good. I appreciate that. Mom would have a hissy fit if Jan showed up out of the blue. I really need to talk to her about all of this first."

"I hope it goes well when you do. Oh, and Star, can I say one more thing?"

"Yeah, sure. What is it, Emma?"

"Don't believe negative thoughts about anyone until you have all the facts."

"Yeah, and I plan to get all the facts, too. I'd better go, Emma. I don't hear the TV in the living room, so I think Mom's probably in her bedroom. I really oughta speak to her now."

"I'll let you go then. Oh, and remember, Star, if you need to talk more about this, just give me a call. Unless I happen to be in the phone shack, you'll get my voice mail. But I'll call you back as soon as I get your message."

"Okay, thanks, Emma. Bye for now."

Star hung up the phone and was about to head for Mom's room when she spotted a note on the kitchen table. She picked it up and read it out loud.

Mike and I are heading to Fort Wayne to see his folks and tell them about our engagement. Since I have next week off from work, and so does Mike, we're planning to stay with his folks until Thursday or Friday. This will give Mike the chance to look at the restaurant he plans to buy there. If it all works out, we'll be moving to Fort Wayne soon after we're married.

I was going to tell you all this at breakfast this morning, but you rushed out of here so fast I didn't get the chance.

There's plenty of food in the fridge, so you shouldn't have to worry about doing any grocery shopping while I'm gone.

I'll see you Thursday evening or sometime Friday.

Love,
Mom

Star's hand shook as she dropped the note to the table. Besides the fact that Mom had taken off without telling her, now she had to wait several days to tell her about Jan. And what if Mom and Mike ended up moving to Fort Wayne? Where would that leave Star? Would they expect her to move there, too? What would happen to Grandma's old house? Would Mom decide to sell it? It wasn't fair. She needed to talk to Mom right now. She needed some answers about Jan.

"Never gonna be the princess, holding tight to my daddy's neck," Star sang as a strangled sob caught in her throat. She paused a minute and swallowed hard. "Never gonna be the apple of his eye. Never gonna walk the aisle hand in hand; a sweet vignette. Never gonna answer all the whys. Ask me what it's like to be connected; ask me why I can't give up control. Ask me how it feels to be protected; ask me who is praying for my soul. Ask me when I knew I'm loved forever. . .never."

CHAPTER 31

Shipshewana

"Hey man, how was your weekend?" Terry asked when Jan climbed into Terry's truck on Monday morning.

"It was good in one way but not so good in another," Jan said with a shake of his head. "You're never gonna believe what I have to tell you."

"What do you mean?"

Pausing a bit to get the words out right, Jan moistened his lips and said, "Saturday, I found my daughter."

"Wow, that's really great news, man!" Terry thumped Jan's shoulder. "Where'd you find her?"

"At Emma Yoder's."

Terry's eyebrows shot up. "Your daughter's Amish?"

"Will you listen to what I'm sayin' here? She's not Amish. She's one of the women I've been learnin' to quilt with these past five weeks."

"Huh?"

"That girl I told you about—the one who calls herself Star—I found out toward the end of class last Saturday that she's my daughter, Beatrice."

Terry released a low whistle. "You've gotta be kidding me!"

"No, I'm not kiddin'." Jan went on to explain about the picture Star had shown the class, and how he had one just like it—only his didn't have his picture torn off.

"Now that's really something!" Terry exclaimed. "I mean, what are the odds that the daughter you never thought you'd see again has been right under your nose these last five weeks?"

"When I found out, that same thought went through my head. Pam called it fate, and Emma said it must be divine intervention." Jan sucked in a deep breath. "I'm not sure what I'd call it, but it sure came as a surprise—for both me and Star."

"I'm really happy for you, man." Terry gave Jan's arm another good thump. "You must feel like you're ten feet tall after bein' reunited with your daughter."

"I am glad I finally got to meet her, but unfortunately, she don't feel the same way about meetin' me."

"How come?"

Jan explained the lie Nancy had told their daughter and how Star had reacted when he'd tried to explain what had happened.

"I'm not sure I'll ever see her again," Jan said with a slow shake of his head. "Emma Yoder called me on Saturday evening and said she'd talked to Star. Asked if she could give me Star's phone number and address, but Star said no." He moaned deeply and rubbed the bridge of his nose. "I feel just sick about this, man. I'd given up all hope of ever findin' Beatrice, and now that I have, she don't want nothin' to do with me."

"If you just give her some time to get used to the idea, I'm sure she'll come around."

"Wish I could believe that, but you didn't see Star's face when she lashed out at me and called me a bum." *And I still can't believe I was actually thinkin' of asking her out—my own daughter, for cryin' out loud,* Jan thought. *But then, how was I to know who Star really was? Whew! I'm sure glad I didn't make that mistake.*

"Maybe once Star talks to her mom about it, Nancy will set the record straight," Terry said with a hopeful expression. "Think about it— this is a lot for your daughter to take in—especially in a short time. I'd say it's pretty major."

"I'd like to believe that Bunny will tell Star the truth, but if she hates me as much as I think she does, I doubt she'll admit that it was her who ran out on our relationship and not me. Even after all these years, I suspect I'm still the bad guy. It's probably why she's never once tried to locate me."

Jan tried to imagine what Star must be feeling. After all, her finding out he was her dad and not just some biker dude who'd come to Emma's to learn how to quilt had to have knocked the wind right out of her sails. Did he dare to believe she might come around after she'd had time to think it all through? Did he dare to hope that Bunny might tell their daughter the truth?

"Just take one day at a time and wait to see what tomorrow brings," Terry said. "That's what my folks are doin' in their relationship right now."

"How are your parents gettin' along these days? I've been meanin' to ask about that but keep forgetting," Jan said, glad for the change of subject. It was better if he focused on something else right now, rather than agonizing over Bunny's betrayal and Star's rejection of him.

"They've started seein' a marriage counselor," Terry replied. "It's gonna take some time and a lot of give-and-take on Mom and Dad's part, but I think if they do what the counselor says, they might get their marriage back on track."

"That's good to hear. 'Course, not everyone who goes for counselin' ends up with a happy marriage. Counselin' sure hasn't seemed to help that bickerin' couple who've been takin' the quilting class with me, although it might be that they aren't doin' everything their counselor says."

Terry grunted and pointed out the front window. "I hate to add to your misery this mornin', but I don't think we're gonna get any roofin' done today, 'cause it's started to rain, and it looks like it's gonna be a gully washer!"

Goshen

When Ruby Lee woke up still fighting the headache that had come upon her the day before, she was surprised to see that Gene was already out of bed. He usually slept in on Mondays because it was his day off, but soon after all the trouble at the church started, Gene's sleeping habits had changed. Sometimes Ruby Lee found him up in the middle of the night pacing the floors. Some days he slept at odd hours and for long periods of time.

When is all this going to end? she wondered as she climbed out of bed and padded over to the window. *Will things ever get better? Will Gene and I know peace and a sense of joy again? I feel like such a hypocrite, singing songs of praise during church, smiling, shaking hands, and pretending that my heart's not breaking, when I really wish I didn't have to be there at all.*

Ruby Lee pressed her nose against the window, barely able to see outside due to the rain coming down in torrents.

"This horrible weather sure matches my mood," she mumbled. "So much for working in the garden today."

She turned from the window, slipped into her robe, and stepped into the hall, where the smell of freshly brewed coffee beckoned her to the kitchen. She found Gene sitting at the kitchen table with his Bible open. When she drew closer, he looked up at her and smiled. "Good morning, my love."

"Mornin'," she mumbled as she reached for a mug and poured herself some coffee.

"How are you feeling? Last night you said you had a headache. Is it gone now?"

Ruby Lee winced as she shook her head. Just the slightest movement made the throbbing even worse. "Hopefully it'll be better once I've had some coffee." She seated herself in the chair across from Gene, added a spoonful of sugar to her cup, and gave it a couple of stirs.

"It's a tension headache, isn't it?" he asked.

"Yeah. It came on me yesterday right after church. This horrible weather we're having doesn't help much either."

"Did someone in our congregation say something to upset you?"

"Nothing directly to me, but I heard a couple of the board members' wives talking in the foyer right before the service started." She frowned. "One of them—Mrs. Randall—said she thought the board should ask you to resign."

Gene nodded slowly as his shoulders slumped. "I figure that'll probably happen at the next board meeting, if not before."

"If you know this, then why don't you resign before they ask you to leave?"

His response came slowly. "You know why, Ruby Lee. The Lord Almighty called me to this church to minister to these people—even the difficult ones." He reached across the table and placed his hand over hers. "God doesn't want us to lose faith or give way to despair. He wants us to keep praying and hope for the best, always trusting Him."

"That's pretty much what Emma Yoder told me last Saturday."

"Well, she gave you some good advice."

"But if the people at our church don't want you anymore. . ." Ruby Lee bit her lip to keep from bursting into tears. What was the point in trying to reason with Gene? They'd had this discussion so many times before.

"You know how much I've been praying about our situation and seeking God's will," he said.

All she could do was nod.

"Well, I've finally reached a decision." Gene paused and looked down at his Bible.

Ruby Lee held her breath and waited for him to continue. *Please, Lord. Please let him say we should leave that church full of ungrateful people.*

Gene pointed to the Bible and smiled. "My answer was here all along."

"What is it?"

" 'Fulfill ye my joy, that ye be likeminded, having the same love, being of one accord, of one mind.' Philippians 2:2," Gene read from the Bible. "If the church board is opposed to us borrowing money to add on to the church, then I, as their leader, need to respect that decision and stop pushing them to do what they feel the church can't afford."

"You're giving up your dream of adding on to the church?"

"That's right."

"But if we don't add on, how will the congregation ever grow? I mean, folks can barely find seats in the sanctuary on Sunday mornings now."

He nodded. "That's true, but there are other things we can do."

"Such as?"

"We can have two services or maybe open up a wall and make use of the room that's now being used for storage, which would let us seat more people."

"So you won't resign and look for another church?" she asked, already knowing the answer.

"Nope." Gene's even, white teeth gleamed as he smiled. "I'm stayin' right here for as long as the good Lord tells me to stay."

"What if the board asks you to leave even after you'd told them you're giving up on the building plans?"

"Then I'll abide by their decision."

Ruby Lee released a sigh of resignation. She had a hunch that once Gene met with the board and told them his decision they would probably not ask him to leave. And if that happened, for Gene's sake, she would continue to support his ministry by being the best wife she could be. She would do it because she loved him and knew it was her responsibility.

Quietly, she bowed her head. *Heavenly Father, I truly do know that You exist, and I ask You to forgive me for doubting Your presence and for losing my faith in people. I know You brought Gene and me here for a reason and that You have a definite plan for our lives. Thank You for that plan and for loving me enough to send Your Son, Jesus, to die for my sins. No matter what happens in the days ahead, help me to trust You in all things.*

CHAPTER 32

Shipshewana

Early Wednesday morning, Emma shivered as she stood on the porch and watched the rain come down. It had begun raining on Monday and had continued to rain all day Tuesday. It wasn't just a light rain either. It had come down in torrents, filling the gutters with so much water that they continually overflowed, leaving the flower beds flooded and puddles scattered across the lawn. Along with the rain, strong winds had blown, until at one point, Emma feared some of her windows might break. But the wind had finally subsided. Now if the rain would just let up.

Sure wish I could get out of the house for a while, Emma thought. She would have enjoyed going to the pond and sitting by the tree where Ivan had carved their initials. She always did her best thinking there, and with all that had been on her mind this week, she had plenty to think and pray about. If the rain let up later today, maybe she could still go to the pond. She hoped so anyway, because she didn't like being cooped up in the house for too long.

Emma was relieved when it quit raining shortly after noon. The fresh air felt good, and she was ready to be outside for a while. So she hitched her horse to her open buggy and headed in the direction of the pond to enjoy her and Ivan's special tree.

Emma didn't know why she felt such a strong need to go there today. Could it be because she'd had a dream about Ivan last night and had awakened this morning with him on her mind?

"Oh Lord, I thank You for all the beauty You created," Emma murmured as she looked up at the pretty blue sky. Even the white, puffy clouds that had formed into such unusual shapes were amazing.

The birds sang a chorus of happy tunes from the trees lining the road, and Emma's horse lifted her head as though sniffing the fresh air and enjoying it, too. Even God's creatures were joyous after the rain. Emma loved how clean everything looked and smelled after a good rainfall and didn't mind if a drip now and then splattered on her lap as it fell from the tree branches overhead.

She hardly knew which way to look. A blaze of orange led her onward as she admired a cluster of tiger lilies growing at the edge of the woods. How grateful she was for all God's creation.

A short time later, Emma guided her horse and buggy up the path leading to the pond. She knew it had been raining hard these last few days but hadn't expected to see so much water everywhere. She giggled to herself, watching a family of bluebirds splashing and bathing in one of the puddles. It even appeared as if the pond had grown to be nearly twice its size. Apparently the ground just couldn't soak all that water in.

Searching for an area that wasn't covered with water, Emma finally located a tree where she could secure her horse. Then, carefully stepping around one puddle after another, she made her way down the path leading to her and Ivan's special tree.

As she approached the spot where it had stood so many years, Emma gasped. "Ach, my! What's happened here?" Their beautiful tree had been uprooted, no doubt from all the wind and rain. It lay across the path, surrounded by mud and leaves, no longer a living, growing tree.

Emma stared, feeling sick at heart. *How long has our tree been down?* she asked herself. *If only I'd come to see it sooner; but then how could I have, feeling the way that I did during my bout with shingles?*

It saddened her to know that there would be no more times of coming here to think and pray while she gazed at the initials Ivan had lovingly carved in the trunk of the tree. Emma knew it was silly, but she felt as though she could burst into tears because such a special memory had been taken from her. She wished she were an artist, so by memory she could sketch and preserve that image of what once had been so special to her and Ivan.

Slowly, she walked to the fallen tree, tears clouding her vision as she stared at those precious initials now facing skyward. Running her fingers over the carved-out bark, Emma remembered once again the kindness that had drawn her to Ivan so many years ago. This place that had given them many wonderful yet simple memories would now be missing a piece of their past.

Emma closed her eyes before leaving, trying to keep an image of their initials imprinted in her mind. She knew that once some time had passed, she'd probably come here again, for it was the *place* that held those special memories, not just the *tree*. For now, though, she'd have to let it sink in that their tree would no longer be here, and that this place would be changed forever.

When the weather improved and everything dried out, someone would probably come along and cut up the tree for firewood. *Well, at least it will go to good use, even though our special initials will be gone,* she told herself, trying to remain positive.

Taking one final look, Emma noticed a few wild irises that had been close to where the tree had been uprooted. Because their bulbs were exposed, she decided to take a few home and put them in one of her flower beds. If they survived, her flower garden would hold yet another memory of something dear to her heart.

Swallowing against the lump in her throat while fighting back more tears of despair, Emma turned and slowly made her way up the path. All she wanted to do was go home, where she could occupy her thoughts with the work she needed to do. She knew from experience that keeping busy was the best remedy for self-pity.

Mishawaka

All was quiet that night as Stuart stepped out onto the deck overlooking their backyard. Following the cooler rain they'd had, the weather had turned muggy and warmer than normal—especially for the beginning of June. Summer would soon be upon them, bringing even hotter, humid weather. So this was simply a taste of what was yet to come.

The tall trees surrounding their yard shaded most of the lawn, but from the deck, the leafy branches didn't obscure the beautiful view they had of the sky. How many times had he and Pam talked about sitting out here on a cool autumn evening or a warm spring night, stargazing while sipping from mugs of hot chocolate and eating s'mores. Somehow those plans were always put on the back burner, and they just never got around to doing it.

This was one of those times the stars looked so close—almost reachable. The fireflies were putting on quite a display as well. Their sparkling lights from the land to the sky seemed to mesh and intertwine with the stars.

Too bad Pam isn't out here enjoying all of this with me, he thought with regret. *But no, she'd rather sulk and refuse to talk to me. Don't see how she thinks we're ever gonna fix our marriage problems this way. For someone who complains about not spending enough time together, she has a funny way of showing she wants to be with me. She must not have been listening last Saturday to the things Emma had to say about marriage. Maybe she doesn't care whether we get our marriage back on track or not. Guess I just need to keep pressing ahead and try to focus on something positive.*

As Stuart continued to watch the twinkling display, he reflected on how well this evening had gone with Devin and Sherry. After supper he'd promised them a game of Frisbee, and then as the sun began to set, he and the kids took a walk through the neighborhood while Pam did the dishes. He'd invited her to go with them, but she'd declined. Was it because she was still miffed at him for wanting to take Devin fishing? Well, she ought to get over it and be glad he wanted to spend time with their boy.

Pulling his thoughts back to the walk he and the kids had taken, Stuart thought about the neighborhood they lived in and how it was nice and spacious with plenty of yard space between each of the homes. As he and the kids had meandered down the streets, outside lights from neighbors' homes glowed as if to invite them in. A few "Hi, how are ya's?" were exchanged with those sitting on their porches and at picnic tables. One of their neighbors had waved as he rolled up the hose that had been left in the yard before the storm. Even though most were near-strangers, it was a friendly area. That had been proven to Stuart and Pam many times when there were emergencies in the neighborhood. People would drop whatever they were doing to lend help where needed, and it made them feel secure knowing they could count on others if it became necessary.

When they'd arrived home from their walk, Stuart had thought about roasting marshmallows, but it was near the kids' bedtime. Much to Stuart's surprise, Sherry and Devin had actually cooperated when Pam said it was time for their baths. Their energy level had been kicked up a notch since the end of the school year. But as bedtime approached, he could see that they were slowly unwinding. After kissing him goodnight, the kids had headed upstairs to their rooms. No doubt it wouldn't be long before they'd drift off to sleep with dreams of summer swimming in their heads.

Pulling up a deck chair and taking a seat, Stuart thought how when he'd brought up the subject of camping last week, he hadn't expected Pam would get so upset, and he still couldn't figure out why she didn't like camping in a tent.

Tent camping was the only kind Stuart had ever known, and he thought it was fun when he could rough it for a few days. Every summer when he was a boy, his parents had taken him and his younger brother, Arnie, camping, and they usually went to a different state park each year. What an adventure it had been, and like most kids, he'd always looked forward to their next family camping trip the following year. Stuart's love of camping grew deeper over time, even though one of their trips could have been proclaimed disastrous.

Stuart shook his head and grinned as he remembered that year, arriving at Mohican State Park much later than they'd planned because Dad had taken a wrong turn and gotten them lost. When they'd finally pulled into their campsite, it was close to midnight, so his folks only had time to put in the crucial stakes to keep the tent in place. They'd decided to jury-rig the porch roof on the tent until morning, while Arnie and Stuart quickly gathered wood for the campfire.

Unfortunately, a terrific thunderstorm hit overnight, with high winds, torrential rains, and plenty of lightning to brighten the sky. It wasn't funny then, and they'd all been pretty scared, but afterward it had made a good story, telling everyone how it went unnoticed that the porch roof had filled up with rainwater. During the storm, Mom and Dad had been more worried about the lightning. The pocket of rainwater was too heavy for the weakly extended porch roof to hold, and before daybreak, the overhang collapsed, sending a flood of water through the whole tent.

Stuart chuckled out loud as he remembered the wet awakening they'd all received that morning. Luckily, it was sunny the next day, and they could hang their sleeping bags and wet clothes on a makeshift clothesline to dry.

Oh brother, he couldn't help thinking. *I can only imagine Pam going through something like that. I can almost hear her squealing right now!*

Thinking about Pam, he let his mind drift to something she'd said to him last week. It had shocked him to learn that Pam's childhood wasn't as rosy as he'd thought, and that she'd resented her father. Maybe tomorrow he would attempt to find out more—if she was willing to talk about it.

As Stuart got up and walked over to the porch railing, he caught sight of a falling star and watched as it fizzled out of sight. "Wish Pam had been here to see that," he muttered.

Growing tired, he turned and was about to go into the house to make sure all the lights were out before going to bed when his cell phone rang. He saw on the screen that it was an employee from work and figured he'd better take the call.

———

Having just put the kids to bed and feeling the need for some fresh air, Pam decided to join Stuart on the porch. Maybe if they spent a few minutes alone, enjoying the cool breeze that usually came up on a hot sultry night, they could communicate without ending up in a fight. It was a worth a try, anyway.

Pam had been pleased when Stuart said he wanted to take a walk around the neighborhood with Sherry and Devin. She'd been tempted to join them but figured it would be good if he spent a little time alone with the kids. Besides, she needed an opportunity to reflect on the things Emma had said during their last quilting class. Pam knew she'd been dwelling on the negative and not appreciating all that she had.

Emma was right, Pam thought. *If I hadn't married Stuart, we wouldn't have the pleasure of raising our two very special children.*

Pam was about to open the screen door when she heard Stuart talking to someone. Had one of the neighbors dropped by? It was getting pretty late in the evening for that.

She peeked through the screen and spotted Stuart near the porch railing with his cell phone up to his ear. Curious to know who it was, she stood quietly off to one side, listening.

"Yeah, this isn't good, and I know what needs to be done," Stuart said into the phone. "I'm going to call a lawyer first thing in the morning. I just don't see any other way."

Heart hammering in her chest, Pam moved away from the door and raced down the hall to their room. She knew things hadn't improved much between them and had been worried that Stuart might leave her, but she hadn't expected it would happen so soon—or that she'd have to hear it like this. Would it help if she told Stuart what she'd just heard and pleaded with him to reconsider? Or would it be better not to fight it—just agree to an amicable divorce? After all, even with all the counseling they'd had, their marriage hadn't improved.

"Oh no," she moaned, nearly choking on the sob rising in her throat, "if we go our separate ways, how will it affect the children?"

CHAPTER 33

Goshen

As Star sat at the kitchen table on Friday evening eating a ham sandwich, a sense of irritation welled in her soul. Mom still wasn't home, and she hadn't even bothered to call. Star didn't have the number for Mike's parents either, and since Mom didn't have a cell phone and Star didn't know Mike's cell number, all she could do was sit here.

How could Mom be so inconsiderate? Star tapped her fingers along the edge of the table. *I just wish she'd get here so I can tell her about Jan. I want to hear what she has to say about all of this. Better yet, I can't wait to see her expression when she hears the big news. I'll bet she'll be as shocked as I was to know that her ex—my dad—has been attending Emma's quilting classes with me for the last five weeks.* She shuddered. *And to think, I even had thoughts about what it would be like if he asked me out. Good grief. . . If Jan had been interested in me, I could have ended up dating my own dad!*

Feeling as if she was about to be sick, Star set her sandwich aside and stood. She was just getting ready to clear the table when the back door swung open and Mom and Mike stepped in. *Oh, great! Now I can't say anything to Mom about Jan until Mr. Wonderful leaves.*

"Where have you been, Mom?" Star asked, feeling as though she'd run out of patience. "I was beginning to think you weren't coming home at all."

Mom giggled like a silly schoolgirl and gave Star a hug. "I told you we'd be back on Thursday or Friday."

"Yeah, but I was hoping it would be sooner, because I really needed to talk to you about—"

"Your mom and I were busy all week, looking at some condos and checking on the details for my new restaurant," Mike said, cutting Star off in midsentence.

"Well, you could have at least called," Star muttered, unable to hide her irritation.

"Sorry," Mom said, "but we got so busy I just lost track of time." She looked up at Mike with an adoring smile that made Star feel even sicker. "We're real excited about his new business venture."

"That's right," Mike agreed. "I'll have to make a few renovations to the building I bought, but it should be ready to open for business by early fall—right after your mom and I get back from our honeymoon."

"Where are you going for that?" Star questioned.

Mom's eyes lit up like twinkling lights on a Christmas tree. "Mike's taking me to Hawaii. Now isn't that great?"

Star nodded, finding Mom's chipper tone an annoyance. She knew it wasn't right to feel this way, but it sickened her to see how happy Mom and Mike seemed to be. He stood close to Mom with his arm around her waist and a sappy-looking grin that stretched ear to ear.

"Then after our trip to Hawaii, your mom and I will be moving to Fort Wayne," Mike said.

So Mom would be getting a trip to Hawaii. How nice for her. She'd said many times that she'd always wanted to go there. Star figured she would probably never make it to Hawaii—or for that matter, anyplace else exciting. Well, at least there'd been no mention of her moving to Fort Wayne with Mom and Mike. That much was good. She'd just have to look for an apartment, because Grandma had left this house to Mom, and Mom would probably sell it and use the money to help buy a condo for her and Mike in Fort Wayne. Star would miss this old house when she moved out, but at least she wouldn't have to live with Mike and Mom and watch them gushing all over each other, while Mike, acting as if he were her father, told Star what she could and couldn't do. She'd live on the street in a cardboard box before she'd put up with that!

"Well, Nancy, think I'll head for home now and let you two visit." Mike bent his head and gave Mom a noisy kiss. "See you tomorrow, sweetie."

Star rubbed a tense spot on her neck and looked away in disgust. She hoped Mike was sincere and really did love Mom, but if he turned out to be anything like the other men Mom had been involved with, Star wouldn't be shocked.

"There's somethin' I need to tell you," Star said to Mom after Mike went out the door.

"Can it wait till tomorrow?" Mom yawned and stretched her arms over her head. "It's been a long day, and I'm really tired, so I'd like to take a bath and go to bed."

Star shook her head determinedly. "No, Mom, it can't wait. This is important, and we need to talk now."

"Okay, but let's make it quick. Like I said, I'm really tired." Mom took a seat at the table, and Star did the same.

"I met my dad last Saturday," Star blurted out.

"Hmm...what was that?" Mom asked as she picked at a piece of lint on the front of her blouse.

"I said I met my dad last Saturday."

Mom jerked her head. "Huh? What did you just say?"

Star released an exasperated groan and repeated what she'd said for the third time.

"You. . .you met your dad?"

"Yeah—Jan Sweet."

Mom jumped like she'd been hit by a bolt of lightning. "Oh brother! This is not what I needed to hear today!" She leaned forward and stared at Star, sweat beading on her forehead. "Have you been searching for him behind my back? You found him somehow and set up a meeting last Saturday—is that what happened?"

Star shook her head. "No, we—"

"Well then, how? Where exactly did you meet Jan, and what makes you think he's your dad?"

Star quickly explained how Jan's identity had been revealed last Saturday and ended by saying, "I can't believe I sat there in Emma's sewing room all that time, never knowing my dad was taking the class with me." She groaned and slowly shook her head. "I think Jan and I had some kind of a connection, Mom. Up until last Saturday, when I found out who he was, I liked the guy, and we sort of seemed to be kindred spirits." Star made no mention of her thoughts concerning the possibility of Jan asking her out. She just wanted to forget she'd ever had that silly notion.

"I can't believe Jan's been living so close to us. If I'd had any idea he lived in the area, I never would have moved here to Goshen."

Star tensed. "Are you saying that if you'd known Jan lived in Shipshewana, you wouldn't have come here to help Grandma when she was sick?"

Mom squirmed in her chair. "Well, I. . ."

"Were you that afraid of seeing him again?"

Mom nodded. "I've been afraid all these years that he'd find you."

"Good grief, Mom, was Jan really that bad of a guy? 'Cause if I'm bein' honest here, he sure doesn't seem that way now."

"Well. . .umm. . .he was a biker and much too wild."

"Did Grandma know about Jan?"

"She knew him when we all lived in Chicago, but when she moved to Indiana a few years after Jan and I split up, I don't think she had any further contact with him. And I'm sure she had no idea he lived anywhere near here, because if she had, she would have said so." Mom's cheeks reddened. "Did Jan. . .uh. . .say anything about me?" she asked in a voice pitched higher than normal.

"Yeah, he had plenty to say."

"Such as?"

"He said your nickname was Bunny. In fact, he has it tattooed on his right arm. Is it true, Mom? Did Jan used to call you Bunny?"

Mom gave a slow nod.

"How come you never told me about your nickname? I would think you would have since I changed my name from Beatrice to Star."

"I didn't think it was important, and since Jan was the only one who ever called me Bunny—"

"Jan said he didn't bail out on us," Star said, cutting Mom off. "Said it was you who left and that he'd tried to find us with no success." Star looked her mother right in the eye. "It's not true, is it, Mom? Jan was lying through his teeth about that, right?"

Mom sat staring at the table for the longest time. Then, with tears gathering in the corners of her eyes, she finally whispered, "No, Star, your dad was telling the truth. I lied to you about that. It was me who left, not him."

Star groaned and leaned forward, until her forehead rested on the table. "Why, Mom?" she asked, nearly choking on the words. "Why'd you leave Jan, and how come you lied and told me it was him who'd run out on us?"

"Well, I. . ."

Star lifted her head and could see Mom was visibly shaken. "All these years, I've been thinking what a bum he must have been to leave us like that. And now, after so much time has gone by, you're telling me different? Is lying what you do best?" Star's tone was caustic, but she didn't care. Mom had disappointed her plenty of times in the past but never more than she had right now.

Mom pushed her chair aside and went to the sink for a glass of water. After she drank it, she returned to the table and sank into her chair with a pathetic little squeak. "Jan and I rode with a motorcycle club, but he took it more seriously than I did. He wanted to ride nearly every weekend, which I was okay with at first." Mom swished her hand from side to side, as though hoping to emphasize her point. "Even after I got pregnant with you, I rode with Jan on a few short trips. But once you were born, I realized it was time to settle down and make a home for my baby."

"Jan said he wanted to marry you and make a home for both of us," Star said.

"Puh! That's what he told me, too, but he was wild and free—not the kind of guy who'd ever settle down. At least that's what I thought at the time." Mom drew in a deep breath and released it with a lingering sigh. "Honestly, Star, by the time you were born, I really didn't care about Jan anymore. It had been fun while it lasted, but I was tired of his biker buddies and sick of riding miles and miles on the back of a stupid motorcycle."

Star listened with interest as Mom continued. "Even on the weekends that Jan decided to stay home with me, someone from the gang always hung around our place." She clutched Star's arm. "Don't you see? I just wanted some peace and quiet in my life. I wanted that for you, too, but I didn't think we'd ever have it if I stayed with Jan. So I took off without telling anyone where I was going, not even my mom. I didn't have any contact with her until two years later—once she'd moved from Chicago and I knew Jan was out of the picture."

Star sat for a while, letting everything Mom said sink in. It was a lot to comprehend, and between what both Jan and Mom had told her, she had a lot to think about. "So what was the reason for you letting me think my dad had left us in the lurch?" she asked. "Why couldn't you have just been honest and told me that you'd run away from him?"

A few tears slipped out of Mom's eyes and splashed onto her crimson cheeks. "I...I didn't want you to think ill of me for taking you away from your dad."

"Oh, you'd rather that I thought ill of him?"

Mom slowly nodded. "I'm the one who had to raise you, so—"

"*Had* to raise me?" Star's voice rose as she clenched her fingers. "Like it was some heavy burden instead of a joy to raise your daughter? Isn't that how it's supposed to be?"

"I didn't see it as a burden, really. I mean, it was hard being on my own and all, but I loved you and wanted your respect, so I just couldn't tell you that I left your dad."

"Like you've ever really cared about having my respect," Star muttered, feeling even more confused and upset.

"What's that supposed to mean?"

Since Star had started telling Mom the way she felt, she figured she might as well say everything that was on her mind. "It means, with the exception of Grandma, I've never felt loved. You always seemed to care more about whatever boyfriend you were with than you did me."

"That's not true, Star. I worked hard so I could give you everything you needed."

"Giving a person what you think they need is not the same as making them feel loved and good about themselves." Star's knuckles turned white as she clenched her fingers even tighter. "You've never encouraged me to sing or write songs; you've never said I was pretty or smart; and whenever you came home with some creep of a boyfriend, you never cared whether I liked him or not!"

"I. . .I guess you're right about that, and unfortunately, most of them were losers. I just didn't make good decisions." Mom's lips quivered as she spoke. "But I think I've finally found the right one this time. Mike really does care about me, and he wants to give me good things."

"Yeah, *you*, Mom—not me. Mike doesn't want to give me anything but a hard time."

"Oh, come on, Star. You know that's not true."

"Isn't it? All the guy's ever done is criticize my clothes, my music, and anything else he can think of to pick at. Never once has he said anything nice about me."

"I'll speak to Mike about that. If he apologizes, will it make you happy?"

"An apology would be nice if it was heartfelt, but since you and Mike will be movin' to Fort Wayne and I'll be looking for an apartment here, I won't have to be around him much, so I don't really care whether he apologizes or not."

Mom sat quietly, rubbing at a stain on the kitchen table.

"So now I know why you lied about my dad leaving," Star said, moving their conversation back to Jan. "What I don't know is why you refused to let me see pictures of him or even tell me his name."

"I didn't want you to ask any more questions about Jan. Worse yet,

I was worried that you might try to find him."

"Would that have been so terrible? Didn't you think I had the right to know my own dad?"

More tears fell onto Mom's face, and she reached for a napkin to wipe them away. "I. . .I was afraid if you ever met your dad, you might like him better than me. I was afraid he might turn you against me or even try to take you away."

"I've gotten to know Jan fairly well during the last several weeks, and he's always seemed nice to me. Even after he told me about you and him and how you'd split, he didn't really say anything mean about you, although I'm sure he could have." Star paused and drew in a deep breath, hoping it would calm her down a bit. "I see now that Jan was just trying to set me straight about the truth. And then I ended up calling him a liar and a bum who walked out on us! He'll probably never forgive me for that."

"I'm truly sorry, Star, and I hope someday you'll forgive me," Mom said tearfully.

Star, unable to accept her mother's apology, slammed her fist down hard on the table, rattling the salt and pepper shakers. "You know what? This is all so ridiculous—like one of those soap operas you watch on TV. I never got to know my dad, my mom's been lying to me all these years, I called my dad a liar when he told me the truth, and now I'm about to be stuck with another stepdad who I can barely stomach!" Star stood so quickly that her chair toppled over. "You know what's really funny about all this?" she added with a sneer. "All of a sudden you're calling me Star. Are you doing that just to try and win me over, Mom?"

"No, I—"

"Boy, I'll tell ya—my life really stinks!" The walls of the house vibrated as Star fled to her room and slammed the door.

Shipshewana

Exhausted from another hard week of roofing, Jan dropped onto his bed and slumped against the pillows. He was thankful for the long hours of work. It kept him too busy to think about the lie Bunny had told Star. But when he closed his eyes, memories of Bunny and how things used to be between them pressed in on him like a stack of roofing shingles.

Jan's mind took him back to the day Bunny had told him she was pregnant. He'd been shocked at first, but after the numbness wore off, he'd actually been excited about the idea of becoming a dad. Being raised an only child, he'd always wished for a brother or sister. Now he'd have a son or daughter to buy toys for, and when the kid was old enough, they could fool around together. He looked forward to holding his baby and going places together as a family. When the kid got older, Jan would teach him to ride a motorcycle, and the three of them would take road trips together. A trip to Disney World or some other amusement park would sure be fun. Jan could only imagine what it would be like to have his own flesh-and-blood child sitting beside him on some crazy amusement ride, where they could laugh and holler like crazy. He figured Bunny would enjoy it, too.

"But none of that ever happened," Jan muttered, as his mind snapped back to the present. Thanks to Bunny running off, he'd been cheated out of knowing and spending time with his daughter all these years. And thanks to Bunny, he was sure that Star hated him.

He moaned. *What should I do about this? If my daughter don't show up at Emma's tomorrow, should I insist that Emma give me Star's address and phone number? Or would it be best if I let all this go and just didn't show up there myself? Maybe it would be better for everyone concerned if I just bowed out of the picture.*

CHAPTER 34

Emma had just finished doing her supper dishes when someone rapped on the back door. Curious to see who it was, she dried her hands on a towel and hurried from the kitchen.

Emma was surprised when she opened the door and discovered Lamar on her porch.

"*Guder owed*, Emma," he said with his usual friendly smile.

"Good evening," Emma replied.

"I have something for you in my *waache*."

"What is it?" she asked, her curiosity piqued as she looked at his wagon.

Lamar crooked his finger. "Come, take a walk with me and see."

Emma stepped off the porch, a little perplexed, and followed Lamar across the yard. When they came to his wagon, he reached into the back and pulled the tarp aside.

Emma gasped when a small wooden table and an image she thought was gone forever came into view, beautifully crafted and preserved for all time.

"See here," Lamar said, pointing to the top of the table. "It's your initials that had been carved in that tree by the pond."

Emma's throat constricted as she struggled with her swirling emotions. "But how? I mean. . . ." She nearly choked and was unable to get the rest of her sentence out.

"I knew about the tree your late husband had carved your initials in because Mary told me. And when you and I met at the pond a few weeks ago, I remembered you saying that you went there sometimes to think and pray."

Emma gave a slow nod. "I was there a few days ago and discovered that the tree had been uprooted by the storm. I figured someone would probably use it for firewood, but it made me feel sad to know that Ivan's and my initials would be destroyed. It was one of the many sweet memories I have of him."

"I understand how that is. When I look at the pretty quilt on my bed that my wife made, it helps to keep her memory alive in here." Lamar placed his hand on his chest.

"So how did this beautiful table come about?" Emma asked.

"Well, you see, when I stopped at the pond a few days ago to see whether it had flooded, I took a walk down the path and discovered that your special tree had been uprooted. Realizing that you'd no doubt miss it, I cut the piece out that had your initials carved in it and made a tabletop from that section. Then I attached it to some table legs I'd already made."

"Danki," Emma said, fighting back tears. "How much do I owe you for this nice table?"

Lamar shook his head. "Not one single penny. I did it to show you how much I care, and seeing your reaction just now is all the payment I need."

"Well, I certainly do appreciate it."

"Shall I take it into the house for you?" he asked.

"Jah, please do."

Lamar lifted the table out of the wagon, and Emma followed him toward the house. She was beginning to see Lamar in a different light, and some of the barriers she'd been hiding behind started to waver. Thinking back, everything about Lamar started coming to light. All he'd ever done was show her kindness, and all she'd ever done was resist it. Maybe if he continued to pursue a relationship with her, she might even consider letting him court her.

"So how'd things go with the quilting class last Saturday?" Lamar asked as they walked through the grass.

"It was interesting, with an unexpected development," she replied.

"How so?"

"Let's get the table into the house, and then I'll tell you all about it while we eat a piece of angel cream pie. How's that sound?"

He grinned at her. "Sounds real good to me."

Mishawaka

"Do you need some help?" Stuart asked when he entered the kitchen and found Pam in front of the sink washing some of their hummingbird feeders. Last year the kids had been fascinated when they'd seen a little hummingbird flitting from one azalea bloom to the next, so this year Pam had purchased a couple of feeders so that Sherry and Devin could watch the hummers up close.

"Guess you can finish washing these.' Pam motioned to the feeders that hadn't been washed. "While you're doing that, I'll fill the clean feeders with the fresh nectar I made a while ago."

He smiled. At least she was speaking to him this evening, even if it wasn't in the friendliest tone.

"How'd your day go with the kids?" Stuart asked, hoping to make more conversation.

She gave a noncommittal shrug.

That's just great. He'd tried speaking to Pam yesterday, asking her to share more about her childhood, but she'd refused to discuss it with him. So much for improving their communication skills like their counselor had asked them to do during their last session.

"Did you do anything special today?" Stuart questioned, still trying to get her to open up. He rinsed out the first feeder, set it on the towel Pam had spread on the counter, and waited for her response.

"I finished all the quilting that needed to be done on my wall hanging while the kids played in the sprinkler to get cooled off. It was a scorcher today."

"Yeah, I know." *Good, she's talking again. I think we might be making some progress now.* "I was glad the air-conditioning was working at the store today. When it went out last year during a heat wave, we had a lot of complaints until we got it fixed."

Pam opened the cupboard door and took out a sack of sugar. "Stuart, I need to ask you something."

"What's that?"

"Are you planning to file for divorce?"

His eyebrows rose. "Not this again, Pam. Why are you asking me that?"

"Because I heard you talking on the phone to someone the other night when you were out on the porch, and you mentioned seeing a lawyer."

Stuart rubbed the bridge of his nose, trying to recall the conversation he'd had with his store employee. "Oh, now I remember. Blaine and I were talking about the fact that someone had fallen in the store the other day, and when he said he thought the lady might try to sue, I said I'd be calling our lawyer."

"Really? That's all there was to it?"

"Yeah, Pam. I'm not filing for a divorce, and I hope you're not thinking of doing it either. The kids need both of us, and we have to keep working on our marriage until things improve."

"You're right, and we will," she said with a look of relief.

For the next few minutes, they worked quietly on the feeders. Stuart was just getting ready to ask more about Pam's childhood, but she spoke first.

"What are you going to do about your wall hanging? You've hardly worked on it at all this week, and Emma's going to show us how to put the binding on tomorrow; then we'll be done."

"I'll work on it when I'm finished washing the feeders."

"You'll never get it done on time. There's too much left to do."

"Then I guess it won't get done." *Why does she have to needle me all the time?* Stuart fumed. *Is it really so important that I finish the stupid wall hanging? Just when I said we needed to keep working on our marriage, and she has to start in on me again.*

He grabbed one of the smaller feeders, and in his frustration, gripped it too hard. *Crack!* The glass shattered.

Stuart winced when he saw blood oozing from the ugly gash in his finger. "Oh no! What did I do?"

When he tried to move his finger and couldn't, he realized what had happened. "We've gotta get to ER fast, 'cause I think the tendon in my finger's been cut!"

As Pam turned on the headlights and pulled their SUV out of the hospital parking lot, a feeling of weariness settled over her like a heavy quilt. The day had started out busy as usual, and she'd had no trouble handling that. Over the years she'd become pretty good at doing projects around the house and taking care of the children. But this evening after Stuart cut his finger, it was all she could do to keep her head on straight and think clearly. Now it was catching up to her.

When they'd left the emergency room and stepped outside, she'd been surprised to see that it was already dark. After they'd arrived at the hospital, she'd lost all track of time. With the paperwork that had to be filled out and then waiting for a doctor to look at Stuart's finger to evaluate what needed to be done, every minute seemed to blend into the next. She just wanted to go home and collapse into bed.

It had really shaken Pam up hearing that Stuart had cut a tendon in his finger and would require surgery on it next week. The fact that he'd cut it while helping her clean the hummingbird feeders made her feel guilty—not to mention that she'd been nagging him about not getting his wall hanging done. If she'd only kept her mouth shut, the accident might not have happened.

"Sure hope the kids are doing okay at the Andersons'," Stuart said, breaking into Pam's thoughts.

"They're fine. I called them while you were with the doctor and told Betty we'd be home as soon as we could," Pam said, looking over at Stuart. "Betty said not to worry, because she and Lewis were enjoying Devin and Sherry so much. She even asked if the kids could spend the night."

Stuart nodded. "That's good."

Pam appreciated the Andersons. It was like having a set of grandparents right next door. Devin and Sherry loved spending time with them and vice versa. Whenever the kids found something interesting in the yard, such as a frog or a grasshopper, they would run next door and show Betty and Lewis as if they'd never seen such creatures before. The Andersons' kids were all grown and out of the house, so when the older couple had an opportunity to spend time with Devin and Sherry, they jumped at the chance. Pam hoped when the kids were grown and raising families of their own, that she and Stuart would be good grandparents.

She swallowed around the lump in her throat. *That is, if we're still married by then.*

Even though Stuart had assured her that he wasn't planning to get a divorce, she feared he might if things didn't get better between them.

"I'm sorry I put you through all of this chaos tonight." Stuart reached over with his good hand and patted Pam's shoulder. "I could see how upset you were in the ER."

Pam nodded and sighed, rubbing her temple. "I'm thankful you didn't lose your finger."

"No more thankful than I am. Just wish they could have done the surgery while we were already at the hospital."

"I guess there's a reason they didn't, Stuart. Don't worry though. Like the doctor said, the surgery will be scheduled for next week, and it will be performed as an outpatient procedure. He said the operation should be no more than an hour, so I'm sure you'll do fine." Pam tried to sound reassuring as she pushed the button to roll down her window. She needed some fresh air to help keep her focused until they got home. "Let me know if that's too much air, and I can put the window up a little."

"Thanks, but the night air feels good."

Pam glanced over at Stuart again and noticed that he was looking at the bandage on his finger. "Does it hurt much?"

"Not really." Stuart shook his head. "I thought it would hurt more than this, but I guess it's still numb from the shot they gave me before they put the temporary stitches in." He paused and laid his hand back in his lap. "Can you believe how crowded that ER was? I was beginning to think they'd never get to me."

Pam was about to comment, but the lump in her throat wouldn't let her get the words out. Her resolve was about gone. It hadn't been easy to mask her fear of Stuart's injury in front of Devin and Sherry and then remain positive for Stuart, getting him to the hospital and waiting in the ER, but now her ability to stay strong was slipping from her grasp.

"Pam, are you all right?"

"Oh Stuart!" Once the tears started, she couldn't get them to stop. It was like floodgates opening, and her vision instantly became blurred. She had no choice but to pull over to the side of the road and turn off the engine. Once she did, the sobs came hard, and it was difficult to catch her breath. She put her head in her hands and cried like there was no tomorrow.

Stuart unbuckled his seat belt and touched her shoulder. "Honey, what's the matter?"

Pam was glad Stuart was being patient with her, because it took a while to calm herself enough to speak again. "I was really scared when I saw so much blood coming from your finger. It was all I could do to keep my head and stay calm in front of the kids." She nearly choked on a hiccup. "All I could think of was getting you to the hospital safely." Another hiccup. "Oh Stuart, I don't know what I'd do if anything ever happened to you."

Stuart moved closer, and Pam had never felt more comforted than when he took her in his arms. Careful not to hurt Stuart's injured finger, her arms tightened around his neck, and she started sobbing all over again.

Once she settled down some, she looked at Stuart, her chin quivering. "If. . .if you only knew how good it feels to have you hold me like this." While Stuart gently smoothed a lock of Pam's hair away from her face, she closed her eyes and felt like a little girl again. "I would have given anything to have my daddy hold me like this when I was scared of all those unseen things you imagine when you're little. All I ever wanted was for him to take notice of me and say that he loved me and was proud of my accomplishments. I could be in the same room, watching TV with him, and he wouldn't even notice that I was there. I thought I did everything right—my grades were good in school, and I never gave my parents any trouble. I would have even gone fishing with him if he'd asked me to, but of course, he never did. When I got older—" Pam took a deep breath, and the rest came out in a whisper. "I finally realized one day that my dad was self-centered and didn't really care about me at all." She didn't think she had any more tears left, but now her weeping came out in a soft whimper.

Stuart held on to Pam and rocked her like a baby. She felt comforted, yet her mind swirled with nagging doubts. After opening up to him like this, would it make any difference in the way he treated her? Things were better between them tonight, but how would they be in the morning?

CHAPTER 35

Goshen

On Saturday morning, Star entered the kitchen and found her mother sitting at the table with a cup of coffee and the newspaper.

"How'd you sleep last night?" Mom asked, looking up at Star.

"Not so well." It was all Star could do to even look at Mom this morning, much less answer any questions.

"Me neither. I kept thinking of all the things we talked about last night, and I want you to know that I truly am sorry."

Star poured herself a cup of coffee and stood staring out the window by the sink.

"I've made an important decision."

Star turned around slowly and looked at Mom. "What's that?"

Mom took a drink of her coffee before saying anything. When she set the cup down, she looked at Star and smiled. "I'm going to give you this old house."

"Huh?"

"I'll have no need of it after Mike and I get married, and I'm sure your grandma would have wanted you to have it rather than it being sold to strangers."

"But what about the money you'd get if you sold the house?" Star questioned.

Mom shook her head. "I'll be well taken care of after Mike and I are married, and since your job doesn't pay much, you really can't afford to get an apartment on your own. If you stay here, you'll have all the memories of Grandma around you, not to mention a comfortable place to live and write your songs without interruptions."

A lump formed in Star's throat. She couldn't believe Mom would actually give her Grandma's house. Maybe Mom did feel some love for her after all. "Thank you. I appreciate that,' Star said tearfully. "Maybe I'll take some voice lessons and learn how to sing a little better, too."

Mom left her seat at the table and gave Star a hug. "You can if you want to, but I think you already sing quite well."

Star sniffed deeply. "You really mean it?"

"Wouldn't have said so if I didn't."

"Do you think I'll ever make it big in the music world?"

Mom shrugged. "I don't know, but I think you should try."

"Yeah, maybe I will."

"So what are you going to do about today?" Mom asked, abruptly changing the subject.

"What do you mean?"

"Are you going to the last quilting class at Emma Yoder's?"

"Sure. Why wouldn't I go?"

"What if Jan's there? What will you say to him?"

"I had trouble sleeping and was thinking about that most of the night."

"And?"

"Now that I know the truth, the first thing I'm gonna do is apologize to Jan for calling him a liar and a bum."

"Then what?"

"Then I'm hoping we can spend some time together outside of the quilt class—get to know each other better and maybe become good friends."

"That'd be nice. I'll be happy for you if that happens, because, Lord knows, I've kept you hating him long enough." Mom's tone was as sincere as the look on her face, and it gave Star a sense of peace. Now she just hoped Jan would accept her apology.

"There's one more thing, Star." Mom took a sip of coffee before she continued. "I'd like the chance to apologize to Jan. He may not believe me, but I do feel terrible about how all this played out. Years ago, I thought I was doing the right thing, but now I see that all I did was bring on a lot of unnecessary hurt, especially to you. You don't know how much I regret it. Things could have been different, and I see that now. So after you've had some time with Jan and have gotten to know him better, I'd like a chance to make things right. He needs to know that our breakup wasn't all his fault and that I'm truly sorry for taking you and running off like I did."

Star placed her hand on Mom's arm. "I accept your apology, and I. . .I forgive you."

"I know I don't deserve it, but thank you for that."

Feeling somewhat better, Star took a seat at the table. She could hardly wait to get to Emma's and speak to Jan.

Mishawaka

Stuart sneaked a look at his wife as she drove them to Emma's for the last quilting class. He saw the glint in Pam's eyes, as though she was deep in thought. He was content with this moment of quiet, amazed at how quickly things had changed between him and Pam.

They say bad things happen for a reason, he thought, recalling the phrase he'd heard some years ago. Nodding his head, he realized there could be some truth to it. It was hard for Stuart not to grin as he recollected the recent turn of events. He remembered how surprised he'd been by Pam's reaction when the mishap had occurred with the hummingbird feeder. She'd appeared to be subdued on the way to the hospital, concentrating on traffic and getting him to the ER safely.

Wanting to stay alert, Stuart hadn't taken the full amount of his pain medicine this morning, so his finger was thumping like crazy with pain. He could ignore the discomfort, though, as he continued to recall the events of last night.

The trip home from the hospital was when Stuart had gotten a real eye-opener. It was like floodgates opening, and once started, nothing could stop Pam's tears. He still couldn't believe all the frustrations and heartache Pam had kept bottled up about her relationship with her dad. It was as if all the tears she'd held in for years couldn't be held back any longer. If he'd only known all this sooner, he'd have understood her better and realized why she felt the way she did about certain situations. Maybe things would have been different between them and not so combative at every turn.

Stuart knew he and Pam still had a ways to go, but he felt confident that they'd reached a milestone last night. He'd looked at Pam with a sense of awe, just as he was doing now, and realized that she really did love him.

And for himself, despite all their ups and downs, there'd never been any doubt of his love for Pam. He might not have shown it in ways she understood, but he'd always loved her. Never more so than he did right now.

Although Stuart knew how hard it had been for Pam, the fact that she'd finally shared those things about her dad made him feel closer to her than ever before. It was a good dose of reality, coming to terms with how for all these years he'd been putting other things above his wife's needs. He was glad they'd stayed up late last night, talking more about the past and their future. They should have been spending more time over the years really talking and listening to each other, rather than arguing and finding fault.

He remembered hearing Paul say during one of their quilting classes that life goes by in a blink, so from now on, Stuart was determined to make a positive change.

"Never thought I'd hear myself say this, but you know what?" he asked, gently stroking Pam's arm.

"What?"

"Even though my finger hurts this morning, I'm actually happy to be going to our little half-stitched quilting club with you."

Pam smiled. "I'm glad."

"Did you remember to bring the plant you potted for Emma?"

"Yes, I did. Earlier I put it in the back of the SUV so we wouldn't forget to take it to her. I hope Emma likes it," Pam added.

"I'm sure she will. Oh, and I forgot to tell you—the little cooler in the backseat—there's something in there for Emma."

"What is it?" she asked.

"Thought maybe she'd like to try some of the wild berries I picked when I went camping last summer. I took one of the containers from the freezer to give to her. Do you think she'll enjoy the berries—maybe bake something with them?"

"Stuart, that was really thoughtful. I'm sure Emma will appreciate the berries, and since she's always baking something, I'll bet she'll put them

to good use." Pam sighed. "You know, today's going to be kind of sad with the classes ending. I've never been good at saying good-bye, and I've grown to know and like Emma so much, it'll be hard to leave her."

"Well, maybe our paths will cross again. Maybe we can stop and visit her when we're in Shipshewana sometime."

"That's a good idea." Pam smiled at Stuart with a look of happiness he hadn't seen in a long time.

The rest of the ride was quiet, but this time, it was more content and peaceful than all the other trips to Emma's had been. Although things weren't perfect between Pam and him, Stuart felt sure they were finally on their way to restoring their marriage.

CHAPTER 36

Shipshewana

Emma stood in the living room, looking happily at her new table and eager to show it to Mary and others in her family. She still couldn't get over Lamar's thoughtfulness in making it for her. Mary had been right—he really was a nice man.

The next time Lamar asks me to go somewhere with him, I should probably accept his invitation, she decided. *Maybe I'll even invite him to join us for supper when I have some of the family over next week.*

Emma's musings halted when she heard a car pull in. She looked out the window, and when she saw that it was Star, she went to the door and opened it.

"Morning," Star said as she stepped onto the porch. "Looks like I'm the first one here."

"That's right. You are. Come in, and we can visit until the others arrive."

Star followed Emma into the house, and when they entered her sewing room, they both took a seat. Emma was pleased to see that Star wasn't wearing her black hooded sweatshirt today. She was dressed in jeans and a white T-shirt, sort of like what Jan usually wore.

"How are you?" Emma asked, hoping Star's anxious appearance didn't mean she'd had a bad week.

"I was pretty stressed-out for most of the week until I talked to my mom—which, by the way, wasn't till she got home last night, because she'd been in Fort Wayne with the guy she plans to marry."

"Did you tell her about Jan and how you'd learned that he was your father?"

"Yeah, and needless to say, she was pretty surprised." Star frowned deeply. "Turns out that Mom lied when she'd said my dad had run out on us shortly after I was born."

"What exactly happened?"

"Mom changed her mind about marrying him. Said she thought he was too wild and had decided that she didn't really love him. So she took off with me and didn't tell Jan or even her mom where she was going."

"Oh my!" Emma couldn't imagine anyone running away like that, but Star's mother was most likely young and very confused back then. And if she thought Jan was too wild, she'd probably done what she felt was right for her and Star at the time. Emma remembered all too well how when people were young, they thought differently, and unfortunately, it sometimes took years for them to realize their mistakes.

"Now what?" Emma asked. "Are you going to tell Jan what your mother said?"

"Definitely. I'm nervous yet anxious to see Jan today. I need to tell him I'm sorry for losing it last week and calling him a liar, among other things."

Emma placed her hand gently on Star's arm. "I'm sure he'll understand and accept your apology. I'm also certain he'll be glad to know that you've spoken to your mother and have learned the truth."

"I sure hope so." Star reached into her jeans' pocket and handed Emma a folded piece of paper.

"What's this?" Emma asked, peering at Star over the top of her glasses.

"It's a song I wrote just for you. Wanted you to know how I feel about the way you've touched my life."

Emma opened the paper, noting that the song was entitled "You Saw Me."

"A lot of layers hide me," Emma read out loud. "Disguise me. . . A shell of sorts to work through my pain. A stack of stories guard me. . . protect me; a trail of tales to keep me safe. But you looked beyond my past and stolen soul. You saw me; you looked beyond the masks and mirrors. . . saw me, and helped me face my faults and fears. When I was hiding, lost behind myself, you saw me."

Tears sprang to Emma's eyes and blurred the words on the page. "Thank you," she said, giving Star a hug. "The words you wrote are meaningful and beautiful. I'm so glad you came to my class, and even happier that you've found your dad."

Star nodded slowly. "Yeah, me too, and I can't wait till he gets here."

Just then another car pulled in, and a few minutes later a knock sounded on the door. When Emma answered it, she found Paul on the porch holding two paper sacks, a manila folder, and his camera.

"It looks like you came with more than your quilting project today," Emma said, smiling up at him.

"That's right, I did." He handed her the manila envelope. "This is for you. Since today is our last class, I wanted you to have something to remember me by. I had my camera in the van last Saturday, and I took the picture before I headed home."

Emma opened the envelope and withdrew an eight-by-ten photo of her barn. Several of her goats were also in the picture, since their pen was near the barn. "This is so nice. Thank you, Paul."

"I have something else as well." Paul reached into the paper sack and removed a package wrapped in foil. "Here are some tamales my sister, Maria, made. I hope you'll enjoy them."

"Oh, I'm sure I will," Emma said, feeling a bit choked up. "I never expected to receive any gifts today." She motioned to Star. "She wrote a special song and gave it to me a few minutes before you arrived."

Star's face reddened as she gave a brief shrug. "It wasn't much."

"It was to me." Emma slipped her arm around Star's waist. "Maybe you'll get one of your songs published someday."

"That would be nice, but I'm not holding my breath, 'cause I've learned from experience that things don't always go the way I'd like them to."

Emma smiled. "Well, let's pray that this time they do."

"I brought this along, too," Paul said, pointing to the camera and moving their conversation in a different direction. "Since it's the last day of our class, I thought it would be nice to take a picture of everyone."

"You're welcome to do that, but I won't be able to be in the picture," Emma said.

"How come?"

"Posing for pictures is frowned upon in my church. We believe it's a sign of pride."

"That's okay," Paul said. "Maybe you could use my camera and take a picture of the six of us who've come to your class to learn quilting."

"That'd be fine. We can do that after everyone gets here," Emma said.

"Oh, before I forget, you'll never guess who sent Sophia a package this week," Paul said, beaming from ear to ear.

"Who?" Star and Emma asked in unison.

"My wife's sister, Carmen."

"Paul, that's wonderful." Emma smiled, thinking this day seemed to be getting better and better.

"Lorinda's folks will be coming to visit us in a few weeks, and I'm anxious to tell them the good news, too. While Carmen may still think I'm to blame for Lorinda's death, at least she's acknowledging Sophia now."

Emma could see how pleased Paul was about this. "You know, Paul, before you arrived, I was getting ready to tell Star that I believe God has a plan for everyone's life," she said. "We don't understand that plan all the time, but sometimes, later on down the road, we can look back and realize why things happened the way they did." Emma knew that applied to her, too.

"I know what you're saying," Paul agreed. "I'm going to keep praying for Carmen and trying to stay in touch. I'm also trusting God that she'll eventually come around."

"I'll be praying for that, too." Emma gave Paul's arm a light pat, and then hearing another car pull up, she went to the window.

Ruby Lee arrived next and gave Emma four beautiful thimbles. Each one had the name of a different season on it, as well as a painted picture—a flower for spring; a sun for summer; an autumn leaf for fall; and a snowflake for winter.

Emma thanked Ruby Lee for her thoughtful gift, and then Ruby Lee told how her husband had met with the church board the previous evening. "Gene agreed to set his plans aside for adding on to the church, and the board members were pleased to hear that," she said. "So for now at least, Gene's going to stay on as their pastor."

"That's a good thing, right?" Star questioned.

"I suppose, but it's going to be hard to put all this behind us." Ruby Lee frowned. "Too much gossip and hurtful things were said about Gene, and I still wish I could give a few of those people a piece of my mind. I've just been so crushed by all of this."

"Psalm 34:18 says, 'The Lord is nigh unto them that are of a broken heart; and saveth such as be of a contrite spirit,'" Emma said.

Ruby Lee nodded. "That's right, and the New International Version of that verse says it this way: 'The Lord is close to the brokenhearted and saves those who are crushed in spirit.' Guess I should take that verse to heart. Sometimes it's hard to forgive and move on, but I know that as a Christian it's what God expects us to do."

Paul nodded in agreement. "God chooses what we go through, but we choose how we go through it."

"I think I'd like to know more about this relationship you three have with the Lord." Star looked over at Ruby Lee. "Would it be all right if I visit your church sometime? Maybe bring Jan along?"

"You want to visit there even after all the negative things I've said about some of the people?"

Star shrugged. "So who says anyone's perfect?"

"You've made a good point," Emma said. "And another thing we need to remember is that anyone who has never tasted what is bitter doesn't know what is sweet. The bad times really do help us remember to appreciate the good."

Another knock sounded on the door. "Would you like me to get it?" Star asked. "It might be Jan."

Emma smiled. "If you like."

When Star returned to the sewing room a few minutes later, Stuart and Pam were with her. Emma was surprised to see that Stuart wore a splint on the index finger of his left hand, but even more surprising was that his other hand held tightly to Pam's.

"What happened to your hand?" Paul asked.

"I had a little accident with a hummingbird feeder. The broken glass cut the tendon in my finger, so now I'll be facing surgery next week." Stuart looked at Pam and smiled. "One good thing came out of it, though."

"What's that?" Ruby Lee asked.

"Pam started crying when she realized how bad my finger was, and I knew then that she really does care about me. We had a good long talk about some things, which also helped. And when we got home from the ER, she stayed up late finishing the quilting part of my wall hanging."

It was Pam's turn to smile. "That's right, and Stuart showed that he loves me, too, when he told me this morning that he plans to buy an RV we can all sleep in whenever we go camping."

Emma was pleased to see that things were going a little better in everyone's lives. Now if Jan would just get here and respond favorably to Star's apology, everything would be nearly perfect. Oh, Emma liked happy endings, and she hoped she would witness one today.

"Pam and I both have something for you," Stuart said. "Mine's some frozen wild berries I picked when I went camping last summer, and Pam's is a plant that she set on your front porch." He grinned and handed Emma a paper sack he'd carried tucked under his arm.

"That's really nice. Thank you both so much." Emma turned toward the kitchen. "I'll just put these in the refrigerator while you all find seats."

When Emma entered the kitchen, she glanced at the clock on the far wall and realized it was fifteen minutes after ten. Since Jan still hadn't shown up, when she returned to her sewing room, she suggested that they get started with the class and wait on taking their picture.

———

As Emma showed everyone how to bind their quilted wall hangings, Star was barely able to concentrate on what was being said. She kept looking at the clock, and as time went on, she became even more concerned. *Where is Jan? Maybe he's not coming today. He's probably upset about the things I said to him last week and doesn't want to see me again.*

"I baked a couple of angel cream pies yesterday," Emma said at around eleven o'clock. "Should we stop for a break and have some now, or would you rather keep working on your wall hangings and have the pie at the end of our class?"

"I'm really not hungry," Star mumbled. "But the rest of you can do whatever you want." She was convinced that Jan wasn't coming. If he was, he would have arrived by now.

Emma smiled sympathetically and offered Star a few comforting words. The others did as well, but as much as Star appreciated their concern, she still felt miserable. All her life she'd wished she could know her father. Now, even though she knew who he was, she was certain that she'd never get the chance to really know him.

"I think we should keep working on our wall hangings and eat when we're done," Ruby Lee said.

Everyone nodded in agreement.

Each of them took turns using the battery-operated sewing machines, and Ruby Lee even tried out Emma's old treadle machine, commenting on how much harder it was to use.

"You're right," Emma agreed, "but once you get a feel for using the treadle, it won't be so difficult, and who knows—you might even think it's fun. I certainly enjoy using that old machine."

Shortly before twelve, everyone had finished binding their wall hangings, so Paul got out his camera and suggested they all gather for the class picture.

Star shook her head. "I'm not in the mood. Besides, Jan isn't here, and without him, it wouldn't really be a class picture."

"I'm real sorry he's not here," Emma said, "but wouldn't you at least like to get a picture of those of you who are here today?"

Star really didn't want to, but reluctantly, she finally agreed. She'd come here today without her hooded sweatshirt but wished now she'd worn it, because she was in a really black mood.

"Let's go outside to take the photograph," Emma suggested. "It's probably not light enough in here for a good picture." She opened the door, and they all stepped onto the porch and struck a pose. Star was the only one not smiling. She just couldn't force her lips to turn up when she felt so sad.

After Paul showed Emma what to do with the camera, she stepped into the yard and was about to take the picture when Jan came trudging up the driveway, huffing and puffing. His arms and face were sweaty, and his clothes were covered with splotches of dirt.

Tears of joy seeped through Star's lashes, but she didn't utter a word. Just waited to see what Jan would say.

"Sorry for bein' late," he said to Emma. "Stupid chain on my bicycle broke, and then I spun out in some gravel and fell off the bike. Fooled around with the chain awhile, but with no tools, it was pretty much hopeless. Since I was determined to get here, I just left the dumb bike there and started walkin'. Then some mangy mutt, who shoulda been home in his pen, chased after me for a time. But when a horse and buggy happened along, the dog gave up on me and started buggin' the horse. Things went from bad to worse after that. The horse was so spooked, it ended up pullin' the buggy into a ditch." Jan stopped and drew in a quick breath. "Well, I couldn't leave the poor Amish woman who was drivin' the buggy alone to deal with all that, so after I'd shooed the dog away, I led the horse outa the ditch and got the woman's buggy back on the road. By that time, I knew I'd missed most of the class, but I had to come anyways, 'cause I needed to see Star, even if it was for the very last time."

"It's okay. You're here now; that's all that matters," Emma said.

Everyone smiled and murmured words of agreement. They, too, seemed happy that Jan had made it before the class ended. But none was happier than Star. She was so glad to see Jan that she almost gave him a hug. Catching herself in time, she just smiled and said, "I'm glad you're here. I was worried you might not come."

Jan shook his head. "I'd actually thought about not comin', but no, I decided I just couldn't do that."

"I need to tell you something," Star said, moving slowly toward him, hands clasped behind her back. Her heart thumped so hard she feared her chest might explode.

"What's that?" he asked with a hopeful expression.

"I spoke with Mom last night, and she admitted that she was the one who took off."

Jan's face broke into a broad smile. "Really?"

Star nodded. "I'm sorry I didn't believe you, but I didn't want to think Mom would lie to me about something as important as this. Can we start over—maybe spend some time together and get to know each other better?" she asked, looking down.

"Yeah, I'd like that. I'd like that a lot." Jan raised Star's chin so she was looking into his eyes. "I'll be getting my driver's license back soon. Think maybe you'd like to go for a ride on my Harley then?"

"Sure, that'd be great. I'd also like the chance to meet your dog.

I've never had a pet, so it would be fun to see what that's like, too." Star went on to tell Jan that when the time was right, her mom would like the chance to make amends with him.

Jan, looking more than a little surprised, nodded and said, "No problem. I'd be glad to talk to Bunny again and try to make things right between us. I know we can never get back what we once had, but if we could be friends, that would mean a lot to me."

"It would mean a lot to me, too," Star said sincerely.

Star and Jan started talking about some other things they'd like to do together until Paul cleared his throat real loud. "Should we take our class picture now so we can have our refreshments?"

"I sure can't be in no picture," Jan said, looking down at the dirt and sweat on his clothes and arms.

"How come? Is it against your religion, too?" Stuart asked.

"Nope, it's nothin' like that, but just look at me, man—I'm a mess!"

"The bathroom's just down the hall," Emma said. "You can go there and get cleaned up, and I'll even let you borrow one of my husband's shirts."

Jan grinned at her. "I'd be much obliged."

"While you're changing and cleaning up, I'll bring out the pie and something for us to drink. Then I'll take a picture of the six of you, and after that we can enjoy the pie while we visit," Emma said.

"Sounds good to me." Jan looked down at Star, and tears welled in his eyes. "Never thought I'd hear myself say this, but somethin' good came from me losin' my driver's license."

"What's that?" she asked.

"Because I lost it and had to serve some time in jail, I was forced to see a probation officer, who said I should find my creative self. And if I hadn't seen Emma's ad and signed up for this class, I never would have met my daughter." Jan smiled at Star in such a special way that she really did feel like his daughter.

"Well, guess I'd better get cleaned up," Jan said, before heading down the hall. When he was halfway there, he turned and called to Star, "Don't go anywhere now, you hear?"

"I wouldn't think of it!" she hollered. Star didn't know what the future might hold for her musical career, but she knew she was grateful for the chance to get to know her dad and was happy that her future would include him.

After Emma found one of Ivan's shirts for Jan to wear, she hurried to the kitchen and was pleased when both Pam and Ruby Lee followed.

"What can we do to help?" Pam asked.

"Let's see now. . . . The pie's on the counter, so if one of you would like to cut it, I'll get out the plates, silverware, and napkins."

"I'll cut the pie," Ruby Lee offered.

Emma looked at Pam. "There's some iced tea in the refrigerator, and glasses are in the cupboard. So if you don't mind, you can take those out to the dining room where we'll sit and eat our refreshments."

Pam smiled. "I don't mind at all."

"You can put them on here." Emma handed Pam a large serving tray.

"I'm going to miss coming here every week," Ruby Lee said as she began slicing the pie.

"I'll miss all of you, too," Emma admitted. "But you're welcome to stop by anytime you like—either for a visit or for help with another quilting project. I'd love to see all of you again."

"You've been a good teacher," Pam said. "And I, for one, have learned a lot coming here—and not just about quilting."

"Me, too," Ruby Lee agreed. "Getting to know everyone and sharing our problems has been good for all of us, I do believe."

"Well, throughout these last six weeks, I've learned quite a bit myself," Emma said. Pam's eyebrows lifted high. "About quilting?"

Emma shook her head. "About people, and how each of us is special in God's eyes. I've also learned to accept help from others whenever I have a need."

"You mean like that nice man who filled in for you when you were sick?" Ruby Lee asked.

"Yes. Lamar's been a big help in many ways, and last night he stopped by with something he made for me."

"What was it?" Pam asked.

"He made a very special table. I'll show it to you after we've had our snack."

"This is ready now." Ruby Lee motioned to the pie she'd cut into equal pieces.

"Then let's get back to the others." Emma led the way to her sewing room, where Stuart, Paul, Jan, and Star sat visiting around the table.

"Can we take the class picture now, before we eat?" Star asked.

Emma nodded. "Let's go outside on the porch."

Pam and Ruby Lee put the pie and iced tea on the dining room table, and everyone filed out the door.

Paul showed Emma again which button to push and reminded her that the camera could focus itself. Then Emma's six students gathered together on the porch while Emma stood in the yard with the camera.

"We may be just a bunch of half-stitched quilters," Jan said as he stood next to Star and smiled, "but we've sure learned some lessons here while gettin' to know and understand each other, and I think we've also learned quite a bit about love."

Star looked over at him and grinned. "I'm really feelin' it right now.

How about you? Are you feelin' it, too?"

Jan gave her a high five. "Yep. Sure am, and I never wanna lose you again." Hesitating a moment, he reached up and put his arm around Star's shoulder. He looked happy when Star moved a bit closer.

Emma held the camera steady and snapped the picture. She planned to place an ad for another quilting class soon and couldn't wait to meet the next set of students God sent her way.

"All right now," she said, smiling as she stepped onto the porch. "Who wants a piece of my angel cream pie?"

Epilogue

One year later

I t's a nice evening, jah?" Lamar said to Emma as they sat on the front porch eating a bowl of homemade strawberry ice cream.

She smiled. "You're right about that, but what makes it even nicer is having someone to share it with."

Lamar's eyes twinkled as he gave her a nod. "Does that mean you're not sorry you married me this spring?"

"Of course not, silly." She reached over and patted his arm affectionately. "The only way I'd ever be disappointed is if you stopped loving me."

He shook his head. "No worries there, 'cause that's never gonna happen."

Emma pushed her feet against the wooden boards on the porch and got the hickory rocker Lamar had given her as a wedding present moving back and forth.

A year ago, she'd been determined never to marry again. But that was before Lamar had won her heart with his kind and gentle ways. She was grateful to have found love a second time and felt that Ivan would be happy for her, too.

"Is there anything you need me to do to help with your quilting class tomorrow?" Lamar asked.

"I was hoping you would show my new students the quilt design you came up with the other day," she replied.

"Jah, sure, I'd be happy to show 'em."

They sat quietly, watching the fireflies rise from the grass and put on their nightly summer show, until a noisy *Vr. . .oom! Vr. . .oom!* shattered their quiet.

When Emma saw two motorcycles coming up the driveway, she knew immediately that it must be Jan Sweet and Star Stephens. They dropped by frequently to visit, as did the others who had come to her first quilting class. Star and Jan may have been cheated out of knowing each other during Star's childhood, but Emma was glad to see how happy they both were now, as they spent a good deal of their free time together. They'd made a trip on their motorcycles to Disney World, and through the help of one of Ruby Lee's friends, Star had gotten two of her songs published. Star's mother, Nancy, now living in Fort Wayne with her husband, Mike, had contacted Jan, and they'd finally made peace. Emma thought the best news of all was that Jan and Star had attended Ruby Lee's church a few times together.

Pam and Stuart Johnston seemed happier, too. According to Pam, since Stuart had purchased an RV, they were spending more time together as a family, which in turn had helped their marriage. They, too, had gone to church several times this past year, which Emma felt certain had also strengthened their marriage.

Paul Ramirez had finished the baby quilt his wife had started before she'd died, and he'd brought little Sophia by on several occasions to see Emma's goats and play with the kittens that had been born earlier this spring. He, too, seemed happy and content and kept in touch with his late wife's family in California. The best news he'd shared was that his sister-in-law had finally come to terms with Lorinda's death and no longer blamed Paul for the accident. Carmen was even planning a trip to Elkhart to see Paul and Sophia sometime this summer.

Ruby Lee Williams, whose husband still ministered to their congregation in Goshen, had stopped by recently and told Emma that their church had grown and its finances had improved so much that the board was now talking about adding on to the building. Emma was glad Ruby Lee and her husband had stuck it out and trusted God to meet the needs of their church. Ruby Lee was glad, too, for she'd admitted to Emma that her faith had been strengthened because of the ordeal.

Emma waved as Jan and Star parked their cycles and headed for the house. Even though she'd taught several more quilt classes over the course of a year, she knew there would always be a special place in her heart for the students from that first quilting class.

She looked over at Lamar and smiled. "Isn't it nice to know that love looks beyond what people are to what they can become?"

He reached for Emma's hand and gave her fingers a gentle squeeze. "That's right, and I'm so glad that the Lord can use us at any age if we're willing."

RECIPE FOR EMMA YODER'S ANGEL CREAM PIE

Ingredients:
1 cup half-and-half
1 cup heavy whipping cream
½ cup sugar
⅛ teaspoon salt
2 tablespoons (slightly rounded) flour
1 teaspoon vanilla
2 egg whites, stiffly beaten
1 (9-inch) unbaked pie shell

Preheat oven to 350 degrees. In a saucepan, combine half-and-half and whipping cream. Warm only slightly. Turn off heat and add, beating with a whisk, sugar, salt, and flour. Add vanilla and fold in stiffly beaten egg whites. Pour into unbaked pie shell. Bake for 45 minutes or until filling is a little shaky.

Discussion Questions

1. Although Emma appreciated help from her family, she didn't want to be a burden and looked for ways to be more independent. What are some things we can do to help family members or friends who have lost a loved one without making them feel as if they're a burden?

2. Sometimes after a person loses a spouse, they shut themselves off to the idea of another marriage, thinking no one could take the place of their deceased loved one. Was Emma too closed to the idea of having a friendship with Lamar? How long do you think a person should wait after the death of a spouse to remarry?

3. Due to the problems they were having at their church, Ruby Lee wanted her husband to get out of the ministry. Is leaving always the best answer when a pastor feels that the congregation is displeased with him? What are some other choices a minister might make instead of leaving a church he has felt called to shepherd?

4. Did Ruby Lee support her husband enough, or was she feeling so much at the end of her rope that she saw no possibility of a positive outcome? What are some ways we can keep our faith strong when going through trying times?

5. Jan, having been deeply hurt when his girlfriend left him, chose not to make any commitments to a woman after that. How can a person deal with rejection and not let it affect future relationships?

6. Pam hid her childhood disappointments from Stuart. Is there ever a time when a person should keep information about their past from their spouse? How did Pam's childhood affect her as an adult? How can a person deal with a scarred childhood and not let it affect their marriage?

7. Communication is important in marriage. Did Stuart and Pam have an honest relationship, or were there too many unspoken feelings? How important is honesty in marriage? What are some ways a married couple can learn to be more honest with each other?

8. In the beginning, Stuart had no understanding of Pam's dislike for camping and fishing. What might he have done to make her more comfortable with the idea? Should he have been willing to stay home more and do other things with the family?

9. Star, having grown up without a father, had abandonment issues and low self-esteem. She also felt that her mother cared more about her own needs than she did Star's. What are some ways a single parent can make sure their children feel loved and secure? How can an adult who grew up with only one parent help themselves to feel more secure?

10. Paul sometimes felt guilty when he left his baby daughter at daycare or with a sitter. How can a parent—especially one who's raising a child alone—deal with feelings of guilt when they have to leave their children with a sitter? Paul also struggled with the fact that his sister-in-law blamed him for his wife's accident. What are some ways we can deal with the pain of being unjustly accused?

11. How do you feel that the Amish people view others outside of their community? Do you think Emma's response to her students was typical for an Amish woman teaching a quilting class? Do you think there's ever a problem of prejudice among the Amish?

12. Was there anything specific you learned from reading this book? Were there any verses of scripture that spoke to your heart?

THE TATTERED QUILT

PROLOGUE

Shipshewana, Indiana

Emma Miller's husband, Lamar, plunked a bottle of suntan lotion on the kitchen table in front of her and said, "How'd you like to take a little *feierdaag* and get away from these chilly days we've been having this fall?"

Her eyes widened. "You want us to go on a holiday?"

"That's right. I was thinking we could go down to Florida for a while. We can rent a place in Pinecraft." Lamar's green eyes sparkled as he drew his fingers through the ends of his full gray beard. "Just think how nice it would be to spend a little time on the beach."

Emma patted Lamar's hand affectionately. "That's a nice idea, but have you forgotten that I recently placed an ad for another six-week quilting class?"

"*Jah*, I know, but no one's answered the ad yet, so maybe you won't have any students this time."

Emma took a sip of hot tea. "I suppose that's a possibility, but I was looking forward to us teaching another class together. Weren't you, Lamar?"

"Of course; all the classes we've taught for the past year and a half have been great." Lamar leaned closer to Emma and touched her arm. "If no one signs up by the end of the week, will you go to Florida with me?"

Emma mulled things over, then finally nodded. "I suppose it would be nice to get a little sunshine and take some long walks on the beach, but we can't go until we get our roof fixed," she quickly added. "With all the rain we've had so far this fall, it could start to leak at any time if we don't get a new roof put on."

Plink! Plunk! Plink! Three drops of water landed in Emma's cup. She looked up at the ceiling and groaned. "Oh dear, I spoke too soon. I'm afraid it's already leaking."

"Not to worry." Lamar gave Emma a wide smile. "I called your roofer friend, Jan Sweet, and he and his coworker will start in on it next week."

Emma reached for her husband's calloused hand and gave his long fingers a tender squeeze. "Is it any wonder I said *jah* when you asked me to marry you? You're such a *schmaert* man."

"And you, Emma dear, are the best wife any man could want." Lamar leaned over and kissed Emma, causing her cheeks to warm. Even after more than a year of marriage, he could still make her blush.

CHAPTER 1

Middlebury, Indiana

Anna Lambright wanted her freedom. She'd turned eighteen a week ago, but her parents were holding her back. Most of the young people she knew had at least started their *rumschpringe*, but not Anna. Her folks held a tight rein and had forbidden Anna to do any of the things other kids did during their running-around years.

"What are they worried about? Do they think I'll get into trouble?" Anna mumbled as she tromped through the damp grass toward the barn to feed the cats. It wasn't fair that she couldn't have the freedom most of her friends had to experience some of the things English teenagers did.

When Anna entered the barn, the pungent odor of hay mixed with horse manure made her sneeze. *If I weren't Amish, what would I be doing right now?* she wondered, rubbing her eyes as they began to itch and water.

To make matters worse, Anna's mother thought Anna should do everything expected of an Amish woman. Anna didn't enjoy cooking, and sewing. They just weren't her thing. She'd tried sewing a dress and had made a mess of it. She couldn't even manage to sew something as simple as a pair of pillowcases without making stupid mistakes. Mom had tried teaching Anna to quilt, but Anna was all thumbs. Her stitches were uneven and much too big.

Anna felt like a misfit. She hadn't been baptized or joined the church yet, so she was free to leave if she wanted to. Only trouble was, where would she go, and how would she support herself? If she left, she'd have to stop working at Dad's window shop, because she was sure he wouldn't let her stay on.

Inside the barn, Anna spotted three cats—one white, one black, and one gray with white paws, sleeping on a bale of straw. As soon as they sensed her presence, they leaped off the bale and zipped across the room to their empty dishes.

"Are you *hungerich*?" Anna asked, reaching for the bag of cat food on a shelf near the door.

Meow! Fluffy, the all-white cat, stuck her nose in one of the empty dishes. The other two cats pawed at Anna's legs.

"Okay, okay, don't be in such a hurry." Anna filled the dishes and then set the food back on the shelf.

While the cats ate, Anna wandered over to the horses' stalls and stopped to watch Cindy, Mom's honey-colored horse, eat the oats Anna's fourteen-year-old brother, Dan, had given the mare a short time ago.

Anna didn't have a horse of her own. She borrowed Mom's whenever she had somewhere to go that was too far to walk or ride her bike. Anna actually preferred riding her bike. It was easier than trying to manage the horse. Even a horse as gentle and easygoing as Cindy could be unpredictable.

One time when Anna had gone to Shipshewana to run some errands for Mom, a motorcycle had spooked Cindy, and Anna had struggled to get the horse back under control. Her mouth went dry just thinking about what could have happened if she hadn't been able to get Cindy settled down. The nervous horse could have crossed into the other lane of traffic, run off the road into someone's fence, or taken off down the road.

Just last month a woman from their community had died in a buggy accident that happened between Middlebury and Shipshewana. Anna figured she'd be safer in a car, although even then there were no guarantees.

"Do you ever feel like breaking out of here and running away?" Anna murmured as the horse finished up with her oats.

Cindy's ears twitched as though in response; then she ambled across the stall and stuck her head over the gate.

Anna scratched behind the mare's ears. "What do you say, girl? Should we escape together?"

"Who are you talking to?" Dan asked, surprising Anna when he came out of nowhere.

"I was talking to Mom's *gaul*, and you shouldn't sneak up on me like that. Where were you anyway?" she asked, turning to look at her blond-haired brother.

"I was up in the hayloft." Dan's blue eyes twinkled, and he grinned at Anna like he'd been doing something special. "I like to go up there to think."

"What were you thinking about?"

He shrugged his broad shoulders. "Nothing really. Just pondering a few things."

Anna tipped her head. "Such as?"

"Wondering what I'll be doing next year, when I graduate from eighth grade."

"I thought you were gonna work for Dad in the window shop."

"I might, but I'm not sure yet. There could be something else I'd enjoy doing more."

Anna could certainly relate to that. Mom and Dad expected her to help out in the shop, answering the phone and taking orders from customers. The only part of the job she enjoyed was being able to use the computer. Because they had to order a lot of things online, they'd been given permission from the church leaders to have a computer in their shop. Of course, they'd never have one in their home. That was against the rules of their Amish church, and Mom and Dad were not about to knowingly break any rules. Anna enjoyed having access to the Internet. When things were slow at the shop, she would take a few moments to explore different websites showing places to visit. She knew without a doubt that spending a good deal of the day on the computer would have been no problem for her, if it were allowed. Anna couldn't believe all the information out there, available by just the click of a mouse.

"Have you ever thought about what it would be like if you didn't join the Amish church?" Anna asked her brother.

Dan shook his head vigorously. "No way! Where would I go? What would I do?" He reached out and stroked Cindy's neck. "Don't think I could be happy if I left our way of life."

Anna didn't say anything. If she told Dan the way she felt, he'd probably blab it to their folks. It was better if she kept her thoughts to herself, at least until she'd made a decision.

"I'd better get back in the house and help Mom with breakfast," Anna said.

"Okay, see ya inside. I've still got a couple of chores I need to do." Dan ambled away.

Anna shook her head. If her brother had chores to do, what was he doing up in the hayloft, thinking about his future? She gave Cindy a good-bye pat and hurried out of the barn.

When Anna stepped into the kitchen, she found Mom in front of their propane stove, stirring a pot of oatmeal. Anna wrinkled her nose. Oatmeal was not one of her favorite breakfast foods.

Anna studied her mother. She was only forty-seven years old but seemed to be aging fast. Maybe it was the fine wrinkles across her forehead, or it could be the dark circles beneath her pale blue eyes. Mom's hair was a mousy brown, and some telltale gray was showing through. Anna hoped she wouldn't look as haggard as Mom when she was in her forties. She hoped her light brown eyes wouldn't lose their sparkle, and that her auburn hair would keep the depth of its color well into her senior years.

"Did you get the cats fed?" Mom asked, breaking into Anna's musings.

Anna nodded. "They were as desperate as usual." She removed her jacket and the woolen scarf she'd worn over her stiff white covering. After hanging them on a wall peg, Anna picked off some cat hairs she noticed clinging to her dress and threw them in the garbage can under the kitchen sink.

"Did you notice how chilly our *wedder* is getting?" Mom questioned.

"Jah, and I don't like cold weather," Anna mumbled as she began setting the table. "Summer doesn't last long enough for me."

"Some chilly or rainy days are what we can expect during the fall. Winter will be here before we know it." Mom flashed Anna a smile. "Before you start setting the table, there's something I want to tell you."

"Oh? What's that?"

"Emma Miller will be starting another six-week quilting class next Saturday, and I signed you up." Mom's smile widened.

Anna's mouth dropped open. "What? Why would you do that? You know I don't sew."

"That's true, and since I haven't been successful at teaching you, I thought maybe Emma would have better luck."

Anna frowned. "But Mom. . ."

"No arguments, now. Your *daed* and I talked this over last night, and we think it's what you need. I went out to the phone shack earlier this morning and left Emma a message, letting her know that you'll be taking part in her next class." Mom patted Anna's shoulder. "If you give yourself a chance, I'm sure you'll learn a lot from Emma. From what I hear, she's a very good teacher. And who knows? You may even enjoy the class."

"Right," Anna muttered under her breath. She'd heard about Emma's quilting classes, and the last thing she wanted to do was sit in a room with a bunch of strangers.

Los Angeles, California

Carmen Lopez had only been out of bed a few minutes, when her telephone rang. She glanced at the clock on her bedside table, wondering who would be calling her at 5:00 a.m. The only reason she was up this early was because she had a story to cover in Santa Monica and wanted to get an early start before the freeway traffic reached its peak during rush hour. There was nothing worse than sitting in a traffic jam with irritated drivers honking their horns and hollering at each other. Carmen always wondered why they did that. Did those people think it would make the vehicles miraculously start moving? Being a reporter, she'd learned very quickly that people liked making statements in any way, shape, or form. Truth was, being engulfed in traffic made her nervous, bringing back the memory of the tragic way her precious sister, Lorinda, had died.

The phone rang a few more times, and Carmen finally picked up the receiver. "Hello," she said, stifling a yawn.

"Carmen, are you awake?"

"Oh, Mr. Lawrence. Yes, I'm up. I'll be heading to Santa Monica soon to cover that story about the recently opened homeless shelter."

"Forget about that. I put Eddie Simpson on it."

Carmen's brows lifted. "You gave my story away?"

"That's right. You don't have time to go to Santa Monica today."

"Yes, I do. I got up plenty early, and—"

"I just booked a flight for you to South Bend, Indiana, and you need to pack. Your plane leaves in four hours."

Carmen frowned. Andrew Lawrence could be a difficult boss at times, and he was a little overbearing, but he'd never pulled her off an assignment and sent another reporter in her place. And he'd never expected her to fly somewhere without giving her advanced notice. "Why are you sending me to Indiana?" she questioned.

"There's been a lot of media hype about the Amish lately, especially with some of the reality shows on TV about Amish kids who've left their families and gone wild," he said. "Since you have connections in Indiana, I figured you'd be the best person to get the lowdown on this. You know—find out why these kids go wild and why their folks look the other way."

"Get the lowdown?" Carmen's eyebrows puckered. "I have no connections in Indiana, sir. And what makes you think I can learn anything firsthand about Amish kids going wild?"

"Your brother-in-law lives there, doesn't he?"

"Well, yes, Paul lives in Elkhart, but—"

"Didn't you mention once that he knew some Amish people?"

"Not in Elkhart, but in Shipshewana," she explained. "Paul took some quilting classes from an Amish woman, but that was over a year ago."

"That's perfect! You can pick the man's brain, nose around the place, ask a lot of questions, and maybe get into a few Amish homes. I'm expecting you to write a good story that'll shed some light on why all Amish kids go wild during their days of running-around. . . ." His voice trailed off. "What is the Pennsylvania Dutch word for it. . .*rumschpringe?*"

"I think that's it, but I'm not sure if Paul has stayed in contact with the Amish woman who taught him to quilt. Also it could take some time to get that kind of information."

"No problem. Take all the time you need."

Carmen blew out her breath. "Mr. Lawrence, I really don't think. . . ."

"It's all set, Carmen. Your flight leaves at nine, so you'd better get packed and hustle yourself to the airport. Give me a call when you get there. Oh, and keep me posted as you gather information. I think this will be a great story. It could even win you a promotion if it's done well, so you'd better not let me down." Mr. Lawrence hung up before Carmen could say anything more.

Carmen sank to the edge of her bed and groaned. She had to admit she was intrigued by this assignment, and if a promotion came from doing it, that would be great. There was just one problem: Even if Paul was still friends with the Amish woman who'd taught him to quilt, there were no guarantees that he would tell Carmen anything. Things had been strained between her and Paul since Lorinda had been killed. For several months after the accident, Carmen had blamed Paul, thinking he could have done something to prevent it. And even though she'd gone to Elkhart once since Lorinda's funeral to see Paul's daughter, Sophia, she and Paul had never really resolved the issue.

It was ironic that Carmen had been thinking about Paul lately. In fact, she couldn't seem to get him out of her mind, no matter how hard she tried. Even before her boss called with this new assignment, her conscience had been bothering her about the strained relationship. Was it right to blame Paul for her sister's death? Was she using him in order to have someone to blame? Could her anger against him just be a cover-up for her own grief? Maybe the best thing to do was apologize to Paul for having blamed him and then ease into the request for him to introduce her to his Amish friend.

Dark brown eyes stared back at Carmen as she smiled at her twenty-four-year-old reflection in the mirror above her dresser. Her hair looked pretty good, even in its tangled state. Just like her sister, Carmen had long black, lustrous hair she could style any way she wanted. As she pulled her thick locks into a ponytail, her plans seemed to fall right into place. She would apologize to Paul. This trip might work right in with the new assignment she'd been given and ease her guilt at the same time. At least it was a step in the right direction.

CHAPTER 2

Mishawaka, Indiana

Blaine Vickers hated his job. Well, maybe not all of it—just when he was asked to do something he didn't feel comfortable with. Like only moments ago when his boss, Stuart Johnston, had asked Blaine to give a demonstration on fly-fishing to a group of wannabe fishermen who'd be visiting the sporting goods store tomorrow afternoon.

"Can't someone else do it?" Blaine asked as he and Stuart entered the break room together.

Stuart shook his head. "None of the other employees knows fly-fishing as well as you, my friend."

Blaine grunted. "But you know I'm not comfortable talking to people."

Stuart gave Blaine's shoulder a quick thump. "What are you talking about? You're a salesman, right? You talk to people every day."

"That's different. I talk to people one-on-one, not in a group setting where all eyes are on me." Blaine had never mentioned it to Stuart, but he hoped to someday own his own fishing tackle store. It wouldn't be a big place like the sporting goods store—just a small place where he'd sell only things fishermen needed. It was probably nothing but a pipe dream, but it was nice to have a goal and something to focus on rather than thinking he'd be stuck working here for the rest of his life. Not that working for Stuart was bad; Blaine just wanted to do his own thing.

Stuart raked his fingers through the back of his curly dark hair. "You'll do fine talking to those people. Don't sell yourself short."

Blaine meandered over to the coffeepot. What choice did he have? Stuart was his boss, and even though they were friends, if he wanted to keep his job he'd have to do what he was told, like it or not.

"Say, Blaine," Stuart said, joining him at the coffeepot, "I'm going fishing at Lake Shipshewana on Saturday. Since you're not scheduled to work that day, why don't you go with me? Unless you're gonna be busy doing something with your lady friend, that is."

Blaine shook his head. "Sue and I broke up a few weeks ago. I thought I'd mentioned it."

"If you did, I must've forgotten. Between staying busy here at the store, going to my kids' games, and trying to keep Pam happy, I can only focus on one thing at a time." Stuart added a spoonful of sugar to his coffee and took a sip. "How come you and Sue broke up? I mean, you've been going out for a few years now, right?"

Blaine sighed. "It's complicated."

"It or Sue?"

"Both." Blaine pulled out a chair and took a seat at the table. He was glad he and Stuart were the only ones in the room, because he wasn't about to spill his guts in front of anyone else. "It's like this—I'm ready to get married, but Sue says she's not. I made the mistake of pushing the issue, and she broke up with me." As Blaine recalled the painful conversation, he rubbed his finger over the small scar on his chin, which had been there since he'd fallen off his bike as a child. "Things were going along fine between Sue and me, but I guess she thought it would mess up our relationship if we made a more serious commitment. For some reason, I think she's afraid of marriage."

"You're right about marriage being a commitment. It takes a lot of work to keep the fires burning." Stuart rubbed the side of his head. "Just ask me. It took months of marital counseling, not to mention six weeks in Emma's quilting classes, for Pam and me to get our act together and put our marriage back on track. But it was worth the effort. Our relationship is a lot stronger now than it was before all that, and we're communicating in a more civilized way."

"You two do seem to be getting along pretty well these days. Maybe it's for the best that Sue and I have gone our separate ways, since we don't see eye to eye on the merits of marriage."

"Yeah, it's better to break things off now than have her decide to bail after you're married."

Blaine sat quietly, drinking his coffee. He was thirty years old and still single. It wasn't that he didn't want to get married, because he did. What really bothered him was when his family got together for holidays and other special events. His two brothers were both married and living in Canada. Seeing how happy Darin and Steve were and watching how their wives looked at them with love and respect, made Blaine envious. He wished he had a wife who'd look at him that way. His sister-in-law, Sandy, adored her husband, not to mention her and Stephen's little boy, Chad, who was four years old, and a miniature replica of his daddy. Even at his young age, Chad seemed to idolize his father, often looking at him like there was no other man on earth. The last time Blaine's family got together for Easter, Darin and his wife,

Michelle, had announced that they were expecting their first child.

Blaine was happy for his brothers, but he couldn't help wondering what it would be like to meet the right person and know she was the one for him. That was what he thought he'd found in Sue, but he'd obviously been wrong. Since their breakup, Blaine had spent a lot of time asking himself if he and Sue had ever been right for each other, or if he had so wanted what his brothers had that he'd been trying to force the relationship to work. Maybe it was best that he'd found out now how Sue felt about marriage. If Sue had agreed to marry him, they might have ended up needing counseling like Stuart and Pam. One thing was for sure: Blaine was tired of going home every night to an empty condo and having a one-way conversation with the fish in his aquarium.

"You know, Stuart," Blaine said, shaking off his thoughts, "I think a day of fishing sounds pretty nice, so if the offer's still open, then yeah, I'd be happy to go with you this Saturday."

"That's great." Stuart thumped Blaine's back. "Say, how about we have a contest to see who can catch the biggest fish?"

"Sure, why not," Blaine said with a shrug. He'd always had good luck fishing, so he was confident that he would catch the biggest fish. "Is there a prize for the winner of this bet?"

"I don't know. Guess there could be. Better yet, let's make the loser pay a consequence."

"What kind of consequence?"

Stuart snapped his fingers. "I've got it! If you catch the biggest fish, I have to buy you a new fishing pole."

Blaine grinned. "That sounds good to me."

"But if I catch the biggest fish, you have to take Emma's next six-week quilting class."

Blaine's mouth opened wide. "You're kidding, right?"

"Nope. You gave me a hard time when Pam forced me to take that class, so it'll be your turn to eat crow."

Blaine chuckled. "I'm not gonna be eating any crow, 'cause I'll catch the biggest fish."

"Does that mean you're agreeing to the bet?"

"Sure, why not?" Blaine smiled to himself. *After all, I'll never have to take those quilting classes.*

Goshen, Indiana

Cheryl Halverson glanced at the calendar on her desk. In two months her grandmother would be celebrating her eighty-eighth birthday, and Cheryl wanted to give Grandma something special. But she couldn't decide what. Grandma didn't need much, not since Cheryl's mother had put her in a nursing home. When Cheryl asked Mom why Grandma couldn't live with her and Dad, Mom said due to the demands of her bank manager job, there was no way she could take care of her aging mother, who needed 'round-the-clock care. Cheryl's mother, Katherine, was fifty-five years old and wasn't ready to give up her job. Cheryl couldn't blame her for that. She didn't know what she'd do without her job as a secretary for an attorney in town. When Cheryl and her boyfriend, Lance, broke up six months ago, moving to Indiana to take this position was what had kept Cheryl going.

"Lance is a creep," she mumbled under her breath. "Wish I'd never met him!" Cheryl and Lance had dated two years, and just when she was sure he would ask her to marry him, she caught him cheating—with her best friend, April Roberts. To add insult to injury, since their breakup, Lance had called Cheryl several times to talk about April and ask her advice about a few things. *Talk about weird,* Cheryl thought, tapping her newly manicured fingernails on her desk. *Who but Lance would be unfeeling enough to call his ex-girlfriend and ask stuff like that? If I ever get involved with another man, I'll need to know I can trust him.*

Glancing once more at the calendar, Cheryl thought about Grandma's birthday. She remembered that her pastor's wife, Ruby Lee Williams, had taken some quilting classes awhile back. *Maybe I could take Grandma's tattered old quilt to Ruby Lee's Amish friend and have it repaired.* For as long as Cheryl could remember, that quilt had been as much a part of her grandmother as the warm smiles and comforting hugs Grandma had always given her.

When Cheryl moved to Indiana, Grandma had given her the quilt to remind her of all the fun times they'd had together. The more Cheryl thought about it, the more she realized it might offer Grandma some comfort to have the quilt now that she was doing so poorly.

Shipshewana

"Where we headed next?" Terry Cooley asked his boss, Jan Sweet. They'd finished tearing the roof off a house in LaGrange that morning and had just entered Shipshewana.

"We need to get started tearing off Emma and Lamar Miller's old roof," Jan replied. "After talking to Lamar the other day, I think he'd like to have it done soon, because if no one signs up for their next quilting class, he's taking Emma on a vacation."

"Where they going?"

"Florida, I think."

"Sounds like a good place to be. Nice, warm sunny beaches. . . Wouldn't mind going there myself for a few weeks." Terry took a drag on his cigarette and flicked the ashes out the driver-side window of his truck.

Jan grunted. "Sure wish you'd give up that nasty habit. It ain't good for your health, ya know."

Terry gripped the steering wheel tightly and kept his focus straight ahead. Jan was not only his boss, but they were good friends, even though Terry was twenty-nine and Jan forty-one. Terry supposed for that reason, Jan thought he could lecture him about his smoking habit, but he wished he'd quit bugging him. Terry was surprised that Jan didn't smoke, too. He had other bad habits, though. He used to drink, not to mention riding his motorcycle too fast. Of course, those days were behind him now. Ever since Jan had been reunited with his daughter, Star, he'd cleaned up his act. That, plus being around Lamar and Emma Miller, had turned Jan into a different man. He was still a bit rough around the edges, but there was a softness to him that hadn't been there before his quilting days. Terry still couldn't get over the fact that Jan had actually made a quilted wall hanging and proudly hung it in his living room. *You'd never catch me at no quilting class*, he thought.

"How are things with Star these days?" Terry asked, offering a change of subject.

Jan turned his head to look at Terry and grinned. "Good. Real good. Whenever we both have a free day, we spend it together."

Terry nodded. "Yeah, I know. That's why you hardly ever go bowling with me anymore."

"What are ya talking about, man? Me and Star went bowling with you and Dottie two weeks ago."

"I don't think taking your daughter bowling hardly counts as a double date."

Jan lifted his broad shoulders. "Never said it did."

"If you'll recall, when I invited you to go bowling, I said you oughta find a date, since I'd be bringing one."

"And I did." Jan smiled. "I don't need to explain that I have a lot of catching up to do with Star."

Terry took another puff from his cigarette. "You got that right."

"You know," Jan said, "I waited over twenty years to find my girl, and now that I have, I plan to spend as much time with her as I can."

"That's fine, but you need a social life, too. I'm sure your daughter has one."

"*Humph!* What would you know about a social life? All you ever do on your day off is bowl, play pool, and ride your Harley."

"For your information I took Dottie out to see a movie last weekend."

"Speaking of your girlfriend, how much longer are you gonna string her along before you pop the big question?"

Terry's brows furrowed. "I ain't stringing Dottie along. I'm not the marrying kind, and Dottie knows that, so things are just fine the way they are between us. Besides, Dottie and I are just good friends, same as you and me—except that she happens to be a female."

Jan shrugged his shoulders. "Whatever."

"Hey, isn't that your nosey old neighbor over there?" Terry said, pointing out the front window at an elderly woman walking along the shoulder of the road, wearing a lime green jacket and floppy beige-colored hat.

Jan nodded. "That's Selma Nash, all right. I see she's picking up aluminum cans, which is better than her running around our neighborhood, making a nuisance of herself."

"Has she been hollering at you about Brutus again?"

"Nope. Not since I started keeping the dog penned up while I'm at work. She likes to tromp around the neighborhood, telling others what she thinks." Jan grunted. "That woman is nothing but a busybody. She needs to get a life that don't involve telling other people what to do."

"Selma's jacket reminds me of that spicy green apple juice Dottie had me drinking the other night. Ugh, that was some nasty stuff!" Terry wrinkled his nose and coughed several times. After he cleared his throat to get the spastic cough under control, he asked, "Why don't you put Selma in her place if she bugs you so much?"

"I've tried, but it hasn't done any good. She can't seem to keep her big nose outta other people's business." Jan paused a moment, rubbing his tattooed arm. "It's sorta like me telling you to quit smoking."

"Yeah, I hear you," Terry retorted. "Maybe Selma has too much time on her hands. Could be if she had something to do, she wouldn't have time to stick her nose where it don't belong."

Just as Terry pulled into Emma and Lamar's yard, Jan slapped his knee. "I've got it! I'll enroll Selma in Emma's next quilting class. It'll occupy her time and give her something to do besides snooping on everyone in the neighborhood and telling 'em what to do."

CHAPTER 3

Selma Nash groaned as she bent to pick up a rubber ball she'd found on her lawn. She'd been out collecting cans all morning, like she did most weeks, and every bone in her sixty-eight-year-old body ached. She shouldn't have to come home and pick up the neighbor children's toys! "What's wrong with their parents?" she mumbled. "Those kids ought to be taught to keep things in their own yard."

Between the dogs and kids on her block, it seemed her yard always had something that shouldn't be in it. Thankfully, Jan Sweet, the burly biker who lived next door, had been keeping his German shepherd penned up when he wasn't at home. The big brute of an animal used to run all over the neighborhood, taking things that weren't his and digging up people's flowers. Of course Jan had replaced the flowers Brutus dug up in Selma's yard, and he'd been compliant when she asked him to keep the mutt at home. But other dogs lived in the neighborhood, and their owners hadn't been as willing to listen.

Selma marched over to the Bennetts' house, which was on the other side of her place, and knocked on the door. When no one answered, she knocked again. Still no response. She'd thought her days of cleaning up after someone had ended when her husband, John, passed away from a heart attack five years ago.

Selma scoffed, remembering how all the complaining in the world hadn't changed her husband's bad habits over the course of their forty-year marriage. All her grumblings hadn't made one iota of a difference, and in hindsight, it had caused a sense of sadness in her every time she thought about how things stood between her and John before he died. It was hard to admit, but she sometimes missed picking up after her husband.

Selma's thoughts went to her daughter, Cora, who'd left home when she turned eighteen.

The last time Selma had seen Cora was when she'd come home for John's funeral, but of course, Cora hadn't stuck around very long. Hadn't even said good-bye to her own mother, for goodness' sake! The spiteful young woman had tossed a rose on her father's casket, jumped in her car, and headed off down the road. It was probably for the best that Cora came back only for the funeral. Selma was so mad at her that any more time spent together would have deteriorated into a series of arguments. Selma tried not to think about it, but many times she asked herself how things would be now if John were still alive.

Heaving a sigh, Selma set the ball on the porch and pulled a notebook and pen from her pocket. She scribbled a quick note and left it with the ball, letting the kid's parents know that if she found any more of his toys in her yard, she'd throw them away. "Guess that's probably a bit harsh," Selma muttered, "but maybe they'll get the point."

She headed back to her house, as a gust of wind blew a cluster of fallen leaves across the grass. She grabbed hold of her hat, fearing it would be blown away. Fall was definitely here, and soon the frigid days of winter would swoop in. When the weather got too cold, it would put an end to her walks, so she'd need to find something else to occupy her time.

Selma stopped at the end of her driveway to check for mail. Yesterday was her birthday, and she hadn't received a single card. Not even from Cora. Of course Selma doubted that she'd hear from her daughter again, yet she kept hoping for a phone call, or at least a letter or card. Maybe it was just as well. If Cora was still part of her life, they'd probably argue all the time. The girl was stubborn and wouldn't listen to anything Selma said. Despite the lack of a close relationship and years that had passed since then, there were moments like this when Selma missed having her daughter around. Of course, she'd never admitted that to anyone, or even talked about Cora. As far as Selma's few friends and neighbors were concerned, she lived alone and had no family.

Shaking her troubling thoughts aside, Selma stepped onto her porch. She was about to open the door, when Jan ambled into the yard and hollered, "Can I talk to you a minute, Selma?"

Selma slowly nodded. She wasn't in the mood to talk to Jan about anything right now—she just wanted to get into the house and fix herself a bowl of soup for lunch.

"What'd you want to talk to me about?" she asked when Jan joined her on the porch.

"Came to give you this." Jan handed Selma an envelope.

Her heart fluttered. Could it be a belated birthday card? Did Jan know that yesterday was her birthday? But how could he know? She'd never mentioned it to him.

With trembling fingers Selma tore the envelope open. What she discovered inside was not a birthday card at all. It was a piece of paper with a woman's name and address written on it.

"Who's Emma Miller, and why are you giving me this?" Selma asked, looking up at Jan through squinted eyes.

"She's the Amish lady I took some quilting classes from a year and a half ago. Only her name was Emma Yoder then. She's married to Lamar Miller now, and they—"

"What's this have to do with me?" Selma couldn't keep the irritation she felt out of her voice. Why was Jan wasting her time? Didn't he realize she had better things to do than stand on the porch and shiver while she stared at a piece of paper with an address of a woman she'd never met?

"I signed you up for Emma's next class." Jan grinned and pointed to the envelope. "So, what do you think about that?"

She pursed her thin lips. "Why would you think I'd want to take a quilting class? I've never said I did, you know."

He lifted his broad shoulders in a brief shrug. "Just thought it might be something you'd enjoy—especially since winter will be here soon, and your work in the yard will come to an end."

Selma stared at the envelope a few seconds more, trying to piece things together. "How much do the quilting lessons cost?"

Jan flapped his big calloused hand. "No need to worry about that. I've got it covered."

"You—you paid for my spot in the class?" she sputtered.

He nodded.

"Why would you do that?"

"Like I said, I thought it'd be something you'd enjoy. The class starts next Saturday. Will you be free to go?"

Selma tapped her chin, thoughtfully mulling things over. "I believe so."

Jan brought his hands together in a clap so loud it caused Selma to jump. "Great! I'm sure you'll enjoy the class as much as I did. Probably more, since you're a woman who likes nice things."

Selma couldn't deny it. Her flower garden was proof enough. Besides, she'd always prided herself on being able to sew, although she'd never made a quilt before. *I'm sure it can't be that hard,* she thought. *I'll bet my quilt will turn out better than anyone else's in the class.*

While Jan's gift wasn't actually a birthday present, it was the best thing that had happened to Selma all week. "Thank you, Jan," she said with a smile she hoped looked sincere. "I think I might enjoy that class, and it'll give me something to look forward to."

Elkhart, Indiana

As Paul Ramirez left his second-grade classroom that afternoon, he thought about the phone call he'd received from his sister-in-law, Carmen, last night. He'd been pleased when she'd said she was in town and wanted to come by Paul's place this evening to visit him and his two-year-old daughter, Sophia. That in itself was a surprise, since things had become strained between Paul and Carmen after Paul's wife died almost two years ago. Paul figured the reason Carmen had only visited once since then was because she hadn't completely forgiven him for not being able to prevent the accident that took Lorinda's life. The other thing that had taken Paul by surprise when Carmen called was that she'd asked if he still visited with the Amish woman who'd taught him how to quilt.

"Yes, I do," Paul had said. "I stop by to see Emma and her husband, Lamar, as often as I can."

There'd been a pause, and then Carmen said, "Could I meet her? I mean, would you be willing to introduce me to Emma?"

Paul had said yes, but he was confused by Carmen's request. Why would she be interested in meeting Emma? And how long would she be in the area? He wished now that he'd thought to ask. Well, she'd be coming by this evening, and he could ask Carmen for details then.

As Paul slid into the driver's seat of his minivan, his thoughts went to Sophia. It would be good for his little girl to spend some time with her aunt. Paul was grateful that his folks as well as his sister, Maria, and her family lived close by. Everyone, including Maria's three girls, doted on Sophia, and of course she loved all the attention. When Lorinda died, it had been difficult for Paul to cope, but with the help of his family and friends, he'd learned to deal with the pain of losing his beloved wife. Of course attending Emma's quilting classes and sharing his feelings with Emma and the other students had been a big help, too.

As Paul drove closer to the Loving Hands Daycare Center, where he dropped Sophia off each morning, he couldn't believe how quickly the leaves had turned color and fallen from the trees lining the street. The only leaves left were from some of the oaks.

Taking his foot off the gas pedal in time to let a squirrel run across the road, he smiled when he noticed that the bushy-tailed critter had a good-sized walnut in its mouth.

Paul pulled into the daycare parking lot and turned off the engine. He was glad things had worked out for Sophia at the daycare. She loved going there, and it made life easier knowing his little girl was content during the day while he taught his second-graders. It hadn't always been that way. Just a year ago, Sophia had cried whenever Paul dropped her off. Since then, she'd become more settled and content being with some of the other children. That eased Paul's guilt for having to leave her each day while he earned a living. If Lorinda were still alive, Sophia would have been home with her mother all day.

Switching his thoughts once more, Paul reflected again on his phone call from Carmen. Maybe he'd take her to meet Emma Saturday morning.

Shipshewana

"I hope you won't be disappointed, but it looks like we won't be making a trip to Florida this fall after all," Emma said to Lamar as he sat in the living room, reading the latest issue of *The Budget*.

He looked up and blinked a couple of times. "Why's that?"

Emma pointed to the sheet of paper she held. "I already have two people signed up for my quilting class, and I have a feeling there will soon be others." She took a seat beside him on the sofa. "I hope you'll be able to help me with the classes again. I'm sure the students would be interested in seeing some of the quilts you've designed, not to mention gaining from your knowledge of quilts."

"I have to admit I'm a little disappointed that we won't be making any trips in the near future. On the other hand, I look forward to seeing who God will send our way." Lamar reached for Emma's hand and gave her fingers a gentle squeeze. "Of course you can count on me to help with the classes."

"*Danki*, Lamar. I always appreciate your help and input in the classes."

"Well now," he said, rising to his feet, "if there's gonna be another class starting next week, then I'd better look through some of my quilts and decide which ones to display in your quilting room."

As Lamar left the room, Emma leaned her head against the sofa cushion and closed her eyes. *Heavenly Father,* she silently prayed, *I don't know the two women who'll be coming to my class on Saturday, nor do I know who else may sign up. But as with all the other students who've come here before, I pray that I can teach them more than just how to quilt.*

CHAPTER 4

Do we have everything we need for class?" Emma asked Lamar as she paced back and forth in the spacious room she used for quilting. Lamar didn't know why, but she seemed a bit nervous today. It was silly, really, since she'd taught several classes since that first one a year and a half ago.

In his usual calm manner, Lamar gave Emma's shoulder a gentle squeeze. "Now try to relax. I'm sure everything will go as well with this class as it has with the others."

Emma sighed. "I hope so."

Lamar motioned to the cup of chamomile tea Emma had placed on the table. "Why don't you finish that before your students arrive? It might help settle your nerves."

Emma took a seat and picked up the cup. "All right, I'll try to relax."

"How many people did you say are signed up for this class?" Lamar questioned.

"As of yesterday, only three—two women and one man."

Lamar rubbed the bridge of his nose. "Seems like the classes are getting smaller. We had only five people for our last class. Maybe folks aren't as interested in quilting as they used to be. Maybe it's time for us to retire."

Emma set her cup down so hard that some of the tea splashed out. "*Ach*, Lamar, I'm not ready to do that. I enjoy teaching others to quilt, and it doesn't matter how many people are in the class. Besides, the smaller classes allow me to give more one-on-one attention to each person."

Lamar sat quietly, then patted Emma's shoulder and said, "You teach them quite well, I might add."

Emma smiled. "I think my students get even more from the class when you help me, Lamar."

Sure hope I won't let you down, Lamar thought, staring at his stiff fingers. With the colder weather, his arthritis was acting up. It was one of the reasons he wanted to vacation in Florida—along with thinking it would be a nice break for both him and Emma. He'd purposely not told Emma about his pain and stiffness because he didn't want her to worry or feel guilty about teaching another quilting class. He just hoped he could get through these next six weeks without letting on.

"Are you certain your Amish friend won't mind us dropping by unannounced?" Carmen asked as she climbed out of Paul's minivan and spotted a large, white house at the end of the driveway.

"I'm sure it'll be fine," Paul said, stepping onto the porch. "Emma's very hospitable, and Sophia and I have come by here many times when Emma didn't expect us. We were always welcomed with open arms."

Carmen didn't know why, but she felt a bit apprehensive. She'd conducted many interviews and never had a nervous stomach before—not even in her early days as a reporter. Today, however, she felt jittery.

She glanced around the yard, and her gaze came to rest on a black, box-shaped buggy parked near the barn. *I wonder how it would feel to ride in one of them,* she mused. Carmen knew from the things she'd read that the horse and buggy were the Amish people's primary mode of transportation.

The *ba-a-a* of a goat drew Carmen's attention to the other side of the yard, where a few goats frolicked in a pen. Nearby were several chickens pecking in the dirt, and just as Carmen and Paul stepped onto the porch, a fluffy white cat streaked across the yard, chasing a smaller orange-and-white cat.

I can't imagine what it would be like to live in this rustic-looking place. It's a far cry from the fast pace of Los Angeles. It might be interesting to be here for a while, but I wonder how long it would take for me to become bored or restless with the solitude.

Carmen stepped to one side as Paul knocked on the door. A short time later, an elderly Amish man with a long gray beard greeted them. His green eyes sparkled as he shook Paul's hand. "It's good to see you. It's been awhile."

Paul grinned widely. "It's good to see you, too, Lamar." He motioned to Carmen. "This is my sister-in-law, Carmen Lopez. She's visiting from California. Carmen, this is Emma's husband, Lamar Miller."

Carmen offered the man her best smile, while shaking his hand. "It's nice to meet you, Mr. Miller."

"Good to meet you, too, and please, call me Lamar." He opened the door wider. "Come in and say hello to Emma. I'm sure she'll be happy to see you," he said.

"If you're busy, we won't stay long," Paul was quick to say. "I just wanted you both to meet Carmen."

"We have a quilting class in an hour, but we can visit till then." Lamar motioned them inside and led the way down the hall. They followed him into a spacious room filled with several sewing machines, an empty quilting frame, and a large table with four chairs on both sides. Several colorful quilts draped over wooden stands were scattered around the room, which was lit by a few overhead gas lanterns. A slightly plump woman wearing a long navy-blue dress and a white cap perched on her head was seated in front of one of the machines. She was so intent on her sewing project that she didn't seem to notice when they came into the room.

"Look who's here," Lamar said, placing his hands on the woman's shoulders.

She turned her head and smiled at Paul. "It's so good to see you," she said, rising from her seat. "Where's that sweet little girl of yours?"

Paul gave the woman a hug. "It's always good to see you, Emma. Sophia is with my sister Maria, this morning." He turned to Carmen and said, "This is Emma Miller. She's the talented woman who taught me how to quilt. Emma, I'd like you to meet my sister-in-law, Carmen Lopez. She lives in Los Angeles, where she works at a newspaper."

Emma smiled as she greeted Carmen with a gentle handshake. "It's nice to meet you."

"I'm happy to meet you, too," Carmen said sincerely. "I was interested when Paul told me you'd taught him how to quilt."

"And she's an excellent teacher," Paul interjected.

Emma's cheeks colored as she dipped her head slightly. "Thank you, Paul. I enjoy sewing, and it's a pleasure for me to teach others how to quilt." She looked up at her husband and smiled. "Now that Lamar's helping me with the classes, people are learning even more."

"Lamar designed all these quilts," Paul said, motioning to the ones on display.

"They're quite impressive." Carmen moved to stand beside a quilt with muted shades of brown and green.

"That one I call Pheasant Trail." Lamar beamed. "It's one of my favorites."

"I can see why." Carmen leaned down to get a closer look. "The details in this quilt are amazing. I wish I could make something like that."

"Have you ever done any quilting?" Emma asked.

Carmen shook her head. "No, but I know how to do some basic sewing. My mother made sure both of her daughters learned how to sew." She glanced at Paul, but he was staring at the floor. Was he thinking about Lorinda and how much he still missed her? Well, Carmen missed her, too. She and Lorinda had been five years apart, but the age difference never mattered; they'd always been close.

As if sensing Carmen's discomfort, Emma touched her arm lightly and said, "Would you care to stay and be part of the class?"

"Oh yes!" Carmen couldn't believe her luck. If she was allowed to sit in on the class, she'd have the perfect opportunity to ask questions about the Amish—maybe even find out some details concerning the young people's time of running-around.

Paul quirked an eyebrow as he looked at Carmen strangely. "You won't learn much in just one class. It took me a full six weeks to be able to make a quilted wall hanging."

"How long will you be in the area, Carmen?" Emma asked.

She shrugged. "I don't know. I guess that will depend on how long my boss allows me to be gone."

"Emma's class goes for six weeks, and that's a long time to be away from work. Staying at a hotel, even an extended stay, like the one you're at now, can be expensive," Paul said before Emma could respond.

"Could you stay in the area for six weeks, Carmen?" Emma questioned.

"Yes, I think so. I'll step outside and give my boss a call." Carmen pulled her cell phone from her purse and scooted out the door.

"Hey, Carmen. How's it going there?" Carmen's boss asked after answering her call.

"Okay, Mr. Lawrence. I'm in Shipshewana, and. . ." Carmen paused and moistened her lips. "I was wondering. . . Would it be all right if I stayed here for six weeks?"

"Six weeks! Why so long?"

Carmen leaned against the porch railing. "I want to take a quilting class."

"Are you kidding me? I sent you there to get a story, not spend your time with a needle and thread." Mr. Lawrence's voice raised a few notches. "This is not a vacation, you know."

"I—I realize that, sir, but the quilting class is held in an Amish woman's home, and I think if I can get acquainted with her, I might be able to find out what I want to know about rumschpringe."

"Is that so?"

"Yes, and if I'm able to take the quilt class, which starts today and ends in six weeks, I'm sure I'll have a good story."

"Well, it better be, because the paper can't afford to send reporters on wild goose chases—especially for that length of time."

"I don't think it'll be a wild goose chase, Mr. Lawrence."

There was a long pause. Then, "Okay, if you think you're going to need six weeks, that's fine. Just make sure you come back with a top-notch story."

"Thanks, I'll do my best. Good-bye, Mr. Lawrence." Carmen hung up, drew in a deep breath, and stepped back into Emma's house.

"It's all set," she said, smiling at Emma. "Just tell me how much I'll owe for the classes, and I can get started today."

Once Emma discussed the price, Carmen turned to Paul and said, "I know you have other things you need to do today, so you can just leave me here and pick me up when the class is over."

Paul stared at her with a look of disbelief, but finally he nodded.

"I can't believe I'm doing this," Blaine mumbled as he parked his SUV on a graveled driveway where a white minivan was about to pull out. If he just hadn't lost that bet with Stuart when they'd gone fishing last Saturday. Blaine had been so sure he would catch the biggest fish that he'd stupidly agreed to take a six-week quilting class if he lost the bet. He'd never expected Stuart to pull a twenty-eight-inch largemouth bass from Lake Shipshewana. If he hadn't actually seen Stuart land the fish, he wouldn't have believed it, but even before his friend pulled the fish out of the water, Blaine knew it was going to be big. It had practically bent Stuart's fishing rod in half, and surprisingly, it didn't break.

Inwardly, Blaine had hoped the fish would roll and detach itself from the hook, but that didn't happen. Why would it? The week had been rotten. Earlier, he'd almost caved in when he'd been forced to give the fly-fishing demonstration to a large group of people. Somehow, dry mouth and all, Blaine had managed to get through it without letting on how uncomfortable he'd felt. And now he was stuck going to a quilting class of all things!

The fish Blaine caught had only been twenty-two inches long. What a disappointment that had been, especially when Stuart looked at Blaine's smaller fish and grinned at him in a teasing way.

Sure wish I could get out of taking this class, Blaine thought. *Maybe I could go inside, sit through the first few minutes, and then develop a sudden headache.*

Blaine was about to get out of his vehicle when his cell phone rang. He glanced at the screen and saw that it was Stuart. *Oh great. What's he doing. . .calling to check up on me?*

Blaine was tempted to let his voice mail answer the call, but changed his mind. If he didn't answer, Stuart would probably think he'd chickened out and wasn't going to take the class after all.

He snapped open his cell phone. "What's up, Stuart? Are you calling to check up on me?" Blaine's tone was harsher than he meant it to be.

"Hey, man, don't get so defensive," Stuart said. "I just wanted to make sure you were able to find Emma's house okay."

"Yeah, I found it. I'm sitting in her driveway right now."

"That's good. I'll be anxious to hear how your first class goes. I'm sure it'll be a walk in the park."

"I'll bet."

"What was that?"

"Nothing." Blaine glanced at his watch. "I'd better go. It's almost ten o'clock, and I sure don't want to be late for class."

"Okay, see you Monday morning."

"'Bye, Stuart." Blaine clicked off his phone and climbed out of his vehicle. He'd just started for the house when an older model Chevy rumbled into the yard. A few minutes later, an elderly woman stepped out. She wore baggy gray slacks, a green turtleneck sweater, and a floppy beige canvas hat. She glanced at him briefly, stuck her nose in the air, and tromped up the porch steps.

"Terrific," Blaine muttered under his breath, running his fingers through his thick, wavy hair. "I'll bet she's here for the quilt class. This is going to be anything but a walk in the park!"

CHAPTER 5

Selma was surprised when a gray-haired Amish man with a long, full beard answered her knock. She'd expected a woman. "Is this the home of Emma Miller?" she asked, eyeing him suspiciously.

He offered her a cheery smile. "That's right. Emma's my wife, and I'm Lamar. Are you one of her quilting students?"

Selma gave a quick nod, thinking he seemed nice enough. "My name is Selma Nash, and I came prepared." She lifted the canvas satchel she'd brought along and gave it a confident pat. "I have everything right here that I'll need to make a quilt."

"Oh, there was no need for you to bring anything," Lamar said. "Emma has all the required supplies. If you'll follow me, I'll lead the way to her quilting room."

Selma clutched her satchel as she walked with Lamar into the next room. Despite what he'd said, she was sure she'd be able to use most of what she had brought along. *Maybe they'll be impressed with all the research I've done beforehand about quilting,* she thought.

As Selma entered the room, she noticed that the inside of the house was as tidy as the outside. She detected a scent of lemon in the air. An older Amish woman sat at the table with a young Hispanic woman, whom Selma assumed was also here to learn how to quilt. But it seemed strange that there were no other students in the room.

"This is Selma Nash," Lamar said to the Amish woman. "She's one of your quilting students."

The woman stood and shook Selma's hand. "I'm Emma Miller, and I'm pleased that you've joined our class." She gestured to the other woman. "This is Carmen Lopez. She's here to learn how to quilt as well."

"Are we the only two people in the class?" Selma asked, feeling rather perplexed as Emma motioned for her to sit in one of the extra chairs.

Before Emma had a chance to respond, the young man Selma had seen outside shuffled into the room. He looked uncomfortable, like he might want to turn and run.

"You must be Blaine Vickers," Emma said, extending her hand.

He gave a brief nod.

"Welcome to our quilting class." Emma motioned to Carmen and then to Selma. "This is Selma Nash and Carmen Lopez, and we're waiting for Anna Lambright to arrive. As soon as she gets here, we'll begin."

Blaine's eyes widened. "So I'm the only guy in the class?"

"You're the only male student," Emma said, "but Lamar will be with us. In fact, he'll be helping me teach the class."

Lamar motioned to one of the quilts in the room. "I've designed many quilts, and I also know quite a bit about the history of quilts."

"I've studied up on them, too," Selma interjected, rather proudly. "As soon as my neighbor, Jan, said he'd paid for me to come to this class, I went straight to the library and checked out a book on Amish quilts."

Selma reached into her satchel and pulled out the book. "See, this one is a Dahlia pattern," she said, flipping through the pages and pointing to one of the pictures. "I love flowers, so that's the kind of quilt I would like to make."

"Perhaps you will someday," Emma said, moving to stand at the head of the table. "But during the next six weeks, I'll be teaching each of you how to make a quilted wall hanging with a simple star pattern combined with Log Cabin quilt blocks with an Eight Point Star layout. The finished square hanging will measure thirty-five inches."

Selma frowned, feeling her forehead wrinkles deepen. "I don't care for that idea. Can't we make the Dahlia or some other floral pattern?"

"Those would be too difficult," Lamar spoke up.

"Well, I'm confident that I could handle any pattern at all, because I'm a proficient seamstress."

"I'm sure Emma has a reason for choosing the simple star pattern," Carmen spoke up. "Since she's the teacher, she obviously knows what's best for us."

Selma glanced at Blaine to see if he was going to comment, but he just stared at the table. He obviously didn't want to be there. *His wife probably forced him to come,* Selma thought. *But then, I wonder why she didn't sign up to take the quilting classes herself.*

"Actually, I chose the pattern for two reasons," Emma said calmly. "First, because it's a bit different from other star patterns. And second, because it will be easy to make. But we'll get into all the details about making the quilt after my other student has arrived."

Selma grunted and folded her arms. "Seems to me if people are going to sign up for a class, the least they can do is be here on time."

"It was the young woman's mother who signed her up," Emma explained. "And I'm thinking perhaps—'

"Maybe she didn't want to come," Selma cut in. "Some daughters can be stubborn like that. They just don't appreciate their mothers."

Everyone looked at Selma with curious expressions, and the room got uncomfortably quiet. Had she said something wrong? Should she explain about her relationship with Cora? No, it was best to leave that alone. After all, it wasn't in her nature to talk about her personal life to a bunch of strangers.

Emma cleared her throat a couple of times, and then she looked over at Lamar and said, "Since Anna's not here yet, why don't you go ahead and share some things about Amish quilts?"

"I'd be pleased to do that." Lamar joined Emma at the head of the table and proceeded to talk about the history of Amish quilts. "Quilt patterns are a reflection of our daily living and can sometimes resemble things found in nature or on the farm." He pointed to one of the quilts on display. "This one I designed myself, and I call it simply, 'Horseshoes.' As you can see, the shape of a horseshoe is patterned throughout."

"How about that one?" Blaine asked, pointing to the quilt closest to him.

"I designed it, too, and it's called 'Pheasant Trail,'" Lamar replied.

"If you ask me, it looks more like 'chicken scratch,'" Selma said with a snort. "Can't you show us some pretty floral designs?"

The room went quiet again, and everyone stared at Selma as if she had pointed ears. What was wrong with these people, anyway? Didn't they want to see something beautiful, or were they content to look at quilts with bland and blah colors?

"You don't have to be so rude," Carmen spoke up with her hands on her slender hips. "I think Lamar's designs are quite unique."

"Yeah, that's right," Blaine agreed. "You shouldn't be putting them down."

Selma's face heated. She had a notion to gather up her things and head out the door. But if she did that, she'd miss out on learning how to make a quilt. "Sorry," she mumbled. "I didn't mean that the quilts weren't nice. I'd just prefer to see something more to my liking."

"The thing about Amish quilts," Emma explained, "is that there's a variety of patterns, which means there is something to fit everyone's taste."

"That's right," Lamar agreed. "Some people prefer the more traditional patterns, like the Lone Star, and some enjoy making something unusual like my Pheasant Trail or Horseshoe pattern."

"When did quilting first begin?" Carmen asked.

"In a traditional sense, not until the 1870s," Lamar replied.

"At first the fabrics were solid and dark, much like our plain choice of clothing." Emma smiled, as she pointed to another quilt made with maroon, brown, and off-white colors. "But later, pastels and whites were added to many of our quilts."

"Do all Amish women quilt?" Selma asked, realizing she'd better stay low-key.

Emma shook her head. "Many do, but some women keep busy with other things and don't have time to quilt."

Selma was about to comment, when the door to the quilting room swung open, and a young, auburn-haired Amish woman rushed in. Her long green dress had several splotches of dirt on it, and there was a large tear near the hem. The stiff white cap on her head was askew, and her cheeks were red as a ripe cherry. "S—sorry I'm late," she panted. "I had a little accident on my bike."

―――――

Emma was relieved that Anna had made it to class, but she felt concern seeing the state of disarray the poor girl was in. "Are you all right?" she asked. "Were you hurt?"

Anna shook her head as she reached up to push her head covering back in place. "I think my knees are scraped up a bit, but I'm okay."

"How'd it happen?" Lamar questioned. "Did you spin out in some gravel, or what?"

Anna frowned. "When a stupid black dog started chasing me and tried to get a hold of my skirt, I got scared and pedaled faster to get away. That's when I lost control of the bike and ran into a ditch beside the road."

"What happened when you fell?" Emma asked. "Did the *hund* bite you?"

"No, but I was afraid he might. Some English man pulled up in his car to see if I was all right, and when he hollered at the dog, it took off like a shot."

"Why don't you go down the hall to our bathroom and make sure you're not bleeding," Emma suggested, noticing the look of embarrassment in Anna's light brown eyes. "Washcloths are in the cabinet, and the bandages are in the medicine chest by the sink."

"I'll do that right now." Anna scurried out of the room, muttering something under her breath.

Poor girl. She's probably self-conscious. Emma turned her attention back to the class, although she wondered how much information she would get through to her students today. They'd gotten a late start, and with Selma's know-it-all attitude, this might be a difficult class to teach. *I've never had one like her before,* Emma thought, cringing inwardly. *Of course it can't be any harder to teach this class than it was my very first one, when I had such a mix of unusual characters.* Emma remembered how surprised she'd been that first day when a young English woman with a sour attitude; a preacher's wife with church problems; a man and his wife struggling with marital discord; a Hispanic teacher, recently widowed; and a tattooed biker on probation had showed up at her door. If she could teach them how to quilt and deal with some of their personal problems, maybe it wouldn't be so hard to work with this group of people. At least she hoped that would be the case. After all, there were just four students. Surely they couldn't all have issues.

I'll need to remind myself to take one week at a time and just do my best, she told herself. *With God's help, nothing is impossible.*

CHAPTER 6

"Sure wish we didn't have to work today," Terry complained as Jan pulled his truck and utility trailer into Emma's yard. "I'd rather be out riding my Harley."

"Same here, but we can't leave those shingles we tore off the Millers' roof yesterday lying in the yard." Jan popped all five fingers on his right hand—a habit he'd started lately. "When we show up here on Monday morning, I want to be able to start on the new roof right away. Of course if we had a gofer things would move along faster."

Terry scratched his head. "A gopher? What are you talking about?"

"You know. Having another guy to take care of the odd stuff, like picking up the old shingles, instead of us having to do it," Jan explained. "Someone who'd bring us stuff when we're working on the roof. Tools and such. Like I said, a gofer." He grinned. "They'd go fer this and go fer that."

Terry chuckled. "Oh yeah. . .that kind of gopher."

Jan thumped Terry's arm. "Well, since we don't have one, I think we oughta get these old shingles picked up."

"Guess you're right. I'll just have to make plans to go riding next Saturday. Do you and Star want to go along?"

Jan shrugged. "I don't know. I'll have to wait and see what she's up to. She may have to work, or she could be in Fort Wayne, visiting her mom and stepdad."

"Do you ever wish you and Bunny could've gotten back together?"

"Sometimes." Jan sighed. "But I guess it's better this way. There was a certain kind of chemistry between me and Bunny when we were teenagers, but after Star was born, her mom changed. She couldn't have really loved me back then if she could just run away and take our baby without looking back or letting me know where she was going. Even if Bunny had tried to start something up with me after Star came back into my life, I don't think I could have ever trusted her again." He groaned. "I'm not sure marriage is even right for me. Think me and my dog, Brutus, are better off without a wife telling us what to do."

"I know what you mean." Terry slapped his knee. "Don't think I'll ever tie the knot." He slowly shook his head. "Not with the way things turned out for my folks."

"It's a shame they split up after being married so many years," Jan said, running his finger over the film of dirt clinging to the dashboard of his truck. "Figured after they'd gone to see a counselor that things might get better."

"Yeah, me, too. They were doing better for a while, but then Dad started drinking pretty heavy, so Mom kicked him out."

Jan gave the fingers on his left hand a good pop. "Life is full of disappointments, ain't it?"

"That's for sure. Sometimes it stinks."

"But some things we just can't change, and right now we'd better quit yammering and get to work." Jan opened the truck door and stepped out.

Terry hopped out, too, and went around and opened the back of the utility trailer. The sooner they got the shingles picked up, the sooner he could return to the single-wide trailer he rented from his uncle Ted. Not that there was anything great waiting for him there. It would just be nice to flake out for the rest of the day. Sometimes he wished he had a home of his own—maybe a log cabin surrounded by trees.

Maybe I oughta look into buying a small piece of land, Terry thought. *Then I could start building a cabin during my free time.* He grabbed some shingles and pitched them into the trailer. *Well, I can't think about that right now. I've got work to do.*

Terry and Jan had only been working a short time, when a sporty-looking, silver-gray car pulled into the yard. A slender young woman with short blond hair worn in a bob stepped out of the car. She was dressed in beige slacks and a rose-colored pullover sweater that showed off her womanly curves. She glanced up at the house, then opened her trunk and removed a cardboard box. Glancing briefly at Terry and Jan, she headed for Emma's house, walking with an air of confidence.

"Now there's a real looker," Terry said, as the woman stepped onto the porch.

Jan rolled his blue eyes. "She's probably here for Emma's quilt class, and don't get any dumb ideas, 'cause she's most likely married. Even if she's not, she looks too sophisticated for a guy like you."

"What are you sayin', man? You think I'm not good enough for someone like her?"

"I ain't saying that at all. Just don't think you'd have anything in common with the woman." Jan motioned to her car. "For crying out loud, she drives a Corvette. How's that compare to your beat-up truck?"

"Well, there's only one way to find out if she's married or not,"

Terry said, ignoring Jan's remark.

"Oh yeah, what's that?"

Terry rubbed his hands briskly together. "I'll go in the house and check things out."

Jan grunted. "Check out what, Terry? Are you just gonna barge into Emma's home and ask the blond-haired chick if she's married? And if she's not, are ya gonna ask her out?"

Terry shrugged. "I might."

"Don't be such a sap. Emma would be shocked if you did something like that, and the cute little blond would probably laugh right in your face."

"Maybe not. Maybe she likes the strong, silent type."

Jan leaned his head back and roared. "You, the silent type? Now that's a good one!"

"Well, maybe I'm not silent all of the time, but I am strong." Terry gave his ponytail a flip and chuckled. "Could be, too, that the pretty little thing likes men with flaming red hair."

Jan pointed to the shingles nearby. "Just get busy picking these up and quit fantasizing."

Terry's eyebrows lifted. "*Fantasizing?* Where'd you pick up a word like that?"

"I ain't stupid, ya know." Jan shook his head. "For your information, being around Star so much and listening to some of the song lyrics she's written has broadened my vocabulary."

Terry bent down and grabbed an armful of shingles. "If you say so."

After heaving the shingles into the bed of the trailer, Terry turned to Jan and said, "Just as soon as we're done here, I think I'll go inside and see what I can find out about the blond. Is that okay with you?"

Jan turned his hands palms up. "Suit yourself. Just don't say I didn't give you fair warning if someone throws you out on your ear. I'd hate to have to say, 'I told you so.'"

When Emma heard a knock on the front door, she turned to Lamar and said, "Would you mind getting that? It's probably Jan. I saw him and Terry pull into the yard a bit ago."

"Sure, no problem. You go on teaching the class, and I'll be back in a minute." Lamar shuffled out of the room, moving at a slower pace than usual. Emma hoped his back wasn't hurting again. He'd had trouble with it since he'd bent the wrong way to pick something up two weeks ago. A few visits to the chiropractor and Lamar said his back felt better, but maybe he just didn't want her to worry.

Turning back to her students, Emma was disappointed that Anna seemed bored. Rather than looking at the samples of material Emma had shown them a few minutes ago, the young woman sat staring out the window as though in a daze.

She doesn't want to be here, Emma thought. *I don't know why Anna's mother thinks I'll be able to teach her to quilt. She won't learn a thing unless she wants to, so the money Ira and Linda spent on the classes for their daughter might be a complete waste. Well, all I can do is try to get through to her and hope for the best.*

When Lamar returned to the quilting room, a slender, attractive woman was with him. Her pretty blond hair reminded Emma of one of her earlier students, Pam Johnston, only this woman's hair was shorter and worn in a bob.

"Emma, this is Cheryl Halverson," Lamar said. "She brought you a quilt."

"It's my grandmother's quilt," Cheryl was quick to explain. "It's in pretty bad condition, and I was wondering if you could repair it for me."

Cheryl set the box she held on one end of the table and opened the lid. When she lifted out a tattered old quilt, Emma slowly shook her head. "Oh my, that does need to be mended."

Lamar's forehead creased. "Can you do it, or is it beyond repair?"

"The ends are quite frayed, and there are several tears, but I think it's salvageable."

Cheryl smiled at Emma with a look of relief.

When Emma opened the quilt more fully, she saw the pattern in it. "Why, this looks like a traditional Amish wedding-ring quilt. Is your grandmother Amish?"

"Oh no," Cheryl said with a shake of her head. "It's a quilt someone gave her when she got married."

"They most likely bought it in an Amish quilt shop," Anna interjected.

Emma was pleased to see the girl taking an interest in the quilt. Well, maybe not an interest, but at least she was offering her opinion.

"Yes, that's probably how it happened alright." Cheryl glanced at Emma's students, sitting around the table with curious expressions. "I apologize if I've interrupted something. I really should have called first and made an appointment to bring the quilt by."

"That's all right. We're having a quilt class," Emma explained. "This is the first one, and we'll meet every Saturday for the next six weeks."

"That sounds interesting."

Emma smiled. "Would you like to join us?"

"Oh, I don't know about that." Cheryl hesitated, tapping her fingernails on the table. "I'm all thumbs when it comes to sewing."

"Join the club," Blaine put in. "None of us here knows anything about making a quilt."

"Except for me," Selma spoke up. "I—I mean, I've never made one, but I do know how to sew. Quite well, I might add."

Emma turned her attention back to Cheryl. "If you'd really like to join the class, we'd be happy to have you."

Cheryl smiled, revealing a small dimple in each of her cheeks. "Yes, I would," she said, taking a seat. "And I'll be happy to pay whatever the cost."

Carmen couldn't believe how kind Emma was to a complete stranger. But then, she'd been kind to her, too. In fact, when Paul had introduced Carmen to Emma, she'd been welcomed as though she was a good friend.

Carmen's conscience pricked her a bit. *If Emma knew the real reason I decided to take this class, she probably wouldn't have been so welcoming. I need to make sure to keep that a secret—from Emma as well as Paul.*

"Now I want to show all of you what your quilted wall hangings will look like when they're done," Emma said, holding up a small colorful quilt with various shades of blue. "We'll begin today by choosing the colors we want and then cutting out the log cabin squares and the points for the star."

Carmen snuck a peek at Selma, just waiting for her to complain about something. What was with that woman, anyway? Did she always walk around wearing a scowl? *She probably doesn't realize how much older it makes her look. She does have beautiful white hair, though.*

Carmen couldn't help wondering what Selma must have looked like years ago and what made her seem so unhappy. Her wrinkles seemed to be a part of the frown embedded on her face. She certainly had the remnants of a nice tan, and if you took away those deeply etched lines, Selma probably hadn't been a bad-looking lady in her younger years.

Regrettably, Carmen could relate in some ways with whatever was making Selma so touchy. She, herself, had things to overcome. And soon, if she wasn't careful, she'd end up looking older than her twenty-four years.

Carmen glanced at Anna as they started picking out colors. She was definitely the age for rumschpringe and seemed to have a chip on her shoulder. Could she be like one of those rebellious teenagers portrayed on the TV show Carmen had seen last week?

Maybe I'll get the chance to question the girl. If not today, then perhaps next Saturday. I'm confident that by the end of six weeks, I'll have my story.

"Okay, man, I'm going inside now," Terry said once he and Jan had finished loading the shingles.

"You're really going into Emma's house?"

"Yeah, that's right."

"What excuse are you gonna use for going in there?" Jan asked.

"I'll ask for a glass of water, or say that I need to use the bathroom. I'm determined to find out if that blond is available."

Jan's eyes narrowed. "Are you serious?"

"Yep."

"Give me a break, man. I mean, you can't just waltz in there and start plying the woman with a bunch of personal questions."

"I'm not gonna ask a bunch of questions. Just need to find out whether she's single or not."

"How do you aim to do that? Are you just gonna introduce yourself and then blurt out, 'Oh, and by the way, are you married?'"

"No way! I'm not dumb enough to do that. I'm gonna get to know the woman first."

"How's that gonna happen in the few minutes you'll be in the house? It don't take that long to drink a glass of water, you know."

Terry rubbed the side of his face. "Hmm. . . You're right. That could be a problem, unless I take a slow drink." He tapped his foot and contemplated things a bit more. Suddenly an idea popped into his head. "I've got it! If I can't get the answers I want right away, then I'll see if Emma has room for one more in her quilting class."

"*Ha! Ha! Ha!* Now that's a good one!" Jan rocked back and forth on his heels, laughing so hard, tears ran down his cheeks.

"It's not funny," Terry mumbled. "If you can learn to quilt, then so can I. And if I find out the little gal's not married, I'm gonna ask her out."

"Well, if you're determined to do this, then I'm going in with you, 'cause this I've just gotta see!"

CHAPTER 7

Shouldn't we have knocked first?" Terry asked when Jan opened Emma's back door and stepped into her kitchen.

"Nope," Jan said, going to the cupboard and getting two glasses down. "When I told Lamar we'd be coming by today to pick up the old shingles, he said if we needed anything, the back door would be unlocked and to just walk right in." He handed Terry one of the glasses. "Here you go."

"Any ideas how I can find out whether the little blond's married or not?"

Jan filled his glass with water and took a drink. "Beats me. This was your dumb idea, so you figure it out."

"Maybe we could go in there and tell Lamar and Emma that we've finished picking up the shingles and will be back Monday morning to start putting on the new roof. Then, maybe one of 'em will introduce us to their quilting students." Terry filled his glass with water, took a drink, and set it on the counter. "But then, even if we are introduced, I'll only know the blond's name, not whether she's married or single."

Jan snickered. "If you wanna know bad enough, I'm sure you'll figure out some way to find out."

Terry rubbed the side of his face. This could be a challenge. He'd have to think fast on his feet. He released his hair from the ponytail, letting it hang loosely around his shoulders. "Do I look okay?"

Jan eyeballed him a few seconds, then shook his head. "I'd put the hair back in the ponytail if I was you."

"How come?"

"Some gals might not like guys with long red hair."

"Well, I can't do nothing about the color, since I was born with it, but if you think it'll improve my chances, I'll put it back the way it was." Terry pulled his hair back and secured it with a rubber band. "Is that better?"

Jan gave a nod. "Looks good to me. Let's go."

Terry picked up his glass and followed Jan into Emma's quilting room, hoping this wasn't a mistake and that the blond wasn't married. If she was, he'd bow out real quick.

When Terry and Jan entered the room, Emma looked up with a startled expression. "Oh, I didn't realize you two had come in. Is there something we can do for you?"

"Just came in for a drink of water," Terry said. He glanced at the cute little blond looking curiously at him, then turned to Lamar, who stood near one of the quilts on display. "Also wanted to tell you that we've got all the old shingles picked up and will be back Monday morning to start on the new roof."

Lamar smiled. "That's great. Thanks for letting us know."

Terry cleared his throat a couple of times, unsure how to proceed. Should he just come right out and ask to be introduced to Emma's quilting students? Hoping for assistance, he poked Jan's back.

Jan glared at him. "Hey, what's up with that?"

"Is something wrong, Jan?" Emma asked, looking at him over the top of her metal-framed glasses.

"Uh, no. I'm good." Terry smiled at Emma and said, "Looks like you're teaching another quilting class."

Emma nodded. An awkward silence filled the room, so facing her students, who sat around the table, she motioned to Jan and said, "This is Jan Sweet. He was one of the students in my very first quilting class."

"That's right, and I can tell you that Emma's one fine teacher," Jan responded. "If you do everything she says, you oughta have a nice wall hanging to take home at the end of six weeks." Jan grinned and winked at Selma Nash. "I'm glad to see ya here today."

She offered him a half smile. "Yes, thanks to your generosity."

Terry nudged Jan again. "Ain't ya gonna introduce me?" he asked, trying to keep his voice low.

With a disgruntled-looking frown, Jan finally said, "This is my friend and coworker, Terry Cooley."

"It's nice to meet you," Terry said, glancing briefly at each of the students, then settling his gaze on the blond.

All heads nodded, but no one offered their names. This wasn't going quite the way Terry had hoped. He'd made it inside, now he sure couldn't leave here without finding out if the blond woman was available or not.

"So, ladies," Terry said smoothly, "what do your husbands think of you taking this class?"

"Actually," Emma spoke up before any of the women could respond, "none of my students are married this time."

"I *was* married," Selma said. "I've been widowed for several years."

Terry knew that already, since Jan had given him the lowdown on his irritating neighbor. But instead of responding, he gave the blond his best smile and hoped she might say something. He was disappointed when she didn't.

"Jan's told me a lot about the quilting class he took," Terry said, pulling his gaze from the blond and glancing back at Emma. "Sounds like he not only learned how to quilt, but had a lot of fun in the process."

"That's true, I did," Jan agreed.

"Well, Emma, if you've got room for one more, think I'd like to sign up," Terry announced.

"We actually have room, don't we, Emma?" Lamar spoke up, moving closer to the table.

"Yes—yes, we do," Emma said, looking a bit flustered as her cheeks turned pink.

Lamar grinned. "It'd be nice for Blaine and me if there was another man in the class."

Terry glanced at the dark-haired guy sitting at the table with his shoulders slumped. He didn't look too thrilled to be here. Maybe it was because he was the only male student.

"You know," Terry said, grinning widely. "Since you do have the room, I'd like to take the class. Can I start today?"

"Of course," Lamar said, pulling out a chair for Terry. "Take a seat and join the others."

Terry looked over at Jan. "Would you mind coming back for me when the class is done?"

Jan gave a nod, looking at Terry as if he'd lost his mind. "Sure, why not?"

Terry rubbed his hands briskly together. "Great! I can't wait to get started!"

"Okay, I'll see ya later then." Jan gave Terry's back a solid thump, said good-bye to Emma and Lamar, and left the room, chuckling as he went out the door.

Sure hope I didn't make a mistake saying I'd do this, Terry thought as he took a seat at the table and checked out all the quilts in the room. It looked like a lot of detailed work went into them, and he wasn't sure he was up to the task of making one. Well, now that he knew the cute little blond was single, he couldn't see any way to ask her out except by taking the quilting class. He might not be interested in getting married, but he was more than eager to go out with someone as good-looking as this little gal. He couldn't help noticing her creamy complexion, slightly turned-up nose, and the thick, long lashes framing her light brown eyes.

He forced himself to concentrate on what Emma was saying, which wasn't easy, since he'd taken a seat right beside the blond-haired beauty.

"Now, class," Emma said, pushing Terry's thoughts aside, "with the templates I just handed out, I'd like you to begin marking the patterned pieces on the back of your fabric with either the dressmaker's chalk or a pencil."

"What do we do after that?" Terry asked, scratching his head. Putting on a new roof seemed like a piece of cake compared to this.

"When you're done marking, you'll cut out the pieces of material you'll be working with." Emma smiled. "Beginning next week, you'll start sewing together the pieces you've cut."

"That sounds like a lot of work," the other guy, sitting across from Terry, said.

He looks as out of place here as I feel, Terry thought. *At least I'm not the only guy here, though. Sure hope this gets better.* He was beginning to question his sanity. The blond might be dating someone already or have no interest in him. Of course Terry's intention was to win her over, and since he'd never had any trouble getting a date before, he was up to the challenge. He wasn't sure about the quilt-making, though.

"It is time-consuming to quilt," Emma said, "but it's well worth the effort. Nowadays, the patterned pieces are usually pieced by machine instead of by hand."

"That's a relief," the Hispanic woman at the end of the table said, heaving a sigh. "I can't imagine having to do everything by hand."

"I'm sure I could do it," Selma spoke up. "I've had a lot of experience mending things by hand."

Selma was the only one Terry knew by name, although he'd never spoken to her before. Most times when he'd gone over to Jan's, the nosy old woman was busy outside, pulling weeds, watering the flowers, or picking up things she didn't think should be in her yard. Terry had noticed that as soon as he pulled into Jan's yard, Selma would suddenly appear in her yard. She always acted as if she was busy with something but kept glancing their way, like a neighborhood snoop. After hearing some of the stories Jan had shared about Selma, Terry had decided it was best to give her a wide berth.

"Mending's not the same as quilting, though," Emma's husband, Lamar, interjected. "I'm sure everyone will find it much easier to use one of Emma's sewing machines."

"I don't know about that," the cute little blond said with a shake of her head. "I've tried using my mother's sewing machine several times and have never gotten the hang of it."

"You look like the type of woman who can do anything she sets her mind to," Terry said, leaning close to her.

She wrinkled her nose, leaned away, and reached for a piece of chalk Emma had placed in the center of the table.

Terry grimaced, while tactfully straightening in his seat. *Do I have bad breath or something? Stupid me, I shoulda put a breath mint in my mouth before I came in here.*

Turning his head and trying to remain inconspicuous, he cupped his hand over his mouth and cleared his throat. For the life of him, Terry couldn't remember what he last ate. Taking a quick glance around at everyone, he was glad Emma still had their full attention. So far so good. No one seemed to be looking at him. Hoping to remain unobserved, Terry expelled a little air into the palm of his hand. Cupping his hand over his nose, he inhaled deeply, and quickly lowered his hand before anyone noticed what he'd done. *Naw, don't think so. My breath smells okay to me. Maybe it's my body that stinks. I could be pretty ripe from cleaning up those shingles. I'll never get to first base with this gal if she won't even talk to me.*

"What will we do after our pieces have been sewn onto the quilt top?" the Hispanic woman asked, giving Terry a sideways glance and raising her eyebrows.

"Then the backing, the batting, and the quilt top will be layered, put into a hoop, and quilted by hand," Emma replied.

Perspiration beaded on Terry's forehead and upper lip. He really had bitten off more than he could chew. If he tried sewing anything, he was sure he'd look like a fool.

"When that step is done, the binding will be put on and your wall hangings will be done," Lamar interjected.

Emma nodded. "You should be able to complete the project in six weeks."

Six whole weeks? Terry groaned inwardly. Short of a miracle, it would probably take him a year to make a quilted wall hanging—if he could make one at all.

Cheryl tried to concentrate on what Emma was telling the class, but it was hard to focus when the red-haired fellow sitting beside her kept saying things to her, while checking her out. At least she thought that was why he kept staring at her and taking every opportunity to lean in closer. Between the two men sitting at the table, the scruffy-looking fellow beside her was the least appealing. Not that Cheryl was looking for another man. But if she was, the nice-looking guy across the table seemed to be more her type. Of course he hadn't said or done anything to make Cheryl think he was interested in her. It was just as well. She didn't need the complications, and she was here for only one reason—to learn from Emma and see that Grandma's quilt got repaired.

They all worked silently for a while, cutting out their squares and points for the stars. Then, reaching into his shirt pocket, Terry pulled out a pack of cigarettes.

Emma's mouth dropped open, and Lamar's bushy gray eyebrows shot straight up.

"Hey, now don't go lighting up in here. You ought to have more respect for Emma than that." The clean-cut guy across the table leveled the redheaded man with a look that could have halted a runaway freight train.

Cheryl felt relief. Earlier, when Terry first sat down, she'd noticed a stale cigarette odor on his clothing, and again, on his breath when he'd move in closer to speak to her. With the allergy she had to smoke, the last thing Cheryl needed was someone blowing smoke in her face.

"Sorry. Guess I wasn't thinking." Terry rose from his chair. "I'll go outside for a smoke."

"Why smoke at all?" Selma asked, wrinkling her nose. "It's a nasty habit, not to mention bad for your health."

"Yeah, well, I enjoy smoking. Besides, it's my health I've gotta worry about, not yours," Terry retorted.

"You don't have to be so rude," Selma huffed, crossing her arms. "A guy like you doesn't even belong in this class."

Neither does a busybody like you, Cheryl thought, watching as Terry hurried from the room.

———

Emma knew she'd have to do something soon with this class, or things would get out of control. She remembered back to her first quilting class, when Jan and Stuart had nearly gotten into a fight because of their hostilities. She couldn't let that happen again.

After Terry returned, Emma remembered that proper introductions hadn't yet been made. "Why don't we start at this end of the table and each of you can share something about yourselves—where you live and anything that might help us get to know you better. After all, we will be spending the next six Saturdays together." She motioned to Carmen. "Would you like to go first?"

Carmen moistened her lips with the tip of her tongue. "My name is Carmen Lopez, and I live in Los Angeles." She hesitated a minute, looking a bit anxious. "I'm visiting my brother-in-law, Paul Ramirez, and his little girl, Sophia. I'm taking the quilt class because it seems—uh—interesting."

Emma nodded. "Paul was part of my first quilting class, and we've become good friends. It's always a joy when he stops by with his little girl." She touched Carmen's shoulder. "Is there anything else you would like to share?"

"I think that's all," Carmen replied, staring down at the table. She appeared to be a bit uncomfortable all of a sudden.

Emma motioned to Anna. "It's your turn."

"There's not much to tell," the young woman mumbled. "My name's Anna Lambright, and I live in Middlebury. I came to the quilt class because my mom signed me up, but I really don't want to be here."

Emma was stunned. She hadn't expected Anna to be so blunt.

"Blaine, why don't you go next?" Lamar suggested, as though sensing Emma's discomfort.

"My name's Blaine Vickers. I work at a sporting goods store in Mishawaka." A patch of pink erupted on Blaine's cheeks. "I'm here because I made a bet with my friend, Stuart, about who could catch the biggest fish. I lost, so now I have to learn how to quilt."

There were a few murmurs from the ladies, and a snicker from Terry, but before anyone could say anything, Emma moved on. "Selma, you're next."

"My name is Selma Nash, and I live here in Shipshewana. I'm here because my neighbor, Jan Sweet, paid for me to take the class. I thought I'd better take advantage of it, because I doubt something like that will ever happen again."

Emma glanced at Lamar, to get his reaction, and he gave her a quick wink. They'd both gotten to know Jan rather well since he'd taken the quilt classes, and they knew that despite his rough exterior, he was a kind, generous man.

Emma then asked Cheryl to introduce herself.

"My name is Cheryl Halverson, and I live in Goshen." She motioned to the tattered quilt she'd brought along. "At the suggestion of my pastor's wife, I brought my grandma's old quilt to Emma for repair. After I got here, I decided to take the quilting class."

"Guess it's my turn." Terry spoke up before Emma had a chance to say he was next. "I'm Terry Cooley, and I also live here in Shipshe." He grinned at Cheryl. "In case you didn't know it, Shipshe's what many of the locals call Shipshewana. Oh, and I'm a roofer by trade."

"What made you decide to join our quilting class?" Lamar asked.

Terry scooted around in his chair, giving his ponytail a quick twist. Then he blew out his breath in a noisy, almost snort. "Well, uh. . . I just thought to myself, if Jan could take the class and like it, then maybe I would, too." He glanced over at Cheryl and grinned. "Thought it might be a chance to make a few new friends as well."

No words were needed as the rhythm of Cheryl's nails clicking on the table spelled out her annoyance with Terry.

Oh dear, Emma thought, seizing the moment to glance out the window, then turning to look at Lamar. His gentle-looking eyes reassured her, even though she couldn't tell what he was thinking. Emma didn't want to feel discouraged, but she couldn't help wondering if this was going to be another challenging class. *If so, Lord, please give me the right words to help these students.*

CHAPTER 8

"How'd things go with the quilt class?" Jan asked Terry as they headed to Emma and Lamar's Monday morning to begin putting on the new roof.

"I would have told you on Saturday if you'd come back to get me," Terry muttered, reaching into his pocket for his cigarettes.

"I couldn't help it. When Star called and said one of her tires went flat, I had to rescue her. I tried calling, but you didn't answer your cell phone, so I left a message."

"I didn't realize my phone was turned off. Then when I did turn it on, the battery was dead. Selma saw me walking home, so she stopped and offered me a ride." Terry groaned. "It was nice of her to drive me home, and it sure beat walking, but that woman nearly drove me nuts with all her snide remarks about nearly everyone in the class. She even had something mean to say about Cheryl."

"Who's Cheryl?" Jan asked.

"That hot-looking blond I plan to take out," Terry proclaimed, blowing rings of smoke.

Jan cranked his head as they drove past the parking lot of the local grocery store.

"Hey! You'd better watch where you're going!" Terry shouted.

"Oh, yeah, sorry. I was checking out that Harley in the parking lot back there."

Terry glanced back at the cycle. "It's a nice one, all right."

"About that date," Jan said, "did you get anywhere with it?"

Terry shook his head. "Not yet."

"Did she show any interest in you at all?"

"No, and I don't wanna rush it. Just give me a chance to work my charm on her."

Jan shook his head. "I still say she's not your type, and I think you're barking up the wrong tree."

"Well, you know what they say...opposites attract." Terry swallowed as he flicked what was left of his cigarette out the window. "She sure is pretty and seems really nice, and I'm definitely attracted to her."

"You know, I do have an ashtray," Jan muttered.

"I didn't think there was room in there. Not with all the gum wrappers and stuff you have jammed inside. When was the last time you cleaned out this truck anyways?" Terry asked.

"Been awhile, I guess."

"Been awhile?" Terry looked at Jan, raising his brows and pointing at the dashboard. "I'll bet I could tell you every burger joint you've stopped at within the last month by all the Styrofoam cups and wrappers you have stuffed up there. It looks like you've been living in this truck."

"S—weet, isn't it?" Jan snickered. "This rig is sorta like my man cave, you know." He poked Terry with his elbow. "Anyways, back to this Cheryl gal. What if the interest you have in her ain't mutual? Then what are you gonna do?"

"Let's change the subject, shall we?"

"Sure, whatever. Why don't you tell me about Selma? How'd she do at the quilt class?"

Terry grunted. "I don't even know why she came. She already knows everything about making a quilt."

Jan's eyebrows furrowed. "She does? Then why she'd agree to take the class?"

"Maybe she didn't want to hurt your feelings. Or maybe she really doesn't know much about quilting and was just trying to act like she does."

Jan gave his index finger a quick pop before grabbing the wheel again. "You know, I'll bet that's it. It don't surprise me, neither. Selma probably acted like a know-it-all to cover up for what she doesn't know. She's one complicated woman."

—————

Selma set her plate of scrambled eggs on the kitchen table and heaved a sigh as she took a seat. Another day of having breakfast and wishing she had someone to share it with. She missed her husband and daughter so much. She couldn't bring John back from the dead, and she'd all but given up on ever seeing Cora again. Selma attended church on a regular basis, yet she had no real friends. Everyone had their own families, like she'd had once, and what would anyone want to do with a lonely old woman?

Selma took a bite of her scrambled eggs and tried not to let images from the past clog her brain like they'd done so many times before. The last thing she wanted to do was stir up old memories. All it did was make her yearn for the past. And she knew all too well that the past was the past, and there was no getting it back.

She glanced at the calendar on the wall near the sink. *Well, at least*

I have another quilting class to go to. I just wish I didn't have to wait until Saturday.

Selma had all of her squares cut out and couldn't wait to start sewing them together. If she weren't afraid of her teacher's reaction, she'd use her own sewing machine and sew them this week instead of waiting to do them during class.

A thump on the back porch drove Selma's thoughts aside, and she pushed away from the table. Since the thump wasn't followed by a knock on the door, she figured it wasn't someone coming to visit. *Don't tell me one of the neighbor kids threw something on my porch.*

Draping a sweater around her shoulders so she wouldn't get chilled, she opened the door and was surprised to see a mangy-looking gray cat staring up at her. *Meow!*

"Go away. Shoo!" Selma clapped her hands, but the cat didn't budge. "Go on now, get!" She stamped her feet and reached for the broom leaning against the wall near her door. "Go back to wherever you belong!"

The cat hissed and bounded off the porch. Selma stepped back inside and slammed the door. "Stupid neighborhood pests," she mumbled. "You'll never catch me owning a cat or a dog!" Shuffling her slipper-covered feet back to the table so she could finish her breakfast, Selma realized that the cat didn't have a collar. Maybe it was just a stray. Well, she hoped it didn't come around her place again!

Mishawaka

"How'd things go at the quilting class?" Stuart asked when Blaine arrived at work Monday morning.

Blaine frowned. "Let's just say that I've had more fun sitting in the dentist's chair than I did during those two grueling hours. And that's saying a lot, because I hate going to the dentist."

"That bad, huh?"

Blaine nodded. "No wonder you dreaded going to that class."

"I did at first," Stuart admitted, "but after I got to know everyone, they kind of became my friends. At least most of them did. I never got that close to the biker or his newfound daughter, though."

"Well, I doubt anyone attending Emma's class will ever be my friend. There were too many people eyeballing me, and it made me sweat."

Stuart's eyebrows lifted. "How many people are taking the class?"

"Six, counting me."

"That's the same number that were in my class. You shouldn't feel nervous around that small of a group. It's not like you're teaching the class or anything."

"I know, but it wasn't just the amount of people there."

"What was it then?"

"I felt some sort of undercurrent going on, and you know I don't like conflict—even when I'm not personally involved."

"What kind of conflict?" Stuart wanted to know.

Blaine leaned against the wall and folded his arms. "Let's see now. . . this white-haired lady, Selma, acted like she knew more than Emma. She was a bit snippy, too. Oh, and the young Amish woman who came in late obviously had a chip on her shoulder and even said she didn't want to be there. Then there was the Hispanic woman who seemed kind of nervous. Oh, and the redheaded roofer was obnoxious and kept trying to hit on the pretty blond woman, who clearly didn't like him or his ashtray aroma."

"So the guy's a smoker, huh?"

"Yeah. He actually tried to light up in Emma's house, but I put a stop to that. He ended up going outside for a smoke, and I was hoping he wouldn't come back."

Stuart laughed. "Sounds like another group of challenging characters for Emma and Lamar to deal with." He gave Blaine's arm a reassuring tap. "Just relax and enjoy the ride. By the end of the six weeks, you might feel differently about things. Believe me, I never thought so at first, but it does get better."

"I doubt that," Blaine muttered. "And I probably won't know any more about quilting than I do right now."

Goshen

Cheryl gripped the steering wheel tightly as she headed for work. She'd awakened with a headache and had thought about calling in sick. But she wasn't going to give in to it. She'd taken an aspirin with a strong cup of coffee and told herself that she could get through the day. Maybe by the time she got to the office, the aspirin would take effect.

As Cheryl drove along, she was thankful that on Friday she'd gotten all her work done and had left her desk clean. She hoped this morning would start out quiet, with only e-mails to answer and phone calls to return. Most likely it would be that way, as long as her boss, Hugh Edwards, hadn't worked on Saturday, like he did on occasion.

Cheryl slipped in one of her favorite Christian CDs and tried to relax. She'd been uptight since she'd attended her first quilt class. When she'd decided to take the class, she hadn't figured that some overbearing guy who smoked like a diesel truck would be sitting beside her, asking a bunch of nonsensical questions.

Cheryl glanced at her cell phone, lying on the leather seat beside her. She'd called her folks Saturday evening, and again on Sunday, wanting to find out how Grandma was doing, but all she'd gotten was her parents' voice mail. She'd left messages every time, but no response. Surely Mom and Dad couldn't both be too busy to call. Had they gone out of town for the weekend? If so, why hadn't they let her know? Cheryl had been tempted to call again this morning, but with the three-hour time difference between Indiana and Portland, Oregon, her folks would still be in bed, assuming they were home.

She drew in a deep breath and exhaled slowly. *I'll try again when I get home this evening. I really want to know how Grandma's doing, and I need to ask Mom not to tell her about the quilt. I want it to be a surprise.*

Just then her phone rang, so she pulled over to answer, hoping it was her mother. Instead, it was her pastor's wife, Ruby Lee.

"Hi, Cheryl," Ruby Lee said cheerfully. "I'm calling to see if Emma was able to fix your grandmother's quilt."

"Yes, she took the quilt in to repair it," Cheryl replied. "Oh, and I ended up signing up for Emma's six-week quilting class."

"I'm glad to hear that. I'm sure you'll enjoy it as much as I did."

"I hope so. I'm not that good with a needle and thread, so I don't know if I can make a wall hanging as beautiful as the one you made when you took Emma's class."

"Now, Cheryl, remember what the Bible says in Philippians 4:13," Ruby Lee reminded. "'I can do all things through Christ which strengtheneth me.'"

Cheryl smiled. "I'll try to remember that. Thanks for the pep talk. I needed it."

"You're welcome. Oh, and one more thing."

"What's that, Ruby Lee?"

"I believe that meeting new people—especially people like Emma and Lamar, will be as good for you as it was for me."

CHAPTER 9

Shipshewana

I've been meaning to ask, how did things go at your quilting class last Saturday?" Emma's daughter Mary questioned as she helped Emma do the dishes. Mary and her family lived next door, but one of the children had been sick last week, so Mary hadn't been over to see Emma for several days. This evening they'd all gotten together at Emma and Lamar's for a haystack supper.

Glancing out the window as the sun settled in the western sky, Emma sighed and placed another clean plate in the dish drainer. "Let's just say the class could have gone better."

"What happened?" Mary asked, reaching for the plate to dry.

Emma lifted her hands from the soapy water and held up one finger. "The first problem was Anna Lambright. She came in late and announced that she didn't want to be there." A second finger came up. "Then there was a lady named Selma Nash, who kept interrupting and acting as if she knew more about quilting than anyone else in the room—including me." Emma extended a third finger. "Jan's friend Terry Cooley was also in the class, and I'm afraid he didn't make a very good impression."

"With you?"

Pushing up her glasses, and leaving a small trail of soap bubbles running toward the tip of her nose, Emma shook her head. "I've met Terry before, so I already knew about his smoking habit. But Cheryl Halverson, who brought her grandmother's quilt for me to fix, ended up sitting right next to Terry." Emma wrinkled her nose. "He smelled like cigarette smoke, which I suspect is why she kept leaning away from him."

"Oh dear." Mary handed Emma a tissue to blot the suds on her nose. "I hope he didn't smoke here in the house."

"He was about to but ended up going outside. Thank goodness Lamar or I didn't have to say anything to Terry about it, because Blaine Vickers, one of the other students, spoke up."

"Who are the others who came to your class?"

"Well, Blaine Vickers is one of Stuart Johnston's friends, and a young woman named Carmen Lopez was also here. She's Paul Ramirez's sister-in-law."

"Sounds like quite a varied group of people," Mary said, reaching for another plate to dry. "Apparently some of them are connected with the first group you had."

"They certainly are. I sure hope things go better during our class tomorrow. I want to be able to help each of my students learn how to quilt."

Mary placed her hand on Emma's arm. "If these classes go like all the others you've taught, I'm sure your students will learn a lot more than quilting from you and Lamar. By the end of six weeks, I can almost count on them being thankful they took your class."

Goshen

Cheryl had just taken a seat at the table to eat the Caesar salad she'd fixed for supper, when her cell phone rang. She was going to ignore it until she realized the call was from her mother.

"Mom, where have you been?" Cheryl asked, reaching for the bottle of ranch dressing to drizzle over her salad. "I've been trying to get a hold of you all week."

"There's no need to be upset, Cheryl," Mom said in a matter-of-fact tone. "Your dad and I needed a little time away, so we went to the beach for a few days."

"To the beach? What about Grandma?" Cheryl's voice rose with each word she spoke. "Who checked up on her while you were gone, and why didn't you let me know you were leaving town?"

"Your uncle Don stopped by the nursing home to make sure she was okay, and we didn't call because going to the beach was a spur-of-the-moment decision."

Cheryl clenched her teeth, forking a crouton and watching it crumble. "I would have appreciated a call. I was worried about you."

"I'm sorry," Mom apologized. "When your dad suggested we go to the beach, I got caught up in the idea and didn't think to call."

"How'd you manage to get time off from the bank?" Mom always used her work as an excuse not to do things with Cheryl, but apparently spending time with Dad was a different matter.

"I had some vacation time coming. Why are you asking so many questions? Don't your dad and I have the right to get away by ourselves once in a while?" Mom sounded upset, and Cheryl knew she'd better not push it any further.

"I'm sorry, Mom. I hope you and Dad had a good time."

"We did. The weather was a bit chilly, but the sun was out, and we had fun walking the beach, looking for shells and agates. You know very well that we don't do something like this often, and it was nice to just go off like we did with no real planning involved." There was a pause. Then Mom said, "How are things going with you?"

"Okay. I found an Amish woman to repair Grandma's quilt, and I signed up to take a six-week quilting class. Please don't tell Grandma I'm having the quilt repaired. I want it to be a special birthday surprise."

"Oh, that's nice, and I won't say a word. Uh, listen, Cheryl, your dad just came in, and I need to talk to him about a few things, so if there's nothing else, I'd better go."

"Sure, Mom. Tell Dad I said hello. Oh, and give Grandma a hug from me when you see her the next time."

"I will. 'Bye, Cheryl."

Cheryl clicked off her phone and stared at her salad. For some reason, she'd lost her appetite. It was just like Mom to be too busy to talk. She never seemed to have enough time for her one and only daughter.

Elkhart

As Carmen stepped onto Paul's porch, her palms grew sweaty. Paul had invited her to join him and Sophia for supper tonight, and even though she looked forward to spending time with her niece, she was nervous about visiting Paul. What if he didn't accept her apology for blaming him for Lorinda's death? What if he quizzed her about the quilt class, and she ended up blurting out the real reason she'd signed up for it? She was sure he'd be upset if he knew she was taking the classes in order to gather research for an article that could shed a bad light on the Amish. And she certainly couldn't mention that she planned to talk privately with Anna Lambright, hoping to get information about her running-around years.

Taking in a quick breath, Carmen rang the doorbell. One glance at the yard told Carmen how the flower beds had been neglected over the past summer. Remnants of weeds where flowers had once bloomed were now dried and bent over.

I'll bet Paul has his hands full, being both mom and dad to Sophia, not to mention his full-time teaching job, Carmen thought. She didn't recall his yard looking so neglected when she'd been here before.

Paul answered the door, wearing a dark blue shirt and a pair of blue jeans. Noting the apron tied around his waist, Carmen suppressed a giggle. She'd never thought of him as the domestic type, but then when he'd had to take on the role of caring for the house, she supposed he'd learned to wear many hats. It couldn't be easy for him raising Sophia on his own. If Carmen lived closer, she would offer to do some things with Sophia. But at least Paul's folks, as well as his sister and her family, lived nearby. From what Paul had said in his e-mails, they often took Sophia to give Paul a break.

"Come in," Paul said, offering Carmen a nervous-looking smile. "You're right on time."

Carmen stepped into the house and removed her coat. "It was nice of you to invite me over. I hope you haven't gone to any trouble preparing the meal."

"Not really," he said, leading the way to his kitchen. Carmen could see it still had Lorinda's touch with the cheery decorations. "I fixed a taco salad for us, and Sophia will have scrambled eggs." He chuckled. "It's one of her favorite things to have for breakfast, but truth is, she likes eggs and could eat them most any time."

"I'm with her on that. Sometimes I like to make breakfast for dinner.

Speaking of Sophia, where is she right now?"

Paul motioned to the door leading to the living room. "In there, watching her favorite TV show with the giant puppets."

Carmen smiled. "I've always enjoyed puppets, too."

"Why don't you go watch the show with her while I get everything on the table?" Paul suggested. "I'll call you when it's ready."

"Are you sure there isn't something I can do to help?"

He shook his head. "I've got it under control."

"Okay." Carmen started out of the room but turned back around. "Uh, Paul, there's something I'd like to say, and if I don't say it now, the evening might go by without another opportunity."

Paul leaned against the counter and folded his arms. "What is it, Carmen?"

She took a step toward him. "I'm sorry for blaming you for Lorinda's death and sorry for not offering more support when she died. I was angry that my sister had been taken from me and needed someone to blame. I realize now that it wasn't your fault, and I don't want there to be hard feelings between us."

Paul stared at the floor. When he lifted his gaze, tears filled his eyes. "Thank you for saying that, Carmen. It means a lot."

Carmen was tempted to give Paul a hug but thought better of it. She wanted to offer comfort, but didn't want him to take it the wrong way. So instead, she merely smiled and said, "I feel better having apologized, and now I'm going to see my sweet little niece."

As Carmen hurried from the room, struggling with tears of her own, she felt a sense of relief for having apologized to Paul. At least that heavy weight had been lifted from her shoulders. Now if she could just get rid of the guilt she felt for not telling him the truth about why she'd come to Indiana.

Middlebury

"How'd things go at work today?" Anna's mother asked as she began dishing up for supper.

"It was okay, I guess." Anna grabbed some silverware from the drawer near the sink and proceeded to finish setting the table.

"Your daed was here almost two hours before you got home," Mom said, reaching around Anna to put a bowl of salad on the table. "Where'd you go after he closed the shop?"

Anna squirmed under her mother's scrutiny. "I. . .uh. . .went to visit one of my friends."

"Which friend, Anna?"

"Mandy Zimmerman."

Mom's eyes narrowed. "You know we don't like you hanging around her. She's a bad influence with all her worldly notions."

Anna went to the cupboard to get down the glasses.

"Mandy's rebellious, too. I wish you would stop seeing her, Anna."

Anger boiled in Anna's chest. *Here we go again. Mom's being critical and telling me what to do.*

"Anna, did you hear what I said?"

"Jah, I heard, but I think I ought to have the right to choose my own friends."

Mom shook her head vigorously. "Not if they're trying to lead you astray."

"Mandy's not doing that. She doesn't push anything on me. She's a lot of fun to be with, and I enjoy our times together." Anna went to the sink, filled a pitcher with cold water, and placed it on the table. "Mom, some of the young people I know are planning a trip to the Fun Spot amusement park tomorrow, and I want to go along."

"You can't, Anna. Have you forgotten about the quilting class?"

"No, but I don't want to go. I'd rather spend the day having fun with my friends than sitting in a room full of weird people and being forced to learn how to quilt."

"I'm sure the other students aren't weird."

"Jah, they are. There's a redheaded guy who tried to light up his cigarette in the Millers' house and an old lady who thinks she knows more than the teacher does. Oh, and then there's—"

Mom held up her hand. "That's enough, Anna. You're going to the quilting class tomorrow, and that's all there is to it. Now go call your sisters and brothers to the supper table."

Anna clenched her fingers so tightly that her nails dug into her palms. Tomorrow morning she would wake up with the flu or a cold, because there was no way she was going back to the quilting class!

CHAPTER 10

The next morning, Anna entered the kitchen, still wearing her robe and slippers. "I can't go to the quilt class today, because I'm *grank*," she announced.

Mom turned from her job at the stove and frowned. "You're sick? What's wrong, Anna? Is it the flu?"

"Umm. . .jah, I think so." Anna hated lying to her mother, but she had to do something to get out of going.

With a worried expression, Mom stepped away from the stove and hurried over to Anna. "You don't have a *fewer*," she said, placing her hand on Anna's forehead. "If you had the flu, I'm sure you'd feel warm. Your cheeks aren't even flushed."

"Well, maybe it's not the flu, but I don't feel well." Anna dropped her gaze to the floor. It was hard to lie to Mom when she was looking at her with such concern. *I shouldn't have let her feel my forehead.*

"Anna, are you pretending to be sick so you don't have to go to the class today?" Mom asked, lifting Anna's chin.

Tears pricked the backs of Anna's eyes, but she held her ground.

"I don't want to go, Mom. I don't like it there, and I don't care if I ever learn how to quilt. I'm not a child, you know—I'm eighteen. I should be able to make my own decisions about something like this."

"I'm sorry you don't like the class, but I think it'll be good for you to learn how to quilt. Your daed and I have already paid for the class, so you need to go." Mom stared at Anna and then added, "Now go get dressed. As soon as breakfast is over and the dishes are done, your daed will hitch his horse to the buggy and take you to Emma's."

"Since you've already paid for the class, why can't Arie go instead of me? She likes to sew."

Mom rolled her eyes. "For goodness' sakes, Anna, your sister doesn't need sewing or quilting lessons. You're the one I've never been able to teach."

"Well, if I have to go, why can't I ride my bike, like I did last week?" Anna asked, knowing she wasn't going to get out of this. She also suspected that Mom didn't trust her to go on her own. She probably thought Anna would skip the class and sneak off for the day with her friends, which was exactly what she would have done if she'd been able to ride her bike.

"Your daed has some errands to run in Shipshewana, so it only makes sense for him to take you—especially if you are feeling poorly."

Anna grimaced. Like she was some sort of a little child, now she was stuck being taken to Emma's and then sitting through another boring class. *Why do Mom and Dad treat me like a baby?* she wondered as she tromped up the stairs to her room. *Can't they see that the more they force me to do things their way, the more determined I am to gain my freedom? If they don't let up on me soon, I might leave home for good!*

———

Shipshewana

"Are you ready for today?" Lamar asked, washing his hands after coming in from tending the goats.

"Jah, I suppose," Emma responded.

When his hands were cleaned and dried, Lamar helped Emma set things out on the sewing table. "I have high hopes that the quilt class will go better today," he said, offering her what he hoped was an encouraging smile. "First classes are always a bit awkward, with everyone getting to know one another."

She gave a slow nod. "I prayed this morning before breakfast that things would go well with the class."

"I prayed the same thing." Lamar placed his hands on Emma's shoulders and looked into her eyes. "Even if things don't go as we might like, I'm sure God will give us the right words to share with our quilting students."

Emma smiled and kissed his cheek. "One thing I've always appreciated about you is your positive attitude. When I'm filled with doubts, you make me feel hopeful."

"Just remember, our hope is in the Lord. Psalm 71:14 reminds us: 'But I will hope continually, and will yet praise thee more and more.'"

"You're right," Emma said. "Danki for that reminder."

"That must be one of our students," Lamar said when a knock sounded on the door. "Would you like me to get it?"

Emma nodded. "Jah, please."

"One of your goats is out," Selma said when Lamar answered her knock. She turned and pointed to the left side of the yard, where a frisky goat nibbled on the grass. "Unless you're trying to replace your lawn mower, you ought to keep that critter in its pen."

Lamar frowned. "Oh great. I must have left the gate open when I fed Emma's goats this morning. Go ahead into the house. Emma's in her sewing room." He hurried past Selma and into the yard, hollering and waving his hands at the goat.

"Sure don't know why anyone would want a bunch of goats. All they do is strip your yard clean, grass and all," Selma muttered as she stepped into the house. "Dogs, cats, goats—they're nothing but a nuisance."

When Selma entered the quilting room, she found Emma sitting at the table with her head bowed. Was she praying or sleeping? Selma waited several seconds, then cleared her throat real loud.

Emma lifted her head and smiled. "Oh, good morning, Selma. I was just getting my thoughts together before teaching the class. How are you today?"

Selma shrugged. "Okay, I guess." She motioned toward the window. "Your husband's outside chasing after one of your goats."

Emma rose from her seat and hurried to the window. "Oh dear, I'll bet it's Maggie again. I hope that critter isn't causing any trouble. She can be an escape artist when she wants to be."

"Lamar said he thought he'd left the gate open when he fed the goats this morning," Selma said, taking a seat at the table.

Emma sighed. "I hope he doesn't have any trouble catching Maggie. She can be a frisky one at times. Do you have any pets, Selma?"

Selma shook her head. "And I don't plan on having any, either."

"Are you allergic to most animals?"

"No, not really. I just can't be bothered with the messes they make."

"Oh, but think of the company a cat or dog offers."

Selma brushed the idea aside. "*Puh!* A barking dog or a yowling cat isn't the kind of company I need. I'd rather be alone than have some animal leaving hair all over my house and making little messes. I just happened to shoo a scraggly-looking cat off my porch this week. You know, once you feed them, they never leave."

Emma opened her mouth, then closed it and looked back out the window.

Selma glanced at the clock on the far wall. It was almost ten o'clock. Were the others going to be late? If so, she would let them know what she thought about that. Like a thorn in her side, tardiness had always been an irritation for her.

———

Cheryl had just gotten out of her car when a truck pulled into Emma's yard. Terry stepped out, puffing on a cigarette.

"Oh great," she mumbled under her breath. She was hoping he might not show up today.

"Are you ready for another lesson?" Terry asked as he approached her.

She took a step back, hoping to avoid the smoke from his cigarette, but it was no use. The smoke wafted up to her nose. She sneezed and coughed at the same time.

"Have you got a cold?" Terry asked, with a look of concern.

She shook her head, while hurrying along. "I'm allergic to cigarette smoke."

"Oops. Sorry about that." Terry dropped the cigarette on the ground and stomped it out. "So how'd your week go?" he asked, following as Cheryl hurried toward the house.

Before Cheryl could respond, an energetic goat zipped right between them. *Ba-a-a!*

"Come back here, Maggie," Lamar panted, red-faced, as he ran after the critter. He looked exhausted, like he might fall over any minute.

"I'll get her!" Terry shouted, tearing across the yard after the goat.

Cheryl stepped onto the porch and watched in amusement as Terry skirted back and forth across the grass in hot pursuit of the lively animal. Lamar stood by watching and catching his breath.

Terry, on the heels of the goat, raced through the front yard, then the side of the house, and back again. It didn't take long for Terry to grow winded as well. *If he didn't smoke he might not be so out of breath,* Cheryl thought.

As she continued to watch, Cheryl knew she would have given up on catching the goat long ago. But Terry was persistent, even when a coughing fit sent him into spasms. Back and forth he and Maggie went, like they were playing some unending game of tag. Finally, as the ornery animal got closer, it seemed that Terry was about to outwit her.

Cheryl's mouth dropped open when Terry took a flying leap, as if he were about to make an impressive tackle, and missed grabbing Maggie's back legs by mere inches. Covering her eyes with her hands, Cheryl peeked through her fingers just in time to see Terry land facedown in a patch of mud.

CHAPTER 11

As Blaine's SUV approached Lake Shipshewana, he fought the urge to stop. The lake was home to native bass and had been named after the chief of a small group of Potawatomi Indians who had used the location for their main camp. It was one of his favorite places to fish, and today the air was crisp yet calm—perfect for fly-fishing. Blaine had seen it many times—those still waters mirroring the azure sky.

Growing up in Canada, where lakes and streams were plentiful, Blaine had developed his love of fishing. He had many fond memories of his parents loading up the family car with picnic foods and fishing poles and taking him and his brothers for a day of fishing. From the first time Blaine could remember going fishing, he was hooked. Fly fishing was his favorite, but any type of fishing provided solitude. Like a true sportsman with heightened senses, nothing went unnoticed.

Blaine made his own lures and had pretty good success with them because they mimicked natural bait. There was nothing like having a pan of fresh-caught trout or bass frying up for dinner. But most times, Blaine just enjoyed catching and releasing, using barbless hooks, so as not to injure the fish. It was the thrill of feeling that tug on his line, reeling it in, and seeing his catch up close. Then, watching as the released fish gave a quick shimmer of its scales before the water swallowed it up in its depths.

Pushing the control to roll down his window, Blaine drew in a deep breath of air. Soon he'd be at the entrance to the turnoff for the lake, and the idea of forgetting about going to Emma's grew more appealing. Would missing one class hurt?

"I'll bet the fish are biting this morning," he said aloud as he hit the button again to close the window. It wasn't fair that he had to go to the stupid class. If he wasn't worried that Stuart would find out, he'd skip it and go fly-fishing instead. But with his luck, Stuart would probably talk to Lamar or Emma this week, and the truth would come out. *I should have known better than to make that stupid bet.*

Blaine thought about the fishing gear in the back of his SUV. He kept it there most of the time so he could fish whenever he got the chance or was in the mood. *Maybe it wouldn't hurt if I stopped and fished for half an hour or so,* he told himself. *I doubt that I'd miss out on much if I arrived at the Millers' a little late.*

Bearing off the main road, Blaine turned his rig into the parking area and shut off the ignition. A few minutes sitting on the dock with his line in the water and he'd feel like a new man.

Terry clambered to his feet, embarrassed that he'd made a fool of himself in front of Cheryl. So much for trying to make a good impression. The worst of it was that he hadn't even caught the stupid goat!

"Are you all right?" Lamar and Cheryl called in unison, as they made their way over to Terry.

"I'm fine. Not hurt. Just dirty and feeling a bit defeated." Terry brushed at the mud on his jeans, wishing he hadn't let his ego get the best of him. "Guess I must look like a real mess."

"Don't worry about that. I appreciate your help. Why don't you go in the house and get cleaned up?" Lamar suggested.

"What about the goat?" Terry asked, unwilling to give up the chase. If he could capture the goat, it might impress Cheryl.

"There's no need for that; looks like Maggie's found her way back into the pen on her own." Lamar pointed to the goat pen, where Maggie scampered about with the other goats. "I just need to go close the gate."

When Lamar headed in that direction, Terry started for the house.

"Are you sure you're okay?" Cheryl asked, catching up with him when he reached the porch.

"Yeah, I'm fine. It's just a good thing my buddy Jan wasn't here to see me make a fool of myself. He'd probably never let me live it down."

"It was just an accident, and you were trying to help." Cheryl offered Terry a sympathetic smile.

He grinned while opening the door for her. Even though Cheryl rolled her eyes, trying to squeeze past him, and then tripped over his big feet, at least she'd seemed concerned about him. Maybe he was making some headway with the pretty blond after all.

As Carmen neared Shipshewana, her thoughts went back to supper at Paul's the night before. The meal was good, and she'd enjoyed getting to know Paul and Sophia better. This visit had been the best so far, being able to spend more time with her niece and not feeling like she had to rush off so quickly. The little girl had taken to Carmen right away and had spent most of the evening sitting on Carmen's lap, while Carmen read from one of Sophia's storybooks. When Paul said it was time for his daughter to go to bed, she'd cried and held her arms out to

Carmen. Then Carmen had helped Sophia change into her pajamas, and afterward, she read the child a bedtime story.

Carmen smiled, reflecting on how she and Paul had tucked Sophia into bed and then spent the rest of the evening drinking coffee, while Carmen shared stories about when she and Lorinda were girls. It was bittersweet, talking about her sister to Paul, and seeing the sad look on his face, but she thought in some way it had brought healing to both of them. Lorinda had been a special woman, and Carmen knew she would always miss her. She was sure that Paul would, too.

Pushing her thoughts aside, Carmen followed a horse and buggy up the Millers' driveway. It stopped near the barn, and Anna stepped down. *Great. This is the perfect time for me to talk to her.*

Carmen parked her rental car and got out. Then she hurried over to Anna, who walked slowly toward the house, head down and shoulders slumped.

"How was your week?" Carmen asked cheerfully.

Anna shrugged and kept walking.

"I noticed you didn't ride your bike today."

Anna motioned to the horse and buggy, pulling out of the driveway. "My dad brought me instead."

Carmen couldn't miss the look of discomfort on Anna's face. She was almost sure the young woman was dealing with some sort of problem.

"I was wondering if you'd like to go to lunch with me after class today," Carmen said as they stepped onto Emma's porch.

Anna's eyebrows arched. "You want to have lunch with me?"

"That's right. I'd like to get to know you better, and it's hard to visit during the quilting class." *At least the kind of visiting I want to do.*

Anna studied Carmen before answering. "That sounds nice, but I can't go to lunch today because Dad will be picking me up as soon as class is over."

"Maybe we can go some other time. Would you be available any time next week?"

Anna looked hesitant, but she finally nodded. "I'd like that. Could you meet me for lunch on Wednesday at Das Dutchman in Middlebury?"

Carmen knew exactly where that restaurant was because she'd had supper there a few nights ago. "Sure, that'd be fine. I'm looking forward to it."

"Me, too." Anna sighed. "Guess we'd better get in there, or they'll be starting the class without us. Not that I'd mind," she quickly added.

That's the second time she's said it, Carmen thought as they entered the house. *Anna Lambright does not want to be here. I hope I can get her to open up to me when we have lunch next week.*

CHAPTER 12

While Terry was in the bathroom cleaning up, Cheryl went to the quilting room to speak with Emma.

"How's my grandma's quilt coming along?" she asked.

"I'm sorry," Emma said, "but I've been busy this week and haven't had much time to work on the quilt. I'm sure I'll be able to get more sewing done on it next week, though," she quickly added.

Cheryl smiled. "I'll be anxious to see the quilt when it's done. And I can't wait to see the expression on Grandma's face when I give it to her."

"Tell me about your grandmother," Emma said, as Cheryl took a seat at the table. "Does she live near you?"

Cheryl shook her head. "Grandma lives in a nursing home in Portland, Oregon. It's not too far from my folks' house, but with Mom and Dad both working all day, they don't go to visit Grandma that often." Cheryl's eyes filled with unwanted tears, and she blinked to keep them from falling onto her cheeks. "I—I don't think Mom really cares that much."

Emma's eyes widened. "About your grandmother?"

Before Cheryl could respond, Terry entered the room and took a seat beside her. His face and hair were wet, and so were the knees of his jeans. Unfortunately, the scrubbing he'd done hadn't removed the odor of smoke from his clothes, but at least the mud was cleaned off.

"So what'd I miss?" Terry asked, leaning close to Cheryl.

Cheryl leaned away. "Nothing. Emma and I were just talking about my grandmother's quilt." She hated to be rude, but the smell of smoke on Terry's clothes made her feel sick.

"Okay. Okay. I can take a hint." Terry leaped out of his chair and found a seat on the other side of the table just as Carmen and Anna entered the room.

Cheryl was relieved when Anna sat on one side of her, but she wished Carmen had taken the seat on the other side instead of sitting at the end, next to Anna. She hoped Terry remained where he was, but when Selma showed up and sat beside her, she wasn't so sure about that. Last week Selma had criticized the way Cheryl held her scissors. Who knew what she might find fault with today?

A few minutes later, Lamar entered the room. "Maggie's back in her pen, and the gate's closed. Hopefully she won't figure out how to get it open," he said to Emma.

She smiled. "You know my Maggie. She's one schmaert little goat."

"Schmaert? What does that mean?" Terry asked.

"It's Pennsylvania Dutch for the word *smart*," Lamar replied.

"Oh, I see. So what's the opposite of schmaert?" Terry questioned.

"*Dumm*," Emma responded.

"That's interesting and all," Selma spoke up, "but we didn't come here to learn a new language. We came to make a quilted wall hanging."

"That's right," Emma agreed, "and we'll get started with today's lesson as soon as Blaine arrives."

Selma wrinkled her nose and grumbled, "Last week Anna came in late, and now Blaine's not here. Can't people be on time? It's inconsiderate when they show up late and make the rest of us wait."

"Have you been out to the phone shack to check for messages this morning?" Emma asked Lamar, ignoring Selma's comment. "Maybe there's one from Blaine, letting us know he won't be here or is running late for some reason."

"I haven't checked yet," Lamar said, "but I'll run out there now. You can begin teaching the class while I'm gone. If Blaine is coming, he can catch up when he gets here."

Emma and her husband are sure patient, Cheryl thought. *If I were teaching this class, I'd call Selma up short for being so rude.*

"I think we should wait to get started until Lamar returns and we know if there's a message from Blaine," Emma said facing the class.

"What are we supposed to do until then?" Selma asked with a look of agitation. "Sit and twiddle our thumbs?"

"Of course not," Emma said, watching Selma take supplies out of her mint-green tote bag. "We can visit and get to know each other a little better."

"Puh!" Selma swiped the air with her hand as if she was after a pesky fly. "I didn't come here to get to know anyone. I came to quilt!"

Emma was taken aback by Selma's rudeness. The poor woman was certainly not the friendly type. "As I said before, we'll begin as soon as Lamar returns from the phone shack." Emma looked over at Terry and smiled. "How was your week?"

"It went fine till I fell in the mud chasing your goat." He leaned his head back and chuckled. "Guess I got what I deserved, thinking I could run faster than that frisky critter."

"If it makes you feel any better, you're not the only one of my students who's gotten bested by Maggie. During my first quilting class, Maggie got out, and Blaine's friend Stuart thought he could catch her. He ended up on his face in the grass. Then your brother-in-law went out to help him," Emma added, looking at Carmen.

"I'm not surprised Paul would do something like that. From the things my sister used to tell me about Paul, he's always been one who likes to help out."

"Yes," Emma agreed. "Paul has many fine qualities, and he was good with Maggie. I never saw that goat react to anyone like she did Paul. She went to him when he held out a handful of grass and didn't resist when he guided her back to her pen. Some people have a special way with animals."

"Jan's good with his dog." Terry spoke up, "but I guess goats ain't my thing."

"No animal is *my* thing," Selma said, wrinkling her nose. "They're nothing but pests."

Feeling the need for a change of subject and wanting her students to get better acquainted, Emma suggested that they go around the table and share something about what they had done during the week. Cheryl, Carmen, and Selma willingly shared a few things, but when Emma asked Anna how her week had gone, she merely shrugged and mumbled, "Same as always."

I wish there was something I could say or do to make Anna open up, Emma thought. *She seems so sullen and withdrawn. Even though Selma's a bit opinionated, at least she's willing to talk.*

Emma was relieved when Lamar returned. "No message from Blaine," he said, "but there was one from my daughter, Katie. She strained her back and asked if I'd give her a ride to the chiropractor's.

It's Dr. Clark's day off, of course, but he kindly said he'd meet us there. Emma, can you manage okay while I take Katie?"

"I'll be fine." Emma patted Lamar's arm. "You go along and help your *dochder*."

"Danki, Emma. I'll see you later." Lamar said good-bye to the class and hurried from the room.

"Since we don't know when or if Blaine will be here, I suppose we'd best get started," Emma said, reaching for a piece of material that had been cut and was ready to sew. "Today we'll begin sewing the pieces of fabric you've already cut. You can take turns using the battery-operated sewing machines, and if anyone wants to try out my treadle machine just let me know and I'll show you how."

"I already know how to use a treadle," Selma announced. "My grandmother had one when I was a girl, and she taught me how to sew on it."

"That's good. Maybe you'd like to use mine today." Emma smiled. "Some of my Amish friends and relatives prefer to use the battery-operated machines or one that's hooked up to a generator, but I've always enjoyed using the treadle."

"My *mamm* uses a treadle machine when she sews, too," Anna said. "But I'm not interested in that."

"You can use one of my battery-operated ones," Emma said, glad that Anna was conversing a bit. Maybe after she'd done some sewing and saw how her wall hanging was taking shape, she'd actually enjoy the class.

"I'd like to try the treadle machine for a few of my patterned pieces," Carmen said.

"Same here," Cheryl agreed.

"Not me," Terry said with a shake of his head. "I'm not even sure I can use the battery-operated machine." He frowned. "I'll probably end up sewing my fingers together instead of the material."

"You'll do fine," Emma said. "I'll make sure of that."

Terry had been fumbling with his pieces of material for ten minutes when Blaine showed up.

"Sorry I'm late," Blaine apologized to Emma. "I stopped at the lake and ended up dropping my line in the water. Guess I sort of lost track of time."

"What do you mean, 'sort of'?" Terry pointed to the clock on the far wall. "You're forty-five minutes late!"

Blaine glanced briefly at the clock; then he smiled at Emma and said, "I caught a largemouth bass, and it's in a bucket on the porch. If you like fish, I'd be happy to give it to you."

Emma nodded. "Lamar and I both like fish, but don't feel obligated to give it to us."

"No, I want to," Blaine insisted. "Should I go out and get it or wait until after class?"

"Just wait until Emma's finished teaching the class," Selma interjected. "In case you haven't noticed, the others have already started sewing, so you'd better take a seat."

Terry looked over at Blaine and said, "You knew you had class today, didn't you?"

Blaine gave a nod. "Of course."

"Then you oughta get your priorities straight, instead of going fishing and showing up late." He plugged his nose. "Phew! No wonder you smell so fishy."

"It's better than reeking of smoke," Blaine countered. "Besides, if you want to catch anything, you have to go when the fish are biting.

And they sure were hungry today," he added. "I caught a bigger fish than the one I'm giving Emma, but it rolled just as I was about to net it, and off went the hook."

Emma was surprised at Blaine's change of mood, and how his face lit up when he talked about fishing. It was nice to see this side of his character, but while she hated to burst his bubble, she'd better do something quick, or these two men who were acting like boys might end up in a fight. It was becoming more obvious to Emma that some sort of duel was going on between Terry and Blaine. She was sure it had nothing to do with Terry's smoking or Blaine's fishing, and everything to do with a certain blond woman in her class.

"Here are the pieces of material you cut out last week," she said, handing them to Blaine. "All you need to do is pin them in place, and you can begin sewing."

Blaine shook his head. "I don't know anything about using a sewing machine."

"I'll show you how," Emma said.

As the others took turns at the sewing machines, Emma instructed Blaine on how to pin his pieces of material together before sewing them. Once she was sure he could handle things on his own, she went to the kitchen to get some refreshments.

She'd just placed some banana bread on a platter, when her nine-year-old granddaughter, Lisa, who lived next door, rushed into the kitchen. "Mama wants to know if you have any *zucker* she can borrow," she told Emma. "We're gonna bake some chocolate-chip *kichlin*, but we don't got enough zucker."

"Of course you can borrow some sugar." Emma lovingly patted Lisa's head, then went to the cupboard and took down the plastic container she kept her sugar in.

"Did you do some baking this morning?" Lisa asked, pointing to the banana bread.

"I made it yesterday," Emma explained. "I'm getting ready to serve it to my quilting students."

Lisa grinned. "Are you gonna teach me how to quilt someday?"

"Of course. Unless your mamm decides she'd rather teach you."

Lisa shook her head. "I'd rather you teach me, *Grossmammi*. You're the bestest quilter in Shipshe."

Emma chuckled. It was nice to know her granddaughter felt that way, but she was sure others could quilt equally well. "I'd better get back to my students now, and you'd better go home. You'll never get any cookies baked if we keep gabbing." She handed the sugar to Lisa, then bent down and kissed her cheek. "I'll see you later this evening when Lamar and I come over for supper."

Lisa nodded and skipped out the door.

Emma was about to carry the tray of banana bread to the other room, when Carmen entered the kitchen. "I came to see if you needed any help," she said.

Emma handed the tray to Carmen. "You can take this into the quilting room, while I get some coffee and mugs."

"Okay." Carmen paused near the kitchen door. "I've been wondering about something, Emma."

"What's that?"

"Since I've been in the area I've heard some things, and one of them is that all Amish young people go through a time of running-around after they finish the eighth grade and are done with their formal schooling."

"That's right. It's called rumschpringe."

"That's what I thought; although I can't pronounce it correctly." Carmen shifted the tray in her hands. "What can you tell me about—"

"I came to tell you that Selma doesn't want any coffee," Lamar said, entering the room. "She said she'd prefer a cup of tea."

"Oh good, you're back. How'd Katie's chiropractic appointment go?"

"It went fine. She's home resting now with an ice pack."

"That's good. Now about Selma's request. . . Did she say what kind of tea she wanted?"

Lamar shook his head. "But to be on the safe side, maybe you should give her a cup of hot water and offer a choice of tea bags."

"That's a good idea." Emma looked at Carmen. "What was it you were about to ask before Lamar came in?"

"It was nothing important. I'll talk to you about it some other time." Carmen hurried from the room.

"Have things gone any better with the class today?" Lamar asked, reaching into the cupboard to get the tin filled with tea bags.

Emma sighed. "Not really. There seems to be some undercurrent going on between Terry and Blaine, and Selma's still a bit overbearing. Then there's Anna. I can't seem to get through to her, Lamar."

"Just give it more time. I'm sure things will improve. This is only the second class." He gave her arm a loving pat. "Remember how it went with your first class, Emma?"

"Jah. It was a bit rocky at first, but as time went on things got better."

"And so they shall again. Just remember to ask God for guidance."

"Yeow!" Blaine hollered. "I stuck my finger with a pin!"

Cheryl reached for her purse. "I have a bandage if you need one."

"Yeah, that'd be good." Blaine smiled at Cheryl in a way that nearly made Terry gag.

Terry rolled his eyes. *I'll bet he did that on purpose, just to get some attention.*

"You need to be careful with pins," Cheryl said as she put the bandage on Blaine's finger.

"I know that now." Blaine pointed to the pieces of material he'd already sewn. "I'm no better at sewing than pinning. Look how crooked my stitches are."

"They're not that bad," Cheryl said, leaning closer to Blaine. "It just takes a little practice to get the hang of it."

Hearing the conversation between the two of them was almost Terry's undoing. It was irritating watching how comfortable Cheryl seemed with this guy who smelled like fish. *I wonder if Cheryl's interested in him. If so, could the feeling be mutual? And Blaine—just look at him.* Terry had noticed before that Blaine didn't make eye contact with anyone much, but he sure wasn't having trouble looking into Cheryl's beautiful, doe-like eyes. The worst part of it was she was looking back.

She does seem to be better suited to him than me. Of course, opposites are supposed to attract, so there might still be some hope, Terry told himself. *If I could just get her to go out with me, maybe she'd see that I'm not half-bad. The biggest problem I see is that I smoke, and since Cheryl's allergic to smoke, that's a strike against me. There's only one thing to do,* he decided, reaching for a piece of banana bread. *I need to quit smoking. But can I do it?*

CHAPTER 13

Elkhart

Would you say that again?" Jan asked as he and Terry headed to a job on Monday morning. "I think I might've been hearing things."

"You heard me. I'm gonna quit smoking."

Jan quirked an eyebrow. "Oh yeah? What made you decide that?"

"Cheryl's allergic to smoke," Terry replied, trying to sound nonchalant. "Don't think she'll ever go out with me if I smell like smoke. Besides, as you've pointed out many times, it's bad for my health."

"Funny, but you've never worried about that before." Jan's deep laughter bounced off the roof of his truck. "Boy you must really have it bad!"

"What do you mean?"

"All the times I've tried to get you to quit, and you've just ignored me."

"That's 'cause I wasn't ready," Terry retorted.

"So you meet some gorgeous blond who you'll probably only date once or twice before you dump her, and suddenly you're ready to throw away your cigarettes? I'll have to see that to believe it."

"You can laugh all you want, but I will quit smoking, and if Cheryl agrees to go out with me, I'm sure I'll wanna date her more than a few times."

"You sound pretty confident. Have you even tried asking her out?"

"No, but I will. . . Next Saturday, in fact."

"And when are you planning to quit smoking?" Jan pointed to the pack of cigarettes in Terry's shirt pocket. "I see you're still toting them around."

"I'll quit as soon as I've smoked my last cigarette."

"When will that be?"

"When I've emptied this pack," Terry said, pulling out a cigarette and lighting up.

"Well, you'd better smoke it up quick then, 'cause there's only four weeks left before your quilt classes end, and that don't leave you much time to win Cheryl over."

"I can do it," Terry said with a vigorous nod. "Just wait and see. Besides, I'll bet I can quit smoking before you get this dirty truck cleaned out."

Jan grunted. "I'd be more worried about your smoking habit than my truck. And you know what?"

"What's that?"

"I think you oughta stop right now, so you have some time to get the smell outta your clothes. I mean, why wait around? If you expect Cheryl to take notice of you, then you oughta get right on it."

"I don't know." Terry scratched his head. "It's not gonna be easy."

"Maybe God wants you to quit. Did you ever think of that?" Jan elbowed Terry in the ribs. "I've invited you to attend church with me and Star many times, but you always come up with some sort of excuse.

Maybe if you sat in church once in a while and let God into your life, you'd have the strength and willpower it takes to quit smoking."

"I'll give it some thought," Terry said, blowing smoke out of his mouth and breathing it back up his nose.

———◇———

Goshen

Cheryl had no more than taken a seat at her desk when the phone rang. "Edwards' Law Firm," she said after she'd picked up the receiver.

"Hey, Cheryl, it's me, Lance."

"Why are you calling me here at work?" Cheryl asked with irritation. She didn't know why her ex-boyfriend would call her at all, much less at her place of employment. She didn't want Mr. Edwards to think she was using the office phone for personal use. He probably wouldn't appreciate it.

"I tried your cell number but all I got was your voice mail," Lance said.

Cheryl reached into her purse and realized that she'd left her cell phone at home. "What do you want, Lance? I have a lot of work staring me in the face and don't have time to talk."

"I won't keep you long, but April's birthday is next week, and I need a suggestion as to what I should buy her."

Cheryl tapped her fingernails on the desk. "Why ask me?"

"You and April used to be good friends—college roommates, in fact. So if anyone should know her likes and dislikes it ought to be you."

"You're the one spending time with her now. April and I don't see each other anymore, so you should be able to figure it out on your own." Cheryl clenched her teeth, struggling to keep her emotions in check.

"I know that, but you used to be best friends, so I thought—"

"Well, you thought wrong. April's your girlfriend, so figure it out.

428

And please, stop calling me!" Cheryl hung up the phone before Lance could say anything more. It was bad enough that he'd dumped her for April. Did he have to rub it in her face?

She grabbed the morning's mail and thumbed through it, anxious to get her mind on something else. As a Christian, Cheryl knew she needed to forgive April and Lance, but with him calling her like this, it was hard to control her temper. Whenever Lance called, it felt like someone had poured salt into her wound. Just when Cheryl thought she was over Lance's rejection and April's betrayal, he'd call again, wanting to know something about April so he could make a good impression.

What was that verse Ruby Lee told me about? Oh yes, "I can do all things through Christ. . . ." I surely ought to be able to take control of my emotions and not get so angry like this. Maybe I should talk to Ruby Lee or Pastor Gene about it.

Middlebury

When Anna arrived at work Monday morning, the first thing she did was boot up the computer to check for e-mails from any of their English customers, who often placed their orders online.

After she'd taken care of that, since no one but her was in the office, she decided to surf the Internet and check out some sites that sold English women's clothes. She was fascinated with the bright colors, fancy scarves, pretty blouses, slacks, and jewelry. One of these days when she went shopping in Goshen, she planned to try on some English clothes. A few of Anna's friends like Mandy, who hadn't yet joined the church, dressed in English clothes whenever they were away from home and out having fun. Anna spent most of her time at work and didn't have much free time to spend away from home, so she hadn't been able to do all the fun things her friends did since they'd gotten out of school.

At least I can look at pretty things online, she mused, admiring a fancy pair of women's platform shoes. The shoes featured suede and tweed uppers, dotted suede details at the heel, and a vintage-looking bow. "Those are amazing," Anna murmured. *Of course I probably wouldn't be able to walk in them without falling over. It'd be fun to try, though.*

Anna had taught herself how to use the online search options, and the more she used the computer, the more fascinated she became. She was amazed at the information available by simply typing in a word or two in the search window. She could visit places she'd only dreamed about, see clothes she longed to wear, and take part in some chat rooms, where she could converse with others outside the scope of her Amish community. Since the computer was in a separate room, away from where the windows were made, Anna used it for her own enjoyment whenever no one else was around. If a customer came in, she could easily minimize whatever page she'd been looking at. And she could usually hear Dad's footsteps when he was approaching the office, so there was time to click out of whatever site she'd been exploring before he discovered what she was up to.

Anna wished she could have a computer at home, but of course that was against their church's rules. And it wasn't bad enough that the church had rules. Mom and Dad had their own set of regulations, which was why Anna felt like a little girl so much of the time. If only they'd give her the chance to explore the English world, she might not feel so frustrated.

"Anna, what are you doing?"

Anna jumped and tried to downsize the website she'd been on. In the process, the mouse flew right off the desk, as Dad's booming voice echoed in her ear.

"*Ach,* Dad, you scared me! I—I didn't hear you come in. I thought you were in the other room."

"I was, but I'm here now, and I don't like what I see!" His finger shook as he pointed at the computer. "I was afraid when I bought that thing that it'd be a temptation for you. Guess I was right because I see that you're looking at fancy English shoes." His forehead creased as he looked at her sternly. "What's it gonna take before you become trustworthy, Anna? You hang around with Mandy even though we don't approve, you've made excuses for not going to church, and now this? I can't believe you, Anna."

Anna dropped her gaze to the floor. "I'm sorry, Dad. I just wanted to see—"

"I know what you wanted to see. You have worldly ways on your mind, and this is not a good thing. I think it'd be best if you let me manage the orders and e-mails from customers from now on. You can work in the back on windows."

"But Dad. . ."

"No buts, Anna. I will not have you, or any of my other *kinner*, using the computer to look at fancy things!" Dad pointed to the other room. "Now go in there and ask your uncle Sam what you can do to help."

Tears welled in Anna's eyes. If she couldn't use the computer anymore, she'd be miserable. It was the only thing she had to look forward to at work every day. She needed to find another job. It was the only way she would be free from so many rules.

Anna squeezed her fingers tightly together. *If Mom and Dad would stop treating me like a child and let me make my own choices, I might not be so interested in fancy things.*

CHAPTER 14

Shipshewana

On Wednesday, shortly before noon, Selma decided to rake the leaves that had fallen from the trees in her front yard. She'd had a late breakfast and wasn't ready to eat lunch, so this seemed like a good time to tackle the job.

When John was still alive, he'd always kept the yard cleaned up, while Selma concentrated on her flower and vegetable gardens. Now the burden of everything fell on her shoulders. It was a lot of work, but she enjoyed being outside, which at least made the time go by quickly.

Selma went to the shed and got out the rake. Then, pushing her floppy-brimmed hat off her forehead a bit, she went right to work. She'd been raking for about thirty minutes when she spotted her neighbor, Frances Porter, who lived across the street, and noticed that she was also raking leaves. Frances was in her forties and worked from home, decorating cakes. Her husband, Earl, was a sales representative for a pharmaceutical company, so he was on the road a lot, leaving many of the chores to Frances and their twelve-year-old daughter, Gretchen. Frances didn't complain, though, at least not to Selma. Of course, most of the neighbors said very little to Selma, unless she spoke to them first.

After Selma had worked her way to the edge of the lawn with her rake, she hollered across the street, "I hope you've insulated your roses against the cold weather we'll soon be having. Some of those leaves in your yard would work well for that."

Frances waved but gave no response. Was she avoiding Selma, or just too busy to talk?

"Humph!" Selma grumbled. "Wouldn't you think she'd have the decency to say she appreciated my suggestion?"

Selma turned aside and continued raking the rest of the leaves. When she was done, she put the rake back in the shed and headed for the house to fix lunch. She'd worked up a hearty appetite, and the thought of that ham sandwich she planned to make sounded pretty good about now.

She'd just started up the porch steps when she spotted that same mangy-looking gray cat she'd chased away the other day, sitting on her porch near the door.

Selma stomped her feet and clapped her hands. "Go on now! Shoo! Shoo!"

The cat tipped its head to one side and let out a loud, *Meow!*

"Don't think you can soft-soap me into feeding you," Selma said, shaking her finger at the cat. "I give out free lunches to no one—least of all to a flea-bitten feline like you!"

Selma reached for the broom she kept near the door, but before she could pick it up, the cat took off like it had been shot out of a cannon.

"Good riddance," Selma muttered as she hurried into the house. "I hope I've scared you enough that you'll never come back here again!"

Mishawaka

Blaine was just getting ready to take his lunch break, when he caught sight of his ex-girlfriend Sue heading his way. *Oh great*, he thought. *I wonder what she wants.*

Sue stepped up to Blaine and touched his arm. "Hi. How are you?"

"Do you really care, or are you just being polite?" he muttered, hoping none of the employees had heard him. The last thing he needed was for word to get out that he'd been rude to a customer. Stuart might be his friend outside of work, but here in the store, all employees were treated equally—and that meant being courteous to every customer.

"Of course I care. We're still friends, right?" she asked, looking up at him with an innocent smile.

"Yeah, sure. Now what can I help you with?" Blaine asked, trying to ignore his rapid heartbeat. Looking at Sue's soft brown eyes and curly auburn hair made him miss what they'd once had together. And it hadn't helped when she'd touched him, either.

"I came to buy a present for my grandfather," Sue replied. "His birthday is next week."

Blaine made a sweeping gesture. "As I'm sure you can see, there are lots of things to choose from here in the store, so why don't you browse around for a while?"

"I was hoping you'd have some suggestions, since you and Grandpa both like to fish."

Blaine's stomach knotted. He'd been convinced that Sue was the right woman for him, and now. . . Well, he just needed to get over her and move on with his life, because there was no point in moping about their breakup and letting it consume him.

"What exactly did you want to get your grandfather?" Blaine questioned.

"I don't know. That's why I asked for your help."

"How about a hunting vest, a hat, or a new fishing pole?" he suggested.

"Maybe. Let's look at those things, and then I'll decide."

"I really don't have time to show you everything," Blaine said, struggling to remain patient. Didn't Sue realize how hard it was for him to be with her? Didn't she care how badly she'd broken his heart by not agreeing to marry him?

She sighed. "Well then, if you'll point me in the right direction, I'll go look for myself."

Blaine showed Sue the sections of the store where she could find the items and then said good-bye and hurried off in the direction of the break room.

When he stepped inside, he saw Stuart sitting at one of the tables with a cup of coffee and a doughnut. It didn't take Stuart long to spot Blaine and wave him over.

"How's it going?" Stuart asked when Blaine took a seat beside him. "You look a little harried right now."

"I'm a lot more than harried; I'm upset." Blaine took a handkerchief from his pocket and wiped his sweaty brow.

"How come?"

Blaine explained about Sue coming into the store and asking his help in choosing a gift for her grandfather. "Wouldn't you think after our breakup that she'd find somewhere else to shop?" he grumbled.

Stuart frowned. "You want to send our customers elsewhere?"

"Just Sue. I wish she'd find a job in some other part of the country so I'd never have to see her again. It's too painful, not to mention a reminder that I must have done something wrong because our relationship failed."

"You didn't do anything wrong."

"Yeah, well, something sure went haywire, or she wouldn't have broken up with me."

"Want to know what I think?" Stuart asked, placing his hand on Blaine's shoulder.

"What's that?"

"You ought to start dating again. It would help get your mind off Sue, and you'd probably smile more often, too."

"I might consider that if there was someone I wanted to ask out."

"What about the pretty little blond you mentioned who's taking Emma's quilt class with you?" Stuart asked. "Didn't you say she was single?"

Blaine nodded. "I'm not sure she'd be interested in going out with me. Besides, I don't know her that well, and we may not have anything in common."

Stuart thumped Blaine's shoulder a couple of times. "There's only one way to find out—ask her out."

"Where would we go?"

"Use your imagination. Take her out to dinner, to the movies, or go bowling. She's bound to like one of those things. And who knows— maybe she's the type who likes to go fishing, the way you and Sue used to do." Stuart took a drink of his coffee. "If you hit it off, she could end up becoming Mrs. Blaine Vickers, and then you can stop worrying about your brothers having families and not you."

Blaine reached for a cup of coffee, savoring the aroma as he lifted it to his lips. "I'll give it some thought."

* * *

Middlebury

Carmen had just entered Das Dutchman restaurant Wednesday afternoon when she spotted Anna near the door. She smiled and touched Anna's arm. "I'm glad you could meet me here today."

"Me, too."

After their hostess seated them at a table along one wall, Anna leaned close to Carmen and whispered, "I'm in big trouble with my dad right now, so I wasn't sure I could meet you at all."

Carmen's ears perked up. "How come you're in trouble?"

Anna proceeded to tell how she'd been caught surfing the Internet and was made to work on windows instead of greeting customers and taking care of orders in the office. "I'm gonna look for a new job," she added.

"What kind of work would you like to do?" Carmen asked.

Anna shrugged. "I'm not sure. I've worked in the window shop ever since I graduated from eighth grade, so I don't really know how to do much else."

Carmen's mouth dropped open. "You didn't go to high school?"

Anna shook her head. "Amish children only get an eighth-grade education."

Carmen wasn't sure how she missed this basic fact, so she decided to question Anna about rumschpringe, asking what it was like to run around with her friends and experience the English world.

"My folks don't approve of most of my friends—especially Mandy Zimmerman—but I still see her whenever I can." Anna sighed. "I can't help but wonder what it'd be like to wear an English dress or a pair of blue jeans, like some of my friends do when they're not at home."

"I saw a little dress shop near the hotel on this property," Carmen said. "Would you like to go there when we're done eating lunch?"

"I wish I could," Anna said wistfully, "but Dad will expect me to be back from lunch by one, so there's no time to look at clothes."

"Maybe we could go on Saturday when we're finished with the

quilting class. Would you be free to do some shopping then?" Carmen asked.

"I–I'm not sure. Maybe, if my dad doesn't take me to Emma's again. Sometimes I feel like running away and never coming back. My parents control my whole life."

Carmen could see by Anna's anxious expression that she wasn't happy. Could her parents be holding such a tight rein on her that she was on the verge of rebellion? Carmen looked forward to visiting with Anna again and getting additional information for the story she planned to write. Maybe there was more to this rumschpringe thing than most people knew about. If so, she planned to find out as much as she possibly could.

Goshen

As Jan directed his truck into town, Terry reached into his pocket and pulled out a cigarette.

"I see you're still smoking," Jan said, looking at Terry with disgust. "I figured you wouldn't be able to hack it."

Terry lit the cigarette and blew the smoke out the open window. "Hey, man, get off my case! I'm doing the best I can with this."

"I don't call blowing smoke out the window doing your best. If you ask me, the only way to quit is to go cold turkey."

"I tried that already. It didn't work. I got shaky, and I couldn't think straight. I just need to taper off."

"Why don't ya try taking only one drag of smoke each time you reach for a cigarette, and then put it out? Maybe that one drag would satisfy you till the next one."

"Guess I could try that, but I don't know. This is harder than I thought."

"It's gonna take you a lot longer to quit if you try to do it with that attitude." Jan reached into his pocket and pulled out a pack of gum. "Here, chew one of these. If you don't quit smoking, your teeth and fingertips will turn yellow."

Terry grunted. "Like gum's gonna take away my craving. It'll probably end up giving me cavities."

"It's sugarless, and it might help you quit smoking. That's what got me over the hump when I used to smoke."

Terry's eyes widened. "When was that? I've never known you to smoke."

"Started when I was sixteen, but I quit before Star was born. I didn't want my little girl breathing any secondhand smoke. That all happened way before I met you."

"But you said Star was less than a year old when her mom ran off with her. I'm surprised you didn't start smoking again after that."

"I was tempted to—many times. But I figured it was a nasty habit, and I hoped Bunny would come to her senses and return to me, so I never went back to smoking."

Terry knew that Bunny was the nickname Jan had given Nancy, his ex-girlfriend. "Guess you've got more willpower than I do," Terry said. "But I'm gonna lick this thing, just wait and see." He popped a piece of gum in his mouth and handed the package back to Jan.

"What are you gonna do if you're still smoking by Saturday?" Jan asked as he turned his truck into the parking lot of the Wal-Mart store in Goshen.

Terry shrugged. "I don't know. Guess I'll chew plenty of breath mints and wear some cologne so I don't smell like smoke." He glanced out the window. "Why are we stopping here?"

"Star's working today, and I want to stop and say hello. You wanna go in with me?"

"Naw. I'll wait for you here. Tell Star I said hi, though."

"Will do." Jan turned off the ignition and hopped out of the truck. "I'll be back soon."

Terry leaned his head back and sat with his eyes closed, thinking about Cheryl and fighting the urge to smoke. Feeling more edgy by the minute, he finally opened his eyes and lit up, making sure to keep his window rolled down so the smoke would blow out. Maybe he wouldn't be able to quit smoking. Maybe he was stupid thinking he could get Cheryl to go out with him. It might be best just to forget the whole thing; then he wouldn't have to take any more quilting lessons. But if he did that, he'd be admitting defeat, and he'd never been a quitter.

"Nope," he muttered, snuffing out the cigarette. "I'm gonna snag a date with Cheryl, and I'll do whatever I need to do in order to make it happen."

CHAPTER 15

I appreciate your taking the time to see me on such short notice," Cheryl said when she entered Ruby Lee and Gene's house Friday evening.

Ruby Lee gave Cheryl a hug. "We had no other plans this evening, and we're always happy to have a visit from any of our parishioners."

"You have a lovely home," Cheryl said, glancing around the cozy but spacious living room. "These hardwood floors are beautiful, and it would be hard to draw me away from those cozy-looking window seats. I don't think I'd get much done, wanting to watch outside all the time."

"We've lived here almost two years, but it still feels new to us." Ruby Lee laughed. "Maybe that's because we lived in a church-owned parsonage for so many years and waited a long time to have a home of our own. About the only thing I've never really gotten used to is the dog next door. He seems to bark at anything that moves—especially the scampering squirrels."

Cheryl sighed. "Where I grew up, outside of Portland, Oregon, my parents had a big backyard, and we were always watching some sort of animal or bird that ventured onto our property. We had squirrels and birds at the feeders my dad built, and occasionally we'd see some deer come out of the woods adjoining our place. They liked to nibble on the shrubbery and grass in the yard."

"That sounds nice, Cheryl," Ruby Lee said as they both went to the window. "Time stands still when I stop to watch the birds at our feeders. The activity there is ongoing." She smiled at Cheryl. "Are there a lot of different birds in Oregon?"

"Oh yes. We have several species, much like you have here. Grandma used to make her own suet, and we'd hang it out during the winter months. The downy woodpeckers and northern flickers loved it." Cheryl pointed to Ruby Lee's backyard. "We have goldfinches, too, like those on your thistle feeders. Some of the birds that came into our yard stayed all year. Other birds came only at certain times of the year. Also, there's a place called the Oaks Bottom Wildlife Refuge, which is about ten minutes from our home. When I was a girl, Grandma and I used to walk the trails there, and we often saw great blue herons and egrets in the small lake and wetlands there. Sometimes we'd even catch a glimpse of a bald eagle flying overhead." Cheryl laughed. "I guess you can tell I could go on and on about the subject of birds and other wildlife."

"I think you and I have a lot in common," Ruby Lee said, lightly tapping Cheryl's arm. "But I guess we'd better get to the reason for your visit this evening." She motioned to the adjoining room. "Gene's in his study. Should we go in there to talk, or would you prefer that he come out here?"

"We can go in there," Cheryl said.

Ruby Lee led the way, and when they entered Gene's study, he turned off his computer and motioned for them to sit down.

"It's good to see you, Ms. Halverson. How are you doing?"

"Please, call me Cheryl." She cleared her throat a couple of times. "To tell you the truth, Pastor Gene, I'm not doing so well."

"What seems to be the problem?"

Cheryl explained her situation with Lance and April and ended by saying that she was still angry and hadn't forgiven them. "I know as a Christian I shouldn't feel this way, but with Lance calling me to ask questions about April, I'm having a hard time dealing with things. I feel like telling him to go jump in a lake. And if I never saw Lance or April again, it would be fine with me. I often find myself wishing I could do something to get even—make them pay for what they did to me."

Gene reached for his Bible, and after thumbing through several pages, he read, " 'Be ye angry and sin not: let not the sun go down upon your wrath.' That's Ephesians 4:26." He flipped back to the Old Testament. "Proverbs 15:1 says: 'A soft answer turneth away wrath: but grievous words stir up anger.'" He closed the Bible and looked directly at Cheryl. "It's our human nature to feel angry sometimes. People hurt us, injustices are done, and sin runs rampant in our world. But it's important to remember not to let our anger consume us or cause us to do something we'll later regret." He paused and laced his fingers together, leaning slightly forward with his elbows on his desk. "Would getting even bring you happiness or change what happened between you and Lance?"

Cheryl shook her head as she swiped at the tears rolling down her cheeks. "No, but I can't forgive their betrayal."

Ruby Lee, who had been sitting quietly beside Cheryl, patted Cheryl's arm. "It's important that we forgive those who have wronged us. Only then will your heart begin to heal."

"My wife's right," Pastor Gene put in. "In Matthew 6:14 we are told: 'If ye forgive men their trespasses, your heavenly Father will also forgive you.'"

Cheryl let Ruby Lee's and the pastor's words sink in. When she felt ready, she said, "You're right, I do need to forgive Lance and April. I also need to ask God to forgive me for the anger and bitterness I've been harboring toward them. If I don't, I know it will destroy my Christian testimony."

"Remember one thing," Ruby Lee said, clasping Cheryl's hand. "You don't have to condone what Lance and April did to you, and you certainly don't have to accept Lance's phone calls. But for complete healing, you may need to let them both know, perhaps through a letter or an e-mail, that you've forgiven them."

"That won't be easy," Cheryl admitted, "but with God's help, I think I can do it."

"There's one more thing I'd like to say before we pray with you," Ruby Lee said.

"What's that?"

"Don't be afraid to begin dating again. Not all men will treat you the way Lance did. When you find the right one, you'll know it. Just make sure he has the same moral values as you."

Cheryl smiled, glad that she'd come here tonight. "Thanks, Ruby Lee, I'll remember that. And thank you, Pastor Gene, for the scripture you shared."

Elkhart

"It's been a long time since I've had pizza," Carmen said, smiling across the table at Paul and Sophia. "Thanks for inviting me to join you tonight."

Paul's eyes twinkled as he tucked a napkin under his daughter's chin. "Once Sophia had her first taste of pizza, coming here to the pizza place became a weekly occurrence. Of course, the fact that her daddy would rather not cook every night played a small role in it, too," he added with a grin.

Carmen laughed and reached for her glass of iced tea, watching Sophia in her high chair, wearing a flowered bib, as she picked the pepperoni off the pizza and ate it first. Her face was a mess, but she was obviously enjoying herself. It was great getting to know Paul, and spending time with his daughter made it that much sweeter. Carmen liked it here in northern Indiana, too. It was different from Los Angeles, with its endless traffic and people rushing about.

"Are you still enjoying the quilt classes you're taking?" Paul asked.

Carmen nodded. "I'm anxious to see how my wall hanging turns out."

"I'm sure it'll be fine. With Emma and Lamar's guidance, I don't think anybody ever leaves one of their classes with a wall hanging they don't like. You'll never meet two nicer people than those good folks, not to mention having the opportunity of making new friends during the course of the six weeks."

"I hope that's the case for me."

"So besides the quilt class last Saturday, what else have you done this week?" Paul asked.

"Oh, I drove around the area, took some pictures, checked out some of the Amish-run stores, and had lunch with Anna Lambright on Wednesday." No way was Carmen going to admit her reason for doing those things.

"Isn't Anna the young Amish woman who's also in Emma's quilt class?" Paul questioned.

Carmen nodded.

"It's nice that you're getting to know some of the others in your class, but I'm surprised it would be the Amish woman and not Cheryl, because it seems like she would have more in common with you than Anna."

"Maybe so, but I'm fascinated with the Amish culture and have enjoyed spending time with Anna." Carmen cringed. Could Paul be on to her? Had he somehow guessed that she planned to write an article about the Amish?

Paul nodded. "You're right; the Amish way of life is fascinating. I think we could learn a lot from the Plain People, and I'm impressed by the way they put God first and care so much for their families."

Carmen reached over and gave Sophia's chubby little leg a gentle squeeze. "I think this little girl is pretty high on her daddy's list." She smiled at Paul. "You're doing a good job raising her. I know Lorinda would be pleased."

Paul sighed. "I hope so. I tend to worry about Sophia, and sometimes I'm a bit overprotective. I often wonder if Lorinda is looking down from heaven and shaking her head when she sees some of the blunders I've made." He chuckled. "Once when I was in a hurry, I tossed Sophia's disposable diaper in the bathroom sink, thinking I'd remember to throw it away after her bath, but I forgot and left it there. The first one to find it was my niece, Lila, who was seven at the time. She and her family had dropped by to visit, and Lila asked to use the bathroom." Paul wrinkled his nose. "Needless to say, my sister, Maria, razzed me about that one."

Carmen chuckled. "We all make silly mistakes."

"True enough, and I've made more than my share." Paul tweaked the end of his daughter's nose. "Isn't that right my little *niña?*"

Sophia giggled and grabbed Paul's thumb.

Carmen smiled. She'd never imagined spending time with Paul and Sophia could be so much fun. And to think, it wouldn't have happened if her boss hadn't sent her on an assignment.

A chill went up Carmen's spine. *I can't let Paul find out why I came.*

He'd never forgive me if he knew I planned to write a negative story about his Amish friends. Sometimes I wonder if I'm doing the right thing. How would I like it if someone were to write a not-so-nice article about my family and our way of life?

Chapter 16

Middlebury

On Saturday morning, Anna was almost out the door, when she remembered that she planned to go shopping with Carmen after the quilting class. "Uh, Mom," she said, poking her head through the kitchen doorway, "I wanted you to know that I'll be a little late getting home this afternoon."

"Why is that?" Mom asked, looking up from where she sat at the table, drinking a cup of tea.

"I want to do some shopping," Ann replied.

"How come?"

Anna grimaced. *Why can't Mom just say, "Oh, all right, have a good time," instead of making me explain everything all the time? Now I have to give some kind of explanation.*

"Mom, will you please fix my hair? A piece of it's sticking out the back of my head covering," Anna's sister Arie said, stepping into the room and rushing over to Mom.

Anna took advantage of the interruption and slipped quickly out the door, relieved that she didn't have to offer her mother an explanation. She was anxious to see Carmen again, but they couldn't go shopping in Shipshewana, where Anna could easily be seen by someone she knew.

Shipshewana

Terry's hands shook as he climbed into his truck and turned on the ignition. He hadn't had a cigarette since yesterday morning, and he struggled with the temptation. Besides being shaky and irritable, he'd had a hard time sleeping last night. What he wouldn't give for a smoke to take the edge off. He'd made sure to use mouthwash and splash on some cologne this morning, hoping to erase any telltale signs of cigarette smoke from the day before. He'd even dressed a little nicer today, choosing some khaki slacks and a beige button-down shirt, instead of his usual jeans and T-shirt. If all went well, he planned to ask Cheryl if she'd go bowling with him tonight.

"Maybe it wouldn't hurt if I just took one drag," Terry said aloud, as though trying to convince himself that it was okay. He opened the glove compartment and removed a pack of cigarettes, then fished around and found a book of matches under an assortment of maps and other things that had been jammed in there. At least his truck wasn't as filthy as Jan's. It just needed a little reorganizing. Terry's rig was old, but he kept it halfway tidy on the inside, and tried to keep the outside clean, too.

Striking the match, and then lighting the cigarette, he sat there awhile, letting the engine idle as he took a drag.

Ahhh. . .that sure feels good. Terry inhaled the air of the cab as it filled with more smoke. Feeling kind of drowsy, he leaned his head against the window and closed his eyes, hoping his urge for a cigarette would ease.

Suddenly, Terry's eyes snapped open. There was a different kind of smoke filling the inside of his truck now. "Oh no!" Terry hollered, turning off the engine and looking down at the seat. A thin pillar of smoke spiraled up from where the smooth vinyl once was. In its place was a hole the size of a quarter, darkened around the edges from the hot ashes still burning in the stuffing of the truck's seat.

Immediately, Terry unbuckled his seat belt, spotted a half-full water bottle that he'd left in the truck, and dumped the water onto the smoldering seat. It did the trick. "Guess that's what I get for taking a drag," he mumbled, rubbing his hand over the gaping hole. Looking at his cigarette pack, he was tempted to throw it out the window. But that would be littering, and with his luck, a cop would probably see him do it, and he'd end up with a fine. He'd toss the cigarettes as soon as he found a garbage can.

"Can't believe this happened," he muttered. Now he'd either have to get the seat re-covered or have the whole thing replaced. Not only that, but he probably smelled like the dickens, too. He really did need to quit smoking.

Terry got out of the truck and walked around for a bit, hoping the fresh air would get rid of the smoky aroma that might be lingering on his clothes.

Getting back into his truck, and sniffing the arm of his shirt, Terry knew if he didn't get going, he'd be late for class. The last thing he wanted was a tongue-lashing from Selma, like she'd given Blaine last week when he'd walked in late. "Well, here goes nothing," Terry said, pulling out into traffic as he popped a piece of peppermint gum in his mouth.

———

Selma peered into her canvas satchel, checking to make sure she had everything she'd need for the quilting class today. Scissors, seam ripper, tape measure, thread, pins, needles, and thimble. Yes, it was all there. Of course, Emma had each of those items available for her students to use, but Selma preferred her own things. She'd ever thought about bringing her portable sewing machine along but knew that wasn't possible since Emma had no electricity in her home. Besides, last week Selma had used Emma's old treadle, and she'd enjoyed the sense of nostalgia from days when her grandmother was alive.

Emma had told them that this week they'd continue to sew the pieces they'd cut out the previous week. Selma looked forward to seeing the wall hanging take shape and couldn't wait for its completion. There was a sense of gratification that came from sewing, just as there was with floral arranging. Selma sometimes missed her position at the flower shop she used to manage, but continuing to work with flowers at home since her retirement three years ago had helped fill the void. Most of the bouquets she put together were for herself, but once a week when the flowers in her yard were blooming, Selma made lovely arrangements for the church she attended. It made her feel good to add some beauty to the table in the entrance; although she wasn't sure how much it was appreciated by others in the congregation. No one except for the pastor's wife had ever said anything to Selma about the flowers she brought.

Pulling her thoughts aside, Selma slipped into her sweater, picked up her satchel, and opened the back door.

Meow! The scraggly gray cat had returned once more, and he darted into the house before Selma could stop him. "Come back here, Scruffy!" she shouted, chasing after the cat as it raced into her kitchen.

The determined feline zipped around the table a couple of times, made a beeline for the hallway, and dashed into Selma's bedroom.

She moaned. If she didn't catch the critter soon, she'd be late. Aggravation tugging at her, Selma set her satchel on the table and headed down the hall. When she entered her bedroom, she gasped. The mangy animal was lying in the middle of her bed, curled up as if he thought he belonged there!

Selma's first instinct was to holler at the cat. But if she did that, he might run, and she'd be on another merry chase. Instead, she tiptoed quietly to the bed, slowly reached out, and scooped the furry cat into her arms. Selma wrinkled her nose, watching as clumps of cat hair floated through the air and onto her clean bedspread.

Prrr... Prrr... Prrr... The cat went limp the moment he was picked up, and nuzzled Selma's neck with his warm nose.

It softened Selma just a bit, but she wouldn't give in. This persistent critter had to go out!

"Why do you keep coming back here when you know you're not welcome?" Selma mumbled after she'd taken the cat outside and placed him on the grass. "Now go back to wherever you belong and stop coming to my house."

The cat looked up at Selma, as if to say, "You know I'll be back." Then it trotted down the driveway with its fluffy tail held high.

I can't figure out why Scruffy doesn't get the hint, Selma mused as she made her way back to the house to get her sewing satchel and use a lint roller on her clothes. She made a mental note to run the vacuum cleaner when she returned.

Does the cat think if he keeps coming around I'll eventually take him in? She shook her head determinedly. *That's never going to happen.*

"Everyone and their horse was at the bakery this morning, and look what I came home with," Lamar announced when he entered the quilting room, where Emma was busy getting things ready for her third class.

She looked up and smiled when she saw the box of doughnuts he held. "What'd they have on sale today?"

Lamar's green eyes twinkled as he grinned at her. "Maple bars and chocolate doughnuts, with vanilla-cream filling."

Emma smiled. "Two of your favorites."

"That's true," he admitted, "but they're not all for me. I plan on sharing."

"I'm glad to hear that. I might like at least one of those tasty-looking maple bars."

"You can have as many as you like, Emma. What I meant to say was, they're not all for us. Thought I'd share them with the quilting class when it's time to take a break today."

"That was thoughtful of you," Emma said. "Especially since all I have to serve are some of the sugar kichlin I made two days ago. I've been busy repairing the quilt for Cheryl's grandmother and haven't had time to do any more baking."

Lamar smacked his lips. "We can have some of those sugar cookies, too."

Emma motioned to the kitchen. "Why don't you put the doughnuts away until it's time to share them with our students?"

"That was my thought exactly, because if I leave them setting out, we'll be tempted to start eating right away, and no one will get much sewing done." Lamar started out of the room, but turned back around. "Isn't it amazing how we often think alike, Emma?"

She nodded. "I'm thankful for that." Emma knew that not all married couples were as compatible as she and Lamar. She felt grateful that God had brought such a kind, loving man into her life. Even though she hadn't planned to remarry after her first husband, Ivan, died, she'd never regretted her decision to marry Lamar.

When Cheryl pulled into the Millers' yard and saw no other cars in the driveway, she figured she must be the first one to arrive. That was unusual, but it was fine with her. She hoped this would give her some time to visit with Emma alone. From the first moment Cheryl had met Emma, she felt comfortable with her. Emma was so kind and easy to talk to. Cheryl felt relaxed around her—almost like she'd known Emma all her life. Maybe that was because, like Cheryl's grandma, Emma was easygoing and didn't just talk about herself. She seemed interested in others.

Not like Mom, Cheryl thought. *Everything always revolves around her job and social activities. Mom could learn a lot if she spent time among the Amish. Maybe she wouldn't be so focused on worldly things.*

Finished with her musings, Cheryl stepped out of the car and headed for the house. She was greeted at the door by Lamar, wearing his usual friendly grin. He, too, made Cheryl feel at ease and welcome in their home.

"Am I early, or is everyone else late today?" Cheryl asked, stepping into the house.

"You're a few minutes early, but I'm kind of surprised some of the others aren't here yet—especially Selma. She's usually the early one."

Cheryl couldn't argue with that. If there was one thing she'd learned about Selma Nash, it was that she liked to be punctual.

"Cheryl's here," Lamar announced as he and Cheryl entered the quilting room.

"Oh good." Emma smiled and motioned for Cheryl to come over to the table. "I did some work on your grandmother's quilt this week, and I want to show you how it's shaping up."

A sense of excitement welled in Cheryl's chest when she took a seat and watched as Emma spread the quilt on the table.

"See here," Emma said, pointing to one section of the quilt, and then another. "I've replaced some of the tattered pieces of material with new ones."

"They look new and yet old. How did you do that, Emma?"

"I used some old pieces of material I had that were still in good condition," Emma explained. "I want to make the quilt look like it did when it was originally purchased."

Cheryl smiled. "It definitely does, and the quilt's taking shape quite nicely. I'm sure Grandma will be pleased when she sees it."

"Will you be going to Oregon to give it to her?" Emma asked. "Or will you mail it and ask your mother to take it to your grandmother?"

"I have some time off from work coming the middle of November, so I'm hoping to take it there myself," Cheryl replied. "I want to give the quilt to Grandma on her birthday." She sighed deeply. "I can't count on Mom to do it. She's always so busy with her job and extracurricular activities. She doesn't even have time to talk to me for more than a few minutes whenever I call. And when I ask about Grandma, Mom either says she's doing okay or that she hasn't visited her in a while." Tears pricked the backs of Cheryl's eyes, and she swallowed around the lump stuck in her throat. "Wouldn't you think she'd want to visit her own mother as often as possible? And I don't understand why she can't take the time to really talk to me."

"I'm sorry, Cheryl." Emma put her hand on Cheryl's trembling shoulder. "It's hard to understand, but some people don't appreciate their family like they should. For me, though, I've always been close to my family. I'm grateful that my daughter Mary lives right next door. I can pop over there anytime I like, and it's always a joy whenever Mary or any of her children drop by here to see us."

"That must be nice," Cheryl acknowledged.

"If your family lives in Oregon, what brought you here?" Emma asked.

Cheryl clasped her fingers tightly together. "My ex-boyfriend is the reason I decided to move. I hoped we'd be married, until Lance admitted that he'd been secretly seeing my best friend, April, and wanted to marry her." She sniffed, struggling not to break down. "I needed a new start, so when the opportunity to work for a lawyer in Goshen came up, I took it."

"You're still hurt by your friends' betrayal, aren't you?" Emma asked. "I can see the pain in your eyes."

Cheryl nodded. "It does hurt, but thanks to my pastor and his wife, Ruby Lee, I've come to realize that I need to forgive Lance and April. In fact, I sent them both an e-mail, saying I'd forgiven them and moved on with my life."

"I'm glad to hear that. I know Ruby Lee, and she's a wise woman," Emma said. "God's Word says a lot about forgiveness. It's the only way we can truly find peace when someone hurts us."

"Ruby Lee thinks I should start dating again," Cheryl said. "But I'm not sure I'm ready for that."

Emma smiled. "You know, after my first husband died, I convinced myself that I'd never fall in love or get married again. Then Lamar came along, and it wasn't long before he won my heart."

"Do you think I should start dating again?"

"It might be a good thing," Emma said. "Of course, that's up to you." She gave Cheryl's arm a gentle squeeze. "Before the others get here, there's one more thing I'd like to say."

"What's that?"

"I have a good ear for listening, so if you ever need to talk about anything, I'm here."

Cheryl smiled. "Thanks, Emma. I appreciate that."

CHAPTER 17

Carmen was relieved when she pulled into Emma's yard and saw Anna parking her bike. Since Anna's father hadn't brought her this time, maybe she'd be free to go shopping after class. Carmen needed the extra time to visit with Anna, in order to find out more about her time of running-around—or perhaps the lack of it. She'd been surprised to learn that Anna's parents were so strict. The bitterness this young woman felt might make a good storyline, and maybe at the same time, Carmen could offer some suggestions to Anna. After all, she remembered her own teen years—those times when she thought she knew more than her parents, while her mom and dad struggled to keep the upper hand.

Now that Carmen was older and looking back, she realized how hard it must have been on her folks, remaining authoritative yet not wanting to let go. But at the same time, Carmen remembered her desire to start doing things on her own and make decisions without needing parental approval. It was a difficult adjustment for any parent and young adult.

For a few years, she and her parents had argued frequently. But once Carmen had proven that she could be trusted, they'd given her more freedom. Looking back on it, she realized that Mom and Dad had done a pretty good job of raising both their daughters. Since Carmen was the youngest, it had been harder for them to let her go, but after some time had passed, they slowly relented and came around to treating her like a responsible adult.

Carmen got out of the car and headed for the house. Anna met her on the porch. "It's good to see you, Anna. Will you be free to go shopping with me after class?" Carmen asked.

Anna bobbed her head. "I told my mom I'd be getting home late and that I had some shopping to do, but she doesn't know I'll be with you."

"Would she disapprove?" Carmen questioned.

"If she knew I planned to try on English clothes, she'd be very upset."

"If you'd rather not do that, I totally understand. I don't want to cause any difficulty for you. If you like, we could just grab a bite of lunch somewhere and visit awhile," Carmen suggested.

Anna shook her head vigorously. "No, I want to go shopping. We can have some lunch when we get to Goshen, if that's okay with you."

"That's fine." Carmen motioned to Anna's bike. "There isn't enough room in my rental car's trunk for that. Do you think Emma would mind if you leave the bike here while we're gone? I can drop you back off when we return from Goshen."

Anna rubbed her chin, looking thoughtful. "I suppose that would be all right. Maybe I could leave it on her porch until we get back. I'll tell Emma that you and I are going out to lunch. That's all she needs to know."

By ten o'clock, everyone but Selma had arrived at Emma's.

"I wonder if something came up for Selma and she couldn't make it today," Emma said to Lamar. "It's not like her to be late."

"Should I check our answering machine and see if she left a message?" Lamar asked.

Emma glanced at the clock. "If she's not here in the next ten minutes, you can go out to the phone shack. In the meantime, would you mind passing out everyone's projects, while I explain what we'll be doing today?"

"Sure, no problem."

While Lamar gave each of the students the patterned pieces they still needed to stitch, Emma explained that they would finish sewing today, and if there was time, they'd cut out the batting. "We may need the entire time to finish sewing the pieces of material you have cut out, though," she added. "And we'll want to take a break at some point, to enjoy the doughnuts and maple bars Lamar bought at the bakery this morning. I also have some cookies to set out."

Terry smacked his lips. "Sounds good. Sure won't turn any of that down. I've always had a thing for maple bars."

"Same here," Cheryl agreed. "Of course I never overindulge on sugary desserts."

"It's nice to know we have something in common." Terry winked at Cheryl.

Blaine cleared his throat real loud. "Can we just get on with our lesson?"

"For a guy who stuck himself with a pin last week, you're sure anxious to do it again," Terry said with an undignified snicker. "Oh, and I'm surprised you're not smelling like fish this morning."

Blaine glared at him. "It'd be better than reeking of cologne. What'd you do, take a bath in it to try and cover up that horrible smell? What is that smell, anyway? Are you smoking a different brand of cigarettes these days?"

Terry sneered back at Blaine. "No, I'm not! Fact is, I'm not smoking at all anymore."

"Oh yeah?"

There they go again, Emma thought. *I really need to put a stop to these snide comments before the situation gets out of control.*

"Terry, Anna, and Carmen, why don't you use the sewing machines first? While you're doing that, Cheryl and Blaine can take turns using my iron to press out the seams on the pieces of material they've already sewn."

"How are we going to do that when you don't have electricity in your home?" Blaine questioned. "Is your iron battery-operated like the sewing machines?"

Emma shook her head. "It's heated with a small propane bottle. I'll fire it up and show you how to use it." She glanced over at Lamar and said, "Maybe you should go out to the phone shack now and see if Selma's left a message for us."

"Jah, I'll do that."

When Lamar left the room, Emma set up her ironing board and lit the propane bottle on the iron, while Terry, Carmen, and Anna took seats in front of the sewing machines.

A few minutes after Emma showed Cheryl how to use the iron, Lamar returned. "There was no message from Selma," he said, "but as I was walking back to the house, her car turned up the driveway, so she should come inside any minute."

A short time later, Selma entered the room, red-faced and looking a bit disheveled.

"Sorry I'm late," she apologized, "but that stray cat I found on my porch last week came back." Selma's thin lips compressed. "Only this time Scruffy got into the house, and I had to chase after him."

Terry chuckled. "Scruffy, is it? Since you've already named the critter, maybe you oughta keep him. That way, you won't have to worry about chasing him off anymore."

"No way!" Selma shook her head. "I can't be bothered with a pet."

"A cat makes a nice companion, and they're really not that much work," Emma said.

"That's right," Cheryl agreed. "The nursing home where my grandma lives has a cat for the residents to enjoy. It's actually been proven that holding or petting an animal can bring down a person's blood pressure."

"My blood pressure's just fine," Selma said with a decisive nod. "Had it checked a few months ago when I had a physical."

"I'd have a cat if I didn't have to be gone from home so much for my job," Carmen interjected.

"We have cats, too," Anna said, "but they stay outside or in the barn because my younger sister, Becky, is allergic to cat dander. I do like to go out and talk to our kitties, though. They always seem to listen."

Emma was pleased that Anna had contributed so much to the conversation. It was a sign that she felt more comfortable with the class.

"Well, I'm not interested in having any pets," Selma said with a note of conviction. "I don't need cat hair all over everything."

Clearly Selma was not in a good mood, so Emma quickly gave her the material she still needed to sew. "Would you like to use my treadle machine again?" Emma asked. "You seemed to enjoy it last week."

Selma gave a quick nod. "That's fine with me."

While everyone worked on their projects, Emma went to the kitchen to put a pot of coffee on the stove. Once it had perked, she would lower the propane level to keep the coffee warm until it was time for refreshments.

Emma rubbed her temples and sighed. She felt like a failure with this class—not in showing her students how to make a quilted wall hanging, but in helping them work through their personal problems. Of course, other than Cheryl, most of them hadn't really opened up to her yet. But Emma suspected that each of them had something they were hiding. She hoped that within the next three weeks they would share their burdens with either her or Lamar. After all, Emma had felt from the very beginning that part of teaching these classes involved mentoring her students emotionally and spiritually. In the meantime, though, she needed to be patient and try to set a good example for all.

As Terry struggled to sew a straight line, his hands trembled and his head felt like it was stuffed with cotton, making it hard to think. Just one full day without a cigarette and he was a basket case. Lighting up in the truck earlier had probably made his symptoms worse, not to mention the bigger problem it had created for him. Now he'd have to spend money to get his truck seat fixed.

Terry would give just about anything to go outside for a smoke, but that was out of the question—especially since he'd announced that he'd quit smoking. Besides, after what had happened with the cigarette he'd dropped in his truck, he knew he really needed to quit, even if a date with Cheryl wasn't in the picture.

Every once in a while, Terry looked up from his sewing and watched Cheryl and Blaine as they took turns using the antiquated iron. They seemed to be talking quite a bit, but with the hum of three battery-operated sewing machines, plus the steady rhythm of the treadle, he couldn't make out what they were saying. Everyone seemed engrossed in what they were doing, and nobody seemed to notice Terry's agitation. *Who knew giving up cigarettes would be so hard? Why couldn't Emma have paired me with Cheryl, instead of putting her with Blaine?*

"Coffee and doughnuts are ready," Emma announced. "Why don't we all gather around the table?"

Terry was hoping to sit beside Cheryl, but Blaine beat him to it. *Rats! At this rate I'll never get to ask her out,* Terry fumed. *Sure can't holler it across the table. Guess I'll have to wait till class is over and catch her at the door.*

Lamar passed the box of doughnuts around, and Emma poured Selma a cup of tea and offered coffee to everyone else.

When Terry picked up his cup, his hand shook so badly that some of the coffee spilled. He jumped up, nearly knocking his doughnut off the table.

"Are you all right? Did you burn yourself?" Emma asked with concern as she handed Terry a napkin.

"Naw, I'm okay," he said, blotting up the mess and trying to make light of the situation. At this rate he'd never make a good impression on Cheryl—especially with the puzzled look she'd just given him. *So much for wearing nicer clothes today,* Terry thought, looking down at the splotches of coffee he'd managed to get on his pants.

"When you come here next week we'll add the batting to your wall hanging and begin the actual quilting process," Emma said. "Does anyone have any questions?"

"Is it all right if I begin the quilting at home?" Selma asked. "I have some batting, so I'm sure I could go ahead on my own."

"I'd rather you not do that," Emma said. "It would put you ahead of the others, and if you made a mistake, you'd have to spend extra time tearing it out."

"I don't think any of us should try working on our wall hangings without Emma's help," Carmen spoke up. "After all, we paid for the lessons, and she's the teacher."

"You know," Lamar added, "when Emma taught her very first class, she let the students take home their quilting projects to work on, but it didn't work out too well for some."

"Well, if that's the way you want it, then I suppose I'll just have to deal with it." Selma folded her arms and stared straight ahead.

No wonder Jan says his neighbor is a pain in the neck, Terry thought. *She's such a know-it-all. I can't understand why she bothered to take this class.*

When everyone finished their snacks, it was time to go, and they all moved toward the door. Terry jumped up from his seat to approach Cheryl, but Blaine got to her first.

"I was wondering, do you like to bowl?" Blaine asked Cheryl as they went out the door.

"I do enjoy bowling, but I'm not very good at it," she replied.

Blaine smiled. "That's okay; I'll coach you. Would you like to go bowling with me this evening?"

"That would be nice. There's a bowling alley in Goshen. Can we meet there around seven?" Cheryl asked, pulling her sweater around her as the October wind blew a chill across the yard.

"Sure, that'd be great." Blaine followed Cheryl out to her car.

Terry gritted his teeth. *That's terrific. Think I might show up at the bowling alley tonight. I wonder how he'd like that.*

CHAPTER 18

Goshen

This is going to be so much fun," Anna said as she and Carmen entered a restaurant on the east side of town. "Thanks for taking the time to spend the afternoon with me."

Carmen smiled. "You're welcome."

After their hostess seated them, and a waitress came to the table to take their orders, Carmen placed her purse in her lap, opened it, and discreetly turned on her portable tape recorder. She wanted to be sure she got everything Anna said to her during their meal. This would be the best time to talk, because when they went shopping it would be harder to converse.

"So is there anything more you can share with me about rumschpringe?" Carmen asked.

"Well, as you know, it's the Amish young people's time before joining the church." Anna paused and took a sip of water. "'Course I'm not sure I'm going to join."

"Is it because you want to do worldly things, or are you unhappy being Amish?" Carmen glanced down at her lap to be sure the tape recorder was working.

"It's not that I have anything against the Amish way of life," Anna replied quietly, looking around, as if afraid someone might hear. "I'm just not sure it's meant for me. I mean, I don't feel accepted by my family."

"Why is that?"

"My folks treat me like a baby." Anna frowned. "Most of my friends do things other than getting together for games and singings. But my parents don't allow me to try anything new."

Carmen leaned forward. "What kind of things?"

Anna shrugged, glancing around again while twirling her napkin around her fingers. Carmen had a hunch this was something Anna didn't want to talk about. *But it's what I want to know. I need to keep pressing until she tells me more.*

"Anna, do your friends drink or do drugs?" Carmen questioned. That was the kind of thing she'd seen on TV, and she needed to know how much of it was true.

"A couple of my friends have done some of those things," Anna admitted. "But most just meet in town and do fun things together."

"What kind of things?" Carmen questioned.

"Some of the girls wear English clothes when they're away from home. Some wear jewelry and makeup, too."

"Have you ever done any of those things?"

The middle-aged waitress came with their orders. "Let me know if you need anything else," she said before turning away from the table.

Anna glanced around nervously, as though someone might be watching her. Then in a timid voice, she said, "I always say a silent prayer before meals. I hope that's all right with you."

"Of course. I'll do that, too." Carmen turned off the tape recorder and bowed her head. Even though she went to church occasionally, she'd never made a habit of praying in public. A silent prayer shouldn't draw as much attention, so she had no problem with bowing her head. However, instead of thinking of something to pray about, a sense of guilt overtook her. She was not only trying to get information for her story from Anna, but she'd invited her out for the afternoon, knowing Anna hadn't gotten permission from her parents.

But how else am I going to get the information I need? Carmen told herself. *I need to keep asking Anna questions for the rest of the afternoon, and sometime this week I'll stop by Emma's and ask her about rumschpringe.*

Shipshewana

Emma had just finished washing the lunch dishes when a knock sounded on the front door. Since Lamar had gone next door to visit Mary's husband, Emma dried her hands and went to see who it was.

When she opened the door, she was surprised to see Pam Johnston on the porch, holding a large paper sack.

"It's good to see you," Emma said, giving Pam a hug. "How have you been?"

"I am doing well, and it's nice to see you, too." Pam smiled, pushing a strand of long blond hair behind her ears. "If you're not too busy right now, I have a favor to ask."

"I was just finishing up with the dishes, but that can wait." Emma opened the door wider and motioned for Pam to come in. "What can I help you with?"

Pam lifted the paper sack. "I'm making a quilted table runner for one of my friends, and I'm having trouble with the binding."

"It's basically the same as you did for the wall hanging you made during the classes you took from me," Emma explained.

"But that was over a year ago," Pam said. "Since I haven't done any quilting since then, I can't remember how I did the binding. I think I'm supposed to sew the strips together at right angles somehow."

"Come into the other room, and I'll show you what to do," Emma said, leading the way.

Pam took the table runner out of the sack and placed it on the table. She'd used material with varied colors of purple and pink and placed them in a simple star pattern.

"This is lovely," Emma said. "You've done a good job so far."

Pam smiled widely, revealing perfectly straight teeth. "Thanks, Emma. That means a lot coming from you. I would have never learned how to quilt if it hadn't been for your patience and expertise."

Emma's face heated with embarrassment. "I enjoy what I do, which is why I've continued teaching quilting classes."

"Speaking of which, how are things going with your new group of students?" Pam asked.

Emma pursed her lips. "Not as well as I'd like, but then it's not the worst class I've ever taught, either."

Pam rolled her eyes. "I'm guessing the class Stuart and I were in was your worst, right?"

Emma gave Pam's arm a tender squeeze. "I wouldn't say worst. I was just new at teaching and wasn't quite prepared for the challenge of instructing such a unique group of people."

"It's true. We were people with problems," Pam said. "And you helped all of us learn a lot more than just how to quilt."

"I hope I can do that with this group of students, too. I'm just a bit worried because, with the exception of Cheryl, no one has really opened up to me yet."

"Do you think they all have a problem?"

Emma nodded. "I believe so."

"I can tell you what Blaine's problem is, if you want to know."

Emma hesitated a minute. As much as she did want to know, she didn't think it would be right to hear it from Pam. It might be like listening to gossip, and she'd always tried to avoid that.

Turning to face Pam directly, Emma smiled and said, "I appreciate the offer, but I think it might be best to see if Blaine chooses to share his burdens with either Lamar or me."

"Oh, I see." Pam's downcast eyes told Emma she was disappointed. "So who are your other students?" Pam asked, quickly revising their topic.

"In addition to Blaine, I have a young Amish woman named Anna. Then there's Cheryl, Carmen, Selma, and Jan's friend, Terry."

Pam snickered. "I've never met Terry, but if he's anything like Jan, I'm sure your class must be quite interesting."

"Oh, it is," Emma admitted. "But then I guess that's why I like the challenge of teaching." She motioned to the quilted table runner Pam had brought. "Now shall we get started with that?"

Goshen

When Cheryl entered the bowling alley that evening, she glanced around but didn't see any sign of Blaine. Well, it wasn't quite seven o'clock, so she'd just take a seat and watch the other bowlers until he showed up. Rubbing her hands, which had gotten quite cold, she realized a pair of gloves would have felt good driving over. It was almost the middle of October, but it felt more like November.

Cheryl watched the activity buzzing around her. The first couple of lanes were reserved for bowling leagues. It looked like the men were against the women. In another lane, an elderly couple seemed to be enjoying themselves.

Looking in the other direction, she noticed a young mother rocking her baby while cheering for her husband after he'd rolled a strike. Cheryl wondered how the baby could sleep with all the noise from people whooping and cheering, balls rolling down the lanes, and pins getting hit and scattering into the pit.

As food smells wafted from the snack bar in the eating area, Cheryl's stomach growled. Several people stood in line, waiting for their orders, while others sat at tables, enjoying the food. She remembered long ago when she'd first bowled with some friends, how good the food at the snack bar had tasted. Maybe she would treat Blaine to a hot dog and a shake after they did a little bowling.

Cheryl took a seat where she could watch the people bowl, but she'd only been there a few minutes when someone tapped her shoulder. She turned her head and was surprised to see Terry.

"How's it going?" he asked, grinning from ear to ear.

"Umm. . .okay. I didn't expect to see you here tonight."

"I come here a lot. Bowling's one of my favorite things to do on a Saturday night." He flopped down in the seat beside her. "Wanna join me in a game?"

She shook her head. "I can't. I'm meeting someone."

Terry quirked an eyebrow. "Blaine?"

Cheryl nodded. "How'd you know?"

"I saw the two of you talking today during class. Figured he might be trying to set up a date. When we went outside afterwards, I heard him ask you to go bowling."

"Oh, so you followed us here?"

"Uh, not really. I actually have bowled here many times."

Cheryl kept her focus on the bowlers in the lane in front of her.

"You thirsty? I could get us a couple of sodas," Terry offered.

"No thanks, I'm fine."

"You like to ride motorcycles?" he asked.

"I don't know. I've never ridden one, although it does sound exciting."

"Wanna try it sometime? I've got a nice bike, and—"

"Oh, there you are," Blaine said, stepping up to Cheryl and touching her arm. "Have you been here long?"

She smiled up at him. "Only a few minutes."

Blaine's forehead wrinkled as he looked at Terry. "What are you doing here?"

Terry lifted his shoulders in a brief shrug. "Came to bowl, same as you. Fact is, I'm meeting my friend Jan and his daughter soon. Any objections?"

Blaine shook his head. "It's a free country." He held his hand out to Cheryl. "Ready to bowl and have some fun?"

She quickly rose to her feet. "Ready as I'll ever be."

CHAPTER 19

Shipshewana

W ould you like a cup of mint tea and one of those chocolate *faasnachtkuche* left over from today?" Emma asked when she entered the living room and found Lamar seated in his recliner near the fireplace.

"That sounds good," he replied, "but I'm surprised there are any doughnuts left."

"Most everyone went for the maple bars," Emma explained.

"Guess I wasn't paying close attention to who ate what. I was more interested in the look on Terry's face when he was watching Blaine talk to Cheryl."

"What kind of a look?" Emma asked.

"Irritation. . .jealousy. . .desperation." Lamar gave his right earlobe a tug. "If I was a betting man, I'd say Terry's interested in Cheryl."

"What about Blaine? Do you think he likes her, too?"

Lamar shrugged. "He acts interested, but not in the same way as Terry. Blaine seems to be. . . Well, he wears kind of a placid expression when he looks at Cheryl. It makes me wonder if he's only showing interest in her to irritate Terry."

"Why would he do that?" Emma questioned.

"I don't know, but I'd like to find out."

"Pam Johnston came by this afternoon, and Blaine's name came up." Emma's glasses slipped down her nose, and she pushed them back into place. "Pam wanted to tell me something about Blaine, but I didn't think it would be right, so I moved our conversation in another direction."

"Maybe I should pay more attention to Blaine," Lamar said. "He might need a friend."

Emma nodded. "You could invite him to go fishing with you sometime. That's something you both have in common."

"That's a good idea, Emma. Maybe we could go some Saturday after class." Lamar rose to his feet. "But enough about your students right now. Let's head out to the kitchen and get our evening snack."

———

Goshen

"What are you doing over there?" Blaine asked when Terry plopped down in the scorekeeper's chair next to him.

"I'm gettin' ready to bowl, same as you. Besides, this is the lane I was assigned," Terry replied with a smirk. At least that was how Blaine interpreted the smug-looking smile on Terry's face. What was the guy really doing here, anyway? Could he have known they were coming and showed up at the bowling alley on purpose, just to make trouble? Did he request the lane next to them, or had it really been assigned?

"Where are your friends?" Blaine asked. "Didn't you say you were meeting them here?"

"I am. They just haven't shown up yet." Terry left his chair and took a seat on the bench beside Cheryl as she put on her bowling shoes. "Do you come here often?" he asked.

She shook her head as she finished tying the shoelaces. "This is my first time since I moved to Goshen. But even when I lived in Oregon, I didn't bowl that often. Back home at our local alley, I remember enjoying the hot dogs and milk shakes and just hanging out with my friends. It's fun to bowl, but I'm really not that good at it, and I've never had lessons."

"I'd be happy to teach you," Terry said, a little too eagerly.

"I'm Cheryl's date, so if there's any teaching to be done, I'm the one who'll be doing it," Blaine called over his shoulder. He'd be glad when Terry's friends arrived. Maybe then he'd mind his own business and quit bothering Cheryl.

Terry didn't seem to notice Blaine's irritation; he was too busy grinning at Cheryl. The guy was clearly interested in her, but Blaine was sure the feeling wasn't mutual. After all, she was too refined for a rough-around-the-edges kind of guy like Terry.

"Would you like me to help you pick out a ball?" Blaine asked, leaving his seat and standing next to Cheryl.

"No thanks, I brought my own," Terry quipped.

Blaine narrowed his eyes. "I was talking to Cheryl."

Cheryl, looking a little flustered, giggled and stood. "Thanks for the offer, Blaine, but I think I can pick out my own ball. I need one that's not too heavy and fits my small fingers." She hurried off toward the rack of balls, leaving Blaine alone with Terry.

"How many years have you been bowling?" Terry asked as he took his bowling ball out of the bag and wiped it down with a small towel.

"I bowled my first game when I was eight years old."

"Guess you must be pretty good at it then."

Blaine gave a nod, watching as Terry put his multicolored bowling ball on the ball return. "I used to play on a league, and my average is 190, but my highest score was 260."

Terry snickered, stuffing the corner of the towel in his back pocket. "That's nothing. My highest score was 275."

"I'll bet," Blaine muttered under his breath.

"What was that?"

"Nothing." Blaine put his own ball on the ball return and seated himself in the scorekeeper's chair again. He was beginning to wish he'd taken Cheryl out to dinner or to see a movie. He'd sure never expected to run into Terry here—not when the guy lived in Shipshewana.

Blaine inserted his and Cheryl's names into the computer scoring system and felt relief when Cheryl returned with her ball, saying she was ready to start bowling.

———

Terry watched as Blaine showed Cheryl how to stand, hold the ball, and make her delivery. Everything was so precise—almost stiff-looking. Not the way Terry would do it, free and easy. *Sure wish it was me teaching her, and not Blaine.*

Terry studied Cheryl as she rolled her ball down the alley. It knocked down three pins and left seven standing.

"It's okay, Cheryl," Blaine said. "I bet you'll pick them up on the next try."

When her bright green ball returned, Cheryl tried again. This time she knocked down three more pins. "Guess it's better than a gutter ball," she said, smiling at Blaine. Then she glanced over at Terry and smiled at him, too. "Is it best for me to aim at the pins or the marks on the floor?"

"Aim at the pins," Blaine said.

Terry shook his head. "I use the marks on the floor mostly."

Cheryl lifted her hands. "That wasn't much help. Guess I'll figure it out for myself. Either way, or doing both, might make it easier."

Boy, she sure is pretty—especially when she smiles, Terry thought. *Sure wish she was my date tonight.*

It was Blaine's turn to bowl, and Cheryl sat beside Terry. As Blaine stepped up to the line, Terry looked over at Cheryl and said, "Look at me over here by myself. I feel like the Lone Ranger."

"Not anymore." Cheryl gestured toward the entrance of the bowling alley. "It looks like your friend Jan just arrived."

Terry swiveled in his seat. Sure enough, Jan was heading his way, and Star was right behind him. When they joined him a short time later, he introduced Star to Cheryl. "And you've already met my boss and good friend, Jan Sweet," Terry added.

———

Cheryl smiled at Star. "It's nice to meet you." The young woman's hair was straight and black, and she sported a small nose ring. Cheryl also noticed a little star tattooed on the young woman's neck, but she wore a radiant smile and seemed quite bubbly.

"Same here," Star said, shaking Cheryl's hand. "Terry's told us all about you."

"It was all good, honest," Terry said, his face turning slightly pink.

It was unexpected to see him blush like that. Cheryl was also surprised to hear that he'd been talking about her. Well, maybe it wasn't just her he'd mentioned to Jan and Star. Terry might have talked about everyone in the class.

"Are we going to bowl, or stand around talking all night?" Blaine asked impatiently. He motioned to Cheryl's ball. "It's your turn now."

"No, it's not," Terry spoke up. "You were about to bowl when Jan and Star showed up."

Blaine's face flamed as he glanced down at the ball in his hands. "Guess you're right."

Cheryl could see how embarrassed Blaine was, so she made light of it. "It's no big deal. I do things like that all the time. The other day at work I went to the copy machine, and after I copied the document I'd taken there, I got distracted when someone asked me a question. Then when I went back to my desk I realized I didn't have the copy I thought I'd made. So back to the copy machine I went, where I discovered that the original, as well as the copy, were still in the machine."

Terry chuckled. "Once, when I was climbing a ladder to get on a roof, I stopped halfway up and couldn't remember what I was going up there for. So I told myself, 'I'm gonna stand right here on this rung till I remember.'" Terry tapped his forehead a couple of times. "I never did figure it out, but after some thought, I couldn't remember if I was going up or down that ladder."

Cheryl laughed. "You made that up, didn't you?"

He winked.

"I think we'd better get back to bowling." Blaine stepped up to the line, made his approach, and let the ball go. He knocked down eight pins, and the two left standing were side by side. "I should be able to get those easily," he said, glancing back at Cheryl.

"I bet you can." She cheered Blaine on.

In the meantime, Terry picked up his ball and stepped up to the line just as Blaine did. They both started their approach and released their balls at the same time.

"That's not good," Star said, glancing at Cheryl and shaking her head. "One of them should have waited for the other to go first. I don't think either of 'em knows anything about bowling courtesy."

Cheryl held her breath as she watched both men's balls roll down the alley toward the pins. Terry's ball, which had been released with a stronger hand, made it there first, knocking down nine pins. Blaine's ball hit his last two pins, and he turned to face Cheryl with a grin.

"Good job," she said, picking up her ball and waiting until Terry finished his turn. He missed the one pin that had been left standing, but instead of getting upset about it, he winked at Cheryl and said, "That was just my practice shot. 'Course practice makes perfect, and nobody's perfect, so really, why practice?"

Cheryl couldn't help but smile. Terry had such a humorous way about him. He was actually kind of a likable guy. Too bad he and Blaine seemed to be at odds with each other. They'd both been acting really testy tonight. "Guess it's my turn to bowl," she said.

The first ball she rolled, knocked down four pins, but on her second try she got three more. After Star took her turn and got a spare, Jan bowled, knocking down all of the pins. Everyone cheered.

Terry and Blaine both jumped up next, grabbed their balls, and lined up, neither of them waiting for the other to go first. Terry glanced briefly at Blaine, then let go of his ball. As it started rolling down the aisle, he shouted, "Come on, baby. . . . Come on. . . . Knock down those pins for me right now!"

Meanwhile, the ball Blaine released glided down the alley, with him coaxing it along. "That's it! That's it! Just a little more to the left."

Terry's ball hit eight pins this time, and Blaine knocked down seven.

"It's time for a spare," Blaine said, looking back at Cheryl.

Terry grabbed his ball and dashed up to the line. Blaine did the same. Once more, they released their balls at the same time.

Thunk! Both men's balls rolled into the gutter without hitting a single pin.

"Rats!" Terry slapped the side of his jeans, and Blaine slunk his way back to his chair.

Cheryl looked at Star and rolled her eyes.

"Men," Star whispered, leaning close to Cheryl. "They always have to show off, and if they don't win, they think it's the end of the world."

Cheryl nodded. To her, bowling, or any other sport, was about having fun. It was obvious that Terry and Blaine took the game more seriously, though.

Star and Cheryl took their turns next, and then Jan. Cheryl watched in fascination as the big burly man bowled one strike, followed by another. Star cheered and so did Terry. But Blaine just sat with his arms folded.

When Star took her next turn, she bowled a strike. Cheryl cheered for her, thinking, *Maybe I should have had her show me a few things about bowling.*

Cheryl went to her purse and dug out a few dollars. "Blaine, would you mind getting me a chocolate milk shake? If they taste anything like the ones back in my hometown, then I can hardly wait to have one. Get yourself something, too," she added, handing him the money. "It's my treat."

"I should be treating you, not the other way around," Blaine said.

"Don't worry about it. You paid for our bowling, so it's the least I can do."

"Okay. I'll be back soon with a couple of chocolate shakes." Casting Terry a quick glance, Blaine hurried away.

For the next two hours they continued to bowl, until Cheryl told Blaine she needed to go. "I plan to attend the early service at church tomorrow morning, so I need to go home and get to bed," she explained.

"Where's your church and what time does it start?" Blaine asked.

Thinking he might want to come, too, she smiled and said, "It starts at 8:45, and the church is here in Goshen. Gene Williams is the pastor, and his wife, Ruby Lee, took one of Emma's quilting classes."

"Oh, I see. Well, if you need to get home, I'll walk you to the car," Blaine said, making no comment about the church or asking for directions.

Disappointed, Cheryl smiled at Star. "It was nice meeting you."

"Same here." Star grinned. "Maybe the two of us can get together and bowl sometime," she whispered. "Without the men."

Cheryl gave a nod. "Sounds like that could be fun." She said good-bye to Jan and told Terry she would see him next Saturday at Emma's. "Oh, and I'm glad you've quit smoking. Keep up the good work," she quickly added.

"I will," he said with a twinkle in his eyes. "Think it'll be worth it."

As Cheryl and Blaine walked toward the door, she glanced over her shoulder and noticed Terry watching her. She couldn't explain it, but something about him was appealing, which was strange, since she hadn't felt that way when they'd first met. While Blaine was nice looking, polite, and seemed to be steady, Terry was funny and had a zest for life. He was different from any man she'd ever known.

When Cheryl stepped into the chilly evening air, a shiver ran through her. *Do I actually wish I'd gone bowling with Terry tonight instead of Blaine? No, that's ridiculous; Terry and I are worlds apart.*

CHAPTER 20

Shipshewana

Selma pulled the covers aside and shivered as she crawled out of bed. It seemed so cold in her bedroom this morning. Could the temperature have dipped lower than usual during the night? Maybe her furnace had quit working.

Wherever Selma could, she stepped on the throw rugs scattered across her bedroom floor, knowing the hardwood would probably be cold. It was the only room in her house, besides the kitchen and bathroom, that didn't have carpeting.

Selma padded across the room in her bare feet and bent down to put her hand in front of the floor vent. *Now that's odd.* Even though the slats were open, no heat was rising through the vent. She slipped into her robe and slippers, then stepped into the hall. It seemed warm enough there, and in the living room as well. She checked both living-room vents and discovered warm air drifting up. It made no sense that the vent in the bedroom wasn't directing heat into the room.

Selma checked a couple more vents—one in the spare bedroom, and one in the dining room. Warm air wafted up from both of them. She felt relief knowing her furnace hadn't given out.

"Guess I'll have to ask someone to crawl under the house and check the heat duct going up to my bedroom," she said aloud. "Maybe it got clogged somehow."

Selma headed for the kitchen to put the teakettle on the stove, and when she stepped into the room, she halted, shocked at the sight before her. That mangy gray cat was sitting in her sink, licking at the slow drip coming from the faucet.

"How in the world did you get in my house, and what are you doing in the sink?" Could she have left the door open last night during the short time she'd gone out to be sure her car was locked? But if the cat had gotten in then, why hadn't she seen it before she'd gone to bed? Maybe the sneaky feline had hidden out somewhere in the house. Whatever the case, Scruffy had to go out!

Meow! The cat looked at Selma as if to say, "Please let me stay in the house."

"I'll give you a bowl of water, but you have to go outside." Selma picked up the cat, unconsciously petting his head.

Prrr. . . Prrr. . . The cat burrowed his nose in Selma's robe and began to knead with his paws.

"Now, none of that, Scruffy," Selma said with a click of her tongue. "You're not going to soft-soap me this morning." She held the cat away from her, while scrutinizing him. *If you could talk, you'd probably tell me plenty*, Selma thought, wondering where this cat must have come from.

She opened the back door, set the cat on the porch, and quickly shut the door. When she returned to the kitchen, she took out a plastic bowl and filled it with lukewarm water. Then she took the bowl outside and placed it on the porch. Seeing that Scruffy was still there, Selma smiled, despite her agitation. If all the mats were combed out of the critter's fur, he wouldn't look half bad. In fact, he was kind of cute, even if he was nearly full grown.

Now don't go getting soft, Selma scolded herself. *I am not keeping this cat.* She opened the door and stepped quickly inside. She needed to eat breakfast and get ready for church, or she'd end up being late. She would deal with the faulty heat vent sometime this week, and she hoped giving the cat some water had not been a mistake. But she had a feeling it already was.

Middlebury

Anna yawned and forced herself to sit up straight, hoping to relieve her aching muscles. They were nearly halfway through Sunday worship, and she really needed a break. She'd wait until the reading of the Scriptures, though. Anna knew that would be when a few other people would slip out to use the restroom or walk around for a bit to get the kinks out of their stiff backs.

Anna barely heard the song being sung, as her mind took her back to yesterday and the time she'd spent with Carmen. She'd enjoyed the afternoon so much, and the interest Carmen had taken in Anna made her feel like she was important. Carmen seemed to care what Anna thought about things and didn't criticize, the way Mom often did. She'd enjoyed sharing information and answering questions Carmen had asked about their Amish traditions. Too bad Carmen didn't live in the area. If she did, she and Anna would probably be friends.

Of course, Anna mused, *Carmen's more educated than I am. She's much prettier, too. I'll bet she thinks I'm really plain.* Nevertheless, no one had ever taken an interest in Anna like Carmen had. It made her feel kind of special.

Anna looked down at her hands, clasped firmly over the skirt of her dark blue dress. *Even though I am plain, I'd still like to be pretty.* Was there such a thing as being pretty and plain at the same time? Anna's grandmother had told Anna on more than one occasion that her auburn hair was pretty. But the freckles dotting Anna's nose made her wish she had a clear, creamy complexion like she'd noticed Cheryl Halverson had.

Anna glanced to her right, where her friend Mandy Zimmerman sat staring out the window of Deacon Lehman's buggy shed, where church was being held today. Mandy looked bored and was probably ready for a break, too. She was a pretty young woman, with shiny blond hair, bright blue eyes, and a bubbly personality. She was also a bit rebellious, although her parents had given her the freedom to experience some worldly things. Mandy's boyfriend, David, had a car, and sometimes took Mandy for rides. Anna, on the other hand, had no boyfriend. She didn't care, though. None of the young men she knew had caught her interest. Besides, she was still young, and there was plenty of time for courting and flirting. Not that Anna wanted to flirt. She'd seen Mandy do it several times, though, with David and a couple of other young men.

Anna's thoughts turned to the piece of jewelry Carmen had bought for her yesterday while they'd been shopping. If Mom and Dad found out she had a fancy bracelet, she'd be in for a lecture, and maybe worse. They might say she couldn't see Carmen anymore outside of the quilt class. Anna was glad she'd hidden the bracelet beneath her underclothes in one of her dresser drawers. Since she cleaned her own room and always gathered up the laundry, she was sure the bracelet wouldn't be discovered.

As the congregation stood for the reading of Scriptures, Anna slipped quietly out and headed for the house. Mandy did the same.

Once in the house, Anna quickly realized there was a lineup in the hallway for the restroom, so she visited with Mandy as they stood in the living room, awaiting their turn.

"I have something to tell you," Anna whispered.

"What is it?" Mandy asked, leaning closer to Anna.

"I went to lunch in Goshen with Carmen Lopez yesterday, and afterward, we did some shopping."

"Carmen's that young Hispanic woman you told me about, right?"

Anna nodded. "Carmen's really nice, and she actually listens when I talk. Not like Mom and Dad. They don't listen or try to understand me at all."

"So what'd you buy when you went shopping?" Mandy asked.

"I didn't buy anything myself, but Carmen bought me a pretty bracelet."

"Why would she do that? She doesn't even know you that well."

Anna sucked in her bottom lip as she mulled things over. "I guess after I shared some things with her about how Mom and Dad have been holding me back, she felt sorry about my situation and decided to give me something nice."

"What'd you do with the bracelet? I'm sure you didn't go home and show your folks."

Anna shook her head. "I hid it in one of my dresser drawers."

"I hope your mamm doesn't find it there."

"I'm sure she won't because she never goes into my room."

Mandy smiled. "I'm anxious to see it. When can you show it to me?"

"How about tomorrow? Maybe we can meet somewhere after I get off work in the afternoon."

"Sounds good," Mandy said. "Let's meet at the Dairy Queen. I've been craving one of those chocolate-and-vanilla-swirl ice-cream cones. Think you can be there by four o'clock?"

Anna nodded, already looking forward to it.

Goshen

When Cheryl stepped into the church foyer, she spotted Ruby Lee, talking with an elderly woman. Cheryl didn't want to interrupt, so she waited until they were done before she joined Ruby Lee. "Guess what?" she asked, giving Ruby Lee a hug. "I took your advice and went on a date last night."

"I'm glad to hear that. Who'd you go out with?"

"Blaine Vickers. He's one of the men taking the quilt class with me." She paused, wondering how much to share with Ruby Lee.

"I sense there's more," Ruby Lee said, touching Cheryl's arm.

Cheryl nodded. "Blaine and I went bowling, and Terry Cooley, who also attends the quilt classes, showed up. He ended up bowling on the lane next to ours."

"Was he invited?"

"No, but he was meeting his friend Jan Sweet and Jan's daughter, Star. They came in after Terry had been there awhile." What Cheryl didn't tell Ruby Lee was that Terry had vied for her attention all evening and that she'd actually enjoyed it. She could hardly admit that to herself, because it didn't seem right that she'd be attracted to someone like Terry.

Ruby Lee smiled. "Sure wish I'd been there. I haven't seen Jan or Star for some time. They kept things quite interesting during our quilting classes, but by the end of our six weeks, we all came to care for each other."

"Terry keeps our classes interesting, too."

"Did I hear my name mentioned?"

Cheryl whirled around, surprised to see Terry, wearing black slacks, a white shirt, and a black leather jacket, standing behind her with a big grin.

"Wh–what are you doing here, Terry?" she stammered. She couldn't get over how different Terry looked today, dressed in nice clothes.

"I overhead you telling Blaine last night that you were going to church this morning."

"I did tell him that, but I didn't say the name of the church, or where it was located—just that it was in Goshen."

"But you did say it was the church Ruby Lee's husband pastored, and since Ruby Lee and Jan took the same quilting class, I figured Jan would know where the church was, so I got the directions from him."

Before Cheryl could respond, Ruby Lee extended her hand to Terry and said, "We always welcome visitors when they come to our church. I'm Ruby Lee. It's nice to meet you, Terry."

"Same here," Terry said, as he shook hands with Ruby Lee. Then he turned back to Cheryl and said, "If you don't mind, I'd like to sit with you during church."

Stunned, Cheryl couldn't seem to find her voice. All she could manage was a quick nod. Had Terry come here to be with her? If so, how did she feel about that?

CHAPTER 21

As Cheryl sat near the back of the church, she wondered what the people around her thought about the redheaded man with a ponytail, seated beside her on the pew. Even though Terry was dressed in nicer clothes today, he still looked a bit rugged. Of course, as she'd heard Pastor Gene say on more than one occasion, "A church is a hospital for sinners, not a home for the saints."

Cheryl thought about how Jesus had spent time with people like Zaccheus, whom many people hated because he was a tax collector. In God's eyes, people were all the same. Stereotyping and bigotry was man's choosing, not God's, and if the people attending this church chose to judge someone because of the way they wore their hair, then shame on them!

That goes for me, too, Cheryl thought. *When I first met Terry, I judged him based on how he looked and because he smoked. I really didn't give myself a chance to get to know him.*

One of the men in the church had just started to give the announcements when Terry leaned over to Cheryl and said, "Can I ask you something?"

Cheryl put her finger to her lips. Apparently Terry hadn't been to church that often. Either that or he didn't know enough to be quiet.

Terry reached for one of the visitor's cards, wrote something on it, and handed it Cheryl.

It read: *Would you go out to lunch with me after the service?*

Cheryl hesitated, then wrote back: *That would be nice.*

Terry couldn't believe his good fortune. He'd not only been able to sit beside Cheryl in church, but now they were eating lunch together at one of his favorite restaurants in Goshen. As far as he was concerned, this was definitely a date!

"This is really good chicken," Cheryl said, taking a bite of the drumstick she held. Terry was glad she wasn't one of those prissy women, afraid to pick up a piece of meat and eat it with her fingers.

He smacked his lips. "You're right about that. But then most of the food they serve here is good."

"Since you're a roofer and get around the area a lot, I imagine you've tried many of the restaurants."

Terry nodded as he reached for his glass of root beer. "When I'm out riding my Harley, I'm able to check out lots of restaurants."

"Do you go riding often?" she queried.

"Yeah, whenever I can." Terry paused to take a drink of his soda. He felt relaxed sitting here with Cheryl and felt no need for a cigarette. Being with her might be the motivation he needed to quit once and for all. "I usually go riding on the weekends, and I probably would have gone today if I hadn't come to church," Terry said, placing his glass on the table.

"So you don't go to church on a regular basis?"

"No, but Jan's always after me to go with him and Star."

"Do they attend church every week?"

Terry shook his head. "Sometimes they hit the road with their cycles. But they go as often as they can," he quickly added. "Jan mentioned one time that if they're near a church during one of their road trips, he and Star will go. Even dressed in their biker clothes, Jan said they've always been welcomed." Terry paused and took a bite of the fried shrimp he'd ordered. "Ruby Lee made me feel comfortable today, so I think I'll start going more regularly, too." He grinned at Cheryl and dipped another piece of shrimp into his cup of cocktail sauce. "I can always go riding on Saturdays, or even Sunday after church."

"I've never ridden a motorcycle before. What it's like?" Cheryl asked.

"Ever gone for a ride in a convertible?"

Cheryl nodded. "My ex-boyfriend had one."

"Well, it's sort of like riding in a convertible, but with no doors. You're open to nothing but the air around you." Terry was glad to know Cheryl had an ex-boyfriend. That meant he had a better chance with her. *Of course, Cheryl might not be interested in a guy like me. She might think Blaine's more her type.*

Cheryl shuddered. "I think I'd be scared to death on a motorcycle."

"Naw, you'd get used to it. It's hard to put into words, except that when I'm on my bike I feel free, like I'm in total charge of what I'm doing. It's great to be able to see everything around me, even the ripples and potholes in the pavement." Terry leaned back in the chair and crossed his arms. "I'm relaxed when I'm riding my Harley, and I enjoy the noise of the wind and even the smells from farms and cars. When I'm out on the open road, just me and my Harley, nothing seems wrong with the world. It's like some people enjoy reading a good book to relax. Well, riding my bike is like that for me. 'Course there are a few things that ain't—I mean, aren't so much fun about riding."

"Like what?" she asked with a curious expression.

"When it rains, it feels like hundreds of needles are hitting my face. Oh, and once a bumblebee crashed into my helmet when I was going at a high speed, and it felt like I'd been hit in the head by a rock. Then, too, after a long ride, my ears sometimes ring for an hour or so. I also learned a good lesson early on."

"What was that?" Cheryl asked, leaning forward.

"When I first got my bike, I thought it'd be neat to let my hair fly free in the wind." Terry scrunched up his face. "Boy was that ever a mistake."

"What happened?"

"When I got home, it took me over an hour to comb out all the tangles. Afterward when I looked at the floor, I thought I'd lost half my hair. 'Course I didn't, but now I never go riding without pulling my hair back into a ponytail."

Cheryl drew in her bottom lip. "I don't think I'd like any of that—especially getting whacked by a bug."

"When you think about it, it's really not so bad. I never ride my Harley without a helmet, and I also have a face shield attached to the helmet to protect my eyes. Over the years, I've found the good that comes from riding my cycle outweighs the bad." Terry snapped his fingers. "Say, I've got an idea."

"What's that?"

"How would you like to follow me back to Shipshe? Then I can give you a ride on the back of my Harley."

"Oh, I don't know. . . .?"

"Aw, come on. It's not as bad as you might think, and you might even enjoy it."

"It does sound intriguing. Do you promise not to go real fast?"

"I won't break the speed limit, if that's what you mean, but we gotta pick up a little speed or we won't get the full enjoyment from the ride."

Cheryl looked down at the outfit she was wearing—a dark green skirt and a creamy off-white blouse. "I'm not dressed for riding."

"If you don't live too far from here, you can go home and change," Terry suggested. "I'll follow you there and wait in my truck till you're ready. Then you can follow me home in your car so you'll have a ride back to Goshen." Terry had thought about offering to give Cheryl a ride in his truck, but the seat still had that hole in it and didn't smell too good. "So what do you say? Should we go for a little joyride today?"

Cheryl sat staring at her plate, but she finally nodded. "Sure, why not? I need a little excitement in my life."

Shipshewana

"Okay, now," Terry said. "You need to keep your feet on the passenger pegs."

"Passenger pegs?"

"The footrests," Terry said, pointing at them.

Cheryl stared at the bike, wondering what in the world had possessed her to agree to go for a ride with Terry. This wasn't the type of thing she would normally do. Up close, his Harley looked bigger than she thought it would. It appeared to be a huge powerhouse on two wheels. And to think she was going to be sitting on that compelling piece of machinery, riding down the open road, with a man she'd felt a great dislike for when they'd first met. *What on earth has gotten into me, agreeing to do something like this?*

Terry handed Cheryl a helmet. "You'll need to wear this."

Cheryl's hair was short enough, so she didn't have to worry about tying it back as she reached for the plain blue helmet. Terry's helmet was a lot fancier. It was almost as colorful as his bowling ball and matched his Harley, which was a fiery red speckled with metallic paint. "What should I hold on to?" Cheryl asked, heart pounding, as she put the helmet on her head and took a seat on the back of the motorcycle.

"Me. You hold on tight to me." Terry grinned down at Cheryl as he stood next to the bike. "And if your back muscles get sore, just lean against the sissy bar behind you. It'll give you some added support."

Cheryl's face warmed as she thought once again, *Oh my, why did I ever agree to this? I must have been out of my mind.*

"Oh, and whenever we're at a stop sign, don't put your feet down; just keep 'em on the pegs. It's my job to make sure the bike stays upright when we're stopped."

Cheryl nodded. "I understand." She was glad she'd made the quick decision to put on her heavier leather shoes instead of the sneakers she'd almost decided to wear.

"One more thing," Terry said, throwing his leg over the bike, "don't wiggle around or shift your weight. Just lean with me, and since you'll be hanging on to me, that should be easy."

"Don't worry," Cheryl said, her voice trembling a bit, "I'll be too scared to do anything but hang on tight."

"You'll be fine; just try to relax and enjoy the ride."

Yeah, right, Cheryl thought. *Sounds like something I heard in a movie once.*

Terry fired up the bike, looking back as Cheryl wrapped her arms snugly around his waist. "By the way," he shouted over the roar of the engine, "you look real good in that helmet."

Cheryl couldn't help smiling. Watching Terry pull his face shield down, she did the same.

As they rode out of Terry's yard, Cheryl couldn't see much of anything except Terry's back. She was also aware of the smell of leather from his jacket, and when they turned onto the road, a drafty wind whipped up the back of her neck. She felt vulnerable, but it was also quite exhilarating. It was nothing like being enclosed in a vehicle, with four sides around her and a roof overhead. And it in no way compared to riding in a convertible.

As they ventured farther onto the open road, Terry picked up speed. Cheryl was glad her helmet had a shield. If not, Terry's ponytail would be slapping her in the face like a horse's tail swatting at flies.

"Whoo-hoo! Isn't this great?" Terry hollered into the wind.

Cheryl was afraid to open her mouth, and she thought for a minute to just lean her forehead against Terry's back and not look at anything at all. At the same time, she didn't want to act like a baby and miss the whole experience, so all she could do was hang on for dear life and try to enjoy this crazy ride.

CHAPTER 22

Selma's eyelids fluttered, but she couldn't quite open them. She'd been having a pleasant dream and didn't want to wake up. But something—she wasn't sure what—seemed to be pulling her awake.

She rolled her head from side to side, snuggling deeper under the blankets. She couldn't remember when she'd slept so well.

Prrr. . . Prrr. . . Something soft and warm pushed at Selma's face.

Selma's eyes snapped open. The furry gray cat was lying on her chest!

"Yikes!' Selma screamed and sat straight up. The cat hissed and leaped off the bed, looking like one of those frightened arched-back Halloween cats.

"How did you get in here?" Selma shouted as the cat raced out of the room. She pulled the covers aside and grimaced when her feet touched the cold floor. Her floor vent still wasn't sending up any heat, and now she had to deal with a cat in the house. This was not a good way to begin her Monday.

Without bothering to put on her slippers and wearing only her nightgown, Selma ran down the hallway, chasing the cat. She caught up with him in the kitchen, where he was crouched near the back door, looking up at her with big, innocent eyes. He looked scared, and Selma almost felt sorry for him. She wondered if someone might have abused the cat, or if he'd learned to defend himself after years of living on his own. She had to admit she had slept quite well last night and wondered if it was due to the warmth and comfort of the cat sleeping on her chest.

No, that can't be, she told herself. *It was the dream I had—that's why I slept so well.* "And you, Mr. Scruffy," she said, picking up the cat, "are going outside, where you belong!"

As Carmen's car approached Emma's house, she thought about how she'd gone to church with Paul and Sophia on Sunday. They'd eaten lunch afterward at a family-style restaurant, then gone to a nearby park. If anyone didn't know better, they might have thought the three of them were a family spending a Sunday afternoon together.

Carmen had enjoyed watching Sophia run and play. She could still hear the little girl's laughter as she sat on the swing, being pushed by Paul and Carmen. Sophia looked so much like her mother, and seeing her on the swing reminded Carmen of the times she and Lorinda were children and enjoyed swinging in their parents' backyard. Carmen looked forward to seeing Paul and Sophia this Saturday evening, when they would have supper at the home of Paul's sister, Maria. Carmen would miss the happy times she'd spent with Paul and Sophia when she went back to California, and she planned to keep in better touch through phone calls and e-mails. Maybe during Paul's summer break, he and Sophia could come to California for a visit. It would be fun to go to the beach and teach Sophia how to build sand castles and search for seashells.

Carmen pulled her thoughts aside as she turned up Emma's driveway and parked the car. When she got out, and started walking toward the house, she spotted Emma's goat Maggie lying on the porch swing, snoozing. The goat looked so cute, Carmen couldn't help but smile. She was sure Maggie had escaped from her pen again, and figured Emma and Lamar didn't realize it.

Carmen walked past the swing and knocked on the front door. Apparently unaware of her presence, Maggie slept on, snoozing like a dog on a lazy summer afternoon. A few seconds later, Lamar came to the door. After Carmen greeted him and said she'd come to visit Emma, she pointed to the porch swing. "Looks like Emma's goat is enjoying herself."

Lamar groaned. "That silly critter can sure be persistent." He opened the door wider. "Emma's in her quilting room, so just go on in. I'd better put Maggie back in her pen."

"Thanks, I will. Oh, and good luck with the goat," Carmen called over her shoulder as she entered the house.

When she stepped into the room, she found Emma working on the tattered old quilt Cheryl had brought for repair.

"I don't mean to interrupt," Carmen said, approaching the sewing machine where Emma sat, "but Lamar said I should come in."

Emma smiled and motioned to the chairs at the sewing table. "What a nice surprise. It's good to see you. Please, make yourself comfortable."

"When I got here, I discovered your goat lying on the porch swing, so Lamar's outside putting her away," Carmen explained. "That animal must keep you and Lamar on your toes."

Emma clicked her tongue while peering over the top of her glasses. "That's my Maggie. I'm beginning to think there's nothing that will keep her in the pen."

Carmen smiled, glancing out the window just in time to see Lamar walking Maggie back to her pen. "She does seem to be quite the escape artist, but I see your husband has everything under control."

"He's good with animals," Emma said. "Maggie can be a handful, but it's hard to stay mad at her. So what brings you by here this morning?" she asked.

"I was hoping we could talk awhile—if you have the time, that is."

"That sounds nice. Would you like a cup of tea?" Emma asked, rising from her chair and setting her sewing aside.

"Don't go to any trouble on my account," Carmen said.

"It's no trouble at all. It's nice that we can visit like this, other than just during the time we spend in the quilt class." Emma smiled and ambled out of the room.

Carmen left her seat and went over to look at the quilt Emma had been working on. Being careful not to touch it, she studied the detailed stitching. Each stitch was evenly spaced, and the pattern, with interlocking patches of color, was quite interesting. A quilting machine couldn't have done it any better than the quality she saw in Emma's work. Carmen remembered Emma saying that the design of this quilt was called Wedding Ring, and that many Amish couples received a quilt like this when they got married.

I wonder if I'll ever get married, Carmen mused. In high school, she'd had a few boyfriends but never gotten serious about any of them. Since her job kept her so busy, she really didn't have time for dating these days. Sometimes, Carmen wished she were married and raising a family or had at least found someone with whom she might want to pursue a meaningful relationship.

"Here we go," Emma said as she entered the room and placed a tray on the table.

Carmen motioned to the quilt. "I know this is old, but I think it's beautiful."

Emma nodded. "I agree. But then, I have a fondness for quilts, so most of them appeal to me."

"I'm glad I decided to take your class," Carmen said. "I'm anxious to see how my wall hanging turns out."

"Do you have a special place you'll want to hang it?" Emma asked.

"I'm thinking of giving it to my niece, Sophia, for her bedroom. The colors I chose are bright, and they nearly match her bedspread and curtains."

"I'm sure she'll appreciate the wall hanging as she gets older, and also the quilt that Paul finished for her after his wife died," Emma said.

Carmen flinched at the mention of her sister. If Lorinda hadn't been killed, she would have finished Sophia's quilt.

"Yes, my sister, Lorinda, had many talents. She could walk circles around me with all she knew how to do." Carmen looked down, wondering if she'd ever get over the loss. "Sophia was cheated, losing her mother before she had a chance to know her." Taking in a quick breath, she continued. "I feel cheated, too, after losing my sister, but I'll certainly make sure I share with my niece all the wonderful memories I've locked away in my heart, growing up with a big sister like Lorinda."

"I'm sure you will, Carmen, and I'm sorry if I've opened up a painful memory for you." Emma put her hand on Carmen's arm, patting it gently. "Your niece is fortunate to have a father like Paul. Even a stranger could see how much he adores his little girl. And from what I've observed, she's pretty lucky to have an aunt like you as well."

"Thank you, Emma. And don't worry, you didn't open any wounds. It's getting easier for me as time goes on to be able to talk about my sister and not get all choked up." Needing to change the subject, Carmen said, "Would you mind if I asked you some questions about the Amish way of life?"

"Of course not. You can ask me anything while we drink our tea."

Emma poured tea into their cups, handed one to Carmen, and took the other for herself.

Carmen took a sip of tea, savoring the delicate aroma and taste of peppermint. "This is really good," she said, letting it roll around on her tongue.

"I'm glad you like it. I grow the mint in my garden, and there was a lot of it this summer."

"I can't have a garden where I live." Carmen sighed. "That's what you get with apartment living."

"Maybe someday you'll have a home of your own." Emma set her cup on the table. "If you have a patio, perhaps you could plant a few herbs in a planter box. They don't need a lot of space. I've planted things in the window box outside the kitchen. It's nice to be able to pick whatever I need without having to walk out to the garden all the time."

"That sounds doable." Carmen's interest was heightened. "I may consider that when I get back home. In Los Angeles, the nights are sometimes cool in the winter months, but the days are pretty mild. In fact, wintertime is our rainiest season. The rest of the year it's quite dry."

"I can't imagine being able to have a year-round garden." Emma paused and took a sip of tea. "Now, on to another subject. What is it you want to know about the Amish life?"

"I've been wondering about rumschpringe. What can you tell me about it?"

Emma tapped her fingers on the edge of the table. "Well, it normally begins around the age of fifteen or sixteen and ends when an Amish young person decides to be baptized and join the church."

"Do most of the youth go wild during that time and do things their parents wouldn't approve of?" Carmen queried, thinking of her boss's insistence that her article focus on wild Amish teens.

"No, not all. In fact, most, at least those in our district, enjoy a time with others their age, where they attend Sunday night singings and get together for volleyball and baseball games. Some take trips together, and some never leave the area during their running-around years."

"So it's not just a bunch of wild parties or Amish young people leaving home to experience things in the world that their parents would disapprove of?"

Emma shook her head. "I'm sure there are a few who do that, but as I said, most of the young people I know have stuck close to home."

"What about their parents?" Carmen asked. "Do they approve of rumschpringe?"

"Some look the other way," Emma admitted, "but other parents hold a tight rein on their children."

"From what Anna's told me, her parents won't give her the freedom to explore the outside world," Carmen said. "Is that healthy?"

Deep wrinkles formed across Emma's forehead as her lips compressed. "It's not really my place to say, but I think they may be making a mistake by holding her back. Anna, like most others her age, is curious about the English world. In my opinion, if she's allowed to experience a few things outside of her community, she might find out, just as my children did, that there's much to appreciate about the Amish way of life."

Carmen mulled things over as she finished her tea. Emma was a wise woman, and this conversation had given Carmen a lot to think about. After learning what she had so far, it would be difficult to write a negative article about the Amish. But if she didn't write it, she could lose her job.

CHAPTER 23

Elkhart

How come you've been so quiet today?" Jan asked as he and Terry removed shingles from the roof of an elderly couple who didn't have much money. Jan had given them a discount, which he often did when someone couldn't pay full price. It was a wonder he made any money at all, but he said that over the years he'd become aware of what a limited income many senior citizens struggled to live on and that it felt good to be able to help out whenever he could.

"Hey, man, did you hear what I said?" Jan repeated. "I asked how come you've been so quiet today."

"Yeah, I heard. I've just been thinking, is all."

"About what?"

"The weekend and how it went."

"If you're talking about Saturday night at the bowling alley, then I can tell you exactly how it went."

Terry tipped his head to one side. "Oh yeah? How's that?"

"You bent over backwards to get Cheryl to pay attention to you instead of her date." Jan grunted. "And you made a complete fool of yourself in the process."

Terry's face heated. "Oh really? What'd I do that made me look like a fool?"

Jan stopped what he was doing and held up one finger. "You tried to out-bowl Blaine, and you both acted like two roosters in a henhouse." Another finger shot up. "You talked more to Cheryl then you did me and Star, and we were the ones you were supposed to be bowling with." Jan held up a third finger, but before he could say anything Terry cut him off.

"Okay, I get it. You're mad because I paid Cheryl some attention." Terry planted his hands against his hips. "Did you forget that I've been trying to get her to go out with me?"

Jan shook his head. "'Course not, but you shouldn't be making a play for her when she's out with another man. That just ain't cool. Anyone watching could see you were pushing too hard, and I wouldn't be surprised if she noticed that, too. If anything, that might have turned her away."

Terry shrugged. "Think what you want to, but I had to get Cheryl to notice me somehow, and you know what? It worked!"

"How so?"

"Cheryl and I had our first date Sunday afternoon."

Jan quirked an eyebrow. "Is that the truth?"

"'Course it is. I showed up at Cheryl's church, and—"

Jan stared at Terry in disbelief. "I'm not hearing this. Did you just say you went to church?"

"That's right, and afterward Cheryl and I went out to lunch." Terry grinned widely. "When we were done eating, we drove back to Shipshe and got my Harley, so Cheryl could take her first ride on a motorcycle."

Jan whistled. "I've gotta hand it to you, buddy. All those crazy stunts you pulled Saturday night must have impressed that little gal. I woulda thought the opposite, though. And going to church. . . Well, if it took trying to land a date with the pretty little blond to get you in church, then I have to say, 'Amen' to that, 'cause I've tried everything but stand on my head to coax you into going to church, and you always come up with some lame excuse."

"You don't have to rub it in." Terry bent down, grabbed an armful of shingles, and tossed them into Jan's utility trailer. "You know what?"

"What?"

"I kinda enjoyed the church service. The preacher read some verses from the Bible that sorta opened my eyes to the truth about some things."

"Such as?"

"He talked about temptation. Even said Jesus was tempted, and that He's able to help those who are tempted." Terry scratched the side of his head. "I think he said the verse was found in Hebrows something or other."

Jan laughed and poked Terry's arm. "It's Hebrews, and it's a great verse for you—especially since you're struggling with the temptation to smoke."

"Yeah. I've been doing a little better with it today, though," Terry said. He patted his pocket. "Been chewing a lot of gum."

"That's good to hear." Jan loaded more shingles into the trailer and paused to wipe his damp forehead. Despite the autumn chill, they'd both worked up quite a sweat. "So where'd you go to church?"

"That church in Goshen, where your friend, Ruby Lee's husband, pastors. That's why I asked you where it was, remember?"

Jan smiled. "Star and I have been there a few times, but we mostly go to a church near my place in Shipshe. Pastor Gene's a good man, and Ruby Lee... Well, she's a sweetheart."

Terry bobbed his head. "She was real friendly and made me feel welcome. When church was over, she introduced me to her husband, and they both said they hoped I'd come back. I even saw a motorcycle in the church parking lot, so I know I'd have something in common with someone in the congregation."

"Think you'll go back?" Jan asked.

"Yeah, I'm pretty sure of it."

"That's good to hear, but you shouldn't be going to church because of Cheryl. There's a lot more to it than that." Jan thumped Terry's shoulder. "Can I offer you a piece of advice?"

"Sure. You usually do," Terry added with a snicker.

"I can see by the starry look in your eyes that you're pretty hyped up about Cheryl. Just be careful you don't get your heart broken. She might have gone out to lunch with you and taken a ride on your Harley, but she went bowling with someone else, so don't get your hopes up."

Terry shrugged. "Don't worry, I'm not. Even if I do go out with Cheryl again, it'll just be for fun 'cause I have no plans of getting serious about anyone."

Jan chuckled and thumped Terry's back. "That's what they all say before they're reeled in."

"Hey, wait up a minute, would you?" Stuart called as Blaine was about to leave the sporting goods store at the end of his workday.

Blaine halted near the door as he put on his hunter-green zip-up jacket. "What's up?"

"I haven't had a chance to talk to you all day and wanted to hear how things went with Cheryl on your bowling date."

"It was okay, I guess," Blaine replied in a nonchalant tone, anxious to get home after a grueling day. He'd been on his feet the entire shift, and between helping customers and stocking shelves, his recliner and a good DVD were all he could think about. Extra shipments of goods were starting to arrive for the upcoming holidays. A busy time of the year for the store was fast approaching, but for now, all Blaine wanted to do was get home and prop up his feet.

"Didn't you enjoy your date at all?" Stuart asked, nudging Blaine's arm.

"Cheryl's nice, but she's not Sue."

Stuart opened the door to let a late shopper out. "Do you think it's fair to compare the two women?"

"Maybe not, but—"

"You need to forget about Sue and get on with your life."

"I guess you're right," Blaine admitted. "And I did enjoy being with Cheryl—at least until Terry showed up and started showing off for her."

"Did she leave with him?" Stuart questioned.

"Well, no, but she didn't leave with me, either. She drove her own car to the bowling alley, and I met her there."

"Was Cheryl impressed with Terry? Did she pay him any attention?"

Blaine shrugged. "I don't know if she was impressed, but she did laugh at his corny jokes."

"Maybe you ought to ask her out again," Stuart suggested. "Take her someplace where Terry's not likely to show up."

"Such as?"

"How about one of the nice restaurants on Winona Lake? Pam really likes it when I take her there. With all the little stores in the village, she could spend hours shopping."

"I don't know. Winona Lake's in Kosciusko County, over an hour away."

Stuart thumped Blaine's back. "Exactly! I mean what are the odds that Terry would show up there?"

"Slim to none, I guess."

"Right. A guy like him probably wouldn't even go to a fancy restaurant, let alone drive that far to get there."

"Hmm. . ." Blaine pondered Stuart's suggestion. "Maybe when I see Cheryl at the next quilting class I'll ask her out to lunch. Better yet, maybe she'd like to go fishing with me sometime." Blaine had never been to Lake Winona, which was south of Mishawaka, but he was game to find new places where he might want to venture for some good fishing. He remembered one of his customers saying he went to Lake Winona every year and rented a cottage there, but Blaine couldn't recall what the man had said about the fishing.

"I don't know about Cheryl, but I know all too well how Pam resented me going fishing so much," Stuart said. "Maybe you'd better stick to taking Cheryl out to lunch for now. Since you'll be at the lake, the subject of fishing might come up, and you can ask her then. And I think it might be better if you asked her out over the phone. That way, Terry won't know about your plans."

Blaine nodded. "You're right. That would be better than asking her during class. I'll give Cheryl a call tonight."

"You're late. What took you so long?" Mandy asked when Anna entered the Dairy Queen and found her friend sitting at a table.

"Sorry, but it couldn't be helped. Dad made me stay longer than usual this afternoon because he had a couple of orders that needed to go out." Anna sank into the seat beside Mandy. "Have you already had your ice-cream cone?"

Mandy shook her head. "I was waiting for you."

Anna smiled. "Good, because I'm hungry and more than ready for a treat. Let's go order our cones now, and then we can visit."

Anna and Mandy returned to their table a few minutes later with chocolate-vanilla swirl cones. "This hits the spot," Anna said, swiping her tongue over the sweet frozen treat. "I love soft ice cream."

"Me, too," Mandy agreed. "Guess this will probably spoil my appetite for supper, but I probably won't eat much of it anyway, because Mom's fixing baked cabbage tonight, and I don't like it."

Anna wrinkled her nose. "Me neither. Besides tasting yucky, cooked cabbage stinks up the house."

"Have you had any luck finding another job yet?" Mandy asked, switching the subject and glancing at the English boys a few tables away.

"No, Dad keeps me so busy at the window shop that there's no time to go looking."

"I'm going down to Sarasota this winter," Mandy announced with a grin. "I'll be working at one of the restaurants outside of Pinecraft." She clasped Anna's arm. "Why don't you come with me? I'll see if I can get you a job there, too."

Anna's eyes widened. "Really? You'd do that for me?"

"Of course. What else are friends for? It would be more fun being there if we were together."

Anna smiled. This might be the opportunity she was hoping for—a chance for a new job—in a place where Mom and Dad couldn't watch every move she made. She'd be able to make her own decisions and not worry about anyone telling her what to do. She had a good head on her shoulders and could never understand why Mom and Dad didn't see that about her.

"So what do you think?" Mandy asked, bumping Anna's arm. "Will you go to Sarasota with me in December? Think about it—it's right by the Gulf, and we could go to the beach during our free time. Imagine getting a tan in December."

"That does sound appealing. Where will you stay while you're there?" Anna asked.

"I'll be renting a small house in Pinecraft." Mandy smiled widely. "Just think how much fun it'll be for us to spend the winter where it's warm."

"I would like to go." Anna paused to finish her cone. "You know what, Mandy?"

"What?"

"If I like it there, I may just stay and never move back."

CHAPTER 24

Shipshewana

Selma turned out the lights in her living room and padded down the hall toward her bedroom, dreading the coolness of the room. She'd called the furnace company, but they said they were swamped and couldn't send a man over until early the next week. Out of desperation, Selma had gone next door to see if Jan might be able to help her out, but he wasn't home; just that big mutt of his, barking and jumping at the fence in his dog run. She knew she shouldn't complain. At least Jan had remedied the problem, and Brutus hadn't found a way to break out of the pen Jan had built for him.

Selma stopped at the linen closet in the hall and grabbed a heavy blanket. The nights had been getting colder lately, and with no heat in her room, she would need the extra blanket. She'd switched to flannel sheets when she'd remade the bed last week, and since then, each morning it was harder to get out of her warm, cozy cocoon.

When Selma entered the bedroom, she placed the blanket on the bed, changed into her nightgown, and turned down the covers. She was about to climb into bed, when she heard an unfamiliar noise. Unexpectedly, the floor vent popped up, and the scruffy cat poked his head through.

Selma jumped. Then, trying hard not to laugh, she shook her finger at the cat and sternly said, "So that's how you've been getting in, is it? You're just full of surprises, aren't you, Scruffy?"

The cat gave a quick *meow!* Then he leaped onto her bed and curled into a tight ball. A few seconds later, seeming quite content, he began to purr, looking as if it would take more than a harsh scolding to change his mind about moving.

Selma couldn't believe how persistent this animal was. It didn't seem to matter how stern she was. Scruffy just wouldn't give up. For some unknown reason, he'd decided to make this his new home, and he didn't seem to care whether Selma liked it or not.

Should I weaken and let Scruffy stay? she wondered. Selma figured if she put the cat out he'd just find his way back in. *Guess I could set a box or one of my bedside tables over the vent, but then he'd probably sit under the house and meow all night.*

Leaning down, so she was eye level with the cat, Selma said quietly, "Okay, Scruffy, you win—you've got yourself a new home."

Middlebury

As Anna got ready for bed, she realized that in her excitement over the possibility of going to Florida in December, she'd forgotten to show Mandy the bracelet Carmen had gotten her. Anna had only been to Florida once, when as a nine-year-old, she'd gone with her grandparents for a few weeks in December. The one thing she remembered most was running barefoot on the white sandy beaches. It had been fun to look for shells, chase the seagulls, and wade in the warm water. Grandpa had even taken a kite along, and on windy days he'd shown Anna how to fly it.

The eighty-degree temperatures in Sarasota felt so good. Not having to bundle up like she would have been doing back home had been a plus, too. Summer had always been Anna's favorite time of the year, and she recalled how different it was to sip milk shakes during the warmth of a winter evening instead of watching snowflakes. On one of those nights, she'd sat with her grandparents on their front porch, watching as lightning illuminated the sky and thunder rumbled.

The idea of going to Sarasota with Mandy was exciting, but one thing bothered Anna. How was she going to tell her folks? They'd never give their blessing, because they thought her place was at home where they could tell her what to do and keep a close watch on her. Anna could already imagine the clash, trying to convince her folks that she should go to Sarasota, while listening to them give all the reasons she shouldn't.

Maybe I should just go and not tell them, Anna thought as she stared at the blank wall across her room. *I could head out during the night, and leave them a note on the kitchen table.* Anna knew that would be a cowardly thing to do, but wouldn't it be better than listening to Mom and Dad list all the reasons it would be wrong for her to go? She could already sense this would become one more wedge pushing her and her parents apart. *I don't need to decide anything right now*, she reminded herself. *December is still two months away.*

Anna went to get her purse, which she'd placed on her dresser when she'd arrived home that afternoon. Reaching inside to get the bracelet Carmen had given her, she was surprised when she couldn't find it. She dug around for a bit, but there was no sign of the bracelet.

Going over to the bed, Anna dumped the contents of her purse onto the quilt, but after sorting through everything, she realized the piece of jewelry wasn't there.

Anna's heart started to pound. What had happened to it? Could one of her siblings have sneaked into her room while she was helping Mom do the dishes and gone through her purse?

She sank to the bed with a moan. *What should I do? I can't accuse anyone when I don't know who did it. And what if I say something and no one admits to taking the bracelet? If Mom and Dad get wind of this, I'll be in trouble for sure.*

Anna pondered the situation. Maybe the best thing to do was snoop around in her siblings' rooms when they weren't there and see if she could locate the missing jewelry. If she didn't find it by the end of the week, she'd have to come right out and ask.

Shipshewana

As Emma followed Lamar down the hall toward their bedroom, she noticed that he was limping and walking slower than usual. Today he'd worked on one of the hickory rockers he made to sell at a local gift store. Perhaps he'd overdone it.

"Are you feeling okay this evening?" Emma asked after they'd entered their room. "I noticed you were limping and wondered if you might be in pain."

Deep wrinkles formed across Lamar's forehead as he turned to face her. "I'm stiff and my joints ache," he admitted, leaning against the dresser for support.

"Did you work too long on the rocker today?"

"Maybe, but I think it's my arthritis flaring up. These cold days we've been having don't help with the stiffness." Lamar rubbed his fingers. "My hands don't work well when my arthritis acts up."

Emma lowered herself to the bed as reality set in. "You wanted to go to Florida because you knew you'd feel better where it's warm, right?"

He nodded slowly as he released the suspenders from his trousers.

"Then why didn't you explain that to me? If I'd only known—"

"You would have agreed to go, even though you wanted to teach another six-week quilting class," he interrupted.

"Jah, that's right. I would have changed my mind had I known the reason."

"Which is why I didn't tell you." He sat beside Emma on the bed. "I knew you were looking forward to teaching another class, and I wouldn't have felt right asking you to give it up on my account."

"Oh Lamar," Emma said, tears welling in her eyes, "you're my husband, and I love you so much."

"I love you, too, Emma." Lamar placed a comforting arm around her shoulders.

"I appreciate you allowing me to teach another class, and I really do feel that the students who've come to my class have been sent for a reason. But your health and your needs come first, so. . ."

Lamar put his finger to her lips. "It's all right, Emma. We have just three more weeks of teaching your students, and maybe after that, if you're willing, we can head to Florida."

She smiled and leaned her head on his shoulder. "I'm more than willing, and if you like, we can spend the entire winter there, where it's nice and warm."

He reached for her hand and gave it a gentle squeeze. "I'm surely blessed to have a *fraa* like you."

Goshen

Cheryl took a seat at her kitchen table and booted up her laptop. While she ate a snack of apples and cheese, she planned to answer any e-mails that had come in over the weekend.

She was about to go online when her cell phone rang. She saw in the caller ID that it was Blaine.

"Hello, Blaine," she said, holding the phone up to her ear.

"Hi, Cheryl. How are you this evening?"

"I'm fine. How are you?"

"Doing okay." After a pause, Blaine cleared his throat a few times. "The reason I'm calling is I was wondering if you have any plans for Saturday."

"Just Emma's quilt class," Cheryl replied.

"I meant Saturday afternoon, when the class is over."

"I have no plans at the moment." Secretly, Cheryl had been hoping Terry might ask her out. As scared as she'd been on the back of his motorcycle, she actually wanted to go for another ride. Now that she knew what to expect, she hoped she could relax and enjoy it more the second time around.

"I'd like to take you out for lunch," Blaine said. "To someplace nice, out of town."

"You've piqued my curiosity. Where did you plan to go?"

"Winona Lake. Have you ever been there?"

"No, but I've heard it's beautiful," Cheryl responded. "And I understand there's a lot to do there."

"Should I go ahead and make reservations?"

"Yes, it sounds nice. I'll look forward to going."

"Great. And I forgot tell you that the restaurant we're going to overlooks the lake. See you Saturday morning at Emma's then."

Cheryl smiled when she hung up the phone. This would be a pleasant change over her boring plans to clean the apartment. She wasn't sure yet what type of relationship Blaine was seeking from her. Did he simply want to be friends, or was he hoping for something more serious? Deep down, she hoped he saw her only as a friend. When she was with Blaine, even though she'd never had any siblings, it felt more like hanging out with a brother rather than being on a date. In any event, eating lunch at a restaurant with a view of the lake would give her a chance to get to know Blaine better. Maybe she would discover that she liked him more than she realized.

CHAPTER 25

Elkhart

"Thank you for inviting me to join you for supper," Carmen told Paul's sister, Maria, when she entered her kitchen Wednesday evening.

Maria smiled. "We're happy to have you, and we're so glad you could join us."

"Is there anything I can do to help?" Carmen asked, looking around the homey room, and feeling a twinge of envy. She'd never realized how much she longed for a house of her own until she'd come to Indiana. Thanks to her job, Carmen was on the road so much she sometimes felt like she didn't have a place to call home.

"You can finish the green salad I started, while I take the enchiladas out of the oven," Maria replied.

"Sure, no problem." Carmen placed a tomato on the cutting board and cut it into small pieces.

"How are you enjoying your quilting class?" Maria questioned.

"It's interesting. I've learned a lot about quilts, and the wall hanging

I'm making is turning out better than I expected," Carmen replied. "At first I was a little nervous about quilting, but now I'm really liking it."

"Paul liked the class when he took it, too." Maria set the dish of enchiladas on the table. "It's been good for him and Sophia having you here. Paul said Sophia lights up when you're in the room."

Carmen felt the heat of a blush. "I've enjoyed spending time with them, too."

"Have you ever considered moving to Elkhart so you could be closer to your niece?" Maria questioned.

"My job's in Los Angeles," Carmen replied.

"I know, but maybe you could get a job as a reporter with one of the newspapers in our area."

"The idea of moving here does have some appeal," Carmen admitted, "but I'm not sure I could find another job I like as well as the one I have now. Besides, I enjoy the warmth of the California sun, and it's only October here, and already I had to buy a warmer coat."

"I know what you mean," Maria said, going to the refrigerator to get the salad dressing. "Of course, some people go south for the winter, but for those of us who have jobs, that's not an option."

"Is supper about ready?" Maria's husband, Hosea, asked, poking his head into the kitchen. "The girls are getting hungry, and Paul and I are having a hard time keeping them under control."

Maria gestured to the table. "We're just about ready, so bring in the crew."

As Carmen helped to get the rest of the things set on the table, she couldn't help wondering what she'd be doing if she were in Los Angeles right now. At first, having her own apartment had been exciting— especially after getting a job at the newspaper. But now, she'd begun to question whether she really wanted to go back to California. Sure, the warm weather was great, but everything that had once been so appealing was slowly losing its zest.

As Paul watched Carmen from across the table, a lump formed in his throat. She reminded him of Lorinda—same dark hair and eyes, and a nose that turned up slightly on the end. It was almost painful to look at her. Even though Carmen was a few years younger than Lorinda, she seemed mature and possessed an air of confidence. She had a special way with Sophia, too, and Paul knew his daughter would miss her aunt Carmen when she returned to California in a few weeks.

I'll miss Carmen, too, Paul admitted to himself. *If only we had more time to spend with her.*

"Are the enchiladas okay?" Maria asked, bumping Paul's arm. "You haven't eaten much on your plate."

"Uh, yes, they're fine." Paul stabbed a piece with his fork.

"Just fine?" Hosea asked, raising his eyebrows. "Usually you can't get enough of my *esposa's* enchiladas."

Paul smiled at Maria. "They're very good. Guess I'm just a slow eater tonight."

"Paul's right," Carmen agreed. "This meal is delicious."

"The girls must think so, too." Maria motioned to Sophia and her two girls sitting near Carmen, eagerly eating their enchiladas.

As the meal continued, the adults talked about the chilly weather that had hit northeastern Indiana, and then the conversation moved to how things were going at the school where Paul taught. After that, Maria asked Carmen what it was like to be a newspaper reporter.

"It's interesting," Carmen said. "There's always something different to report."

"I imagine there's a lot more happening in Los Angeles than here," Paul said.

"There can be," Carmen responded, "but I'm often asked to travel to other places to cover news stories. My favorite ones to write about are human-interest stories, where I get to meet different people."

Paul listened with interest as Carmen explained more about her job. He could see that she was passionate about her work, and it made him doubt that she would ever give up her life in Los Angeles.

"I don't know about anyone else, but I'm so full I couldn't eat another bite," Hosea said, pushing away from the table. "Paul, would you like to join me in the living room to watch the evening news?"

Paul shook his head, snapping out of his thoughts. "You go ahead. Think I'll help Maria with the dishes. It'll be like old times when we were kids."

"I'd be happy to help Maria," Carmen was quick to say.

"That's okay," Paul said. "Why don't you spend some time with Sophia and the girls? Maria and I used to make a good team when we did the dishes together." He stood and started clearing away the dishes. Truth was, he'd hoped for a little one-on-one time with his sister this evening.

When Carmen, Hosea, and the girls left the kitchen, Maria filled the sink with warm water and added some liquid detergent. "You know," she said, smiling at Paul, "some people might think it's strange that a busy woman like me doesn't own a dishwasher, but I actually enjoy washing the dishes by hand."

Paul chuckled and reached for a clean towel, in readiness to dry. "I guess you take after our mother. I can't remember how many times I've heard Mom say over the years, 'I'll never own a dishwasher; they're just not for me.'"

"Like mother, like daughter," Maria said with a laugh. She glanced over at Paul as she placed some clean dishes in the drainer. "I sense you have something you'd like to talk about."

He nodded slowly. "You know me so well."

"What's on your mind?"

"Carmen." Paul lowered his voice. "Ever since she came here, she's been on my mind."

"I'm not surprised," Maria said, handing him another dish to dry. "She looks a lot like Lorinda."

"You're right, but it's more than that. I really enjoy being with her, and. . ." Paul's voice trailed off as he swiped the dish towel over the clean plate.

"Are you falling for her? Is that what you're saying?"

Paul shrugged his shoulders. "I–I'm not sure. I just know that being with Carmen makes me feel happier than I've been in a long time. Do you think it could be just because I miss Lorinda so much? Or could I actually be falling in love again?"

"Only you know that," Maria said in a big-sister tone of voice. "But if you'd like my opinion, I think you should spend as much time with Carmen as you can—maybe take her out a few times, just the two of you. If there is something brewing between you, you'll know soon enough."

"If Carmen and I go out by ourselves, would you be willing to watch Sophia?" he asked.

"Of course. The girls love spending time with their cousin."

Paul knew he didn't have much time since Carmen would be leaving in a few weeks. "All right then," he said. "I'm going to ask her out."

Goshen

Think I'll call Mom and see how Grandma's doing, Cheryl thought, glancing at the clock on her kitchen wall. It was almost ten, which meant it would be seven in Portland, so maybe she could catch her folks at home.

Cheryl reached for the phone and punched in her folks' number. Her father answered on the third ring.

"Hi, Dad. How are you doing?"

"I'm fine, Cheryl. How about you?"

"Doing good and keeping busy as usual." Cheryl switched the phone to her other ear. "Is Mom there?"

"No, she's at her garden club meeting. Should I ask her to call when she gets home?"

"No, that's okay. I'm just calling to see how Grandma's doing, and I'm sure you can tell me that."

"She's about the same. Doesn't say much when we go to the nursing home to see her, and she seems to be getting weaker."

"I'm sorry to hear that. As soon as Emma finishes Grandma's quilt and I'm done with the quilt classes, I'll be coming there to see Grandma. Maybe seeing that her quilt has been repaired will perk her up."

"I wouldn't count on it, Cheryl. I'm not even sure she'll know who you are."

"Why wouldn't she? Grandma knew me when I went to see her before I moved here."

"Some days she's fine, but other times she doesn't seem to know your mother. That's one reason we don't go as often to see her."

"I think Grandma needs people around here—people she knows and loves." Cheryl fought the urge to go see Grandma right away, but she wanted to wait until she could take the quilt for her birthday. She felt sure it would make a difference.

"If there's nothing else, I'd better hang up," Dad said. "There's a game show coming on TV that I want to watch."

"Okay, Dad. Have a nice evening." *I can't believe Mom doesn't visit Grandma very often. How can she be so selfish and unfeeling?*

When Cheryl hung up, she decided to check her e-mails before going to bed. She found one from April, with an invitation to her and Lance's wedding the first week of December. To add insult to injury, April had asked Cheryl to be one of her bridesmaids.

Cheryl grimaced. *The nerve of some people. If they think I'm about to go to their wedding, after what they did to me. . . What I should do is e-mail them back and give them a piece of my mind!*

"Be angry and sin not." The verse of scripture Ruby Lee had quoted to Cheryl a few weeks ago, came to mind. *Okay, I won't give them a piece of mind. But I'm not going to the wedding. It would be too painful. I'll send them an RSVP that I won't be attending.*

Middlebury

Anna slipped out of bed and tiptoed down the hall toward her sister Susan's bedroom. She should be asleep by now, and this was the perfect chance for Anna to search for her bracelet. She'd already looked in Arie's and Becky's rooms while they were helping Mom do the supper dishes. She would have checked Susan's room during that time, too, but Susan had been in there playing.

Holding a flashlight in one hand, Anna quietly opened the door. She shined the beam of light toward the bed, and when she saw that her sister was sleeping, she padded across the floor to Susan's dresser. The first drawer squeaked when she opened it, and she held her breath, hoping she hadn't awakened Susan. Hearing nothing, she pulled it the rest of the way out and rummaged through Susan's clothes. No bracelet there.

Anna continued to pull out drawers and look through each one, but there was no sign of her bracelet. *Let me think—where else could I look?*

Being as quiet as possible, she made her way to the closet and opened the door. Several of Susan's toys were on the floor, along with some shoes, a pair of rubber boots, and a jar of marbles. Anna thought it was strange that a young girl would collect marbles, but then Susan was a bit of a tomboy.

Anna knelt on the floor, where she discovered a stack of shoe boxes near the back of the closet. She opened the first one and saw that it was full of feathers. The second box held a collection of dried flowers, and the third box was full of pictures Susan had drawn of horses, cows, and chickens. Anna frowned. *Maybe Susan didn't take my bracelet after all.*

There was one more shoe box, and when Anna opened it, she gasped. Hidden under several pieces of paper, she found her bracelet. *So Susan must have gone through my purse, discovered the piece of jewelry, and hidden it here. Should I wake her and ask about it right now, or wait till morning? Or would it be better if I just took the bracelet and said nothing?*

Anna remained on her knees, contemplating things a bit longer. Then she snatched the bracelet and hurried out of Susan's room. She would decide what to do about this in the morning.

CHAPTER 26

Anna studied her youngest sister from across the breakfast table, wondering what she was thinking. Did Susan know the bracelet she'd taken from Anna's purse was no longer in her possession? Her face revealed no telltale sign of guilt or unease as she ate a slice of toast and giggled with their sister Becky about hiding from Arie earlier this morning.

Anna had planned to confront Susan about the bracelet on Thursday, but due to her work schedule and Susan being in school all week, she wasn't given the opportunity. If she didn't do it soon, however, it would be time to leave for the quilting class, so she was determined to speak to Susan after breakfast. Since it was Arie's and Becky's turn to do the dishes, and Susan would probably go outside to play after their meal, Anna decided that would be the best time to catch her. She was sure Susan hadn't told Mom about the bracelet, because if she had, Mom would surely have said something. Not only that, but if Susan had mentioned the jewelry to Mom, she would have had to admit that she'd snuck into Anna's room, gone through her purse, and taken the bracelet.

Anna ate her ham and eggs in silence, and as soon as breakfast was over, she cleared her dishes, grabbed her sweater, and followed Susan out the back door. Anna waited until her sister was a safe distance from the house. Then she hurried across the yard to where Susan knelt on the grass, petting a black-and-white kitten.

When Susan saw Anna approaching, she jumped up and started to move away. "Wait a minute. I need to talk to you," Anna said, placing her hand firmly on her sister's shoulder.

Susan looked up at Anna with a wary expression. "About what?"

"I think you know," Anna said sternly. "You took something of mine, and you had no right. You shouldn't have been in my purse."

Susan dropped her gaze as the kitten pawed at the hem of her dress. "I–I'm sorry, Anna. I was looking for some gum, and when I found the bracelet, I thought it was pretty, so I put it in a shoebox where I keep some special things." Her lower lip trembled. "You're not gonna tell Mom and Dad are you? I'd be in big trouble if they knew what I did."

Anna shook her head. "I won't say a thing, but you must promise never to do anything like that again. It's not right to take something that doesn't belong to you."

"I—I know. I'll go up to my room and get the bracelet right now."

"You don't have to do that," Anna said. "I already found it and took it back."

Susan's eyes widened. "You snuck into my room?"

Anna wasn't sure what to say. She'd just given her sister a lecture about sneaking into her own room and messing with her belongings, yet she'd done the same thing. "I suspected you had taken the bracelet," she said, carefully choosing her words. "So on Wednesday night after I was sure you were asleep, I went to your room to look around and found the bracelet in the shoe box in your closet."

"Guess we're even now," Susan said. "I took your bracelet, and you snuck into my room." Picking up the kitten, she skipped off toward the barn.

Anna sucked in a deep breath. *That went well enough. Now I'll either need to find a safe hiding place for the bracelet or give it back to Carmen.*

Shipshewana

Cheryl had just stepped out of her car when she heard the familiar roar of an engine. Turning, she saw Terry pull into Emma's yard on his motorcycle. When he turned off the engine and removed his helmet, he waved. She felt her face flush, which seemed to be happening a lot lately, especially whenever Terry was around.

"How you doing?" he called, swinging his leg over the cycle and pushing it toward the big tree to park it.

Cheryl waited until he'd put the kickstand down and caught up to her, then she smiled and said, "I'm fine. How about you?"

"Doing good, but I'll be better if you'll agree to go riding with me after class today," he said with a lopsided grin.

"I'm sorry, Terry," Cheryl said with regret, "but Blaine and I made plans for this afternoon."

Terry's smile faded. "Oh, I see. Guess that's what I get for waiting till the last minute to ask." He kicked a small stone with the toe of his boot and sent it skittering up the driveway. When they reached Emma's front porch, Terry stopped and turned to face Cheryl. "How about tomorrow afternoon? Would you want to get something to eat after church and then go for another ride on my Harley?" When Cheryl hesitated, he quickly added, "Or did the first ride freak you out too much?"

"I was scared at first," Cheryl admitted, "but once I got used to being on the bike, it was kind of fun." She hesitated, biting her lip. "Actually,

I was hoping you'd ask me out again." Her eyes widened, and she stepped back, regretting what she'd just said. Cheryl had never been that forward before—not even with her former boyfriend.

Cheryl held her breath and waited for Terry's response, knowing if she tried to explain, it could be even more embarrassing.

"You were?" Terry's smile returned. "Does that mean you'll go out with me tomorrow?"

Cheryl nodded and quickly stepped into the house. For a twenty-eight-year-old woman who was normally quite confident, she felt shy all of a sudden and needed to put a little space between herself and Terry. Aside from her reservations, Cheryl had enjoyed Terry's company last Sunday and figured she probably would again. Besides it was fun to be dating again—especially when she had two very different men taking an interest in her.

Following Cheryl, Terry was about to enter Emma's house, when Selma showed up. He waited, holding the door for her.

"I'm not late, am I?" Selma asked as she stepped onto the porch, panting as though short of breath.

"Well, if you are, then I must be, too," Terry responded with a teasing grin.

Selma's forehead wrinkled. "I slept longer than I'd planned this morning, and then—" She stopped talking and brushed a hand across her beige-colored slacks, where a glob of gray fur was stuck. Picking the hair off her pants and blowing it from her fingers, she watched as the air took the fluff and floated it into Emma's yard.

"Is that cat hair?" Terry questioned, remembering Selma's comment about not wanting any pets. He hadn't forgotten that Selma thought four-legged creatures were a nuisance.

Selma sheepishly nodded. "Yes, it is cat hair."

"Is that from the same stray cat you were telling our quilting class about? Scruffy, was it?"

Her cheeks reddened. "Yes, that's the cat that's been hanging around my place, and he's been getting into the house through the vent in my bedroom floor. To make matters worse, for the last several days I haven't had any heat coming up from that vent."

"Did you call the furnace company?" Terry asked as he and Selma entered the house.

She nodded. "But they haven't made it out to my house yet."

"Want me to take a look?" Terry offered. "I could follow you home after class."

"I don't have a basement, so you'd have to crawl under the house and you'd probably get dirty."

Terry shrugged. "That's no big deal. Being a roofer, I get dirty almost every day."

Selma's thin lips formed a smile. "Thanks, I'd appreciate that."

Crawling under Selma's house sure wouldn't be as much fun as going out with Cheryl, but at least Terry would be doing a good deed. He'd learned from Jan how good it felt to do something helpful for the older generation. He figured, too, that keeping busy today would take his mind off Cheryl and her date with Blaine.

CHAPTER 27

"Good morning," Emma said after everyone had taken their seats around the sewing table. "Today we'll begin the quilting process, and if anyone has a question as we go along, please don't hesitate to ask."

Terry's hand shot up.

"What's your question, Terry?" Emma asked.

"Will we be using the sewing machines again? I had a hard time holding the material straight while I tried to sew last week."

Emma shook her head. "The quilting is done by hand with a needle and thread. Now, will everyone please place your work on the table?"

After the students did as Emma asked, she explained that the quilting process was stitching three layers of material together. "But before we begin the actual process, you'll need to cut a piece of cotton batting approximately two inches larger than your quilt top on all sides," Emma said. "The excess batting and backing will be trimmed even with the quilt top after all the quilting stitches have been completed."

Everyone watched as she and Lamar demonstrated.

"Now, in order to create a smooth, even quilting surface, all three layers of the quilt need to be put in a frame," Emma continued. "For a larger quilt you would need a quilting frame that could stretch and hold the entire quilt at one time. But since your wall hangings are much smaller than a full-sized quilt, you can use a frame that's similar to a large embroidery hoop." She held up one of the small frames she'd placed on the table. "It's important when using this type of hoop to baste the entire quilt together through all three layers. This will keep the layers evenly stretched while you're quilting. Just be sure you don't quilt over the basting, or it will be difficult to remove later on."

Emma waited patiently until each person had cut out their batting. Then Lamar stepped forward and said, "The next step will be to mark the design you want on your quilt top. But if you only want to outline the patches you've sewn with quilting, then no marking is necessary. You'll just need to quilt close to the seam so the patch will be emphasized."

Emma went on to explain about needle size, saying that it was best to try several and see which one seemed the most comfortable to handle. She also stated that the use of a snugly fitting thimble worn on the middle finger of the hand used for pushing the quilting needle was necessary, since the needle would have to be poked through three layers of fabric repeatedly. She then demonstrated on a quilt patch, showing how to pull the needle and thread through the material to create the quilting pattern. "The stitches should be tiny and even," Emma said. "They need to be snug, but not so tight that they'll cause the material to pucker."

Terry groaned. "That sounds hard, and look—I've already stitched my shirtsleeve to a piece of the material," he said, lifting his arm. "Guess I shouldn't have gone ahead of the others." Wanting to look a little nicer today, he'd worn a pale green shirt with long sleeves, but now he wished he'd worn a T-shirt. "At the rate I'm going, I'll probably mess my whole wall hanging up. Since this is the fourth class, I thought I'd be doing better by now."

"Don't worry, it takes time, and that's why Lamar and I are here to help you," Emma said. "For now, rather than worrying about the size of the stitches, just try to concentrate on making them straight."

"Better let me take a look at that shirtsleeve," Lamar spoke up, walking to Terry's side of the table. "I'll just cut the material off for you, and it's nothing to get riled about. At one time or another we've all had an unforgettable moment when trying something new. I'll bet someday you'll look back at this and laugh."

Terry held his wrist out to Lamar and watched as he quickly detached the material and loose threads. When Lamar was finished, Terry glanced over at Cheryl, who sat across the table from him. She was already pinning her batting to the patterned pieces of material she'd sewn last week, and from the smile on her face, he figured she was enjoying the whole process.

Quilting ain't for me, Terry thought as he fumbled with his pieces of material, trying to get them placed and stitched on the batting he'd cut. *I doubt I'll be looking back and laughing at anything that has to do with quilting. If it hadn't been for wanting to ask Cheryl out, I'd never have taken this class.*

Terry studied Cheryl's pretty face and golden-blond hair. She was a real looker, all right; but it was more than Cheryl's looks that had made Terry decide to ask her out again. Having spent last Sunday afternoon with her, Terry quickly realized that he was drawn to her personality. He liked hearing her laugh when he said something funny and was impressed with her caring attitude. Cheryl had also been such a good sport about riding on the back of his Harley. He appreciated that she didn't judge him because of the way he dressed or wore his hair, either.

Terry glanced over at Blaine, sitting beside Cheryl with a Cheshire cat grin on his face. *I'll bet he loved it when I stitched my shirtsleeve to that piece of cloth. Well, I guess it was pretty funny. Blaine's probably better for Cheryl,* Terry thought with regret. *If I had a lick of sense I'd back off, but if I did that, I'd never get the chance to really know her. Nope. I'm going out with her again tomorrow and see where it goes from there.*

Carmen glanced at Selma, who sat beside her. She was smiling and appeared much happier this morning. Up until today, she'd been so sullen. *I wonder what happened to bring on the change? Guess it wouldn't be right to ask, but it's sure an improvement.* Watching Selma as she sewed and hummed to herself, made Carmen feel happy, too.

Carmen turned her attention to Anna, sitting on the other side of the table. Even though she was doing a good job of quilting, her droopy eyelids and slumped shoulders made her appear to be sad. Had something happened at home? Did she have an argument with her parents or one of her siblings? Carmen hoped she could talk to Anna after class. Whatever was bothering the girl, Carmen was sure she wouldn't want to discuss it in front of the others. Maybe Anna would open up to her. After all, she had told Carmen some things about her parents and shared her feelings about them. But knowing Anna trusted her bothered Carmen, too, because she'd begun to question her motives in writing the negative article about the Amish.

"How are you doing?" Emma asked, placing her hands on Carmen's shoulders. "Are you getting the feel for quilting yet?"

Glad for the interruption, Carmen smiled up at Emma. "It's not as hard as I thought it would be, but it is slow and tedious."

Emma nodded. "It's good to go slow at first, though. That way you'll be able to get more even stitches. But remember, the more you do it, the easier it will get."

"I'm glad I signed up for this class," Carmen said. "Not just to learn to quilt, but to get to know you, Emma."

"My wife's easy to get to know, because she cares so much about people," Lamar spoke up from across the room, where he'd gone to get more pins for Blaine.

"And so do you," Emma said, smiling at Lamar when he returned to the table.

He grinned back at her. "Guess that's why we make such a good team."

Carmen couldn't help feeling a bit envious. It was obvious that Emma and Lamar were deeply in love. What she wouldn't give to find that kind of happiness with a man. *Lorinda and Paul had a special relationship,* she thought. *If she hadn't been killed, they might have had another child by now, and I'd be an auntie again.*

Carmen thought about the phone call she'd had from Paul last night, asking if she would join him for dinner tonight. He'd said Maria would watch Sophia, so it would just be the two of them. Carmen looked forward to spending some time alone with Paul. He was easygoing, kind, and quite good-looking. It was no wonder Lorinda had fallen in love with him. Given the chance, Carmen thought she could fall in love with Paul; although she doubted he'd ever feel that way about her. Besides the fact that Carmen was Lorinda's sister, her home and job were clear across the country. It was just a silly dream to think that anything romantic could develop between her and Paul, yet she couldn't stop thinking about it. In fact, the more Carmen tried to talk herself out of those possibilities, the more her mind kept going in that direction. Once more, Carmen wondered how Paul would feel if he knew the real reason she was here. What would he think of her then?

Blaine fidgeted in his chair, anxious for today's class to be over. Even though he was finally getting the hang of it, he was bored with quilting.

"How's it going?" Lamar asked, taking a seat beside Blaine.

"Okay, I guess, but sewing's not really my thing." He glanced around to see if anyone was listening.

"What is your thing?"

"That's easy; it's fishing."

"I enjoy fishing, too," Lamar said. "In fact, when the weather is nice I go to Lake Shipshewana every chance I get."

"Same here. It's a wonder we've never bumped into each other there." Blaine smiled, wondering why the two of them had never struck up a conversation about fishing before. The class would have been less boring if they had. "No matter what time of day, I can't think of anything I'd rather be doing than sitting at the lake with my fishing pole in the water."

"How about the two of us going fishing this afternoon?" Lamar suggested.

"As nice as that sounds, I've made other arrangements for today," Blaine said, with a feeling of regret. "If the weather's decent, maybe we could go next week after class."

Lamar gave a nod. "That sounds like a plan."

When class was over, Anna hurried out the door behind Carmen. "I need to tell you something," she said as they stepped into the yard.

"What is it?" Carmen asked, halting her footsteps.

"It's about that bracelet you gave me." Anna dropped her gaze to the ground. This was harder than she thought it would be. "As much as I'd like to, I—I just can't keep it."

"How come?"

"One of my sisters found it in my purse, and I'm afraid if I keep it my folks will find out." Anna shifted nervously from one foot to the other. "I appreciate that you bought it for me, and I hope you'll understand, but I need to give the bracelet back to you."

"I'll take it back on one condition," Carmen said as Anna handed her the bracelet.

"What's that?"

"If you'll allow me to buy you something else."

Anna shook her head. "That's okay; I don't really need anything."

"Oh please. I'd really like to get you something," Carmen insisted. "Is there anything special you'd like?"

Anna shook her head. "I'm fine, really."

Carmen looked disappointed, but she smiled and said, "Let me know if you change your mind."

Terry grimaced as he watched Cheryl leave her car parked in Emma's driveway and get into Blaine's SUV. It was hard to see her go off with Blaine when he wished she was leaving with him. He consoled himself with the thought that he'd see Cheryl tomorrow at church and then they'd spend the afternoon together. Right now he needed to head over to Selma's and take a look under her house. After that, he was anxious to take a ride on his Harley. He'd been struggling with an urge to smoke all morning and hoped that getting out on the open road might clear his head. Some days, Terry wondered if he'd ever lick his smoking habit, but because of Cheryl, he had a reason to conquer his addiction. She was a positive influence on his life in more ways than one. He actually found himself saying a little prayer that it would all work out.

CHAPTER 28

After Emma and Lamar finished eating their lunch, she returned to her quilting room to work on the quilt for Cheryl's grandma. Taking a seat in front of her quilting frame, she studied the colorful quilt. A lump formed in her throat as she thought about the gift of love Cheryl wanted to bestow on her ailing grandmother. Emma hoped she could get it done in time for Cheryl to take to Oregon for her grandmother's birthday. *I wish I could be there to see the look of surprise on the old woman's face when Cheryl presents her with the quilt,* she thought. *If Oregon wasn't so far away, I'd ask if I could accompany Cheryl to the nursing home where her grandmother lives.*

"Are you sure you should be working on that quilt right now?" Lamar asked when he entered the room.

Emma peered at him over the top of her glasses. "What do you mean?"

"You look tired. I think you've been doing too much lately." Lamar grabbed a chair, pulled it close to Emma, and took a seat. "I don't want you to get sick or end up with a case of the shingles like you had a year ago in the spring."

"I appreciate your concern," Emma said sweetly, "but I'm just fine. If I get tired, I'll go take a nap."

"I have a better idea," Lamar said. "Why don't the two of us take a ride to Lake Shipshewana? We can either walk around for a bit or just sit on a bench and watch people fish. It's a bit chilly outside, but not too cold yet, so it should be just right for a little relaxation together and a chance for some fresh air."

"Wouldn't you rather go alone, so you can fish?" she asked, knowing how much her husband enjoyed his time at the lake and the opportunity to bring home his catch for supper.

"That'd be nice, but I've made plans to go fishing with Blaine after class next week, so I can wait till then." Lamar leaned over and kissed Emma's cheek. "I'd like to spend this afternoon with you. It's a good day to be out among nature."

Emma smiled. "A trip to the lake does sound nice. I'll set the quilt aside for now, and return to it after we get back. Why don't I fix a thermos of hot chocolate and take along some of those kichlin I baked yesterday?"

Lamar smacked his lips. "That sounds *wunderbaar*."

⸻

As Terry lay on his back under Selma's house, he noticed a large rip in the foil-wrapped ductwork. He shined his flashlight around, wondering how the ductwork had gotten torn. Then he noticed several paw prints on the ground. They didn't look like those made by a cat, so he figured a family of raccoons might have been under the house and torn the ductwork open for warmth. Of course, Selma's cat had probably taken advantage of it, too, and found a way to get inside.

Terry crawled back out, went into Selma's house, and told her what he'd found.

"Can it be fixed?" she asked, scrunching up her face with a look of despair.

"Yeah, but I'll have to run to the hardware store to get some duct tape and aluminum wrap."

"I hate to put you to all that trouble," she said.

He shook his head. "It's no trouble, and it won't take me long. I'll just hop on my cycle and be back in a flash."

Selma opened her purse and handed Terry a fifty-dollar bill. "Will this be enough?"

"Yeah, that's plenty. I'll bring back the change."

"While you're gone, I'll fix some lunch," Selma offered.

"There's no need to do that," Terry said, shaking his head. "Don't want to put you to any trouble."

"It won't be any trouble at all, and it's the least I can do to repay your kindness," she insisted.

Terry shrugged. "Okay, if you insist."

When Terry returned from the hardware store, he went back under the house and fixed the torn ductwork while Selma scurried around the kitchen, setting the table and putting things out to make ham-and-cheese sandwiches. It wasn't often she had anyone to share a meal with in her home, so she looked forward to visiting with Terry as they ate lunch together.

When Terry returned to the house a short time later, she motioned to the table. "Like I promised, I have everything ready."

Terry grabbed the end of his ponytail and twisted it around his fingers a few times as he leaned against the counter in her kitchen. "I really don't need any payment for doing a good deed, but since I am kinda hungry, I'll be glad to take you up on that offer."

Selma smiled and gestured to the hallway outside of the kitchen. "You can wash up in the bathroom at the end of the hall."

Terry gave a nod and hurried down the hall.

Selma went to the refrigerator and took out mustard, mayonnaise, and pickles. By the time she'd placed them on the table and added a bag of potato chips, Terry was back.

"That's a nice picture of you I saw sitting on the bookshelf just inside the living room," Terry said. "How long ago was it taken?"

"That's actually my daughter, Cora, and the photo was taken some time ago," Selma said. "Would you like a bowl of soup to go with the sandwiches? I have some leftover chicken noodle soup in the refrigerator I can heat up."

"Thanks anyway, but a sandwich will be plenty for me." He grinned and pointed to the chips. "I might have some of those, too."

"Take all the chips you want." Selma gestured to the chair at the head of the table. "Have a seat, and I'll get you something to drink. Would you like coffee, milk, or apple cider? I don't have any soda pop."

"A glass of milk would be great," Terry replied, taking a seat at the table.

Selma poured Terry's milk and a glass of cider for herself. Then she took a seat across from him and opened the bag of chips. While they ate, they discussed the quilting class.

"I think everyone's wall hanging but mine will turn out good." Terry moaned. "I stink at sewing."

"It takes practice and patience," Selma said.

"Yeah, well, I probably won't sew another thing after the classes are done." Terry reached for his glass of milk and took a drink. "Don't even know what I'm gonna do with the wall hanging."

"Maybe you could give it to someone—your parents, perhaps?"

Terry shook his head. "Nope. My folks split up a few months ago, and I doubt either of 'em would want the wall hanging."

"I'm sorry to hear that. I'm glad my husband stayed true to me right up till the day he died." Selma sighed. "I wish I could say the same for my daughter, though."

"Did she separate from her husband?" Terry asked.

"Cora's not married. She left home several years ago, and I haven't seen her since my husband died."

"That really stinks." Terry took a bite of sandwich. "I can sorta relate to what you said, though. I have two sisters—Faye and Jenny—but rarely see 'em."

"Do they live out of state?" Selma questioned, adding a few chips to the inside of her sandwich. It was the way she'd been eating them since she was a girl.

"Naw. Faye lives in LaGrange, and Jenny lives in Goshen. They're too busy with their own lives to pay much attention to me." Terry's forehead wrinkled. "'Course they don't care for the way I look, so that might be part of the reason they don't come around much."

"Maybe it's your long hair your sisters don't appreciate."

"My hair ain't that long." Terry gave his ponytail a flip. "It's only shoulder-length when I'm wearing it down."

"Have you ever considered cutting it?"

"Never gave it much thought." Terry grabbed a few more chips. "Why, do you think I should?"

Selma shrugged. "I don't know; maybe." Truthfully, she'd never been fond of long hair on a man. Anything past the ears seemed too long to her. But then she was a bit old-fashioned. At least that was what Cora had always said.

"Maybe I will cut my hair someday," Terry said, reaching for another piece of bread, "but right now I like it this way."

"What about Cheryl? Does she like the way you wear your hair?"

Terry blinked a couple of times. "Uh—I'm not sure. What made you ask?"

Selma lifted her gaze toward the ceiling. "It's fairly obvious that you're smitten with her."

"So tell me about your daughter," Terry said. He obviously didn't want to talk about Cheryl. "How come she doesn't make contact with you?"

"We don't see things the same way." Selma's voice dropped to a near whisper. Whenever she looked at Cora's picture, her beautiful brown eyes seemed to bore right through her. But Selma couldn't get rid of the photo. It was all she had to remind her of the little girl who used to live here, whom she still loved but couldn't reach. "Cora has never liked me telling her what to do," she explained. "So she takes the easy road and avoids me."

"Guess we have something in common then," Terry said. "We both have family members who want nothing to do with us."

Winona Lake, Indiana

"This seems like a nice enough place," Cheryl told Blaine as they entered the BoatHouse Restaurant. Looking around, she noticed right away the welcoming décor.

"Yeah, my boss, Stuart, told me about it. Said the restaurant has great year-round lakeside dining, not to mention some pretty good food." Blaine patted his stomach. "Since it's way past lunchtime, I'm more than ready to eat."

Cheryl smiled as the hostess seated them in a booth near a window with a gorgeous view of the lake. Sliding into their seats, she felt like they had the whole place to themselves, with the high-backed booths separating them from the rest of the patrons. "It was worth the drive down here, don't you think?" she asked Blaine.

He nodded and perused the menu the hostess had given them before leaving their table. "Would you like some fried calamari, mozzarella wedges, or a battered veggie platter as a starter?"

"If I had an appetizer, I'd probably be too full to eat anything else." Cheryl studied the soups and salads on the menu. "The oriental chicken salad sounds good."

"What else would you like?" Blaine asked.

"Just the salad will be enough."

He studied her from across the table. "If you eat like that all the time, no wonder you're so thin."

Cheryl laughed lightly, feeling the heat of a blush.

Blaine tapped the menu with his index finger. "Think I'll have a shrimp cocktail and the Asian cashew chicken. I'll probably get a side order of sweet potato fries, too."

When their waitress returned, they gave her their orders; then Blaine started talking about the lake again. "From what Stuart's said, Winona Lake is a great shopping spot for anyone looking for unusual things like pottery, jewelry, wood carvings, and handmade silverware. After we finish eating, maybe you'd like to browse some of the shops while I check out the lake for the best fishing spots."

"Are you planning to fish today?" Cheryl questioned. She wondered if he hadn't brought her here just so he could spend the afternoon fishing.

"No, not today, but if I decide this is a good place to fish for bass, I might try it out sometime. Do you like to fish?" he asked.

"No, not really."

"Oh, I see." Blaine's frown revealed his disappointment. "So is it okay with you if I check out some fishing spots while you shop?"

She nodded. "Sure, that's fine." Truthfully, Cheryl didn't think this was much of a date if they went their separate ways after lunch, but she chose not to make a big deal out of it. Besides, it would give her a chance to look for some things she hadn't been able to find anywhere else. She might find something nice to give Grandma for her birthday, in case Emma didn't get the quilt done on time.

As they ate, Blaine talked about fishing, while Cheryl stared out the window. She tried to act interested at first, but it was obvious that Blaine's mind was on fishing, not her. Cheryl found herself drawn to the beauty of the lake and the cottages dotting the shoreline. She wondered what it would be like to wake up every morning and watch the sun rise as it reflected across the lake.

"Look at this." Cheryl motioned to the pamphlet she'd found propped up with the dessert specials, explaining the history of the restaurant. "It says here that this restaurant was built on the same foundation as the cafeteria that was constructed here in the 1940s, when the original boathouse was removed."

"Hmm. . . That's interesting."

Cheryl kept reading as Blaine finished eating his fries. "And get this. The original boathouse was built way back in 1895. It also says that in the 1960s, the cafeteria was converted to a roller skating rink."

"Is that so?" Blaine reached for his glass of orange soda and took a drink.

"I'll bet it was fun to roller skate here by the lake." Cheryl looked up from the brochure and realized that Blaine, now gazing out the window, was no more interested in the history of the restaurant than she was with his fishing stories. She couldn't help wondering why he never asked anything about her. Their conversation today, as well as the other times they'd talked, seemed pretty one-sided. Maybe she'd made a mistake agreeing to go out with him again.

When the meal was over, Blaine said he would meet Cheryl where his SUV was parked, in two hours.

"That's fine. I'll see you then." Cheryl hurried off toward one of the stores.

She felt guilty for feeling this way, but she actually looked forward to being alone for a while. It wasn't that Blaine was unpleasant; they just didn't have much in common. *Maybe I haven't given Blaine a fair chance,* Cheryl thought. *Guess I could try fishing with him sometime; although sitting in a boat with a fishing pole really isn't my thing.*

CHAPTER 29

Shipshewana

D espite the chill in the air, the lake is beautiful today," Emma said, looking at the pristine waters as Lamar helped her out of the buggy. "I'm glad you suggested we come here this afternoon."

Lamar's eyes twinkled. "I thought we both needed a little break, and there's nothing like fresh lake air to make one feel energized. Look there, toward the center of the lake," he said with the excitement of a young boy.

Emma turned her attention to the geese Lamar was pointing at.

"Good thing we brought some bread along. Maybe we can entice them over to the shoreline so we can feed 'em."

Breathing deeply of the fresh air, Emma watched as the majestic-looking birds glided quietly over the surface, making small ripples in the lake's calm waters. Lamar had been right—the air was crisp and clean smelling. As always, Lamar looked at the positive side of things. She thought back to when she'd first met him and how in the beginning, she had avoided spending time with him. It didn't take long for Lamar to worm his way into her heart, however, and she was glad she'd agreed to become his wife. Others, including their families, said they complemented each other.

I think it's true, Emma mused, glancing at Lamar as he secured their horse to a nearby tree. *I certainly enjoy his company, and we work well together at home and teaching the quilting classes.*

As they walked down the path, Emma's thoughts shifted, reflecting on all the times she'd come to the lake with her first husband and how Ivan had carved their initials in a tree that stood in this very spot until a storm took it down. As difficult as it had been losing Ivan, Emma knew that she'd been blessed in both of her marriages. That special old tree was gone, but thanks to Lamar cutting out the piece of wood with the initials in it, Emma had a beautiful table that would someday become a cherished heirloom for her children and grandchildren.

Emma knew the importance of passing things on to the next generation. That's why she'd taught her daughters and granddaughters how to sew and quilt. Since Mary lived close to Emma, she often came over so she and Emma could do some quilting together. It was fun having someone to quilt with while getting caught up on one another's lives.

"How did you think things went with the class today?" Lamar asked, bringing Emma's thoughts to a halt.

Emma sighed. "Okay, I guess, but I wish Anna would open up to me. She seemed even more sullen than usual this morning."

"She does seem to be catching on to quilting, though," Lamar observed.

"Jah, but I'm concerned because Anna doesn't say much to anyone except Carmen." Emma stopped walking and turned to face Lamar. "I have a hunch that young woman is not going to join the Amish church."

"What makes you think that?"

"She has a chip on her shoulder and seems to be dissatisfied with the Amish way of life. I recognize it because when I was a young girl that's how I felt."

Lamar's mouth gaped open. "Oh Emma, I find it hard to believe that you ever had a chip on your shoulder or were dissatisfied being Amish."

"It's true. I was restless and rebellious and almost ran off with my boyfriend, but I came to my senses in time." Emma's face heated just thinking about it. Even after all these years she felt shame for what she'd put her parents through.

"Maybe you should share this with Anna," Lamar suggested. "Let her know that you understand what she's going through."

"I would if she'd open up to me, but I can hardly bring up the subject for no reason at all."

Lamar took Emma's hand and gave it a gentle squeeze. "I think we should pray about this, don't you?"

Emma nodded. She'd been praying for Anna, as well as her other five students, and would continue to do so.

———

Winona Lake

Blaine left the Lakehouse store, where he'd spent the last half hour looking at various items involving water sports, and headed for his SUV to wait for Cheryl. After talking to a fisherman he'd met in the store, he'd learned that Winona Lake was known as one of the better bass fisheries in northern Indiana. He'd also been told that it was best to fish during the early morning hours before any power boats hit the water. The thing that made him want to come back the most was learning that in addition to largemouth bass, there were also walleye and bluegills. The man had said the shallower water of the lake was best fished from a kayak with a flat bottom because the thick vegetation that grew there could create a problem for motor boats.

Blaine glanced around the parking lot, then over toward one of the shops. *Where is she, anyway?* he wondered, looking at his watch. *Cheryl should have been here by now. What could be keeping her?* Blaine pulled out his cell phone to call her and frowned. *That's great; my battery's dead. Think I'd better drive past some of the shops and see if I can spot her.*

———

Cheryl stepped out of the Whetstone Woodenware shop and headed for the parking lot where Blaine's vehicle was parked. She'd spent a little more time in the shop than she'd planned, but at least she'd found a nice hand-carved soup ladle to give her mother for Christmas. She'd also purchased a set of wooden salad tongs for herself. Since Cheryl's dad loved coffee, she'd bought him a wooden scoop for measuring out coffee grounds. She wished she'd been able to spend a little more time in that shop, but she was already late.

As Cheryl switched her bag of purchases to the other hand, she looked for the spot where Blaine had parked his SUV before they'd gone to eat. *What's going on? Blaine's vehicle isn't there. Did he move it? Could I be mistaken about where he parked it?*

Feeling a sense of panic, Cheryl dashed up and down the aisles of parked cars, searching for Blaine's rig, but to no avail. Out of breath, she halted and looked at her watch. She'd gotten here fifteen minutes later than when they'd agreed to meet, so at least she wasn't too far off the mark. But then, she started blaming herself. *This is my fault. I should have been paying attention to what time it was and spent less time shopping.* Was it possible that Blain had become impatient and left without her?

Was he capable of doing such a thing?

Why didn't he call me? Cheryl fretted, reaching into her purse to retrieve her cell phone. When she didn't find it there, she remembered having set it on her dresser this morning to charge the battery. "That's just great; I left home without it," she mumbled, looking both ways and wondering what direction to take.

As Terry approached Winona Lake on his Harley, he lowered his speed. The resort town looked busy today, with many cars lining the streets. Even the parking lots were full. He saw several boats on the lake and people walking from shop to shop.

Terry hadn't planned on coming to the area today, but after he'd left Selma's and taken to the road, he'd just kept going, enjoying the ride. Winona Lake was where he ended up.

Think I'll look for a spot to park my cycle and then head into one of the restaurants for something to eat, Terry thought. The sandwiches he'd eaten at Selma's had filled him for a time, but he'd worked up an appetite riding down here from Shipshewana.

When Terry turned onto the next street, he spotted a blond-haired woman coming out of a parking lot. She looked kind of like Cheryl. After doing a double-take, he realized it *was* Cheryl!

Terry pulled his cycle next to her and stopped. She gave him a blank look at first, but then her mouth formed an O. "Terry, wh–what are you doing here?" she stammered.

"After I finished helping Selma with a little problem she had, I decided to take a ride, and this is where I ended up. It's a nice fall day for a road trip, fresh air and all. I've been here before, but not for some time." He studied Cheryl a bit and noticed that her face was red and her forehead glistened with sweat. "What are you doing here?

And where's Mr. Clean? I thought the two of you had a date this afternoon."

"We did, but we went our separate ways after lunch and were supposed to meet back at his car. But when I got there, Blaine's SUV was gone." Cheryl's forehead wrinkled. "And I wish you wouldn't call him 'Mr. Clean.'"

Ignoring her last comment, Terry said, "Where'd the guy go? Don't tell me he went home without you."

"I—I don't know. I'm worried that he might have, because if Blaine was still here, I'm sure his vehicle would be in the lot. Why else would he have moved it?"

Terry shook his head and muttered, "Some date he turned out to be. I've done a lot of things I'm not proud of in my life, but I've never left a date stranded."

"Do you have a cell phone?" she asked. "I need to call him."

Terry shook his head. "No cell phone for me today. I forgot and left it home this morning. Where's your cell phone?"

She frowned. "I left it at home."

"Well, if you need a ride, I'd be happy to give you a lift," Terry offered. "I always carry an extra helmet with me."

Cheryl hesitated, but finally nodded. "Thanks, I appreciate that, but what about my package? How am I supposed to carry it if I'm holding on to you?"

"That's not a problem." Terry pointed to the saddlebags on the back of his cycle. "Just stick it in there."

"Okay, but if you don't mind, I'd like to ride around town once or twice and see if we can spot Blaine's vehicle. Before we head home, I just want to be sure he's not still here someplace, looking for me."

"Sure, we can do that. But if we don't see the guy, then I say we head outta here. We can stop on the way back to Emma's, where you left your car, for a bite to eat. I was gonna eat here, but I can wait."

———

Blaine had driven past all the shops in town several times, but there was no sign of Cheryl. Since his cell phone was dead, he'd gone to a pay phone and tried to call her, but all he'd gotten was Cheryl's voice mail. This was frustrating, and he wasn't sure what to do. Cheryl had to be somewhere in town, and he sure couldn't leave without her, so he decided to go back to the parking lot where they were supposed to meet and check one more time. If Cheryl wasn't there, he'd leave the SUV parked and walk into every single shop until he found her.

A few minutes later, Blaine pulled into the parking lot. The spot he'd been in before was taken, but there was another slot a few cars away. He didn't see any sign of Cheryl, however. Pulling into the empty spot, he turned off the ignition and got out. *Guess I'd better head for the shops*, he told himself.

Blaine had only walked a short distance when he heard the roar of a motorcycle. Looking to his right, he spotted a guy on a Harley, and a woman with blond hair on the back. She held on to the biker's waist as they headed out, in the opposite direction. Blaine blinked a couple of times and stared in disbelief as realization set it in. Even with his helmet on, he could see it was the redheaded roofer from the quilting class driving the bike, and Cheryl, with wisps of blond hair sticking out from under her blue helmet, was his passenger on the back!

CHAPTER 30

Blaine's hands shook as he stood on the sidewalk and watched Terry's bike disappear out of town. *The nerve of that guy, running off with my date! I'll bet he had it planned all along. For all I know, Cheryl might have been in on it, too. I wonder if she told him we were coming here today?*

If Blaine hadn't been so far from his vehicle, he would have gone after them. But trying to catch up to the fast-moving motorcycle would be a challenge, and with his luck, he'd probably end up with a speeding ticket.

Stuffing both hands into his jacket pockets, Blaine walked back to the place where he'd left his rig and continued to mull things over. *Should I try calling Cheryl when I get home and demand to know why she rode off with Terry, or do I just let it go and forget about her?*

Blaine wished now that he hadn't taken Stuart's advice and asked Cheryl out in the first place. Terry had shown up on their first date at the bowling alley, and now again today! *Strange coincidence, if you ask me. Or is it?* Blaine hated feeling this way, but what else could he think?

"Maybe I should give up on women," Blaine mumbled as he approached his car. His track record wasn't good. First Sue walked out of his life, and now it appeared as if Cheryl had done the same without even giving them a chance to get to know each other.

Of course, Blaine thought as he opened the vehicle door and slid in behind the wheel, *I haven't really tried to get to know Cheryl.*

He remembered that back at the restaurant most of their conversation during lunch had been about him. He'd barely listened when Cheryl read the history of the BoatHouse Restaurant. Since it didn't have anything to do with fishing, he hadn't been that interested. Still, he should have at least made some effort to be involved in the conversation.

Blaine decided he would give Cheryl a call when he got home. Perhaps he'd jumped to conclusions, and she'd been looking for him while he'd gone looking for her and thought he'd left. He hoped that was the case and that she hadn't planned to meet Terry the whole time.

Shipshewana

When Anna left Emma's after the quilt class, she pedaled her bike around Shipshewana for a while, feeling sorry for herself. It wasn't just that she'd been forced to give up the beautiful bracelet. She felt sad because there were only two weeks left of the quilting classes, which meant Carmen would be going back to California. Anna would miss the talks they'd had, although she really didn't know a lot about Carmen. During the times they'd spent together, Anna had mostly talked about herself. Of course, that was partly due to Carmen asking so many questions about the Amish way of life. Anna wondered why Carmen was so curious. Of course, Anna was curious about things concerning the English life, and more times than not, she found herself wishing she could wear beautiful garments like Carmen's instead of her plain clothes.

Knowing she should be getting home before Dad came looking for her, Anna turned her bicycle in the direction of Middlebury. She'd have to offer an excuse for being late, and the only thing she could think to say was that she'd been hungry after class and had gone to a restaurant in Shipshewana for something to eat. It wouldn't really be a lie, since she had eaten a hamburger and chocolate shake at one of the restaurants.

As Anna continued to pedal toward home, she thought about her decision to move to Sarasota. If she'd kept the bracelet Carmen had given her, she could have taken it with her. Oh well, it was too late for regrets.

Anna thought once again about the best way to tell her folks that she'd be leaving the first week of December. She knew they wouldn't be in favor of her going to Florida with Mandy, but she was old enough now to make her own decisions.

———

When Lamar turned their horse and buggy onto the driveway, he handed Emma the reins and said, "Think I'll hop out and check the mail. It'll save me a trip walking out after I put the horse and buggy away."

"Would you rather I get the mail?" Emma asked.

He shook his head. "That's okay, I'll do it. No need for you to get out."

Emma smiled as she watched Lamar climb down from the buggy and walk to the mailbox by the side of the road. He was always so thoughtful and considerate.

When Lamar returned to the buggy, he handed Emma a stack of mail and took up the reins.

As they headed up the driveway toward the barn, Emma thumbed through the mail. She smiled when she saw a letter from her sister Rachel, who lived in Middlefield, Ohio. Tearing open the envelope and quickly reading Rachel's note, Emma's smile widened.

"What's that big grin about?" Lamar asked. "I'm guessing whatever you opened is not a bill."

"No, it's not. It's a letter from my sister Rachel, and she's coming for a visit."

"How nice. When will she arrive?"

"In two weeks. It's been almost a year since I've seen her, so I'm looking forward to her visit." Emma placed Rachel's letter in with the rest of the mail and sighed. "The only thing that concerns me is that there are still two more quilting classes to go, and the quilt for Cheryl's grandmother isn't done yet. So I may not have enough time to clean house and get things ready for Rachel's visit."

Lamar reached over and patted Emma's hand. "Not to worry; I'll help as much as I can. I'm sure Mary and your granddaughters will, too."

Selma stood at the door, looking out and calling for Scruffy. She hadn't seen any sign of the cat since early this morning and was beginning to worry. *Could he have returned to wherever he came from?* she wondered. *Maybe he wasn't really looking for a new home. It could be that he was lost and just needed someplace to get in out of the cold.* Selma hated to admit it, but she missed the pesky cat. His gray-colored coat had looked better after she'd combed out the mats, and she had even given him a collar with a small bell so she could tell where he was in the house.

"Guess that's what I get for letting the critter worm his way into my house and heart," Selma muttered, closing the door. It seemed like she was destined to lose everyone she cared about—even a pet. It was as if

"What's that?"

"Are you seeing anyone? I—I mean, do you have a steady boyfriend?"

She shook her head. "Why do you ask?"

"Oh, just curious. I figured a beautiful woman like you would have at least one guy who was serious about her."

"No, not really," she said.

Paul couldn't explain it, but he felt relieved knowing Carmen wasn't dating anyone.

His thoughts were interrupted when their waitress returned with two plates of turkey, mashed potatoes, and green beans. *I wonder how Carmen would respond if I asked her to stay in Indiana?* Shaking the notion aside, Paul picked up his fork and started eating. No matter how much he wished it wasn't so, Carmen's job and her home were in California. He needed to keep his focus on something else and quit wishing for the impossible.

CHAPTER 31

Goshen

For the beginning of a workweek, traffic was light. In Cheryl's eyes this was always a good thing, aside from the fact that her job was only a fifteen-minute drive from where she lived. Following two days off, Monday mornings were hard enough, especially when it had been a good weekend, like the past one was.

As Cheryl headed to work, all she could think about was how the weekend had gone, and how much she'd enjoyed being with Terry again. They'd stopped at a café on the way back from Winona Lake, but since Cheryl was still full from the lunch she'd had earlier, she'd sipped iced tea and visited with Terry while he ate a burger and fries. She'd enjoyed listening as he told her about some of his biking trips and was pleased when he asked her some questions about growing up near the Oregon coast. Not like Blaine, who hadn't asked Cheryl anything about her past or personal life. In fact, her conversations with Blaine in no way compared to her time spent with Terry. The two men were as different as day and night.

Cheryl was fairly sure Mom and Dad wouldn't approve of Terry because he was such a free spirit, but that was what intrigued her the most. She knew, too, that Dad wouldn't like Terry's long hair. Cheryl couldn't really explain it, but she felt more comfortable with Terry than any other man she'd dated. When she'd first met him, a few things about him irritated her, but the more time she spent with Terry, the more he seemed to be growing on her.

On Sunday, Terry had come to church again. This time, he'd seemed more relaxed and had even taken part in the singing. Ruby Lee had led the music and chosen several lively choruses. Cheryl had snuck a peek at Terry during the praise-and-worship time and was happy to see him clapping along and grinning as they worshiped the Lord. After church, Cheryl and Terry had gone out for lunch and ended the day with another ride on his Harley. Only this time, Jan and his daughter, Star, joined them—for church, as well as lunch and the three-hour road trip. Cheryl had been exhausted when she went home that evening but had felt exhilarated at the same time. She'd never imagined riding on the back of a motorcycle could be so much fun.

Having Star along had put Cheryl more at ease on the bike, but she didn't think she'd ever want to ride a motorcycle by herself the way Star did—not even if it had a fancy custom paint job. Cheryl had to admit, the starbursts in bright neon colors fit Star's personality, as well as her name.

The only downside of the weekend had been the misunderstanding with Blaine. After she'd arrived home that evening, she'd received a phone call from Blaine, asking why she hadn't waited for him and saying he'd seen her ride off with Terry. He'd sounded upset, but once Cheryl explained what had happened and said she thought he'd left town without her, Blaine seemed to understand.

I probably shouldn't compare Terry and Blaine, Cheryl told herself as she pulled into her parking space behind the attorney's office. *But Terry has a sense of humor, and he makes me laugh. In comparison, Blaine seems kind of boring.*

Mishawaka

"How was your weekend?" Stuart asked when he met up with Blaine in the parking lot of the sporting goods store.

Blaine frowned. "Let's just say it wasn't the best."

"What happened?"

"I took Cheryl to lunch at that restaurant in Winona Lake on Saturday, like you suggested, and it didn't turn out so well."

"Was it the service or the food?" Stuart questioned.

"Neither. What ruined the day was when Cheryl left with Terry."

Stuart's eyebrows shot up. "Terry Cooley?"

"Yeah. They rode out of town on his motorcycle."

"I don't get it. If Cheryl went to Winona Lake with you, how'd she end up with Terry?"

"At first I thought they'd pre-planned the whole thing," Blaine said as they started walking toward the store. "But then I called Cheryl Saturday night, and she said when she'd gone back to the parking lot to meet me and discovered that my rig was gone, she panicked and thought I'd left town without her."

Stuart rubbed his chin. "Why would she have to meet you? I thought you were together."

"We were during lunch, but afterwards Cheryl went shopping while I checked on some fishing spots in the area."

Stuart stopped walking and squinted his eyes. "You're kidding, right?"

"No, I'm not. I've never fished in that area and wanted to know what the lake has to offer."

Stuart thumped Blaine's back. "If you want my opinion, you should have gone shopping with Cheryl and done fish scouting on your own time. Women like it when men go shopping with them. Pam sure does."

Blaine shook his head. "Sue never wanted me to go shopping with her."

"Sue...Sue...Sue. You've got to quit thinking about her, my friend. That relationship's over, and you need to move on."

"I know that, but I'm not sure Cheryl's the right woman for me," Blaine said as they entered the building. "She seems to like Terry better anyhow, so I think I'm gonna back off."

Shipshewana

Emma had just taken a seat at her sewing machine to begin working on the binding of the quilt for Cheryl's grandmother when her daughter Mary entered the room.

"I see you're still busy with that old quilt," Mary said, moving to stand beside Emma's chair.

Emma nodded. "I need to get it done before the final class so Cheryl can take it to Oregon for her grandma's birthday." She drew in a deep breath and blew it out quickly. "But I need to get busy cleaning the house so everything will be ready when Rachel arrives. At times like this, it seems there just aren't enough hours in the day."

Mary placed her hand on Emma's shoulder. "Listen, Mom, I've been thinking about this ever since yesterday when you told me about Aunt Rachel coming. I want to reassure you that I'll do all I can to help get the house ready in time. In fact, I don't think you need to do anything. Just concentrate on teaching your last two classes and getting that quilt done on time, and leave the cleaning to me and the girls."

Emma stood and gave her daughter a hug. "Danki, Mary. I don't know what I'd do without you. I know you have your hands full at your home, too."

Mary smiled. "You're welcome, Mom. And don't worry about me. Remember, helping each other when there's a need is what family is for."

———

"You're sure wearing a big grin today," Jan said as he and Terry headed down the road in his truck toward the small town of Emma to bid on a roofing job. "Are you still flying high from your date with Cheryl yesterday?"

Terry nodded, popping a piece of bubble gum in his mouth. "I can't help it, man. There's something special about Cheryl. I feel like a different person since I met her."

Jan looked over at Terry and grinned. "You act like a different person, too. Never seen you so happy and eager to please any woman before. You've got it bad, don't you?"

Terry shrugged. "I don't know. Maybe. I just really like being with her, and she makes me feel. . .well. . .special—like she really cares about me."

Jan gave the steering wheel a rap. "The question is, do you care for her?"

Terry clenched his fingers. "Just said I do, didn't I?"

"But do you care enough for Cheryl to set your fears about marriage aside?"

"Who said anything about marriage?"

"I did, and I said it 'cause if you really like Cheryl and you keep going out with her, eventually she's gonna expect some sort of commitment."

Terry winced and tried to change the subject. "Hey, I wonder if

Emma Miller has ever been to the town of Emma." He slapped his knee, watching Jan roll his eyes. "All kidding aside, let's stop at the little Emma Café for lunch today. I hear they have some really good pizza and home-cooked meals."

"Sounds good, but I'm not letting you off the hook that easy, pal," Jan said. "Seriously now, friend-to-friend, think about what I said, and don't make the same mistakes I have in the past."

Terry didn't want to think about making a serious commitment right now. He was just getting to know Cheryl and really hadn't thought much beyond that. Could he set his fears about marriage aside and continue to pursue a relationship with Cheryl that might lead to commitment, or would it better if he broke things off now before one or both of them got hurt?

Selma had just finished the breakfast dishes when she heard the tinkling of a bell, followed by a distinctive *meow!*

She dried her hands on a dish towel and hurried to open the back door. Scruffy sat on her porch, but her heart gave a lurch when she saw blood and realized that the poor cat was bleeding.

"Oh my!" Selma gasped, scooping the cat up and taking him inside. "What happened to you, Scruffy?"

Without so much as a second thought, Selma placed the cat on the kitchen counter so she could see how badly he was hurt. All sorts of things went through her mind. Did Scruffy get hit by a car? Had he been in a fight with another cat, or maybe a dog? Was it possible that some wild animal had attacked the cat?

Meow! The cat looked up at her as if to say, "Please help me."

After a quick examination, Selma discovered several lacerations and knew Scruffy needed to see the vet. Stitches might be needed, so there was no time to waste. Dr. Benson would know what to do. While she was there, Selma would ask about preventive shots the cat might need, even though she had no idea if Scruffy had received any before.

She hurried to the utility room, where she grabbed a cardboard box and an old towel. Wrapping the towel around Scruffy, she lifted him from the countertop and carefully placed him in the box. Then, after calling the vet and saying it was an emergency, Selma grabbed her car keys and purse, while mentally figuring out the quickest route to the animal clinic. Hoisting the box and looking down at poor Scruffy, she closed the door behind her. Selma wasn't sure how the cat would react when she put him in the box, but so far, so good. She sighed with relief when Scruffy curled into a ball and purred as if he understood that she was taking him to a place where he would be helped.

Dear Lord, Selma silently prayed as she hurried across the yard to get her car, *please let this poor cat be okay.* From that moment on, Selma knew for sure that Scruffy was here to stay.

CHAPTER 32

Shipshewana

Selma sat in her rocking chair, looking down at Scruffy, who was sound asleep in the wicker bed she'd prepared for him after returning from the vet's yesterday. The poor cat had several gashes that needed to be stitched, but Selma was thankful his injuries weren't any worse. Dr. Benson had said it looked like Scruffy might have tangled with another cat, which made Selma wonder how that other cat had fared.

Dr. Benson had given Selma some pills to mix in Scruffy's food that would help with infection. He'd also given Scruffy a shot and suggested that Selma get the cat neutered as soon as he'd recovered from his injuries, as it might make him less apt to fight. The doctor said he thought Scruffy was about six months old. When Selma went back with the cat for his follow-up appointment in two weeks, he would get the needed shots, and Selma would set up another appointment for his surgery.

Selma reached down, and when she stroked Scruffy's silky head, his left ear twitched, but he didn't open his eyes. The cat hadn't done much more than sleep since she'd brought him home. At least early this morning she'd been able to get him to drink some water and eat a little food. The vet said not to worry if Scruffy didn't have much of an appetite and seemed to sleep a lot. Those were some of the side effects from the medication he'd been given. Plus, the cat was sore from the sutures, which was another good reason to keep him calm and quiet.

As Selma continued to look at the slumbering cat, she wished she could take away his pain. "You'll be okay, boy," she whispered, petting Scruffy's head. "You have a home with me for as long as you like."

The cat emitted a soft purr, and Selma sighed contentedly. It felt kind of nice to know that someone needed her, even though it was an animal. She hadn't experienced that in a long time.

Topeka, Indiana

Carmen had been driving around Amish Country all afternoon, stopping to talk to a few Amish people and watching them interact with each other in the various Amish-run stores. She needed to start writing her article soon but had been procrastinating.

As she parked in front of another Amish store, she thought about the good time she'd had with Paul last Saturday evening. In fact, she found herself daydreaming about him a lot lately. If she closed her eyes, she could almost see his smiling face, hear the laughter in his voice, and smell his musky aftershave.

She also thought about precious little Sophia and how every time the little girl saw Carmen, she would reach out her arms to her. Until she'd gotten to know her niece, Carmen had never desired to be a mother. Now, the idea of having a child of her own would be like a dream come true.

Carmen's cell phone rang, interrupting her musings. She glanced at the caller ID and grimaced. It was her boss—probably calling to check up on her again. She thought about letting it go into voice mail but knew she'd be prolonging the inevitable. Mr. Lawrence was a persistent man and would no doubt keep calling until she finally answered.

"Hello, Mr. Lawrence," Carmen said, holding the phone up to her ear.

"Hey, Carmen. I'm calling to see how things are going. Have you got that article finished yet?"

"No, I'm still working on it, and I thought you said I could have the full six weeks."

"I did say that, but there was another TV show on about the Amish last night, and I thought this would be a good time to publish the article on wild Amish teenagers and their parents who look the other way while the kids do whatever they want."

"It's not like that, Mr. Lawrence. From what I've found out—"

"So how soon can you have the article done?" he asked, cutting her off.

"I—I don't know. I'm going to need a little more time to gather information."

"Well, good grief, you've been there for four and a half weeks. I'd think by now you ought to know something."

"I have learned a lot," Carmen said, "but not enough to write the story yet. I promise I'll have something written up soon."

"How soon?"

Doesn't he ever let up? Carmen pressed her hands together until her veins protruded. "I need another week and a half. Can you give me that long to complete the story?" she asked, trying her best to sound cheerful.

Silence. Then he said, "Okay. A week and a half, that's all. I expect a story on my desk by then, and it had better be a good one, Carmen, or you'll be back to writing news about the freeway traffic." Mr. Lawrence hung up without even saying good-bye.

Carmen let her head fall forward onto the steering wheel and groaned. *I need to write that article, no matter how much I don't want to. If I don't, I may lose my job. But how can I in good conscience write the negative article he wants me to when it's not even true that all Amish kids go wild into drinking, drugs, and sex during their running-around years?*

Middlebury

"Mom, Dad, there's something I need to tell you," Anna said after her family sat down to eat supper.

"Can it wait till we're done eating?" Dad asked. "I've been working hard all day and am really tired, so I'd like to eat without a bunch of noisy conversation."

Anna nodded. "Sure, Dad, it can wait." *Maybe it's better this way,* she decided. *It would probably be best to talk to Mom and Dad privately, rather than in front of my sisters and brothers. I'm just anxious to get this over with.*

Earlier that day while working at the window shop, Anna had decided to tell her folks that she planned to go to Florida with Mandy in December. She was tired of keeping her plans bottled up inside and knew the longer she waited, the harder it would be. She hoped that for once they would understand her feelings and accept her decision to leave home and strike out on her own.

As Anna began eating, her stomach tightened. She wasn't sure she'd be able to finish her meal. The longer she waited to say what was on her mind, the more she questioned her decision to tell Mom and Dad tonight. Would it hurt to wait awhile longer—maybe until after the last quilting class? By then, she'd have her wall hanging done and could give it to Mom as a sort of peace offering.

When the meal was over and her siblings had left the kitchen, Anna began helping Mom clear the table. She'd just placed the first stack of dishes in the sink, when Dad spoke up. "Anna, what was it you wanted to talk to me and your mamm about?"

Anna swallowed hard and turned to face him. "It was nothing important. It can wait till another time," she said, hoping the trembling she felt in her body didn't show in her voice.

"Now's a good time for me." Dad leaned back in his chair and clasped his hands behind his head. "Take a seat, Anna, and tell us what's on your mind."

Anna hesitated, and then looked at Mom, hoping she'd come to her rescue and say she didn't need to talk about anything tonight. But Mom took a seat at the table and motioned for Anna to do the same.

"Is this about the bracelet that young woman from the quilting class gave you?" Mom asked after Anna had seated herself in the chair next to her.

Anna gasped. "H–how do you know about that?"

"Susan told us," Dad announced. "She also admitted that she took the bracelet from your purse and put it in a shoe box in her closet, but that you found it there and took it back." He released his hands from behind his head, leaned forward slightly, and stared hard at Anna. "Why would you feel the need to have a fancy bracelet?"

"I—I didn't feel the need," Anna stammered. "Carmen gave it to me as a gift, and I—"

"And you just couldn't say no?"

Dad's piercing gaze made Anna shiver, and she quickly looked away.

"So was the bracelet what you wanted to tell us about?" Mom asked, reaching over to touch Anna's arm.

Anna knew bringing up Florida right now would cause a rift, and she wasn't prepared to deal with an uproar. As she tried to think of something to say, a cry from her youngest sister arose from the next room.

"Mom, Susan knocked your pretty vase on the floor!" Becky shouted.

Anna watched with relief as both her parents jumped up from their chairs and headed for the living room.

While Mom and Dad were gone, Anna got up and quickly finished washing the dishes. When that chore was done, she went up to her room and shut the door. A headache had been coming on all afternoon, and now her head was thumping so hard she could hardly think.

I'm going to bed, she told herself. All she wanted was to get rid of the pain in her head and blot out what she knew would be coming when she finally found the nerve to tell Mom and Dad she was leaving.

CHAPTER 33

Shipshewana

T oday was Emma's fifth quilting class, and Terry looked forward to going. Not because he liked to quilt, but he was anxious to see Cheryl again and hopefully go to lunch with her after the class. He hoped by getting there early he'd be able to sit beside her while they worked at the sewing table. It wouldn't set well with him if Blaine got there first and nabbed that chair. As far as Terry was concerned, after what Blaine had pulled last Saturday, leaving Cheryl without a ride home, she shouldn't give him the time of day.

Terry had just parked his truck and gotten out, when "Mr. Clean's" SUV pulled in. As soon as Blaine hopped out, Terry marched up to him and said, "I can't believe you'd have the nerve to show your face here this morning."

Blaine blinked, taking a step back. "Wh–what do you mean?"

"You left Cheryl alone without a ride home last Saturday, remember?"

Blaine's eyes narrowed as he came forward, poking his finger into Terry's chest. "As I recall, you stole my date."

Keeping a lid on his temper, Terry looked Blaine right in the eye and calmly said, "You were nowhere around, so what was I supposed to do, leave her stranded?"

Blaine shook his head. "Do you really think I'd leave her alone like that, without transportation? I can't believe you'd confront me with a statement like that."

"Look," Terry said, trying to smooth things over and not wanting to provoke a fight, "I was only trying to help by giving her a lift."

"Well, you could have helped a lot more if you hadn't shown up and whisked Cheryl away. Eventually, we'd have found each other, and then I would have taken her home."

Cheryl joined them on the porch just then. Terry was surprised; he'd been so intent on his discussion with Blaine, he hadn't heard her car pull in.

"Do you really need to rehash this again? I thought I'd explained all this to you on the phone last weekend," she said, looking at Blaine.

"Whatever," he said with a brief shrug before heading into the house.

Cheryl looked at Terry with questioning eyes. "I just got in on the end of your conversation with Blaine. Was he giving you a hard time about last Saturday?"

Avoiding the fact that he'd been the one who'd confronted Blaine, Terry nodded. "Yeah, but it's okay. We didn't come to blows or anything, so no harm was done."

"Well, you don't have to worry about Blaine. I'm not going out with him again."

"You're not?"

She shook her head. "We really don't have anything in common, and I don't enjoy being with him the way I do you. For some reason, Blaine and I couldn't seem to connect." Cheryl lowered her gaze, while Terry watched a blush appear on her beautiful face. "With you, I feel like I have a connection," she said in a voice barely above a whisper.

Terry felt ten feet tall. Yet he was uncomfortable about expressing to Cheryl how he felt about her. "So does that mean you'll go out to lunch with me after class this afternoon?" he asked, trying to sound casual.

"That would be nice. I'd be happy to go."

Carmen entered Emma's quilting room, feeling a bit nervous and distracted. All she could think about was how she felt forced to write a story that wasn't true about the precious Amish friends she had made. *I don't think I can do it,* she told herself. *I need to write the truth, not something that will please my editor. For now, though, I have to quit thinking about this and focus on something else.* Carmen took a seat on one side of the table. Paul would be coming by after class with his daughter, because they'd made plans to take Sophia for a carousel ride at the Davis Mercantile in Shipshewana, so that was something to look forward to.

From what Carmen had read in a brochure she'd picked up, the carousel had been fully restored and featured hand-carved farm animals. Later they'd be going to the Red Wagon, a toy store also in the Davis Mercantile. She was sure Sophia would be excited about that. Paul had mentioned that he would treat them to lunch at the Daily Bread, where several Amish-style dishes were served. Carmen hoped if there was time that they could stop by the Scrapyard, where a variety of scrapbooking supplies were sold. With all the pictures she'd taken here in Amish Country, not to mention the ones of Paul and

Sophia, Carmen had decided to begin a scrapbook, as a remembrance of this special trip.

———

As Emma stood at the head of the table, ready to teach the class, she felt concern. Terry and Cheryl were the only ones smiling, and she figured that was because they were sitting together. It was interesting to see how their attitudes had changed toward one another from the first quilting class until now. They'd obviously set whatever differences they had aside and found some things they enjoyed about each other.

Sort of like how it was with Lamar and me, Emma mused.

She turned her attention to the others. Blaine's shoulders sagged, as if in defeat; Carmen appeared agitated as she twisted her finger around the ends of her hair. Anna, whose eyes were red and puffy, appeared to have been recently crying. Selma hadn't arrived yet, and Emma hoped that when she came in today, she'd be in a good mood.

Emma was about to begin the class, when Selma finally showed up. Instead of the usual lime-green attire, Selma wore a pretty fall sweatshirt with light brown slacks. Her sweatshirt wasn't plain, either. It had a delicate white collar and on the front was an image of a maple tree in vivid colors with a hay-filled wagon underneath. Nestled on top of the bales of hay was a cat, much like the one Selma had described that she'd taken in.

"You look nice and fallish today," Emma complimented. "That's a pretty top you're wearing."

"Thank you," Selma answered. "Sorry I'm a little late, but my cat got into a fight with another cat, and I spent some extra time this morning getting him to eat his food."

"I'm sorry to hear that," Emma said with concern. "Is the cat going to be okay?"

Selma nodded. "The vet stitched his wounds and gave him an antibiotic, so as long as I keep him inside and quiet until he heals, Scruffy should be fine."

"That's good to hear," Terry spoke up. "That little critter's a mighty nice cat."

Selma smiled, looking perkier than Emma had seen her before. "I didn't think so at first, but he's sort of grown on me." Selma turned her attention to Emma again. "Did I miss anything by being late?"

Emma shook her head. "I was about to tell the others what we'd be doing today."

"I hope we're going to continue quilting," Cheryl said, "because I'm not finished with that part of mine yet."

"Neither am I," Terry agreed. "And I'm all thumbs, so I'm not sure I'll ever get it done."

"I'll help you with it," Lamar volunteered. "You, too, Blaine," he quickly added.

Blaine perked up a bit. "Thanks, Lamar, I appreciate that. And I'm really looking forward to going fishing with you after class today."

"Same here," Lamar said. "Let's hope the fish will be biting this afternoon. Oh, and by the way, Emma made us some sandwiches to take along."

Blaine smiled at Emma. "Thanks, that was nice of you."

"I was happy to do it," Emma responded. She was glad to see that Blaine's attitude had improved. She'd noticed that he still seemed a bit withdrawn around everyone and hoped going fishing with Lamar might loosen Blaine up a bit. Now if she could just see a smile from Carmen and Anna.

"Today we'll finish the quilting part of your wall hangings and then get the bindings pinned in place," Emma said. "Next week we will sew the bindings, and your wall hangings will be completed."

With Lamar's help, Emma handed everyone's project to them, along with pins, needles, thread, thimbles, and large embroidery hoops. While everyone worked, she went around to make sure the women were doing okay, while Lamar supervised the men. After each of them finished quilting, Emma showed how to cut and pin the binding. Following that, she suggested they take a break for refreshments.

"That sounds good to me," Terry said, rubbing his hands together. "What have you got for us this time, Emma?"

She smiled. "I made some apple crumb bread. And if any of you want the recipe for it, I'll gladly share."

Cheryl and Selma's hands shot up, but the others just sat there. Well, maybe after they tasted it, they would change their minds.

During their refreshment break, Emma told Cheryl that she was making progress on her grandmother's quilt. "I'm sure I'll have it done for you by next week," Emma said.

Cheryl smiled. "I'm looking forward to seeing the quilt and anxious to give it to Grandma when I go there for her birthday."

"How long will you be gone?" Terry asked.

"Probably just a few days," Cheryl responded. "Unless my boss gives me some extra time off, I can't be away from work too long, so I'll fly to Portland on a Friday morning, and return to Indiana Monday or Tuesday of the following week. I don't have my plane tickets bought yet, though. I'm waiting to hear from my mother about the date for Grandma's party. We may have it on a different day than her actual birthday in order to work around my parents' busy schedules."

"I hope your grandmother appreciates you coming for her birthday," Selma spoke up. "I didn't even get a phone call or a card from my daughter on my last birthday." She sniffed and blinked a couple of times, as though trying to hold back tears. "Cora hates me, and it's probably my own fault."

The room got deathly quiet. Emma glanced at Lamar to get his reaction, but he said nothing. Since everyone looked so uncomfortable, Emma felt she had to say something. Placing her hand on Selma's trembling shoulder, she quietly said, "Would you like to talk about it?"

Selma drew in a quick breath and released it with a shuddering sigh. "Cora left home after she graduated from high school, and the only time's she's been back was for her father's funeral. She never calls or writes, and whenever I've called her, she's always cut me off, saying she's too busy to talk."

"Why'd your daughter leave home?" Lamar asked.

Selma's voice quavered. "For years, my husband and I didn't think we could have any children, but then in my late thirties, we were blessed with a daughter." She dabbed at her tears. "Everything was wonderful when Cora was little. We did lots of fun things together. But as time went by, we started to disagree about things. Cora excelled in the business courses she took during high school, and John and I thought she should go to college to better her skills, so that one day she might get a job in management. I managed a flower shop during that time, and I loved my job, but Cora was satisfied with just doing office work." Selma paused again and blotted her tears with the tissue Emma handed her. "Cora said I was hard on her and expected too much and that I wanted her to be just like me. All I really wanted was for my daughter to reach her full potential." Selma drew in a deep breath and continued. "I'm afraid Cora was right. I didn't listen to what she wanted, and there were other issues, too. Even with my husband, I looked for the negative instead of the positive. I've wished so many times that I could go back and change things."

"That's what my folks do with me, too," Anna interjected. She pursed her lips. "They don't really listen to my feelings or hopes for the future. I talk, but they don't listen, if you know what I mean. That's why I'm planning to. . ." Her voice trailed off.

"What are you planning to do?" Emma questioned.

Anna shook her head. "Nothing. I shouldn't have said anything."

Standing at the head of the table, Emma looked at each of her students. "In 1 John 4:12, it says: 'If we love one another, God dwelleth in us, and his love is perfected in us.'"

"That's a good verse," Lamar added. "It reminds us of the importance of loving others—and that includes our families, whom we often take for granted. Just because we don't always see things the same way doesn't mean we should give up on someone in our family or shut them out of our lives." He smiled at Selma. "In hindsight, I think we all wish we could go back and do things differently. But then, if we've learned something from the experience, that's important, don't you think?"

Selma nodded slowly.

"Would you like a piece of advice?" he asked.

Selma nodded once more.

"Get in touch with your daughter as soon as possible and let her know how much you love her. If you've done something to offend her, apologize and ask if you can start over."

"That's excellent advice," Emma agreed. She turned to face Anna. "You might need to think about that as well, where your parents are concerned."

"You don't understand," Anna said, choking on a sob. "Nothing I do pleases Mom and Dad. They want to keep me a little girl forever, never letting me make my own choices. Well, I have made my choice, and today I'm going to start doing what will make me happy!" She jumped up, grabbed her sweater and purse, and raced out of the house, leaving everyone in the room with their mouths hanging open.

CHAPTER 34

W hy don't we take your car when we go out to lunch?" Terry suggested as he and Cheryl left Emma's house. "You probably wouldn't want to ride in my truck."

"Don't worry about me," Cheryl said with a shake of her head. "I don't mind riding in a truck."

"Okay, but I've gotta warn ya, my truck's kinda noisy."

"Then I guess I'll just have to talk a little louder," she said with a chuckle.

Terry grinned and opened the door on the passenger side for her to get in.

"Your truck's not so bad," Cheryl said as she climbed in and looked around. "In fact, you keep it pretty nice inside compared to some I've seen." She ran her hand over the leather seat.

"Well, you haven't heard the engine yet. And to be honest, the inside of my truck doesn't always look this good," Terry admitted.

"You could have fooled me. Even this bench seat looks brand new."

"Actually, it is. I had it replaced a few weeks ago, which is what prompted me to clean out the truck." Terry chuckled. "Couldn't have a cluttered truck with a brand-new seat."

Cheryl smiled. "I know what you mean. When I get something new for my apartment, it almost always triggers me into buying something else. Guess I get that from my mom. She used to drive Dad crazy every time he did some kind of improvement or repairs to the house. I remember the time she asked him to paint the living room. After it was done, Mom wanted all new furniture and pictures for the room because the walls looked so clean and nice." Cheryl giggled, as she reminisced. "She said the old stuff just wouldn't do."

As they drove out of Emma's yard, Terry glanced at Cheryl and said, "Speaking of nice—I think you're pretty nice, and easy to please."

She smiled, feeling the heat of a blush erupt on her cheeks. "I try to be, but I'm sure my parents might say otherwise. When I was a little girl, my dad said I was spoiled."

"How come? Did your folks give you everything you wanted?"

Cheryl shook her head. "Far from it. But my grandma sort of spoiled me. Not with gifts so much, but by giving me lots of attention—something I didn't get much of from Mom or Dad."

"I'm surprised at that. Didn't you mention when we went out to lunch last week that you're an only child?"

Cheryl nodded.

"Everyone I know who grew up without brothers and sisters pretty much had their parents all to themselves."

"Well, that wasn't the case for me. Dad kept busy at work, and so did Mom. And when they weren't working, they were involved in some activity that took them away from home. If they could work it into their schedule, which wasn't very often, they'd try to spend some time with me. But even then, I never felt special. I think they were just trying to fulfill their parental duty." Cheryl sighed. "That's why I spent a lot of my childhood with Grandma, and it's how we became so close."

"Is this the same grandma who owns the quilt you're having Emma fix?" Terry questioned.

"Yes, it is. Grandma Donelson is my mother's mom, and when my grandpa passed away ten years ago, Grandma moved in with us. We became even closer after that. She's in a nursing home in Portland now, not far from where my parents live."

"What about your dad's parents? Are they both still living?"

"Yes, but they live in Idaho, so I don't get to see them much." Cheryl nodded at Terry. "What about you? Are your grandparents alive, and if so, do they live nearby?"

"My dad's folks are both dead, and my mom's parents live in Oklahoma. I know I should, but I don't keep in touch with them much." Terry pulled into a gas station. "I hope your stomach can hold out for lunch a while longer, 'cause this old truck needs some gas."

She smiled. "I think I'll make it."

Terry turned off the ignition and hopped out of the truck. While he pumped the gas, Cheryl reached into her purse, pulled out her cell phone, and turned up the volume. She'd had it muted during the quilting class, not wishing to disturb anyone should it go off. As she was putting the phone back into her purse, a package of mints fell out. When she leaned over to pick it up, she discovered a pack of cigarettes on the floor of the truck.

"That's just great," Cheryl mumbled. "Terry's obviously started smoking again." *Or maybe he never quit and just managed to hide it well. I can't date a guy who smokes, not with my allergies.*

When Terry got back in the truck, Cheryl held the cigarettes out to him. "What's this? I thought you said you'd quit smoking."

His eyebrows shot up. "I did. Those ain't mine. They're not even the brand I used to smoke."

"Oh really? Whose cigarettes are they, then?"

"I picked up a hitchhiker on the way to class this morning, and the guy tried to light up, but I told him, 'Not in my truck.' I'm guessing he must have left his cigarettes when I dropped him off. You do believe me, don't you?" he asked, looking anxiously at Cheryl. "By the way, I didn't explain this before, but that's why I had to put a new seat in this truck. Because of my smoking, I burned a hole in the old seat. That bad habit was a costly one, and I found out the hard way that it's expensive in more ways than one."

Cheryl sat trying to process all of this. She wanted to believe Terry and hoped he was telling the truth, because she would never get involved with another man who wasn't honest with her.

Terry reached for her hand. "I'm not lying, honest."

"Okay," she said, relaxing a bit. "I'll take you at your word."

"Sure is a nice day to be at the lake," Lamar remarked as he and Blaine sat at a picnic table, eating the lunch Emma had prepared for them.

Blaine nodded eagerly as he bit into his roast beef sandwich. "Like I said before, for me, there's nothing like being in the fresh air near a body of water, where the fish are just waiting to be caught. Even if I don't catch any fish, there's nothing I enjoy more than being out here like this. It sort of helps clear my head and allows me to put aside any problems I have."

Lamar chuckled. "I like to fish, too. It's very relaxing, but I'd give it up if Emma asked me to."

Blaine's forehead wrinkled. "You're kidding, right?"

"Nope. Nothing and no one is as special to me as my dear wife."

"Does Emma ever go fishing with you?" Blaine asked.

"She has a few times, but she usually keeps busy making the quilts she sells to one of our local quilt shops. When I go fishing, it's most often with my son-in-law or one of his boys."

Blaine was about to comment, when his cell phone rang. "Drat! I forgot to turn that stupid thing off." He glanced at the caller ID and blinked when he realized it was Sue calling. *I wonder what she wants. Guess I'd better answer it and find out.*

Flipping his phone open, Blaine said, "Hello."

"Hi, Blaine, it's Sue."

"Yeah, I knew that when I saw your name on my caller ID."

"Are you busy right now?" she asked.

"I'm eating lunch with a friend."

There was a pause. "Are you on a date?"

"What? No. I'm with Lamar Miller, and we're at Lake Shipshewana." *Not that it's any of your business,* Blaine thought with irritation.

"Oh, I see. Well, I won't keep you, but there's something I wanted to say."

"What's that?"

"I ran into Stuart and Pam at the mall last night. They were shopping with their kids, and Stuart mentioned that you'd been taking some quilting classes. I never pictured you doing something like that."

"It's true. Stuart got me into it with a bet we stupidly made."

"Yes, he mentioned that. Stuart also said you've been seeing a woman you met there, and I. . .I was wondering if you're getting serious about her."

"At this point, I can't really say. Cheryl and I have only gone out a few times." Blaine wasn't about to admit to Sue that he wasn't planning to see Cheryl anymore. No point in giving her the satisfaction. Besides, why did she care? Their relationship was over.

"Oh, I see."

Blaine wasn't sure how to read Sue's tone of voice. Was she jealous? Did she wish that she and Blaine were still dating? Did he dare to ask? No, that would be setting himself up to get hurt again.

"Look, Sue, I really can't talk anymore."

"Okay, sure. I'll let you get back to your lunch. Good-bye, Blaine."

"Bye, Sue." *Please don't call again; it hurts too much.* Blaine turned off his cell phone and stuffed it in his shirt pocket. Then he grabbed his can of soda pop and took a drink.

"Sorry for the interruption," he said, setting his empty can down. "That was my ex-girlfriend, Sue."

"You still care for her, don't you?" Lamar asked.

"What makes you think that?"

"I can see it on your face."

Blaine didn't know why, but he ended up telling Lamar all about Sue and how she'd turned down his marriage proposal, and they'd broken up.

"Would you like a piece of advice?" Lamar asked.

Blaine shrugged. "I guess so." With the eager expression on Lamar's face, he figured the elderly man was just waiting to give his opinion.

"Sue must still have some feelings for you, or she wouldn't have questioned you about Cheryl."

"You really think so?"

Lamar gave a nod. "If you love this woman, then maybe you shouldn't give up on her." Lamar reached into the picnic basket for another sandwich and handed it to Blaine. "You know, when I first started caring for Emma, she wouldn't give me the time of day."

"So what'd you do?" Blaine asked, his interest piqued.

"I kept pursuing her—did nice things for her and hung around till she couldn't say no." Lamar snickered. "It was a challenge at first, but well worth the wait. Now Emma and I are quite happy together."

Blaine smiled. "That's obvious. You two seem like you were made for each other—as some might say, you're soul mates."

Lamar bobbed his head. "But we wouldn't be married today if I hadn't made an effort to win Emma's heart. So I'm thinking maybe you gave up too soon on winning the hand of the woman you love."

"Maybe so, but I don't think pursing Sue is a good idea because she might turn me away, and I don't want to be hurt again."

"Well, you'll never know unless you try, and since Sue called, my guess is she misses you."

"I'll give it some thought," Blaine said. "But we came here to do some fishing today, so why don't we get to it?"

"Hey, Anna, come with me to the women's restroom," Mandy said when Anna met her at the 5 & 20 Restaurant after she'd left Emma's quilting class. She held up a paper sack. "I want to show you something."

Curious to know what her friend had in the bag, Anna followed Mandy into the restroom.

Once inside, Mandy opened the sack and pulled out two pairs of jeans, two knit tops, and a pair of lightweight jackets. She gave one set of clothes to Anna. "Put these on, and take down your hair. We're gonna spend the rest of the day as English girls."

"Doing what?" Anna asked, her heart beating with excitement. Here was a chance to see what it felt like to look English, but even so, she was apprehensive.

"Let's start by having a couple of burgers for lunch, and then we'll go shopping for some makeup and jewelry."

Anna's eyes widened. "What if someone sees us? As much as I'd like to do what you suggested, I don't want my folks to find out. It was bad enough they found out about the bracelet Carmen gave me. It would be a hundred times worse if they learned that I was walking around Shipshe wearing makeup and dressed in English clothes."

Mandy laughed and poked Anna's arm. "You worry too much. With our hair down and wearing these clothes and some makeup, no one's gonna know who we are."

"They might, and I'm not willing to take that chance. Especially when we're so close to home."

"No problem. We'll go to Elkhart or Goshen and have a fun day there."

"How are we supposed to get there, Mandy? Either of those towns are a long ways for us to ride on our bikes."

Her friend nodded. "You're right, which is why I thought we could hitchhike."

Anna shook her head vigorously. "No way! Hitchhiking could be dangerous."

Mandy pulled a cell phone out of her purse. "Okay, worrywart, if you don't want to hitchhike, then I'll call my brother, James, and ask him to give us a ride."

James, still going through his running-around years, had bought a car. And Mandy, being the free spirit she was, had a cell phone her folks knew nothing about.

"Well, what do you say?" Mandy nudged Anna's arm again. "Should I give James a call or what?"

Anna nodded. She'd wanted to experience the English world, so she'd take a chance and go with Mandy today.

CHAPTER 35

Goshen

While sitting in a booth beside Mandy, at a burger place in town, Anna stared down at her English clothes. It felt strange to be wearing them, and the jeans felt a bit tight, but it was kind of fun and exciting; especially once she'd looked in the mirror and realized how cute the clothes looked on her. Since Anna had never worn makeup before, Mandy had shown her how to apply it. Anna was amazed at how the eyeliner and mascara made her eyes look bigger.

It had worked out well that Mandy's brother had been able to give them a ride to Goshen, where they were less apt to be seen by anyone they knew. Of course, as Mandy pointed out, with the makeup and jewelry they wore, even if they were seen by someone they knew, they might not be recognized.

"Look over there," Mandy whispered, leaning close to Anna's ear. "See those cute guys at the table near the door? They're watching us."

Anna glanced in that direction. Two young men, one with blond hair and the other with coal-black hair, stared at them with big grins. Before Anna could comment, the one with blond hair left his seat and strolled across the room, stopping in front of Anna and Mandy's table. The other fellow followed, and they both plunked down on the other side of the booth.

"You girls live in Goshen?" the dark-haired boy asked. "Don't think I've seen you around this burger joint before."

Mandy rolled her eyes. "Goshen's a big town, and there are lots of fast-food restaurants, so what are the odds that you'd have seen us before?"

The boy leaned his head back and laughed. "Guess you're right about that." He looked at Anna and winked. "I'm Bill. What's your name, sweetie?"

Anna's cheeks warmed, but before she could reply, Mandy quickly said, "She's Anna, and I'm Mandy."

Bill motioned to his blond-haired friend. "This is my buddy, Tony, and we've been watching you two ever since you came in."

Tony grinned and winked at Mandy. "How'd you like to spend the rest of the day with us? We promise to show you a good time."

Anna held her breath and waited to hear how Mandy would respond. She hoped she wouldn't say yes, because the way these two guys looked at them—like hungry animals—made Anna nervous. She also noticed the outline of a pack of cigarettes stuffed inside the sleeve of Tony's T-shirt. She shuddered to think how she and Mandy would react if these boys insisted that they smoke with them. Anna had never smoked a cigarette before; she had no desire to, either. Just the smell of cigarette smoke made her head feel stuffed up.

"We appreciate the offer," Mandy said smoothly, "but my friend and I have other plans for the day."

"What kind of plans?" Bill asked.

"We're going shopping," Anna interjected.

Tony smiled. "Shopping, is it? Well, maybe we'll just tag along then."

Oh no, Anna thought. *How are we going to get away from these two? I really don't want to go anywhere with them.*

Mandy smiled, tipping her head. "Feel free to go with us if you want, but you might get bored."

"I don't think so," Tony said with a quick shake of his head. "Who could be bored hanging around two girls as hot-looking as you?"

Anna cringed. All of a sudden, she didn't feel so cute. This day wasn't turning out the way she'd hoped. She had merely wanted to have a little fun wearing English clothes, and she wished she could make Tony and Bill go away. She feared that if she and Mandy went anywhere with these two, things could turn out badly.

"Aren't we supposed to meet James soon?" Anna asked, looking at her friend.

Mandy nodded. "Oh, that's right. I'd almost forgot." She smiled at Tony and sweetly added, "Maybe we'll see you some other time."

Bill frowned, but Tony merely shrugged and said, "Well, if you've got another date, you should have just said so."

Anna was about to say that James wasn't her date, but changed her mind. If the guys thought she or Mandy had a boyfriend, they'd probably leave them alone.

Tony stood and stuffed his hands in his jean's pocket. "We'll be sitting over there, in case you change your mind."

As Tony and Bill sauntered off, Anna blew out her breath in relief. "I'm glad they went back to their table. I didn't like the way those two looked at us, and I didn't want to go anywhere with them, did you?"

Mandy shrugged her slim shoulders. "It might have been kinda fun, but with James coming to pick us up in a few hours, it wouldn't have worked out so well."

"I hope they don't come back over here," Anna said, feeling kind of shaky inside. "Worse yet, what if they follow us when we do our shopping?"

Mandy leaned close to Anna and whispered, "I think I know a way we can sneak out of here without them knowing."

"Really? How?"

Mandy smiled. "Come with me to the ladies' room, and I'll show you." Moments later, two young women in Plain clothes slipped unnoticed out of the restaurant.

Elkhart

"This has been such a nice day," Paul told Carmen as he lifted Sophia off the carousel.

She nodded enthusiastically. "I'm going to miss all the fun times I've had with you and Sophia when I go back to California."

Then don't go, Paul thought, but he didn't voice the words.

"Why don't you and Sophia come out to see me during your spring break next year?" Carmen suggested. She bent down and gave Paul's daughter a kiss on the cheek. "You'd like that, wouldn't you, little one?"

Sophia giggled, and the look of adoration Paul saw on her face as she lifted her hands up to Carmen, put a lump in his throat. "Sophia's going to miss you, and so am I," he said, making eye contact with Carmen.

"I'll miss you both, as well." Carmen took one of Sophia's hands and Paul clasped the other one as they walked past several shops in the Davis Mercantile. When they came to the scrapbooking store, Carmen suggested that Paul take Sophia to the toy store while she bought a few scrapbooking supplies.

"That's probably a good idea," Paul said. "If we all go in, Sophia will get restless."

Carmen smiled. "We can either meet outside the scrapbook store, or if I get done before you do, I'll join you in the toy store in twenty minutes or so."

"Sounds good." Paul bent down and scooped his daughter into his arms. "Off we go, little one. Let's find you a new toy."

Carmen had been looking at scrapbooking supplies about twenty minutes, when her cell phone rang. When she saw that it was her boss, she reluctantly answered the phone. *He doesn't give up,* she couldn't help thinking.

"How's it going, Carmen?" Mr. Lawrence asked. "Have you got that story wrapped up yet?"

"Not quite, but by the time I get back to the office, I'll have that story about the Amish and how they let their young people go wild during their time of rumschpringe."

"Okay, but I may not be here when you do," he said. "I have to take my wife to see her niece who just had a baby, so if I'm not here, just give your story to the assistant editor, Mike, and he can look it over before it goes to press."

"Okay. Have a good trip, Mr. Lawrence."

Carmen had no more than hung up, when out of nowhere, Paul, with Sophia perched on his shoulders, stepped up to her. "Who were you talking to, and what's this about writing a story on the Amish?"

Caught off guard, and realizing that Paul had obviously heard her conversation with Mr. Lawrence, Carmen swallowed hard and moistened her lips with the tip of her tongue. "Umm. . .I thought you took Sophia to the toy store."

"Never mind that. What's this about?" Paul asked again, pointing to Carmen's cell phone.

Unsure of where to begin, Carmen drew a deep breath. "Let me explain."

"Yes, please do. I'm all ears."

Quickly, Carmen told Paul that she'd been sent to Indiana to write a story for the newspaper in Los Angeles that would shed some light on the topic of rumschpringe and why the parents of Amish young people allowed them to run wild during that time.

Paul frowned, while shaking his head. "So the whole time you've been taking Emma's quilting classes, and spending time on your own with Anna Lambright, you've been gleaning information for your story?"

Carmen nodded, hoping to explain a little more. "But it's turned out to be more than that, Paul. During the time I've been here, I've come to—"

Paul held up his hand. "You don't need to say anything more; I get the picture. You've used my Amish friends to get the story you want, and now you're going to shed a bad light on the Amish way of life."

"It's not like that. I really—"

"I don't want to talk about this," Paul said. "If you're done shopping, I'll drop you off at your hotel and you can say good-bye to Sophia, because we won't be seeing you again before you return to California." Paul lifted Sophia from his shoulders and held her in his arms.

Carmen cringed at the way he looked at her and recoiled at his next verbal blow.

"I'm really disappointed in you, Carmen. I never thought you'd stoop so low. And all those months I had to live with you thinking the accident that killed my beloved wife was my fault. . .well, I should have known from that what kind of a person you really are."

Paul's icy stare and the tone of his voice was enough to make Carmen know that she'd lost his respect. No matter what she said, he wouldn't listen.

I should not have agreed to do that story, she thought with regret. *No matter what I say or do, Paul will never trust me.*

———

Middlebury

James picked up Anna and Mandy later than expected, and by the time they got back to Shipshewana, Anna really had to hustle to get home, riding her bike, which she'd left locked to the bike rack outside the 5 & 20 restaurant.

When Anna walked into her house, flushed from the hard ride, she found Mom and Dad in the living room. Dad was reading the newspaper, while Mom knitted on the prayer shawl she'd started a few weeks ago.

"You've been gone most of the day, Anna," Mom said, setting her paper aside. "Where have you been?"

"I went to lunch and then did some shopping with Mandy." Anna plopped down in the empty chair across from her parents.

"You know we don't approve of you hanging around that girl," Dad said, looking at Anna over the top of his reading glasses.

"Mandy's a good friend," Annie defended, grasping the arms of her chair. Then throwing caution to the wind, she leaned forward and blurted, "I'm going to Sarasota, Florida, with Mandy in December." There, it was out, and she felt a sense of relief for finding the courage to finally say it—that is until she saw her parents' reactions.

Dad's face turned beet red, and he slapped his hand down on the end table next to the sofa so hard that Mom's knitting yarn fell off and unraveled as it rolled across the floor.

"Anna Lambright, I forbid you to go!" he shouted. "And if you leave here against our wishes, you may as well stay in Sarasota and never come back!"

"I'm an adult now, and I have a right to make my own decisions," Anna argued. "I need some time to decide whether I want to join the Amish church or not." Tears stung Anna's eyes as she abruptly stood. What was the point in trying to explain? "I'm sorry you feel that way, Dad, but there was no good time to tell you this. I figured you'd react this way, but my mind is made up." Unable to say anything more, Anna ran up the stairs to her room, slamming the door behind her.

CHAPTER 36

As the week went by, Emma became more excited. Her sister was supposed to arrive on Friday but had called and said that due to a few extra stops her driver had made, she'd be a day late, and that Emma should expect her to arrive sometime Saturday.

"I hope Rachel gets here after the quilting class today," Emma told Lamar as they sat at the kitchen table Saturday morning, drinking coffee. "I want to give her my undivided attention, and if she comes in the middle of class, I won't be able to do that."

Lamar placed his hand on Emma's arm and gave it a tender squeeze. "Try not to fret. Rachel will get here when she's supposed to get here, and if happens to be when in you're in the middle of teaching your class, then you can introduce her to everyone."

Emma smiled. "That's true, and since she's also a quilter, she might enjoy seeing what my students have been doing."

"Speaking of which," Lamar said, rising from his chair, "I hear the roar of a motorcycle, so I'm guessing Terry must be here."

When Terry pulled his cycle into Emma's yard, he noticed that no other vehicles were there. He figured he was probably early, but that was okay because if the class went longer than normal today, he'd have to leave early. He'd be heading out for a three-day fund-raiser bike trip this afternoon and didn't want to be late meeting up with Jan and Star, along with the rest of the people who'd be riding with them. This fund-raiser was to help a family who'd recently lost everything when their house burned down. Since Terry had gone to school with the man, he wanted to help out in any way he could. In fact, he and Jan had offered to help rebuild the family's house, as had many of their biker buddies.

Terry stood on the porch a few minutes, watching for Cheryl's car. He hoped she would get here soon, so he could tell her about his plans. If she didn't, he'd try to sneak in a few words with her during class.

After waiting several more minutes and seeing Selma, Blaine, Anna, and Carmen show up, Terry finally gave up and went inside, too.

Emma smiled as everyone took a seat around the table. "Today we'll finish the binding on your wall hangings," she said. "But I think we should wait until Cheryl gets here."

Terry glanced at his cell phone to check the time. "I'm in a hurry, so if you don't mind, I'd like to start sewing right away."

"Go right ahead. Lamar can help you finish up," Emma responded. "The rest of you are free to do the same. Cheryl's wall hanging is almost done, so when she gets here I'm sure it won't take her long to finish it."

Goshen

Cheryl had forgotten to set her alarm, so she was already running late, but just as she climbed into her car, her cell phone rang. Seeing that it was her mother, she quickly answered the phone. "Hi, Mom. How's Grandma doing?"

"I was there the other day, and she didn't know who I was. I'm not sure it'll do any good to have a party for her."

"With or without a party, I'm still coming for her birthday," Cheryl said.

"Have you booked your flight yet?"

"No, but I'm going to do that as soon as I get home from the quilting class today. I should have done it sooner, but I've been watching for a cheaper rate, and there hasn't been any." Cheryl took a deep breath. "Do you think she'll recognize me?"

Mom sighed. "I don't know."

"I'll give you a call as soon as I get my tickets booked so you or Dad will know when to pick me up."

"All right, Cheryl. We'll talk to you soon."

Cheryl's heart was heavy as she clicked off the phone. She was tempted to skip Emma's class today, but it was the last one, and she really wanted to finish her wall hanging. She'd also planned to have lunch with Terry. If those weren't reasons enough, Emma had promised she'd have Grandma's quilt done today, so Cheryl needed to pick it up. Maybe once Grandma saw her old quilt again, she would regain some memories.

———

"Thanks for helping me get this done so fast, Lamar," Terry said, looking at the clock on the far wall and knowing he had to leave soon. Cheryl still hadn't arrived, and he hoped he would have time to explain why he had to cancel their lunch date today. Lately, Terry had been so wrapped up in wanting to be with Cheryl, it had taken him by surprise when Jan reminded him that the charity ride was this weekend.

"Are you doing something special this afternoon?" Lamar asked, placing Terry's finished wall hanging in a cardboard box.

"Yeah, I have plans with a few of my biker friends. We're going on a road trip for a few days to help a friend in need, and I just found out this morning that we're supposed to leave this afternoon."

"Are you finished up?" Emma asked, walking over as Lamar handed Terry the box.

Terry nodded. "I hate to do this, but as I was telling Lamar, I've got a trip to take and need to get going. Is it okay if I leave my wall hanging here till I get back?"

"Certainly," Emma said.

He smiled at her. "Just want you to know that I appreciate all you and Lamar have done in helping me make the wall hanging." He rubbed his forehead. "This sure isn't the way I wanted to leave on our last day of class, and I didn't even get to see Cheryl and explain why I have to postpone our lunch plans."

"Don't worry about it." Lamar put his hand on Terry's shoulder. "When she gets here, we'll explain things to her. Just be safe on that trip, and have fun."

"I'll ask Lamar to fill me in on this trip you're taking," Emma said. "But while you're still here, I need to tell everyone something."

When Emma had the class's attention, she began to explain. "I know this is the last day of class, but with my sister arriving today, I want to spend as much time with her as possible, so I was thinking of setting another time when we can all get together and visit awhile. Would two weeks from today work for all of you? I'll make a dessert, of course," she quickly added.

Everyone agreed, except Carmen, who said she had to return to California.

"I hate to run off like this," Terry said, looking at Emma, "but I'll catch up with you when we get back together here." With that, Terry hollered, "See you all soon," and headed out the door.

Terry hopped on his cycle and started the engine. Revving up the engine and knocking the kickstand back with his foot, he headed out. He thought this road trip might serve a twofold purpose. Besides raising money for a needy family, it would give him some time to clear his head so he could deal with all the things he'd been thinking about concerning Cheryl and where their relationship might be headed.

As Emma and Lamar supervised the students, Emma began to worry. Not only was Cheryl late for class, but Rachel wasn't here yet, either. She hoped Rachel's driver hadn't run into bad weather or experienced any problems with her vehicle.

Lord, please bring my sister and Cheryl here safely, Emma silently prayed, *and help me not to worry so much.*

Needing to focus on something else, Emma moved across the room to help Carmen, who'd just dropped a package of pins. As she approached the sewing machine where Carmen sat, she noticed that the young woman's hands were shaking, and her eyes were rimmed with tears.

"Oh dear, what's wrong?" Emma asked. "There's no reason to be upset about dropping those pins."

"It. . .it's not the pins," Carmen said, sniffing. "I've done something I'm not proud of, and I think I've ruined my relationship with Paul."

Emma placed her hands on Carmen's trembling shoulders. "I'm sure whatever you did can't be that bad."

Carmen bobbed her head, while swiping at the tears running down her cheeks. "Yes, it is."

Emma didn't want to pry, but she thought it might help if Carmen talked about it. She was on the verge of asking, when a knock sounded on the door. Lamar said he would get it, and he returned moments later holding a suitcase, with Rachel at his side.

Emma hurried across the room and gave her sister a hug. "Oh Rachel! It's so good to see you!"

Rachel nodded, her pale blue eyes sparkling with the joy she obviously felt. Then she looked around the room and said, "I can see that you're busy right now, so I won't interrupt. Lamar can show me to my room."

"Nonsense," Emma said with a shake of her head. "I want you to meet my quilting students." She took Rachel's arm and led her around the room, introducing her to each one. By this time, Carmen had dried her eyes and looked a little perkier. When Rachel reached out and shook Carmen's hand, Carmen smiled and said, "It's nice to meet you."

Thinking this might be a good time to take a break, Emma announced that she was going to the kitchen to get some refreshments.

"I'll help you," Rachel said, following Emma into the other room.

When they returned with a tray of cookies, coffee, and iced tea, Emma was pleased to see that Cheryl had finally arrived, after being over an hour late. The young woman's face looked drawn, and Emma suspected that she, too, might be upset about something.

"Sorry I'm so late," Cheryl said, turning to Emma. "I forgot to set my alarm last night, and then I got a call from my mother." She paused a moment and drew in a sharp breath. "My grandma's not doing well, so I'm anxious to go home to see her." Cheryl's voice trailed off and she dropped her gaze to the floor.

"I'm so sorry to hear that," Emma said, gently touching Cheryl's arm. "I have the quilt ready for you, so you'll be able to take it when you go. In fact, I'll get it right now."

While Emma went after the quilt, Cheryl glanced at the empty seat, then noticed Lamar heading her way.

"Are you looking for Terry?" he asked.

"Yes. How'd you know? Didn't he make it to class today?"

"He was here, and you missed him by about fifteen minutes," Lamar explained. "He had to leave early because he was meeting his friends. Seems like they're going on some sort of bike ride for a couple of days. He said he'd call you when he gets back."

Just then Emma returned with the quilt. She asked Lamar to hold one corner, while she held the other, so Cheryl could see how it had turned out.

"Oh, it's beautiful," Cheryl murmured. "I think Grandma's going to be pleased."

Rachel, who stood off to one side, moved forward. She stared at the quilt and gasped. "Ach, my! This isn't *meechlich*!" she said, lifting her eyebrows in obvious surprise as she brought her hand up to her mouth.

"What isn't possible?" Emma questioned, watching as her sister drew closer to the quilt and examined every detail.

"The *gwilt*. It belonged to our sister Betty."

"Why would you think that?" Emma asked.

"See here," Rachel said, touching the underneath side on one corner of the quilt. "Those are Betty's initials. I remember when she embroidered them there."

"Betty?" Cheryl said, her eyes opening wide.

Rachel nodded. "She's our oldest sister, but she left the faith and moved away when she was eighteen years old."

Emma's lips pursed as she stared at the quilt. "I've never met Betty. She left home shortly before I was born. I'd only heard my family talk about Betty a few times, but I know from what little had been said that it hurt our parents deeply when Betty left. And in all those years, she never returned or made any contact with our family. I can't imagine how I would have felt if one of my children had done that."

Emma turned to Cheryl. "I wonder how your grandmother ended up with our sister's quilt. Do you know where or from whom she bought it?"

Cheryl stood motionless, as though in a daze. In a barely audible voice, she squeaked, "Betty is my grandmother's name. I don't know how it's possible, Emma, but I think Grandma might be your sister."

CHAPTER 37

Portland, Oregon

E mma's excitement rose as she followed Cheryl and Rachel off the train. Needing to find out if Cheryl's grandmother was their sister Betty, Cheryl had booked train tickets for all three of them, since Emma and Rachel weren't allowed to fly. Spending two days on the train gave them time to visit and let all that they'd learned sink in. Cheryl seemed especially thrilled to find out that Emma might actually be her great-aunt.

The train trip had been pleasant for Emma, except for the worry she felt about the health of Cheryl's grandmother. The scenery had been beautiful as they'd headed west, zipping through the central states, then the mountainous areas, until they'd ended up here in Portland.

"Oh, there's my folks." Cheryl motioned to the middle-aged couple walking toward them. After she'd hugged her parents, she introduced Emma and Rachel.

"So if what Cheryl told me on the phone is true, then you two would be my aunts," Cheryl's mother, Katherine, said, giving Emma and Rachel a hug. "I wasn't aware that my mother had any sisters. She's never said much about her past, and when I asked about her childhood, I was told that she had no family. I figured that meant no siblings."

"I was only seven years old when Betty left home, but I remember that she was upset about something," Rachel said as they headed toward the baggage claim area. "Later on, our folks explained that Betty wanted to live in the modern world and thought our ways were old-fashioned. Betty and Dad had words, and he said if she left home she shouldn't come back." Rachel sighed deeply. "I suppose she took him at his word, because we never heard from her again. I remember Mama crying many times over losing Betty."

Reflecting on all of this, Emma thought of Anna and how dissatisfied she seemed with her life. She hoped for Anna's sake, as well as her parents', that she wouldn't decide to leave the Amish faith. *When I get home, I'll talk to Anna and her parents,* she decided. *They need to have more understanding where Anna is concerned, and Anna needs to appreciate her family. Maybe our story will open their eyes.*

"Let's get your luggage put in my van, and we'll be on our way to the nursing home," Cheryl's father said. "I'm sure you ladies are as anxious as Cheryl is to see Betty."

Shipshewana

"Have you talked to Cheryl since we got back from our road trip?" Jan asked as he and Terry pulled into a gas station to fill up Jan's truck.

Terry shook his head. "I've tried leaving several messages, but she doesn't respond. I even drove over to her apartment last night, but she wasn't there." He gripped the edge of his seat, fighting the sudden urge for a cigarette, which he hadn't felt for several weeks. "Man,

I hope Cheryl's not mad at me."

"Why would she be mad?"

"'Cause I left Emma's early last Saturday without telling her why. I had hoped I could explain to her in person that I'd totally forgotten about the charity ride we'd planned. All I could think about was going to lunch with Cheryl again." Terry heaved a sigh as he rubbed the bridge of his nose. "My heart must be clogging my brain these days."

Jan opened the truck door. "Didn't you say that Lamar told you Cheryl had gone to see her grandmother, whose health isn't good?"

"Yeah, that's right."

"Cheryl's probably busy with things and hasn't checked her messages."

"Maybe so.

"Well, I'd better get the gas pumped or we'll never get to our next job."

While Jan filled the gas tank, Terry pulled out his cell phone and tried calling Cheryl. All he got was her voice mail again. He left a message: "Hi, Cheryl, it's Terry. I've been trying to get a hold of you for the last three days. Could you please call me back as soon as you get this message?"

Los Angeles

"What is this?" Mr. Lawrence asked, slamming the morning's newspaper down on Carmen's desk.

"If you're referring to my article, then it is what it is," she said, meeting his steely gaze. Carmen wondered why she worked for this harsh, demanding man.

"Of course I'm referring to your article!" He pointed a bony finger at the newspaper. "This was not written the way it was supposed to be, Ms. Lopez, and I can't believe Mike let it be published in my absence."

"I wrote the truth as I saw it. Isn't that what a good reporter is supposed to do?"

His face reddened. "Humph! Just how much digging did you really do?"

"I spoke to several Amish people while I was in Indiana and got to know some personally."

"You made those people sound like a bunch of saints."

Carmen shook her head vigorously. "I did not. I made them sound as they are—a kind, gentle people, who deal with their problems by relying on each other for support, while maintaining their strong moral values. They put God first in all things and hold their family members in high regard." Carmen paused for a breath. "They live life simply and by their own choice, not because they're forced to. Do they have problems? Certainly. But then don't we all?"

"That's all fine, well, and good," he said, leaning on the desk, "but an article like this isn't sensational enough. I was hoping for something juicy and shocking, like the things we've heard on the news, where some Amish have gone bad."

Carmen's jaw clenched. "So what you're saying is, if one person, no matter what his nationality or faith, does something wrong, that makes all people of that group bad?"

He shifted his stance. "Well, no, but—"

"But you're unhappy with me because I made this a positive article and not a negative one, is that right?"

He nodded.

Carmen took another deep breath. "I know a lot of readers out there want nothing more than to read about bad things happening to people. But with the way the world is these days, I believe many more people want to read about the good things that happen."

He opened his mouth, but Carmen rushed on. "Everyone has things going on in their own lives, and I know, at least for me, that I'd rather hear about pleasant things and noble situations. You know—something noteworthy. There are a lot of decent folks in the world, but for some reason, the majority of things we see on TV and read about in the paper dwell on the bad stuff that happens. If that's what sells, then I'm not sure I want to be a part of it anymore."

"This newspaper is about selling papers, Carmen," Mr. Lawrence reminded. "And my reporters will do whatever it takes to get good stories."

"I'm sorry you feel that way." She rose from her desk. "As of this moment, I'm turning in my resignation."

"Well, that's good, because if you hadn't quit, I would have fired you."

Breathing deeply to calm her nerves, Carmen forced a smile and said, "I'll clean out my desk and be gone before the end of the day."

CHAPTER 38

Portland

A lump formed in Cheryl's throat as she and her mother stood next to Grandma's bed. Grandma's eyes were closed, and she seemed unaware of their presence. It was quite warm in the room, but Grandma was covered with a blanket. Even so, Cheryl could see the outline of her body, which looked small and fragile. It was upsetting to see how frail Grandma had gotten since the last time they'd been together. Was it only a few years ago that she'd been so perky?

"Mom, wake up," Cheryl's mother said, gently shaking Grandma's shoulder.

Grandma's eyes opened, and she blinked a couple of times. "Katherine?

"Yes, Mom. I'm here with Cheryl, and we've brought some guests along." Cheryl's mother motioned to Emma and Rachel, who stood off to one side.

Grandma gave no indication that she saw them, as she stared at

Cheryl with a blank expression.

"Grandma, do you know how I am?" Cheryl asked, leaning in close to be sure Grandma could see her face.

Grandma studied Cheryl a few more seconds, then gave a slow nod. "You're my granddaughter."

Cheryl breathed a sigh of relief. She glanced at Mom and saw tears in her eyes. Did she feel guilty for being too busy to spend time with her own mother?

"Grandma, I want to introduce you to some very special people," Cheryl said, motioning for Emma and Rachel to move closer to the bed. "I think you might already know them. They're sisters, and their names are Emma and Rachel."

"When you were young, was your name Betty Bontrager?" Rachel asked, leaning close to Grandma's bed.

Grandma's eyelids fluttered.

"Did you grow up in Middlebury, Indiana? Were your parents named Homer and Doris?" Emma softly questioned, standing next to Rachel.

Grandma released a shuddering breath and coughed, while trying to sit up.

With Cheryl on one side, and her mother on the other, they eased two pillows behind Grandma's back and helped her get into a sitting position.

"There, Grandma, is that better?" Cheryl asked, holding her grandmother's hand.

Grandma nodded as tears filled her eyes. "Do I know you?" she asked, looking at Emma and then Rachel.

"Our parents were Homer and Doris Bontrager," Rachel repeated. "Our oldest sister's name was Betty."

Grandma covered her mouth as a heart-wrenching sob tore from her throat. "I. . .I'm that Betty. I never thought I'd see any of my family again." She looked at Cheryl and her mother. "I. . .I mean, the family I was born into," she said, lifting a shaky hand to swipe at the tears dripping onto her weathered cheeks.

Concerned for her grandmother, Cheryl stepped between Emma and Rachel. "I think this might be a bit too much for her. Maybe we should slow down and let her process things."

Cheryl was amazed that Grandma, whose memory was failing, seemed to remember these details now. Perhaps she'd longed to see her family so badly that it had been ever present on her mind.

Before Emma or Rachel could respond to Cheryl's request to slow down, Grandma shook her head and said, "No, let them go on."

"Whatever happened? Why'd you stay away all those years?" Rachel asked, tears dribbling down her own wrinkled cheeks. "Our mother's heart was broken, you know."

Even with Cheryl's comforting touch, Grandma continued to sob as she rocked back and forth. "I didn't want to stay away. I. . .I was scared. I prayed that we'd all be together someday, but Papa said he never wanted to see me again. I was afraid if I came back I wouldn't be welcome, and I couldn't handle the rejection." Grandma drew in a shuddering breath. "Staying away and having no contact with my family seemed easier, but I never forgot them."

Emma took Grandma's other hand. "It's too late to change the past, but we've been given a second chance. The Lord led us to you, and for that I'm so thankful." She took a seat in one of the chairs near Grandma's bed, and motioned for Rachel to do the same. "Now let's not waste a minute. I want to get better acquainted with the sister I never knew."

Cheryl placed the box with the quilt in it at the foot of Grandma's bed. "I have something I'd like to give you." She lifted the lid, removed the quilt, and gently covered Grandma with it. "Happy birthday, Grandma."

"It's my old quilt!" More tears fell as Grandma stroked the edge of her quilt with loving hands. "But it's not tattered anymore. It's even more beautiful than when my mother gave it to me. How did this happen?"

Cheryl explained that she'd taken the quilt to Emma to be repaired, and then told Grandma the details of how Rachel had recognized the quilt and they'd figured out that Grandma must be their long-lost sister.

Tears were shed all around, as two happy sisters, a mother, and her daughter, gathered around Grandma's bed. Cheryl knew that for the rest of her life she would cherish this special moment and the story of how the once-tattered quilt had brought them all together.

Mishawaka

After fixing himself a microwave dinner of macaroni and cheese, Blaine decided to relax in his recliner the rest of the evening. This was the night he usually watched a program about fishing.

Tonight's show featured rainbow trout and had been filmed in the Finger Lakes region of New York. Any other time, Blaine would have quickly become engrossed in a program like this, but unfortunately, all he could think about was the conversation he'd had with Lamar, concerning Sue.

Why did Sue call me like that? he wondered for the umpteenth time. *And why did she want to know about me going out with Cheryl?*

"Women," Blaine muttered as he stared at the TV. "They sure can be hard to figure out."

The phone rang, startling him out of his thoughts. Caller ID told him it was his brother Darin.

"Hello," Blaine answered, wondering what his brother wanted.

"Hey, Blaine. How ya doing?" Darin's voice sounded full of excitement. "It's been awhile since we talked. Hope things are going good for you."

"I'm doing fine. How about you?"

"I have some great news. I'm a dad!" Darin shouted.

Had nine months gone by already? Blaine wondered, holding the phone away from his ear.

"Michelle went into labor this morning, and at 4:35 this afternoon, our baby boy was born. Can you believe it? I'm officially a dad!"

"That's great, Darin. How are Michelle and the baby doing? Oh, and what'd you name your son?"

"They're both doing great. We named him Caleb Vickers, and he weighs a little under seven pounds."

Blaine listened as his brother told how great it had been to be there when the baby was born. He was happy for Darin and Michelle but felt envious. He could almost foresee the next visit when his family got together. It would most likely be at Thanksgiving or Christmas, which wasn't too far off. There would be more questions about him, of course. Had he met anyone yet? Did he ever plan to settle down and have a family of his own?

Blaine would love to have a family someday, but it didn't just happen out of the blue—although at times he wished his soul mate would suddenly appear.

Blaine listened awhile longer as his brother nearly talked his ear off. Finally Darin said he'd better hang up because he had several other calls to make.

When Blaine hung up, he grabbed the remote and clicked off the TV. *Man, my life is the pits!*

Elkhart

Carmen had been gone less than a week, but it felt much longer to Paul. He hadn't said it out loud, but he really missed her.

Why did she have to betray my trust? Paul fumed as he sat at his desk, prepared to boot up his computer. If only she hadn't come here to write a negative story about the Amish. They got enough negative press coverage—much of it exaggerated or based on untruths. The majority of Amish people were humble, hardworking, and living their lives as their ancestors had done. As was so often the case, when one of their kind did something wrong and it made the news, many people began to think that all Amish were bad.

Think I'll go online and see if I can find the story Carmen wrote for the newspaper she works for, Paul decided. *I'd like to see how damaging it was.*

After finding the Los Angeles newspaper's website, he did a search for Carmen's story. Sure enough, there it was, in the News section: "Amish Values" by Carmen Lopez.

Oh boy, here it comes. She's going to start bashing the Amish values. Paul read the story out loud: "There are many myths about rumschpringe, which is a time for Amish young people to decide whether they want to join the Amish church. Most Amish youth don't leave home during this time. Amish parents do not encourage their children to break the church rules, but to behave morally during their running-around years. Some stories about rumschpringe portray it as a time of wild parties and experimentation with drugs and alcohol. This kind of behavior is an exception rather than the norm. Some groups of Amish young people may meet in town and change into 'English' clothes. The girls may even wear makeup or try on jewelry, and Amish boys may buy a car during this time. But many own horses and buggies, which they use to court a young woman. Dating among the Amish typically involves attending Sunday night 'singings,' participating in games and activities with others their age, and having the young man visit in the young woman's home. The key purpose for rumschpringe is for Amish young people to decide if they want to join the Amish church."

Paul leaned in closer and murmured, "She got that right."

Dropping to the next paragraph, he continued to read: "Although some young people choose to separate themselves from the Amish way of life, almost ninety percent of Amish teenagers eventually choose to be baptized and join the Amish church. Those who choose to leave are not shunned unless they have already joined the church and then choose to break away. Amish communities and individual families vary in their views of the best response to offer during rumschpringe. Some parents allow certain behaviors, while others hold a tighter rein."

Paul nodded as he continued to read. "During my recent six-week stay in northeastern Indiana, I got to know several Amish people quite well and observed their customs. It's the opinion of this reporter that Amish parents do not condone wild or immoral behavior, and they do try to monitor their young people's actions. The Amish I came to know and respect put God first in their lives and have strong family values. Most of us 'Englishers,' as the Amish often refer to those who are not Amish, could learn a lot from the Amish way of life, where simplicity and a devotion to God are the foundation of their faith."

"Well, what do you know?" Feeling as though all the air had been sucked out of his lungs, Paul leaned back in his chair with a groan. He sat running his fingers through his hair, then stood and began to pace, wrestling with what he should do. He'd misjudged Carmen. She hadn't written a negative story, after all. It was quite the opposite.

Paul returned to his chair and bowed his head, asking for God's guidance in all of this. A still, small voice seemed to be saying, "Call her!"

With no hesitation, Paul reached for the phone and quickly punched in Carmen's number. He just hoped it wasn't too late and that she would accept his apology.

CHAPTER 39

Shipshewana

"It's sure nice to have you back. How was your trip?" Lamar asked after he'd helped Emma's driver carry hers and Rachel's luggage to the house.

"It was good, but we're both exhausted," Emma said, squeezing Lamar's hand.

Rachel nodded. "It was a worthwhile trip, however."

"Two weeks is a long time to be gone from home, but I'm glad it worked out for you to spend time there and get to know your long-lost *schweschder*," Lamar said.

"I know," Emma agreed, "and what a joy it was to discover that one of my special quilting students is actually my great-niece. It's no wonder Cheryl and I felt a connection. I keep thinking if we had gone to Florida instead of staying here and holding another quilting class, I may have never met my sister Betty or discovered that I had a niece and a great-niece I knew nothing about."

"Did you connect with Cheryl's mother, as well?" Lamar asked.

Emma sighed. "Not like I did with Cheryl, but Katherine, who was equally surprised to learn that she had Amish relatives, did seem to appreciate getting to know me and Rachel, and I look forward to corresponding with her in the days ahead."

"Same here," Rachel agreed.

"And how is your sister doing?" Lamar questioned.

"Not well, but better than when we arrived in Portland," Rachel interjected. "I think our reunion gave her a lift, and we promised to keep in touch through letters and phone calls. I just hope her memory doesn't go."

"Maybe we can plan a trip there sometime," Lamar said, placing Emma's suitcase in the entryway.

"I wouldn't want to travel that far during the winter months, but if Betty's up to company in the spring, we might think about going then." Emma smiled at Lamar and then turned to Rachel. "Lamar and I are planning to spend the winter months in Sarasota, Florida."

Rachel's blue eyes brightened. "Will you be staying in Pinecraft?"

Emma nodded. "Lamar has a cousin who owns a house there, and he said we could rent it for a reasonable price."

"That will be nice," Rachel said. "Maybe I'll drop down and visit sometime during your stay."

Emma smiled. "We'd welcome that, wouldn't we, Lamar?"

He bobbed his head. "Emma and I are always open to having company."

"What will you do while you're in Florida?" Rachel questioned.

"Oh, I don't know," Emma replied. "We'll probably do some sightseeing and get to know the area and the people. We have several friends who've relocated to that area and some who go there for the winter months, so it'll be nice to visit with them as well. And of course it will be wunderbaar to spend some time on the beach, soaking up the sun and looking for shells."

"That's right," Lamar agreed, "and I'm looking forward to doing some fishing."

Rachel touched Emma's arm. "Do you think you might teach a quilting class while you're there?"

"Oh, I don't know about that," Emma said. "I'd really planned on just taking it easy all winter."

"Well, I certainly don't blame you. We all need that from time to time." Rachel yawned. "Now, if you'll excuse me, I think I need to take it easy for a spell. If you don't mind, I'm going upstairs to rest for a bit."

"No problem," Emma said. "I'd do the same if my students weren't coming over today, but I did promise them that we would all get together one last time to share how everyone's doing."

As Rachel left the room to head upstairs, a knock sounded on the door. "I'll see who it is," Lamar said as Emma took a seat. A few seconds later, he was back with Carmen at his side.

"Now this is a pleasant surprise," Emma said, smiling. "I thought you'd gone back to California."

"I did, but I came back." Carmen dropped her gaze as she shifted her weight from one foot to the other.

"If you two will excuse me, I need to go feed the goats and then check for any phone messages that may have been left this morning," Lamar said, glancing at Emma. Did he sense that Carmen wanted to speak with her alone?

Carmen waited until he left the room, and then she leaned against the table as if needing a little support. "I need to tell you something, Emma."

"Oh, what's that?"

"Before you say anything, please hear me out. I came here to take your quilting classes under false pretenses."

Emma blinked. "I'm not sure what you mean."

"I came to Indiana to do a story on the Amish—a negative story that would shed a bad light on rumschpringe."

"Oh my!" Emma clasped her hand over her mouth. "I had no idea you came here for that. Is this the reason you were asking me so many questions about our young people and their running-around years?"

Carmen nodded, her eyes filling with tears. "After getting to know you and Anna, I came to realize that things weren't as I'd thought them to be, and I just couldn't write the story the way my boss wanted me to." She paused, reached into her purse, and pulled out a newspaper. Handing it to Emma, Carmen said, "Here's the story I ended up writing, and it's the one that went to print, although my boss wasn't happy about it."

Emma repositioned her reading glasses and read the article slowly, to be sure she didn't miss anything. When she was done, she looked up at Carmen and said, "That was a nice article. You didn't show us as being perfect, but neither did you shed a bad light on us, the way some reporters have done. That's not to say that some of the things written about certain Amish people haven't been true. Unfortunately, there are bad people in all walks of life."

"Not you, though, Emma," Carmen said, touching Emma's shoulder. "You're one of the kindest, most thoughtful women I've ever met."

"Does Paul know about this article?" Emma asked, pointing to the paper.

Carmen shook her head. "He knows I planned to write it, but as the negative article my boss wanted me to compose. Paul doesn't know anything about the one I actually wrote. When he found out I was sent here to write a damaging article, he was very upset and accused me of taking advantage of you." She sniffed and swiped at the tears running down her flushed cheeks. "I'm afraid he won't let me see Sophia anymore, and I was hoping that—"

"That something might develop between you and Paul?" Emma interrupted.

Carmen nodded. "I've come to care for them both so much, and if there was anything I could do to make things right, I surely would."

"You already have."

Carmen jumped at the sound of Paul's voice. "Paul, where did you come from?" she squeaked.

"I just got here—came to see Lamar and Emma," Paul said as he strode into the room, holding Sophia's hand.

As soon as the little girl saw Carmen, she squealed and ran toward her. Carmen opened her arms and gave Sophia a hug.

Emma smiled. It was obvious the child loved Carmen as much as Carmen did her. "You know," Emma said, "I think I'll go out to the kitchen and fix some refreshments. If you'll excuse me, I'll be back soon."

"Do you need some help?" Carmen asked.

"No, I can manage. Just stay and visit with Paul, and I'll take Sophia with me." Emma took the child's hand and ushered her out of the room.

Carmen turned to Paul, and was about to say something, but he spoke first. "Carmen, before you try to explain anything, I have a few things I'd like to say."

"Go ahead, Paul."

"I've been trying to call you, but all I ever got was your voice mail."

"That's because I'm not home; I'm here," she said, feeling a bit apprehensive. Was he going to chastise her again for her betrayal? What could he say to her that he hadn't said before?

"I'm surprised you're here," Paul said. "I thought you were still in California."

"I was, but I came back so I could take care of a few matters," she replied, her defenses rising.

"Well, believe me, I'm glad you're here, because I read your article online and need to apologize for the things I said before you left for California."

Blinking, Carmen could hardly believe her ears. "I accept your apology," she said, feeling a great weight lifting off her shoulders, "but I'm really the one who needs to apologize. When I came here on this assignment, I had no idea what to expect or that I'd meet such wonderful Amish people, like Emma, Lamar, and Anna." Carmen looked into Paul's eyes. "I wasn't thinking about how all this would hurt you and Sophia. I–I care for you both." She didn't dare say how much.

"We care for you, too," he said, taking her hand. "And if I had my way, you'd stay in Indiana and forgot about California."

Carmen smiled up at him. "That's good to hear, because I've quit my job at the newspaper there and have found one at the newspaper in Goshen."

Paul's eyes widened as a genuine smile stretched across his face. "Now that is good news!"

Sophia was seated in the high chair in Emma's kitchen, happily eating a cookie with a glass of milk, so Emma decided to take the rest of the cookies into the living room to share with Carmen and Paul. She'd just stepped into the hall when she saw the young couple holding hands and looking lovingly at each other. *Better not disturb them right now,* she decided. *Think I'll give them a little more time alone.*

Emma had no more than reentered the kitchen, when Lamar came in from outside. "Look who just arrived," he said, motioning to Anna, who followed close behind.

"Oh Anna, it's good that you came today. Carmen is in the living room with Paul." Emma gestured to Sophia, sitting in the high chair. "This is Paul's little girl, Sophia."

Just as Emma said her name, Sophia looked up and gave Anna a big grin.

"She's so cute," Anna exclaimed.

Emma smiled, watching as Anna walked over to Sophia and tickled her under the chin.

"I'm going back outside," Lamar said. "I plumb forgot about checking for phone messages."

When Lamar went out the door, Emma turned to Anna and said, "How have you been?"

Anna's cheeks colored. "It's hard to explain, because I'm still confused, but I think my eyes have been opened to some things."

"Oh? What kind of things?" Emma asked.

"Lately I've been feeling like I need to get away someplace on my own. And I've had an opportunity to go to Florida with my friend Mandy in December." Anna stopped talking, as if to regroup her thoughts; then she slowly shook her head. "I thought this would be my chance to get out on my own for a bit. I wanted a taste of something different—maybe even try out the English way of life. Then two weeks ago, after our last quilting class, Mandy and I went to Goshen and we dressed in English clothes, let our hair down, and even wore some makeup. It was fun until a couple of English fellows came into the restaurant and wouldn't leave us alone."

"Did anything happen?" Emma asked with concern.

"No, thank goodness," Anna replied. "Mandy and I slipped into the restroom, washed off the makeup, and changed back into our Amish clothes. Somehow we were able to slip back out without those guys even recognizing us."

"I'm glad to hear that," Emma said, placing a comforting hand on Anna's arm.

"When I got home that evening," Anna continued, "and told my folks who I was with, Dad yelled and Mom's face turned red. They never did approve of me hanging around with Mandy, but she's my best friend. Then I got angry and blurted out to Mom and Dad that I was going to Florida, and that my mind was made up."

Emma almost knew what was coming next. It sounded all too familiar after recently hearing her sister Betty's side of the story, but she let Anna go on telling her what had happened.

"So when I said that, Dad told me if I went to Florida, I could just stay there and never come back." Anna's chin quivered, and her eyes filled with tears. "How could Dad say something like that to me?"

"I'm sure he didn't mean it, Anna. He was only speaking out of anger and concern."

Anna sighed. "Well, ever since then, Dad and I are hardly talking, and Mom is so upset she keeps begging me not to go. I'm so confused and don't know how to fix things between us. If I don't go to Florida and get some experience on my own, I don't think things will ever change for me here at home."

"I understand," Emma said, giving Anna a hug. Then she quickly told her about meeting her oldest sister for the first time, and how and why Betty had left home. She then stated, "Betty's decision to leave home, and our parents' response to it, affected everyone. If you're going to leave home and think you'll want to come back, then you should tell your parents that. In fact, I think it would be good if you tell them everything you've told me just now, Anna. And if you like, I'd be happy to speak with your Mom and Dad, too."

"Would you really do that for me?" Anna asked.

Emma nodded. "I had it in my mind to do that anyway. Since Lamar and I have decided to spend our winter in Sarasota, I'll let your parents know that we'll be there in case you need anything. That might set their minds at ease."

Anna smiled as she dried her tears. "Danki, Emma. I think that would help, and I'll look forward to seeing you in Florida."

Emma motioned to the door leading to the living room. "As I mentioned, Carmen's here, and I'm sure she'll be happy to see you, so why don't you go in and say hello?"

"Okay, I will." Anna started out of the room but turned back around. "I'm glad I talked to you, and I appreciate your concern and support." She pivoted around and hurried down the hall.

Seeing that Sophia had smudges of cookie on her face, Emma went to the sink and wet a paper towel. She'd just finished cleaning the little girl up when Lamar entered the kitchen.

"I just checked our phone messages," he said, "and there was one from Blaine."

"Oh, what'd he say?" Emma asked, lifting Sophia down from the high chair.

"Well, first he wanted to let us know that he'd become an uncle again. Seems his brother Darin and his wife, just had their first *boppli*—a little boy."

"Isn't that nice?" Emma smiled. "I'll bet Blaine is excited.

"He was and said he'd be heading up to Canada around the holidays when all his family will be together." Lamar paused before continuing. "Guess what else?"

"There's more?" Emma asked.

Lamar gave a nod. "Blaine also said that he wouldn't be able to come here today because he's meeting Sue for coffee."

Emma quirked an eyebrow. "Isn't she Blaine's ex-girlfriend?"

Lamar nodded. "Guess she wants to get back together, and at my suggestion, Blaine's giving her a second chance."

Emma tweaked her husband's nose. "Is that so? And I thought I was the only matchmaker in this family."

"Oh really? Who, might I ask, have you been trying to get together?"

Emma gestured to Sophia. "Her daed's in our living room right now, talking to Carmen."

Lamar's eyes twinkled. "Ah, I see. And I'm guessing you had something to do with that?"

"Well, I didn't set it up, if that's what you mean, but after Carmen showed up, Paul and Sophia came by. When I saw that Paul had some things he wanted to say to Carmen, I brought Sophia in here so the two of them could talk in private." Emma's voice lowered to a whisper. "I peeked in on them a few minutes ago, and they were holding hands. Anna, in fact, just went to join them. And by the way, Anna opened up to me, and we had a good talk."

Lamar grinned. "That's *gut*, jah?"

"Yes, it's very good on both accounts."

A knock sounded on the back door, and Lamar called, "Come in, it's open!"

Selma stepped in, smiling from ear to ear. "I'm not late, am I?" she asked.

"No, Carmen and Anna are here, and they're in the living room with Paul," Emma replied.

"And Blaine's not going to be able to make it," Lamar added.

"Well, there's something I want to share with you," Selma said, clasping Emma's arm. "I called my daughter last night, and we had a long talk. I apologized to Cora for the things I've said in the past that hurt her, and she said she was sorry for leaving home and not keeping in touch with me."

"Oh, that's wonderful," Emma said, giving Selma a hug. "I'm happy to hear that things are working out between you and your daughter."

"It's because of you, Emma," Selma said, tears gathering in the corners of her eyes. "You taught me more than just how to quilt. You helped me realize the importance of loving and accepting others."

Emma smiled. "I think we all learned a lot from each other during our quilting classes."

The roar of an engine drew Emma's attention to the kitchen window.

"Sounds like Terry and Cheryl are here," Lamar said with a chuckle. "I'll let them in."

When Cheryl and Terry entered the kitchen, Emma knew immediately that they had worked things out, for they wore huge smiles on their faces.

"Cheryl told me the good news," Terry said, stepping up to Emma. "Special things seem to happen when folks take your quilting classes. Jan found his daughter during one of your classes, and now Cheryl's found her great-aunt and you've found your sister." Terry, looking into Cheryl's eyes, smiled and took her hand. "I found you, and it's almost too good to be true."

Emma was surprised to see that Terry had cut his hair and was dressed in nicer clothes. He obviously wanted to make a good impression on Cheryl.

Lamar winked at Emma, and she winked right back. She knew

beyond a shadow of a doubt that this would not be the last group of would-be quilters she would teach. Whether it was here in Indiana or in Florida during the winter, she knew that God would send the right people at just the right time.

Emma's Apple-Crumb Bread

Ingredients:
- ½ cup butter
- 1 cup sugar
- 2 eggs
- 1 teaspoon baking soda dissolved in 2 tablespoons milk
- 2 cups flour
- ½ teaspoon salt
- 1 teaspoon vanilla
- 1½ cups chopped apples

Topping:
- 1 teaspoon cinnamon
- 2 tablespoons butter
- 4 tablespoons flour
- 2 tablespoons brown sugar

Preheat oven to 325 degrees. Cream together in a bowl the butter, sugar, and eggs. Add the baking soda dissolved in 2 tablespoons milk. Finally, add in the flour, salt, vanilla, and chopped apples. Pour into a 9" x 5½" greased bread pan. Combine topping ingredients and sprinkle over top of bread batter. Bake for 1 hour.

Discussion Questions

1. In this story, Anna was dissatisfied with her life and wanted to leave home to try out the "English" way of life. Why do you think some teenagers (Amish or English) are anxious to leave home and strike out on their own?

2. Due to his parents' breakup, Terry feared marriage and commitment. How can a person whose life has been affected by a breakup learn to have a meaningful relationship without fear or worry that it will happen to them?

3. After Carmen was asked to write an article that would shed a negative light on the Amish, she came to realize that things weren't quite the way she thought they were. Have you ever been asked to do something you believed would please your boss or brighten your career and then realized what you'd been asked to do was wrong? How did you handle the situation?

4. Blaine felt uncomfortable in a group setting—especially when he was expected to do something unfamiliar to him, such as quilting. Have you ever been afraid to try something new for fear of saying or doing something foolish? How can we help ourselves or someone we know get over feeling self-conscious when trying something new?

5. Selma had been holding a grudge ever since her daughter left home. This compounded her fear of rejection and lowered her self-esteem, making it difficult to develop a relationship with others.

Has a fear of rejection ever kept you from reaching out to others?

6. Cheryl was an only child and felt all alone growing up due to the lack of her parents' attention. Have you ever felt that way? What are some ways we can deal with painful childhood memories or feelings of rejection from our parents?

7. Was it fate or God's intervention that kept Emma and Lamar from going to Florida too soon? Has a reverse decision ever opened a door to something unexpected in your life?

8. Carmen felt that too much of the news was based on negative events. Would you rather read about tragedies and other people's problems, or do you prefer to read about the good things people do or that happen to them? Does hearing about other people's problems make ours seem any less?

9. Lamar tried to hide from Emma the fact that his arthritis was acting up. Do you think spouses should ever keep things about their health from each other?

10. At times Emma felt like she was not getting through to her students or helping them with their personal problems. She didn't want to pry, but she hoped they would feel free to share with her so she could help mentor them as she'd done with several other people who had previously come to her home to learn to quilt. What are some ways we can minister to others without prying into their personal lives?

THE
HEALING
QUILT

CHAPTER 1

Sarasota, Florida

Seating herself on a weathered, wooden bench, Emma Miller gazed at the waves lapping gently against the shore. The soothing scene almost lulled her to sleep. Lido Beach was peaceful on this early January morning, and there weren't many people milling about yet. It almost felt as if she and Lamar had the whole beach to themselves. This morning after breakfast, Lamar had talked her into catching the bus and coming here so they could enjoy the beach before it got too crowded.

Wiggling her bare toes in the sand, Emma watched as her husband rolled his trousers up to his knees and waded into the crystal-clear, turquoise water. Lamar seemed happy and contented, and thanks to the balmy weather, his arthritis didn't bother him nearly so much.

Lamar was definitely getting around more easily, and that made it worth moving down here for the winter.

Unfortunately, after only two weeks of living in their newly purchased vacation home inside the village of Pinecraft, Emma was bored. Sure, there was plenty to do. They could visit other Amish and Mennonites; spend time on the beach looking for shells; or ride their three-wheeler bikes to the park or one of the many stores and restaurants in the area, since horse and buggies were not allowed. But Emma wanted more. She needed something meaningful and constructive to do.

"Come join me," Lamar called, looking eagerly at Emma. "The water's warm, and there are lots of shells!" His thick gray hair and matching beard stood in stark contrast to the turquoise-blue water behind him.

Emma smiled and waved in response. She wasn't in the mood to get her dress wet this morning. For that matter, she wasn't in the mood for much of anything just now. Emma missed her family and friends in Shipshewana, Indiana. She even missed the cold, wintry days, sitting by the fire with a cup of hot coffee while she worked on one of her quilting projects. Fortunately, Emma's daughter, Mary, and her family lived next door and were keeping an eye on Emma and Lamar's Indiana home, as well as feeding and caring for Emma's goats.

Emma's sister, Rachel, had planned to come down for a few weeks, but one of Rachel's daughters was sick, and she'd gone to her house to help out while she recuperated, so she might not make it, after all. Emma couldn't help feeling disappointed.

Maybe I should call Mary and ask her to send me some of my quilting supplies, Emma thought. *It would be good to have something productive to do while we are here.*

"Emma, aren't you going to join me?" Lamar hollered, holding up a large shell he'd found. "You oughta come and take a look at this one. It's the best shell yet!"

"Maybe later," she called in response.

Lamar waded out of the water and plodded across the white sand, stopping in front of Emma. "Is something wrong? You usually enjoy looking for shells with me."

Making circles in the sand with her big toe, Emma sighed. "I do, Lamar, and don't take this wrong, but I wish there was more for me to do than come here to the beach or bike around Pinecraft, where I end up talking to people about family back home. I need something meaningful to do with my time."

He took a seat on the bench beside her and placed the colorful shell in her lap. "Why don't you teach some quilting classes? We talked about that before we left Indiana."

She gave a slow nod. "*Jah*, that idea was mentioned, but I'm not sure there would be enough interest in quilting here in Florida. At home where so many tourists come to learn about the Amish, people are eager to learn how to quilt. Here where it's warm and sunny most of the winter, people are probably more interested in spending time on the beach and being involved in other outdoor activities."

"You won't know if you don't try." He patted her arm affectionately. "Why don't we run an ad in the local newspaper and put some flyers up around the area? Maybe you could talk to the owner of the quilt shop on Bahia Vista Street and see if you could teach your classes there."

Emma shook her head. "If I'm going to teach quilting, I prefer that it be done in our own home, where it's less formal and people will feel more relaxed."

"I understand," Lamar said. "And if it's meant for you to have another six-week quilting class, then people will come."

Emma pursed her lips as she mulled over the idea. "If I did hold some quilting classes, would you be willing to help me again?"

"Of course. I can explain the history of quilts at the introductory class and be there to help out whenever I'm needed. It'll be a little different in our new surroundings. I'm sure I'll enjoy it as much as I have all the other times I've helped you teach back home." Lamar smiled, his green eyes twinkling like fireflies on a summer's night. "It will be interesting to see who God sends to our classes this time around."

Emma nodded, anticipation welling in her soul. "Okay then. Let's start advertising right away."

Chicago, Illinois

Bruce "B.J." Jensen stood in front of the easel he'd set up near the window in his studio. He tipped his head, scrutinizing his most recent painting— ocean waves lapping against the shore as the sun began to set.

B.J. frowned. He hadn't been to the ocean since his wife, Brenda, died five years ago. For that matter, he hadn't been anywhere outside of Chicago since then. At first his responsibilities as an art teacher had kept him tied to home. After he retired a year ago, freelance jobs kept him too busy to travel. But he was running out of time. Pretty soon, if he didn't see some of the things he'd been wanting to, it would be too late.

He stared out the window at the fresh-fallen snow. B.J. had always loved winter and appreciated that he lived where all four seasons could be enjoyed. But this year for the first time, the snow and bitter cold winds Chicago was known for really bothered B.J., and he was ready for a change.

If only I had more time, he thought with regret. *Time to see all the things I've missed and time to spend with my family and friends.*

B.J. had been diagnosed with cancer two years ago—just a few days after his sixtieth birthday. Recently, he'd found out that the cancer had spread from his throat to other parts of his body. But he hadn't told his daughters, Robyn and Jill; they both had busy lives of their own, and he didn't want them to worry. They thought the cancer surgery had been successful and that he was in remission. He didn't have the heart to tell them the truth. Knowing his daughters, they'd set everything aside to take care of him. B.J. didn't want that. He didn't want their sympathy, either. Maybe when he reached the final stages he would tell them. Until then, he planned to live each day to its fullest, while seeing and doing some of the things he'd always wanted to do. First off would be a trip to Sarasota, Florida, to see the Gulf of Mexico and paint some beautiful scenes on the beach.

Sarasota

Kyle Wilson stopped near the living-room couch. His fifteen-year-old daughter, Erika, sat in her wheelchair in front of the window facing the bay. She seemed so forlorn, with head down and shoulders slumped. But then, that was nothing new for her these days. Once full of life and unafraid, Erika was a different person now. She'd been despondent for more than a year—ever since her accident.

Kyle reflected on the event that had left his only child paralyzed from the waist down. Erika had invited two of her friends over to swim in their pool. They'd had a great time, laughing, splashing each other, and taking turns competing on the diving board.

Erika had learned to swim when she was a young girl. Kyle and his wife, Gayle, had nicknamed her "tadpole" because she loved the water so much. Last year when Erika turned fourteen, her interest turned to diving and trying different techniques off the springboard. Kyle was truly amazed at how fearless his daughter had been. She'd seemed to be good at everything, no matter what she attempted.

Kyle's throat constricted as he recalled how the accident happened....

"Come on, Erika, it's getting late, and you're tired. I think you'd better get out of the pool."

"In a few minutes, Dad. I just wanna do one more dive," Erika protested. "It's called a 'forward reverse.'"

Kyle could almost feel her eagerness as she climbed out of the pool and clambered up the diving-board ladder, so he let it go. He watched as Erika stood forward on the board, staring down at the pool's blue depth, her honey-blond hair pulled back in a ponytail, with water still dripping off the ends. As she leaped into the air, her body arching backward, it was like watching in slow-motion as her head and shoulders cleared the board.

Kyle held his breath. His daughter's fluid motion seemed to go perfectly. But instead of Erika's body straightening out after clearing the board, she made a wrong move. Her body came out of the arc at an odd angle, throwing her off-balance.

Kyle stared in horror as Erika's back and legs hit the board with a terrible crack. He watched helplessly as she bounced off the board and let out a scream as she fell into the water. Something had gone terribly wrong.

He leaped out of his chair, knowing he had to get his precious daughter help as quickly as possible.

———

Sweat beaded on Kyle's forehead as his mind snapped back to the present. *It's my fault she's crippled,* he berated himself for the umpteenth time. *If only I'd insisted she quit for the day, before she did that stupid dive. If I'd known what Erika had in mind, I would have stopped her before it was too late. I'm a doctor who treats many children every year, but I couldn't help my own daughter because the damage to her spine could not be fixed.*

Kyle clenched his fingers until his nails dug into the palms of his hands. Erika's accident had been the second traumatic event he'd faced in a relatively short time. Kyle's beautiful wife had died a year earlier from injuries she'd sustained when her car was broadsided by a truck. Truth was, Kyle felt guilty about Gayle's accident, too. She'd asked him to run to the store that rainy evening to pick up some baking soda she'd forgotten when she'd gone shopping earlier in the day. Gayle had all the other ingredients she needed to make a batch of chocolate chip cookies, Kyle's favorite. But Kyle had said he was too tired after a long day at the hospital to run to the store. So Gayle had gone out on her own. If Kyle had been driving the car, he might have avoided the accident. Even if he'd been the one killed, Erika would at least still have her mother.

Kyle rubbed a pulsating spot on his forehead. He knew all the *if onlys* and *what ifs* wouldn't change the facts, but it was hard not to be consumed by guilt—especially when he'd had to watch his daughter struggle with her disability. Erika needed something to look forward to each day—something meaningful to do with her time. He'd tried to interest her in some creative projects she could do from her wheelchair—like making beaded jewelry and painting—but she'd flatly refused. She wasn't even interested in playing her violin anymore. Gone was her dream of becoming a high school cheerleader, swimming, and going to dances. Erika seemed to think her life was over, and that grieved him immensely.

Should I force the issue and hire someone to come in and teach Erika something despite her objections? he wondered. *Would she cooperate if I did?*

The phone rang, startling Kyle out of his musings.

"I'll get it, Dad," Erika said, seeming to notice him for the first time. "At least answering the phone is something I can manage."

Kyle couldn't help noticing her sarcastic tone. Did she really feel that she wasn't capable of doing anything more than answering the telephone?

Dear Lord, he silently prayed. *Please help me find something beneficial for my daughter to do.*

"Come here, girl!" Kim Morris called as her dog frolicked on the beach, kicking up sand. The black-and-tan German shepherd ignored her and chased after a seagull.

Kim clapped her hands. "Stop that, Maddie, right now!"

Apparently tired of chasing the gull, Maddie darted in the direction of a young boy playing in the sand with his bucket and shovel. Thinking the child might be frightened by the dog, Kim picked up a stick and called Maddie again. "Come on, girl, let's play fetch!"

Woof! Woof! Maddie raced to Kim's side, eagerly wagging her tail.

Kim flung the stick into the water and laughed as Maddie darted in after it. The dog might be six years old, but she had the energy of a pup.

Coming out of the water and bounding across the sand, Maddie dropped the stick a few inches from Kim's bare toes. Kim grunted and picked it up. She would toss it a few more times, and then it would be time to get off the beach. It wouldn't be good if she were late to work her first day on the job. Being fairly new to the area, Kim was glad she'd been hired as a waitress at a restaurant a short distance from the small community known as Pinecraft. A lot of Amish and Mennonites lived in Pinecraft, either full- or part-time, and she'd been told that the restaurant business during the winter months was always the best because of so many visitors.

I just hope I don't lose this job because of my klutziness, Kim thought as she gave the stick another good toss, and Maddie tore after it. *I can't live on unemployment forever, and I need this job if I'm gonna start a new life for myself.*

Kim had moved from her home state of North Carolina to Sarasota a few months ago, hoping to start a new life with her boyfriend, Darrell. But things hadn't worked out, and they'd broken up. Rather than moving back home and admitting to her folks that she'd lost another boyfriend, Kim had decided to stay in Florida and make the best of the situation.

Since she loved the beach and enjoyed year-round warmer weather, she thought she could be happy living here, even without Darrell. Kim's track record with men wasn't that good, and she was beginning to doubt whether she'd ever find the right one. For now, though, she needed to settle into her new job, make a few friends, and find something creative to do in her spare time. Hopefully, this would give her life more meaning. Making friends shouldn't be that difficult, as she'd always been a people person. Finding something creative to do shouldn't be that hard, either. The thing Kim worried about most was keeping her job, but with determination to do her best, she was sure that would work out, too. At least she hoped it would. If it didn't, she might be forced to return to North Carolina, and that would mean admitting to her folks that she'd failed again.

CHAPTER 2

Phyllis Barstow smiled across the dinner table at her husband, Mike. "How'd it go on the boat today?" she questioned.

"The fishing went fine, but my boat started acting up. If it keeps on, I'll have to take it in for an evaluation. Things are busy right now, with all the visitors in town, and I can't afford to lose any business." He took a drink of his lemonade.

"Well, don't take any chances with the boat," Phyllis cautioned. "I don't want you getting stranded in the middle of the gulf or the bay—especially with a boat full of people."

Mike pulled his fingers through the ends of his dark, wavy hair. "You worry too much, Phyllis. I'm not gonna get stranded." He finished his pancakes, pushed away from the table, and stood. "I need to get going. See you this evening, hon." He gave Phyllis a quick peck on the cheek, grabbed the lunch she'd packed for him, and raced out the back door.

Phyllis sighed. Mike had become a workaholic. His charter fishing boat seemed to be his life these days, and his relationship with her was no longer at the top of his list. Even though she went on the boat with him sometimes to help out, it wasn't the same as spending time alone with her husband, since Mike was busy with the people who paid him to take them fishing.

Ever since their twin girls, Elaine and Elizabeth, had gone off to college, Phyllis had been trying to get Mike to pay more attention to her. But work always came first. She was forty-five and he was forty-six, and since they weren't getting any younger, she hated to see him pulling away from her—especially when a boat and fish were what seemed to be coming between them.

Phyllis reached for her cup of coffee and drank the last of it. *What I need is something fun and creative to do that won't leave me smelling like fish.* She tapped her fingers along the edge of the table. *Maybe I should take that quilting class I read about on the bulletin board at the supermarket the other day. At least it would be something to look forward to, and it would give me the opportunity to be creative.*

She reached for the phone. *Think I'll give the teacher a call and see if she has room in her class for one more student. This will certainly be an adventure. . .something I've never done before.*

As Noreen Webber drove home from her hair appointment, a sense of satisfaction welled in her soul. She had wanted a red sports car since she was eighteen years old and had finally purchased one last week, on her sixty-fifth birthday. The car not only looked cute, but it had all the bells and whistles. She'd waited a long time to have the car of her dreams, and just sitting in the vehicle, not to mention driving it, caused her to feel like a teenager again. So much so, that it made her wish she was young again and could flirt the next time she saw a good-looking guy.

Better get my head out of the clouds and come down to earth, because I think my flirting days are over. Noreen glanced in her rearview mirror to see if her hair looked as good as she hoped. Yes, every hair was in place, and Noreen's stylist had done a good job with the new cut and style. She knew it was vain, but if she was going to drive a sports car, then she wanted to look as young as possible.

At least I can enjoy driving it for a few good years—until I'm either too old, or the desire to own a sporty-looking car passes, she told herself. *In the meantime, I'm going to dress and think as young as I can. Who knows, maybe some nice-looking man will ask me out. I'm not looking to get married again, but it might be kind of fun to start dating. If I were to find the right man, I might even consider marriage again.*

Noreen, a widow for the last five years, had retired from teaching high school English two years ago. She'd been married to her husband, Ben, for forty years, until he died unexpectedly from a heart attack. The first couple of years after his death had been hard, but Noreen's job kept her going. Now that she was retired, she felt like a fish out of water, and always seemed to be searching for something meaningful to do. Her only child, Todd, whom she and Ben had adopted, was married and lived in Texas, so Noreen only saw him a few times a year. Todd's wife, Kara, had been previously married and had two young boys, whom Todd was helping her raise. They'd invited Noreen to move to Texas, but she liked the warmer weather in Florida and preferred not to move.

Noreen often filled her lonely hours walking on the beach. She also volunteered a few days a week at a local children's hospital and took as many creative classes as she could, just to have something fun to do, and so she could be around people. This morning, Noreen had seen an ad in the local newspaper about a six-week quilting class being offered by a woman who lived in the village of Pinecraft. She was seriously considering signing up for it. Quilting was one thing Noreen hadn't tried yet, and she was sure it would be interesting.

A horn honked from behind, pulling Noreen out of her musings. "Don't be in such a hurry," she mumbled. "The light hasn't been green that long. People shouldn't be so impatient."

The car behind her sped up, and as it came alongside her on the right, the horn tooted again.

"What is your problem?" Noreen glanced over at the driver, and her face warmed when she realized it was Tina, one of the nurses at the hospital where she volunteered. Tina pointed at Noreen's car and mouthed, "Nice. Is it new?"

Noreen smiled and nodded. She'd obviously misjudged the horn honking. Tina had simply been trying to get Noreen's attention.

Tina waved and moved on up the street in her minivan. Noreen looked forward to telling Tina, as well as the other nurses, about her new car when she went to the hospital next Monday morning. At least it would give her something exciting to talk about. Maybe she would mention the quilt class she was thinking about taking, too.

As Jennifer Owen sat on a wooden bench, waiting for the bus, she watched the traffic go by and thought about the situation she and her husband, Randy, were in. They'd been having a tough time since Randy lost his job, and she worried that if he didn't find something soon they wouldn't be able to keep up with their monthly bills. And in nine weeks, their first baby was due, but they didn't have any health insurance.

Jennifer, a hairdresser, had wanted to find a job at one of the local hair salons, but she'd had morning sickness during the first half of her pregnancy and knew she'd never make it through a workday without getting sick, so Randy had insisted she not work at this time. That had been before he'd lost his job working as a cook in a local Italian restaurant. It wasn't that the owner was displeased with Randy's cooking; the business was struggling and had to close. So for the last two months, they'd been living on Randy's unemployment checks and what little they'd managed to put away in their savings.

Jennifer tried to remain positive for Randy's sake, but she was scared. If Randy didn't find a position in one of the local restaurants soon, they might not be able to continue paying the rent on their small, two-bedroom home.

Today, like every other day since Randy lost his job, he'd scoured the want-ads and checked at the local unemployment office for a cook's position. Then he'd gone out looking for work. Since Randy's older model pickup was in for some repairs, he'd taken Jennifer's car. That left her to take the bus to the nearest pharmacy and pick up a few necessary things.

Jennifer felt fortunate to have a husband like Randy, who wanted to provide for his family. Her sister, Maggie, wasn't that lucky. Maggie's husband, Brad, sat around the house all day, drinking beer and smoking cigarettes, while his wife went to work cleaning people's houses. Well, at least Maggie wasn't expecting a baby, and they only had two mouths to feed.

"Would you mind if I sit here?" a young Amish woman asked as she approached.

Jennifer smiled. "No, not at all."

"Have you been waiting long?"

Jennifer looked at her watch. "Oh, five minutes or so."

They sat silently for a while; then Jennifer asked, "Do you live around here?"

"No, I live in Pinecraft, but I came over to this area early this morning to do some shopping. How about you? Do you live close by?"

Jennifer nodded. "Our house is right there—the white one with blue trim across the street. I don't normally take the bus, but my husband needed my car today so he could look for a job."

"What kind of work does your husband do?" the young woman questioned.

"He's a cook."

"It must be kind of scary to be unemployed, especially when you're expecting a baby," she said, glancing at Jennifer's stomach.

"Yes," Jennifer admitted. "We have some money saved up, but it won't last long if he doesn't find a job soon." She folded her hands across her stomach and gave it a gentle pat. "I saw an ad in the paper this morning, placed by a woman who lives in Pinecraft. She'll be teaching some quilting classes in a few weeks, and if I had extra money right now, I'd take the classes. It would nice to make a special quilt for our baby." She sighed. "Unless Randy gets a job in the next week, I can't even think about taking that class."

The bus pulled up. Jennifer thought she might continue talking with the Amish woman once they got on the bus, but there were no seats together. So she made her way down the aisle and took a seat beside an elderly woman, eager to get off her feet. She was glad she didn't have to take the bus on a regular basis, but if things didn't change, she and Randy might have to sell one of their vehicles.

CHAPTER 3

Two weeks later

T here's something I forgot to tell you," Lamar said as he and Emma sat across from each other at the kitchen table Saturday morning.

"What's that?" she asked, reaching for her cup of tea.

"Yesterday, when I met Amos Troyer for coffee at the restaurant up the street, Anna Lambright was our waitress."

"Oh? How's she doing?"

"Seems fine. Said she really likes it here." Lamar added a spoonful of sugar to his coffee and stirred it around. "It's good that she's keeping in contact with her folks, though. I hope they've finally accepted the fact that she wants to try living in Sarasota."

Tapping her fingers absently against her chin, Emma stared out the kitchen window, gazing at the oranges hanging on the tree in their small backyard. "Looks like the Honeybells are about ready to be picked," she mentioned. "Maybe we can offer some to those who attend our quilt class."

"That's a good idea, Emma," Lamar said. "The neighbor next door said those oranges are good eating in January, and I'm sure we'll have more than enough to share with our students."

Emma nodded as she continued to stare absently out the window, tapping her fingers.

"Are you *naerfich* about today's quilting class? You seem kind of stressed this morning," Lamar commented.

"I'm not really nervous," she replied. "Just a little concerned."

"About what?"

"Whether teaching quilting classes here in Pinecraft is a good idea."

Lamar's thick gray eyebrows lifted high on his forehead. "Why wouldn't it be? It didn't take long for six people to sign up for the class, so there must be some interest."

"I suppose that's true," Emma agreed, "but our home here is much smaller than our place in Shipshewana, so we'll be a bit cramped. We barely have room for the table our students will sit at, and the two sewing machines we bought, plus the one I borrowed, take up even more space in our small dining room."

"It'll all work out, you'll see." Lamar left his seat and patted Emma's shoulder affectionately. "I have a feeling that, just like all our other classes, God has directed these six new students to our home for a special reason."

She smiled and relaxed a bit. "You're probably right, Lamar. I hope and pray we will not only be able to teach each of our new students how to quilt, but that God will give us the wisdom to meet their needs."

Erika Wilson folded her arms and stared out the side window of her father's van. She couldn't believe he had signed her up to take a quilting class, and without even asking if she wanted to go. Now they were heading across town to Pinecraft, and she had no say in it. Truth was, Erika hadn't had much say about anything since her accident. Dad made all the decisions, and she was stuck in her wheelchair, forced to do whatever he said. It wasn't fair! Life wasn't fair—at least her life.

If her legs weren't paralyzed, she would be able to do all sorts of fun things with her friends. Now, whenever Lynne and Becky came over to see her, all they could do was sit and talk, watch TV, or play a computer game. No more swimming, bike riding, water skiing, dancing, roller boarding, or cheerleading—all the things Erika used to love to do. She'd practiced so diligently, hoping it would help when the time came for cheerleader tryouts. But that, as well as everything else, had been squashed from her life. She'd tried to be happy for her friends when they told her they had been picked for the squad, but that made it even harder to be around them lately. Erika's fun, teenaged years had been stolen from her, and there was no way to get them back.

How does Dad think me learning to quilt can make up for all the things I can't do? I hate the idea of quilting. It's for old ladies, not someone like me. Erika swiped at her cheeks, her fingers wet with salty tears. *I feel like an old lady, stuck in this chair. Dad may as well put me away in a nursing home, because I'm not good for much of anything but sitting around, staring out the window, and wishing I could turn back the clock to the minutes before I stupidly got on that diving board.*

"You're awfully quiet back there," Dad called from the front seat of their van.

Erika continued to stare out the window, feeling sorry for herself. She noticed some birds fly past the van and was envious because they were free.

"I know you're not thrilled about going to the quilting class, Erika, but I think if you give it a chance, you'll have a good time."

"I doubt it," she muttered.

"Don't be so negative."

"Kids my age don't learn how to quilt."

"I'll bet Amish girls do," he countered.

Erika grunted. "I'm not Amish."

"Well, just give it a try, okay?"

"Do I have a choice? You're the one in control these days."

Dad thumped the steering wheel with the palm of his hand. "I don't like your attitude, Erika, or your tone of voice. Now I want you to go to that class this morning with a smile on your face. Is that understood?"

Erika frowned. "Don't see why I have to smile about something I don't wanna do."

"I'm not asking you to smile about the quilting class. I just want you to be pleasant and try to have a positive attitude. Can you do that for me, Erika?"

"I–I'll try," she murmured. *But I don't have to like it.*

B.J. felt a sense of apprehension as he drove along Bahia Vista Street in the convertible he'd rented, following his GPS to the address of the quilting class he'd signed up for after arriving in Sarasota. Although he was interested in the design of Amish quilts and thought he'd like to create a painting of one, he was sure he'd be the only man in the class and would probably feel foolish.

Well, what does it matter? he asked himself. *I don't have long to live, so I may as well enjoy whatever time I have left and do the things I want to do, no matter how ridiculous I may look or feel.*

B.J.'s thoughts turned to his daughters back home. They knew he was here, but he'd only told them that he was going to Florida to enjoy the beach and warm weather and hoped to get some painting done.

Neither Jill nor Robyn had any idea he was taking a quilt class. He still felt guilty for not telling them his cancer had returned, but he'd convinced himself that for now, at least, it was for the best.

As B.J. turned up the street leading to Emma and Lamar Miller's house, he made a decision. If he was able to learn how to quilt, he would make Diane, his ten-year-old granddaughter, a quilted wall hanging so she could remember him after he was gone.

When Noreen pulled her sports car in front of the house where the quilt class was supposed to take place, she spotted a silver convertible with the top up, parked in the driveway. *Well, someone here has good taste in vehicles,* she thought.

She'd just opened her car door when a baldheaded man, who looked to be in his early sixties, got out of the convertible. He glanced her way and nodded. "Are you here for the quilting classes?"

"Yes, I am, and I'm really looking forward to it," she responded.

"Same here."

Her eyebrows lifted. "You want to learn how to quilt?"

"That's right; I'm an artist, and because of all the unusual designs in the quilts I've seen, I'm hoping to paint a picture of one." The man's voice was deep and sounded a bit gravely, but he had a pleasant smile.

Noreen still thought it was a bit strange that a man would want to learn how to quilt, even if he was an artist, but she figured, *Each to his own.*

"Shall we go inside and meet the teacher?" he asked, moving toward the house.

She gave a nod. *Having a man in the class should make things interesting.*

CHAPTER 4

Phyllis Barstow had just stepped onto the porch of a small Amish home in Pinecraft, when a noisy motorcycle pulled up to the curb. She frowned. *What's a biker doing in a place like this? I'm sure he's not planning to take the quilting class.*

Phyllis shook her head, glancing at the other cars parked in the driveway. *There won't be any men in this class—just a bunch of women like me, looking for something fun and creative to do. The biker's probably lost and asking for directions.*

Watching as the biker climbed off the cycle and removed his helmet, Phyllis was surprised to see that it wasn't a man at all. The thirty-something woman pulled her fingers through the ends of her wavy blond hair, grabbed a satchel from the back of the bike, and started up the walk leading to the house. Removing the elastic band that held the rest of her hair back, she gave her head a good shake, and more waves fell into place. When the young woman reached the porch, she smiled at Phyllis. "You here for the quilt class?"

Phyllis nodded. "Are you?"

"Sure am, and I'm glad the classes are being held on Saturdays, 'cause right now I have the weekends off."

"Where do you work?" Phyllis asked.

"At the restaurant a few blocks up on Bahia Vista Street." The young woman extended her hand. "I'm Kim Morris."

"Phyllis Barstow. It's nice to meet you. Shall we go inside and see who else came?"

"Hello everyone," Emma said as she and Lamar stood in front of the table where their six students sat—five in the folding chairs she'd provided, and the teenage girl in her wheelchair. "I'm Emma Miller, and this is my husband, Lamar."

Lamar stepped forward and smiled. "It's nice to have all of you here."

Everyone nodded—everyone but the teenage girl, that is.

"Why don't you take turns introducing yourself?" Emma suggested. "Oh, and please tell us the reason you signed up for this class. We can start with you," she said, smiling at the petite blond-haired woman sporting a nice suntan.

"My name is Kim Morris, and I'm taking this class to make some new friends and do something creative."

"Thank you, Kim." Emma motioned to the next person, who happened to be the only man. In the past, there had been at least two men in Emma's classes.

The man, looking more than a bit uncomfortable, said in a gravelly sounding voice, "My name is B.J. I'm an artist, and I thought it'd be fun to learn about the color and design of quilts. I may try to paint a picture of one as well."

"Lamar is an artist, too," Emma said. "He's designed a good many quilts."

Lamar's cheeks reddened. "I don't really consider myself an artist. I just enjoy coming up with various designs that depict many things." He motioned to the older woman who sat next to B.J. "Now it's your turn."

She rubbed her hands briskly together, as though eager to speak. "My name is Noreen Webber, and like Kim, I'm taking this class to make some new friends."

Emma was surprised that the woman made no mention of wanting to learn how to quilt. If she came here only to make friends, then she probably wouldn't get much out of the class. She could have made friends just as easily by doing something else.

"Guess I'm next," the young pregnant woman with long black hair and dark brown eyes, spoke up. "My name is Jennifer Owen, and I'm here because someone graciously paid for me to take this class."

"That was nice. Was it a friend or relative?" Kim asked.

Jennifer shrugged. "I don't know. My husband's a cook, but he lost his job awhile back, so I'd given up on the idea of taking this class. Then, two days ago I found an anonymous note in my mailbox, saying I was signed up to take the quilt classes and that they had been paid for." Jennifer paused and rubbed her stomach. "I'm expecting our first child in seven weeks, and I would love to know how to make a quilt for the baby."

Emma smiled and nodded. "Lamar and I are glad you're here." Then she motioned to the middle-aged woman with shoulder-length auburn hair, sitting across the table. "Would you please tell us your name and why you signed up for this class?"

"I'm Phyllis Barstow, and I'm eager to learn something new. My husband has a charter fishing boat service, and since he's out on the water so much, it leaves me a lot of time to explore some creative things. I've done some sewing and several craft projects over the years, so I'm looking forward to learning how to quilt."

Emma glanced at the teenage girl in the wheelchair. "What is your name, dear?"

The girl mumbled something in a voice barely above a whisper.

Emma leaned closer. "What was that?"

"I said my name's Erika. Erika Wilson."

"And what brings you here?" Lamar questioned.

She turned her head to look at him. "I don't wanna be here, but my dad made me come."

Emma cringed, remembering how Anna Lambright's mother had forced her to take Emma's quilting classes last fall. The young Amish woman had made it clear from the start that she didn't want to learn how to quilt. If Erika was here against her will, she might not learn a thing.

Perhaps I should speak to her father when he comes to pick Erika up after class, Emma thought. *If I'm unable to find a way to make Erika enjoy the class, maybe she shouldn't be here. But it's not my decision to make. Her father paid for the class, and he obviously thinks this is something his daughter needs, so I'll do my best to teach her.*

"Should I go ahead and explain about the history of Amish quilts now?" Lamar asked, breaking into Emma's thoughts.

"What? Oh yes, why don't you do that?" Emma's face heated, and she took a seat beside Kim as Lamar began to talk.

"The existence of quilts among the Amish began as early as the 1830s, although the quilts back then were much plainer than those being made now," he explained. "During that time the Amish used quilts as simple coverings for their beds."

"That's right," Emma agreed. "In the early days, most Amish made their quilts using simple materials from one color. Later, they began sewing several colored pieces of cloth into a variety of patterns."

"The earlier designs were basic rectangles and squares, but as time went on, more colorful, bold patterns were used," Lamar put in. "An older Amish quilt can be identified by its simple design, with less decoration than the Amish quilts that are made today." He continued to talk about the variety of colors and numerous designs in Amish quilts, and ended his talk by saying, "The Amish not only make quilts for their homes, to give others, or to sell, but they often donate quilts to be auctioned at local benefit events to help those in need. It's a gift of their time, and by giving, a demonstration of their love for others is shown. Owning an Amish quilt has a special meaning, reminding us that since the beginning of our church, we've been taught the same priorities: God first and family second."

Lamar picked up one of the quilts on display. "This one I designed myself. I call it, 'Pebbles on the beach.'"

"That's beautiful," Phyllis said as Lamar brought it closer to the table. "I've always enjoyed living near the water, and I guess that's a good thing, since my husband fishes for a living."

"My wife has a few other quilts she'd like to show you," Lamar said.

Emma stood, and with Lamar's help, held up the first quilt. "Here's another pattern that reflects the beauty of the ocean. It's called, 'Ocean Waves,'" she explained.

"I really like that one." Kim smiled. "My dog, Maddie, loves to frolic in the waves."

"What kind of dog do you have?" B.J. questioned.

"Maddie is a German shepherd, and I think she loves the beach as much as I do." Kim chuckled, her laugh lines deepening. "Her favorite thing is chasing seagulls, but she also enjoys prancing through the waves and playing fetch with whatever I throw her."

Everyone smiled. Everyone but Erika, that is. She just sat with her arms folded, looking bored with it all.

"What's that pattern called?" Jennifer asked, pointing to a quilt Emma had draped over a wooden rack.

Emma smiled. It was good to see her students taking an interest in the quilts. "That one is the dahlia pattern. As you can see, it has a three-dimensional effect from the gathered petals surrounding the center of each star-shaped flower."

"I think I'd like to try painting that quilt," B.J. said. "I like the unusual design and muted fall colors."

"Now that Lamar has explained the history of Amish quilts, and we've shown you several quilt designs, I'll explain what we're going to do with the quilted wall hangings you'll be learning to make." Emma motioned to the bolts of material stacked on the table. "As you can see, I have lots of fabric to choose from, and I always ask my students to begin with a simple star pattern for their first project."

Noreen frowned. "I thought we were going to learn how to make a full-sized quilt. I want one to put on my bed."

"You need to become well-acquainted with the basics of quilting first," Lamar said.

"That's right," Emma agreed. "By the time you finish these classes, you'll know the basics of quilting, so you should be able to make a larger quilt if you want. Of course, you may use whatever colored material you like for your wall hangings, which will make each of them distinct." She held up a smaller quilt with various shades of green. "I wanted to show you what your quilted wall hangings will look like when they're done. You'll begin today by choosing the colors you want and then cutting out the log cabin squares and the points for the star."

"Before we do that, why don't we take a break for some of the tasty cookies Emma made this morning?" Lamar suggested. "When we're finishing eating, everyone can choose their material and cut out the patterned pieces."

Kim smacked her lips, while patting her stomach. "That sounds good to me. I'm always ready for a snack."

Everyone but Erika nodded. The girl sat with a scowl on her face.

Dear Lord, please show me how to get through to her, Emma prayed. *I believe this young girl needs to know how much You love and care for her, and maybe that will be revealed to her during one of our classes.*

CHAPTER 5

When Emma and Lamar returned from the kitchen with a plate of cookies and a pot of coffee, B.J.'s stomach growled. He hadn't felt up to eating breakfast, but now he was actually hungry.

When he'd been taking chemo, he'd had no appetite, and often got sick to his stomach. Then there was the hair loss and the unrelenting fatigue. He could handle being bald, since many men his age shared that condition. But between being nauseous and feeling so tired he could barely cross a room, he had concluded that the treatments were worse than the cancer itself.

Then B.J. had been told that his cancer was beginning to spread. He'd decided to quit chemo and live out the rest of his life trying natural alternative treatments that would hopefully strengthen his immune system. He knew taking supplements and eating right probably wouldn't cure his illness, but they might make him feel better and possibly give him a little more time on earth. Even if they didn't, it was his body and his life, and he planned to die *his* way, without family members or doctors telling him what to do.

"These are really good cookies. What do you call them?" Kim asked, bumping B.J.'s arm as she reached for another one from the plate in the center of the table. "Oops! Sorry about that."

"It's okay. No harm done," he replied.

"They're raisin molasses," Emma said, pushing a stray piece of gray hair back under her head covering. "They were my favorite cookies when I was a girl, and my mother taught me to make them as soon as I was old enough to learn how to cook."

"Well, they get my vote," B.J. said, licking his lips. "Haven't had cookies this good since my wife died five years ago."

"So you're a widower?" Noreen's question sounded more like a statement. Then she quickly added, "Isn't that a coincidence? I lost my husband five years ago, too."

"Sorry for your loss," B.J. mumbled around another cookie.

"What did your wife die from?" Jennifer asked.

B.J. clenched his fingers. He didn't want to talk about this, especially with people he'd only met. "She had a heart attack a few days after her fifty-fifth birthday."

"My husband, Ben, died on the operating table," Noreen said, dropping her gaze to the table. "He, too, had a heart attack, but the doctors couldn't save him."

Feeling the need for a change of subject, and realizing that all eyes and ears seemed to be focused on him, B.J. looked at Lamar and said, "Would you mind if I stayed a few minutes after class and photographed some of your quilts?"

"The Amish don't like people to take their picture," Erika spoke up, glaring at B.J. as though he had said something horrible.

"I wouldn't be taking their picture," B.J. countered. "Only the quilts."

"I have no problem with that," Lamar said. "And just to be clear, here in Pinecraft some Amish, especially the younger ones who haven't joined the church, don't seem to mind if someone snaps their picture, although most won't actually pose for a photo."

Erika folded her arms. "Well, I think it's rude to take pictures of people who are different than you."

"We're not really so different," Emma spoke up. "We just dress modestly and live a different lifestyle than some people." She motioned to her plain green dress.

B.J. wondered if Erika's remark had more to do with herself than Emma or Lamar. He had a feeling the young woman felt self-conscious about being in that wheelchair. He was tempted to ask how she'd lost the use of her legs but thought better of it. Just as he didn't want to talk about his cancer or his wife's death, Erika might not like talking about her disability.

"If everyone has finished their refreshments, I think we should get back to our quilting lesson," Emma said. "I'll demonstrate how to use a template, and you can begin by marking the design on your pieces of fabric, using dressmaker's chalk or a pencil. When that's done, you'll need to cut out your patterns."

"What will we do after that?" Phyllis questioned.

"In the next step, called piecing, you will stitch the patterned pieces together onto the quilt top, which will also need to be cut," Emma explained. "Now, the quilt top is usually pieced by machine. Then later, the backing, batting, and quilt top will be layered, put into a frame, and quilted by hand. Of course, we won't do all that in one day. It will be spread out over the course of six weeks."

"Now using the templates," Emma continued, "I'd like you to begin marking the patterned pieces on the back of your fabric. When you're done, you'll need to cut out the pieces of material you'll be working with." Emma smiled. "Next week, you can sew the pieces you've cut."

Perspiration beaded on B.J.'s forehead. Maybe he was in over his head. If he tried using one of the sewing machines, he'd probably end up making a fool of himself.

"What will we do during our last class?" Kim asked.

B.J. rolled his eyes. Talk about skipping ahead! Couldn't the little blond take the classes one at a time without having to know what was coming next?

"You'll put the binding on, and then your wall hangings will be done," Lamar responded.

Everyone worked silently until it was time to go home. When Erika's father came to pick her up, he asked how things had gone, and B.J. overheard Erika whisper, "I'm not coming back next week."

It's just as well, B.J. thought. *She obviously doesn't want to learn how to quilt.* B.J. reached for his camera bag. *I, on the other hand, want to know everything I can about quilts.*

When Phyllis arrived home that afternoon, she was surprised to see her husband lying in the hammock on their porch.

"What are you doing home so early?" she asked, taking a seat in the wicker chair across from him.

"The motor on my boat gave out. Had to have the boat towed to shore, and now it's outta commission till the motor can either be fixed or replaced." Mike groaned. "This is not what I need right now."

Phyllis's eyebrows shot up. "Oh Mike, if it can't be repaired, can we afford a new motor?"

"Doesn't matter. I need the motor to run the boat, and I need the boat to take people out fishing. The boat will be dry-docked for several weeks, so I may as well make the best of it." He yawned and stretched his arms over his head. "Haven't you been saying I work too hard and you wanted us to take a vacation?"

She pursed her lips. "If you're out of work, we can't afford a vacation. Besides, I've already paid for the quilting class, and I'm committed to finishing it."

"If we're not gonna take a vacation, then I guess I'll get caught up on my sleep, 'cause I've been pretty tired lately." Mike closed his eyes and clasped his hands behind his head. "Wake me when supper's ready."

Phyllis groaned inwardly. Mike finally had some time off, and now they couldn't afford to go anywhere. She wished she hadn't signed up for the quilting classes. *Well, I've already paid for the class, and it'll only tie me up one day a week,* she reminded herself. *Maybe the rest of the week Mike and I can find something enjoyable to do that doesn't cost any money. If nothing else, we can spend some time on the beach.*

"How'd the job hunting go?" Jennifer asked just as her husband, Randy, said, "How'd the quilting class go?"

She giggled. "Should I answer your question, or do you want to go first?"

Randy bent to kiss her, his light brown hair falling forward and brushing her cheek. "Your face is glowing, Jen. Does that mean you had a good time today?"

"Oh yes," she said sincerely. "Emma and Lamar Miller are the nicest couple, and they have the cutest little house. I even saw an orange tree in their backyard." She touched his arm. "Oh, and I learned a lot about the history of Amish quilts."

"Is that all? I thought you went there to make a quilt."

"We did begin working on our wall hangings, but Lamar thought it would be good if we understood a bit about the background of Amish quilts." Jennifer flipped the ends of her hair over her shoulder and started pulling it up to make a ponytail. "It was really quite interesting—almost as intriguing as the people who are taking the class with me."

"What do you mean?" Randy asked, taking a seat on the couch.

She tucked in beside him, securing the rubber band around her ponytail. "Well, besides me, there were three other women: Kim, Phyllis, and Noreen. Then there was a teenage girl in a wheelchair. Her name is Erika, and she had a negative attitude. There was also a man who's an artist. I'm not sure what his real name is, but he introduced himself as B.J."

Randy's mouth opened slightly. "I'm surprised a guy would want to learn how to quilt."

"He said he's interested in painting a picture of a quilt, and he even stayed after class to photograph a few that Emma and Lamar had on display."

"What about the girl in the wheelchair?" Randy questioned. "What was she doin' there?"

"She said her dad made her come, and it was obvious that she didn't want to be there."

"That doesn't surprise me." Randy shook his head. "Most teenagers have other things they'd rather be doin' besides sitting in a room with a bunch of women and one weird man, listening to the history of quilts."

"B.J. isn't weird," Jennifer said protectively, although she had no idea why she felt the need to defend a man she barely knew. "If I had to wager a guess, I'd say that the reason Erika's dad made her take the class is because he wants her to learn something creative."

"Maybe you're right." Randy reached for Jennifer's hand. "Now, in answer to your question about the job hunting, I had no luck at all today. None of the restaurants in Sarasota need a cook right now. I'm thinkin' I may have to start looking in Bradenton or one of the other towns nearby."

"Maybe we should go back to Pennsylvania and move in with one of our folks," she suggested.

He shook his head vigorously. "No way! I like the warm weather here, and I sure don't miss those January temperatures in Pennsylvania. Besides, we moved to Sarasota for a new start and to be on our own, and one way or the other, we're gonna make it work."

Chapter 6

Monday evening, B.J. sat in the living room of the small cottage he'd rented near the beach, looking at the pictures he'd taken of Lamar and Emma's quilts after class on Saturday. He was pleased with how the photos had turned out and was even more impressed with the vivid shades and unusual designs. After B.J had taken the photos, he'd stayed awhile longer, visiting with Lamar and Emma. They'd even invited him to stay for lunch.

What a nice couple, B.J. thought. They had a welcoming home that reminded him of his grandparent's house, where tempting aromas used to drift from the kitchen whenever Grandma had spent the day baking.

B.J. had considered sharing his health situation with the Millers during lunch but decided there wasn't much point to that, since they couldn't do anything to change his situation. They'd probably pity him, and B.J. didn't want that. Sympathy wouldn't change the fact that he was dying, nor would it make him feel better. He just wanted to make whatever time he had left seem as normal as possible.

B.J.'s cell phone rang, pulling his thoughts aside. He checked the caller ID. It was one of his daughters. "Hey, Jill. What's up?"

"Hi, Dad. I'm calling to see how you're doing."

"I'm fine. How are you and the family?"

"We're all good. Kenny and Diane miss their grandpa, though. When are you coming home?"

B.J. chuckled. "I've only been here a few days, and the quilt class I'm taking is for six weeks, so. . ."

"You're taking a quilt class?"

"Yeah, I know. It's not the kind of thing you'd expect me to do, huh?"

"It sure isn't. What made you decide to take up quilting, Dad?"

He laughed again, hoping it didn't sound forced. "I'm not planning to become a quilter, if that's what you're thinking. I just thought it would be interesting to learn how they're made. I'm also hoping to do a few paintings of Amish quilts. Oh, and I took some pictures the other day after my first lesson. I'm using them as my guide while I paint."

"Oh, I see. Well, the quilts I saw when we visited Arthur, Illinois, were beautiful, so I'm sure your paintings will be, too."

"I hope so." B.J. drew in a quick breath as he sank into a chair. Right about now, he felt as if he could use a nap.

"Are you sure you're feeling okay?" Jill asked. "You sound tired, Dad."

"Guess I am a little," B.J. admitted, picking up the picture of Jill and her sister, Robyn, that he'd brought along. *How much more time do I have to spend with them?* he wondered. *Should I have come here to Florida, knowing my time could be short?*

Shaking his thoughts aside, B.J. said, "I got up early this morning to walk on the beach, and I've spent the rest of the day painting a seascape. I want to finish that before I get started on a quilt painting."

"Sounds like you're having fun."

"Sure am. That's why I came down here—to have fun and enjoy the sun." B.J. stifled a yawn and put the framed picture back on the table.

"I'll let you go, Dad, so you can rest. Talk to you again soon."

"Okay, Jill. Tell the kids and your sister I said hello." B.J. clicked off the phone and dropped his head forward into his hands. He felt like a heel keeping the truth from his daughters, but he wasn't ready to tell them just yet.

"Hi, I'm Anna Lambright," a young Amish woman with auburn hair peeking out from under her white head covering said to Kim.

Kim slipped on her work apron and extended her hand. She had the dinner shift this evening and had arrived at the restaurant a short time ago. "It's nice to meet you, Anna. I'm Kim Morris. I assume you're a waitress here, too?"

Anna nodded. "I've been working here for the last couple of months. I moved down from Middlebury, Indiana, with my friend Mandy Zimmerman."

"Does Mandy work here, too?" Kim asked.

"Yes, but she worked the morning shift today."

Kim smiled. "Maybe I'll get the chance to meet her sometime."

"I'm sure you will. We often have our shifts switched around, so one of these days you and Mandy will probably work the same hours."

"Did your whole family move to Sarasota?" Kim questioned.

"No, they live in Middlebury, and I doubt that any of them would ever move here," Anna replied. "My folks didn't want me to move, but a woman I took quilting lessons from talked to them about it. After she explained that she and her husband were coming down here for the winter and would keep an eye on me, they finally agreed that I could go." Anna's eyebrows lowered. "I really don't need anyone watching out for me. I'm nineteen years old, and I can take care of myself."

"You took quilting lessons?" Kim asked.

"Yeah, but not 'cause I wanted to. My mom signed me up for the class."

"I'm taking quilting lessons, too," Kim said enthusiastically. "From an Amish lady who lives in Pinecraft."

"Her name wouldn't be Emma Miller, would it?"

"As a matter of fact, it is."

"Emma's the one who taught me how to quilt—only it was at her home in Shipshewana, Indiana," Anna said. "She and her husband, Lamar, bought a place down here because Lamar has arthritis and needed to get out of the cold winter weather."

"That makes good sense." Kim glanced at her watch. "It's been nice talking to you, Anna, but I'd better get to work."

"Same here." Anna gave Kim's arm a tap. "See you around."

Kim gave a nod, then moved into the dining room. Anna seemed nice. She hoped she would have the opportunity to get to know her better.

Noreen tapped her foot impatiently, glancing around the room and then back at her watch. She'd come to this Amish-style restaurant for supper and had been sitting at a table for ten minutes, waiting for a waitress. The place was crowded, and maybe they were short-handed, but that was no excuse for poor service. If someone didn't come to her table in the next five minutes, she was leaving.

Finally, a young woman with short blond hair stepped up to her and said, "Have you had a chance to look over the menu?"

"Yes, I certainly have." Noreen studied the woman's face. "Say, didn't

I meet you at the quilt class last Saturday?"

"Yes, I'm Kim, and your name is Noreen, right?"

Noreen nodded. "I didn't realize you worked at this restaurant. I've been here several times and never saw you waiting tables before."

Kim smiled cheerfully. "I started a few weeks ago." She motioned to the menu. "Have you decided what you want to eat or drink?"

"I'd like the chicken pot pie with a dinner salad. Oh, and a glass of unsweetened iced tea with a slice of lemon."

"Okay, I'll put your order in right away," Kim said before hurrying away.

Noreen sighed. She hoped Kim didn't take as long to bring her meal as she had to wait on her. She may have said something to her about it if it hadn't been for the fact that she and Kim were taking the same quilting class. Kim seemed like a nice person, and there was no point in causing dissension between them, especially since they'd be spending the next five Saturdays together.

Noreen glanced around the dining room again, wondering if she knew anyone else here. She didn't recognize anyone in the sea of faces.

A short time later, Kim returned with a glass of iced tea, which she placed on the table.

Noreen picked it up and took a drink. "Eww. . .there's sweetener in this. If you'll recall, I asked for unsweetened tea."

Kim's cheeks reddened. "I am so sorry about that. I must have written it wrong on the order pad. I'll get you another one right away." She picked up the glass and hurried away.

Noreen crossed her arms and stared at the table. At this rate she'd never get anything.

Finally Kim showed up again. "Here you are, Noreen." When she reached over to set the glass down, it wobbled and tipped, spilling some of the iced tea onto the table. The next thing Noreen knew, the icy cold liquid had dribbled onto her beige-colored slacks. "Oh no," she groaned, heat rising to her cheeks. "This is probably going to leave a nasty stain!"

"I'm sorry again." Kim grabbed some napkins and began wiping up the tea on the table, as Noreen blotted her slacks. "If you can't get the stain out, I'll buy you a new pair of slacks. Just please don't say anything to my boss."

Noreen could tell from the way Kim glanced over her shoulder that she was fearful of losing her job. "I won't say anything," Noreen promised. "Just relax. If I can't get the stain out, I'll let you know when we meet at the quilt class this Saturday."

"Oh, thank you. I don't know what I'd do if I lost this job." Kim blew out her breath with obvious relief.

"Would you please pass the parmesan cheese?" Phyllis asked her husband as they sat on their deck together, eating supper.

Mike stared absently at his plate of spaghetti.

"Did you hear what I said, Mike? I asked you to pass the cheese."

"Oh yeah, sure." He handed her the jar and leaned back in his chair with a groan. "I know you worked hard making supper, honey, but I'm not really hungry tonight."

"I've noticed you've been tossing and turning in your sleep lately. Are you still stressing over your boat?" Phyllis questioned.

Mike grunted. "How can I not be stressed? There's more wrong with it than I was originally told, and now it looks like it's gonna be out of commission for at least five weeks. Maybe longer."

"Try not to worry," she said. "We have enough in our savings to get us by till you're able to start working again."

"It's not just the money, Phyllis. I'm bored out of mind. All this sitting around doing nothing is making me feel like a slug." He thumped his stomach. "Think I'm gaining weight, too. All I seem to want to do is nibble. Then I'm not hungry at mealtime."

The phone rang, interrupting their conversation. "Want me to get it?" Phyllis asked, rising from her seat.

Mike nodded. "I don't feel like talking to anyone right now."

Phyllis hurried into the other room. When she returned several minutes later, her brows were furrowed.

"What's wrong, honey?" Mike asked. "You look upset."

"It's my sister, Penny. She slipped on the wet grass when she went out to get the mail this morning and broke her leg."

"That's too bad." Mike reached for his glass of water and took a drink. "Is she gonna be okay?"

"I'm sure her leg will heal, but she'll be wearing a cast for six weeks and could really use some assistance." Phyllis placed her hand on Mike's shoulder. "Would you mind very much if I went there to help out?"

"How long would you be gone?" he asked.

"Until she's out of her cast and able to get around on her own. Would you like to go with me, Mike? It might be a good time for you to get away while your boat is being fixed."

He shook his head. "Think I need to stick around here in case the boat gets fixed sooner than expected."

"Do you have any objections if I go? Penny said she'd pay for my plane ticket to North Dakota, but I'd be there for several weeks. Do you think you can survive without me for that long?"

"You go ahead and take care of your sister; that's important—especially since she lives alone. I'll miss you, of course, but I think I can manage okay while you're gone."

Phyllis smiled. "Great. I'll call Penny back and let her know." She started for the door but turned back around. "Oh. I forgot about the quilting class."

"Just call the teacher and tell her something's come up and you can't finish the class."

"But I paid for it already, Mike." Phyllis moved back to the table. "Would you go in my place?"

"To the quilt class?"

"Of course. That's what I was talking about. Weren't you listening, Mike?"

"Yeah, I was listening."

"Then would you finish the classes for me?"

His eyebrows shot up. "You're kidding, right?"

"No, I'm not. You don't have much else to do while you're waiting for the boat to be fixed, so I thought—"

Mike held up his hand. "Well, you thought wrong. I don't know a thing about quilting, Phyllis."

"Neither do I, but I was planning to learn, and if you go in my place, you can show me what you've learned after I get home. Just think, Mike, we could quilt together and maybe make one for each of our daughters for Christmas next year." She leaned over and kissed his neck. "If you do this for me, when your boat gets fixed and you get your next paying customer, I'll go out with you and act as your bait boy."

He hesitated but finally nodded. "All right then, it's a deal. After all, how hard can quilting be?"

CHAPTER 7

Emma had just taken a seat at her sewing machine to begin work on a quilt, when Lamar came into the room. "I know you're busy, but could I talk to you for a minute, Emma?" he asked.

"Of course." She set her sewing aside and turned to face him. "I wanted to ask you something, too, but you go first."

He shifted his weight a couple of times, like he did whenever he was nervous or unsure of something.

Emma felt immediate concern. "What is it, Lamar? Is something wrong?"

He shook his head. "Not wrong; I just have a favor to ask."

"What's that?"

"My friend Melvin Weaver wants to hire a driver and go down to Venice tomorrow to look for sharks' teeth, and he invited me to go along."

"But tomorrow is Saturday—our second quilt class, remember?" Emma reminded.

"I haven't forgotten," he said, scrubbing his hand down the side of his bearded face. "I just thought. . . . Well, if you think you can get along without me tomorrow, I'd like to go with Melvin. If not, then I'll go some other time. Maybe you and I can hire a driver and look for sharks' teeth together. Doesn't that sound like fun to you?"

"It's okay, Lamar. You go ahead. I'll manage without your help on Saturday. After all, before I married you, I used to teach the classes on my own. And as far as me hunting for sharks' teeth. . . Well, I've heard how it's done, and the idea of standing in the surf, sifting through the sand with a bulky scoop, seems like hard work to me. Think I'd rather stay here and quilt." Emma pursed her lips. "My only concern about you being gone this Saturday is that it'll mean B.J. will be the only man in class. He might feel uncomfortable with that."

Lamar's forehead wrinkled. "I never thought of that. Maybe it would be better if I stayed here to help you. I can go hunting for sharks' teeth some other time."

"Are you sure about that?" Emma asked. "I don't like to disappoint you."

"It's okay, really," he said with a nod of his head. "I promised to help you teach this group of quilters, and that's what I'm gonna do. I'll get in touch with Melvin and take a rain check with him on that."

Emma smiled. Like her first husband, Ivan, Lamar was a kind, caring man. She felt fortunate to have found love a second time.

"Now what was it you were going to ask me?" Lamar questioned, turning to look out the window.

"I was going to ask if you could pick some of the oranges from our tree later today or even tomorrow morning. I thought it would be nice to share some of them with everyone at the quilt class."

"Sure thing. I was just about ready to pick us each one for a snack later on. If they're ripe enough, I'll pick some in the morning for everyone." Lamar rubbed his hands briskly together. "Weren't we lucky that this house had an orange tree in the backyard?"

Emma nodded. "It'll be nice to send a healthy snack home with everyone tomorrow after class."

Mike groaned as he rolled out of bed on Saturday morning, rubbing his eyes to clear his vision. He couldn't believe he'd agreed to take Phyllis's place at the quilt class in Pinecraft. "I must have been out of mind," he muttered. The only good thing was that Phyllis had told him one of the teachers was a man and that another man was also taking the class, so Mike figured that might help him feel less out of place. Of course, he didn't know a thing about sewing, nor did he want to know how to quilt. No matter what Phyllis thought, as far as Mike was concerned, anything that involved a needle and thread was for women, not a man who felt more at home on his boat than anywhere else.

Mike's cell phone rang, and he picked it up off the dresser. After checking the caller ID, and realizing it was Phyllis, he answered. "Hi, honey. How's your sister doing?"

"Penny's still in a lot of pain, but she's so appreciative that I'm here to help out. Thanks for allowing me to do this, Mike."

"Sure, no problem."

"I called to remind you about the quilt class," she said. "It starts at ten this morning."

"Yeah, yeah, I know, and don't worry, I won't be late. Wouldn't wanna miss one minute of that exciting class."

"Are you being sarcastic?"

" 'Course not," Mike lied. "I'm looking forward to learning how to quilt." *In a "dreading it more than coming down with the flu" kind of way,* he mentally added.

"When I get home I'll be anxious to hear about everything you've learned."

"Let's hope I'm able to learn anything at all," he muttered.

"What was that?"

"Oh, nothing. Listen, Phyllis, I'd better get going or I *will* be late for the class."

"Okay. Talk to you again soon, Mike."

"Bye, hon." Mike clicked off his phone and sank to the edge of the bed. *Sure hope my boat's up and running soon. That'll give me a good excuse to quit going to the quilt classes.*

Goshen, Indiana

"Guess who I talked to last night," Jan Sweet said to his twenty-one-year-old daughter, Star. He'd just arrived at Star's house to pick her up for a motorcycle ride. They'd be meeting his buddy Terry and Terry's girlfriend, Cheryl, later on this morning. First, though, Star had offered to fix Jan breakfast.

"Who'd you talk to?" Star asked, motioning for Jan to take a seat at the table.

"Emma Miller. She and Lamar are spending the winter in Sarasota, you know."

Star smiled, pushing her long dark hair away from her eyes. "That's nice. Are they enjoying the warm weather down there?"

"I think so, but Emma said she misses her friends and family here in Indiana." Jan flopped into a chair. "I miss Emma and Lamar, too. Miss stopping by their place for a visit and some of Emma's tasty homemade treats." He smacked his lips. "That angel cream pie she made for our quilting class was the best. You oughta get the recipe from her and make it for your old dad sometime."

Star rolled her coffee-colored eyes. "You're not old, but I'm not really into baking pies. Just wait until Emma gets home and then you can ask her to make you one."

"But that won't be till spring," Jan complained. "Don't think I can wait that long."

"Well, you don't have much choice." Star handed him a cup of coffee, then went to the stove to begin cooking their eggs.

"I don't know about that. Thought it might be fun to take a run down to Florida sometime soon. Would you like to go with me, Star?"

She looked at him over her shoulder. "Are you serious, Dad?"

Jan nodded. "We could head down to Sarasota to see the Millers and enjoy some time on the beach." He winked at Star. "It might be more fun if we just drop in and surprise them, though."

"Do you think they'd appreciate that?"

"Ah, sure. Emma and Lamar are good sports. I'm sure they'd be happy to see us."

"When were you thinking of going?" Star asked.

"I can't go right away 'cause I'm in the middle of a roofing job, and I need to get it done soon, before we get snow or heavy rain. It's been a fairly mild winter so far, which has been good for business, but I'm sure it won't last forever." Jan paused. "I should get the job finished up in a day or two though."

"So when did you want to go?" she persisted.

"I could wait a few weeks. Would you be able to get time off from your job by then?" he asked. "I'll leave Brutus with Terry, so the dog won't be a problem."

"I do have a couple weeks' vacation coming," she said. "When I go to work Monday morning, should I put in for the time off?"

"Yeah, why don't you?" Jan leaned back in his chair, locking his fingers behind his head. "This will be great, kiddo. I can hardly wait to go."

"Will we ride down there on our motorcycles, or did you plan to take your truck?" Star asked.

"If the weather cooperates, I think we oughta ride our bikes. It'll be more fun that way, and I can hardly wait to see the look on Emma and Lamar's faces when we show up."

Sarasota

Lamar whistled as he headed out the back door to pick some oranges. It was a beautiful Saturday morning—the kind of day that made a person feel alive and raring to go. He paused in the yard a few minutes, breathing in the fresh clean air.

On a morning like this, it's hard to imagine bad things going on in the world, he thought. Lamar hadn't told Emma, because he didn't want her to worry, but earlier in the week when he'd gone to the store to pick up a few things, he'd overhead someone say there had been some robberies in a neighborhood not far from where they lived. A few people had been robbed in broad daylight, right in their own backyard. After hearing that, Lamar had been keeping his wallet in the house whenever he went into the yard.

Lamar reflected on the economy, and how so many folks were struggling to find good ways to make it through life's hardships, while others, like this group of thieves, had turned to crime and stealing from others, perhaps to survive. He sent up a silent prayer as he gazed into the deep blue sky, then headed toward the orange tree.

Lamar remembered how he and Emma had enjoyed their juicy oranges for a snack yesterday. There was nothing like eating fresh fruit picked right off the tree. The oranges were so sweet, and he was happy they could share some with their quilting students.

Continuing to whistle, Lamar started putting oranges, still wet from the morning's dew, into his basket. *It doesn't get any better than this,* he thought, lifting his face to the sun.

Suddenly, he realized that the birds were silent. That seemed a bit odd. Usually, the yard was full of birds chirping out a chorus of welcome to Lamar as soon as he stepped into the yard.

"Stay where you are, and don't move a muscle!" a male voice said sternly.

Lamar froze in his tracks, watching a drop of dew fall from one of the oranges, as if in slow motion, and then splatter on top of his shoe.

Another male voice said firmly, "Don't turn around; just stay where you are."

Lamar's heartbeat picked up speed. All he could think about was his dear wife, Emma. *Am I about to be robbed? What should I do? I don't want to do or say anything to anger these men. The back door's not even locked. What if they barge inside and hurt Emma?*

As if to send his wife a silent message that only she could hear, Lamar whispered, "Please, Emma, stay in the house and lock the door."

CHAPTER 8

Emma hummed softly as she removed a coffee cake from the oven. She planned to serve it to her students during the quilting class. Last week, she'd served cookies, and everyone seemed to enjoy them, so she hoped the cake would be just as well received.

Squinting over the top of her metal-framed glasses as she placed the cake on a cooling rack, Emma wondered what was taking Lamar so long to pick the basket of oranges. He'd been out there at least half an hour already. Maybe she should check on him. First, though, she would get out the plates and forks and put them on the counter for when dessert would be served. Once Lamar brought the oranges in, she would peel a few to serve with the cake.

Emma took a platter from the cupboard and placed it on the table. Then, remembering that she had some grapes in the refrigerator, she got them out as well. She stood there a moment, tapping her finger against her lips, while looking around the kitchen. There really wasn't much else to do, so she decided to peek out the window to check on Lamar, knowing he should have that basket pretty much filled with oranges by now. She was almost to the slightly open window, when she heard someone outside speaking rather loudly.

"I'll walk to him slowly from behind," a stranger's voice hollered.

"Okay. I'll approach him from the front," a second man said.

What's going on out there? Emma wondered. When she reached the window, she gasped. Emma could not believe the scene unfolding right there in their own backyard.

"Okay, I got him!" the man yelled. "Quick, bring me the electrical tape."

Lamar had been standing there, still as a statue and struggling not to turn around to get a good look at the person who'd told him to remain where he was, while waiting for "who knew what" to happen. Were these men going to tie him up, tape his mouth shut, and then go into the house and rob them? *But wait a minute,* he thought. *That guy just said, "I got him," yet I'm still standing here untouched.*

Lamar couldn't take it any longer. It seemed like forever that he'd been standing in the same position, unmoving like the men had told him. He was getting a cramp in his leg, and just as he was about to turn around, someone tapped his shoulder and said, "Okay, sir, it's safe now."

Safe? Lamar whirled around, and was about to demand that the young man wearing a white T-shirt and blue jeans tell him what was going on. Instead, he froze, staring in disbelief at the sight in front of him.

"Sorry if I scared you, sir, but I didn't want anything to happen to you," the man said in a soothing voice. "My partner and I have been lookin' for this fella since yesterday, when a call came in that he was spotted in your neighborhood."

Lamar blinked a couple of times, unable to believe his eyes. Was he really seeing what he thought he was? Just then, he saw Emma coming out the back door, then running toward him with eyes wide, looking as astonished as he felt. There, by the side of the house was another man wearing jeans and a T-shirt, hunkered down and sitting on top of a large alligator, of all things.

"I wanted to get his mouth taped shut before I felt it was safe enough for you to move," the first man said to Lamar. Then glancing at Emma, he added, "We have a truck parked around the corner that we'll put the gator in to relocate it to another area." He extended his hand. "By the way, the name's Jack, and that's Rusty over there, sittin' on the gator. We do this for a living, capturing and relocating wild animals. Bet you never expected to see one of those creatures in your backyard this morning, did you?"

"No, I sure didn't," Lamar said, slowly letting out some air as he put his arm around Emma's waist. It felt like he'd been holding his breath for hours instead of minutes. He could feel his limbs finally relaxing, relieved that it wasn't a robbery after all.

"Oh Lamar," Emma cried, her cheeks turning pink, "you could have been hurt! What if that alligator had attacked you?"

"The good Lord was with me, that's for sure," Lamar answered, looking at the eight-foot gator and shaking his head. "Guess he blended in so well with all the greenery by the house that I never even saw him lying there. When I came outside, he didn't make a sound. Of course," Lamar continued with a nervous laugh, "I had my mind on those oranges getting picked."

"Where did that alligator come from?" Emma asked Jack.

"We got a report there'd been one seen over in the pond by the golf course not far from here, and when we went to capture it, the gator was nowhere to be found."

"Oh my! I guess he decided to do some exploring." Emma looked up at Lamar with a wide-eyed expression.

Lamar nodded, while gently patting her arm.

"Come on, Jack. It's time to get this guy moved. You better go get the truck," Rusty said, still sitting on top of the gator.

"Sorry I had to meet you folks this way, but I'm glad everything went good with no mishaps," Jack said. "Have a good day, and if you see some of your neighbors, let 'em know the creature was captured. This morning we were going door to door, letting people know a gator was roaming about, and just as we were coming to notify you, Rusty and I spotted the creature in your yard."

"I'm glad you did, 'cause I sure wouldn't have known what to do," Lamar replied, swiping at the trickle of sweat above his brows as he and Emma stood there watching. "You take care now, and thanks." It was amazing how big that alligator was, yet it lay there, fairly calm, letting Rusty hold it down.

"Don't worry, folks; I've done this hundreds of times," Rusty assured them. "Once you tape their mouth shut, they remain pretty quiet."

"Please be careful anyway," Lamar said to Rusty as he and Emma started walking toward the house.

"Wait. Aren't you forgetting something?" Emma asked, brushing his arm with her hand.

Lamar laughed as he went back to get the basket of oranges. "Just wait till our quilters hear about this." He stopped walking and sniffed the air. "By the way, Emma, do I smell the aroma of coffee cake coming through the open window?"

She smiled and nodded. "But you can't have any till it's time to serve refreshments."

"That's okay," Lamar said, looking down at the basket he held. "I can always have one of these juicy oranges if I get a craving for something sweet before then.”

———

“I guess we need to remind ourselves that we’re in Florida, not Indiana, and there are a few critters here that we don’t have back home,” Emma said as they entered the house.

Lamar nodded. “I thought of that the other day, when I spotted a gecko crawling along the windowsill outside our bedroom. We need to make sure we keep the screens in place on all the doors and windows so none of the outdoor critters can make their way inside.”

“That’s a good idea,” Emma agreed. “If I found a gecko crawling around in here, I’d probably fall on my face trying to catch the little creature.”

Lamar chuckled. “They do move quite fast.”

“And I don’t move like I used to, either,” Emma said as they made their way into the dining room, where the quilt class would be held.

“Do you need my help with anything before our students arrive?” Lamar asked.

“No, I think everything’s pretty much ready.” A knock sounded on the front door. “Now I wonder who that could be,” Emma said. “It’s too early for any of our students to be here.”

“Well, there’s only one way to find out.” Lamar went to the door and opened it.

Anna Lambright stepped in with red cheeks and tears in her eyes. “Anna, what’s wrong?” Emma asked, rushing to the young woman’s side.

“My folks are pressuring me again to move back home. I thought they understood why I wanted to live here, but now they’ve started badgering me.” Anna sniffed. “I know you spoke to them before I left Indiana, but will you talk to them again, Emma? Please make them see that I'm a grown woman with a life of my own."

Emma put her arm around Anna's trembling shoulders. "I'm so sorry, Anna. I thought your parents were fine with the idea of you being in Sarasota. They know Lamar and I are here to help with anything you might need, but perhaps it would be good if I remind them of that."

Anna bobbed her head. "I think the thing that set them off was when they read an article in the paper about some robberies that had been going on down here. They're worried I might not be safe." She paused to blow her nose on the tissue Emma handed her. "They don't realize I'm not a little girl anymore. Besides, robberies can happen anywhere."

"That's true. It seems like no one is safe these days," Lamar put in. "However, we can't hide out in our homes or stop living. We need to use caution and ask God to keep His protecting hand upon us." He looked over at Emma. "We can certainly attest to that, right, Emma?"

She nodded, and was about to tell Anna what had just happened in their backyard, when another knock sounded on the door. While Lamar went to answer it, Emma motioned for Anna to take a seat. "Our quilt class doesn't start for another forty-five minutes, so why don't we visit awhile? I'm anxious to hear how your job at the restaurant is going."

Anna smiled and took a seat at the table. "For me it's going good, but not so much for one of the other waitresses."

"Oh, why is that?"

Before Anna could respond, Lamar entered the room, pushing Erika in her wheelchair.

"Sorry for showing up early," the young girl mumbled. "There was an emergency at the hospital, and my dad had to go, so the woman who Dad hired as my caregiver dropped me off now 'cause she has a hair appointment. I hope that's okay."

"It's not a problem at all," Emma said. She was pleased to see that

Erika had come back. After last week, she'd half expected a call from Erika's dad saying Erika had dropped out of the class. "Since you're here early, you can join us and our Amish friend for a glass of freshly squeezed lemonade before the others in our class arrive. It'll give us a chance to get better acquainted."

Erika glanced at Anna, then back at Emma. "Something cold does sound good."

Emma introduced Anna and Erika; then she excused herself to get the lemonade. Lamar went with her, and as they left the room, Emma said a silent prayer for both young women, asking God to show them the path He wanted them to take. She felt certain that each of these young women had a special purpose in life.

CHAPTER 9

Erika knew it was rude, but she couldn't help staring at Anna. Not only was she dressed in Amish clothes, like Emma, but she was young and had two good legs. As far as Erika could tell, Anna might be a little older than her, but not by much.

Anna didn't know how lucky she was. Erika envied people, especially those who were close to her age and weren't bound to a wheelchair. They didn't have to worry about the rest of their lives; they still had dreams they could live out, that would hopefully come true. Erika wondered, in her condition, if she was destined to be alone for the rest of her life. Who would want to be strapped down by someone in a wheelchair? And what would she do if she did fall in love with a man someday? Could she expect him to commit to a relationship, knowing he would always have to do certain things for her? That was the burden she'd placed on her dad, as well as the woman he'd hired as Erika's caregiver.

The silence in the room was thick, as neither Erika nor Anna spoke to each other, while waiting on Emma's return.

A short time later, Emma came back with glasses of lemonade for them. She placed them on the table and was about to sit down, when Anna suddenly stood, gave Emma a hug, and said she needed to go.

Is Anna as uncomfortable around me as I am her? Erika wondered. *Does she feel sorry for me, sitting here in my wheelchair, not saying a word?* She grasped the armrests on her chair tightly and clenched her teeth. *Well, I don't need her pity.*

Anna started for the door, hesitated, then glanced quickly at Erika. "It was nice meeting you. I'm sure you'll enjoy the quilting classes, 'cause Emma and Lamar are good teachers." Then she turned and rushed out the door.

Emma stood several seconds, watching out the window as Anna made her way out of the yard. Then she turned to Erika and said, "How was your week?"

Erika shrugged, running her finger down the side of the wet, cold glass of lemonade. "Same as usual. I wake up in the morning, and whether I'm at school or home, I sit in my wheelchair the rest of the day. Dad and my caregiver, Mrs. Drew, take care of most of my needs, so I've pretty much got it made, wouldn't you say?"

Emma, as though sensing Erika's frustration, gently touched her shoulders and said, "I'm sure it must be hard for you, and I'm hoping that by taking this class. . ."

"As I've said before, I really don't care about learning how to quilt. I'm only here because my dad insisted I come." Erika gulped down some of her drink, thinking how good the lemonade tasted. *I bet Emma made this herself. It sure doesn't taste like the store-bought kind.*

"You know," Emma said, motioning to the front door, "when Anna took my class up in Shipshewana last year, she didn't want to learn how to quilt, either."

"Then why'd she come?" Erika asked, after taking another swallow of lemonade

"Her mother signed her up for the class." Emma's glasses slipped to the end of her nose, and she paused to push them in place. "Anna wasn't interested in sewing at home, and her mother hoped I could teach her."

"That's interesting, but what's that got to do with me?"

"Take this napkin and wrap it around your glass. It will soak up some of the moisture." Emma smiled and then continued. "Even though Anna didn't want to come to the class at first, eventually she liked it, and she learned to quilt."

Erika didn't respond, just wrapped the napkin around the glass and finished her drink. She hoped the others would get here soon so they could get on with the class, because the sooner it was done, the sooner she could go home to the solitude of her room, which was fast becoming her only safe place.

———

Maybe I've said enough, Emma thought. *It might be better to just show Erika kindness and do the best I can at teaching her to quilt. Once she discovers that she can do it, she might find it enjoyable and realize she can do something useful.*

"If you'll excuse me a minute, Erika, I need to go back to the kitchen," Emma said. "Lamar's still in there, and I need to make sure he isn't sampling the snack I prepared for our quilt class today."

"Go right ahead," Erika responded in a sullen tone.

Emma hurried to the kitchen, where she found Lamar at the table, peeling an orange. "I was hoping you weren't testing the coffee cake," she said, taking a seat beside him.

He wrinkled his nose. "Nope. I knew better than that. Don't want to do anything to get my *fraa* riled at me."

"It would take a lot more than you eating a piece of my coffee cake to get your wife riled," Emma said. "Now, if you ate the whole thing that would be an entirely different matter."

"Figured, to play it safe, I couldn't get into much trouble if I just had an orange." He glanced at the doorway leading to the other room. "Is everything okay with Erika? She seems pretty down-in-the-mouth today."

"I'm afraid you're right," Emma agreed. "She doesn't want to be here, but I think the real problem may lie in the fact that she has no self-esteem."

"Guess that might be the case, all right." Lamar bit into a piece of orange, sending a spray of juice in Emma's direction. "Oops! Sorry about that."

"No harm done." Emma grabbed a napkin and blotted the juice that had sprayed her apron. "Getting back to Erika, I can understand why she'd be depressed and feel as though she has no self-worth, but there are other people in the world who are worse off than her."

"That's true," Lamar agreed.

"I feel as though Erika has come to us for a reason, and I hope there's something we can do to help her."

"God will give us the right words at the right time; He always has," Lamar said. "And who knows, Emma, a breakthrough for Erika might come about because of something that someone else says or does, rather than through one of us."

Emma nodded. "I'm fortunate to have married a man as *schmaert* as you."

Lamar grinned, bouncing his bushy eyebrows up and down. "Well, I did convince you to marry me, so I must be fairly smart."

"It's nice to see you this morning," Kim said as she and Noreen stepped onto the Millers' front porch.

"Same here," Noreen said with a nod.

"I've been wondering if you were able to get that tea stain out of your slacks," Kim said.

"As a matter of fact, I was," Noreen replied. "I used cold water and some Stain Stick, and it came right out."

Kim blew out her breath. "That's a relief."

"Would you like a friendly piece of advice?" Noreen asked.

"Sure."

"During my college days, I worked as a waitress for a while, and one thing I tried to remember was to be careful with the food and beverages I carried to and from the table. Some customers wouldn't be as nice as I was about a waitress spilling something on their clothes, and if you want to keep your job, you have to be on your toes."

"Yes, I know, but accidents can happen."

"And it's your job to make sure that they don't." Noreen pursed her lips. "Otherwise, you could end up getting fired. In my day, I saw that happen more than once."

Kim cringed. While Noreen had kept quiet about her spilling the tea, she figured if something like that should happen to Noreen again while Kim was waiting on her, she would tell Kim's boss. Kim had a hunch that Noreen wasn't one who gave people a second chance.

Kim wasn't normally so klutzy—only when she got nervous or overly stressed. Hopefully things would go better for her at the restaurant once she relaxed and felt more comfortable with her new job.

"Guess we'd better get inside," Kim said, knocking on the front door. "I don't know if everyone else is here or not, but we don't want to hold up the quilting class."

Soon after Kim and Noreen showed up, Jennifer arrived.

"Are you feeling all right? You look tired today," Emma said, feeling concern when she noticed the dark circles beneath the young woman's brown eyes.

"I didn't sleep well last night," Jennifer said. "The baby kept kicking, and I couldn't seem to find a comfortable position."

"I remember when I was carrying my youngest daughter, Mary," Emma said. "She used to get the hiccups, and that would wake me out of a sound sleep." She gave Jennifer's arm a tender squeeze. "Once that *boppli* comes, you'll forget about any discomforts you had before she was born."

Jennifer tipped her head curiously. "Boppli? Is that another name for baby?"

Emma's face heated as she slowly nodded. "It's Pennsylvania Dutch, and even when I'm talking English I sometimes forget and say something in our traditional Amish language."

"It'd be fun to learn a few Pennsylvania Dutch words," Kim spoke up. "Would you teach us, Emma?"

"I'd be happy to," Emma replied. "Maybe I can do that during our refreshment time. Right now, though, I think we need to get started with our quilting lesson."

"But B.J. and Phyllis aren't here yet," Lamar said. "Don't you think we should wait for them?"

Emma touched her hot cheeks. "Of course. How silly of me." She didn't know why she felt so flustered this morning. Maybe it was because of the scare they'd had earlier with the alligator in their yard. That was enough to put anyone's nerves on edge.

Emma glanced at the clock, and noticed that it was almost ten. She hoped her last two students weren't going to be late. If they didn't get started soon, they would fall behind schedule, and she wanted everyone to finish their quilted wall hanging by the end of the sixth lesson. "I guess we can wait a few more minutes to get started," she said, "but if B.J. and Phyllis aren't here by ten fifteen, we'll need to begin without them."

"While we're waiting, Emma, why don't we tell these ladies about our exciting morning?" Lamar said.

"Since it actually happened to you, I'll let you tell them," Emma replied.

Everyone, even Erika this time, focused on Lamar as he proceeded to share the story about the alligator that had entered their yard and been captured by the two men. When he got to the part about Rusty sitting on the gator, Erika's eyes widened. "That guy must have been very brave or incredibly stupid," she said. "Even when I had two good legs, I would never have done anything like that."

"Each of us has different fears and things we feel brave about," Lamar said. "It's just a matter of what we're willing to do."

"That's right," Kim agreed. "Some people are afraid to ride a motorcycle, but I'm not the least bit scared when I'm riding mine."

"Two of our previous quilters from Indiana own cycles," Lamar interjected. "I don't think they're afraid to ride, but they do use caution."

Kim bobbed her head. "Same here. One thing I always remember is to wear my helmet. I've seen some bikers go without it, but in my opinion, that's just asking for trouble."

"Is there anything you've ever done that others might be afraid to try?" Emma asked, looking at Jennifer.

A wide smile spread across the young woman's face. "Before Randy and I got married, I loved to water-ski. Of course, I'd never try that now. It wouldn't be safe for the boppli." Jennifer patted her stomach, and looking at Emma, she grinned. "Did I pronounce that word right?"

Emma smiled and nodded.

"Why don't you go next?" Lamar said, motioning to Noreen. "Is there something you do that others might be afraid to try?"

"Not unless you count teaching high school English. Some people might be afraid of that." Noreen paused, snickering quietly. "Now I recently did something that surprised even me. Imagine a sixty-five-year-old woman like myself buying a sports car. But I did, even though I'm still trying to figure out why." She lifted her gaze to the ceiling, rolling her hazel-colored eyes.

Everyone laughed. Everyone but Erika, who sat staring at her hands, clasped firmly in her lap. Emma thought about asking the girl if there was anything she'd ever done that would seem frightening to others, but decided against it. If Erika wanted to open up, she would.

As if she were able to read Emma's thoughts, Erika suddenly blurted, "I was never afraid of anything till I tried a new dive. It went horribly wrong, and I ended up with a spinal cord injury." She lifted her chin in a defiant pose, although Emma noticed tears glistening in the girl's pretty blue eyes. "Guess that's what I get for showin' off when I should have listened to my dad when he said I should get out of the pool. Some people might believe I got just what I deserved for doing the dive, and they'd probably be right about that."

"Blaming yourself is not the answer," Emma said. "In the Bible we are told to forgive others, and I believe that means we need to forgive ourselves as well."

"I know what the Bible says; my dad and I go to church every Sunday," Erika said with a huff. "So you don't need to preach at me."

Emma's heart went out to Erika. It was obvious that she held herself accountable for the accident that had left her legs paralyzed. Worse than that, Erika thought she deserved her physical limitations. She saw them as a punishment for disobeying her dad. No doubt that was the reason for her negative attitude and cutting remarks.

I won't say anything more to her about this right now, Emma thought, *but I can certainly pray for Erika and ask God to bring healing to her young heart.*

CHAPTER 10

Emma was about to have the class begin sewing their quilt squares, when she heard footsteps on the porch. "That must be B.J. or Phyllis," she said to Lamar.

"Whoever it is, I'll let them in." He moved toward the door.

When Lamar returned a few minutes later, B.J. was at his side.

"Sorry I'm late," B.J. apologized. "Guess I was more tired than I thought last night, because I slept right through the alarm this morning."

Seeing the look of exhaustion on the man's face, Emma became concerned. "Are you feeling alright?" she questioned.

"I'm fine. Just tired is all." B.J. took a seat at the table, next to Noreen. "Did I miss anything?" he asked.

"Not really. Emma was waiting until you and Phyllis got here," Noreen replied. "I wonder what her excuse is for being late."

"Maybe something unexpected came up," Emma was quick to say in

Phyllis's defense. "I'm sure if she wasn't able to be here she would have called."

Noreen shook her head with a look of disgust. "In the world we live in today, it seems that many people aren't dependable and only live for themselves. Why, the other day my neighbor's teenage son was supposed to mow my lawn, but he never showed up."

"Did you call to see what happened?" Kim asked.

"Of course I called. His mother said he'd gone off with his friends to watch a ball game." Noreen's forehead wrinkled. "That's just one example of the lack of dependability I was talking about."

Emma tapped her hand gently against the table. "Once Phyllis gets here, I'll explain what she needs to do with her quilt squares, but I think the rest of you should get started now." She hoped Noreen wouldn't make any negative comments when Phyllis arrived. Noreen and Erika's catty remarks brought tension into the room.

Noreen's face tightened as she looked at her watch. "We're already fifteen minutes behind, so we may end up needing to stay longer today."

"If that turns out to be the case, then any of you who wish to, can stay as long as you need to after class." Emma motioned to the three sewing machines on the other side of the room. "You'll have to take turns using the machines."

"What should we do while we're waiting our turn?" Jennifer questioned.

"You can either visit with the others who are waiting or start cutting out your batting, which is what I had planned for you to do next Saturday."

"We don't want to get ahead of things," Noreen said with a click of her tongue. "But then there's not really much for us to visit about, since we barely know one another."

"That's how you'll get to know each other," Lamar spoke up. "All of our students in the past became well acquainted by the end of six weeks. In fact, some even became close friends, and last fall one of our students' friendships turned to romance."

"How interesting." Noreen glanced quickly at B.J. and smiled.

Emma wondered if Noreen thought there might be a chance for her to find romance in this class. *Now wouldn't that be something?* she thought, smiling to herself.

"Actually one of our students signed up for the class just so he could get to know a pretty young woman who'd come to learn how to quilt," Lamar interjected.

"How'd it work out?" Kim asked, leaning slightly forward in her seat.

"It didn't start out too well," Lamar said. "Terry was a bit overbearing at first, and Cheryl didn't want anything to do with him." He looked over at Emma and grinned. "Eventually, Terry won Cheryl's heart."

"I didn't come here for love or romance," Noreen said, "but if by chance it were to happen, I wouldn't turn it down." She gave B.J. another quick glance, but he wasn't looking her way.

Is something going on here? Emma wondered. *Could Noreen be interested in B.J.? Or maybe it's just my imagination, because they barely know each other.*

"I'm definitely not interested in romance," Kim said. "With romance comes heartache, and I've had my share of that already."

"Are we done with all this silly talk about love and romance?" Erika asked, frowning. "I thought we came here to learn how to quilt."

"And so we shall," Emma said. "Why don't I get Jennifer, Noreen, and Erika started on the sewing machines, and the rest of you can visit with Lamar? I'm sure he'd be happy to tell you more about the quilts he's designed."

Lamar gave a nod. "I'm always eager to talk about quilts."

Erika groaned. "I'd like to know how you think I'm supposed to use one of the sewing machines when they all have foot pedals to make the machine go. In case you've forgotten, my legs are paralyzed."

Emma's face warmed, and quickly spread to her neck. "Oh dear, I hadn't thought about that. Perhaps Kim would be willing sit beside you and operate the pedals while you guide the material under the pressure foot to sew the seams."

"I'd be happy to do that while we're here," Kim said, "but what will Erika do when she's at home and wants to start another quilt or do some other type of sewing?"

Erika shook her head. "That won't be a problem because after I finish this wall hanging, I don't plan to do any more sewing. As I've said, I'm only doing it to please my dad, and when I'm done, I'm done. In fact, if I never see another needle and thread, it'll be soon enough for me."

Emma cringed. With that negative attitude, Erika might be hard to reach. *But I won't quit trying,* she told herself. *We still have four more classes, and every time Erika comes to our home, I'll make an effort.*

———

"I still can't believe I agreed to do this," Mike grumbled as he parked his car in front of a small cream-colored house in Pinecraft, bearing the address his wife had given him. A few other cars were parked there, along with a motorcycle. *I wonder who rides that,* he thought as he stepped down from his SUV. *I can't believe anyone who rides a bike would be interested in quilts. Maybe it's some poor guy whose wife talked him into coming here like me. Well, here goes nothing.*

Mike tromped up the porch steps and knocked on the door. A few minutes later, an Amish man with a head full of thick, gray hair and a matching beard greeted him. "May I help you?"

"Uh, yeah, I'm here for the quilt class."

The man's bushy eyebrows furrowed. "Excuse me?"

"I'm here for the quilt class. This is the right place, isn't it?" Mike questioned.

"Well, yes, we are holding a quilt class here today, but it's the second class, and we weren't expecting any new students."

"I don't think you understand." Mike tapped his foot impatiently. "I'm here to take my wife's place in the class."

"Who is your wife?"

"Phyllis Barstow. I'm her husband, Mike."

"I'm Lamar Miller." He extended his hand. "My wife, Emma, and I met Phyllis last week when she came for the first lesson."

"Well, she won't be back," Mike said. "Her sister broke her leg, and Phyllis went to Fargo, North Dakota, to take care of her. She asked me to come here in her place and learn how to quilt." *And I stupidly said yes,* he silently added.

"Oh, I see." Lamar opened the door wider. "Come inside, and I'll introduce you to my wife and the others in our class."

As Mike stepped into the house, he caught sight of a small gecko skirting along the baseboard. He didn't pay it much mind, knowing the critter was harmless and good for catching bugs.

Mike's thoughts shifted when he followed Lamar into a room where four women sat at sewing machines, while an Amish woman and a bald, older man were seated at a table in the center of the room.

"Everyone, this is Phyllis Barstow's husband, Mike," Lamar announced. "Phyllis had to go to North Dakota to help her sister who has a broken leg, so Mike's here to take her place."

The Amish woman smiled and rose from her chair. "I'm sorry Phyllis won't be able to complete the class, but it's nice that you can be here to learn how to quilt."

"Yeah, I can hardly wait," Mike muttered under his breath.

"My name is Emma Miller, and these are the quilt squares your wife cut out last week," Emma said, handing Mike a plastic sack. "We are in the process of stitching the squares together now, and I'd be happy to help you with that."

"It's a good thing, too, 'cause I don't know the first thing about sewing," Mike said, wondering once more why he'd agreed to do this. It wasn't likely that he would learn anything he could show Phyllis when she returned. He'd probably make a mess of her wall hanging.

Emma smiled. "It's okay. I'm here to teach you, Mike, and we're glad to have you in our class."

Lamar nodded in agreement.

"I'm not sure I'm even teachable." Mike swiped at the trickle of sweat rolling down the side of his head. "Now give me a fishing pole, some bait, and a hook, and I'm good to go, but I'm not the least bit comfortable with a needle and thread."

The baldheaded man at the table chuckled. "Well, you're in good company then, because other than appreciating the beauty of quilts, I don't know anything about sewing, either."

After Emma introduced each of the students to Mike, he took a seat at the table between her and B.J. He was about to take Phyllis's quilt squares out of the bag he'd been given, when the older woman, Noreen, let out an ear-piercing scream.

"What's wrong?" Emma asked, scrunching her brows.

"Look. . .over there!" Noreen, her eyes wide with obvious fear, pointed to the wall closest to her. "Get it! Get it! I can't stand creepy-crawlies in the house."

"If someone will help me corner the critter, I think we can catch him pretty quick," Lamar said, moving toward the gecko.

Mike, being the sportsman that he was, jumped up right away. "No problem. I bet I can catch him," he hollered as he took up the chase.

After Lamar and Mike pursued the gecko unsuccessfully, B.J. got into the act. "Come back here," he panted, red-faced and gasping for breath as the gecko eluded his grasp and slithered up the wall. The poor man looked exhausted. Winded and coughing, he finally had to quit.

"Are you okay?" Noreen asked, a look of concern etched on her face.

"I—I'm fine. Just a bit winded is all." B.J. flopped into a chair. "Guess that's proof that I'm not as young as I used to be."

Mike made another pass at the gecko, but missed again and fell on his face.

"Maybe I can help." Kim dashed across the room and quickly snagged the critter in the palm of her hand. Everyone but the girl in the wheelchair cheered.

Mike clambered to his feet a bit too quickly and had to steady himself until a wave of dizziness passed. He was embarrassed that he'd made a fool of himself in front of the class, but figured the wooziness had been caused by jerking his head too fast while in hot pursuit of the gecko. Mike had the strength and agility to reel in a big fish when he went out on his boat, but he couldn't even catch a little lizard. And to be shown up by a woman, no less! He really felt like an idiot. This was not a good way to begin his first quilting class, and he could only imagine how the next hour would go.

CHAPTER 11

After Kim put the gecko outside, the class continued, and the topic of the alligator that had been in the Millers' yard came up again.

"I still can't get over that," Kim said, sitting down at the sewing machine beside Erika once more. "A little gecko is one thing, but I don't know what I would have done if I'd been in your shoes, Lamar. Think I would have run straight for the house, screaming all the way."

"I'd have probably passed out on the lawn," Noreen put in as she finished up with her bit of sewing.

"Back home all we ever had to deal with was my goat, Maggie, getting out of her pen." Emma chuckled. "I guess here we need to be a little more careful when we step into the yard."

"Most gators don't show up in people's backyards unless there's a body of water nearby," Mike said as he laid out the quilt squares his wife had cut the previous week.

That guy seems like a know-it-all to me, Kim thought as she continued helping Erika by pressing on the foot pedal for her. *I don't think he really wants to be here, either. But then neither does Erika, so that has to make it hard on our teachers.*

"I just thought of something," Emma said, coming up beside Erika and Kim. "What if we put the foot pedal for the electric sewing machine up on the cabinet next to the machine? Then, Erika, you can press down on it with your elbow, which would give you both hands free to guide your material under the presser foot."

"That's a good idea," Kim said before Erika could respond. "Don't know why I didn't think of it myself."

"I—I guess I could give it a try," Erika said, with a dubious expression.

As Emma placed the foot pedal on the cabinet and showed Erika what to do, Kim began pinning her own quilt squares together, while glancing over at Jennifer. The young woman seemed nice and was eager to learn how to quilt. Jennifer didn't say a lot, though, and Kim wondered if she was shy or just didn't have much to talk about.

If I was in her place and expecting a baby, that would be all I talked about, Kim mused. At the age of thirty-six, she'd all but given up on marriage and having a family of her own. Oh, she'd dated a few men over the years, but none had been willing to make a commitment, and a few she'd broken up with because she knew they weren't good husband material. Most of the men she'd gone out with were either selfish, had nothing in common with her, or wanted more than she was willing to offer. Kim had made a pledge when she was a teenager to remain pure and give herself only to the man she would marry. But since marriage and children probably weren't in her future, she'd put her focus on other things—riding her motorcycle, walking her dog on the beach, and being cheerful to all her customers at the restaurant.

Kim's thoughts were interrupted when Emma touched her shoulder and asked, "How's it going?"

"Okay, I guess. It just takes awhile to get all the squares pinned in place."

"That's true," Emma agreed, "but once you get the blocks sewn together, your wall hanging will start to take shape."

Kim sighed. "I've been trying to decide what to do with it after I'm done."

"I'm going to hang mine in my living room," Noreen said. "I know just the place for it, too."

"Mine's going in the baby's room," Jennifer spoke up. "That's why I chose pastel colors in shades of pink."

"Does that mean you're having a girl?" Noreen questioned.

"Yes. At least that's what the ultrasound showed." Jennifer's shoulders drooped. "I just hope my husband finds a job before the baby comes."

"What does he do for a living?" This question came from B.J.

"He's a cook, and a mighty fine one, too." Jennifer smiled. "The only good thing about Randy being out of work is that now he cooks most of our meals. I'd gladly take that responsibility over again, though, if he could only find a job."

Kim was glad Jennifer was opening up, but she felt sorry for the young mother-to-be. Maybe there were some benefits in being single. At least she only had to worry about supporting herself and taking care of her dog.

"I'm thankful that someone gave me the gift of this class," Jennifer went on to say. "I just wish I knew who it was so I could thank them for it." She looked over at Emma with a hopeful expression. "Do you know who it was?"

Emma adjusted her head covering, which was slightly askew. "The person who paid for your class wishes to remain anonymous and said they felt it was more of a blessing to keep it that way."

"Someone left a box of food on our front porch the other day, too, and there was no note attached," Jennifer said. "I'm beginning to see that God is providing for Randy and me in many ways."

"We'll be praying for you, dear," Emma said. "Try to keep a positive attitude while waiting for God to provide your husband a job."

———

As Noreen worked at the sewing machine, she was glad that she had something to do. She'd felt a little foolish, making such a fuss about the lizard—especially after thinking about that big alligator in Emma and Lamar's backyard. She would have had a conniption, seeing such a creature anywhere close to her home.

Noreen's mind drifted to the envelope that had come in this morning's mail. She'd been hoping to hear from her son, Todd, or his wife, Kara, but guessed they were busy with their lives in Texas, because the letter wasn't from them. She understood that Todd and Kara had busy lives of their own, but she missed them and would have gone to visit more often but didn't want to intrude.

Two years after Noreen married her husband, Ben, and they'd found out they couldn't have children of their own, they'd been given the opportunity to adopt Todd. What a wonderful life they'd had raising their boy. All those years when Todd was growing up, they had been a threesome, doing so many things together—simple things like camping, fishing, and going on picnics. They'd also enjoyed going to some of the local festivals every year. Of all the fun things to do at festivals, Todd usually went for the pony rides. In fact, from a very young age, he'd been interested in horses. To follow his dreams, after graduating from high school, he'd gone to Texas to stay with a friend, where he'd learned about ranching. Eventually he'd married Kara, and they'd been living in

Texas ever since, working on the ranch where they'd met. In addition to their ranch duties, they had Kara's boys, Nolan, who was ten, and Garrett, age twelve, to raise.

After Ben died, Noreen had felt totally alone, especially given that they had been married for forty years, but she didn't want to burden her son or make him feel obligated to her. She wanted Todd and his wife to pursue their dream of someday owning their own ranch. So Noreen decided to move forward, pushing herself to learn how to cope with living alone. It was hard at first, but she made it a point to get on with her life. She had been a teacher for all those years and used to give her students pep talks when they seemed fearful about their future. Now it was her turn to give herself a pep talk. After all, she wasn't the only woman in the world who'd lost her husband.

Thinking back to the letter she'd received this morning, Noreen was glad it hadn't been a piece of junk mail, like she so often found in her mailbox. Instead, the return address revealed it was from Monica Adams, a former student. Every now and then Noreen received notes from students letting her know what was happening in their lives. She'd put off opening Monica's note until later today so she wouldn't be late to class.

"Is everyone ready to take a break for some refreshments?" Emma's question broke into Noreen's thoughts. She glanced at her watch and realized it was already eleven o'clock.

"I made some coffee cake, and Lamar picked oranges from our tree in the backyard this morning," Emma said, smiling at the class.

"Both sound good to me," Noreen said, putting her sewing away, while several others bobbed their heads in agreement. Not Mike, though. He sat there, wrinkling his nose.

"I'm allergic to oranges," Mike informed Emma. "So I'll pass on those.

Sure don't want to break out with a case of hives."

"No, that wouldn't be good," Emma said. "Would you like some of my coffee cake, though?"

Mike nodded eagerly. "That suits me just fine. I didn't have much for breakfast this morning so I'm feelin' kinda hungry right now." He rose from his chair to follow Emma into the kitchen, thinking he might get to taste some of that cake before anyone else. But he'd only taken a few steps when he felt kind of shaky and broke out in a sweat.

"Oh, great, not this again," Mike groaned, grabbing the back of B.J.'s chair as everything blurred before him. He'd felt this way when he'd first woken up this morning and figured he might be coming down with the flu. He'd felt better once he'd had a cup of coffee and a doughnut, however.

"Are you okay?" Lamar asked, taking hold of Mike's arm. "Is it too hot in here? Should I open a window or door?"

"No, I'm fine. Just feeling a little woozy is all."

Lamar quickly pulled out an empty chair and instructed Mike to sit down. "Try to relax and take some deep breaths. I'll open a window to let in some fresh air. Hopefully, that will help you cool down."

Mike did as Lamar suggested. As he sat, fanning his face with his hands, while blinking his eyes to clear them, he could only imagine what Phyllis would say if she knew what was happening to him right now.

What is happening to me? Mike wondered. *I felt fine when I first got here, except for feeling a bit woozy when I got out of the car. Why do I feel so horrible now? Are these spells a warning of some kind?*

CHAPTER 12

S hould we call 911?" Noreen asked, concerned about Mike's strange behavior. "You might be having a heart attack." She remembered too well how her husband had collapsed on the floor of their living room when his heart gave out. And even though she'd called for help, and they'd performed surgery at the hospital, it had been too late for Ben. She hated to think that might be the case with this man, too.

Mike shook his head determinedly. "There's no need for that. I feel a little weak and shaky is all, but I'm sure I'll be okay once I have something to eat."

"It might be a case of low blood sugar," Erika spoke up. "I've heard my dad talk about patients who've actually passed out when their blood sugar dropped, mostly because they hadn't eaten. You oughta make an appointment with your doctor and have it checked out."

Mike flapped his hand. "Don't think there's any need for that. I'm sure it'll pass."

Men can be so stubborn, Noreen thought. *I'll bet if Mike's wife was here, she would insist that he see a doctor today.*

"Erika's right," Lamar said, "but in the meantime, I'll get Emma, and we'll see that you get something to eat." He hurried into the kitchen, as Mike continued to breathe deeply, while keeping his head between his knees.

"We have a problem in the other room," Lamar said when he entered the kitchen where Emma stood at the counter cutting the coffee cake.

Emma turned to face him. "What kind of problem? Is someone having trouble with one of the sewing machines?"

Lamar shook his head. "Mike isn't feeling well. Said he felt shaky, and he's sweating profusely. I was afraid he might pass out so I opened some windows and had him sit down to rest."

"Oh dear! We'd better call for help right away." Emma moved quickly across the room, where the telephone sat on the roll-top desk. At a time such as this, she was glad the Amish were allowed to have electricity and telephones in their homes here in Pinecraft.

Lamar stepped between Emma and the desk. "Mike doesn't want us to call for help. He thinks he just needs to eat something, and Erika mentioned, too, that it could be a drop in his blood sugar."

"Well, if that's the case, then some cake might help." Emma handed the platter to Lamar, then she grabbed some paper plates and forks and followed him into the other room. Immediately she cut a piece of cake and offered it to Mike.

"Thanks," he said, quickly wolfing it down. "Boy, that sure tasted good. And you know what? Think I'm feelin' better already. A little food was probably all I needed."

"I'll bet it's your blood sugar, alright," Erika said, nodding her head.

"Eating something sweet brought it up real quick. If you find out you have hypoglycemia it could turn to diabetes, and of course, you'll have to watch what you eat."

"Well now, aren't you just the little doctor?" Mike's eyes narrowed. "I'm sure I don't have that. I just needed to eat something, and I feel fine now, so you can quit badgering me."

"I wasn't." Erika frowned. "Oh, never mind. I'll keep my opinions to myself from now on. It's your health anyway, not mine."

Feeling the need to break the tension, Emma quickly said, "I'll go to the kitchen and get the tray of orange slices now. Then we can sit around the table and eat our snack while we get better acquainted." She rushed back to the kitchen and was surprised when Noreen followed.

"Men can be so pigheaded sometimes," Noreen muttered. "If my husband hadn't been too stubborn to see the doctor for annual checkups, he might still be alive." Her lips compressed, as a frown etched her forehead. "One time I made Ben an appointment, and he got really mad. He even said I was treating him like a little boy."

"That must have been upsetting," Emma acknowledged. "But when a grown person doesn't want to do something, there isn't much anyone can do about it. Sometimes the more we say, the more they refuse to listen."

"I guess that's true. I just wish. . . ." Noreen's voice trailed off, and then she said, "Can I help you with anything, Emma?"

"Well, let's see. . . ." Emma glanced at the refrigerator. "There's a pitcher of iced tea in there, so if you want to bring that in, along with the paper cups on the counter, that would be appreciated."

"I'd be happy to." Noreen smiled as she moved across the room.

Emma was glad Noreen seemed in better spirits. Sometimes rehashing the past, especially something that couldn't be undone, brought a person down. If there was one thing Emma had learned in her sixty-seven years, it was the importance of focusing on the positive and making the most of each day. She hoped by their actions and words that she and Lamar would be able to share that with this group of quilters, just as they had done with all the other classes they'd taught.

When Emma returned to the dining room, she was relieved to see that Mike looked better and was visiting with B.J. as though nothing had happened. It upset her to think that someone in her class wasn't feeling well. Fortunately, it didn't seem to be serious. But if it had been, she would have definitely called for help, despite any objections on Mike's part.

"Those are some really nice shells in that jar over there," Kim mentioned, as everyone enjoyed their refreshments. "Someone must like to comb the beach as much as I do."

Lamar grinned widely. "That would be me. Of course, I think Emma likes beach combing, too. Right, Emma?"

"Yes, it's relaxing; just like working in my flower beds back home." Emma glanced at Erika. "Do you enjoy going to the beach?"

"Not really." Erika frowned. "I mean, what's fun about sitting in a wheelchair staring at the water?"

"I often sit on a bench and watch the waves," Emma said, hoping to bring Erika out of her negativity. "I like that even more than searching for things on the beach. It's also interesting to watch people, especially children when they find something fascinating."

"I do that sometimes, too," Kim interjected. "Of course, if I sit for too long, my dog, Maddie, nudges me with her nose, wanting to play."

"What about the rest of you?" Lamar asked. "Do you all enjoy the beach?"

"I do," B.J. was quick to say. "I like to watch the sunset and try to capture all the vivid colors on canvas."

"Randy and I enjoy the beach," Jennifer said. "It's one of the few things we can do that doesn't cost money."

"Sometimes I think the things that are out there, free to enjoy, are more meaningful than anything else," Emma added. Her heart went out to Jennifer. She remembered back to the days when she and her first husband, Ivan, were newlyweds and struggled financially. If not for the help of their family and friends, some days they might not have had enough money to put food on the table.

Maybe there's something we could do to help Jennifer and Randy, Emma thought. *The very least we can do is give them some food. I hope they won't be too proud to accept it.*

"What about the Amish words you promised to teach us?" Kim asked.

"Oh, that's right. I did say we would do that." Emma looked at Lamar. "Should I share one, or would you like to?"

"You go ahead, Emma."

"Well, the Pennsylvania-Dutch word for children is *kinner.*"

"And for *thank you*, we would say *danki*," Lamar interjected.

"That's interesting and all," Noreen spoke up, "but this is taking up time, and I think we should get back to work on our quilts."

"You're right," Emma agreed. "There's more sewing to be done on your quilt squares." She looked over at Mike. "Are you feeling up to trying out one of the sewing machines?"

"Sure. But I'll probably end up stitching my shirt instead of the material," he said with a shrug.

"I'm sure you'll do fine," Emma said, remembering how a couple of her previous students had done that very thing. "I'll show you everything you need to do."

While Jennifer pinned more of her squares together, she visited with Kim. "Are you married?" she asked.

Kim shook her head. "Don't you remember last week when I mentioned that I wasn't looking for love or romance?"

"Oh, that's right. Guess I forgot."

"I don't even have a serious boyfriend right now, but maybe it's better that way," Kim said.

"You have such a nice smile, and you seem so easygoing. I wouldn't have been surprised if you had a husband and a few kids."

Kim leaned her head back and laughed. "I'm so far from that, it's not even funny."

"Do you like kids?"

"Oh sure, but it's not likely that I'll ever have any of my own." Kim picked up another pin and stuck it in place. "It's not that I don't wish for it, but I'm thirty-six years old, and even if I got married in the next few years, I'm too old to start a family."

"My mother was thirty-two when she had me," Jennifer said.

"Are you the youngest child in your family, or did your mother have more kids after you?" Kim questioned.

"I'm the oldest, and I have three younger sisters still living at home."

"Your mom had more courage than me," Kim said. "If I don't get married in the next year or so, I'm giving up on the idea of having any kids."

Jennifer touched Kim's arm. "You never know. Mr. Right could be just around the corner. Or he might be the next customer you wait on at the restaurant. Stranger things have been known to happen."

"My last boyfriend, Darrell. . . Well, let me put it this way—I thought we had a good thing going, and that he was 'the one.' I was so sure of

Darrell's love that I moved from my home in North Carolina to Florida, thinking we could start a new life together." Kim slowly shook her head. "Believe me, I've never done anything that huge before." She paused to pin a few more pieces of her quilt blocks together. "Everything went along smoothly for a while, but then things turned sour and Darrell broke up with me. It only took a few months to know our relationship was going nowhere and that Darrell wasn't the 'Mr. Right' I thought he was."

"Do you have any family here in Florida?" Jennifer asked.

"Nope. My parents are living in North Carolina, and my brother, Jimmy, is in the navy, and currently stationed in Bremerton, Washington. I miss my family, but I stay in touch through phone calls, text messages, and e-mails."

"Have you thought about moving back home?"

"Yeah, many times, but if I did, it'd be like admitting that I failed. I refuse to turn tail and run back home. I want to try and make a go of it here." Kim smiled. "Thank goodness for my dog, Maddie. She and I have fallen into somewhat of a routine, and it's comforting to know she won't desert me."

"I guess sometimes things happen to make us think about what we really want in life," Jennifer said. "Don't give up, Kim. I'm convinced that there's someone in this world for everyone."

Kim snickered. "I don't think it'll be anyone like the crotchety man I waited on yesterday. I wouldn't give him a second glance, even though he was sort of good-looking."

"How come?"

"He got mad because I dribbled some ketchup on his plate when I was handing him the bottle. I don't know why he'd complain about that. He was having eggs and hash browns, and who doesn't like a little ketchup with that?"

"I'm sure you won him over with your winning smile."

"Maybe. At least he didn't say anything to my boss about the incident."

"Did he leave you a tip?"

Kim shook her head. "Guess he thought I oughta pay for my flub-up, so the only thing he left was his dirty napkin, dotted with ketchup."

Jennifer snickered and gently squeezed Kim's arm. "I like you, Kim. You make me laugh."

"Thanks," Kim said. "I enjoy being able to bring humor into people's lives, and I like it when someone makes me laugh, too."

Everyone worked in silence awhile, until Noreen announced that it was time for her to go. "I haven't even read my mail from this morning yet, and I have a hair appointment this afternoon that I don't want to miss." She patted the sides of her hair. "I'm having some color put on to cover my gray, so I don't want to be late."

"I think we're about done for the day anyway," Emma said. "During our next class we'll finish stitching the quilt patches, and then hopefully get the batting cut out."

"Great. I'll see you all next Saturday then," Noreen said, gathering her things and hurrying out the door.

"My ride's here," Erika said when a wheelchair-accessible van pulled up in front of the Millers' house.

Everyone else said their good-byes, and Lamar reminded Mike that if he had another dizzy spell, he should call the doctor.

"Yeah, I'll do that," Mike agreed on his way out the door.

Jennifer had a feeling that he probably wouldn't do it—not unless his wife came home and made the appointment for him. She thought about how Randy relied on her for things like that. He would put off going to the dentist until he had a toothache, unless Jennifer made him an appointment for a cleaning and checkup. *Men are alike in many ways,* she thought, heading for the door.

"Oh, Jennifer, would you wait a minute?" Emma called.

Jennifer halted and turned back around.

"I was wondering if you would like a bag of oranges to take home," Emma said. "We also have some extra lemons we'd be happy to share with you."

"That'd be great. With the way Randy likes to cook, I'm sure he'll put the lemons to good use."

"How about some of those ginger cookies you made the other day?" Lamar said to Emma. "We still have plenty left, and you and I sure aren't going to eat them all."

A lump formed in Jennifer's throat. Emma and her husband were so kind and generous. To show her appreciation, she gave Emma a hug.

"Lamar and I will be praying that your husband finds the right job soon," Emma said. "In the meantime, if there's anything we can do for you, please don't hesitate to ask."

"Thanks, I'm grateful for your concern."

"Now, let me help you carry the fruit and cookies out to your car," Lamar offered.

"See you next week," Emma said. "And don't forget our offer of help."

Jennifer nodded, then hurried out the door. She couldn't believe what a nice couple they were. Too bad everyone didn't have such a generous spirit. If they did, the world would be a better place.

CHAPTER 13

When Jennifer arrived home from the quilt class, she found Randy sitting on the couch in the living room with his feet propped on the coffee table, staring into space.

"What are you doing here?" she asked, setting her tote bag on the floor. "I thought you had a job interview today."

He grunted. "I did, but when I got to the restaurant I was told that they'd already found a cook, so they didn't ask me one question about my previous experience."

"Then why'd they want to interview you?" Jennifer questioned, taking a seat beside him. She couldn't imagine being called to an interview and then being told that the position had already been filled. That just didn't seem fair!

Randy shrugged like it didn't matter, but Jennifer knew from his dejected expression that it did.

"Guess maybe they interviewed the other cook first, liked what he said, and hired him on the spot." Randy squeezed his hands together. "You'd think they would have at least talked to me first and then decided who was best suited to the job. Whoever heard of doing interviews like that, anyways? And wouldn't you think they'd give everyone a fair chance? They just wasted my time!" He slapped the newspaper lying on the sofa beside him. "I've looked through the want ads till my eyes hurt, and there are no positions for a cook available in this town right now. At the rate things are going, we'll starve to death before I find a job."

Jennifer leaned over and gave him a hug. She felt bad seeing her husband like this, but maybe it was good for him to vent a bit. It wasn't healthy to keep things bottled up. "I know you're upset, and it's understandable, too, but we need to keep a positive attitude and never give up."

"I won't give up," he said, shaking his head, "but I'm not sure I can think positive thoughts right now."

Jennifer sighed, wondering what it would take to get Randy out of his slump.

"How'd it go at the quilt class today?" he asked.

"It went okay. When I got ready to leave, Emma and Lamar Miller gave me a sack of oranges and lemons, as well as a container of cookies. They're out in the car, so if you don't mind getting them. . ."

"Fruit and cookies, huh?" He snorted. "Like we can live on those!"

"We still have some food in the house, Randy." Jennifer took hold of his hand. "I think what the Millers gave us was a nice gesture, don't you?"

"I'm sure they meant well, but we don't need anyone's charity. I accepted it when someone paid for your quilt class, and then when my brother sent us some money so we could get new tires for your car, but now we're accepting food handouts, too? When's it gonna end, Jennifer?

If things get any worse, we may have to sell one of our vehicles."

"I think we should be grateful for whatever help we receive."

"Well, if we're gonna take charity, then I'd at least like to do something nice in return."

"Like what?" she questioned.

"Maybe we could have Emma and Lamar over for dinner some evening. Of course, we can't do that till I've found a job and we can buy a decent cut of meat."

Jennifer sighed. "I don't think the Millers would expect an expensive meal. Maybe you could barbecue some burgers or make a big taco salad."

"I'll give it some thought." Randy rose to his feet. "Guess I'd better get those oranges and lemons brought in before they shrivel up from the heat. It may be the dead of winter and cold as an iceberg in some places, but here in Sarasota, it's hot enough to cook a hot dog on the roof of your car."

Jennifer snickered. She was glad her husband hadn't lost his sense of humor, despite all they'd been going through with the loss of his job.

"Say, Randy, I've been thinking," she said before he headed outside. "Since we still don't have a crib for the baby, why don't we go to one of the thrift stores in the area soon and see if we can find one? They might have some other baby things in good condition, too."

He shook his head. "I don't want our baby girl to have a bunch of used furniture or hand-me-down clothes. She deserves better than that."

"We can't afford to buy anything new right now," Jennifer argued. "Your unemployment check just doesn't go very far."

"How well I know it. Let's wait another week or so and see if I find a job before we look at any of the thrift stores, okay?"

She nodded slowly. "Whatever you think's best."

Noreen entered her house and flopped into the recliner with a moan. She'd gone to the styling salon after the quilt class today, and been told that her stylist had gotten sick and gone home. Noreen could have rescheduled, but since she didn't know how long her stylist would be sick, she decided to stop at a store on the way home and buy a box of hair color. She'd never attempted to color her own hair but figured it couldn't be that difficult. She would fix herself some lunch, read this morning's mail, then do her hair.

Moving to the kitchen, where she'd left the stack of mail, Noreen opened up the letter from her former student Monica:

Dear Mrs. Webber:

I hope this note finds you well. The reason I'm writing is to let you know that the high school class I graduated from is having its twentieth reunion in three weeks and we're inviting many of our teachers to be at the function. I realize this isn't the time of year for most reunions, but we couldn't get the school auditorium when we want it, so the committee decided to have the event this month instead. Please let me know if you'll be able to come

Sincerely,
Monica Adams

"Of course I'll come," Noreen said aloud. It would be great to see some of her old students again, as well as her teacher friend, Ruth Bates, who would no doubt also get an invitation. Noreen would give Ruth a call later on to see if she was planning to go.

One more reason to get the gray out of my hair so I don't look so old, she thought.

After shampooing and towel-drying her hair, Noreen stepped up to the bathroom mirror. She blinked in disbelief, and her mouth dropped open. Her hair was darker, alright, and yes, the gray was gone, but it was darker than it had ever been in her life! The color looked so stark, even against her tanned skin. Had she bought the wrong shade of brown or left it on too long?

Bending over to fish the empty box from the garbage, Noreen gasped. She didn't know how she had missed it before, but the color listed on the box was black, not brown!

Tears pooled in Noreen's eyes. "I look ridiculous like this. What was I thinking? I shouldn't have colored my own hair. I should have waited till Lynn came back to work. How can I go anywhere in public looking like this?" she wailed.

Goshen

With a sense of excitement, Jan knocked on Star's door.

"Come in, Dad!" Star hollered from inside the house.

He stepped in and smiled when he found his daughter in the living room, holding her guitar. "Hey, how'd you know it was me at the door?" he asked.

"Are you kidding me?" Star grinned. "I could hear your motorcycle comin' from a block away."

Jan chuckled. "Yeah, I'll bet. If you were playing your guitar you probably couldn't hear much other than that." He winked at her. "More'n likely it was my heavy boots clompin' up your front steps that told you it was me."

She placed the guitar on the sofa and poked his arm. "You got me there, Dad."

Jan draped his leather jacket over the back of a chair and took a seat beside her on the sofa. "So, are you ready to leave this cold weather behind for a few weeks and head to sunny Florida in the morning?"

She drew in her bottom lip. "Uh, I was gonna call you about this, but now that you're here, I can give you the bad news to your face."

His forehead wrinkled. "What bad news?"

"I can't go to Florida with you."

"How come? You're not sick, I hope."

"No, it's nothing like that. I can't get the two weeks off that I have coming right now."

He smacked the side of his head. "Oh great! Why not?"

"When I went to work this morning, the boss informed me that Shawn Prentiss, one of the guys who stocks shelves, had an emergency appendectomy, so that leaves them shorthanded. He asked me to wait a few weeks to take my vacation—until they can hire someone to take Shawn's place, because he probably won't be back for at least six weeks."

"I'm sorry to hear that," Jan said. "Guess we'll put our Florida plans on hold till you're free to go then."

Star shook her head. "Two weeks from now the weather could improve and you might have some roofing jobs. I think you oughta go on the trip without me, and if my boss hires someone to take Shawn's place soon, then I'll hop on a plane and join you in Sarasota. Since I won't be ridin' my bike, we can double up on yours and get around that way. Or maybe I can rent one once I get to Florida."

Jan gave his beard a sharp pull, mulling things over. He really didn't want to go without Star, but she had that look of determination he'd come to know so well, and he figured if he said no, she'd argue with him the rest of the day.

"Well, okay, if you're sure," he finally said.

Star gave a quick nod. "I'm not happy about having to stay behind, or for that matter, even flying down there, but I'd be a little nervous cycling all the way to Florida by myself. Most of all, though, I'd feel worse if you didn't go ahead."

"No, I wouldn't want you comin' all that way alone on your bike." He gave her a hug. "You have a good head on your shoulders, and I'm glad you came back into my life when you did."

"Same here." She hugged him back. "You need to promise me one thing."

"What's that?"

"Don't ride your bike too fast; remember to stop for a break every few hours; and call me every night so I'll know how you're doing."

He tweaked the end of her nose, lightly brushing her gold nose ring with his little finger. "That was three things, and you said one."

She giggled and poked his arm playfully. "Okay, so I lied. Seriously, though, I really do want you to call when you stop for the night. Oh, and when you get to Sarasota, I'll want to know that you've arrived safely."

"Yes, Mother," Jan teased, leaning his head against the back of the sofa. "I'll keep you posted every step of the way, but it's sure not gonna be the same without you on this road trip. You're my favorite cycling partner."

CHAPTER 14

*B*ong! *Bong! Bong! Bong! Bong!*

Emma's eyes snapped open, and she cast a quick glance at the clock on the far wall. After doing some mending this afternoon, she'd relaxed in her recliner for a while. Then, unable to keep her eyes open, she'd fallen asleep. Now it was five o'clock.

"That noisy clock you bought the other day has just let me know that it's time to start supper," Emma said to Lamar, who sat on the sofa nearby, reading the newspaper. She yawned and stretched her arms over her head.

"Sorry about that," Lamar apologized. "When I found the clock in the secondhand store, I didn't realize it would be so loud. I can turn the ringer off if you'd like."

"*Danki*. It might be better if you did." Emma expelled another noisy yawn.

"Did you have a nice nap?" Lamar stifled a yawn, then laughed.

"Hearing you yawn makes me feel the need to yawn, too."

"Jah, hearing someone yawn can be quite contagious." Emma grinned. "When I was a young girl, I and a bunch of my classmates were supposed to be quietly reading, while our teacher Sara Beiler graded papers. Some of us got mischievous and took turns yawning, and in no time we had the teacher yawning, too. Sara never caught on to what we were doing, and it was all we *kinner* could do to keep from laughing out loud. We were lucky that day that we didn't get in trouble."

Lamar clucked his tongue. "My, my, you were a little dickens when you were young," he teased.

"Oh, you know, it was just kid stuff." Emma yawned once more and covered her mouth with the palm of her hand. "I don't know why, but I've been tired ever since our quilt class ended today."

"Tired physically or emotionally?" Lamar asked.

"I think it's more emotional than anything," she said. "It's difficult to see others struggling and not be able to do anything about it."

"Is there anyone in particular you're thinking of?"

She nodded. "Jennifer, for one. She's on the brink of becoming a new mother and shouldn't have to worry about how she and her husband are going to provide for their baby when it comes."

"We can give them some more food," Lamar suggested. "Or maybe buy them a gift card they can use at one of the grocery stores in their neighborhood."

"That's a good idea. I think we should do that. Unfortunately, just seeing that they have food in the cupboards won't pay their bills."

"We could give them some money, I suppose."

Emma removed her glasses and cleaned a spot that was smudged. "I'm not opposed to that idea, Lamar, but I think from what Jennifer's said, her husband might take offense if we gave them money. Maybe if we knew them better. . ."

"I wish I knew of some restaurant that needed a cook," Lamar said. "I'd surely put in a good word for Jennifer's husband." He rose to his feet. "Speaking of restaurants, why don't we go to that nice one up the street, where Anna and Kim work? It'll save you from having to cook this evening."

"Oh, I don't mind cooking; I'll just keep it simple. I appreciate your offer, Lamar, but I really don't feel like going out this evening."

"Okay. I'll turn the clock's ringer off, and then we can go to the kitchen and I'll help you fix whatever you want."

"We have some cold meat loaf and potato salad in the refrigerator, so maybe I'll make a fruit salad to go with those and use some of our juicy oranges. I also have some strawberries and pineapple that I purchased at the produce market the other day, so that can be our dessert."

"Sounds good. We haven't had fruit salad in a while," Lamar said. "I can help by slicing up whatever fruit you want to use."

Emma smiled. Once more, she was reminded of how fortunate she was to be married to such a kind, thoughtful man.

As dinnertime approached, Mike started feeling kind of shaky again. After returning from the quilt class, he'd spent the afternoon working in the yard and hadn't taken time to eat lunch. A few times he'd had to stop when fatigue overtook him.

"Big mistake for not eating sooner," Mike muttered, reaching for a jar of peanut butter from the refrigerator. Since he didn't have the energy to cook anything tonight, a peanut butter and jelly sandwich would have to suffice. It was something he could make quickly and get into his stomach, which was growling loudly.

Mike got out the bread and slathered peanut butter on one piece and jelly on the other. Then he poured himself a glass of milk and took a seat at the table. He'd just taken his first bite, when the telephone rang.

"Oh great," he mumbled. "It's probably some irritating advertising call. Those always seem to come in around dinnertime." Mike was tempted to ignore it, but on the chance that it might be his wife, he left the table and went to check the caller ID. Sure enough, it was Phyllis.

"Hi, hon," he said, mouth still full of sandwich.

"Did I catch you in the middle of supper?" Phyllis asked.

"Not so much." He moved back to the table and took a drink of milk. "Just having a peanut butter and jelly sandwich."

"That's all you're eating for supper?"

"Yeah, but it fills the hole." Mike took another drink and gulped it down, looking out the window toward the bay.

"Are you okay? You don't sound like your usual self tonight."

"Naw, I'm fine. Just tired is all. Guess I overdid it doing yard work today." Mike reached for the sandwich and took a bite. His shakiness had subsided some, but he still felt kind of weak. No way was he going to tell Phyllis that, though. She'd be torn between coming home to look after him and taking care of her sister.

"How'd the quilt class go today?" she asked.

"Fine. How's Penny doing?"

"Okay, but she's not ready to be on her own yet. She really appreciates me being here, especially with the snowstorm we're having right now. I think it's a blizzard, actually." Phyllis paused briefly. "I'm glad Penny has a generator. So many people here are without power, but Penny's prepared for something like this." She laughed lightly. "My big sis always did have a good head on her shoulders."

"I hope you two stay put and don't go anywhere. You're not used to driving in the snow—especially with someone else's vehicle," Mike said with concern. "Sure wish I was there with you right now."

"We're managing okay. The weather station's been warning people about this blizzard for a few days, so I went out and got some extra groceries the other day," Phyllis said. "Penny doesn't live far from the store, and I truly think everyone goes there just for the bread and milk. There was hardly any left in the store when I got there. Anyhow, Mike, I'm glad I thought to bring along some warmer clothes for this trip." She laughed. "I'd feel like a Popsicle if I'd only brought shorts and sandals."

"Guess people prepare for a snowstorm a little differently than when we get ready for a hurricane. At least up north, they don't have to board up the house or move inland," Mike said.

"You're right about that. It's sort of exciting to see all this snow, but at the same time, I really miss you and can't wait to get home. I'm starting to forget what that warm sunshine feels like, and I sure miss smelling the ocean breeze."

"I'll take our warm winters over those frigid ones any day." Mike grabbed a napkin and swiped at the sweat on his forehead. Even though he'd eaten half the sandwich, he still didn't feel right. His skin felt clammy. Now, along with everything else, the area around his mouth tingled a bit. *What in the world is going on with me?* Mike wondered. What he really wanted to do was head to the living room and lie down on the couch.

"Mike, are you listening to me?"

"Uh, what was that?"

"I was wondering if you've heard anything about your boat yet."

"Nope, nothing recently, but the last time I checked I was told it would be a few more weeks." He took a seat at the table.

"I'll let you go so you can finish your sandwich. I'll call again in a few days."

Mike said good-bye to Phyllis and grabbed the other half of his sandwich. *Maybe come Monday morning I will call the doctor,* he decided. *It doesn't make sense the way I've been feeling today, and I really would like to know if there's something seriously wrong.*

"How'd your day go, sweetie?" Kyle asked as he and Erika sat at the kitchen table, eating the pepperoni pizza he'd brought home for supper. It wasn't the healthiest meal, but it was quick and easy. Besides, it was Erika's favorite kind of pizza.

"My day was the same as usual," she mumbled around a piece. "How was yours?"

"Exhausting." He reached for his glass of water. "Never had so many emergencies all in one day."

"Accidents or kids who are sick?" she asked.

"Both."

Erika grunted. "Life stinks, and folks just need to get used to it. I'd hate to be a doctor and see people hurting all the time."

I watch you hurting, he thought. *Sometimes that's worse than anything I see at the hospital, Erika. I'd give anything if I could give you back the ability to walk.*

"How'd the quilt class go today?" Kyle asked, feeling the need to change the subject before he gave in to the blame game again.

"Well, it wasn't quite as boring as the week before."

"Oh? What happened?"

"A gecko got into the Millers' house and gave a couple of people a merry chase." Erika reached for her glass of lemonade. "Oh, and one of the women had to drop out of the class to take care of her sister who has a broken leg, so her husband took her place."

"That was nice of him."

Erika wrinkled her nose. "I don't think he really wanted to be there, and he especially wasn't having fun when he almost passed out."

Kyle's eyebrows lifted. "What brought that about?"

Erika shrugged. "I'm not sure, but he seemed to feel better after he ate some of Emma's coffee cake. I told him I thought he should see a doctor,'cause he could have low blood sugar."

"That's possible, but of course, it could have been something else causing his symptoms. I'm glad you suggested he see a doctor, though. That was good thinking on your part."

"I'm not stupid, Dad."

His face heated. "Never said you were. Why do you always have to get so defensive, Erika?"

"I'm not. And why do you always treat me like a baby?"

Because you act like one sometimes. Of course, Kyle didn't voice his thoughts. Erika would have really gotten defensive.

"Let's not argue," Kyle said, reaching for another slice of pizza. "I don't have the energy to spar with you tonight."

Her lips compressed, but she made no comment. Kyle was beginning to think he would never get through to his daughter. He could only hope and pray that someone else could.

———

As B.J. sat on the porch of the bungalow he'd rented, watching the waves lap against the shore, he reflected on the debilitating fatigue he often felt, and wondered if his cancer had worsened. He remembered his doctor back home telling him that if he wasn't going to continue his treatments, then he needed to get his affairs in order and try to enjoy whatever time he had left.

And that's just what I'm doing, B.J. thought. Since he'd come to Sarasota, he'd developed a more positive outlook than when he'd been diagnosed with cancer. Maybe it was because the warm sunshine felt so good. Or it could be a renewed interest in his artwork since he'd begun taking the quilting classes. Either way, B.J. was living life the way he wanted, and by learning how to quilt, he hoped to hand down something special to his granddaughter when he left this old earth.

B.J.'s thoughts turned to his friend Sam Murphy, whom he'd met at the oncologist's office during one of his appointments. He'd talked to Sam on the phone last night and learned that Sam's cancer was getting worse. Sam sounded as though he'd given up when he told B.J. that his doctor had said he probably had about three or four months to live.

"Why do well-meaning doctors think they have to tell their patients how long it will be till they kick off?" B.J. muttered after taking a sip of his iced tea. He just wanted to live each day to the fullest, and not think about what lay ahead. After all, everyone had to die sometime—some sooner than others.

B.J. pulled out his hanky and blotted a splotch of tea that had dribbled out of his glass and landed on the front of his shirt. *If God wanted us to know the exact day of our death, He would have had it written on our birth certificate or something.*

A seagull screeched overhead—*reep, reep, reep*—and B.J. lifted his gaze upward, watching as the noisy bird flittered around, chasing another gull. When the gulls flew out above the water, B.J.'s thoughts turned to his friend again.

Sam had mentioned how supportive his family had been since hearing of his diagnosis. He said he didn't think he could make it without their encouragement. Sam's daughter had even told him that being there to help him was the least she could do for all the sacrifices he'd made during her childhood. She counted it a privilege to be there for him.

It might be a privilege for Sam's daughter, B.J, thought, *but maybe she's not as busy as my daughters are They both have their own lives to live, and there is no way I'm going to get in the way of that. I don't want anyone feeling obligated to take care of me.*

He reached for his glass and took one final drink. *Maybe I'll get lucky and die in my sleep; then I won't have to worry about this any longer. That would solve the nasty little problem for everyone.*

CHAPTER 15

Noreen yawned and pulled the pillow over her head, hoping to drown out the sound of the neighbor's yappy dog. But the terrier kept barking, and the pillow did little to diffuse the irritating sound. Ever since her neighbor had purchased the puppy last week, Noreen had begun to lose sleep. That dog's yipping had probably scared every bird away, too.

Despite Noreen's irritation, she felt sorry for the mutt. It was a cute little pup, not much bigger than a rabbit. Didn't those neighbors know they shouldn't leave an animal that young alone in the yard? What if it found a way under the fence and ventured off their property? If the dog got out, it could get hit by a car or someone might steal it. Worse yet, what if an alligator got it? Noreen shivered, remembering the Millers' incident with the gator.

I may have to approach those people if their dog continues to bark and whine all the time, Noreen told herself. She didn't know the middle-aged couple on that side of her house very well, but she hoped they were reasonable people and would see the importance of keeping their puppy safe, even if they weren't concerned about the dog's barking.

With an exasperated sigh, she threw the covers aside and crawled out of bed. Stopping in front of her dresser to look at herself in the mirror, she frowned. Today was Tuesday, and it had been three days since she'd colored her hair. In spite of several washings, it was still just as dark as it had been on Saturday.

Self-conscious about the way she looked Noreen had skipped church Sunday morning and remained in her house all day yesterday, too. She certainly couldn't keep hiding from the world, however. Noreen liked to keep busy and enjoyed her freedom to go someplace whenever she felt like it.

Unless I plan to stay here indefinitely, guess I'd better find an appropriate hat or scarf to cover my head.

Noreen thought about Emma Miller and the stiff white head covering she wore. *If I had a hat like that to wear, I could sprinkle a little cornstarch in the front of my hair, to resemble the gray that used to be there, and no one would be any the wiser.*

She chuckled, her dour mood briefly dispelled as she pictured what she would look like wearing an Amish woman's hat. *I'd have to find an Amish dress to wear, too, or I'd really look ridiculous.*

Dismissing that thought, Noreen opened one of her dresser drawers and rifled through some colorful scarves. She tried on a few, but none covered her hair adequately. Next, she opened her closet door and took down all the hats on the shelf. After trying each of them on, she determined that nothing looked good enough to wear. Her only option was to go shopping for a new hat or scarf. If she found something that covered her hair sufficiently, she would wear it to the quilting class this Saturday. Since the school reunion was still a few weeks away, her hair would hopefully look better by then. If not, she may forget about going. Noreen stuck her tongue out at her reflection in the mirror. *Too bad it's not a Halloween party instead of a quilting class, because I'd certainly fit in.*

———

Knowing she had to be at work at noon, Kim had decided to get up early and take Maddie for a romp on the beach. The dog had spent the last hour running up and down, kicking up the sand and chasing seagulls, while Kim looked for shells. On one of her days off, she hoped to drive down to Venice to look for sharks' teeth. She'd heard they were there in abundance and thought it would be fun.

Too bad I don't have anyone to go with me, she thought. *It would be more fun that way. Guess I'll put the idea on hold for now.*

Kim kicked off her sandals and squatted beside a clump of broken shells. The shimmery white sand felt cool as her toes wiggled below the surface. While looking up every once in a while to watch Maddie play, Kim sifted through the sand, hoping to find some good shells that weren't broken. She was happy to have found a few, and then, digging deeper, her fingers touched something smooth and round.

"What's this?" she murmured, pulling the item up through the sand.

Turning it over in her hand, she soon realized it was a man's ring. Continuing to look it over, she saw the initials *B.W.* engraved on the inside of the gold band. A black onyx stone was mounted in the middle of the setting, and it had some sort of an emblem on one of the sides, with what looked like the inscription of a year on the other.

I'll bet this is someone's high school class ring, Kim thought as she examined it closer. The ring was a bit worn, so it was hard to tell what the lettering was around the insignia. Kim couldn't make out the year, either, but she was fairly sure it was a school ring.

I wonder how long this has been buried in the sand.

Hearing a shrill whistle, Kim looked up and saw a tall, bearded man with shaggy brown hair, wearing jeans and a biker's vest, and with a leather band around his head. He appeared to be heading her way. *Oh great. I wonder what he wants,* she thought, standing as she slipped the ring into the pocket of her shorts.

"Do you know who that dog over there belongs to?" he asked, pointing at Maddie, who'd just darted into the surf.

"She's mine. Why do you ask?"

"Well, she's got something in her mouth, and I don't think she oughta be running free on the beach. Don't you have a leash for her?"

Irritation welled in Kim's chest. Just who did this guy think he was talking to her like that? He didn't even know her and had no right to say anything about her dog.

"Maddie is fine; she's just having fun. Probably found a piece of driftwood to play with," she countered.

The biker took off his sunglasses and placed them on top of his head. "I think it's a bird—probably a gull."

Kim gasped. "Is—is it dead?"

He shrugged his broad shoulders. "Beats me. But if I were you, I'd go find out."

Kim hesitated a minute, then tromped to the edge of the water. "Maddie, come here, right now! And let that bird go!"

To Kim's relief, Maddie plodded out of the water and did as she was told, dropping the gull at her feet. The bird, although shaken, appeared to be unharmed and eventually flew off toward the sea.

"So your dog's name is Maddie, huh?"

Kim glanced over her shoulder and saw the burly man moving closer to her. *Oh great. Now what? I wish he'd go away.*

"Did you hear what I said? I asked if the dog's name is—"

"I heard, and yes, her name is Maddie."

When the guy squatted down and reached out to stroke Maddie's head, Kim noticed he had the word *Bunny* tattooed on his arm. She was tempted to ask him about it but didn't want to prolong this conversation.

"I've got a German shepherd, too," he said. "Fact is, my dog, Brutus, could probably pass for your dog's twin brother."

"Where is your dog?" Kim asked, clipping Maddie's leash to her collar.

"He's in Shipshe. My friend Terry's takin' care of Brutus while I'm gone, which suits me fine 'cause they really get along."

Kim tipped her head as she pushed a pile of sand back and forth with her big toe. "Shipshe?"

"Yeah, Shipshewana, Indiana. That's where I live. Took some time off work to come down here so I could visit some friends and spend a little time on the beach." He thrust out his hand. "The name's Jan. Jan Sweet."

Kim fought the urge to laugh out loud but kept her frown in place. She'd never heard Jan for a guy's name before. It sure didn't fit this big brawny fellow. He'd probably had a hard time living with a name like that and most likely been teased about it.

Jan could tell by her pinched expression that the cute little blond was miffed at him. Maybe she wasn't used to some stranger barging in and asking about her dog. Maybe she thought he was coming on to her and using the dog as an excuse to make conversation. *Or she could be thinking I'm just a nosey fellow who oughta mind his own business. Guess these days one can't be too careful, though.*

When the pretty lady didn't accept Jan's friendly gesture or offer her name, he lowered his hand and began petting the dog again. "How old is she, and how long have you had her?" he asked.

"She's six years old. I got her at the pound a month ago. Now if you'll excuse me, I need to get going 'cause I'm scheduled to work at noon, and I don't wanna be late." Clutching the dog's leash, she marched off in the opposite direction, leaving Jan by himself.

He watched her walk away and grinned when she glanced back at him briefly before heading off the beach. Seeing the German shepherd made Jan feel a bit homesick. He'd only been gone two days and had arrived in Sarasota early this morning. Already, he missed Brutus. Even more so, he missed Star and wished she could have come along with him. Traveling on the open road, just him and his Harley, was usually pure pleasure. Not this time, though. During the two days he'd spent traveling, all he'd thought about was his daughter and how he missed riding with her. At one point, Jan had been tempted to turn around and head back home but decided against it because he really wanted to see Emma and Lamar and find out how they were doing. Besides, for the last several months, he'd put in long hours with roofing jobs and really needed a break not only from the work, but from the cold weather they'd had recently in northeastern Indiana.

Putting his sunglasses back on, Jan stared out at the sparkling blue water, enjoying the warmth of the sun on his face and arms. It was a far cry from the frigid temperatures back home. The sounds were different here, too.

Closing his eyes, Jan listened as the waves splashed against the shore, while seagulls cried in unison as they flew overhead. Some of their calls sounded like high-pitched laughing. In the distance, Jan could have sworn he heard a ship's horn.

He opened his eyes, and looking across the water, he saw no sign of any ships. Maybe he'd just imagined it.

Jan breathed deeply, enjoying the smell of the salty air and hearing some kids' laughter as they played along the shore. It seemed like everyone he saw here wore smiles. It made Jan feel carefree, like he was a kid again. He'd have to put on his shorts or swimsuit and come back soon so he could swim or just lie around on the beach. Right now, though, he was anxious to head over to the Millers' and see how they were doing.

CHAPTER 16

Emma had just started making ham and cheese sandwiches for lunch, when a knock sounded on the front door. Since Lamar was in the backyard picking some lemons, she set the bread aside and went to answer the door.

Fully expecting to see one of her neighbors, Emma was shocked when she discovered Jan Sweet on their porch.

"Surprise!" Jan said with a twinkle in his blue eyes. "Bet you never expected to see me here in Pinecraft, did you?"

Emma reached out and gave Jan a hug. "No, I surely didn't. When did you get here, and how long can you stay?" She motioned to Jan's motorcycle, parked in the driveway. "Now don't tell me you rode that all the way from Shipshewana."

He chuckled. "One question at a time please, Emma."

Holding the door open for him, she smiled, feeling her cheeks warm. "Come inside, and I'll start over with the questions. Have you had lunch yet? I was just getting ready to fix ham and cheese sandwiches for Lamar and me, and we'd love to have you join us," she said, leading the way to the kitchen. "Lamar's out back right now, picking lemons, but oh my, is he ever going to be surprised to see you, Jan. In fact, I can't get over it myself."

"I don't want you to go to any trouble on my account," Jan said, leaning against the counter near the sink, "but a sandwich does sound pretty good about now."

"It's no bother at all; there's plenty of ham and cheese." She motioned to the table. "Take a seat, and we can visit while I finish making the sandwiches."

Jan did as Emma suggested, and a few seconds later, Lamar came in through the back door. He took a few steps, halted, and his face broke into a wide smile. "Well, look who's here! This is sure a surprise. What brings you to Sarasota, Jan?"

Jan stood and shook Lamar's hand. "Came to see you and Emma, of course. Thought it'd be nice to get a little sunshine, too," he added with a grin.

"Sure can't blame you for that," Lamar said, handing two fat lemons to Emma. "Can you stay and join us for lunch, Jan? We've got some catching up to do."

"I already invited him," Emma said.

"She didn't have to twist my arm too hard, either." Jan seated himself at the table again.

"How long are you here for?" Lamar questioned.

"A couple of weeks. Star will be joining me then, and we'll stay for a week or so after that. She would have ridden down with me on her bike, but she had to fill in for someone at work and couldn't get the time off."

"Oh, my, I hope she's not planning to ride down here on her

motorcycle all by herself," Emma said, feeling concern. She knew that some English folks thought it was dangerous for the Amish to use horses and buggies for their main mode of transportation, but she thought it would be a lot more dangerous to ride a motorcycle.

Jan shook his head. "Star will be catching a plane when she comes down to Florida, so you don't have to worry about that."

Emma blew out her breath, while slathering some mayonnaise on the bread. "That's a relief. It's just not safe for a young woman to be traveling alone these days—especially on the open road."

"Do you have a place to stay while you're in Sarasota?" Lamar asked, looking at Jan.

"Not yet, but I thought I'd look for a cheap hotel. Since I'm gonna be here awhile, I don't want anything too expensive."

"Why don't you stay here with us?" Emma and Lamar said in unison.

Emma chortled. "It seems that my husband and I are thinking alike. You know, Jan, we have an extra bedroom, and we'd love to have you as our guest."

"I appreciate the offer, but that's too much to ask."

"No, it's not," Emma said, vigorously shaking her head. "We'd enjoy having you stay with us, and we'd be disappointed if you didn't."

"Emma's right." Lamar agreed. "It'll give us a chance to get caught up with each other's lives and find out how things are going back home."

Emma put the finishing touch on the sandwiches. "It's all settled then. As soon as we're done eating, you can bring your things into the house."

"Now, how can I refuse an offer like that?" Jan gave them a wide smile. "Once Star gets here, I'll find us a hotel."

"That won't be necessary," Emma was quick to say. "Our living-room couch pulls out into a bed, so one of you can sleep right there."

"We're gonna bow for silent prayer now," Lamar said when Emma set the platter of sandwiches on the table and took a seat. "But if you'd rather pray out loud, Jan, that's fine with us, too."

Jan shook his head. "Naw, that's okay. I'm a believer, and I go to church whenever I can, but I ain't really comfortable prayin' out loud. So I'll just bow my head and say a silent prayer with you and Emma."

"That'll be just fine," Lamar said, casting Emma a smile.

All heads bowed, and when they'd finished praying, Emma jumped up and said, "Oh dear, I forgot the iced tea." She hurried across the room and returned a few minutes later with a tray that held a pitcher of iced tea, three glasses, and several lemon slices. She also placed a bag of potato chips on the table.

"I don't really need those." Lamar thumped his stomach. "Just a sandwich and the tea will be enough for me."

Emma sat down and scooted the bag of chips close to Jan's plate. "I'll bet you'd like some, though, right?"

With an eager expression, he grabbed a handful of chips. "It sure is great to see you folks again. How have you been anyways? Are you happy being here for the winter?"

"We sure are," Lamar said. "I love spending time on the beach, and the warm weather has been good for my aches and pains."

"That's great news." Jan grabbed a sandwich and took a bite. "So what do you enjoy about Sarasota, Emma? Do you also like to spend time on the beach?"

"It is nice," she admitted, "but I think Lamar enjoys it more than I do."

"Don't forget to tell Jan about the excitement we had here not long ago," Lamar said, stirring a slice of lemon around in his tea.

"Oh Jan, wait till you hear this." Emma leaned forward, eager to share with Jan. "You won't believe it, but we had an alligator in our backyard. Lamar should probably be the one to tell you about it, though, since he was out back when the gator was discovered."

Jan's eyes widened. "Wow, really? What happened?"

Emma watched Jan's expression as Lamar described the incident, including that he'd been thinking it was a robbery in progress. Hearing about that morning all over again made her feel as though it had happened to someone else instead of right in their own yard. Emma smiled as Lamar ended his story by telling how Jake and Rusty captured and relocated animals for a living.

"I'll give it to those two men," Lamar said, shaking his head, "because they sure knew what they were doing and handled the situation with ease. I could never have done that."

"Wow!" Jan exclaimed. "You were lucky those guys showed up when they did, and doubly fortunate it wasn't a robbery."

"I couldn't agree with you more," Emma said. "Everything turned out fine for all of us. Even for the alligator, since it was removed safely and relocated."

"You'll have to show me where the alligator was," Jan said. "I'd like to go out and look at your fruit trees, too. Never saw a lemon tree before."

"Neither had we till we came to Florida, and we have an orange tree, too." Emma took a handful of chips and placed them on her plate. "Oh, and that's not all the excitement, either. The other day one of our neighbors told us that the robbers had been caught, so that was a big relief."

"I'm glad you're both safe," Jan said, gulping down the rest of his tea.

"So are we," Emma agreed.

"We'll take a walk outside after lunch," Lamar said. "So, what's new in Shipshe, Jan?"

"Not a whole lot, really. Terry and Cheryl are still going out, and. . . Well, I probably shouldn't say anything since nothing's official, but Terry's planning to ask Cheryl to marry him."

Emma clapped her hands. "Oh, that is good news! I hope they don't get married this winter, though. We'd love to be there for the wedding."

"Since he hasn't even asked her yet, it's not likely they'd tie the knot before spring, or it could even be summer or fall." Jan grabbed a few more chips.

"What about some of our other quilting students?" Emma questioned as she poured Jan more tea. "Do you have news on any of them?"

"Yep. Paul and Carmen got married a few weeks ago."

"We knew about that, because we got an invitation to their wedding," Emma said. "I just hope they understood why we couldn't be there."

"I'm sure they did." Jan swiped his napkin over his mouth where some mayonnaise had stuck to his lip. "Oh, and another bit of news. Blaine got engaged to Sue, and he'll soon be opening his own fishing tackle store."

Emma looked over at Lamar and smiled. "It's good hearing such happy news about people who have come to our classes, isn't it?"

"Jah, it sure is," Lamar agreed. He pointed to the potato chips. "If you don't mind passing me the bag, Jan, think I'll have a few, after all."

"Have you heard anything from Stuart and Pam Johnston?" Emma asked.

Jan shook his head. "But I did see Ruby Lee a week ago, Sunday, when Star and I went to church."

"How's she doing?" Emma asked.

"Great. Things are going well at her husband's church, and they've been getting even more new people."

"I'm glad to hear that." Emma got up from the table and returned with a plate of raisin molasses cookies. "Are you ready for dessert?" she asked, placing the cookies in front of Jan.

"Sure thing!" he took three and plopped them on his plate.

"Did Emma tell you that we're teaching another quilting class?" Lamar asked.

Jan's mouth formed an O. "Really? Here in this house?"

"That's right," Emma said. "This place is much smaller than our home in Indiana, but we've been hosting our classes in the dining room, and it's working out just fine. We'll be having our third class this Saturday."

"Well, I'll be sure to make myself scarce," Jan said after he'd eaten the cookies. "Sure don't wanna be in the way while you're teachin'."

"Don't worry about that," Emma said. "You're welcome to join us if you want. You could share your own quilting experience with our new class."

Jan shook his head. "Think I'll pass on that, but I will have another cookie. These are sure good."

Emma smiled. "Thanks. They're one of Lamar's favorites."

Jan thumped his stomach. "I can already see that I'll have to go on a diet after this trip. You're too good of a cook, Emma."

She felt the heat of a blush on her cheeks. "You're just being nice."

"No, it's the truth."

Emma looked forward to having Jan stay with them over the next couple of weeks. It would be like old times, even if he didn't sit in on any of their quilting classes.

Randy had spent the morning job hunting again, this time in Bradenton, with no prospects at all. The longer he went without a job, the more discouraged he felt. *Maybe I should call my brother and see if he can help us out,* he thought as he thrust his hands into his pants pocket and ambled down the sidewalk. *But if I did that, it'd be like admitting defeat. I'll find something soon; I just have to.*

As Randy turned the corner, heading back to his pickup, he spotted a baby crib in one of the store windows. Pink and blue balloons waved in the breeze, as if welcoming customers inside. A big banner hung above the store's entrance, advertising a sale, including some merchandise at 50 percent off.

Think I'll go in and take a look around, he decided. *Maybe I'll find something nice that's been marked down.*

Entering the store, Randy meandered around, checking out all the baby things—several styles of cribs, playpens, car seats, strollers, and even some musical mobiles. Their baby girl would need all of those things.

He walked over to study the cribs. He'd never realized there were so many types. There were convertible cribs in all different wood grain selections. Some even had changing tables attached. There were also portable cribs, mini-cribs, and the usual standard crib.

Randy stood there smiling. He really liked the convertible crib, crafted in a deep cherry, like it was made for a princess. But that one was way overpriced. Another crib caught his eye, with a big "half price" sign attached. It was all white, and he realized it would work just as well as the more expensive one. He could just picture his beautiful baby girl lying in that crib, sleeping soundly and sucking her thumb.

While contemplating the different cribs, Randy came to the conclusion that a convertible crib would be more cost effective. When needed, the crib could be switched into a toddler bed. That way they wouldn't have to buy another piece of furniture when the baby was old enough to go from a crib to a bed. It was like buying two beds in one and would save them money in the long run.

Once he'd decided on the white crib, he spotted a matching dresser that could also be used as a changing table. A pink teddy bear sat in the crib, just beckoning him to buy it. After Randy put the bear in his cart, he wrote the item numbers down for the crib and dresser so he could tell the sales clerk after he'd finished shopping.

As he made his way around the store, Randy saw many other neat things. He picked out two sets of sheets for the crib—one with teddy bears and the other a plain pink. He spotted a mobile with different animals dangling from the center, and that also went into his shopping cart. Then he found a car seat, stroller, and a wind-up swing to put the baby in.

What kid wouldn't love that? Randy thought before he noticed a clerk and told her the item numbers of the furniture he wanted to purchase. He was going to love being a daddy, and no matter how hard he had to work, he'd make sure his daughter wanted for nothing. Of course, that would all depend on him finding a job.

Randy's hand slipped into his pocket, and after pulling out his wallet, he removed a credit card and approached the checkout line. *I may not have a job or any extra cash right now, but I can charge all the things our daughter will need. Maybe by the time the bill comes, I'll have found a job.*

CHAPTER 17

For the past hour, Jennifer had been sitting at the kitchen table, going over their bills and trying to balance their checkbook. Even with the small amount they had left in their savings plus Randy's unemployment check, their money wouldn't last long. It was a good thing they hadn't charged anything lately, because their credit card was close to being maxed out. *If Randy could just find a job,* she thought. *This is not a good time for us to be bringing a baby into the world. If I'd only known eight-and-a-half months ago that we'd be going through financial struggles like this. . .*

"Come see what I bought today, honey!" Randy shouted from the living room.

Jennifer jumped. She'd been so busy fretting about their finances that she hadn't even heard him come in. If he'd bought something, maybe that meant he'd found a job.

When Jennifer stepped into the living room, she halted, barely able to believe her eyes. There was baby stuff everywhere!

"What did you do, win the lottery?" she asked, with her mouth gaping open.

He grinned widely. "'Course not, sweetie. I'm not that lucky. I never win anything."

"Then how. . ."

"I used my credit card to buy these things for the baby."

"What?" Jennifer shouted as her hands started to shake. "How could you do something so foolish? Don't you care that we're already in debt up to our necks?"

Randy dropped his gaze to the floor. "I want our child to have new things, and I just thought. . . ."

"Well, you thought wrong. I've spent the last hour trying to juggle our bills and pay the ones that are overdue, and we certainly can't afford to add anything more to our credit card. As nice as all this looks, you'll have to take everything back."

"But Jennifer, the baby will be here in a few weeks, and we need to be ready. Don't you want to see what all I bought?"

"No, I don't, and we can't afford any of it. As I said the other day, we can look for some used furniture and other baby things and only get what we absolutely need." Jennifer's tone softened when she saw the look of disappointment on her husband's face. "Even if you found a job tomorrow, we wouldn't have enough money for all this. We have too many bills that need to be paid." She moved closer to Randy and touched his arm. "I'm sorry, but these things really do need to go back."

Randy shuffled his feet a few times, and he finally nodded. "You're right. I made a hasty decision and got carried away. I'll load the stuff into my truck and head back to the store right now."

Mike stared blankly at the magazine he'd picked up, feeling more nervous as each minute ticked by. He'd called his doctor's office yesterday, and since someone had cancelled their appointment, he'd been able to get in this afternoon. Now, as he sat in the waiting room, he'd begun to worry. What if something was seriously wrong? What if he couldn't run his charter boat business any longer due to ill health? How would he provide for Phyllis? But he had to know what was causing him to feel so lousy, and if it was bad news, he'd figure out how to deal with it, just like he always had when he'd been dealt a bad hand. Life was full of ups and downs, disappointments, and unexpected disruptions to one's plans, but that didn't mean a person should give up.

As Mike had learned at an early age from his dad's example, it was how a man handled situations that proved his worth. A guy could whine about the injustices of life, or he could buck up and make the best of the situation.

That's what I'll have to do if the doctor tells me there's something seriously wrong, Mike told himself. *I will not wimp out on my wife, and I won't give in to self-pity because that won't solve a thing.* Still, Mike hoped he didn't have diabetes. How could he possibly give himself a shot if he had to be on insulin? He hated needles, and he liked sweet foods. The last thing he wanted was to be mindful of everything he ate.

"Mr. Barstow, we are ready to see you now."

Mike rose from his seat and followed the nurse into one of the examining rooms. She got his weight, took his vitals, and asked several questions about the symptoms he'd been having. Then she left Mike alone in the room to wait for the doctor.

Several minutes went by, and Mike grew more fidgety. He'd always hated waiting for things. He figured the doctor was busy, but if that was the case, why did the nurse call him in when she did? *If I was missing work on the count of sitting here, I'd be really upset,* he fumed.

Finally, Dr. Ackerman stepped into the room. "It's nice to see you, Mr. Barstow. I hear you're having some problems."

"Yeah." Mike quickly explained about the shakiness, sweating, and dizziness he'd experienced, and ended by saying that with each episode, he'd felt better after eating.

"The first thing I'm going to do is order some blood tests, and I'll also do a physical today." The doctor filled out a lab form and handed it to Mike. "Get this done in the morning, and go in fasting. Don't eat or drink anything but water after midnight tonight. I want to check your blood sugar level, among other things. Oh, and please stop at the front desk on your way out and make an appointment to see me the middle of next week. Your lab work should be back by then." He motioned to the examining table. "Have a seat up there, and I'll check you out."

Mike did as he asked. No matter how things turned out, he was not saying anything to Phyllis about this until he had to. There was no point in worrying her about something she could do nothing about.

Sure wish I didn't have to return all this stuff, Randy fumed as he entered the store. *But I know Jennifer's right; we really can't afford to get any further in debt. She's probably still mad at me for doing something so stupid.*

"I need to return everything I bought earlier today," Randy told the salesclerk who had waited on him earlier.

"You're kidding, right?" She squinted, looking at Randy as if he'd said something horrible. "What's the problem, sir?"

Randy couldn't seem to swallow his pride and admit that he couldn't afford these things. There was no way he'd own up to that. "Uh. . .well, a funny thing happened," he stammered, trying to come up with a good excuse. "See, when I got back home, my wife was all excited and said she'd just gotten a phone call from her parents." Since the clerk didn't know

Randy or Jennifer, or any of their families for that matter, he continued to add to the story. "My in-laws are coming to see us soon, and they said they'd be bringing all sorts of things for the baby, including furniture." Randy coughed, and then feeling his face heat up, he added, "So, until I see what they're bringing us, there's no point in me keeping any of these items. Sorry about that."

"Come with me then," the clerk said in a tone of irritation. "I'll start the refund process." Suddenly, the clerk stopped and swung around, causing Randy to almost bump into her. "I hope you remembered to bring your receipt, because we can't do a refund without it."

"I did; it's right here." Randy held up the yellow slip. "Oh, and I'm gonna need some help bringing in the bigger items that are out in my truck."

"I'll call someone to help you with that." The clerk's furrowed brows let Randy know she was anything but pleased about this.

For cryin' out loud, Randy fumed. *I'm sure I'm not the first customer who's ever brought anything back.*

As Randy headed out the door, he caught sight of a sign telling about a contest to win some free baby things, including furniture. He was surprised he hadn't seen it before. Could he have walked right past it? Or maybe the contest hadn't been posted until after he'd left the store earlier today.

Guess it wouldn't hurt for me to fill out the form and enter the contest, he decided. *Although I don't know why; I've never won anything before.*

Randy stopped, filled out the form, and dropped it into the box. *Maybe I should have chewed some gum and stuck it on my entry form,* he thought. *That way, whoever draws the winning name would be more apt to pull mine out 'cause it'd probably stick to his finger.*

Randy shook his head. *Now that was a crazy thought, and it'd be cheating, besides. What's come over me, anyway? First I made up a lie to the salesclerk about why I returned all the baby stuff, and now I'm thinking of how to cheat my way into winning a drawing. I need to get a grip.*

CHAPTER 18

"How about I take you two out for supper tonight?" Jan suggested as he, Lamar, and Emma sat on the front porch, enjoying the sunshine late Thursday afternoon.

"Oh, you don't have to do that," said Emma. "I'm more than happy to fix supper for us here."

"You've already provided several meals since I got here, not to mention letting me stay in your spare room," Jan reminded them.

"We're happy to do it." Lamar turned to Emma. "Aren't we?"

She bobbed her head. "Most definitely."

"Even so, I'd like to treat you folks to a meal out once in a while, and unless you've already got something started for supper, we can start by going out tonight."

Emma reached over and patted Jan's hand. "Alright then, if you insist. So, where would you like to go?"

"That's up to you," Jan replied. "I haven't been here long enough to know of any good places to eat. Do you guys have a favorite restaurant?" He patted his stomach and chuckled. "As you might guess, I enjoy most any kind of food."

"We could go to the restaurant up the street, where Kim and Anna work," Lamar suggested.

"Who are Kim and Anna?" Jan wanted to know.

"Anna is Amish, and she's from one of our earlier quilting classes—the one your friend Terry was in."

"Oh yeah. If I remember right, Anna moved down here with a friend."

"That's correct. She's working as a waitress at a restaurant nearby. Kim is one of my current quilting students." Emma smiled. "Oh, and she's single and drives a motorcycle. She's also quite pretty, so you might be interested in meeting her."

Jan shook his head. "Naw, I don't think so, Emma. I'm gettin' along just fine without a woman to complicate my life."

"*Wie geht's*, Lamar and Emma?" an elderly Amish man asked, interrupting their conversation as he approached, leading a small dog on a leash.

Lamar waved. "Hello, Abe. We're doing fine. How are you?"

"Doin' as well as any eighty-year-old can." Abe grinned. "I've been meaning to stop by. Thought maybe we could head over to Pinecraft Park for a game of shuffleboard some time."

"Sounds good to me," Lamar responded with a nod.

"Heard you had a gator in your yard."

"Jah. It was quite an experience. When we get together for shuffleboard, I'll tell you all about it." Lamar motioned to Jan. "Abe, this is our good friend, Jan Sweet. He's from our hometown in Shipshewana, and he'll be staying with us for a while."

"Pleased to meet you, Jan." Abe nodded as his little beagle hound yanked on the leash.

Jan gave a saluting wave. "Same here."

"Don't blame you for coming down south to get away from the cold weather. My wife, Linda, and I come from Ohio, and we just couldn't take the cold winters anymore. So five years ago, we sold everything and moved to sunny Florida." Abe grinned and gave his full gray beard a quick tug. "We've never regretted it, neither."

"I'll bet, too," Lamar said with a nod. "Emma and I probably won't sell our home in Shipshe, but it's nice to know we have a place here where we can spend our winters."

"If I get to likin' this weather too much, I might be tempted to stay in Florida," Jan commented. "I could ride my bike all winter and never have to worry about dealin' with snow. 'Course, I ain't likely to move, since my business and my daughter are in Indiana."

"I see you have a new walking partner, Abe," Emma commented.

He gave a nod. "Jah, that's right."

"That's a cute little dog. What's its name?" Emma questioned.

"This is Button. We just got her yesterday." Abe squatted down and pet the dog's head. "Never thought we'd get another dog, but we used to have a beagle when we lived in Ohio. Shortly before we moved here, old Gus got real sick, and we had to have him put to sleep. It was one of the hardest things Linda and I ever did, and because of it, we vowed never to get another pet. We didn't think we could go through that again, but the longer we've been down here, the more we've missed the fun we had with Gus all those years, so we finally talked ourselves into getting another dog."

"She certainly is cute." Emma giggled, watching Button chew on Abe's shoelaces. "She's so tiny. How old is she, Abe?"

"She's actually ten weeks old, but she's a miniature beagle and won't get as big as most standard beagles." Abe bent down to pick up the pup and stood. Button started licking his face right away. "Linda and I have to get used to a puppy all over again. We kinda forgot, with Gus being so laid back, how rambunctious a little one like this can be."

Everyone laughed as Button tried to grab the brim of Abe's straw hat. "Guess I'd better get going," he said. "As you can see, Button is getting impatient and looking for something to eat. In one day's time the little stinker ruined two pairs of my socks." Abe's chest moved rhythmically as he chuckled. "I suppose it could be a good thing, though. Linda won't have to get after me to pick up my things. Anyway, it's good seeing you, Emma and Lamar, and we'll get together soon." He looked over at Jan and smiled. "Nice meeting you."

"Likewise," Jan responded.

"Tell your wife I said hello," Emma called as Abe, carrying the puppy, headed down the road.

"Looks to me like that pup's got his master eating out of the palm of his hand." Lamar laughed. "I think Button has won my friend Abe's heart."

"He seems like a nice neighbor," Jan commented. "Are all the folks here in Pinecraft as friendly as Abe?"

"Pretty much," Emma said. "This is a good neighborhood, and it's a comfort to know there are dependable people who'll keep an eye on our place here when we're back home in Indiana."

"Too bad you couldn't train an alligator to be a watchdog," Jan teased. "You'd never have to worry about being robbed, that's for sure."

"You've got that right." Emma snickered. "Well, how about we head to the restaurant now? It's close enough that we can walk, and I don't know about you men, but my stomach's starting to growl."

"My appetite is growing, too," Lamar said, getting up and folding his chair.

"I was hoping you'd say that," Jan agreed. "Let's go have us a nice evening, and as you Amish like to say, 'Let's eat ourselves full!'"

Goshen

Star paced the living-room floor, fretting because she hadn't heard from her dad, other than one brief call after he'd arrived in Sarasota. She'd left him a couple of messages, but he hadn't returned any of her calls. Wasn't he checking his voice mail? And what all was he doing down there? Surely he would have caught up on visiting with Emma and Lamar by now.

She slapped the side of her head. *What was I thinking? I should have gotten the Millers' phone number from Dad before he left home. Think I'm gonna try calling his cell number again, 'cause I'm getting tired of waiting around and worrying that something might have happened to him.*

Star grabbed her cell phone and punched in her dad's number, frowning when she got his voice mail again.

"Dad, this is Star. I've been trying to call you, and I don't know why you haven't responded. Please call me back as soon as you can."

Star clicked off and sank into a chair. *This wouldn't be happening if I'd gone to Florida with Dad. Sure hope everything's okay. If I don't hear something from him soon, I'm gonna ditch my job and hop on the next plane to Sarasota.*

Sarasota

"How are things going with you?" Anna Lambright asked as she passed Kim on the way to the kitchen to pick up an order.

"Well, I've only dropped one plate and spilled a glass of milk so far, but other than that, things are going great," Kim replied with a grin. "I'm surprised no one's complained to the boss about me being such a klutz."

Anna touched Kim's arm. "I'm sure the customers know you don't do it on purpose. Besides, you're so polite and friendly to everyone, and that goes a long ways."

"I hope you're right, because I can't afford to lose this job."

"Me neither." Anna inhaled deeply. "The last thing I want is to feel forced to go home and listen to my folks say, 'I told you so.'"

"Are they still giving you a hard time about being down here?"

"They've let up for now, but I think it's because Emma called and had a talk with my mom," Anna said. "It's sad to say, but Mom and Dad will listen to Emma before they will me. They've never given me much credit for doing the right thing or being able to take care of myself."

"I think a lot of parents are like that when it comes to their young people getting out on their own."

"Don't they want us to have our own lives? I mean, shouldn't I have the right to make decisions and choose where I want to live?"

Kim nodded. "I think everyone deserves that privilege."

They reached the kitchen, and their conversation ended as they both picked up their orders.

Kim had just served a middle-aged couple their meal, when she turned to her right and saw Emma and Lamar Miller seated at a booth.

She blinked rapidly, unable to believe her eyes. Sitting across from them was the biker she'd met on the beach! *What in the world are they doing with him?* Well, she would know soon enough, because that was one of her tables.

Jan studied the menu they'd been given when they'd first sat down. There were so many choices, but his gaze kept going back to the buffet island to his left. He'd scoped it out on the way in and decided that if he didn't find something he liked better on the menu he'd go for the buffet. In addition to several kinds of meat, it offered mashed potatoes, scalloped potatoes, stuffing, a pasta dish, three vegetable choices, and everything one needed to build a hearty salad. Jan had eyeballed a couple of dessert items on the buffet, too, so he knew there was no chance of him leaving here hungry. Unless he used some restraint, he figured he'd be miserable when he walked out the door.

"Emma. Lamar. It's good to see you."

Jan jerked his head at the sound of a woman's voice. He looked away from the menu, and when he recognized the cute little blond he'd met on the beach, his mouth dropped open.

"We were hoping you might be working tonight," Emma said, smiling at their waitress. She turned to Jan and said, "This is Kim Morris, one of our quilting students. Kim, I'd like you to meet our good friend, Jan Sweet."

Kim stood several seconds, staring at Jan like he had two heads. "You—you're that guy I met on the beach."

He nodded. "Sure never expected to see you again. How's your dog?"

Kim's lips compressed. "Maddie is fine. And for your information, I take good care of her."

Jan shrugged. "Never said you didn't. I was just pointing out that—"

"Do you two know each other?" Lamar interrupted.

"Sort of," Jan mumbled. "We met on the beach the first day I got here. I had no idea you and Emma knew her, though."

"How do you know the Millers?" Kim asked, looking at Jan with a curious expression.

"I took Emma's quilting classes before she and Lamar were married."

Kim blinked. "Really? I'm surprised that—"

"That someone like me would want to learn how to quilt?"

Kim's face reddened. "Well, you don't exactly seem like the type."

Jan snickered. "There's a lot about me that I'm sure would surprise you."

"Jan is staying at our place while he's here on vacation," Emma said. "So I'm sure you two will have a chance to get better acquainted."

Jan jiggled his eyebrows, feeling kind of playful all of a sudden. Remembering back to last fall when Terry had taken Emma's quilting class so he could get to know Cheryl and ask her for a date, Jan was beginning to understand his friend's reasoning. But he could see from Kim's disgruntled expression that the last thing she wanted was to get to know him better. Well, like it or not, she'd better get used to the idea, because come Saturday, Jan planned to stick around and be part of the quilting class.

CHAPTER 19

J an knew the quilt class would be starting soon, so he decided to check his voice mail before the students arrived. "Stupid phone! How did all these messages get on here without me knowing it?" Jan muttered to himself. He was surprised to find that most of them were from Star. Feeling guilty when he heard how upset she was, he gave her a call. When he got her voice mail, he figured she was probably at work, so he left a message. "Hi, Star, it's me. Sorry I missed all your calls. I just discovered that my phone was muted, so I never heard it ring. Haven't checked my messages for a few days, either. I've been staying with Emma and Lamar. They have a spare room and said they were glad to have me here with them. We've been having a great time catching up on things."

Jan was tempted to mention that he'd met Kim, but decided against it. He didn't even know Kim that well, and if he told Star that he planned to hang around during the quilting class in order to get to know Kim, she'd probably tease him. *If my buddy Terry knew, he'd give me a hard time about it, that's for sure.* There'd be no end to Terry's ribbing.

Slipping his cell phone into his jeans pocket, Jan stepped out of the guest room and joined Emma and Lamar in the dining room. "All ready for the quilting class?" he asked, looking at the colorful quilt Lamar had draped over a wooden rack.

"Yes, we sure are," Emma replied. "So what are your plans for the day?"

Jan pulled his fingers through the ends of his beard. "If you don't mind, think I'd like to stick around during the class."

Emma's fingers touched her parted lips. "Really, Jan? I thought you didn't want to sit in on the class."

Yeah, but that was before I knew the pretty blond I met on the beach was one of your quilting students, Jan mused. Of course, he didn't voice his thoughts.

"Well, I thought it over and changed my mind. Decided it might be kind of fun to meet your new quilting students." Jan wasn't about to admit that the only reason he'd decided to hang around for the class was so he could get to know Kim better. He could barely admit that to himself.

One by one, the students arrived, and Emma watched with curiosity at Jan's eager expression when Kim showed up. Was it possible that he had more than a passing interest in the young woman?

Now, wouldn't that be something? Emma thought. *Jan's friend Terry has a special woman in his life now, and it would be nice if Jan found someone, too. Well, I'd best not meddle. If it's the Lord's will for Jan and Kim to be together, He will put it all in place.*

After everyone had gathered around the table, Emma introduced Jan and explained that he had been one of her first quilting students.

She didn't mention, however, that the reason he had come to her class was because his probation officer had suggested it as a creative outlet. If Jan wanted to share that information, it was up to him.

"How do you like it here in sunny Florida?" Mike asked, looking at Jan.

"It's great! I'm likin' the warmth, not to mention the company." Jan winked at Emma and grinned at Lamar. Then he cast a quick look in Kim's direction and smiled at her, too. "So far, I've met some real nice people."

"How long are you planning to stay?" Noreen questioned.

"My daughter, Star, is planning to join me when her vacation starts in two weeks, and we'll probably hang around another week or two after that."

"What about your wife? Will she be coming to Sarasota, too?" Kim questioned.

Jan shook his head. "Don't have a wife. Star's mom and me split up over twenty years ago, when Star was less than a year old."

"Oh, I see." Kim turned to Emma. "What are we going to do on our quilting projects today?"

"You'll continue to sew your pieces of fabric together, and then I'll show you how to cut out the batting," Emma replied. "While you're waiting your turn to use a sewing machine, you can either talk with Lamar about some of the other quilt patterns he's designed or visit among yourselves."

"I've come up with several new ideas for patterns recently," Lamar said, rubbing his hands together. "I think my trips to the beach are giving me inspiration to create some new designs."

"I feel that way, too," B.J. interjected. "Only my designs are on canvas."

"So you're an artist?" Jan questioned.

B.J. nodded. "When I was a boy, my dad used to brag about my artistic abilities, and my mother said I was born with a paintbrush in my hand."

Jan chuckled. "My folks always said I was born to ride a motorcycle 'cause I liked my first bike with training wheels so much."

Kim perked right up. "Is that your Harley I saw parked in the driveway?"

"You bet it is."

"Kim has a motorcycle, too," Emma said, even though she'd already mentioned that fact to Jan.

Jan blinked his eyes rapidly, then a slow smile spread across his face. "That's cool! Do you mind if I go out and take a look at it right now?"

Kim hesitated at first, but then she said, "Guess that'd be okay. Since Noreen, B.J., and Erika are using the sewing machines right now, I'll go check out your bike, too." Kim looked at Emma. "Is that okay with you?"

"I have no objections at all," Emma said.

Jan jumped up, and Kim did the same, then they both rushed out the door.

Emma couldn't help feeling pleased. Maybe there was some hope for Jan and Kim to become a couple. They had their bikes in common, at least.

"That's sure a nice bike," Jan said, after he'd checked out Kim's black Harley with pink stripes. "I see you even have a helmet to match. That's pretty cool!"

"Your bike is nice, too," she said, motioning to Jan's black-and-silver motorcycle. "It's bigger than mine and looks like it'd be good for long road trips."

"Yeah, and since there's room enough for two, sometimes Star rides with me. She has her own bike, but I decided to add a sissy bar to mine.

That way when she or someone else rides with me, it's more comfortable for their back."

They talked motorcycle stuff for a while, and then Jan gathered up his nerve and asked if Kim would like to get a bite to eat with him after class. "We could either ride our own bikes, or double up on mine. Maybe we could grab a burger and fries at a fast-food place and then head to the beach."

Kim looked up at him, tucking a stray piece of blond hair behind her ear. "I—I don't know about that. . . ."

"Do you have other plans for this afternoon?"

"No, not really, but if I went I'd have to take my own bike. So when we got ready to leave the beach I could just head straight home rather than coming all the way back here to get my bike. I'd have to keep my eye on the time because of Maddie, too. It's bad enough that she's home by herself when I'm at work, and I hate leaving her in the outside pen too long, because she barks, which irritates the neighbors."

Jan grunted. "I can relate to that. But it's better to have the dog penned up than running around the neighborhood causing trouble. I went through that with my dog already and almost lost him because he took off from the yard. So I finally had to pen him up while I was at work, and it's been much better that way."

"That's true for Maddie, too." Kim glanced at her watch. "I can't believe we've been out here almost thirty minutes. I didn't realize we'd been talking that long."

"Sorry," Jan apologized. He resisted the temptation to reach out and twirl Kim's fallen curl around his index finger. Tucking his hands in his jeans pocket, he said, "It's probably my fault, for flappin' my gums. Sure hope I didn't cause you to miss anything important in there."

"I'm sure it's fine," Kim said. "It's most likely my turn to use one of the sewing machines, though."

"Uh, before we go inside, you never really did say if you'll go to the beach and have lunch with me today."

"Sure, why not?" she said with a nod.

As they turned and headed for the house, Jan couldn't keep from smiling all the way. He was anxious for the class to be over so he and Kim could be on their way. He'd never imagined coming to Florida and meeting someone like her. Things like this just didn't happen to him. Of course, he figured nothing would come of it—not with them living several states apart. Besides, Kim would probably turn out to be like all the other women Jan had dated—a passing fancy.

CHAPTER 20

How are you feeling today?" Lamar asked Mike as he sat at the table, waiting his turn to use one of the sewing machines.

Mike shrugged. "I'm okay, I guess. Better than last week. But then I've been eating regular meals, which I think has helped."

"That's good to hear," Lamar said. "You gave us all a pretty good scare when you got dizzy and shaky last Saturday."

"Yeah, I had another spell at home, so I made an appointment and got in to see my doctor within a few days."

"How did that go?"

"The doc said he wasn't able to give me a diagnosis yet, but he did a thorough exam and sent me to get some blood tests. I should know something when I go in next week."

"It's good that you went," Lamar said. "Emma and I will be anxious to hear the results of your tests, and I certainly hope it's nothing serious. Of course, we'll be praying for you, Mike."

"Thanks." Mike couldn't believe Lamar's concern. Most people who didn't know a person that well probably wouldn't have even thought to ask how he was doing, much less offered to pray for him. Mike was beginning to realize that Emma and Lamar were caring people who lived their religion and showed it to others by what they said and did.

Maybe when Phyllis gets home, the two of us ought to start going to church, he decided. *She's mentioned it a few times, but I've always been too tired or too busy to go. Between now and then, it probably wouldn't hurt if I said a few prayers of my own, 'cause I'm nervous about the outcome of my blood tests.*

"Sorry for taking so long," Kim apologized to Emma after she and Jan had returned to the house. "We got a little carried away talking about our bikes."

"That's okay," Emma said. "The machines are free now, and you're just in time to start sewing."

Kim smiled. "Oh good. I'll get right at it then."

While Kim went to one of the sewing machines, Jan meandered over to the table where B.J. sat with Noreen and Erika. He seemed genuinely interested in what they were doing. Though she resisted the idea, Kim had to admit, there was something about Jan that intrigued her.

I can't believe I agreed to go out with him after class, Kim thought as she took her seat at the sewing machine. *I barely know Jan, and since he's not from around here, there's no chance of us ever getting to really know each other or develop a relationship. Maybe that's for the best,* she decided. *Less chance of any romantic involvement that could lead to another dead end for me. Well, I've already said yes to his invitation, so I may as well go and try to enjoy the afternoon.*

Kim started working on her quilt squares, and at the same time, she thought about the day she'd met Jan on the beach and how irritated she had been when he said she ought to keep an eye on her dog. But after visiting with him outside by their bikes, she'd seen him in a different light and actually found herself yearning to know him better, even though he would be leaving in a few weeks.

I can't worry about this right now, Kim told herself. *I need to concentrate on making my wall hanging.*

At eleven o'clock, Emma suggested that everyone take a break for refreshments.

"What'd you fix for us today?" Mike asked. "I hope it's not oranges again."

Emma shook her head. "I made a couple of strawberry pies, and there's also a fruit platter with strawberries, bananas, and grapes."

"Guess to be safe, I'd better stick to the fruit and leave the pies alone," Mike said.

"That's good thinking." Lamar gave Mike's shoulder a squeeze.

"While I'm getting the refreshments, the rest of you can visit or keep working on your squares," Emma said, starting for the kitchen door.

"I'll help you with that." Jennifer left her seat and followed Emma to the kitchen.

"How did your week go?" Emma asked as she took the pies from the refrigerator. "Did your husband find a job yet?"

Jennifer's shoulder drooped as she slowly shook her head. "Randy's getting really discouraged, and he proved that when he did something totally out of character the other day."

"What happened?"

"He charged up a bunch of furniture and other things for the baby that we really can't afford."

"Oh dear." Emma placed the pies on the table. "How will you pay for everything if he doesn't find a job soon?"

"Even if Randy found a job today, we'd have a long ways to go in catching up with our bills. But we don't have to worry about paying for the baby things, because I insisted that he return them." Jennifer sank into a chair and lowered her head. "I felt bad for him. He seemed so proud and happy when he showed me what he'd gotten for the baby. This whole situation with him being out of work is taking a toll on our marriage."

Emma remained silent as she let Jennifer continue.

"I couldn't let even more money problems get in the way of us trying to keep it all together. If I wasn't due to have a baby in a few weeks, I'd go back to the styling salon where I used to work, but even if I could, I wouldn't make enough to support us and the baby."

Emma placed her hands on Jennifer's trembling shoulders. "I know it isn't much, but I have a box of food I want to send home with you today."

"I appreciate it," Jennifer said tearfully, "but I'm not sure how Randy will respond to that. He'll probably see it as a handout, because he's too proud to admit that we need help."

"Would you like me to ask Lamar to speak to your husband?"

Jennifer sniffed. "That might help—if Randy's willing to listen." She paused and wiped her nose on a tissue she'd pulled from her pocket. "You know, Emma, when I got home from your class last week and showed Randy the fruit and cookies you'd sent home with me, he said he'd like to have you and Lamar for supper sometime to say thanks for your kindness."

Emma flapped her hand. "What we did was nothing big, and no thanks is needed."

"But if you came for supper, it would give Lamar a chance to talk to Randy," Jennifer said.

Emma nodded slowly. "You might be right about that. If you'll let us know what night would work best for you, we'll plan to be there."

"Any night this week should be fine. Why don't we make it Friday?"

"Friday would be good for us," Emma responded.

Jennifer tapped her fingers along the edge of the table. "I hate to even ask this, but do you think your friend Jan would feel bad if he wasn't included? It's not that I would mind having him," she quickly added. "I just don't think Randy would open up to Lamar if someone else was there."

"I understand," Emma said. "And I'm sure Jan won't mind fending for himself that evening. Maybe he'll even have a date by then."

"This pie is sure good, Emma," Jan said as everyone sat around the table, enjoying the refreshments Emma had provided.

"Thanks, I'm glad you like it." Emma looked over at Noreen, and her gaze came to rest on the green scarf she'd worn around her head in turban fashion today. Emma had been tempted to ask about it but didn't want to be rude.

Perhaps Noreen couldn't get her hair to look the way she wanted this morning, Emma thought. *Maybe she had what I've heard some Englishers call a bad hair day. Well, it's Noreen's right to wear whatever she wants. After all, I wear my head covering, and no one here has questioned me about it.*

"Tell us more about your artwork, B.J.," Lamar said. "Are you self-taught, or have you had professional lessons?"

"I painted and drew pictures on my own throughout my childhood and teen years," B.J. said, "but after high school I went to college and majored in art."

"What school did you go to?" Erika asked. It was the first time today that she'd joined in the conversation.

"The college was in New York," B.J. replied.

"So is that where you're originally from?" Erika questioned.

B.J. shook his head. "I grew up in Columbus, Ohio."

"Did you say 'Columbus'?" Noreen asked with a curious expression.

"That's right, but after I graduated from college, I didn't move back home. Took a job as an art teacher in Chicago, which is where I still live."

"What a coincidence," Noreen said. "My sister and I grew up in Columbus."

"Really?" B.J. reached for a cluster of grapes.

"That's right. We lived on the north side of town."

B.J.'s eyebrows lifted. "That's interesting. So did I."

"I'm curious," Noreen said, leaning slightly forward. "What does B.J. stand for?"

"Bruce Jensen," he replied. "But I've gone by B.J. since I was in college, when some of my friends started calling me that."

"Did you say Bruce Jensen?" Noreen's mouth twisted at the corners, and she stared at him as though in disbelief.

He gave a quick nod.

"Did you by any chance have a girlfriend in high school whose name was Judy Hanson?"

B.J.'s face blanched. "Why, yes, I did. What made you ask that question?"

Noreen lips quivered. "Judy was my sister, and you're obviously the man who broke her heart." She pushed back her chair with such force that it nearly toppled to the floor. "I'm sorry, Emma, but I have to go!" Noreen quickly gathered up her things and rushed out the door.

CHAPTER 21

"How many times are you going to clean things in here?" Lamar asked as he watched Emma scrub the kitchen counters. "I think they're clean enough, don't you?"

"You're right, Lamar, but staying busy helps when something's on my mind."

"And what would that be?"

Emma dropped the sponge into the sink and turned to face him. "I'm upset with how things turned out today, and I'm beginning to think we'll never be able to help any of our students."

"Now don't you go thinkin' negative thoughts like that," Lamar said with a shake of his head. "Things aren't really that bad."

"Are you serious?" Emma leaned against the counter and folded her arms. "Not only is Erika still being very negative, but Jennifer shared with me how depressed her husband has become because he's still unemployed. All I could do was offer her some food."

"I'm sure she appreciated it, Emma."

"I know, but it just didn't seem like enough. I don't have any answers for her, and I wish we could do more."

"Well, you said Jennifer invited us to their house for supper on Friday night, so maybe we can take them another box of food."

"That's a good idea, and I'm sure it will help some." Emma sighed deeply. "I'm also worried about Mike. I could see how anxious he was about his health, yet he wouldn't really open up and share his fears."

"He talked some to me," Lamar informed her. "I think he'll feel better once he gets the results of his blood test next week."

"I hope it's nothing serious," Emma said. "And with his wife away, I'm sure Mike feels even worse."

"You're probably right," Lamar agreed. "I told Mike we'd be praying for him."

"That's good, Lamar. We also need to pray for B.J. and Noreen. He looked devastated when Noreen yelled at him, and she seemed terribly upset when she ran out of our home."

Lamar tugged on his ear. "I wonder what was up with that."

"Apparently B.J. did something to hurt Noreen's sister, and Noreen's angry about it." Emma slowly shook her head. "We've never had a class like this, Lamar. Everyone has a problem, but no one seems willing to say much about it, or ask for our help."

"They don't need to ask," Lamar reminded. "We just need to be there and offer our support. Remember all the other classes? Even though we had our doubts at first, in the end, things turned out for the best."

"That's true, and I have to remember that God seldom swoops down and fixes everything. Some things take time, and people need to be willing to allow Him to help them cope and manage their problems."

"Well said. And you know, Emma, one good thing did happen today," Lamar commented.

"What was that?"

"I do believe that Jan may have found himself a lady friend."

Emma smiled. "I think you could be right about that."

"What a beautiful day it is to be on the beach," Kim remarked as she and Jan sat on a bench facing the water, eating burgers and fries. "For me, this is the best part of living in Florida, having the gulf and its beaches so close at hand."

"Think I could get used to this kind of life." Jan tossed a fry to a squawking seagull and laughed when three more gulls moved in and tried to grab it.

"If you like it here, why don't you relocate?" Kim asked.

He shook his head. "I can't. I'm a roofer, and my business is in northeast Indiana."

"You could start over. That's what I did when I left my home in Raleigh, North Carolina. Of course, I didn't have my own business to worry about."

Jan threw several more of his fries on the sand and watched as the hungry birds attacked. "It'd be hard to start over with a new business here. I'd probably have some stiff competition in an area as big as Sarasota and the surrounding towns, and it would take some time to get my name out there."

"I suppose you're right." Kim finished her burger and leaned back with eyes closed and head tilted toward the sun. "My advice is to enjoy every moment of your vacation. By the time you leave, you'll be nice and relaxed and probably go home with a really nice tan."

Jan gave no reply. He didn't give a rip about getting tan or being relaxed.

When he'd first met Kim on the beach with her dog, he'd been intrigued. Now, he just wanted to spend the time he had left in Sarasota getting to know the perky little blond sitting next to him. He couldn't take his eyes off her, and almost choked on a french fry, seeing Kim's face lifted toward the sun. Her smooth tan skin and those long, thick eyelashes lying against her cheeks were almost his undoing. Her silky hair coming loose from behind her ears and gently bobbing with the warm breezes made him wish once again that he could wrap a strand of it around his finger.

"Are you all right?" Kim asked when she opened her eyes. "You're looking at me strangely."

Jan coughed and swallowed to regain his composure. "Yep, I'm just fine. Those dumb seagulls made me laugh and I almost choked." *Boy, did that sound stupid,* he thought. *But I couldn't come right out and tell her the truth.*

"Yes, they are crazy birds." Kim pointed toward the water. "Would you look at that?"

"What is it?" he asked.

"There's a dog out there, standing on a paddle board, and a woman is pushing it along." She giggled. "Don't think I've ever seen anything like that before."

Jan smiled. "Guess it takes all kinds."

"You're right. That's what makes the world such an interesting place." Kim closed her eyes again. "It feels so good to just sit here and soak up the sun. I feel totally relaxed."

"Same here." Jan thought about how he and Kim had ridden their own bikes to Lido Beach, which meant they couldn't visit on the way. It didn't matter, though. Ever since they'd first stepped onto the sand, they'd been talking pretty much nonstop. They'd shared things about their families, jobs, and what kinds of things they enjoyed doing just for fun. Jan couldn't remember when he'd felt this comfortable with a woman—not even with Star's mother, Nancy, whom he'd nicknamed Bunny. He'd only spent part of a day with Kim, and already he felt as if he'd known her for years. He'd been attracted to Nancy physically, but their personalities were as different as fire and ice. Even better, he and Kim had a lot in common. They both owned motorcycles, liked to bowl, enjoyed eating pizza, and ironically, they each owned German shepherds.

What a shame they lived so many miles apart. Why couldn't he have found a gal like Kim back home? Even if they established a friendship while he was here, it would probably end when he returned to Indiana. It would be too hard to have a long-distance relationship. Phone calls weren't the same as spending actual time together.

Appealing as it sounds, I sure can't pull up stakes and move down here, Jan reminded himself as he took a drink of root beer.

"You're awfully quiet," Kim said, opening her eyes. "Are you bored with my company now?"

Jan jerked his head. "What? No! Just the opposite, in fact."

She smiled. "Does that mean you've enjoyed being with me as much as I have you?"

He gave a nod, pleased that she'd said what he'd been thinking.

"Can I ask you something?"

"Sure thing. What do you want to know?"

Kim pointed to his arm—the one with "Bunny" tattooed on it. "I'm curious about that name."

"It's a nickname for someone I used to date—my daughter's mother, in fact." Jan slapped the side of his head. "I didn't have much in the way of brains when I had that tattoo done. Guess I figured I'd spend the rest of my life with Bunny."

"Things don't always turn out the way we think they will," she said.

"Nope, they sure don't."

They sat quietly for a while, watching kids squealing with excitement as they ran out to meet the water, and couples walking hand-in-hand along the sandy beach. Turning to Kim, Jan touched her arm briefly and said, "Would you be willing to go out with me again? Maybe we could go bowling, catch a movie, have another picnic on the beach, or take a ride on our bikes."

"That sounds like fun."

"Which one?" he asked, tipping his head.

"Everything you suggested."

He snapped his fingers. "Great! Let's do all four."

"All in one day?" Her eyebrows lifted.

"Sure, why not? We could start by taking another ride on our bikes and come back here to the beach. We can lie in the sun, splash around in the water, and eat some lunch. Then we can take in an afternoon show and end the day at the bowling alley."

"Whoa now! That all sounds nice, but maybe we should space those things out a bit. I have a job, you know, and don't forget about Maddie. I don't like leaving her alone for long hours."

"Maybe we can do something together on your next day off, and either take Maddie along or just not be gone all day."

"My next day off is tomorrow. Since it's Sunday, the restaurant will be closed, but I did plan on going to church in the morning. Guess I could go to the early service though."

"Would you mind if I tag along?" Jan asked.

"No, not at all. I'd enjoy the company."

"I hope you don't think I'm bein' too pushy," he said, "but since I'll only be here a few weeks before my daughter joins me. . ."

"Oh, that's right. You did say something earlier about her coming here."

"Is that a problem?"

"No, of course not. I'd like to meet her."

He grinned. "And you shall, 'cause I'm sure Star will enjoy meeting you, too."

"Guess what, Randy?" Jennifer asked when she arrived home from class and found him sitting slumped on the front porch.

"I have no idea," he mumbled. "And I don't feel like guessin' neither. Just tell me, okay? I'm not in the mood for guessing games."

"There was a new guy in our class this morning—a friend of Lamar and Emma's. He's a big, rugged-looking biker, and he drove all the way down here from Shipshewana, Indiana."

Randy lifted his head and shrugged. "So, what's that to me?'

"Nothing personal, but I thought you might be interested in hearing about—"

"Sorry, but I'm not."

Jennifer winced. She hated seeing her husband in such a sullen mood. And she didn't have to ask the reason for it. He'd obviously spent the day job hunting and had come up empty-handed again.

"There's a box in the trunk of my car," Jennifer said. "It's a gift from the Millers."

"What'd they give you this time?" he asked, glancing at her car parked in their driveway.

"It's full of food, but I didn't look inside to see what all is in it."

"Humph! You know how much I hate handouts."

"I don't like to accept charity from others, either, but in our situation, we need all the help we can get."

"Yeah, you're right about that. Guess we'd better have them over for supper to show our appreciation. Why don't you give 'em a call and see if they're free to come over one evening this week?"

"Actually, I already invited them. I suggested Friday night, and Emma said that would be fine." Jennifer placed her hands on Randy's shoulders. "We can just keep it simple, okay?"

"Sure, whatever." He rose to his feet. "I'll go get the box out of the car, and then we can figure out what I should fix for our guests."

"I cannot believe the man I thought was so nice is actually my sister's old boyfriend!" Noreen fumed as she drove through town. She had gone shopping after she'd left Emma and Lamar's, like she always did whenever she was upset, but it had only fueled her anger. Seeing herself in the store mirrors, wearing a turban on her head, had only added to her anxiety. She was glad no one had asked her about it at the quilting class. She would have been mortified to admit what she'd done to her hair, let alone allowing them to see the dark color.

The color of my hair is nothing compared to the agony Bruce put my poor sister through when he broke up with her, Noreen told herself. *Didn't he even care that she was carrying his child? Judy was just a teenager, in the prime of her life. She hadn't even finished high school yet.*

Noreen gripped the steering wheel so hard her fingers ached, as the memories from the past flooded her mind. *Apparently all he cared about was running off to college and forgetting his responsibilities to the innocent young woman he'd taken advantage of. And to think, my sister thought she loved that man! If Judy were still alive, I'd make Bruce meet her face-to-face and beg for her forgiveness. But it's too late for that. Thanks to that man, Judy is gone, and I'll never let him meet the child he abandoned before the innocent baby came into this world.*

CHAPTER 22

Erika sat in her wheelchair near the front door, dressed in her church clothes but not wanting to go. She dreaded having people stare at her with pity or worse yet say something they thought would cheer her up. According to Dad, those well-meaning folks had her best interests at heart, but she didn't want their words of encouragement. Even though she was sure they might mean well and want to cheer her up, what they said had the opposite effect.

Last Sunday, while sitting in the greeting area of church waiting for Dad, Erika overhead some of her friends talking about the fun they were having at their high school games. It was basketball season, and being junior varsity cheerleaders, her friends accompanied the team to all of the games.

Erika's first intention was to go over and join them, but after hearing their conversation, she decided against it. Not wishing the girls to see her, she'd repositioned her wheelchair to the corner where a large artificial plant sat. That way she could eavesdrop, while peeking through the plant's dusty leaves, without her friends noticing. It ended up being a mistake, because hearing the excitement in their voices as they chatted about the latest game became painful. But stuck behind the plant, she had no choice but to remain where she was and listen.

So far, their basketball team had an unbeaten season, and the next game was against their biggest rival. They'd never won a game against that school, but maybe this year things would be different. At one time that would have meant something to Erika, but now, she couldn't care less. She dreaded the pep rally the school would have on the afternoon of the approaching game. Because she was in a wheelchair, she'd have to sit conspicuously alongside the bleachers in the gymnasium. The thought of being forced to watch her friends go through their cheering routines made Erika even more miserable. Knowing she should be out there helping to rouse school spirit caused her to feel worthless and apart from everyone else.

Erika closed her eyes, remembering how she and her friends had tried out for the cheering squad. They'd all looked forward to high school with anticipation of what it would it bring, but what happened to her that summer changed everything.

I would have made the squad if not for my diving accident, she thought, opening her eyes.

Erika dreaded going to high school and church. *Sure wish I could get out of going today. I'm so tired of it all.*

When Dad came out of his bedroom, he smiled at Erika and said, "Ready to go?"

She shook her head. "Can't we do something else today? I get tired of going to church every Sunday and seeing the same people with fake smiles on their faces."

Dad's face tightened. "They're not fake smiles, Erika."

"Well, the things they say to me seem phony."

He shook his head. "You're just too sensitive."

She folded her arms. "You would say that. You never agree with me about anything."

"That's not true, and you know it."

She gave no reply. *It wouldn't matter what I said. Dad always thinks he's right.*

"We're not staying home from church," Dad said, "but we can do something fun afterward."

"Like what?"

"How about we go to the beach? It's a beautiful sunny day, and—"

"No thanks. There's nothing for me to do on the beach anymore." Erika frowned. "I can't swim or even play in the sand, and it's no picnic to sit there and watch others have all the fun."

Dad knelt on the floor in front of her chair and took hold of Erika's hands. "I understand how you feel, but—"

"No, you don't." Tears gathered in Erika's eyes, and she blinked, in an attempt to keep them from dripping onto her cheeks. "Everyone says they understand just to try and make me feel better, but nobody with two good legs could possibly know how I feel."

"I'm trying, Erika." Dad patted her arm and stood. "I just wish you could find something that would give you pleasure and bring meaning to your life. I'd hoped the quilting class might do that for you."

She wrinkled her nose in disgust. "Those people are weird, Dad."

He scowled at her. "I know Emma and Lamar dress different than we do, but I don't think they're weird."

"I wasn't talking about them. I meant the other quilting students." Shaking her head, Erika muttered, "Yesterday there was a biker in the class, with a scruffy beard and several tattoos. He's from Indiana, and

I guess he'll be staying with Emma and Lamar for a while."

"Don't be so judgmental, Erika. He might be a nice man."

"Whatever." She turned her wheelchair toward the front door. "If we have to go to church this morning then let's get it over with. There's a new computer game I wanna try out this afternoon."

Dad smiled. "That's good. I'm glad you have something to look forward to."

Erika shrugged.

"Are you sure you don't mind me bringing Maddie along?" Kim asked Jan as they headed to the beach in her little red car, which they had also taken to church.

"Nope. Don't mind a'tall. That way, she won't have to be locked up all day." Maddie lay on the seat between them, and Jan reached over and stroked the dog's head. "My dog, Brutus, likes to go places with me, too, whenever I take my truck. If I had him with me now, I'll bet when we got to the beach he'd have a ball traipsing through the water and be chasin' after every seagull he saw."

"How'd you end up with Brutus?" Kim asked.

"Got him from a friend of mine when he was just a pup. I remember you said you got Maddie at the pound."

"Yeah. I'd read an article in the paper that the Humane Society was asking for help. After breaking up with my boyfriend, I was feeling kind of down and thought doing something helpful might get me out of my mood." Kim paused, noticing that Jan was watching her intently. "I bought a few sacks of dog food to donate, and after arriving at the animal shelter, I ended up looking at all the animals," she continued. "I was shocked to see so many that needed a good home. And well, to make a long story short, Maddie and I seemed to connect, and I felt like

I was saving her life." Kim smiled. "Little did that dog know that she actually saved mine."

"I know exactly what you mean," Jan agreed. "Brutus is almost like family to me."

"Maybe sometime you can come to Florida in your truck and bring your dog along," Kim said, feeling Jan out to see if he had any interest in returning to Sarasota and hoping he did.

"Maybe so, only driving the truck wouldn't be near as much fun as ridin' my bike."

"Tell me more about your daughter," Kim said. "What's she like, and what interests does she have?"

A huge smile spread across Jan's face. "Star's amazing. She sings and plays the guitar. Oh, and she writes most of her own music."

"That's impressive. Has she ever had any of her songs published?"

"Yeah, a couple, but I'm hopin' she'll get a few more breaks, 'cause she's got a talent that deserves to be recognized."

"Sounds like Star is a special young woman. I'm sure you're proud of her."

Jan bobbed his head. "You got that right. Every chance we get, we spend time together."

Kim smiled. Jan might look a bit rough around the edges, but even after knowing him for such a short time, she could tell he had a heart of gold. She'd been surprised yesterday when he'd shared several things about his past, including how Star's mother had run off with her when she was a baby. It was sad to think that Jan had been cheated out of the opportunity to be a father to his only daughter until they'd met by chance during one of Emma's quilting classes.

Kim didn't understand how any mother could have taken her child and run from the child's father, unless they were being abused. Even though she didn't know Jan all that well, she felt sure that wasn't the case. From what Jan had said yesterday, Star's mother was kind of a flake who'd gone from one relationship to another, while Jan had wanted to settle down and raise a family.

I can relate to that, Kim thought with regret. *But none of the men I've dated have had marriage on their mind.* She glanced at Jan out of the corner of her eye as he continued to pet Maddie. *I'd better not get my hopes up about Jan, either, because with the miles between our homes, it's not likely that our relationship will go very far.*

As B.J. sat on a wooden bench at the beach, painting a picture, he thought about Noreen being his ex-girlfriend's older sister. He'd met Noreen a couple of times before she got married and moved away, but Judy had called her sister "Norrie," so he didn't realize her name was actually Noreen. Not that he would have recognized Noreen when they'd met that first day of the quilting class, even if she had used the same first name. B.J. and Noreen had both changed quite a bit over the years.

A sense of regret welled in his soul. He'd almost forgotten about his high school sweetheart until her name was mentioned. B.J. and Judy had been serious about each other back then, and he'd thought he might even marry her someday, but his folks had put an end to the relationship, telling Bruce that he was too young to get serious and that he had his whole life and a career ahead of him. They insisted that he break things off with Judy and sent him away to college. When he came home at the end of his first year, he was surprised to learn that Judy and her family had moved, and no one seemed to know where they'd gone. His folks said it was for the best, that he could do better than a girl like Judy. Well, he'd found a good woman when he met Brenda, who'd later become his wife, but he'd never compared her to Judy. Not until now, at least.

Judy was a lot like B.J.—kind of shy and reserved—and she had a creative side. She wrote poems and short stories, which she'd often shared with him when they were alone. Brenda had been B.J.'s opposite, yet he'd been attracted to her from the moment they'd met at a party thrown by one of their mutual college friends. Brenda had been outgoing and talkative. He remembered how his mother, after meeting Brenda, had called her a social butterfly. His mom and dad had encouraged the relationship from the beginning, and B.J. hadn't objected because he was attracted to Brenda's magnetic personality and good looks. Her jet-black hair and sparkling blue eyes could have turned any man's head.

Judy, on the other hand, was rather plain, although not unattractive. She had light brown hair, which she wore in a ponytail much of the time, and didn't care about the latest fashion trends. She was down-to-earth and always looked on the bright side of things.

I wonder where Judy is now. B.J. pondered. *Noreen left Emma and Lamar's in such a hurry yesterday, I didn't get the chance to ask. I'll question Noreen about Judy when I see her at the next class, though. I'd like to reconnect with Judy—for old time's sake.*

Well, enough with the reminiscing, B.J. told himself. *I came here to paint, not dwell on the past.*

"Hey, isn't that B.J. from the quilting class over there on that bench?" Jan asked as he and Kim, leading Maddie on her leash, made their way across the white sandy beach.

She shielded her eyes and looked in the direction Jan was pointing. "You're right. That is B.J. It looks like he's painting something. See that easel in front of him?"

Jan nodded. "Should we go say hi?"

"I don't know. Do you think he'd mind if we interrupted him?"

"Guess we might disrupt his concentration," Jan said. "But what if he sees us over here and thinks we're snubbing him?"

"You're right. We don't want to be unsociable," Kim responded. "Besides, I'd kinda like to see what he's painting."

"Same here. Let's go on over then."

As they approached B.J., Maddie started pulling on her leash.

"All right, girl, but don't run off too far." Kim bent down and unhooked the leash from the dog's collar.

Jan snickered as Maddie let out an excited bark and dashed into the water. Kim would be lucky if she ever got the dog back on her leash.

"I see we're not the only ones from our class who enjoys this beach," Kim said, stepping up to B.J. "It's nice to see you today."

He smiled up at her and then nodded at Jan. "I heard you two talking yesterday about going to the beach, but I thought you planned to do that after class," he said.

"Oh, we did." Kim smiled at Jan. "We enjoyed it so much, we decided to come back again today after church."

"It's a good day to be here," B.J. said with a nod. "Nice and warm, with just a slight breeze. It's a perfect opportunity to get some painting done."

Jan studied the painting, already in progress. The ocean scene featured seagulls swooping close to the waves, and a couple of boats on the horizon. "You do nice work," he said, gesturing to the easel.

B.J. smiled. "I did an ocean scene from my studio in Chicago, but it's much better to paint here by the water. I think it helps to put more feeling into my work."

"It's beautiful." Kim looked closely at the painting. "I can almost feel the spray from the waves you've painted. You captured everything perfectly."

"Thanks. I do my best."

Jan was tempted to bring up the topic of Noreen, and what had gone down at the quilting class yesterday but thought better of it. It was none of his business, and if B.J. wanted to talk about it, he would.

From the choice words coming from Noreen before she'd stormed out of the Millers' house, Jan figured B.J. must have done something pretty bad. *Guess everyone has said or done something in the past that they're not proud of,* he thought. *I know I've done my fair share of flubbing things. I have to wonder, though—if what B.J. did was so bad, why didn't Noreen stick around to discuss it with him? It'll be interesting to see if she shows up for class this Saturday. Well, I'm gonna be there, that's for sure. Not to see what goes down between B.J. and Noreen, but so I can spend more time with Kim.*

CHAPTER 23

How are things in North Dakota?" Mike asked as he sat in the living room Friday evening, talking to his wife on the phone. Mike was all settled in his easy chair and breathed deeply the aroma of the coffee he'd just brewed. With the TV on mute, he used the remote to flip through the channels, not really paying attention to what was on the screen, trying to focus on what Phyllis was saying.

"A little better than the last time we talked. It's not snowing right now, and it's good to have the power on again. Even though Penny has that backup generator, it's nice to have everything running off the main grid again." After a pause, Phyllis said, "How are things with you?"

"Okay." Mike gnawed on his lower lip, contemplating whether to tell his wife that he'd seen the doctor and gotten the results of his blood test. Would it be best to tell her now or wait until she got home? If he told her now she would worry about him. If he waited to tell her the news, she'd be upset. It was a no-win situation. He'd rather face a group of disappointed fisherman than explain his issues to Phyllis.

"Mike, are you still there?"

"Uh, yeah. Just thinking is all."

"About what?"

"Umm. . .there's something I need to tell you." He pointed the remote, turning off the TV, then reached for his coffee cup, blowing on the steam still rising from it.

"What is it, Mike?"

"I've been having a little problem lately, so I went to see the doctor last week, and—"

"What? And you're just now getting around to telling me that?" Phyllis's voice rose. "What's wrong, Mike? Have you been sick?"

"No, not really. Well, kind of, I guess."

"What's that supposed to mean?"

"I've felt kind of weird and shaky lately. So I finally went to see the doctor, and he had me go in for some blood tests. I got the results yesterday."

"You got the results a day ago, and you're just now telling me about it?" Mike winced when he heard the frustration in Phyllis's voice.

"Calm down, honey," he said, trying to keep his own voice composed. "I knew if I told you that, I'd get this reaction."

"So you figured it'd be best not to tell me at all?"

"That's not it. I just didn't want to worry you, Phyllis, especially while you're helping your sister."

"Well, it's too late for that, because I am worried. What was the outcome of your tests?"

"I have pre-diabetes, but—"

"Diabetes? Oh, Mike, no!"

He grimaced. "I wish you'd stop interrupting and let me tell you everything the doctor said."

"Sorry. I'm listening."

"I don't have full-blown diabetes yet. According to the blood tests, I'm in the early stages, and the doctor seems to think that if I exercise regularly and watch my diet I may never get to the place where I have to take pills or insulin shots."

She blew out her breath. "That's a relief. You really had me worried. Of course, you'll have to follow through and do as the doctor said."

"Yeah, I know. It's gonna be hard for me to give up sweets, though."

"There are many delicious desserts made with sugar-free ingredients," she said. "When I get home, I'll try a few recipes and see what you like. In the meantime, promise me that you'll be good and eat right."

"Yes, Mama."

"I'm serious, Mike."

"I know, hon, and I promise to toe the mark."

"So how's the quilt class going?" she asked, her tone relaxing some.

"Fine. Some big biker fella who's a friend of the Millers joined us last week. Guess he took one of their classes up in Shipshewana, Indiana."

Phyllis snickered. "I can't picture Emma and Lamar becoming friends with a biker."

"It was a surprise to me as well, but those two are the nicest people. I think they could be friends with anyone—except maybe some hardened criminal who nobody could reach."

"Just from my first meeting with Emma and Lamar, it wouldn't surprise me if, were they ever to meet such a person, they'd try to reach out to him in kindness."

Mike laughed. "You could be right about that."

"Thanks for the ride," Lamar told their driver when he dropped them off at Jennifer and Randy's place that evening. "We'll give you a call when we're ready to come home."

"Oh, let's not forget the box of food we have in the trunk," Emma said as she stepped out of the car. They'd filled the box with flour, sugar, cereal, bread, eggs, pasta, milk, and several packages of meat. She hoped Randy and Jennifer would graciously accept their gift.

Lamar lifted the box, and they headed up the porch stairs. Emma reached out to knock, but the door swung open before her knuckles connected with the wood.

"It's good to see you. Please, come in." Jennifer greeted them with a cheery smile.

"Since you wouldn't let us bring anything to contribute to the meal, we brought you this," Lamar said as they followed Jennifer into the house.

"What is it?" she questioned.

"Just a few more items of food we thought you could use." Emma smiled. "And please don't say no, because we have plenty of food in our pantry, and we surely don't want to take this box home."

"We appreciate your thoughtfulness; isn't that right, Randy?" Jennifer asked, gesturing to the box after her husband stepped into the room.

He shook hands with Emma and Lamar, then looked into the box. "You're giving us more food?"

Lamar nodded. "It's just a little something to help out."

Randy hesitated but finally nodded. "Thanks, we appreciate it."

"While Randy takes the box to the kitchen, why don't the rest of us go into the living room so we can visit before supper's ready?" Jennifer suggested, holding the small of her back as she led the way to the other room.

Emma and Lamar took a seat on the couch, and Jennifer sat in the rocking chair across from them, rubbing her stomach.

"You look tired, Jennifer. How has your week been going?" Emma asked, feeling concern.

Jennifer patted her ever-growing stomach. "This little girl has been pretty active lately, and I'm not sleeping as well as I should."

"I'm sorry to hear that," Emma said. "How much longer until the baby comes?"

"Just four more weeks, unless I'm late." Jennifer gave her stomach a couple more pats. "I think our baby is anxious to be born, because she seems to be kicking all the time."

"Some babies can be pretty active," Emma said. "I remember when I was expecting my daughter, Mary, she often got the hiccups, and it would wake me during the night."

"I just checked the oven, and supper's ready," Randy said, joining them in the living room. "I hope you folks like enchiladas."

"Can't say that I've ever had them," Lamar spoke up. "But I'm willing to try anything."

Emma and Lamar rose from their seats and followed Jennifer and Randy into the small but cozy dining room. Emma could see that Jennifer had set the table with her best china, and a pretty floral centerpiece sat in the middle of the table.

After they all took seats, Lamar said, "At home, Emma and I usually offer a silent prayer, but here in your house we'd be pleased if you prayed out loud."

Jennifer glanced at Randy, and his ears turned red. "Uh, yeah, well. . . Jennifer, why don't you pray for the meal?"

Jennifer fingered her napkin. Emma wasn't sure whether this young couple felt uncomfortable praying in front of others, or if they normally didn't pray before a meal, but she sensed the awkwardness of the moment. To ease the tension, she quickly said, "Or maybe you'd prefer that we all pray silently instead."

"No, it's fine; I'll pray for the meal," Jennifer said. After everyone bowed their heads, she prayed in a soft-spoken voice, "Dear Lord, I thank You for this food, and for the hands that prepared it. I also want to thank Emma and Lamar, who have been patiently teaching me to quilt and generously gave us some food. In Jesus' name, amen."

When everyone opened their eyes, Jennifer passed the tossed green salad around the table, followed by the dish of enchiladas.

"This certainly smells good," Emma said, spooning some of the Mexican dish onto her plate.

"You're right about that," Lamar agreed. "And if it tastes as good as it smells, I think we're in for a treat."

While Emma poured some dressing over her salad, Lamar took a bite of enchilada. As he chewed, his face, neck, and ears turned red. Coughing, he quickly reached for his glass of water.

"What's wrong?" Jennifer asked, looking at Lamar with concern. "Did you swallow incorrectly, or is it too spicy for you?"

Gasping for breath, Lamar croaked, "It—it's hotter than anything I've ever tasted."

Jennifer took a taste, then quickly spit it back onto the plate. Her forehead wrinkled as she looked sternly at Randy. "What did you do to the enchiladas? They're hotter than a blazing furnace!"

Randy's brows furrowed. "I–I don't know what happened. Thought I'd poured just the right amount of picante sauce over the top of them. And it was the mild kind, not hot."

"I've never tasted anything this hot that's supposed to be mild." Jennifer grabbed her glass of water and took a drink.

Emma stared at her plate. She was glad she hadn't tasted her enchilada yet. If it was hot enough to affect Lamar and Jennifer as it did, she'd probably have choked to death.

"I'm going to get the jar of sauce." Randy rose from the table and left the room. When he returned with the jar, he placed it on the table and pointed to the label. "See, it says right here that it's mild."

"Maybe you should taste it," Jennifer suggested.

Randy opened the lid, stuck his spoon inside, and put the whole spoonful in his mouth. "Yow! That's anything but mild!" He coughed, sputtered, and gulped down his glass of water.

"That jar of sauce must have been mislabeled," Jennifer said. "You should take it back to the store."

"I'll do that tomorrow," Randy said, "but right now we need something else to eat, so I'll grill some burgers with the package of ground beef that was in the box the Millers gave us." He looked across the table at Emma and Lamar. "I'm really sorry about this. It wasn't a good way to repay your kindness."

Lamar waved a hand. "Don't worry about it, Randy. Barbecued burgers will be just fine." He pushed his chair aside and stood. "In fact, I'd enjoy helping you grill them, and while we're doing that, it'll give us a chance to chat."

Randy gave a nod. "Sounds good to me. Let's get that grill started."

Emma smiled. She was glad to see Randy relax a bit and be willing to accept, not only the food they'd brought, but Lamar's help.

"I'm glad you suggested we go bowling tonight," Kim said when Jan picked up his ball and got ready to take his turn.

He smiled and nodded. "Back home, bowling is one of my favorite things to do on a Friday night."

"Do you have a bowling partner?"

"Star usually goes along, and sometimes we bowl against my friend Terry and his girlfriend, Cheryl." Jan wiggled his eyebrows playfully. "It's kinda fun to compete and see who can rack up the most pins."

"Well, you won't have to worry about that tonight, 'cause even though I enjoy bowling, I'm not very good at it," Kim said. "I'll probably have more gutter balls than strikes."

"Let's not worry about competing." Jan grinned. "I just wanna have fun and get to know you better."

Kim gave a nod. "Same here."

As they took turns bowling and keeping score, Jan appreciated what a good sport Kim was. She never got upset when she messed up, and even when he made a strike or a spare, she cheered him on. He found himself liking her more all the time, and that scared him. Could he trust Kim not to break his heart the way Star's mom had?

I've gotta quit thinking like this, Jan told himself. *In the short time I've known her, I can already tell that Kim is nothing like Nancy.*

Jan glanced to his right and saw a middle-aged man dressed all in black sitting on a bench at one of the alleys up from them. The guy had thick dark hair and sideburns, and of all things, he was wearing sunglasses.

Jan nudged Kim and snickered. "Look over there. I think an Elvis-wanna-be is in the building."

Kim looked that way and laughed. "You're so funny, Jan. No wonder I'm having such a good time tonight."

He wiggled his eyebrows again, stifling a belly laugh. "Thank you. Thank you very much."

As the evening progressed, Kim found herself enjoying her time with Jan more than she'd ever expected. Not only had he offered her some bowling tips, but even when she rolled a few gutter balls, he never made fun of her.

When they finished bowling, they headed out to an Asian restaurant Kim had been meaning to try. Each table had its own chef, who cooked the meal on an open hibachi grill right in front of them. After he'd cut the tails off the shrimp, he flipped them into his white chef's hat, adding a bit of humor to the whole experience.

Kim glanced over at Jan and could see by his broad smile that he was having a good time and enjoying the meal. She liked his easygoing, positive attitude, and wished once more that Jan didn't have to return to Indiana when his vacation was over. *When I've worked at the restaurant long enough for some vacation time, maybe I'll take a trip to Shipshewana and see where Jan lives,* she thought. *Who knows—I might even like it there and decide to stay.*

CHAPTER 24

"How'd your date with Kim go last night?" Lamar asked as he, Emma, and Jan sat at the kitchen table Saturday morning, eating breakfast.

Jan grinned widely. "Good. Really good." He reached for his glass of freshly squeezed orange juice. "I like her a lot."

Emma looked at Lamar and smiled when he winked at her. It was good to see Jan in such good spirits. He'd been through a lot over the years and deserved to be happy. Emma couldn't help but wonder, though, how Jan and Kim could keep their relationship going once Jan returned home. Also, things seemed to be moving rather quickly between the two, and that concerned her a bit. She hoped no one would end up getting hurt.

"Say, Jan, I've been wanting to make a trip to Venice to look for sharks' teeth," Lamar said. "Would that be something you'd be interested in doing?"

Jan nodded enthusiastically. "You bet! When did you wanna go?"

"Anytime you'd like. 'Course, it can't be on a Saturday, because of the quilt classes, and then, Sunday is our day for church."

"No problem. We can make the trip whenever you want. I'll have to see about renting a car, though, since I only have my motorcycle with me." Jan smacked his forehead. "Hey, here's an idea. I could get a sidecar and have it attached to my bike. Wouldn't it be fun to tool around together that way? Emma, you could ride in the sidecar, and Lamar can sit behind me on the bike. How far is it from here to the Venice beaches?"

"I'd say about twenty miles or so," Lamar replied. "I'm not sure we'd want to travel the way you suggested, though. Emma and I are a little old for that sort of thing. Right, Emma?"

She gave a decisive nod.

"Not a problem," Jan said. "I'll see about renting a car for the day. That way there'll be plenty of room for all three of us to go."

"You two don't need to worry about me. Just go ahead and have fun," Emma said. "I'll be perfectly fine here at home while you're gone. Oh, and maybe you could see if one of our drivers will take you to Venice. That would probably be cheaper than Jan renting a car."

"Aw, come on, Emma, you've gotta go along. I thought I'd invite Kim to join us, and it'll be more fun if you're there, too." Jan reached for his cup and took a drink. "Hey, I've got it!" he said, nearly choking on his coffee. "Kim has a motorcycle, but she also owns a car. I'll bet anything she'd be willing to drive us there."

Emma didn't really care about looking for sharks' teeth, but it would be nice to visit with Kim, walk the beach, and search for pretty shells. "Okay, if Kim goes, then I will, too." Emma blew out a puff of air. "I feel better knowing we'll be taking a car. I just can't see myself riding in one of those sidecar things."

"I understand, but I haven't ditched the idea of getting a sidecar. I'd actually like to see how my bike maneuvers with one of those on. While I'm here in Florida, I may get one installed before I head home. That is, if I can find a dealer around here that sells 'em." Jan rubbed the bridge of his nose. "If I got a sidecar, Star could ride in that on the way home instead of sitting on the back of my bike, like we'd planned for her to do. Might be more comfortable on the long trip. And since I hate leaving Brutus at home so much, or having to ask someone to watch him when I go on some motorcycle trips, he could ride along." He chuckled. "Can't you just see my dog sittin' next to me in a sidecar? I wonder how he'd look wearing goggles."

They all laughed. "That would surely be something, alright," Emma agreed.

Jan rubbed his hands together. "Now back to goin' to the beach in Venice. Here's another thought. Maybe we should wait till Star gets here. I think lookin' for sharks' teeth would be something she'd enjoy doing, and it'd be a chance for her to get acquainted with Kim."

"That's a good idea, Jan." Emma smiled, looking at Lamar, who was nodding his head in agreement. "It will be so nice to see Star again, but Jan, don't you think you should ask Kim first, if she would mind driving us all to Venice?"

"'Course I'll ask, but I'm almost sure she won't mind." Jan gave his left earlobe a tug. "In the short time I've known Kim, I've found her to be real easygoing. In fact, if she was here right now, I can almost bet she'd have already suggested taking her car."

Emma reached for her cup of tea and took a sip. *If Jan wants Star to get to know Kim, then he must be getting serious about her already. Now, wouldn't that be something if Kim decided to move to Indiana and she and Jan got married? It would be a pleasure to have another one of my quilting students living nearby so we could visit once in a while.*

Emma enjoyed staying in touch with her previous students. It was nice to see some of the quilting projects they had done on their own—not to mention keeping up with what was going on in their lives. Just the other day she'd received a letter from Pam Johnston, who'd attended Emma's first class. Pam mentioned that she and Stuart were planning to take their children to Disney World during their spring break and said if Emma and Lamar were still in Florida, they might come down to see them, since Orlando was only a few hours' drive from Sarasota.

We'll be going home in the spring, Emma thought. *I need to be close to my family there and could never be happy staying here on a permanent basis. Oh, I hope Lamar doesn't get any ideas about living here year-round.*

"Emma, did you hear what I said?" Lamar asked, nudging her arm.

"Uh, sorry, I didn't. Guess I was deep in thought. Would you please repeat it, Lamar?"

"I asked if there's anything you need me to do before our students get here this morning?"

"Thank you, but I think everything we need has been set out." Emma turned to Jan and said, "Will you be joining us again today?"

He gave a quick nod. "Wouldn't miss it!"

Goshen

Star picked up her guitar and took a seat on the end of her bed. It had been awhile since she'd composed a new song, and since she didn't have to work this morning, it was a good time to come up with some words that would express the way she felt about her dad. Star wished she and Jan could gain back the twenty years they'd lost when her mom had taken her and run off, but that wasn't possible. What mattered was the time they had to be together now and in the future.

Star was glad her dad didn't have a serious girlfriend. It was probably selfish, but she wanted him all to herself. It was bad enough she had to share him with Brutus. The mutt always seemed to be vying for his master's attention—especially when Jan had been away from home for a while. She could only imagine how the dog would carry on when Jan returned from Florida. He'd probably become Jan's shadow for several days.

"Though we can't turn back the hands of time, we have the future to look forward to," Star sang as she strummed her guitar. "Like grains of sand slipping through our fingers..."

Star's cell phone whistled, letting her know she had a call. She placed the guitar on the bed and picked up the phone. Looking at the caller ID, she smiled, pleased to see it was her dad.

"Hey, stranger, what's up? I haven't heard from you for a few days."

"Sorry about that," he said. "I've been occupied."

"Doing what?" she asked.

"Helping out at Emma and Lamar's and spending time with Kim. She's the cute little gal I told you about—the one who's taking the quilt class and has a German shepherd named Maddie."

"Oh, I see." Star hoped her dad wasn't getting serious about Kim, because a long-distance relationship wouldn't work. Besides, he didn't need a woman to complicate his life and come between them.

"I was gonna wait to tell you this when you got here, Star, but I think I've found the perfect woman."

Star lifted her gaze toward the ceiling. "Yeah, Dad, right. You barely know this Kim person."

"I realize that, but we have a lot in common, and it's like... Well, it feels as if we're soul mates."

Star's fingers clenched the phone. "No way, Dad! You can't know that in such a short time."

He grunted. "You're not being very supportive, but I'm sure you'll feel differently once you've met Kim."

"I doubt it," she mumbled.

"What was that?"

"Nothing. I've gotta go now, Dad. I'm busy." Star hated to hang up so soon, but this conversation was not what she'd expected. Her dad's announcement had really thrown her for a loop.

"That's okay. I need to hang up anyway. The quilt class will be starting soon, and I don't wanna miss it."

"Okay, whatever."

"I'll pick you up at the airport next Thursday," he said. "Oh, and Star. . ."

"Yeah, Dad?"

"I'm looking forward to seeing you."

"Same here. Bye, Dad."

When Star clicked off her cell phone she flopped back on the bed with a moan. Dad thought he was in love with a woman he hardly knew. *Well, when I get to Sarasota, things will change. I'll talk some sense into Dad and make him see what a mistake he's making. And if trying to reason with him doesn't work, then I'll have to take more drastic measures, because I can't let that woman come between me and my dad!*

Sarasota

"Is Jennifer here yet?" Kim asked Emma, after she'd entered the Millers' house. "There's something I want to tell her."

"Not yet, but I'm sure she'll be here soon," Emma replied.

"Hey, Kim, I'm glad you're here," Jan said with an eager expression as he sauntered into the room. "There's something I'd like to ask you."

"Oh, what's that?"

"Lamar mentioned this morning that he'd like to go down to Venice to look for sharks' teeth, and I thought if you'd like to go along that you might be willing to drive us all there, since you have a car."

Kim smiled. "That sounds like fun, and it's actually something I've been wanting to do. So yeah, I'd be happy to drive you there."

"We'll help with the gas," Lamar spoke up.

"Oh, don't worry about that," Kim responded with a wave of her hand. "It'll be my pleasure."

Emma shook her head. "If we're going along, then we insist on helping out with the gas."

"We can talk about that when the time comes. When did you want to go to Venice?" Kim asked, directing her question to Jan.

"Any day you have off," Jan replied. "But I'd like to wait till Star gets here, 'cause I think she'd enjoy looking for sharks' teeth, too."

"When did you say your daughter will get here?" Kim asked.

"She's flying in on Thursday."

"That's perfect. I have next Friday off," Kim said. "Would that be a good day for all of you?"

Lamar nodded, and so did Emma.

"That's great!" Jan bumped shoulders with Kim. "I can hardly wait."

"Same here," she agreed. "I'm anxious to meet your daughter. Oh, and Emma, we'll have to put our heads together and take a few things along for a picnic lunch. Maybe we can eat right there on the beach. I think it'll be a terrific day."

"I hope I'm not late," Jennifer said when she entered the Millers' house a short time later. "I don't know why, but the traffic was terrible this morning."

"You're not late at all. Only Kim and Jan are here, but Jan's in the spare room right now, and Kim's in the dining room at the table," Emma said. "You can go right in if you want to."

Jennifer hesitated a minute. "Before I do, I was wondering if Lamar suffered any ill effects from Randy's spicy enchiladas."

Emma shook her head. "No, he's fine. I don't think he ate enough of it to cause any real distress."

"That's good to hear. Randy was so embarrassed by what he did."

Emma patted Jennifer's arm. "Well, he needn't have been, because it wasn't his fault."

"I know, but Randy's a cook, and he always tries to do his best." Jennifer held her hands tightly at her sides as her eyebrows pulled together. "I think the longer he's unemployed, and the closer it comes for me to have the baby, the more worried he becomes. If he doesn't find a job soon, we may have to leave Sarasota and move in with one of our parents."

"Would that be such a bad thing?" Emma questioned.

Jennifer nodded. "It would be admitting defeat, and since our parents aren't well off, us moving in with them would cause a hardship."

"Hopefully, it won't come to that. I know it's hard, but try to keep a positive attitude and trust God," Emma said. "One of my favorite verses of scripture is Proverbs 30:5: 'Every word of God is pure: he is a shield unto them that put their trust in him.'"

Jennifer smiled. "That's the same verse Lamar quoted to Randy when they were outside grilling the burgers. Randy shared that with me after you folks left. He said Lamar gave him a pep talk about how important it is to trust God, even when things look hopeless." Jennifer gave Emma a hug.

"We're pleased that you have both shared your feelings with us. That helps us know how to pray." Emma paused. "Oh, and before I forget,

Kim wants to talk to you. Why don't we go in to see her now?"

When they entered the dining room, Jennifer took a seat in an empty chair next to Kim.

Kim turned and clasped Jennifer's arm. "I'm glad you're here. I wanted you to know that the restaurant where I work is looking for a cook."

A sense of hope welled in Jennifer's chest. "Really? Have they interviewed anyone yet?"

"I don't know. I stopped over at the restaurant before coming here to pick up my paycheck, since I forgot to get it after work yesterday." Kim's cheeks turned pink. "Guess I was too excited about my bowling date with Jan. Anyway, I think you should call your husband now and let him know about the job. He should go over there as soon as possible to apply."

"You can use our phone in the kitchen," Emma spoke up.

"Thanks." Jennifer hurried from the room. Maybe this would be the day that her prayers were answered.

CHAPTER 25

"I can't believe I'm wearing this stupid turban again," Noreen fumed as she drove down Bahia Vista toward Pinecraft. She'd washed her hair several times during the week, but the color hadn't faded much at all.

Well, at least the neighbor's dog had quit yapping so much, and she was grateful for that.

Noreen grimaced as another thought popped into her head. *I dread having to face Bruce Jensen again today.*

When Noreen first met the man, she'd thought he was nice and perhaps even her type. *I could have made the same mistake my sister did if I'd become involved with him,* she thought. *I'll bet he never loved Judy, or he wouldn't have run out on her when he found out she was carrying his child. Instead, he ran off to college in another state, never giving a second thought to my sister or their baby.*

The closer Noreen got to Pinecraft, the more upset she became. Well, she wasn't going to let Bruce keep her from finishing the wall hanging she'd started. She just wouldn't talk to him about Judy. Better yet, maybe she would bring it up at the Millers' today and embarrass B.J. in front of the whole class!

When B.J. pulled in front of the Millers' house, he spotted Noreen getting out of her car. "Oh, great," he mumbled. "The last thing I need is a confrontation with her out here in the yard." He did want to talk to her, though, because he had some questions to ask about Judy. But he figured it would be better to wait until after class. Maybe he would invite Noreen to lunch, where they could talk privately without the rest of the quilting students listening in on their conversation.

B.J. slunk down in his seat, hoping she wouldn't notice him. If he waited until Noreen went inside the house before making his appearance he might be better off. He glanced at the driveway and saw Kim's motorcycle and a few other vehicles and knew everyone else had probably arrived.

Looking back at the house, B.J. relaxed a bit when he saw Noreen go inside. He waited a few more minutes before getting out of the car. As he walked slowly up the walk to the porch, a van pulled in.

B.J. watched as Erika's father lifted her wheelchair from the van and placed her in it. He felt sorry for the girl. Her life had been altered by an accident that could have been avoided, and now her activities were restricted and she was bound to that chair.

Life isn't fair, B.J. thought. A person never knew what was around the next bend. They could be in an accident, become terminally ill, or lose all their possessions due to some horrible disaster. There were times when he wondered if it would have been better if he'd never been born.

Enough with the negative thoughts. It's time to go inside.

B.J. glanced across the table and noticed Noreen's scowl. He wished she'd quit looking at him with that sourpuss expression. Did she hate him that much for breaking up with her sister? Why couldn't she let go of the past? *It's just so petty,* he thought.

In an effort to avoid Noreen's piercing gaze, B.J. turned to face Mike, who sat on his right. "How'd your week go?"

Mike shrugged. "Okay, I guess."

"Did you get the results of your blood tests?" Lamar questioned from where he sat at the head of the table.

Mike nodded. "Found out I have pre-diabetes, but the doc said if I watch what I eat and exercise regularly, my blood sugar numbers should improve."

"That's good to hear," Lamar said, smiling.

B.J. nodded. He wished what was wrong with him could be controlled by diet and exercise. *Try not to think about it,* he reminded himself. *Just live each day as it comes and enjoy every moment you have left on earth.*

"I got in touch with Randy, and he's going over to the restaurant right now to see about that job," Jennifer said as she returned to the room and took a seat beside Kim.

Kim patted Jennifer's arm in a motherly fashion. "I hope it all works out."

"Yeah, me too. It gives me a ray of hope, at least."

"Please let us know how it all turns out," Emma said.

"Yes, I will."

"Well, now that we're all here, we'd better get started. Today we'll be cutting out the batting for your wall hangings, and then we'll begin the quilting process."

"Oh great. More sewing on that dumb sewing machine." Erika wrinkled her nose, like some foul order had permeated the room. "I had a hard time holding the material straight last week when I sewed the pieces of material together." It was the first thing the girl had said since she'd gotten here, and as usual, it was something negative.

"Actually, the quilting will be done by hand, with a needle and thread," Emma explained. "But before we begin the actual process, you'll each need to cut a piece of cotton batting about two inches larger on all sides than your quilt top."

"The excess batting will be trimmed even with the quilt top after the quilting stitches have been done," Lamar interjected.

B.J. and the rest of the class watched as Lamar and Emma demonstrated how it should be done.

"I'll explain the details of the quilting process once you've all cut out your batting," Emma went on to say. "So let's begin that now."

Everyone did as she asked, and as they cut, Noreen looked over at B.J. and said, "You're doing it wrong. The piece you cut is too small." She clicked her tongue. "I suppose some people can't do anything right."

"What's that supposed to mean?" B.J. asked.

"Nothing," she mumbled.

They worked awhile longer, then Noreen turned to B.J. and said, "You sure messed up where my sister was concerned."

"I was going to wait until we could talk in private," B.J. said, "but since you brought the subject up, I'd like to know what I did to Judy that was so terrible. I mean, a guy ought to have the right to break up with a girl without her sister carrying a grudge all these years and treating him like he's got the plague."

Noreen set her work aside and glared at B.J. "Since you obviously don't mind the whole class knowing about your sordid past, I'll tell you exactly what you did to Judy."

The room became quiet as B.J. leaned closer to Noreen and said,

"Please do."

"First of all, you took advantage of my sister's innocence and talked her into sleeping with you."

Seeing the look of shock on everyone's face, B.J. wished there was a hole in the floor so he could crawl into it and hide. This was so embarrassing!

B.J. was about to offer an explanation, but Noreen spoke again. "When you found out that Judy was carrying your child, why did you run off to college to fulfill your dream of becoming an artist? Couldn't you have stayed in Columbus and taken responsibility for your actions?"

The shock of hearing this sent B.J.'s mind whirling. He couldn't deny that he and Judy had been intimate, but she'd never told him she was pregnant. He'd broken up with her because his parents said if he didn't they wouldn't pay for his schooling, and he'd really wanted a degree in art. What a shock to learn that Judy had been carrying his child.

Noreen's finger trembled as she shook it at B.J. "Choosing your career over my sister was pretty selfish, don't you think?"

"If I had known Judy was pregnant, I would have married her."

"I'll bet you would."

"You have to believe me," he said. "I'm not the kind of man who would shirk his responsibilities." Sweat beaded on B.J.'s forehead as a sense of panic welled in his chest. "Give me the chance to apologize to Judy and meet our child. Please tell me where she lives, or at least give me her phone number."

Noreen shook her head. "It's too late for that. Judy is gone, and so is your son."

CHAPTER 26

B.J.'s eyes widened as his mouth dropped open. "I—I have a son?"

Heat flooded Noreen's face, and she covered her mouth with the palm of her hand. She hadn't planned to let Bruce know that he had a son, but she couldn't take back what she'd said. She would have to be careful not to tell Bruce any more, for her sister's ex-boyfriend had no right to know anything about his son. Worse yet, if the truth came out, Judy's son would be crushed, and Noreen feared it might ruin her relationship with him.

"Where is Judy, and where is our boy?" B.J. asked in an emotion-filled voice.

Noreen drew in a calming voice. All eyes and ears seemed to be upon her, and she wished she could crawl under the table. "My sister is dead. She died from complications during childbirth." She choked back the sob rising in her throat. Even after all these years, it was difficult to talk about. Now, with the father of Judy's son staring at her from across the table, it was more painful than she ever thought possible.

B.J. winced as though he'd been slapped. "I—I'm so sorry about Judy. I had no idea. Why didn't someone tell me this?"

"Would you have cared?" Noreen asked, searching through her tote bag for a tissue.

"Of course I would, and I still do." He paused and clutched his chest, as though in pain. "What about the baby? Did he die, too?"

Noreen was tempted to say that Bruce's son had also died, but she had a feeling he'd be able to see through her lie. "Judy's baby was adopted by a good family," she said, blowing her nose and dropping her gaze to the table.

"Do you know who they are? Do you have any information about the boy's whereabouts?"

"No, I do not, and I don't want to talk about this anymore." Dabbing at the moisture beneath her eyes, Noreen picked up her scissors to finish cutting the batting.

B.J.'s eyes narrowed. "I think you do know where he is. I have a feeling you're keeping it from me."

She shook her head vigorously. "I've told you all that I know. If you had wanted to be a part of your son's life, then you shouldn't have run off like you did."

His jaw clenched. "I told you I did not know Judy was pregnant."

Mike cleared his throat real loud, and everyone turned to look at him. "It's obvious that you two have some issues, but this isn't the place to be airing them out. The rest of us came here to learn how to quilt, and you're taking up our time with your personal problems. You oughta deal with all of this after class. I can't speak for everyone else, but you two going back and forth at each other is making me uncomfortable."

"Mike is right," Erika spoke up. "This isn't the place to be airing out your differences."

"Actually, it might be exactly the place," Jan interjected. "During the quilt classes I took at Emma's home up in Shipshe, everyone in the class had some sort of problem. We were all like a bunch of broken shells on the beach, and it seemed like there was no way to put the pieces together. But once we started talkin' about things, we felt better." Jan looked at Emma and smiled. "Our special teacher here not only taught us how to quilt, but gave us spiritual guidance as well."

"I take no credit for that," Emma was quick to say. "It was the Lord, guiding and directing my words. And because my students were open to change, He was able to heal hearts and give those who'd been hurting a new perspective." She paused a moment. "In Ezekiel 34:16 it says, 'I will seek that which was lost, and bring again that which was driven away, and will bind up that which was broken, and will strengthen that which was sick, saith the Lord God.'"

"That's a great verse, Emma," Jan said. "I think many of your students, includin' yours truly, were broken people in need of healing."

Noreen's shoulders stiffened, wishing she could flee the room. Well, she'd run out last week, but she wouldn't do it again. It would be a sign of weakness. "I don't need any guidance, or a new perspective," she muttered. "I signed up for these classes to learn how to quilt, and for no other reason. So let's get on with our lesson."

Emma looked at Lamar, hoping he might say something, but all he gave was a quick nod. Assuming that meant she should proceed with the lesson, Emma waited while everyone worked on their batting, and she sent up a silent prayer that this class would end on a good note. She never dreamed her quilt classes would hold so many surprises, but it seemed that each one of them had so far. Well, at least these quilting students were finally beginning to open up. She just hoped it would end with healing. For now, though, she needed to concentrate on teaching today's lesson.

Once Emma saw that everyone had finished cutting their batting, she held up one of the small wooden frames Lamar had made. "In order to create a smooth, even quilting surface, all three layers of your quilt will need to be put in a frame like this," she said. "If you were making a larger quilt, you would need a quilting frame that could stretch the entire quilt at one time." Emma paused to be sure everyone was listening; then she continued. "Since your wall hangings are much smaller than a full-size quilt, you can use a smaller frame such as this."

"That looks sort of like the embroidery hoop I've seen my grandma use," Jennifer said.

Emma nodded. "That's correct, and it's important when using this type of hoop to baste your entire quilt together through all three layers. This will keep the layers stretched tightly while you are quilting."

"Just be sure you don't quilt over the basting," Lamar added. "Because it will be hard to remove later on." He snickered. "Oh, and be careful not to stitch your blouse or shirt to the quilt, like one of our previous students did."

Jan rolled his eyes. "I'll bet it was my buddy Terry. That sounds like something he'd end up doing."

"You're right. That did happen to Terry," Emma agreed.

Jan slapped his knee. "Figured as much."

Emma then told the class about needle sizes, pointing out that it was best to try several and see which one seemed the most comfortable to use. "It's also a good idea to use a thimble on your middle finger for pushing the quilting needle, because the needle has to go through three layers of fabric to create the quilting pattern." Following that, she passed around a tray full of various thimbles. "Now, if everyone will choose a needle and thimble, you can begin the quilting process."

Emma waited until everyone had done as she asked, the whole time watching the body language between Noreen and B.J. They obviously both carried a lot of pain, and perhaps some serious regrets. She hoped they would be able to work it out and prayed that God would show Lamar and her if there was anything they could do. The Lord seemed to be using this quilt class already, by bringing B.J. and Noreen together after all these years. It had happened before, when Star and Jan learned they were father and daughter during Emma's first set of quilting classes. Then last year, Emma had been reunited with her sister, Betty, whom she hadn't even known about. Surely it was no coincidence in how that had all happened. If Noreen and B.J. could just set their hostilities aside and talk things through, perhaps their reunion might turn into something good.

Setting aside her thoughts, Emma explained that the next step would be to mark the design they wanted on their quilt top. "However," she added, "if you just want to outline the patches you've sewn with quilting stitches, no marking is necessary."

"You'll need to quilt close to the seam so the patch will be emphasized," Lamar interjected. "Oh, and don't forget, your stitches should be small and even. They also need to be snug but not so tight that they'll cause any puckering."

"I'll demonstrate on my own quilt patch," Emma said, picking it up and showing everyone the correct way to pull the needle and thread through the material to create the quilting pattern.

Mike's forehead wrinkled. "That looks too hard for me. My hands are big and the only thing I've ever sewn is a button on my shirt—and Phyllis had to help me with that."

"Speaking of Phyllis, how is her sister doing these days?" Emma asked.

"Better, but her leg's not healed well enough so she can be on her own yet," Mike replied. "They've been having some nasty weather in North Dakota lately, so Phyllis won't come home until she's sure Penny can manage okay without her."

"That's understandable," Kim spoke up. "It would be bad enough to be laid up with a broken leg, but trying to get around on crutches while wearing a cast could be dangerous, not to mention difficult."

"You've got that right," Mike agreed.

"Can we get back to our lesson now?" Noreen looked at Emma. "Will we be expected to finish the quilting process today?"

Emma shook her head. "Whatever you don't get done can be finished next week. During our final lesson, you will finish your wall hanging by putting the binding on." Emma glanced at B.J., who now seemed almost subdued as he continued to work on his project. "Now if any of you needs help today, just let either Lamar or me know." Emma motioned to Jan, sitting close to Kim. "I'm sure Jan would be willing to help out, too, since he's taken the class and is familiar with the procedure."

"I'd be more than willing to help." Jan smiled at Kim. "So don't hesitate to ask if you need anything."

She smiled in return. "Thanks, Jan. If I keep sticking myself with this needle, I may turn the whole project over to you."

He shook his head. "Naw, you're doin' just fine."

Emma moved over to stand beside Erika. "How are things going with you? Are you getting the feel for quilting?"

Erika shrugged. "I guess so. It seems easy enough."

"Not for me," Mike said. "I'm all thumbs. Some people think baiting a hook is hard, but that's nothin' compared to quilting."

"It just takes practice," Emma said. She gave Erika's shoulders a tender squeeze. "What you've done so far looks very nice. I think you have a knack for quilting."

Erika looked over her shoulder at Emma, and the faintest smile crossed her lips. "Thanks."

At least that's a step in the right direction, Emma thought as she moved back to the head of the table. *Now if we could just help Noreen and B.J. resolve their differences, I'd feel a lot better about things today.*

CHAPTER 27

At eleven o'clock, Emma suggested that everyone stop quilting and she served a snack of orange slices, fresh strawberries, and banana bread. That was fine with Jennifer. Her back was beginning to ache from sitting so long, and it made her uncomfortable to witness the undercurrent going on between B.J. and Noreen. Every time B.J. asked Emma a question or needed help with his stitching, Noreen said something derogatory.

That poor man, Jennifer thought as she bit into a juicy strawberry. *I wonder if he and Noreen can work out their differences. Everyone makes mistakes. Besides, it doesn't sound like B.J. knew anything about the consequences of his actions years ago.*

Walking around for a bit to get the kinks out of her legs and back, Jennifer looked around the tidy room that Emma kept. A battery-operated clock on one wall, a quilted wall hanging on another—and then there were the sewing machines, lined up in a row along the windowed wall, with the table they'd all been sitting around in the center of the room. There was no clutter, for everything in the room seemed to have a purpose.

Jennifer pressed on the small of her back, and it relieved the pain somewhat. She was definitely ready for this baby to be born.

Her thoughts shifted as she looked at the clock on the far wall. She could hardly wait to get home today to talk to Randy and find out how things went at the restaurant. She was almost afraid to ask, but oh, how she hoped he'd gotten that job.

"If everyone is finished with their refreshments you can continue working on your quilting projects," Emma instructed her students.

"I'm finished and ready to get back to work." Noreen pushed away from the table. "But let me help you carry the empty plates to the kitchen."

Emma's first thought was to tell Noreen that she could manage the dishes on her own, but thinking this would be a good opportunity to speak with her about B.J., she changed her mind. "Thank you, Noreen. I appreciate that."

"I can carry some dishes, too," Kim spoke up.

"That's alright," Emma said with a shake of her head. "I appreciate your offer to help, but there aren't many dishes, so I think Noreen and I can manage just fine."

"Oh, okay." Kim sat back down, and Emma and Noreen gathered up the dishes and left the room.

When they entered the kitchen, Emma told Noreen that she could put the dishes in the sink. "I'll wash them later this afternoon."

"How do you deal with not having a dishwasher?" Noreen asked, looking around the room.

Emma laughed. "I can't miss what I've never had. Why, I've been washing dishes by hand since I was a young girl. When my sister, Rachel, and I were too short to reach the sink, we had stools to stand on."

Noreen grimaced. "Before I got married, I used to wash dishes by hand, too, but it was definitely not my favorite thing to do."

"I guess we all have chores we'd rather not do."

Noreen gave a nod. "I suppose I should go back and get busy on my wall hanging. I don't want to get behind."

When Noreen started for the door, Emma quickly said, "Before you go, there's something I'd like to say."

"What's that, Emma?" Noreen asked, turning to face her.

Emma moistened her lips with the tip of her tongue, hoping her words would be well-received. "I don't mean to interfere, and I'm not trying to stick my nose in where it doesn't belong, but I wanted you to know that should you need to talk about your situation with B.J., I'm here to listen."

Lowering her gaze to the floor, Noreen quietly said, "I'll keep that in mind." Then she hurried into the next room.

Emma stayed in the kitchen a few moments longer, offering a prayer on Noreen's behalf. She obviously didn't want to discuss the situation, so Emma would just keep praying.

———

"You're doin' a great job with that," Jan said, leaning over Kim's shoulder.

She smiled up at him. "Thanks. The stitching is a little tedious, but it's fun to be creative like this."

"I know what you mean," he agreed. "When I took Emma's quilting class, on the advice of my probation officer, I think some of the other students thought it was kinda weird to see a big guy like me with a needle and thread in his hands."

"You were on probation?" Erika jumped into the conversation.

Jan gave a nod.

"What'd you do?"

"Got busted for a DUI. Do you know what that means, Erika?"

She rolled her eyes. "Of course I do. I may be disabled, but I'm not stupid."

"Never said you were." Jan grunted. "You're too sensitive about bein' in that wheelchair, if you ask me."

"Well, I didn't ask," she shot back.

Emma quickly stepped forward and said, "We only have a few minutes left today, so if anyone has a question, now is a good time to ask."

Erika lifted her hand.

"What's your question?" Emma asked.

"What are we supposed to do with our wall hangings after they're done?"

"Whatever you like." Emma smiled. "I'm sure most of you will want to keep yours, but of course, if you want to give the finished project to someone as a gift, that's perfectly fine, too."

"I might give mine to the hospital where my dad works," Erika said. "I think it would look nice hanging in the waiting room inside the children's wing. That's why I'm including a smiley face in the center of my wall hanging."

"That's an excellent idea," Lamar spoke up. "Don't you think so, Emma?"

Emma nodded. It was good to see Erika coming out of her shell. And the fact that she wanted to give her wall hanging away was a good indication that she was thinking beyond her own struggles.

"Erika, now that you know how to sew, maybe you could make some other things the children at the hospital could enjoy," Emma said.

Erika tipped her head. "Like what?"

"What about some cloth dolls?" Jennifer suggested. "I'll bet any of the little girl patients would like to have a doll to play with and cuddle."

"That's a good idea. What do you think about that, Erika?" Emma questioned.

Erika shrugged. "I'll give it some thought."

Well, at least she didn't say no, Emma thought.

When Emma announced that class was over for the day, Noreen gathered up her things and skirted out the door. B.J. felt a sense of panic. He needed to talk to Noreen and try to find out more about his son. He felt sure she was hiding something.

Mumbling a quick good-bye to Emma and Lamar, B.J. rushed out the door. Seeing that Noreen was already at her car and about to get in, he hollered, "Please, wait, Noreen! I need to speak with you."

Ignoring him, she jerked the car door open, but she dropped her purse and half of the belongings fell out. She bent to pick it up, throwing the contents back in, giving B.J. time to step up to her car.

"Here, you forgot this," B.J. said, bending down to get the tube of lipstick that had rolled slightly under her car.

"I saw it." Noreen grabbed the tube when he handed it to her and threw it in her purse. B.J. noticed how she wouldn't even look at him, even though they were hunkered down, face-to-face.

"What are you afraid of, Noreen?" he asked. "Why won't you tell me more about Judy's death and the child you said was adopted?"

As Noreen rose to her feet, the turban on her head caught on the edge of the car door and ripped right off. "Oh no!" she gasped, as her midnight-black tresses tumbled out. "Now look what you made me do!"

B.J. bent to pick up the turban that had fallen on the ground. If he hadn't been so concerned about getting answers from her about Judy and their child, he might have laughed, seeing Noreen standing there like that. Laughing at her was the last thing he wanted to do, however. She was already mad enough at him. No wonder she'd worn the turban to the last two quilt classes. Apparently she'd dyed her hair black and didn't want any of the quilting students to see it. Well, he couldn't blame her for that. It looked terrible!

"Give me that!" Noreen snatched the turban out of B.J.'s hands, hopped into her car, and slammed the door. Then she started her engine and peeled out of the driveway in a spray of gravel. B.J.'s shoulders slumped. At this rate he would never get the answers he sought.

As Jennifer headed for home, she thought about everything that had happened during the quilt class. If it hadn't been for the tension between Noreen and B.J., she would have enjoyed herself, for she found quilting to be a stress reliever.

After I finish the wall hanging, I'll get started on a quilt for the baby, she decided. *And when Randy gets a job and there's more money coming in, maybe I can make a queen-sized quilt for our bed.*

Jennifer turned on the radio and hummed along to a couple of her favorite tunes. It made the drive less boring. Her ankles were a little swollen from sitting so long this morning, so she decided to get some things done at home and move around more this afternoon.

When she finally pulled into her driveway, she was relieved to see Randy's truck. Anxious to hear about his job interview, Jennifer climbed out of the car and stepped onto the front porch. "Now, what is this?" she murmured, picking up a small box lying near the door. It had a picture of a crib mobile inside on it. *I wonder where that came from.*

Stepping inside, Jennifer halted. In the middle of the living-room floor sat Randy, surrounded by baby furniture and unopened boxes. She couldn't believe it! "What is going on, Randy? All these things must have cost a fortune!"

"I know, I know. It's a lot to take in," Randy said, looking around the room. "But don't get upset, because I—"

"I was just going to ask where the little box by our door came from, and now I see all of this! Did you go back to the store and charge a bunch of baby things again?" Jennifer's jaw clenched as she awaited his answer.

Randy shook his head. "Calm down, Jen, and let me explain. I found them on the front porch when I got back from the restaurant this morning. I must have forgotten to bring in that smaller box you found. I have no idea where it all came from, and seeing all of this surprised me as much as it did you." Randy paused a moment and stood. "But before we talk about this more, just listen to this, honey." He reached for her hand. "I got the cook's position at the restaurant on Bahia Vista Street! Isn't that great news?"

She relaxed a bit and started to giggle. "Oh Randy, what an answer to prayer! After I called you about the job opening, I could hardly wait to get home to see how it went." Jennifer hugged him tightly, then rested her head against his chest, her whole body relaxing.

"Maybe things are starting to look up for us now," he said.

Leaning back to look at his face, Jennifer nodded tearfully. "I'm so glad about your new job, and I'm anxious to hear all the details, but first, what about all these baby things? How did they end up on our porch?"

"I don't know. There was no note or anything. But let's not worry about who gave us these gifts," he said, resting his chin on top of her head. "Someone obviously wanted us to have all this furniture, and we can sure use it. Wow, I can't believe that two good things happened today."

Jennifer smiled. "I'm grateful for the baby things and relieved that you didn't charge them. I just wish I knew who to thank."

"Me too, but let's just be thankful, okay?" Randy tilted her face up toward his and kissed her.

CHAPTER 28

I *wonder if I could have won that drawing for baby furniture that I entered,* Randy thought as he left the house Thursday morning to head to his new job. He hadn't given it much thought until now, but if he had won the drawing, then all the baby things that had been left on their porch would make sense.

I've still got plenty of time till I have to be at the restaurant, so think I'll stop by the store on my way to work and ask who won that drawing.

Monday had been Randy's first day on the job. He'd worked the breakfast and lunch shifts, and things had gone well. The owners of the restaurant were nice and had even stopped by the kitchen to tell him that several customers that morning had mentioned how good the food was. He hadn't been working a week yet, and already he was getting compliments. Boy, did that feel good, and to be working again felt even better.

Things seem to be looking up for us, Randy mused, turning onto the street where the store was located. *Since I have a job now, I don't have to worry about our bills, and the nursery is full of everything we'll need for the baby. Now all we need to do is try to be patient and wait for our little girl to be born.* He glanced at his reflection in the rearview mirror. *I wonder if she'll look like Jennifer or have more of my traits. Sure hope she doesn't end up with a nose that's a bit too long, like mine. Our little girl should have a cute turned-up nose, like her mother's.*

Randy parked his truck near the store and headed inside. He hoped he wouldn't encounter the salesclerk who'd been miffed when he'd returned the original baby furnishings. He couldn't really blame her for that. Most likely the sale personnel worked on commission, and she'd made a sale and lost it just as fast on the same day.

When Randy spotted a clerk in the baby section, he was relieved that it was a different woman. He stepped up to the counter and asked about the drawing that had recently been held. "I'm thinkin' I may have won, because last Saturday a bunch of baby items were left on our front porch."

"The winner would have been notified by phone first," the middle-aged clerk said. "Then once the address was verified, you would have been asked to come to the store to pick up your items."

Randy scratched his head. "Are you sure about that? I mean, if someone from the store tried to call and we weren't home, maybe the baby things were delivered and left on our porch."

"That wouldn't have happened."

"Can you at least tell me who the winner was?" Randy asked.

"Sorry, but I don't have access to that information, and even if I did, I would not be permitted to give it out. As I said before, if it had been you, there would have been a phone call."

"Okay, thanks for your time." Randy turned and hurried out of the store. This whole thing really had him puzzled. If he hadn't won the drawing, then who had left all that stuff at their home?

"Good morning," Anna Lambright said as she passed Kim near the breakfast buffet at the restaurant.

"Morning." Kim smiled. "I've missed seeing you. Guess that's what happens when we work different shifts."

Anna nodded. "I actually prefer the morning shift. It gives me a chance to get some afternoon sun on the beach. Have you been there lately?"

"Since tomorrow's my day off, I'll be going to Caspersen Beach in Venice with Emma, Lamar, Jan, and his daughter, Star." Kim smiled. "We're going to look for sharks' teeth, and I'm really looking forward to that."

"I didn't realize Jan's daughter was in Sarasota."

"She's supposed to arrive today. Jan should be picking her up soon."

"So you'll get to meet her for the first time?"

"Yes, and I'll admit, I'm a little nervous about it. But if she's anything like Jan, I'm sure she'll be nice."

Anna poked Kim's arm playfully. "You like him a lot, don't you? I can see it by the gleam in your eyes."

Kim laughed self-consciously. "Does it really show?"

"Yeah, but that's okay. If being with Jan makes you happy, that's a good thing."

"Thanks. Well, guess we both need to get to work. We don't want any of our customers complaining because they had to wait too long for their orders this morning."

"We sure don't. If I don't talk to you before, have a nice time at the beach tomorrow. I'll be thinking about you when I'm here working."

"I'm sure you'll get your chance to go to the beach again soon."

"You're right. My friend Mandy and I hope to go to Siesta Keys Beach." Anna gave Kim's arm a light tap. "See you later."

As Kim went to the kitchen to turn in her order, she thought about Jan and how much she'd come to care for him in such a short time. She was almost sure he felt the same way, because of the expression in his eyes when he looked at her.

I wonder if he's holding back because he knows he'll be going home in a few weeks. Maybe that's why Jan hasn't tried to kiss me, she thought. *He might not want to give me hope that there could be anything more than just a passing friendship between us. It's gonna be hard, but I need to accept that fact and be prepared for when he leaves.*

Jan parked his motorcycle in the parking lot and sprinted for the airport terminal. Star's plane should be arriving any minute, and he wanted to be waiting for her. He was anxious to see Star and glad they would get an opportunity to spend some time together here in the warmer climate.

Jan didn't have long to wait, for a few minutes later, he spotted Star heading his way. Her dark brown hair bounced in rhythm with each step as she came closer, and her face broke into a wide smile when she saw him. Was it Jan's imagination, or did his daughter look a bit older today? It hadn't been that long since he'd last seen Star, so he couldn't quite tell what the change really was.

"Hey, Dad, it's good to see you," she said, giving him a hug.

"It's great to see you, too, kiddo. I've missed you a lot."

"Ditto."

"If you don't have any checked luggage to pick up, we can head out to the parking lot." Jan gestured to the door leading outside.

"Nope. I knew I'd be riding home on the back of your bike, so everything I need is right here," she said, pointing to her backpack.

"That's great. Let's get going then."

As they walked across the parking lot, Jan looked over at his daughter. "I can't put my finger on it, but there's somethin' different about you."

"Do you like it?" Star fluffed up her hair. "Thought I'd go with a shorter style, and I got a body wave, too. It's a bit bouncy, but I really like the change."

"It's cute, Star. Yeah, real cute. Makes you look older, too."

"Well, it's time I start looking my age. I'm in my twenties now and can't look like a teenager forever."

Jan would have given anything to have been a part of Star's teenage years. He had missed out on so much of her life. It was hard not to look back and be full or regrets, but he knew he had to put the past to rest as best as he could. Star was back in his life now, and going forward was all that mattered. No more would he be missing out on anything pertaining to his daughter's life, and he looked forward to every bit of it.

When they reached the spot where Jan's motorcycle was parked, Star's eyebrows squeezed together. "What's this for?" she asked, pointing to the new sidecar Jan had purchased on Monday. "I hope you don't think I'm ridin' in that."

"Only if you want to. Thought you could put your backpack in the sidecar and then ride on the back of the bike with me. But when we head for home in two weeks, you might be more comfortable riding in the sidecar than on the back of the bike."

She shook her head vigorously. "No way, Dad! Sidecars are for old ladies and dogs."

He chuckled. "That's the main reason I got it, Star. Thought it'd be fun to give Brutus a ride."

Star rolled her eyes and whacked his arm. "You're gettin' strange ideas in your old age, Dad."

He grinned. "Not so strange, really. Think I'm just gettin' more settled."

Star shook her head, pulling her curls aside and clipping them at the back of her head. "Don't think you'll ever be settled. You're a free spirit, just like me."

"Can't I be a free spirit and settled at the same time?" he asked after they had put on their helmets. "Look at you. You're already making changes, like your hair."

"Yeah, right. So, are we going straight to Emma and Lamar's? It'll be nice to see them."

"Yep. We're goin' there right now. They're looking forward to seeing you, too. Oh, and Star, I've made plans for us to do something fun tomorrow with Emma and Lamar."

"What's that?"

"We'll be driving down to one of the beaches in Venice to look for sharks' teeth. Doesn't that sound like fun?"

"Sure, I guess so. But how are we gonna get there? There sure isn't room in your sidecar for both Emma and Lamar."

"Kim will be driving us in her car."

Star's body stiffened as she held her hands rigidly at her sides. "Kim's going, too?"

"Yeah. It'll be a good chance for the two of you to get acquainted."

"Who says I want to get to know her? I mean, she's really nothing to me."

"Well, she is to me, and I want you to know her."

"Let's get going," Star said, nudging Jan's arm. "I'm hot, tired, and hungry to boot."

"I'm sure Emma will have lunch waiting for us when we get there,"

Jan called over his shoulder as they took their seats on the bike. Turning on the engine, he headed out of the airport parking lot. He didn't care for Star's attitude toward Kim. It seemed as if she didn't want to meet his new girlfriend.

Kim is my girlfriend, isn't she? Jan asked himself as they sailed down the road. *Sure seems like it to me.*

Chapter 29

Sitting in the backseat of Kim's car between Emma and Lamar, Star clenched her teeth. The vehicle was small, and she felt cramped and couldn't see out either of the side windows. She had to settle for looking straight ahead, watching Kim's eyes in the rearview mirror as she drove them down Highway 41 toward Venice.

Star was usually uncomfortable when someone else was driving, and today was no exception. It didn't help that Kim kept glancing at Dad as they held a conversation. It was sickening to watch her dad smiling, nodding, and hanging on every word Kim said. Kim was no better. She kept laughing at the stupid little jokes and corny stories Dad told as they traveled along. Star would be glad when they got to Venice so she could get out of the car and be on the beach. *If Dad keeps acting like a teenager with a crush, I'll lose my appetite.*

"You're awfully quiet," Emma said, gently patting Star's arm. "Are you feeling okay today?"

"I'm fine. Just tired is all."

"That's understandable. We did get up pretty early this morning, not to mention the hours you traveled yesterday on the plane."

"I'll be fine." Star studied Emma. She was wearing a navy blue dress, black shoes, and black stockings, and her white head covering was neatly in place.

Lamar was dressed in a pale blue shirt and a pair of denim-looking trousers held up with black suspenders. His straw hat rested in his hands and would no doubt offer him shade when the sun heated things up later today.

Star's dad, on the other hand, had on a pair of jeans, with his swim trunks underneath. He also wore one of his biker vests, which covered his back and chest, leaving his muscular arms showing. Star wondered if he'd worn it to show off for Kim.

She glanced down at the black shorts she'd worn, along with a light beige tank top. At her dad's insistence, she'd brought her swimsuit along but doubted that she'd wear it. She'd rather lie on the beach and soak up the sun than go swimming. Star thought she might also try some song-writing. She'd brought along a notebook and pen, in case she became inspired by the sound of the waves or seagulls that would no doubt be soaring overhead. If she kept busy with that, maybe she wouldn't be expected to make conversation with Kim.

"I should have let you sit by the window," Emma said, breaking into Star's musings. "You've never been to Florida before, and there's so much to see on this route we are taking. Have you ever been along a coastline like this?"

Star shook her head. "I saw it from the plane when I was flying down here, but I've never been to the beach on the gulf before."

"Today should be fun for you then," Lamar interjected. "Before too long, you'll be able to walk right out and put your feet in the water."

"I'm anxious to see it," Star admitted. "The closest thing to big water I've ever seen was Lake Superior when Mom and I lived in Minneapolis. It was only one time, though, when Mom was dating some guy from Duluth. He took us to a place called Two Harbors for the day."

"The lakes make up a large body of water, too," Lamar said. "It's a lot like the ocean when you're looking out toward the horizon and all you can see is water. Ocean waves are a lot bigger than what you'd see on a lake, though."

Star nodded. "I remember there were small waves on Lake Superior."

"Going to the lake sounds like a nice memory for you," Emma commented.

"It was a memory alright." Star remembered how she'd felt like a nuisance that day, so long ago. It had been pretty clear Mom's boyfriend Eddie wanted Mom all to himself. *Thank goodness Mom broke that relationship off quickly.*

Star wondered how things would go today between her dad and Kim. Would Kim resent her and act like she was in the way? Well, Star would make sure she wasn't in the way, because she had little to say to Kim. And if she said what was really on her mind, she would upset both Kim and Dad.

Feeling drowsier, Star leaned her head back against the seat and closed her eyes. "Wake me when we get there," she murmured.

Venice, Florida

"According to my GPS, this is the place," Kim said, pulling into the parking lot at Caspersen Beach. "And look, there are restrooms and a place to wash the sand off our feet, so that'll be handy."

Everyone climbed out of the car, and while Emma and Lamar

stretched their legs and Star headed for the restrooms, Jan went around to open the trunk, where they'd stowed all their beach supplies and picnic basket. He and Kim had purchased some beach chairs, in addition to two special scoops with long handles they could take turns using when they searched for sharks' teeth in the shallow part of the surf. Jan could hardly wait to try out one of those contraptions.

"I'm glad I brought plenty of sunscreen along," Kim said, joining him at the back of the car. "From the looks of the sky, and feeling how warm it is already this morning, I'm guessing we're in for a pretty hot day."

Jan patted his jeans. "Which is why I am wearing my swim trunks under here—so I can get cooled off in the water if I get too hot and sweaty."

"I'd thought about bringing my swimsuit," Kim said, "but I knew Emma wouldn't be wearing one, and knowing that the Amish dress modestly, I didn't want to offend her or Lamar." She glanced down at her turquoise shorts and rose-colored, sleeveless top. "Even this outfit, I wasn't too sure about."

"Aw, you look fine," Jan said. *More than fine,* he mentally added. "Star wore shorts today, too, so you're not alone, and I'm sure neither Emma nor Lamar will be offended."

Kim smiled. "Your daughter's a pretty young woman, Jan."

"Yeah. I think she got her mother's good looks, 'cause I still have mine." Jan chuckled and winked at Kim.

She swatted his arm playfully. "Seriously, I'm glad Star's here. I hope she and I will have a chance to really visit today. Since you and I were talking in the front seat on the way here, and she was sitting in the back, I didn't get the opportunity to ask her any questions." She paused while Jan reached into the trunk and took out the beach chairs. "I took

US 41 so Star could see more of the scenery along the way. Maybe I should have suggested that she sit up front with me. Except for what I overhead her telling Emma and Lamar about the lake, I don't think she said much else."

Jan removed the rest of their things from the trunk. "Since we plan to spend a good portion of the day on the beach, you two will have lots of time to get acquainted. I'm sure you'll get to know her, so don't worry."

Between them, Jan and Kim managed to grab most of the things. Lamar carried the beach umbrellas, Star had the picnic basket, and Emma tucked an old quilt under her arm as they left the parking lot and headed down the path to the beach. "Good thing we thought to bring the umbrellas along," Jan added. "It'll be nice to have a shady place to get out of the sun for a while. And just listen. . . Think I can already hear the waves calling to me."

Sarasota

B.J. stared at the painting he'd started a few days ago. It was another beach scene, with the sun setting over the water in a rainbow of glorious colors. If he got it finished in time, it would make a nice thank-you gift for Emma and Lamar, which he hoped to give them at the last quilting class. So far, the seascape looked pretty good, and he was happy that he'd captured the colors just right, but something seemed to be missing. He just needed to figure out what and then add it in. Well, if he didn't get it done before the last class, he'd finish it when he returned home and mail it to them. He hadn't noticed many pictures on the walls in the Millers' house, but hoped Emma and Lamar would like this one. Trouble was, he had so little energy this week. *Probably the cancer taking its toll on me,* he decided. He'd felt better when he'd first arrived in Sarasota, and thought there might be some hope for him after all. But for the last few days, he'd felt his body weakening, and it made him wonder if it had been a mistake to leave Chicago and come here. Maybe he should have continued with his cancer treatments. The vitamins and herbs he'd tried so far hadn't done much to make him feel better. Perhaps he just needed to give them more time, or maybe he'd waited too long after his cancer diagnosis to try the more natural approach. Either way, B.J. knew he was in trouble, because he had coughed up blood the other day, and that wasn't a good sign. But he had to keep fighting and pressing on. In addition to the wall hanging he wanted to finish for his granddaughter and the painting for the Millers, B.J. had a son out there somewhere whom he wished to meet.

B.J. left his easel, turned on the CD player for some relaxing music, and reclined in his chair. *I just wish Noreen would talk to me without getting hot under the collar. I wonder what would happen if I looked up her phone number and gave her a call. But that might make her even angrier than she already is.*

Just then, B.J.'s cell phone rang. Glancing at the caller ID, he saw that it was his daughter, Robyn. B.J. hated to ignore Robyn's call, but the last thing he wanted to do was deal with her asking how he was doing. He dreaded the thought of telling his daughters the truth about his cancer, but sooner or later it would have to come out. He wasn't sure what would be worse: explaining that his cancer was spreading, or telling Jill and Robyn they had a stepbrother, who until recently, B.J. had known nothing about.

Finally, the phone quit ringing, and B.J. sat with his eyes closed, thinking things through. If he didn't get anywhere with Noreen this Saturday at the quilt class, then he would follow her home so they could talk.

The phone rang, startling Noreen as she sat in her recliner, half-asleep. She pulled herself out of the chair and went to answer it. "Hello."

"Hi, Mom. How's it going?"

Noreen yawned. "Uh, fine. How are you, Todd?"

"Doin' good. I didn't wake you, I hope."

"It's okay. I was just resting my eyes a bit. It's good to hear your voice, Son."

"Same here, Mom. Say, the reason I'm calling is Kara and I have some time off, and it's been awhile since we've seen you, so we thought we'd come to Sarasota for a visit."

Noreen's heartbeat quickened. As much as she wanted to see Todd and his wife, now wasn't a good time. Not with Bruce asking so many questions about Judy's son.

"Mom, did you hear what I said?"

"Umm. . .yes, I did."

"So, is it okay if we come down to see you?"

Think, Noreen, think. She swallowed hard. "Well, I'm kind of busy right now."

"Doing what?" he questioned.

"I'm taking a quilt class, and there are still two more lessons, so. . ."

"Are you tied up with the class every day of the week?"

"Well, no, but. . ."

"Kara and I can fend for ourselves while you're at the class. It'll give us some time to hang out on the beach or explore a few things in Sarasota that we haven't seen before."

"O–okay, if you're sure," Noreen finally conceded, unable to think of any other excuse. Her son and daughter-in-law meant the world to her, and she really did want to see them. It had been way too long since their last visit. Noreen just hoped Todd hadn't noticed her hesitancy.

She would just have to make sure Todd and Kara never met B.J. while they were visiting, because she certainly wasn't going to mention him.

CHAPTER 30

Venice

Your dad mentioned that you sing and play the guitar," Kim said, in an attempt to make conversation with Star. The women had been sitting on the old quilt Emma had brought along, while the men took a walk up the beach. So far, Star hadn't said more than a few words, not even to Emma.

Star merely shrugged, as she sifted grains of sand through her fingers.

Thank goodness Emma is here, Kim thought. *I feel invisible to Star.*

"Star not only plays and sings, but she's an accomplished songwriter," Emma put in. "In fact, she's had two of her songs published."

"That's awesome. I'll bet your dad's really proud of you."

"Yeah, I suppose," Star muttered, making no eye contact with Kim.

"I've always wanted to learn to play the guitar," Kim said, hoping Star would at least look at her. "Maybe you could teach me sometime."

Star pursed her lips. "That might be kinda hard since you live in

854

Florida, and we live up north."

"Maybe you could give Kim a few lessons before you go home," Emma suggested.

Star shook her head, looking back at Emma. "No can do. I didn't bring my guitar."

"Lamar has an old one you can borrow," Emma said.

Star's eyebrows shot up. "Lamar plays the guitar? I didn't think Amish people could own any musical instruments."

"Is that true?" Kim asked, turning to look at Emma.

"Some Amish do play the guitar or harmonica, but not in church. Sometimes when we get together with friends or family members we sing, and someone might play their guitar or harmonica," Emma explained. "Some of our young people have even been known to use a battery-operated keyboard."

Star whistled. "Now that's a surprise."

Emma laughed. "We're not entirely old-fashioned in our ways, and we do like to have fun when we gather with family and friends."

"You're right, Emma," Kim agreed. "I've witnessed that during our quilting classes whenever Lamar has teased you or told a joke."

Emma smiled. "My husband's a good man, and he's brought much joy into my life." She motioned to the men, who'd moved even farther down the beach. "Jan is a good man, too, and I think even in the short time you've known each other, he's come to care a good deal for you, Kim."

Kim glanced over at Star to gauge her reaction, but the young woman just sat, swirling her fingers in the sand.

A dragonfly darted between them, and flicking it away, Star rose to her feet. "Think I'm gonna take a walk down the beach a ways."

"Would you like some company?" Kim called as Star started to walk away. She thought this might be a good chance for them to talk privately and hopefully break the ice.

Star shook her head and kept walking in the opposite direction of the men.

"Oh great. My hopes of getting to know Star seem to be going nowhere." Kim leaned back on her elbows and sighed. "I'm afraid Jan's daughter doesn't like me very much. I think she might be upset that her dad's spending time with me."

Emma gave Kim's arm a tender pat. "She hasn't had the chance to get to know you yet. Just give her some time, and I'm sure she'll warm up to the idea of you and Jan seeing each other."

Kim drew in a deep breath and released it slowly. "I hope so, but then maybe it doesn't matter."

"What do you mean?"

"Jan and Star will be going back to Indiana in a few weeks, and then I'll probably never see them again." Kim slowly shook her head. "It's a shame, too, because even in the short time I've known Jan, I have really come to care for him."

Emma nodded. "I figured as much, but if things are meant to work out between you, then they will."

"I wish I had your confidence." Kim shaded her eyes as she watched Jan and Lamar turn and head back in their direction, and then remembering she'd put her sunglasses in her tote bag, she reached inside and put them on. "I sometimes have a hard time making decisions and don't always make right choices," she admitted. "I wish I had a guidebook that would show me what to do."

"Actually, there is," Emma said. "It's the Bible, and in Proverbs 3:6 it says, 'In all thy ways acknowledge him, and he shall direct thy paths.'" Emma crossed her ankles and clasped her fingers around one knee.

"When Lamar and I first met, I was confused about our relationship, but after praying about it, the Lord showed me what to do. If you trust God, and seek His will, He will show you what to do concerning Jan and his daughter."

Kim smiled. Emma was a wise woman with a heart for people. Sitting here, the old quilt beneath them, made Kim feel relaxed and hopeful. It almost felt like a healing quilt. She was glad she'd chosen to take Emma's quilting classes. But choice had nothing to do with her relationship with Jan. Things had just seemed to happen in the short time they'd known each other, and now she had strong feelings for him and wasn't sure what to do. *Will I be able to turn those feelings off once he goes back to Indiana?* she wondered. *I guess Emma's right; I need to pray about this.*

"Have you found any yet?" Jan called to Lamar, after they'd gathered up the long-handled scoops and waded into the water in search of sharks' teeth.

"Just a few. How's it going with you?"

"Not too bad. Found a couple of good ones, I think." Jan gestured to the plastic bag in his hand. "Got a few shells in there, too." He was glad he'd stripped down to his swim trunks. Otherwise, his jeans would be as wet as Lamar's trousers. Even though Lamar had rolled them up to his knees, his trousers were wet almost up to his waist from the waves washing in.

Jan watched with interest as a turtle came out of the water, walked up the beach, and meandered along the path that led to the road. A lot of interesting things could be found here on Caspersen Beach.

"Sure am glad that fella we ran into up the beach showed us what to do, or I probably wouldn't have found any sharks' teeth at all," Jan said, lifting his long-handled scoop to see what all he'd trapped.

Lamar straightened and rubbed the small of his back. "I don't know about you, but I'm about ready to take a little break. Why don't you see if either Kim or Star would like to take my place for a while?"

"I can't ask Star right now." Jan pointed down the beach. "Look, she's way down there, sittin' on a rock by the water. I'll see if Kim wants to try her hand at this, though. It's a lot of fun, and I'll bet she'd enjoy it as much as I do."

Jan followed Lamar to the place where Kim and Emma sat and knelt beside them on the sand so he wouldn't mess up Emma's quilt.

"Take a look at all the fossilized sharks' teeth we've found," Lamar said, holding his bag open for Emma to see.

Emma's eyes widened. "Oh my! Some of them are so small; I don't know how you even spotted them."

"They get trapped in the scooper," Lamar explained. "But I'll have to admit, it was hard to see some of those littler ones."

Jan showed Kim what was inside his plastic bag.

Her eyebrows lifted. "Wow, those are sure impressive! The only thing I've ever found on the beach that looked that interesting was a man's ring."

"Really? Where'd you find that?" Jan asked.

"On Lido Beach a few weeks ago. It had some initials carved in it. I think it may have been someone's class ring."

"What did you do with it?" Emma questioned.

"Took it home and put in my jewelry box." Kim pushed a wayward strand of hair off her forehead. "I'd return the ring to its rightful owner if I knew who it belonged to."

"Maybe you oughta take it to a jewelry shop and see if it's worth some money," Jan suggested.

Kim shook her head. "Think I'll hang on to it for now. Or maybe I'll run an ad in the paper about it."

"Why don't you bring it to class with you?" Emma said. "I'm curious to see what it looks like."

Kim gave a nod. "If I don't forget, I will."

"Right now, how'd you like to use one of the scoops and try to find some sharks' teeth with me?" Jan asked Kim.

"That sounds like fun, but if you and Lamar want to keep looking, I can wait."

"That's okay," Lamar was quick to say. "I'm ready to take a break. Bending over like that and then lifting the handle of the scoop made my back ache a bit." He smiled at Emma. "I know it's not lunchtime yet, but I could sure use a snack."

Emma smiled and motioned to their lunch basket. "I think that could be arranged."

Jan reached out his hand and helped Kim to her feet. Then Lamar handed her his scoop. "Now you need to show Jan how it's done," Lamar teased.

Kim laughed. "Emma and Lamar are sure great," she commented as she and Jan walked toward the water.

"You got that right." Jan glanced down the beach and saw that Star was still there. *She's not very sociable today,* he thought. *Maybe she just needs some time alone. She's probably enjoying the warm sun and salty air. Sure wouldn't be gettin' that if she was at home right now.*

As Star sat on a large rock with her legs outstretched, she couldn't help but enjoy the cool water as it splashed gently over her bare feet. Hearing a helicopter buzz overhead, she looked up. When it moved out of sight, she noticed several pelicans skimming the water as though searching for fish. It was funny to watch them fly straight up then dive right down to snatch their prey.

A slight breeze lifted the bangs from her forehead as she shielded her eyes from the glare of the sun. Glancing up the beach a ways, she saw her dad and Kim in the water, looking for sharks' teeth, no doubt.

Star pulled her hair back and secured it with a clippie. Her hair wasn't as long as it had been before, but there was still enough to clip back, letting the shorter ends fall free. She'd hated sitting there on Emma's old quilt as Kim plied her with questions and couldn't wait to get off by herself so she think and try to enjoy the day.

Glancing at the water again, she noticed farther out, where it appeared to be deeper, a group of teenagers laughing and shouting to each other as they frolicked in the waves.

I wonder what it would have been like to have had friends to hang out with when I was their age, Star mused. She thought about her own teen years and how she'd preferred to be a loner rather than making friends. She could almost hear her mom saying, "You've pushed people away most of your life. No wonder you have no friends."

Star hated to admit it, but Mom was right. She did push most people away. She'd seen too many complications where having friends was concerned. They could be friends one minute and turn on you the next. Star's dad was like having a best friend, but that was different. She knew him well enough to know he'd never turn on her. But he was doing a good job of ignoring her today.

Star drew her knees up to her chest, watching in disgust when her dad put his arm around Kim's waist. She nearly gagged when he kissed Kim on the mouth. Didn't he care that Lamar and Emma were sitting on the quilt, no doubt watching them?

After knowing the Millers as long as he has, Dad oughta realize that married Amish couples like them never display that kind of affection in public. And what in the world is he thinking, getting involved with Kim? If she's falling for him, the way I think he is her, then he's gonna break her heart when we go back home. Maybe Mom was right when she told me that Dad walked out on us when I was a baby. Maybe he lied when he said it was Mom who took me and ran off.

Looking away, Star knew her thoughts were running amok. Mom had already admitted that she'd been the one to leave. Still, it did seem odd that after all these years, her dad had never had a serious relationship with a woman.

Could there be a deep-seated reason for that? Star wondered. *Maybe he's never really gotten over his feelings for Mom.* She shook her head, trying to clear her jumbled thoughts. Even if that were the case, Star's mother was married now and living in Fort Wayne, Indiana, so it was too late for her and Jan to become a couple again.

Star glanced up the beach once more and saw Dad and Kim with their heads together, apparently looking at something in one of their scoops.

I don't know what I'm going to do about this, Star fumed, *but I've gotta think of something before Dad gets some dumb idea about moving to Florida.*

"This is hard work," Kim said as she dumped a scoopful of shells onto the sand. "And it's difficult to see if there are any sharks' teeth in all the debris." Truth was, she still felt a bit breathless after Jan's kiss. If the tender way he'd looked at her before the kiss was any indication of the way he felt, he had fallen for her as hard as she had for him.

"After you've scooped up some stuff, try lifting the wire basket in and out of the water to rinse the sand off, and then shake it back and forth. Most of the bits and pieces you don't want will sift right through the basket, hopefully leaving just the good things behind."

"For a guy who's never done this before, you sure know a lot about it," Kim said.

Jan smiled. "Guess I'm just a quick learner."

"Lamar seemed to be enjoying himself when he was out in the water with you," Kim mentioned. "It was fun to watch him plodding through the water with his pants rolled up to his knees."

"Yeah." Jan chuckled. "He said he's been wantin' to do this ever since he and Emma came down for the winter. I'm glad he invited us to come along."

"I wish I could have brought Maddie with us today," Kim said wistfully. "She would have had fun, too. But there wasn't room in the car for her, so I asked one of my neighbors to check on her for me today."

"We'll have to bring Maddie along the next time we go to the beach," Jan said. "I'll bet Star would enjoy seeing your dog, too. Especially since she looks so much like my Brutus."

Kim turned to look down the beach to where Star had been sitting and noticed that she wasn't there anymore. Then she spotted her seated on the quilt beside Emma and Lamar. They were chatting away like best friends.

I wish she would visit with me like that, Kim thought. *I'll never get to know Jan's daughter if she won't converse with me.*

Kim's thoughts were halted when someone started shouting. Looking out at the water, where some teenagers had been swimming, she noticed that they seemed to be out pretty far. At first, she thought they were just fooling around, but then one of them hollered, "Help! Help! My friend is drowning!"

With no hesitation, Jan dropped his scoop, jumped into an oncoming wave, and started swimming out to the kids.

Kim stood on the shore, hands sweating and heart racing as she grabbed Jan's scooper. She hoped Jan was a strong swimmer and that the kid he was trying to save wouldn't pull him down.

CHAPTER 31

What's going on? What's my dad doing?" Star asked Emma and Lamar when she caught sight of Jan swimming out through the waves. "He sure can't be looking for sharks' teeth way out there."

"I—I don't know." Emma placed her hands parallel with her eyebrows, gazing out to where Star was pointing. "It looks like there are some young people out there, and Jan seems to be swimming in their direction. She turned to Lamar. "Can you tell what's going on?" The sun was at an angle that made the water glare back, and each ripple and wave glistened in the sun's reflection, making it hard to see.

Lamar shook his head, shading his eyes. "Not from this far, Emma. My vision isn't as good as it used to be."

"Mine either," she said. "And my glasses are only for close-up work."

"Well, my eyes are good, and I don't like what I see!" Star clambered to her feet.

Just then, Kim came running up from the water's edge, red-faced and panting. "Someone's in trouble out there, and Jan went to help, but we need to call for assistance right away." Dropping to her knees, she reached for her canvas tote, which she'd left on the quilt, and rummaged through it for her cell phone.

A sense of panic welled up in Star's soul, and with her heart pounding, she dashed to the shoreline. *Dear God, please don't let my dad drown. I need him so bad!*

————

"Maybe I should swim out and see if I can help Jan," Lamar said, starting to rise from the quilt.

Emma clasped his arm as he helped her get up. "Oh Lamar, I wish you wouldn't try to do that. I don't think you're up to something so strenuous."

Lamar frowned. "I can't just stand here and do nothing, and I'm not a *schwechlich mann*, you know."

"Of course you're not a weakly man," Emma was quick to say. "That's not what I meant."

Lamar folded his arms. "Sure sounded like it to me, but it doesn't matter. All that matters now is that they need help."

"Let's wait and see if Jan needs any assistance," Kim said after she'd made the 911 call. "If he does, then I'll swim out there myself. Ever since I was little I've been like a fish in the water."

"I guess that would be best," Lamar conceded. "Sounds like you're a stronger swimmer than me."

They stood watching while another small crowd of people gathered, pointing and observing as Jan swam toward the teens. A middle-aged man ran up to them and offered to call 911.

"Thank you, sir, but I already have," Kim answered and scurried back down to the water's edge to stand near Star.

"Oh dear." Emma sighed. She felt so helpless. She had heard the concern in Kim's usual bubbly voice. *And poor Star. She must be frantic with worry about her father right now.* All Emma could do was pray and hope for the best.

———

As Jan swam out to the drowning victim, he mentally recounted all that he'd learned during his training as a lifeguard shortly after graduating from high school. *Enter the water. Approach the victim from behind so he doesn't pull you down. Place your arms under the victim's armpits and bend your arms back so they're pointing at yourself, and hold on tight.*

Even though it had been more than twenty years, the instructions Jan learned back then had stuck with him. Thanks to his job as a roofer, he was in pretty fair shape physically. There was no doubt that swimming against this current was tiring.

Jan approached the teenage boy, who was now bobbing up and down, while gulping in water and gasping for air, and his training took over. He did everything just like he'd been taught. Jan pushed aside any fears about what could be swimming beneath the waters around them and concentrated fully on the boy.

The kid was in a panic, of course, and Jan had to remind him over and over to calm down. "Try to relax. You're gonna be okay. Trust me. I've got you."

Drawing in a deep breath, Jan swam toward shore, pulling the boy along. As he drew closer, he spotted Star and Kim standing near the edge of the water.

"I called 911, so help should be here soon," Kim said as Jan laid the nearly unconscious boy on the sand.

"Good," Jan panted. "But we can't wait for help to arrive. The kid could have water in his lungs, and he needs mouth-to-mouth resuscitation right now."

"I'll do it, Dad," Star volunteered, falling to her knees in order to help. "I've had CPR training. Besides, you look exhausted and oughta rest for a while."

"Star's right," Kim agreed, getting on the other side of the boy. "If necessary, she and I can take turns with the resuscitation."

Jan couldn't argue with their assessment, so he flopped down on the sand to catch his breath and watched as the women took over. Jan cast a quick glance toward the ocean and caught sight of a dolphin not far from where the teens had been. Looking back at the teenaged boy, he sent up a silent prayer, asking for the kid to be okay.

Emma and Lamar, as well as the other teenagers who had been in the water, gathered around with anxious expressions. Star turned the young man's head to one side, allowing the water he'd swallowed to drain from his mouth and nose. Then she turned his head back to the center and began mouth-to-mouth resuscitation, while Kim checked the boy's pulse. The small crowd of people that had quickly congregated stood far enough back to give them room.

Jan accepted a bottle of water that a middle-aged man offered him and said thanks when asked if he was alright. "Yeah, I'm okay." It was plain that everyone around was concerned.

When the boy started to breathe and cough, the crowd sighed with relief. Jan was hopeful that the kid would make it now.

A short time later, sirens wailed in the distance. Hopefully, the boy hadn't taken in too much water and wouldn't end up with complications.

Sarasota

Mike had just taken a seat on his front porch, to read the paper and enjoy the sun, when a sporty-looking black car pulled onto his driveway. A few minutes later, Mike's older brother, Keith, who lived in Orlando, got out of the car.

"Hey, Brother, it's good to see you!" Mike set his newspaper aside and stood. "What brought you to Sarasota today?"

Keith stepped onto the porch, and the brothers shook hands, then drew each other in for a hug and slap on the back. Afterward, Keith groaned as he sank into the wicker chair next to Mike's. "I was hoping you'd be here, because I need to talk."

Mike moved his chair closer to Keith's and sat down. He'd never seen his brother look so serious. "You seem upset. Is something wrong?" he asked, giving Keith his full attention.

Keith nodded, pulling his fingers through the ends of his thick blond hair. "I'm just gonna come right out and say it. Gina's left me."

Mike bolted upright, feeling as though an electrical current had been shot through him. "You're kidding, right?"

Keith slowly shook his head. "Wish I was."

"But why? What happened?" Mike could hardly believe his sister-in-law would have done such a thing. His brother had gotten married later in life, concentrating on getting settled into his career first. Gina was quite a bit younger than Keith, but from the beginning of their relationship she seemed to adore Keith. He'd given her everything she could have asked for—a big house, fancy car, and money to satisfy all of her whims. It made no sense that she would leave.

"Gina says I'm never around—that I'm not there for her and the kids anymore." Keith reached up and massaged the back of his neck. "She's seeing the clown who coaches Robbie's Little League team. Says he's more of a father to our son that I've ever been. Besides, the guy is a good-looking dude. At least, she thinks he is. Now tell me, how can I compete with that?" He moaned, leaning forward as though in great pain. "I just don't get it. I've worked hard all these years so my wife and kids could have nice things. They've wanted for nothing, and this is the thanks I get. I feel like I've been kicked in the teeth."

"I don't know what to say, Keith, except I'm sorry. Is there a chance you can win her back?"

"I don't think so. Gina made it pretty clear that she's done with me."

"Have you thought about going to see a marriage counselor?" Mike asked. "Would Gina be willing to try that?"

Keith shook his head. "I'm not about to let some shrink get inside my head. Besides, Gina's pretty involved with this baseball geek, and I doubt she'd agree to go for counseling. I think it's too late. I'm not sure how I could have been so dense, but I never even saw this coming."

"You ought to at least give counseling a try," Mike said, rising to his feet. "You can't walk away from fifteen years of marriage."

"You're right. It's tough. But if divorce is what she wants, then who am I to stand in her way?"

Irritation welled in Mike's soul as he glanced out at the bay. "It doesn't sound to me like you care that much if you're not willing to fight for your marriage."

"I do care," Keith snapped back. "It's just that Gina wants me to give up my career and hang around at home all the time."

"Maybe you should cut back on your hours at work," Mike suggested.

Keith looked at Mike like he'd taken leave of his senses. "No way. I'm not willing to do that. I've worked too hard to get where I am today. Not to mention having recently been offered a big promotion."

Mike knew that his brother's job as a sales rep for a big Orlando company put him on the road a lot. Last Christmas Mike had overhead Gina telling Phyllis that Keith was gone so much that she was beginning to feel like a widow. What had shocked him most that day was when Phyllis responded by saying that she could completely understood because she thought Mike cared more about his boat than he did her. At the time, Mike had brushed it off, thinking the women were overdramatizing. He'd rationalized his need to be on his boat so much. After all, didn't working long hours to give his wife nice things count for anything? Surely she should be able to figure out that his desire to make a good living proved how much he cared for her.

But hearing about his brother's situation caused Mike to stop and think about his own life and what was truly important to him. All these years Mike had thought his brother had the perfect life—a great career, good money, and a wife and kids who adored him. From as far back as Mike could remember he'd wanted to be successful like his older brother, but now he asked himself if success was really that important.

It was hard to figure people out or understand the logic behind their thinking, but Mike knew one thing for sure: he didn't want his own marriage to end up like Keith and Gina's. He'd been blinded by what he thought his brother had. When Phyllis got home, Mike planned to spend less time on the boat and more time with her.

CHAPTER 32

"Hey, kiddo, how'd you sleep last night?" Jan asked when Star came out of the bathroom on Saturday morning, rubbing her eyes.

She frowned as she stretched her muscles and tilted her head from side to side. "I would've slept a whole lot better in a bed instead of on the couch."

"Why don't you take the spare room, and I'll sleep on the couch. I offered to do that when you first got here."

Star shook her head. "Naw, the couch only makes into a double bed, and the bed in the guest room is a queen. You need that bigger bed more than I do, Dad." She released a noisy sigh. "I don't see why we can't stay in a hotel instead of here with Emma and Lamar."

"They invited us to stay with them, Star, and I don't wanna hurt their feelings," Jan explained in a low voice so the Millers wouldn't hear. "You know as well as I do what good people they are, and sleeping on the couch a few more nights isn't going to hurt you. Besides, with the

871

money we're saving, it'll give us more to spend on the way home."

"I guess you're right on both counts, but when are we leaving?" she asked with a hopeful expression.

"Thought we'd head out the Monday morning after the last quilting class. That'll give us plenty of time to make it home before you have to be back at work."

"What about your business, Dad? Don't you think you should go home sooner, in case a big roofing job comes in?"

Jan shook his head. "Terry's there. If something develops, he can handle it on his own. Besides, with the cold weather they're having up north, it's not likely that anyone's gonna want their roof replaced till spring."

"Guess you're right about that, too."

Jan paused before heading to the kitchen, where the aroma of fresh coffee beckoned him. "I know I told you this on the way home from the beach, but I'm real proud of the way you revived that boy who almost drowned."

"What I did was nothing, Dad. You were the hero, going out there to rescue him. When the boy's parents tracked you down afterward to say thanks, I could tell they thought you were a hero, too."

"I just followed my instincts. Sure couldn't stand there and let the kid drown." Jan smiled. "I was relieved when his parents said their son was going to be okay. That could have ended in disaster."

"Yeah, I know." Star took a few steps and halted. "Before we go into the kitchen, could I ask you a question, Dad?"

"Sure thing, kiddo, you can ask me anything."

She moistened her lips with the tip of her tongue. "It's about Kim."

"What about her?"

"I've been wondering how serious you two are about each other.

I saw you kiss her when we were at the beach in Venice, and. . ."

"I like her very much, Star," Jan was quick to say. "Kim and I have a lot in common, and I enjoy bein' with her more than any woman I've ever met." He bumped Star's arm playfully. "Present company excluded, of course."

Star dropped her gaze to the floor. "I see."

Jan put his thumb under her chin and lifted it until she was looking directly at him. "You're not jealous, I hope."

"No. Uh, yeah, maybe I am a little."

"Well, don't be. You're my daughter, and no one will ever come between us. You are still my number-one girl, and that'll never change. For the rest of the time we're here, I hope you'll give Kim a chance to get to know you better, because she's feeling some negative vibes coming from you." Jan pulled Star close and kissed her forehead. "Now let's get in there and see if Emma has breakfast ready, 'cause the Saturday quilters will be here soon."

"Don't see why we have to be here for that," Star complained. "Can't the two of us do something fun today? We could check out Siesta Key Beach or join one of those sightseeing tours at the marina."

"We'll do something fun after the class," he said. "I want to be here to see how things go, and maybe help out if I'm needed."

She grunted. "I thought the Millers were teaching the class."

He tweaked the end of her nose. "They are, smarty, but I want to be there in case Emma and Lamar get busy and someone has a question or needs extra help."

Star rolled her eyes. "Someone, like Kim?"

He shrugged. "Maybe."

Star opened her mouth as if to respond, but Emma called to them from the kitchen. "If you two are ready, breakfast is on the table."

Jan nudged Star's arm. "Guess we'd better get in there. We can talk later."

———·———

Noreen's hands felt clammy as she gripped the steering wheel. She dreaded going to the Millers' house for the fifth quilting class, because she hated the thought of seeing B.J. again. And knowing Todd and Kara would be here next week made her all the more apprehensive. If only they would wait to come for a visit until B.J. went back to Chicago. *I should be dancing on air knowing that my son and his wife are coming for a visit. Instead, I'm dreading it,* Noreen fumed. The more she thought about it, the more upset she became. *Bruce Jensen is messing everything up. I shouldn't be surprised, though; he's good at it.*

"I know one thing," Noreen barked, hitting the steering wheel to affirm her decision. "No matter how much prying B.J. does, he will never know about Todd!"

She looked in the rearview mirror, and grimaced at her reflection. Since B.J. had seen her hair last week when her turban fell off, she figured there was no point in wearing it again today, as he might say something about it in front of the others.

I don't know why I care what he thinks or doesn't think, Noreen scolded herself. Besides, she'd seen her hairdresser this week, gotten her hair cut, and had some highlights put in, which had toned down the black a bit. Her hair wasn't to her liking yet, but at least it looked better than when she'd first put that awful color in.

Glancing at her gas gauge, Noreen realized she'd let her tank get low, so she pulled into the nearest gas station. It wasn't like her to let it go below half. Her only excuse was that she'd been under so much stress and wasn't thinking clearly or paying attention to details, the way she normally did.

Noreen got out of her car, and as she pumped the gas, she thought about the class reunion she'd been invited to attend this evening. Ever since she'd dyed her hair, she'd struggled with whether to go or not. Through all Noreen's years of teaching, her hair had never been as dark as it was now. But was that a good reason to stay home? Most likely, the students wouldn't remember how her hair had looked back then, unless they got out their class yearbooks and checked out the teachers' photos.

If I don't go, I will miss seeing some of my old students, and any of my coworkers who might also be there, she told herself. *No, I'm going, even if I look like an old fool. Even if just for a few hours, maybe the enjoyment of seeing everyone again will take my mind off everything else that's been happening in my life lately.*

When B.J. arrived at the Millers', Noreen was just getting out of her car. He fully intended to ask her about Judy's son again, but by the time he'd gotten out of his car, she was already on the porch. He noticed everyone's vehicles were there, and most likely, the other quilters were waiting for them. Even so, while he had this opportunity, B.J. wanted to try once more to get some answers from Noreen.

Maybe Emma won't answer the door right away, and I'll get to Noreen before she goes into the house, B.J. thought as he made his way slowly across the yard. He was more tired than usual today and couldn't walk as fast as he normally did. There was no doubt that his illness was taking a toll on him, and he was powerless to stop it.

"Please don't start badgering me again," Noreen snapped when B.J. stepped onto the porch. "As I told you before, I don't know where Judy's son is, and I don't want to talk about this anymore. I just hope you can live with the fact that you took advantage of an innocent girl." Her mouth quivered. "If Judy hadn't gotten pregnant, she'd still be alive today."

"You don't know that," B.J. shot back, taking deep, deliberate breaths to slow his racing heart. "People die from many causes." *Like cancer,* he mentally added, gripping the porch railing, so he wouldn't lose his balance.

Now don't let me fall apart in front of Noreen. B.J. willed his weakened body to keep going, as he fought to overcome a dizzy spell.

Noreen turned her back on him and said nothing, just knocked on the door.

"I know you blame me for your sister's death, and if there was anything I could do to change the past, I surely would. Please try to understand," he implored. "Judy and I were both young, and I was still living under my parents' roof. I was just a teenaged boy, but if I'd known about everything, I wouldn't have left like I did. Please listen to me, Noreen." B.J. didn't like talking to someone's back, especially when they gave no response, but he continued anyway. "What teenage kid doesn't make mistakes? I'm not trying to make excuses for myself, but I had no idea about any of what happened. Not about Judy being pregnant, her having the baby, or about her death."

Noreen continued to ignore him and was practically pounding on the Millers' front door.

"Just try to put yourself in my place, Noreen," B.J. said, hoping she would finally realize what it was like for him to find out about his and Judy's child after all these years.

Noreen turned around suddenly, and looked as if she were about to say something, when Emma, with her usual cheery smile, opened the door. "Good morning. I'm glad you're both here."

When they entered the house, Emma looked at Noreen and her eyes widened. "Oh, you've done something different with your hair."

Noreen's cheeks turned pink. "Uh, yes. I changed the color and had it cut a bit shorter."

As worn out as he felt, B.J. stifled a laugh, and then hastily coughed to cover it up. Emma's shocked expression said it all. But she didn't laugh, either—just invited them to join the others at the table. Even in his own misery, B.J. could still find humor in this situation, and he couldn't wait to see the reaction of the other quilters when they saw Noreen's hair.

CHAPTER 33

It's good to see you all here," Emma said as she looked at everyone seated around her table. "I hope each of you have had a good week."

A few heads bobbed, but Noreen, looking as if she had eaten a sour cherry, said nothing, and neither did B.J., who sat with his shoulders slumped and head down. It tugged at Emma's heartstrings, making her wish once again that there was something she could do to help these two. But she didn't want to be pushy. If they wanted her or Lamar's help, surely they would ask.

"We had an interesting Friday," Kim spoke up with enthusiasm. "Jan saved a boy from drowning."

"Really? Wow! Tell us about it," Jennifer said, leaning forward with a wide-eyed expression.

Jan shrugged his shoulders. "It was nothin' really. Just did what most anyone woulda done."

"You're being modest," Lamar interjected. "Out of everyone on the beach, you were the only one who swam out to rescue the boy. You gave it no thought, just jumped into action."

"That's right, and you could have drowned in the process," Kim said.

"Well, I'm perfectly fine, and so is the boy." Jan smiled at Kim. "And don't forget, you and Star took turns reviving the kid till the paramedics got there."

"Who's Star?" Erika asked.

"She's my daughter," Jan replied. "She flew down here from Indiana so we could spend some time together, see some sites in Florida, and visit our friends, Emma and Lamar."

"By the way, where is Star today?" Kim questioned. "I thought she might join our quilting class."

"She took my bike and headed out to see what Sarasota's all about."

"It's a shame she didn't stick around. Didn't you say she was in the quilting class you took, Jan?"

He nodded.

"I invited her to join us," Emma said, "but she said she'd rather do something else." Emma gestured to the wall hangings everyone had begun quilting the previous week. "I think we'd better get busy now and continue with the quilting process. Since next week is our final class, we'll do the binding that day, and then you can take home your finished projects."

Mike cleared his throat before speaking. "Phyllis called last night, and she'll be coming home on Monday, so she'll be able to attend the class next Saturday."

"That will be nice," Emma said, smiling. "Then you can show her everything you've learned about quilting."

"I'd thought about just letting her take my place but changed my mind," Mike said. "Something happened this past week that made me realize I don't spend enough time with my wife. I'm gonna change all that when Phyllis gets home. There's a lot of lost time to make up for."

───

While everyone quilted, Jan sat beside Kim, watching as she moved her needle in and out of the material like she'd been doing it all her life. *Wish I didn't have to go home a week from Monday*, he thought with regret. *I'd like to stay longer and spend more time with Kim. I could check with Terry, I guess. If we don't have any houses to roof in the next few weeks, maybe I could hang around Sarasota awhile longer.*

Jan stroked the ends of his beard as he contemplated the idea. *But then Star has to get back to her job, so unless she'd be willing to fly back to Indiana alone rather than riding home with me, I don't see any way I can stay here longer. Maybe I'll discuss it with her later today.*

Jan's thoughts took him back to the quilting classes he'd taken with Emma's first group of students. It had been during their fifth class that he'd learned Star was his daughter. And now, being here in this quilt class had brought another special person into his life. He fixed his gaze on Kim once more and smiled. She really was a special gal.

───

At eleven o'clock, Emma excused herself to get refreshments, and Lamar went with her. They returned several minutes later with some chocolate chip cookies and a tray with crackers and cheese.

"Delicious as usual," Jan said, biting into one of the cookies and smacking his lips.

Noreen rolled her eyes. *That man is so ill-mannered. I don't understand what pretty little Kim sees in him.* She accepted the cup of tea Emma handed her. *Each to his own, I suppose, but a man like that would never appeal to me.*

She glanced at B.J. *I can't believe I was actually attracted to that man when I met him at the first quilting class. But not anymore. My sister was sure taken with him, though, and I'm not sure why. Of course, he was much younger then, and from what Judy said, he was quite good-looking. It's strange, but B.J. looks much older today than he did on the first day of our class.*

Noreen studied B.J.'s face, noting the dark circles beneath his eyes, which appeared almost sunken today. *Maybe he hasn't been sleeping well lately,* she thought. *Or perhaps he isn't taking good care of himself.*

"Oh Emma," Kim spoke up, "I brought that old ring I told you about yesterday—the one I found on Lido Beach."

Emma moved closer to where Kim sat, on the left side of Noreen. "Oh yes, that's right. I'd like to see it."

Kim reached into her tote bag and withdrew a small box. Then she opened it and handed a ring to Emma.

"You're right," Emma said, turning it over in her hand. "I see some initials engraved in the band. It's hard to make them out, since they are pretty worn, but it looks like the letters B and W."

Noreen almost choked on her tea when she heard what Emma had said. "Why, those were my husband's initials. May I see the ring?"

Emma looked at Kim, and when she nodded, she handed Noreen the ring.

Noreen studied it a few seconds and gasped. "This was my husband's! He lost it in the sand a few weeks after we moved to Sarasota." Tears welled in her eyes. "I would know this ring anywhere, and I can't believe you found it."

"Wow! What are the odds of that happening? I can't fathom it myself." Kim left her seat and held out her hand to Noreen. "Here you go. Take the box, too." She paused a moment, then quickly added, "You don't know how close I came to advertising the ring in the Lost and

Found section of the newspaper."

"Thank you so much. I can't begin to tell you how much this means to me," Noreen said with feeling. "After we'd gone back to the beach the next day to see if we could find Ben's ring and then searched for hours, we finally gave up. We thought it was lost forever, or that someone might have found the ring and kept it." She sniffed and wiped the tears from her cheeks. "Oh, this has truly made my day."

"I think Kim finding it was meant to be," Emma said, patting Noreen's shoulder.

"That's right," Lamar agreed. "God works in mysterious ways."

"We've been blessed this week, too," Jennifer put in. "Someone left us a lot of baby things, but we don't know who to thank for it."

"Some people like to do things in secret, and they don't want any thanks," Jan said, reaching for another cookie.

"Would anyone care for some cheese and crackers?" Emma asked, motioning to the other tray.

"I'll take a few," Mike responded. "Now that I'm restricted from eating a lot of sugary things, other foods that are better for me taste pretty good."

Emma handed the tray to Mike, and after he'd taken a few crackers, she passed it to Erika. "I'd rather have a cookie," the young woman said.

"Here you go." Jan passed the cookie plate down to Erika.

"What about you, B.J.?" Emma asked. "Would you like crackers or cookies?"

B.J. shook his head. "No thanks, I'm not really. . ." His words were cut off when a coughing fit overtook him. He quickly pulled a hanky from his pocket and held it over his mouth.

"Are you okay? Would you like a glass of water?" Emma asked, wearing a look of concern, as did everyone else in the class. Even Noreen thought his cough sounded pretty bad.

He lowered his hand, and Noreen gasped when she saw a splotch of blood in his hanky.

"Oh my! B.J., you're bleeding!" Kim exclaimed.

B.J. nodded slowly and looked from person to person, stopping at Noreen and holding her gaze. "I have cancer." He paused and drew in a quick breath. "Short of a miracle, it won't be long till I'm dead."

CHAPTER 34

After B.J.'s surprise announcement, the whole room went silent, filled with strong emotions. He hadn't meant to blurt out that he was dying. *If I just hadn't coughed up blood,* he thought with regret, *no one would have been any the wiser.* Now he had to deal with their sympathetic expressions as they processed the idea that one of their fellow quilting students would soon be checking out of this world.

B.J. almost knew how they felt and experienced sorrow for them in the awkwardness of the moment. He was sure they probably felt the same way, only for a different reason. Realizing that the outcome of his cancer was coming sooner, rather than later, was still hard for him to grasp, even after all this time. It wasn't fair. Lately, there'd been some days that B.J. thought for certain would be his last. But on other days, everything seemed right with the world, and it felt like his cancer was just a bad dream.

Thinking back, he realized that he'd wasted a lot of time moaning and groaning about having a bad cold or the twenty-four-hour flu. If he'd only known then what he knew now. Unfortunately, he understood the meaning of misery, and not just the part about having cancer. Maybe though, in spite of everything, there was a little ray of sunshine. B.J. wasn't sure why this had happened, but for weeks now, his senses had become more heightened. Could it be because his spirit knew there was so little time left? Like this morning when B.J. witnessed a beautiful sunrise. If it hadn't been for the need to get to the quilt class, he would have gathered up all his art supplies and headed to the beach to capture more clearly the morning's rosy dawn on canvas.

Ironically, B.J.'s favorite song from when he and Judy had dated was playing on the radio this morning. Even after all these years, he hadn't forgotten a single word of those lyrics. Were these little signs of awareness a clue that his death was closer than he thought? It just couldn't be. Not yet, anyway. B.J. needed more time. He had to say good-bye to his daughters, and he really wanted to find his son.

"I'm sorry to hear about your illness," Lamar said, moving across the room and placing his hands on B.J.'s shoulders. "We had no idea you were dealing with health issues, but now that we know, we will certainly be praying for you."

Emma bobbed her head in agreement, obviously left speechless with this news about one of her quilters.

"If you knew you were sick, how come you left your home in Chicago and came to Florida?" Mike questioned.

"It was on my bucket list," B.J. replied. "And when I got here and found out about the quilt class, I decided I'd like to make a wall hanging to give my only granddaughter. Hopefully, it'll be something she can remember me by."

"I'm surprised your daughters didn't talk you out of coming," Kim commented. "If I'd been sick when I left home, my parents would have pitched a fit."

B.J. drew in a couple of shallow breaths. "Neither of my girls knows that my cancer is terminal. When I left home, they thought I was doing better—that my cancer was in remission."

"So you lied to them, huh?" The blunt question came from Erika, who as usual, had kept pretty quiet during the first half of the class.

B.J. shook his head. "I didn't actually lie. Just didn't tell them the whole truth."

"My dad always says when you know something important but keep it from someone, it's the same as lying," Erika said.

"From your point of view, I can see that," B.J. responded, remembering when his daughters were Erika's age. "But from a parent's position, it's not so easy to reveal something this major to their kids. My daughters are very sensitive and even more so since their mother's death. As their father, it's only natural that I want to protect them from any kind of pain, especially news as serious as this."

"I can understand that," Jan interjected. "If I was in your position, I'd have a hard time tellin' Star about my illness."

B.J. sighed, picking up a pencil lying close by and tapping it on the table. While the room went quiet again, and B.J. thought about this a bit more, he realized what he must do and came to a final conclusion. "You know, Erika, maybe you're right. I probably should have told my children. No matter how you look at this, it'll be distressing all the way around. Some days I feel ready for the outcome of this, but when it comes to my children, I'm not ready to say good-bye. Even though I don't know how to easily handle it when I go home, I plan to break the news to my daughters."

"Psalm 46:1 says, 'God is our refuge and strength, a very present help in trouble,'" Emma said, her eyes tearing up. "He will give you the strength that you need to tell them, and we'll certainly be praying for you."

B.J. gave a slight nod. "Thanks, I appreciate what you said."

———

As Noreen sipped her tea, she reflected on all that B.J. had shared. Just because she felt vengeful, was it right to keep the truth from him about his and Judy's son? Was it fair to Todd not to let him know about his birth father and mother?

But if I tell B.J. or Todd, what good would it do? she wondered. *If B.J. really is dying, what's the point in revealing the truth? They would no more than get to know each other, and B.J. would be gone. Maybe it's better if I remain quiet about this.*

Noreen's gaze came to rest on the zippered pocket of her purse where she'd put her husband's ring. She couldn't help wishing Ben were here now to tell her what to do. He'd always had a way of knowing what was best and had set Noreen straight many times when her feelings ran amuck. But Ben wasn't here, and Noreen knew she had to make this decision on her own.

"B.J., do you feel up to continuing with the class today?" Emma asked. "You look awfully tired. Maybe you should go back to the place you've been renting and rest."

"Better yet," Lamar interjected, "you should go to the hospital or clinic and be checked out."

B.J. shook his head with a determined expression. "I came here to complete a wall hanging, and no matter how rotten I feel, I'm going to get it done."

That man is so stubborn, Noreen thought. *But then, I guess most men have a determined spirit when it comes to getting something done.* For a minute, when B.J. had first announced that he was ill, Noreen wanted to say that he deserved it. But her conscience quickly reminded her that it was wrong to think such thoughts, and pity for the man took over.

"If you need help with your quilting, I'm here to assist," Emma said, smiling at B.J. before she got up to open the curtains wider, letting more sunshine into the room.

"I appreciate that," he said with a nod.

Noreen could see by B.J.'s pained expression that he wasn't feeling well. *I think he's trying to put on a brave front, but B.J. shouldn't even be here today,* she thought. *I hope he goes home to his family so they can take care of him.*

Star felt relief when she pulled up to the Millers' house and saw no cars. She and Dad could take off on his bike and do something together. While she'd been driving around by herself, Star had discovered that Sarasota had a zoo. Thinking it would be something fun for her and Dad to do, she'd waited until shortly after noon, when she was pretty sure the quilters would be gone, to return to Emma and Lamar's.

After parking her dad's bike in the driveway, Star removed her helmet and sprinted up to the house. *Guess I'd better change into some shorts. Maybe I'll work on my tan while Dad and I are walking around at the zoo.*

When she stepped inside, Star found Emma and Lamar in the kitchen, eating lunch.

"You're just in time to join us. There's ham and cheese for a sandwich." Emma motioned to everything set on the table. "Let me get you a plate."

Star shook her head. "I appreciate the offer, but I'm hoping Dad and I can go to the zoo today, and I thought we'd catch a quick bite on the way. I just need to change into something a little cooler. It's really warming up out there."

"I'm sorry, Star, but your dad's not here," Emma said. "He and Kim decided to take her dog for a run on the beach."

"You're kidding, right?" Star mumbled. Then seeing their serious expressions, she realized that Emma was telling the truth. "That's just great! Dad didn't even have the decency to tell me he was going."

"Jan didn't know this morning," Lamar spoke up. "I heard him and Kim talking about it during class. Guess it was something they decided to do on the spur of the moment."

Star frowned. "Well, he could've at least called and let me know. Seems like he cares more about Kim than he does me."

Emma left her seat at the table and gave Star a hug. "I'm sure that's not true, dear. I know from the things Jan's said that he loves you very much. He's a different person now that you're back in his life."

"He has a funny way of showing it," Star said as she walked over to the window to look out. With her chin sticking out stubbornly, she turned back to the Millers and said, "Believe me, I get it. This change in Dad has nothing to do with me."

"I'm not making excuses for Jan," Lamar said, "but the two of you will be leaving soon, and he probably wants to spend as much time with Kim before then as he can."

"Whatever." Star turned away, struggling not to give in to the tears pushing at the back of her eyes. "That Kim!" she fumed. "She's ruining everything. I should have known better than to come here to Florida, thinking I'd have Dad all to myself."

"Aren't you going to join us for lunch?" Emma asked as Star moved toward the door.

Star shook her head. "No thanks. I've lost my appetite." Without saying anything more, she rushed out of the room. *For two cents I'd book a plane ticket today and head back to Indiana. What point is there in waiting to ride home with Dad, anyways?*

CHAPTER 35

J an laughed as Kim's dog darted into the surf, chasing a couple of seagulls. "I'll bet if my Brutus was here now, he'd be right in there with Maddie, havin' the time of his life."

"I'll bet, too," Kim said. "It would be fun to get our two dogs together sometime," she added.

Jan nodded. "Why don't we take a seat over there?" He motioned to the only wooden bench on this stretch of beach. "As long as Maddie doesn't stray too far, you should be able to keep an eye on her from there."

"Sounds like a plan." Kim followed Jan to the bench.

As soon as they sat down, he reached over and took Kim's hand. "I know it hasn't been that long since we first met, but I feel like I've known you for a long time."

She smiled. "Same here. I've felt it from that first day we ate lunch on the beach together."

Jan swiped at the sweat on the back of his neck, feeling nervous all of a sudden. "I really enjoy being with you, and I think if we had more time. . ." He stopped talking and drew her into his arms for a kiss that took his breath away. How was he ever going to say good-bye to this woman who had stolen his heart in such a short time? He couldn't ask Kim to give up her job and move to Shipshewana, and he couldn't give up his business and move here.

"Our friendship doesn't have to end after you leave," Kim said when the kiss ended. "We can keep in touch through phone calls, text messages, and e-mails."

"The phone calls I can do," Jan replied, "but I ain't that computer savvy, and my cell phone's just the basic kind, so I can't send text messages, either."

"After I've worked at the restaurant long enough to get some vacation time, maybe I can make a trip to Shipshewana to visit you," Kim said.

"I'd like that." Jan bobbed his head. "And I'll come back to Florida to see you again, too."

Who knows, he thought, *maybe after Kim visits Shipshewana she'll like it there well enough to stay. She could always get a job at one of the restaurants in the area.* Jan didn't voice his thoughts, though. He figured it would be better to wait until she visited and saw whether she liked it there or not. Maybe Kim was thinking the same thing and would suggest that he move to Florida.

It was hard not to let his thoughts run away with him, but he decided to keep these things to himself for now. Nonetheless, Jan couldn't stop himself from wondering what it would be like if he were married to Kim. Would she be okay with the small house he lived in? Would their dogs get along? Could Star accept Kim as her stepmother?

I wonder if my neighbor Selma would like Kim? Jan mused. Selma was hard to please, and it had taken him awhile to win over the elderly woman. But paying for her to take one of Emma's quilt classes had done the trick. Ever since then, she'd been sweet as cotton candy and had even brought Brutus a few doggie treats.

"Say, isn't that Erika Wilson over there?" Kim asked, breaking into Jan's thoughts.

He turned and looked in the direction she was pointing, where a teenage girl sat in a wheelchair with larger-than-normal wheels— apparently made for use on the beach. A man was crouched in the sand beside her. "I think you're right, Kim. That does look like Erika. I'm guessin' that's her dad with her."

Kim smiled. "I'm glad to see her here. From some of the things Erika has said during our quilting classes, it doesn't sound like she does much for fun."

———

"Now you'll have to admit," Dad said, grinning at Erika, "it feels pretty good to be here on the beach."

She grimaced. "Going to the beach might be fun if I had two good legs and could play in the water or run through the sand. Instead, I'm just sitting here wishing for something I can't have."

"While it's true that you can't run or walk anymore, you still have your senses of taste, smell, hearing, touch, and sight. Unlike that group of children over there," Dad said, gesturing to his right.

Erika turned her head and was surprised to see that the children Dad was referring to were holding on to a rope. "What are they doing?" she asked.

"Looks to me like those kids are blind. See that young man over there? He's leading them down the beach, using the rope so none of them wander off."

Erika's eyebrows shot up. "If they're blind, why would they come to the beach? I mean, they can't see the color of the sand or watch the waves."

"That's true," Dad said, "but they can smell the sea air, hear the roar of the waves, and listen to the call of the gulls overhead. Those children can also feel the warmth of the sand beneath their feet, as well as the breeze coming off the gulf." Dad smiled. "Just listen to the sound of their laughter. It's obvious that they are having the time of their lives."

Erika reflected on that. She watched as one blond-haired little boy tugged on the rope to get everyone to stop. The child couldn't have been more than six or seven years old, yet he seemed thrilled to share with the others what he'd felt beneath his feet when he shouted, "The sand feels warm!" Then bending to pick something up, he turned the item over and over in his small hands.

From where Erika sat, she could see that it was a seashell. The young boy continued holding the shell and turning it every which way. He seemed to be using his fingers to touch each part of it. Then he said something to the little girl next to him and passed it over to her.

Erika watched as the girl, with dark hair full of curls, held the shell and became familiar with it, just as the young boy had done. She even held the shell up to her nose, apparently smelling it. Then she passed it on to the next child in line, and each one did the same, until all the children had taken a turn holding, touching, and smelling the shell. The last boy held the seashell up to his ear and said something to the rest. Then the children passed the shell around again, and this time, everyone held it to their ear.

Erika was impressed watching all of this and realized that if the sightless children could enjoy their time on the beach without seeing, than she could do the same without the use of her legs. "Guess maybe I need to appreciate things more and quit feeling sorry for myself," she murmured.

"At least I can see how beautiful it is here, where some of those poor kids may never have seen anything in their lives." Erika couldn't imagine what it must be like to have never experienced the gift of sight.

Dad took her hand and gave it a gentle squeeze. "Now that's the old Erika talking."

Erika glanced down and noticed something in the sand below her footrest. She repositioned the wheelchair and reached down to pull a seashell out of the sand. It reminded Erika of a snail-like creature she'd seen on a cartoon years ago. The dull white on the outside of the shell couldn't compare to its interior of smooth light pink. On one end were rows of little spikes that decreased to a smaller single point.

Erika ran her fingers over the surface, and then she held the shell up to her ear, just as the sightless children had done.

Dad looked at her and smiled.

She grinned back at him. "It's a great day to be alive and here on the beach."

"You look miserable, honey. Is there something I can do to make you more comfortable?" Randy asked as he and Jennifer sat on the couch watching TV.

"Not unless you can make the baby come early." She placed both hands on her stomach and leaned slightly forward. "I feel top heavy, and it's hard to find a comfortable position anymore. My back is just one big ache."

Randy rubbed the small of Jennifer's back. "Your due date's still two weeks away, so it's probably best if the baby doesn't come early."

She sighed deeply. "You're right; I'm just anxious for her to get here."

"So am I, Jen. And I'm thankful I have a job now, because I was beginning to think I would never find one."

"I knew you would, but I'll admit I was worried that we might go under financially. I was beginning to think we might have to move back home and live with one of our parents."

Randy shook his head vigorously. "I would have borrowed the money from my brother, Fred, before even considering moving into my parents' home. Dad's health isn't good, and the last thing they need are three more mouths to feed."

She nodded slowly. "My folks aren't much better off—not with having kids still living at home."

Randy clasped her hand. "We don't have to worry about that now. Thanks to an anonymous donor, our baby has everything she'll need." He realized now that his pride had gotten in the way when he'd first lost his job, but the evening they'd had the Millers for supper had made him see things in a different light. Talking with Lamar had helped Randy's attitude improve, and now that he had a job, things looked more hopeful for him and Jennifer than they had in a long time.

"Yes, we have much to be grateful for. I just hope and pray that when our little girl is born she'll be healthy and that the delivery will go smoothly."

"Don't be nervous," Randy said, hoping to relieve her anxiety. "I'll be with you through the whole process."

"I'm thankful for that, because I don't think I could do it without you." Jennifer paused and tipped her head. "What was that?"

"What was what? I didn't hear anything."

"It sounded like someone stepped onto our front porch."

Randy listened intently. Sure enough, there was a thump, followed by the sound of footsteps.

"Guess I'd better go see who it is," he said, rising from the couch.

Randy opened the door just in time to see a young Amish woman running away from the house. He glanced down and noticed a box of food on the porch. Cupping his hands around his mouth, he hollered, "Hey, did you leave this box on our porch?"

The young woman kept going, until she climbed into the passenger's side of a car parked down the street.

Randy squinted. She looked familiar—like one of the Amish waitresses he'd seen at work. But if it was her, why would she leave a box of food on their doorstep?

He bent down, picked up the box, and stepped back into the house. If he saw the Amish waitress at the restaurant when he went to work on Monday, he would ask if she was the one who'd left the food.

CHAPTER 36

B.J. yawned as he lay curled up on the couch. Today had been tiring, and he'd done nothing but rest since he got home from the quilting class this afternoon. Exhausted as he was, B.J. felt somewhat relieved that he'd let slip to the other quilters how cancer was slowly robbing his life. He hadn't felt that way at first, but after thinking things through, he'd come to realize that keeping his illness to himself had done him no good. Telling the quilters about it had sort of prepared him for giving the news to Robyn and Jill.

B.J. had left the Millers' today without saying anything more to Noreen and had given up asking her anything about his and Judy's son. She either didn't know the whereabouts of the boy or didn't want to tell him. As difficult as it was, he had to accept her choice.

Guess it shouldn't really matter, he told himself. *With the way my health is failing, even if I did know my son's whereabouts, I doubt I'd have the energy to go see him. It'll take all my strength just to get on a plane and*

*return to Chicago, where my daughters are waiting. Maybe I should ask one
of them to come down here and accompany me home. It'd be easier than trying
to make it on my own.*

B.J. rolled from his side onto his back and stared at the ceiling.
He'd had a good life with Brenda, raising their two beautiful daughters,
and he was grateful for that. He'd also been blessed with grandchildren.
Why then, did he feel the need to meet the young man who might
never have been told about his biological father?

"I need to let this go," B.J. murmured. "Even if I did get to meet my
son, I don't have enough time left to really get to know him."

B.J. squeezed his eyes tightly shut. *God, if You're real, please give me a
sense of peace about this.*

"It's good to see you," Noreen's friend and fellow teacher Ruth Bates
said when Noreen neared the entrance of the high school gymnasium.

"It's good to see you, too." Noreen gave her friend a hug. Still feeling
a bit self-conscious about her hair, she said, "I almost didn't come to this
reunion, but I'm glad I did."

Ruth looked at Noreen strangely. "Why wouldn't you come?"

Noreen explained about the hair color she'd put on, then quickly
added, "I guess that's what I get for not looking at the color on the box
closely enough."

Ruth laughed. "Things like that have happened to the best of us.
You look fine, Noreen, so I wouldn't worry about it."

Noreen relaxed a bit. "I appreciate the affirmation, because this has
been kind of a trying week for me."

"I'm sorry to hear that. If you'd like to talk about it, I have a listening ear."

Noreen shook her head. "It's a personal matter, and nothing I can discuss right now, but your prayers would be appreciated."

"I can certainly do that." Ruth gave Noreen's arm a gentle squeeze.

As they made their way into the gym, which had been decorated with colored balloons and streamers, a young woman came up to Noreen. "So glad you could be here tonight, Mrs. Webber."

Noreen thought the woman looked familiar, but she couldn't quite place her.

"You don't recognize me, do you?" the woman said, as a few other students joined her. "I'm Karen Rasmussen, the girl who spent more time in the principal's office than she did in your class."

Noreen recalled that Karen had been one of her most challenging students, always talking when she should have been listening, and making wisecracks about what some of the other girls in class wore. Back then, Karen ran with a rowdy group that thought nothing of skipping school or cutting up in class. To look at the young woman now, one would never know she'd been a wild child during her high school years.

"If it weren't for your patience and persistence, I probably would have flunked English and might never have graduated high school and gone to college," Karen said, resting her hand on Noreen's arm.

Noreen smiled. "People change, and if I had even the slightest bit of influence on any of my students, then I'm grateful."

"We are the ones who should be grateful," a well-groomed, auburn-haired man spoke up. "You were one of the best teachers at this school, and you always treated everyone with fairness."

Noreen swallowed hard, fighting the urge to give in to tears. Until this moment, she'd never realized that she had impacted any of her students' lives. Hearing their praise and seeing how well these two young people had obviously turned out lifted Noreen's spirits. For the first time since she'd found out who B.J. was, Noreen felt a sense of joy in her heart and maybe even hope for the future.

Jan whistled as he stepped onto the Millers' front porch that evening. Kim had just dropped him off after they'd spent most of the day together, and he was in an exceptionally good mood. He knew for certain that Kim's feelings about their relationship matched his.

Jan noticed his motorcycle parked in the driveway, so that meant Star must be here. Maybe the two of them could go out for a late bite to eat.

Stepping into the house, Jan spotted Emma and Lamar sitting in the living room with grim expressions.

"What's up?" Jan asked. "You two look like you've lost your best friend."

"Star's gone," Emma said, slowly shaking her head.

Jan's forehead wrinkled. "What do you mean she's gone? Where'd she go?"

"She left you a note," Lamar said. "It's on the kitchen table."

Jan hesitated, then took off for the kitchen. He scooped up Star's note from the table and read it silently.

Dad,

Since you would obviously rather be with Kim than me, I decided to go home. I was able to get a flight this afternoon, and one of Emma and Lamar's English friends is taking me to the airport. There's no need to try and stop me, because by the time you read this, I'll be on a plane heading for the airport in South Bend, Indiana.

Star

Stunned by his daughter's words, Jan rushed back to the living room. Waving Star's note in the air, he stepped in front of Emma and Lamar. "Do either of you know anything about this?" he asked. "Did Star say anything to you before she left?"

"Star is upset about Kim," Emma said. "We tried to talk her out of going, but she's convinced that Kim is coming between you two."

"How so?"

Emma sighed. "Think about it, Jan. Since Star got here, how much time have you actually spent with her?"

He shrugged. "Not a whole lot, I guess."

"Remember, Jan," Emma said, "for a good many years, Star was cheated out of having a father, and then just when you were developing a solid relationship with her, along comes Kim. Now, Star feels threatened."

Jan sank into the chair across from them. "She oughta know I love her and that Kim's not tryin' to come between us."

"I'm sure Kim isn't doing it intentionally," Lamar said, "but Star isn't ready to share you with anyone. Not this soon anyway. And if you want my opinion, things are moving pretty fast with you and Kim."

Jan rubbed his temples as he contemplated their words. He felt like he was being forced to choose between Star and Kim. "I can't lose the relationship I've established with my daughter," he said. "Guess the only thing I can do right now is break things off with Kim. If it's meant to be, then maybe somewhere down the road things will work out for Kim and me. Right now, though, I need to think of what's best for Star."

"We understand, and we'll be praying for your situation," Lamar said.

Emma nodded in agreement.

Jan was tempted to call Kim and talk to her about this, but decided it would be best if he discussed things face-to-face. Rising from his chair, he turned to the Millers and said, "Guess I'd better head over to Kim's house right now, 'cause there's no point in putting this off. Then tomorrow morning, I'll be heading for home so I can set things straight with Star."

Kim had just brought Maddie inside for the night and was thinking of going to bed, when she heard the unmistakable roar of a motorcycle pull up out front. A few minutes later, there was a knock on the door.

Woof! Woof! Maddie's tail wagged when Kim opened the door and Jan stepped into the house. Kim smiled, thinking she wasn't the only one happy to see Jan.

"This is an unexpected surprise. Did you forget something in my car, Jan?"

He shook his head. "We need to talk."

"You so look serious," Kim said, noting the deep wrinkles in Jan's forehead. "Is something wrong?"

"Yeah, I'm afraid there is."

With a sense of apprehension creeping up her spine, Kim motioned to the couch. "Let's have a seat and you can tell me about it."

"While we were at the beach today, my daughter got a plane ticket and flew back to Indiana." Jan sank to the couch, scrubbing a hand over his bearded face. "She thinks I don't care about her anymore."

"Is it because of me?" Kim asked, dreading the answer.

He gave a quick nod. "Star's jealous of our relationship, and I guess that's my fault. I really blew it, 'cause I haven't paid her enough attention since she came down here to join me for what was supposed to be our vacation together."

Kim placed her hand on his arm. "I'm sorry, Jan. I shouldn't have taken up so much of your time."

"It ain't your fault," he was quick to say. "I'm the one who messed things up with Star." Jan leaned forward, with his elbows on his knees. "There's no easy way to say this, Kim, but I think it'd be best if you and I break things off before we get too serious about each other."

It's too late for that, Kim thought. She knew it was probably too soon, but she'd foolishly allowed herself to become serious about Jan and had even fantasized about having a permanent relationship with him.

Deciding that it would be best not to let Jan know how crushed she was by this, Kim forced a smile, sat straight up, and said, "I understand. Your relationship with your daughter should come first, and I wish you both well."

"This ain't easy for me, you know," Jan said, "because I really do care about you." He leaned over and kissed Kim's cheek. "Maybe someday, when Star's more secure in our relationship. . ."

Kim held up her hand. "It's okay. You don't have to make any promises that you may not be able to keep."

Jan didn't say anything as he stood and moved toward the door. He'd barely grasped the knob, when he turned back around. "It's been great getting to know you, Kim, and no matter what happens in the future, I want you to know that I'll never forget you or the time we've spent together."

Barely able to speak because of her swollen throat, all Kim could do was give him her bravest smile and whisper, "Same here. Take care."

Jan bent to pet Maddie, as she had followed him to the door. "Take good care of Kim, now, you hear?"

As though understanding what he'd said, Maddie licked his hand, while her tail wagged furiously. When Jan went out the door, the dog slunk to the corner of the room, plopped down, and let out a pathetic whimper.

Tears streaming down her hot cheeks, Kim buried her face and sobbed, soaking the pillow she held. Like most dogs when they sensed things about people, Maddie got up and came to rest her head on Kim's knee.

"Just when I thought I'd found the perfect guy, all my hopes and dreams have been dashed," Kim cried. "Maybe I am destined to live with a broken heart." She got down on the floor and, holding her dog tightly, continued to sob.

CHAPTER 37

On Monday, after Mike fixed himself a high-protein drink as a mid-morning snack, he received a phone call telling him his boat was ready.

Mike smiled. His boat could finally be put back in the water. That meant he could start taking calls from people who wanted to hire him to take them fishing.

For the past several weeks he'd had to turn everyone away. He'd not only missed the cash flow but time spent on the water. Even sitting out on the deck of their house where he had a nice view of the bay gave Mike a sense of yearning to be on his boat.

Think I was born to be on the water, he mused. But the example of his brother's situation had made Mike realize that he couldn't be on the water all the time just to make money. A lot of things in his life were going to change.

Glancing at his watch, Mike realized it was almost time to head to the airport so he could pick up Phyllis. She'd called Saturday evening to give him her flight details.

"Sure can't wait to see her," Mike said before hurriedly finishing his protein drink.

Kim's hand shook as she turned in another customer's lunch order. She hadn't slept well over the weekend, and really wasn't up to working today. But it wouldn't be right to call the restaurant this morning and give them that excuse. She needed to save her sick-time benefits for when she was really ill, and not for jangled nerves, which she hoped to get under control. Besides, working and being around people might help take her mind off Jan and the fact that he'd left for Shipshewana yesterday morning. Kim knew that unless Star gave her blessing, there was no chance of her and Jan ever having a permanent relationship.

"Are you okay?" Anna Lambright asked as she joined Kim near the breakfast buffet. "I couldn't help but notice that you dropped a bowl of soup awhile ago, and then soon afterward you spilled coffee on the floor."

"Don't remind me. I've been a ball of nerves all day, and I also messed up someone's order and forgot to take 'em the beverage they wanted. In trying to make it right, I offered them a free dessert." Kim sighed, bringing her hands to her forehead. "I was doing better, but now I fear that if I keep doing things like that, I really could lose my job."

"What's wrong? Just having an off day, or did something happen over the weekend to upset you?" Anna questioned.

"I can't take the time to go into details right now," Kim whispered, "but the bottom line is this: Jan and I won't be seeing each other anymore."

"How come?"

"His daughter flew back to Indiana on Saturday, and Jan headed out on his motorcycle Sunday morning. He's probably getting close to home by now."

"I'm sorry to hear that," Anna said, giving Kim's arm a little squeeze. "You seemed so happy when you started seeing Jan."

"I was, but I guess it wasn't meant to be. I'll be fine, though. You needn't worry about me." *Yeah, right. Who am I kidding?* Kim asked herself. She knew in her heart that losing Jan was not going to be an easy thing. With Jan, it was different from any of her other failed relationships. She guessed she'd just have to take one day at a time and try to make the best of her situation.

Anna looked like she was about to say more, when the new cook, Randy, stepped up to them. He stared at Anna with a peculiar expression. "Mind if I speak to you for a minute?"

Anna squirmed nervously but slowly nodded.

"I'll see you later," Kim said to Anna, before heading for the kitchen. *I wonder why Randy wants to talk to Anna. Could she have messed up someone's order?*

"Uh, unless it's something important, I really don't have time to talk," Anna said, taking a few steps away from Randy, then glancing at one of her customers, who was obviously trying to get her attention.

Randy held his ground. The customer could wait a minute. "It is important. Someone's been leaving things on our front porch. And the other day I found a box of food there, and someone who looked like you was running down the sidewalk and getting into a car. Was it you, Anna? Are you the one who's been leaving things on our porch?"

Anna lowered her head. "Yes," she quietly said.

"Really? How come?"

"Because I knew you'd been out of work, and I wanted to help out," she explained, lifting her gaze to meet his. "I'd hoped that when I left them there, you'd either be gone or wouldn't hear me step onto the porch."

"But how did you know about our situation? I never met you till I came to work here."

"I met your wife several weeks ago, when we were waiting to catch a bus. We started a conversation, and she ended up telling me about your job loss. She also mentioned that she'd wanted to take Emma's quilting class but couldn't afford it."

Randy's eyebrows shot up. "You paid for Jennifer's quilting classes, too?"

Anna nodded.

"But why? You didn't even know my wife."

"That's true, but when I lived in Indiana, I took Emma's class, and it helped me in so many ways. I was hoping that if Jennifer took the class she would also benefit from it."

"So you know Emma and Lamar Miller?"

"Yes."

"Do they know about the things you've done for us?"

"Not everything. Emma knows I paid for Jennifer's quilting classes. I wanted all the other things I've done to be anonymous."

"How'd you get our address?"

"When I met Jennifer the day we were waiting for the bus, she pointed to your house, so I memorized the address and put the quilt class ticket in the mail, marked 'Dear Friend.' Then whenever I stopped to see the Millers, Emma kept me informed on how you and Jennifer were doing."

"I see." Randy scratched the side of his head. "I still don't get why a complete stranger would spend their hard-earned money on people they don't even know. Was it you, by chance, who got us those baby things? If it was, all that stuff must have cost you a fortune."

"Not really. I entered a drawing at a store here in Sarasota, with the idea that if I won I would give the baby things to you and Jennifer." Anna smiled. "I've never won anything before, so I was surprised when the store called and said my name had been drawn. Since I had no way of delivering the baby things myself, I asked a friend who has a truck to drop them off."

Randy wasn't sure what to say. He'd never had anyone who was almost a complete stranger do something so nice. "Thank you, Anna. I appreciate everything you did," he said, blinking rapidly as his eyes grew misty. "But now I'm wondering, did you have something to do with me getting the job here, too?"

Anna shook her head. "Kim is the one who found out that they needed a cook, and I believe she told Jennifer about it during one of the quilting classes."

"Then I guess I have her to thank, too, and I'll do it right now." Randy turned aside, feeling eternally grateful. It was nice to know there were still some people who cared about others and wanted to help out. Someday, when he got the chance, he would return the favor—if not to Anna or Kim, then to someone else who had a need.

"Are you sure you don't want to go over to Pinecraft Park and watch me play shuffleboard with some of the men?" Lamar asked as Emma threaded her sewing machine.

"No thanks," she said. "I want to get some sewing done this afternoon, but you go ahead."

He bent to give her a peck on the check. "Okay. I'll see you later then."

Several minutes after Lamar left, a knock sounded on the front door. Emma set her sewing aside and went to answer it. She was surprised to see Noreen on the porch.

"It's good to see you. Please, come in." Emma opened the door wider.

"I hope I'm not interrupting anything," Noreen said. "But if you're not too busy, I need to talk."

"I was sewing, but I'm never too busy to visit." Emma led the way to the living room and invited Noreen to take a seat.

"Thank you." Noreen held something out for Emma. "I went to Lido Beach this morning, to do a little soul searching, and found this pretty seashell while I was there. I thought maybe you'd like to have it."

"Oh, that's a nice one." Emma took the pretty salmon-colored shell. "They call these conch shells, right?"

"That's correct. This one I believe is a horse conch, and it's actually Florida's state shell."

"That's interesting. I didn't realize Florida had a state shell," Emma said, walking over to the built-in shelf in the corner of the room. "Think I'll put it right here."

"Those are the types of seashells you'll see kids holding up to their ears," Noreen said. "In fact, I do it, too."

Emma smiled and took a seat beside Noreen on the couch. "I have a hunch that many other adults do, as well."

"When I was a girl, my family lived in Columbus, Ohio, and one summer our parents took Judy and me on vacation, here in Sarasota. We had so much fun that week, especially since it was the first time we'd seen the Gulf of Mexico." Noreen stared off into space, as though reliving the past. "We loved jumping the waves, and every morning we'd head for the beach to look for seashells. One day Judy found a shell similar to the one I gave you, only bigger. Daddy told us if we held the shell to our ear we could hear the ocean inside." Noreen looked back at Emma and said tearfully, "I still have Judy's seashell sitting on the coffee table in my living room."

"That's a pleasant memory," Emma said, feeling touched that Noreen had opened up to her like that. "I'm glad you shared it with me, and I can see that it's still very special to you."

"Yes, I guess it is," Noreen answered, straightening her shoulders. "Talking about seashells isn't why I came here today, though."

"Why did you come?" Emma asked.

"I needed to talk to you about something quite serious."

"Oh?"

"I did a lot of thinking over the weekend—about B.J."

Emma sighed deeply. "I felt sad hearing about his cancer. It must have been difficult for him to take the quilting classes when he'd been feeling so poorly."

Noreen gave a nod. "I feel the same way. He must have great inner strength to complete the wall hanging for his granddaughter. It sort of made me see B.J. in a different light." Noreen paused, took a deep breath, and looked straight into Emma's eyes. "I haven't been completely honest with B.J. about his and my sister's baby."

"Oh?" Emma folded her hands and waited for Noreen to continue. She could tell by the woman's pinched expression that this was a difficult subject to talk about.

"I do know where B.J.'s son is living, but I didn't want B.J. to know because I was angry with him for breaking up with Judy. It devastated my sister, and I didn't think B.J. deserved to know the truth because he'd hurt Judy so bad. I also blamed him for her death, because she died giving birth to his baby." Noreen's voice faltered, and she squeezed her eyes shut.

"And now?" Emma coaxed.

"After thinking things through, and realizing that B.J. doesn't have long to live, I'm wondering if it would best to let B.J. meet his son."

"Would that be possible?" Emma questioned. "Do you know where the young man lives, and have you spoken with him about this?"

Noreen drew in a long breath and released it in one quick puff. "B.J.'s son is named Todd. He's my adopted son."

"The son you said lives in Texas?" Emma asked in surprise.

"Yes, but Todd and his wife are coming to see me. They'll arrive this Wednesday." Noreen paused again and dabbed at the tears rolling down her cheeks. "Do you think I'd be doing the right thing if I told Todd about his biological father, and then let him decide whether or not he wants to meet B.J.?"

Emma mulled things over. Then she finally nodded and said, "Yes, I think that's the wise thing to do."

CHAPTER 38

Goshen

When Jan approached Star's house on Wednesday morning, he was relieved to see that both her motorcycle and car were parked in the driveway. That meant she must be here. When he'd arrived home late Monday night he'd called and left her a message, but she hadn't responded. He'd called again on Tuesday, but still no reply. Could her voice mail be full? Was the battery dead on her cell phone? Or was his daughter ignoring his calls on purpose? He hoped that wasn't the case.

Figuring that Wednesday was usually one of Star's days off, he'd taken the chance and driven to Goshen to talk to her face-to-face. That would be better than a phone call anyhow.

Jan parked his truck, got out, and glanced up at the stately old house. Star had inherited the place when her grandma died and her mom got married and moved to Ft. Wayne. He was glad Star had ended up with the house. She'd had a rough childhood and deserved a cozy place to call her own. Even though Star had been fortunate enough to have a couple of her song lyrics published and had even been offered the chance to move to Nashville, she'd decided to stay here, to be close to Jan.

How could I even think of establishing a permanent relationship with Kim if Star's not on board? Jan thought. *My daughter comes first, no matter what.*

He took the stairs two at a time and rapped on the door. Several minutes went by, then Star, holding her guitar, finally answered.

"Dad! I'm surprised to see you. Figured you'd still be in Sarasota."

"Headed for home after I got your note." Jan's lips compressed. "In case you've forgotten, you were supposed to be with me on the trip home."

"Yeah, that was the plan all right, but that was before I realized you'd rather be with Kim than me," she said, frowning deeply.

"Didn't you get my phone messages?" he asked.

She shook her head. "Turned the volume down when I went to see a movie the other night. Guess I forget to turn it back up."

"I left you a message saying I'd broken things off with Kim, and that I didn't want things to change between you and me."

Star's eyes widened. "Really?"

"Yeah, and I'm sorry for messin' up our vacation, Star." Jan turned his head to glance at the rain that had begun to fall. "Can I come in, before I get wet?"

"Yeah, sure." Star opened the door wider and Jan stepped into the house.

As Jan wiped his feet on the doormat, Star propped her guitar in the corner of the living room. "Would you like some coffee?" she asked. "I don't have any made right now, but it won't take long to fix."

"Sure, that would taste good," he responded. "But none of that flavored kind."

Star smirked and went to the kitchen, while Jan took a seat on the couch. She returned a short time later with two steaming cups of coffee.

"Boy that was quick! My coffeemaker takes forever to make a pot of brew. How'd you make this so fast?" Jan asked as he blew on his cup and took a tentative sip. "I know this isn't instant coffee; it's good and strong, just the way I like it."

"I got a new coffee machine that uses the pods. You can make a single cup of coffee in seconds." Star sipped some from her own mug. "Vanilla's my favorite flavor, but I bought a box of the bold coffee, since I knew that's what you like best."

"Well now, don't that beat all?" Jan said, shaking his head. "Never knew any coffeemaker could work that fast."

"You can even get hot chocolate and tea in the pods. And apple cider," Star added as she seated herself beside him.

Jan drank a little more coffee, then he turned to her and said, "You know how much I love you, don't you, Star?"

"I love you, too, Dad, but I was afraid if you kept seeing Kim that you might end up moving to Florida."

He shook his head. "Not a chance. My business is here, and so are you." Jan hoped his tone sounded upbeat so Star wouldn't think he had any regrets. Truth was, he didn't regret his decision to stay in Indiana; what he felt bad about was breaking things off with Kim.

Sarasota

"I know it's none of my business, but I feel like calling Star and talking to her about Jan and Kim," Emma said as she and Lamar sat in their backyard watching several wild parrots eat at the feeders Lamar had put up. They were such colorful birds and fun to observe. One was even hanging upside-down, as if showing off to the others.

Lamar touched Emma's arm. "I'm not sure it would do any good to talk to Star about Kim. Besides, it's up to Jan to work things out with his daughter, don't you think?"

Emma sighed. "I suppose, but I feel sorry for Kim. When we were at the restaurant for supper last night and she waited on us, couldn't you see how upset she was?"

"She got our order confused with someone else's. Is that what you mean?"

"It did show that she had her mind somewhere else," Emma said, "but there was a look of sadness in Kim's eyes that wasn't there before. I think she misses Jan a lot and is disappointed that he went home a week earlier than he'd planned."

Lamar reached for the glass of lemonade Emma had placed on the table between them and took a drink. When he finished, he turned to Emma and said, "Why don't we pray about it for now? Then in a week or so, if you feel the Lord is telling you to talk to Star, you can give her a call."

Emma smiled as she gave a nod. "As usual, you're full of *gscheidheit*."

"My wisdom comes from God," Lamar said, after taking another drink from his glass. "And I'm not the only wise person in this house. You have given godly counsel to many of your students since you began teaching quilting."

Emma pursed her lips. "That may be true for some in this group of quilters, but I don't feel like I've helped them resolve any of their problems. Some, at least, seem to be solving them on their own."

"Maybe that's a good thing, Emma," Lamar said. "I like seeing people realize they might be wrong about something or working to change their ways. People influence people all the time, not just by what they say, but by example." He patted her arm. "You know what, Emma?"

"What's that?"

"I'm thinking our students have been influenced in many ways by your example and how you get along with everyone."

She smiled and clasped his hand. "I am trying to be a Christian example in all that I do and say, but I admit that sometimes I fall short."

"We all do, Emma. That's because we're human. Guess the main thing to remember is to commit our life to Christ and ask Him to guide us in all we say and do."

Emma pinched the bridge of her nose. "Oh Lamar, there are so many people in our world, and those He's brought to our class are but a few. How I hope He will heal their hurts and touch their lives in some special way."

"He will, Emma, if they're open to it." Lamar took Emma's hand. "Now, let's pray."

"It sure is good to be home," Phyllis told Mike as they sat together on the deck, watching the boats in the bay. "I'm not used to that bitter North Dakota winter weather. I thought I was going to freeze to death when I took Penny's dog out to do his business during the blizzard. Thank goodness the dog didn't waste any time."

"When you told me about it, I worried about you and felt guilty for being here where I could enjoy the sun," Mike replied. "More than once I thought I should have gone with you."

Phyllis shook her head. "I managed fine helping my sister, and she's well-equipped for handling weather-related emergencies. I was glad you were here so you could take the quilt class in my place." She reached for his hand. "I'm looking forward to going to the last class with you this Saturday and can't wait to see how your wall hanging turned out."

"Well, don't expect too much," Mike said. "I'm all thumbs when it comes to a needle and thread. Even with Emma's help, my quilted project doesn't look nearly as good as it would if you had made it."

"That doesn't matter." Phyllis squeezed his fingers. "The important thing is that you were willing to take the class in my place and did your best."

Mike's cell phone rang, interrupting their conversation. "I'd better get this, honey. It could be a work-related call."

"That's fine," she said. "And while you're doing that, I'll go inside and fix our lunch."

When Mike answered the phone, a man came on, asking if Mike could take him and two other men fishing on Saturday. Mike was on the urge of saying yes when he remembered his promise to go to the quilt class with Phyllis. "Sorry," he said, "but I can't take you out on Saturday. If you can wait till Monday morning, I'll be free then."

"That won't work," the man said. "Saturday's the only day the three of us can all go. If you can't do it then, we'll call another charter boat service."

"I understand." Mike hung up the phone, struggling with mixed emotions. It had been hard saying no—especially when he really wanted to go out on his boat—but he knew it wouldn't be right to let Phyllis down. Besides, he'd promised himself that he would spend more time with her and less time on the boat and that he'd limit his work to just five days a week.

Guess learning not to be such a workaholic is gonna take some time, Mike thought as he leaned back in his chair. *But if spending more time with Phyllis will strengthen my marriage, then it'll be worth every minute.*

———

Noreen had just checked the roast warming in the oven, knowing Todd and Kara would arrive soon, when she heard a car pull up. Peeking out the window, her heartbeat picked up speed when she saw that it was them. Any other time, Noreen would have been full of excitement having her son and his wife come for a visit. But today she felt a bit rattled and full of apprehension. *Please let this all work out,* she prayed as she removed her apron and stopped by the hallway mirror to take a quick look at her reflection.

"It's sure good to see you, Mom," Todd said when he and Kara entered the house a few minutes later.

Noreen hugged them both. "It's good to see you, too. How are the children?"

"Doing well," Kara replied. "Since the boys are in school right now, they're staying with friends while we're gone."

"I'll look forward to seeing them the next time," Noreen said.

Todd, looking more handsome than ever with his dark hair and brown eyes, looked at Noreen and blinked. "What'd you do to your hair? It's darker than I've ever seen it before."

Noreen's face heated. "It's a long story, and I'll explain later. Right now, let's get your things brought into the house, and we can visit while we eat supper. You haven't eaten yet, I hope."

"We knew it was getting close to supper, and Todd said he was sure you'd have something waiting for us." Kara pushed a strand of her shoulder-length blond hair behind her ear and smiled.

"From what I can smell, I'm sure it's gonna be good," Todd said, sniffing toward the kitchen. "My mouth's watering already, Mom."

While Todd brought in their suitcases, Kara and Noreen set the table. When Todd returned, and they were all seated around the dining-room table, Noreen offered thanks for their meal, and for Todd and Kara's safe travels. Then she passed the food.

"If this roast is half as good as it smells, I'm definitely having seconds." Todd winked at Noreen.

"The potatoes and carrots look yummy, too," Kara commented. "You shouldn't have gone to so much trouble, Noreen."

"It was nothing, really," Noreen said, almost dropping the basket of rolls as she handed it to Kara. "Cooking a roast in the oven with potatoes and carrots doesn't take much effort, but it's one of my favorite supper dishes. Of course, I don't have it much anymore," she added. "Cooking for one isn't much fun, so I either eat something simple like salad, soup, or a sandwich, or I sometimes go out for a meal."

"It has to be lonely for you living here by yourself," Todd said. "Why don't you reconsider and move to Texas so you can be closer to us?"

Noreen shook her head. "We've had this discussion before, Son. Sarasota is my home, and I'm not ready to leave it right now. Maybe someday. We'll see."

"Okay, Mom, I understand." Todd reached for the salt shaker. "Just remember, you're welcome to come visit us anytime."

"Yes, and I will."

As they continued their meal, they talked about other things—the weather, politics, and what Todd and Kara wanted to do while they were visiting Sarasota.

When everyone was done, Noreen got up from the table to clear the dishes, but Kara said she would take care of that so Noreen could visit with Todd while they enjoyed some coffee.

"What's new in your life these days, Mom?" Todd asked, before taking a sip of his coffee.

Noreen shifted uneasily in her chair. Was this a good time to tell Todd about B.J., or should she wait a few days?

"Is something wrong? You're squirming around like you're nervous, Mom."

Noreen drew in a deep breath, unsure of how to begin. "There's something I need to tell you, Todd."

"What's that?"

She moistened her lips with the tip of her tongue. "You've known you were adopted ever since you were a boy. Your dad and I never kept that from you."

"Right. You both said you thought I ought to know."

Noreen grabbed a napkin and balled it up in her hands, damp with perspiration. This was much harder than she'd thought it would be. "There's...um...something else that you don't know."

He leaned slightly forward. "What's that?"

"Your birth mother, whose name was Judy, died giving birth to you, and...well...Judy was my sister."

Todd's forehead wrinkled. "My birth mother was your sister?"

Noreen nodded slowly.

The room became deathly quiet. Kara stopped doing the dishes and moved closer to the table. "So you're actually Todd's aunt?" she asked Noreen.

"Yes, that's right."

"Why didn't you tell me this before?" Todd's voice sounded strained, and a vein on the side of his neck bulged. "Did you think I couldn't handle it?"

"It wasn't that. I was afraid if I revealed the truth that your father might somehow find out."

"Dad didn't know who my birth mother was?" Todd's eyebrows drew together.

"Oh, he knew alright. It was your flesh-and-blood father I didn't want to know about you."

"I'm confused, Mom. Who is my real father, and why didn't you want him to know about me?"

Noreen squirmed under Todd's scrutiny as she explained about B.J. "And now, after all these years, B.J., whose real name is Bruce Jensen, made a sudden appearance. He's been attending the quilting classes with me, but I didn't know it was him at first. The truth of his identity came out later on."

"Does he know about me?" Todd asked, sitting back in his chair, while Kara came and stood behind him, placing her hands on his shoulders. They were obviously quite shocked by this unexpected news.

"He didn't know Judy was pregnant or that she'd given birth to a son until I let it slip during one of our quilting classes." Noreen drew in a deep breath to help steady her nerves. "The thing is, B.J. has cancer, and according to him, he doesn't have long to live. So I was wondering if... Would you be willing to meet B.J. after the quilt class this Saturday?"

Todd sat several seconds, reaching back and touching his wife's hands. "I—I don't know. I'll have to think about it."

CHAPTER 39

When the quilting students arrived on Saturday morning, Emma was happy to see that, with the exception of B.J., they'd all finished with the quilted part of their wall hangings and were ready to put the bindings on. She was also pleased that Mike's wife was with him.

"It's good to have you back with us, Phyllis," Emma said.

Phyllis smiled. "I'm glad I could be here for the last class. From what Mike has said, he's enjoyed getting to know all of you and has learned a lot while taking the classes."

Emma felt relieved because at first Mike hadn't seemed comfortable.

She glanced at Erika and noticed that the young woman wore a genuine smile this morning. Apparently, she was happy to be here as well.

Maybe Lamar and I have done some good while teaching this class, Emma thought as she placed several pairs of scissors on the table, along with the material each person would use for their binding. At least everyone had learned the basics of quilting, and they all seemed to have enjoyed the class.

Emma looked at Kim, who was chatting with Jennifer. She was probably still hurting over her breakup with Jan, yet she tried to remain cheerful and interested in what the others were saying.

What a shame, Emma thought. *I had hoped things would work out for her and Jan. I wish Star would have given herself the chance to get to know Kim better. I'm sure she would have realized what a sweet person she is.*

"Emma, did you hear what I said?"

Emma jumped at the sound of Lamar's voice, close to her ear.

"Uh. . .what was that?"

"I asked if you were going to explain to the students how to put their bindings on, or would you rather that I do it?"

"Oh, I was just going to do that," Emma replied, feeling a bit flustered. She knew better than to let her mind wander like that—especially during one of their quilting classes. It was important to stay focused, and for the rest of the class, that's what she planned to do.

First Emma explained how to cut, pin, and sew the binding to the edge of the wall hangings. Then, since B.J. had fallen behind last week because he wasn't feeling well, Emma offered to help him finish his quilting, while the others took turns using the sewing machines to put their bindings on.

B.J. smiled, although it appeared to be strained. He was obviously not feeling well again this morning, and Emma's heart went out to him. She knew that illness, injuries, financial problems, and many other painful things were a part of life, but it was hard to see people suffer, and she wished there was something she could do to make things better for B.J. She hoped, too, that as soon as today's class was over, the poor man would make plans to return to Chicago to be with his daughters. He really needed their support during a time such as this. His illness was not something he should have to face alone.

Noreen worked quietly at one of the sewing machines, every once in a while glancing at her watch and wondering if Todd would show up. This morning he'd agreed to see B.J., so she'd given him Emma and Lamar's address and said he should come by at the end of class. She didn't want to interrupt their final lesson, and knew that Todd meeting B.J. could end up to be quite an emotional experience.

Maybe it would have been better if I'd suggested some other place for Todd and B.J. to meet, she thought. She'd chosen the Millers' home because she knew they were good people and would have wise counsel to offer should things get sticky or too emotionally charged.

How different things would have been for me and Ben if Judy had married Bruce Jensen and they'd raised Todd themselves, Noreen continued to muse. *Judy and Bruce were really young back then, so marriage and raising a child would have been a struggle for them, but Ben and I would have helped in any way we could.*

Noreen had always wondered why things happened the way they did. Was there some big master plan for everyone's life? It was true Judy would have struggled even if B.J. hadn't been informed and she'd tried to raise the baby alone. Noreen knew that she and Ben would have given Judy a home and helped to make things easier for her and the baby.

But Noreen was certain of one thing: she had no regrets about raising Todd. She and Ben had been able to give their son a stable home. And if they hadn't adopted Judy's son, they would have missed out on the privilege and joy of raising him.

She lifted her gaze from the strip of material she'd been sewing and looked at B.J., who sat at the table beside Emma. She was pinning B.J.'s binding in place while he watched. Lines of fatigue etched his forehead, and the sparkle that had been in his eyes during the first quilt class was gone. The poor man probably wasn't feeling well and wished he was home in bed.

Should I say something to B.J.? Noreen wondered. *Maybe give him a heads-up that his son will be coming to meet him? Or would it better to wait and let him be surprised?*

Noreen's thoughts were halted when Jennifer, sitting at the sewing machine next to hers, groaned. Feeling concern, Noreen pivoted in her seat and said, "Are you okay?"

Jennifer rubbed the small of her back. "My lower back hurts this morning, and I'm having a hard time finding a comfortable position."

"I'm almost done with my binding now," Noreen said. "Would you like me to finish yours so you can sit on the couch and rest?"

Jennifer shook her head. "I appreciate the offer, but I'll be okay."

The truth was, Jennifer wasn't okay. She'd been having sharp pains in her back since she got up this morning, and they seemed to be getting worse, no matter what position she was in. Could these pains mean she was in labor? Oh, surely not. Contractions were supposed to be felt in the stomach, not the back. Then again, as she recalled during one of her childbirth classes, their instructor had mentioned that some women had back pain during labor.

I'm sure I'm not one of them, though, she thought. *My back just hurts because I'm so top-heavy up front.*

"If everyone's ready for a break, I'll bring some snacks in now," Emma said, rising from her seat at the table.

"I'll help you," Jennifer volunteered. She hoped that standing and moving around for a while might ease the pain in her back.

When they entered the kitchen, Emma placed a container filled with cookies on the table, and also a tray. "If you'd like to put the cookies on the tray," she told Jennifer, "I'll cut up some cheese and apple slices. Those will be better for Mike than cookies."

Jennifer nodded. "Oh, and Emma, I wanted to tell you that Randy and I found out who left the things on our porch," Jennifer said as she placed several cookies on the tray.

Emma's eyes widened. "Oh?"

"She's a young Amish woman who works as a waitress at the restaurant where Randy works now. Her name is Anna Lambright. Randy said you know her, right?"

Emma's cheeks colored. "As a matter of fact, I do. Anna used to live in Middlebury, Indiana, and she was a student in one of my quilting classes."

"Did you know she was secretly helping us?" Jennifer questioned further.

"I knew she'd paid for your classes, but she asked me not say anything." Emma put the cheese she'd cut on a second platter. "Anna went through some problems with her folks before she moved to Sarasota, and because of it, she's become sensitive to other people's needs," Emma explained. "I hope you and Randy were able to accept her gifts without reservation."

"We both felt funny about it at first, like we did when you and Lamar gave us food," Jennifer admitted. "But after thinking things through, we realized that we needed to appreciate what had been done for us and not let our pride stand in the way."

Emma began cutting the apples. "We all tend to be prideful at times, but God teaches us about the importance of humility. I believe that includes being willing to accept help from others."

"I agree." Jennifer picked up the tray of cookies. "Should I take these into the other room now?"

Emma nodded. "I'll follow as soon as I'm finished with the apples."

Jennifer had just entered the living room, when a sharp pain stabbed her lower back, this time, radiating around to her stomach. *So much for feeling better when I'm on my feet,* she thought, wincing.

"How did everyone's week go?" Lamar asked as they all sat around the table eating their snacks.

"Mine was good," Erika spoke up. "Last Saturday after class, Dad and I went to the beach. While we were there, we saw a group of sightless children being led on a rope." Erika's dimples deepened when she smiled. "Then one of their helpers, who I know from high school, came over and talked to me. After we visited awhile, I found out that they're in need of volunteers at the blind school, so I offered to tutor a few kids who are having trouble in math."

Emma left her seat and stood behind Erika. "I'm pleased to hear that, and I'm sure your help will be greatly appreciated," she said, placing her hands on Erika's shoulders. It did Emma's heart good to hear the enthusiasm in the young woman's voice and see the look of joy on her face. While she knew she couldn't take any credit for this, Emma was glad Erika had made a turnaround from her negative attitude and found some purpose for her life. She prayed that God would guide and direct Erika in the years ahead to do His will and make the best of her situation. If there was one thing Emma had learned over the years, it was that most people, including those who were faced with physical limitations, had the ability to do something positive with their lives.

Emma noticed that Jennifer's face was screwed up as though she were in pain. "What's wrong, Jennifer?" she asked with concern.

Jennifer took a deep breath and placed her hands against her back.

"I—I think I'm in labor."

Just then, there was a knock on the front door. Emma hurried to answer it, and as she was about to ask the tall dark-haired young man who stood on her porch if she could help him, he said in a deep voice, "Is Bruce Jensen here? I was told that he's my father, and I need to speak to him."

CHAPTER 40

Goshen

Star had just come out of the grocery store, when she spotted Ruby Lee Williams in the parking lot. Ruby Lee had taken the same quilting class as Star, and they'd gotten to know each other quite well. Ruby Lee's husband, Gene, was a minister, and Star attended his church whenever she could, along with her dad.

"Hey, how's it going?" Star asked, joining Ruby Lee at the trunk of her car, where she was loading several sacks of groceries.

Ruby Lee turned and smiled. "It's going well, Star. How are things with you?"

"Okay, I guess."

"I heard you and your dad went to Florida. How was your trip? Did you have a good time?"

Star shrugged her shoulders. "The beaches were nice, and the weather was warm, but Dad and I didn't spend much time together."

Ruby Lee's dark eyebrows lifted slightly. "Really? How come?

I thought the reason for the trip was so you two could spend some quality time together."

"That's what I thought, too, but Dad had other ideas."

"Such as?"

Star folded her arms. "Dad met this woman named Kim, and he spent most of his time with her instead of me. You should have seen 'em, Ruby Lee. They acted like a couple of lovesick teenagers." Star stuck her finger in her mouth and made a gagging sound. "It was just plain sickening."

Ruby Lee's surprised expression turned to one of joy. "So Jan has a girlfriend now? I think that's wonderful, don't you?"

A cold wind blew across the parking lot, causing Star to shiver. "Not really. I told Dad in a note how upset I was because he seemed to care more about Kim than me."

"What'd he say about that?"

"Said it wasn't true, and that he didn't want anything to get in the way of our father-daughter relationship, so he broke things off with Kim."

Ruby Lee tipped her head. "And you're okay with that?"

"Sure, why not? I mean, Kim lives in Sarasota, and Dad lives here, so a long-distance relationship would have been dumb."

Stopping to make more room in the trunk, Ruby Lee removed the last sack of groceries from her cart. After slamming the lid shut, she clasped Star's arm, looking her right in the eyes. "I can understand the way you feel to a point, but don't you think you're being rather selfish trying to keep your dad from falling in love and making a life with the woman he loves?"

Star rubbed the back of her neck, where the frigid wind seemed to have settled. "He loved my mom once, but when she walked out of his life he got over it."

"That's not the point, Star," Ruby Lee said gently. "I think I know Jan pretty well, and I don't believe for one minute that he would push you out of his life if he fell in love and got married. There's room enough in that big heart of his to love more than one person, and I personally think you ought to give him the freedom to date and fall in love with whomever he chooses."

Star dropped her gaze to the ground, suddenly feeling like a heel. "I know Dad's been miserable since he got home, and I suppose it's my fault. Guess maybe I oughta do something to make it right. I just hope it won't backfire in my face."

Sarasota

Emma had just called the restaurant to let Randy know that Jennifer was in labor and had no more than hung up the telephone when it rang, startling her. Too much was happening too fast here today, and her stomach quivered from all the excitement. First, Jennifer going into labor, and then the young man showing up, proclaiming to be B.J.'s son. It was a bit overwhelming.

"Emma, aren't you going to answer that?" Lamar asked, gesturing to the phone, still ringing.

"Jah, of course." Emma picked up the phone and was surprised to hear Star on the other end.

"I hope I'm not calling at a bad time," Star said, "but I was wondering if you had Kim's phone number. I need to talk to her about something."

"I do have her number, but Kim is here at the house right now, so would you like me to put her on?" Emma asked.

"Sure, that'd be great."

Emma called Kim to the phone, and after Kim had taken the receiver, Emma moved back to the living room where Noreen, B.J., and the young dark-haired man stood near the door. She glanced quickly at Jennifer, now lying on the couch, waiting for Randy to come. Mike's wife, Phyllis, sat nearby, offering encouraging words to the expectant mother, while Erika and Mike looked on with concerned expressions.

"What's this about you being my son?" B.J. asked, stepping up to the young man who had shown up a few minutes ago. Could it be possible, or was this some kind of a hoax?

"This is my adopted son, and he's yours and Judy's boy," Noreen spoke up.

B.J.'s throat constricted as he stared at Todd, noting that the young man had some of his own characteristics—thick dark hair, like he'd once had, oval face, and slender build. However, he had Judy's dark brown eyes and dimples.

"I'm happy to meet you," B.J. said, extending his trembling hand to Todd. Then he turned back to face Noreen. "I thought you didn't know where my son was."

"I—I'm sorry, and I'm ashamed of myself, but I lied."

"Why'd you keep it from me?" B.J. rasped, feeling weak and shaky.

"I didn't think you had the right to know because I blamed you for Judy's death."

"And now?"

"After I learned of your illness, and thought things through, I changed my mind." Tears welled in Noreen's eyes. "God spoke to my heart, and I realized it wasn't right to keep the truth from you any longer."

B.J. swallowed hard, barely able to keep his own tears from falling. He looked back at Todd and said, "If I'd known about you, I never would have broken up with your mother or gone off to another state to attend college. I would have stayed in Columbus and done the right thing by Judy."

"When Mom and Dad found out Judy was pregnant, they sent her to me and Ben, since we lived here in Sarasota by then, and they knew that nobody in Columbus would be any the wiser," Noreen interjected.

"Did you plan to adopt me from the very beginning?" Todd asked, turning to face Noreen.

She shook her head. "But after Judy died, we knew adoption was the best thing for you, as well as us, since we truly wanted you, Son." Noreen touched Todd's arm. "We never regretted it, either. You were a blessing to both Ben and me. We loved you as if you were our flesh-and-blood son."

"Todd, I'm sorry I didn't have the opportunity to know you during your growing-up years," B.J. said, barely able to speak around the lump in his throat. "I have many regrets, but so little time. If only we had more opportunity to get to know each other. I'd like you to meet your half sisters, too."

"My wife and I will be here visiting Mom for another week," Todd said. "I think we should spend that time getting to know each other, don't you?"

B.J. bobbed his head. "I'd like that, too. I had planned to return to Chicago early next week, but it can wait a few more days. Getting acquainted with my son takes priority over everything else right now."

After a slight hesitation, Todd took his father into his arms. To B.J., nothing had ever felt better. His son's strength was just what he needed as he stood enveloped in the young man's arms, and Noreen stood by, her cheeks damp with tears.

Emma, seeing that things seemed to be working out between B.J., Noreen, and Todd, moved back to the couch to see how Jennifer was doing.

"I hope Randy gets here soon," Jennifer said, looking up at Emma with wrinkled brows. "I'm a little scared."

Pulling a chair over to be near Jennifer, Emma sat down and held Jennifer's hand. "Having a baby for the first time is always a bit frightening since you're not completely sure of what all to expect. But once that little girl is in your arms, you'll forget everything else and concentrate fully on her."

"Thank you, Emma," Jennifer said, squeezing Emma's fingers when another pain started. "They told us the same thing during the birthing classes."

A few minutes later, Randy burst into the room. Emma hadn't heard him enter the house but figured Lamar must have let him in.

"I came as soon as I got the call," Randy said, dropping to his knees in front of the couch. Taking his wife's other hand, he asked, "How far apart are the pains?"

"Kim was timing them for me before she went to the kitchen to take a phone call, and they were about six minutes apart." Jennifer clenched her teeth. "It feels like the pains might be coming even closer now."

"Time to go the hospital." Randy helped Jennifer to her feet and led her toward the door.

"Please call and let us know once the baby is born," Emma called after them.

"Will do!" Randy said over his shoulder as he steadied Jennifer, going out the door.

A short time later, Kim returned from the kitchen, wearing a huge smile. "You'll never guess what Star said. She apologized for causing the breakup between me and her dad and said that after talking with her pastor's wife she realized it wasn't right to stand in the way of Jan's happiness. She also said she was sorry for not getting to know me or even giving me a chance to be her friend."

"I'm pleased to hear that," Emma said.

"And so am I," Lamar agreed.

"Star also said that if her dad was going to have a special person in his life, she was glad it was someone like me," Kim added, squeezing her hands together.

Emma smiled. "That's wonderful. I was hoping Star would realize that Jan having a relationship with you wouldn't affect the way he feels about her."

"And you know what else?"

"What's that?"

"Star invited me to come visit them, and as soon as I get some time off, I'm going to do just that." Kim eyes brightened. "When I get home this afternoon I'm going to give Jan a call. I'm just so happy I could burst!"

"*Ach*, my!" Emma exclaimed, looking at Lamar. "Such excitement we've had here today."

That evening while Emma was preparing supper, the telephone rang. Lamar stepped into the kitchen to answer it.

Trying not to eavesdrop, Emma kept stirring the kettle of chicken-corn soup.

A few minutes later, Lamar hung up the phone and joined Emma at the stove. "That was Randy. Jennifer had the baby, and they named her Anna." He grinned. "I think they chose that name because Anna Lambright was their secret gift-giver."

"That's *wunderbaar*!" Emma drew in a deep breath and released it slowly.

"It seems they made it to the hospital in time, because little Anna was born a few hours later," Lamar added. "Randy said she weighed almost seven pounds and is nineteen inches long."

"Randy and Jennifer have been blessed in so many ways. And now, they've received the biggest blessing of all—a precious baby girl." Emma remembered the joy she'd felt when her own children were born. "How grateful I am that we've had the privilege of not only teaching, but getting to know so many of our students. I pray that God will bless this group of quilters in very special ways."

EPILOGUE

Shipshewana
Six months later

T hink I'll meander down to the mailbox and see if the mail's come yet," Lamar said as he and Emma sat on their front porch, watching their goats frolic in the pen.

"That's a good idea," Emma said. "I'm hoping to hear something from my sister in Oregon, letting us know if she's feeling up to us coming for another visit later this fall. They'd visited Betty in the spring, and Emma had been pleased to see how well she was doing. It was hard to believe that just a year ago, her dear sister had been so ill she barely recognized anyone. *The power of love can work miracles,* Emma thought.

Lamar patted Emma's arm. "I'll be back soon with the mail."

Emma watched as he made his way down the driveway, walking easily and without a limp. They'd had a good time in Florida, but she was glad they were home now, close to their family and friends. Being in the warmer weather all winter had helped the symptoms of Lamar's arthritis, but of course, the weather was warm here in Indiana now, too.

939

But, in a few months when it turned cold again, they would catch the Pioneer Trails bus and head for their Florida home.

Emma leaned her head against the back of her chair and listened to the twitter of the birds, while a slight breeze tickled her nose. *God has surely blessed us,* she thought.

When Lamar returned with a handful of mail, as well as a large package the mailman had left in the phone shack, he handed the envelopes to Emma and set the package on the porch. "Looks like there's a letter from Noreen Webber and one from your sister's daughter, too."

"Oh, that's good." Emma took the mail and eagerly opened the first letter. "We've been invited for a family get-together next month in Portland," she said after she'd read her niece's letter. "Do you think we can go, Lamar?"

He gave a nod. "Don't see why not. Cheryl and Terry's and Jan and Kim's double wedding is in two weeks, so it won't interfere." He grinned. "I'm almost sure that some of our earlier quilting students will be at the wedding, too."

"I wouldn't be surprised."

Lamar gave Emma the other letter. "Guess you'd better see what Noreen has to say."

Emma tore open the envelope and tears pooled in her eyes as she read it aloud:

> *"Dear Emma and Lamar,*
>
> *"It's with sadness that I'm writing to tell you of B.J.'s passing. His funeral was last week, and Todd and I went to Chicago for the service. It was a sad time for all, but Todd had the chance to get to know his half sisters, and they plan to stay in touch.*
>
> *"I've kept in contact with the others from our quilting class.*

Mike and Phyllis recently returned from a trip to Hawaii.
Jennifer and Randy are doing well, and their
sweet little girl is growing like a weed. Kim, as I'm sure
you know, will be getting married soon. Oh, and I saw Erika the
other day at the children's hospital, where I volunteer. In addition
to doing some tutoring at the blind school, Erika has been making
cloth dolls to give to the children at the hospital.

"As for myself, I'm keeping busy with my volunteer work, and
more recently, I've gotten involved with a seniors' group and have
even gone on a few dates with a very nice man.

"I feel, as I'm sure the others who attended our class do, grateful
to you and Lamar for your kindness, patience, and the Christian
example you showed each of us during our quilting classes. I can
honestly say that I learned a lot more than quilting while attending
your classes. I've been able to let go of the anger I felt all those years
towards B.J., and it feels as if a great weight has been lifted from
my shoulders.

"Many blessings to you and yours,
"Noreen

"P.S. Almost forgot to mention that before I left Illinois, B.J.'s
daughter Jill gave me a picture of a seascape her father had started
painting while he was in Florida. He finished it after he returned
to Chicago, but due to his weakened condition, he never got it
mailed. Jill said her dad wanted you folks to have it and asked that
I get it to you. It should be arriving at your place soon."

"I wonder if that's what's in there," Emma said, gesturing to the package.

"Well, let's take a look." Lamar opened the box and removed some wrapping paper. Then he lifted the most beautiful painting out for

Emma to see.

"Ach, my! It's just lovely," Emma gasped as her eyes focused on the seascape, to which had been added a quilt similar to one that Lamar had designed and showed the class. It was spread out on the beach, and the colors from the setting sun cast a rosy appearance across the quilt. At the top of the picture, engraved in the frame were the words: THE HEALING QUILT.

Tears welled in Emma's eyes and she sniffed deeply. "Oh Lamar, even in B.J.'s darkest hour, he remembered us. Wasn't that thoughtful of him?"

"Jah, it certainly was," Lamar agreed.

Emma clasped her hands lightly together, gazing at the painting through watery eyes. "I'm looking forward to the days ahead, knowing that with God at the center of our lives, we will continue to be blessed, as we allow the Lord to help us bless others."

Emma's Raisin Molasses Cookies

2 cups raisins
1 cup shortening
½ cup sugar
2 eggs
1½ cups molasses
4 cups flour
3 teaspoons baking powder
½ teaspoon baking soda
1 teaspoon salt
2 teaspoons cinnamon
2 teaspoons ginger

Preheat oven to 350 degrees. Rinse and drain raisins. In a mixing bowl, cream shortening and sugar. Add eggs and beat well. Blend in molasses. Sift flour with baking powder, baking soda, salt, cinnamon, and ginger. Blend into creamed mixture. Stir in raisins. Drop by teaspoons onto greased cookie sheet and bake for 15 to 18 minutes. Yields about 6 dozen cookies.

DISCUSSION QUESTIONS

1. Emma agreed to spend the winter in Florida because of Lamar's arthritis, but she missed her family in Indiana and soon became bored. What are some ways we can deal with being separated from family and friends?

2. B.J. hid his health issues from his family, wanting to spare them the truth for as long as possible. Is there ever a time when it's right for someone to keep something like that from their family?

3. Since losing the ability to walk, Erika Wilson had no confidence in herself and felt as if she was worthless. Have you or someone you know ever felt that way? What are some ways we can offer encouragement to a person with a disability?

4. Noreen struggled to forgive B.J. for hurting her sister in the past. Was Noreen justified in feeling bitter toward B.J.? What does the Bible say about forgiveness?

5. Star, having been reunited with her father two years ago, felt jealous when he showed an interest in Kim. What are some ways an adult child can deal with their parents' desire to date again?

6. Mike Barstow was a workaholic and wanted to be on his boat all the time. Do you or someone you know tend to work too much, neglecting your personal relationships in exchange for your job? What are some things we can do to curb the desire to work all the time?

How can we find more time to spend with our family and friends?

7. When Kim felt nervous, she was a bit klutzy, which often resulted in minor accidents on the job. Yet because of her friendliness, Kim's customers liked her and didn't complain to her boss. Has a waitress ever given you the wrong order or spilled something on you or the table? How did you handle the situation?

8. Noreen had a secret she was keeping about her sister's child. Do you think an adopted child has the right to meet his birth parents if possible? How should an adoptive parent respond when their child wants to look for their birth parents?

9. Erika took a risk the day she had the diving accident. After doing several previous dives, she was tired, yet chose to do one more dive to show off for her friends. Erika's father urged her to get out of the pool, but when Erika did the dive anyway, it ended in a serious accident that changed her life. Would you take a chance, of any sort, doing something risky that could possibly cause permanent injury to yourself?

10. Kyle didn't try to stop his daughter from doing one more dive, even though he knew she was tired. After the accident that left Erika paralyzed from the waist down, he felt guilty. As a parent, do you find it hard to allow your children, especially as teenagers, to make their own decisions, even though you feel their decisions are wrong or risky? When should a parent step in and say no to what their child wants to do?

11. Jennifer's husband, Randy, was discouraged when he couldn't find a job. What are some ways we can help someone who is unemployed, yet actively looking for work, without making them feel inadequate or indebted to us?

12. Jennifer and Randy were being helped by a stranger. Would you be able to accept such generous gifts from someone you didn't know? If you had been Jennifer, would you have been able to take the quilting class, knowing someone had paid for your class, while the rest of the quilters had to pay for their own?

13. This story was set in the small community known as Pinecraft, which is part of Sarasota, Florida. What differences did you see in the way the Amish live there, from other Amish communities in different parts of the country?

14. Emma sometimes quoted different Bible verses to her students. Were there any verses of scripture in the book that spoke to your heart? If so, in what way?

ABOUT THE AUTHOR

New York Times bestselling author Wanda E. Brunstetter became fascinated with the Amish way of life when she first visited her husband's Mennonite relatives living in Pennsylvania. Wanda and her husband, Richard, live in Washington State but take every opportunity to visit Amish settlements throughout the States, where they have many Amish friends. Wanda and Richard have been blessed with two grown children, six grandchildren, and two great-grandchildren. In her spare time, Wanda enjoys beachcombing, ventriloquism, gardening, photography, knitting, and having fun with her family.

To learn more about Wanda, visit her website at www.wandabrunstetter.com.

OTHER BOOKS BY WANDA E. BRUNSTETTER

Adult Fiction

The Prairie State Friends Series
The Decision
The Gift
The Half-Stitched Amish Quilting Club
The Tattered Quilt
The Healing Quilt

The Discovery Saga
Goodbye to Yesterday
The Silence of Winter
The Hope of Spring
The Pieces of Summer
A Revelation in Autumn
A Vow for Always

Kentucky Brothers Series
The Journey
The Healing
The Struggle

Brides of Lehigh Canal Series
Kelly's Chance
Betsy's Return
Sarah's Choice

Indiana Cousins Series
A Cousin's Promise
A Cousin's Prayer
A Cousin's Challenge

Sisters of Holmes County Series
A Sister's Secret
A Sister's Test
A Sister's Hope

Brides of Webster County Series
Going Home
Dear to Me
On Her Own
Allison's Journey

Daughters of Lancaster County Series
The Storekeeper's Daughter
The Quilter's Daughter
The Bishop's Daughter

Brides of Lancaster County Series
A Merry Heart
Looking for a Miracle
Plain and Fancy
The Hope Chest

Amish White Christmas Pie
Lydia's Charm
Love Finds a Home
Love Finds a Way
Woman of Courage

Children's Fiction

Double Trouble
What a Pair!
Bumpy Ride Ahead

Bubble Troubles

Green Fever

Humble Pie

Rachel Yoder—Always Trouble Somewhere 8-Book Series

The Wisdom of Solomon

Nonfiction

Wanda E. Brunstetter's Amish Friends Cookbook

Wanda E. Brunstetter's Amish Friends Cookbook Vol. 2

The Best of Amish Friends Cookbook Collection

Wanda E. Brunstetter's Desserts Cookbook

Wanda E. Brunstetter's Amish Christmas Cookbook

The Simple Life Devotional

A Celebration of the Simple Life Devotional

Portrait of Amish Life—with Richard Brunstetter

Simple Life Perpetual Calendar—with Richard Brunstetter

Let's Keep In Touch!

Want to know what Wanda's up to and be the first to hear about new releases, specials, the latest news, and more? Like Wanda on Facebook!

 Visit facebook.com/WandaBrunstetterFans

Now Available!

THE
DISCOVERY SAGA
COLLECTION

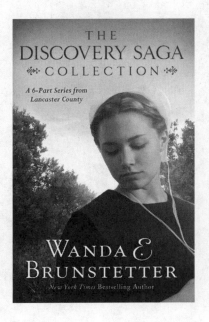